THIN AIR

 DEL REY · NEW YORK

THIN
AIR

RICHARD K. MORGAN

Published in the United States by Del Rey, an imprint of Random House, a division of Penguin Random House LLC, New York.

Del Rey and the House colophon are registered trademarks of Penguin Random House LLC.

Originally published in the United Kingdom by Gollancz, a division of the Orion Publishing Group, London.

Library of Congress Cataloging-in-Publication Data

Names: Morgan, Richard K., author.
Title: Thin air / Richard K. Morgan.
Description: New York: Del Rey, 2018.
Identifiers: LCCN 2018031284 | ISBN 9780345493125 (hardback) |
ISBN 9781101885369 (ebook)
Subjects: | BISAC: FICTION / Horror. | FICTION / Westerns.
| GSAFD: Science fiction. | Horror fiction.
Classification: LCC PR6113.O748 T47 2018 | DDC 823/.92—dc23
LC record available at https://lccn.loc.gov/2018031284

Printed in the United States of America on acid-free paper

randomhousebooks.com

2 4 6 8 9 7 5 3 1

First US Edition

Designed by Debbie Glasserman

IN MEMORY OF GILBERT SCOTT

Musician, Craftsman, Friend.

His demons were some of the worst I've seen.
But he fought them long and hard,
he took the endless battle for granted, and
he never once understood the depths of strength, courage,
and determination he brought daily to the fight.

In the time and space won in that fight,
he found a way to make beautiful things.

Without a frontier from which to breathe new life, the spirit that gave rise to the progressive humanistic culture that America has represented for the past two centuries is fading. The issue is not just one of national loss—human progress needs a vanguard and no replacement is in sight.

The creation of a new frontier thus presents itself as America's and humanity's greatest social need . . .

I believe that humanity's new frontier can only be on Mars.

—Robert Zubrin, *The Case for Mars*

Far from the heroic and romantic heraldry that customarily is used to symbolize the European settlement of the Americas, the emblem most congruent with reality would be a pyramid of skulls.

—David E. Stannard, *American Holocaust*

[A]n imagined order is always in danger of collapse, because it depends on myths, and myths vanish once people stop believing in them.

—Yuval Noah Harari, *Sapiens*

PART I
BLACK
HATCH
BLUES

Wake Up will habitually be accompanied by coinciding sensations of exhilaration, obsessive focus, stress tension, and mild nausea. These conditions are part and parcel of the work and must be handled as such. You are running-hot—get used to it.

(Also part and parcel of the work—context you Wake Up into is likely going, or has already gone, completely to shit.)

—Blond Vaisutis
Overrider Induction Manual—
Informal Veteran Comments Appended

ONE

IT WAS EARLY evening when I hit the Mariner Strip, and up in the Lamina they were trying again for rain. With limited success, I'd say. Got this thin, cold stop-start drizzle weeping down out of a paprika sky.

I didn't have the detail on it; I'd been too busy. Some newly written subroutine was what I'd heard, something consulted in from the edgy end of the industry, coded and cooked and cut loose somewhere up there amid the vast shifting gossamer layers that keep the Valley warm. Must have had some solid marketing muscle behind it, too, because the streets were crowded for a midweek night. When the rain kicked in, it felt like the whole city jammed up to watch. Everywhere you turned—people stopping to crane their necks and gawk.

I spared the sky a sour glance of my own, didn't stop. Shoulder on instead, keep the pace through stalled knots of rubberneckers and ecogeeks talking shit. Anyone looking to actually get wet behind this shit would likely be waiting a while. In the pushy seduction of the marketing, people tend to forget—nothing falls fast on Mars. And new code or not, this attempt at downpour wasn't going to be breaking any basic laws of physics. Mostly, the promised rain just floated and blew around overhead, scornful of the halfhearted gravity, tinged in the dying light to a blood-red spray.

Pretty to look at, sure. But some of us had places to be.

The Strip loomed around me—five-story Settlement-era facades in scarred antique nanocrete, repair protocols long exhausted. These days the inert surfaces are lathered by decades of storm wind and grit into something that looks more like flat expanses of coral at low tide than anything you'd call human-made. Back in the day, the COLIN engineers were all about huddling down—they ran the build either side of a broad channel dug out between the exposed foundations, mirror-image structures rising on either side. Sixty meters wide, that channel, and three kilometers long, bent just a little out of true to take advantage of existing fault-line geology in the Valley floor. Once upon a time it housed hydroponic gardens and manicured recreational spaces for the original colonists, all of it roofed in under glass. Parks, velodromes, a couple of small amphitheaters, and a sports field—even, they tell me, a swimming pool or three. Free access for all.

Imagine that.

Now the roof is gone, and so is the rest of it. Knocked down, torn out, cleared away. What they left in its place is a scuffed and littered sunken boulevard, tangled up with barrows and street stalls, all vying to shift the cheapest product to the crowd. *Get it while it's hot, people, get it now!* Last season's discounted coding spikes, semismart jewelry, branded Marstech, faked or stolen—it'd have to be at those prices—and fast food, lots of it, steaming from myriad different woks and pans. Street chemists hang about on the fringes, pushing Twenty Tailored Ways to Get Out of Your Head in a Hurry; street boys and girls stand at corners, flexing a more basic route to the same escape. You could argue, I guess, that you're still in a recreational space of sorts. But it's a pretty gaunt and garish spirit of fun that stalks the Strip these days, and if you ran into it, you wouldn't want to meet its eye.

For those chasing that particular ghost regardless, you reach bottom via long escalator tunnels hacked inelegantly right through the original structure—there's one at the end of most of the cross streets where they back up to the stretch of Settlement-era build, hemming it in on both sides with architecture altogether less hunkered and hermetic, conceived for a generation that could suddenly Go Outside. The cross streets end, the expansive aspirational leap and soar of the Outdoor New butts up abruptly against the somber, ragged backsides of the Settlement Old. You step on the escalators under big cowled openings in the worn nanocrete, and the endless alloy belt ride carries you through and down.

Or—if you're new to Mars, fresh off the shuttle, or some kind of nostalgia freak—you do the loud tourist thing and ride the gargantuan antique cargo elevators at either end of the channel. Twinned thousand-square-meter loading platforms, still pistoning massively up and down like the breath in slow lungs, smooth as the day they were put in. Got these tacky fake-historical stand-clear messages blaring out on a looped track from bullhorn speakers along the safety railing. Rotating yellow warning cherries, the whole deal. The grimy heavy engineering prowess of the old High Frontier, preserved today for your jaded delectation.

Either way—platforms or endlessly moving covered stairways—you're left with pretty much the same sensation. You're easing down slowly, sinking into the belly of something huge and probably hazardous to your health.

Fine by me.

I'd taken the escalator down from the end of Crane Alley, which put me about a klick away from where I wanted to be—slow going with the weather geeks clogging up the flow. And as I came out under the exit cowl, against all the odds, there was some genuine street-level rain to contend with. It slapped my face as I moved through the crowds; it dampened my collar. Put an unaccustomed beading of moisture on my brow and the backs of my hands. Felt pretty good, but then, so did everything else right now.

Three days awake and running-hot.

Over my head, early lights were coming on behind long-redundant storm slits in the upper levels of the build, hinting at sultry mysteries within. Club names and logos clung to the antique architecture like a plague of gigantic luminescent beetles and centipedes. And across the drizzling sky, the first of the 'branegels spread their almost invisible soap-bubble wings. Silver flurries of preliminary static shivered down their surfaces, like coughing to clear your throat. The images shook out, and the long night's video pimping began.

I'd thought maybe, with the shuttle in from Earth and just docked that morning, we'd have some ultratripper montages or standard profile spots for Vector Red and Horkan Kumba Ultra. But tonight the rainmaker publicity led the parade—moody intense footage of taut young bodies cavorting on nighttime streets in a rainstorm the likes of which no one around here would ever get within 50 million kilometers of seeing for real. Thin dark clothing drenched through, ripped and torn, a kind of favela-chic thing, clinging to curves and declivities, molded round nipples teased erect, framing cold cuts and slices of water-beaded flesh. Marketing copy bannered repeatedly across the pan-and-grab footage—

PARTICLE SLAM DUNK—GET WET, WHY DON'T YOU! A JOINT CODING VENTURE, BROUGHT TO YOU BY PARTICLE SLAM, IN CAPITAL PARTNERSHIP WITH THE COLONY INITIATIVE.

Yeah, COLIN strikes again—ubiquitous, all-powerful corporate midwives to mankind in space. A couple of centuries back, when they kicked off their efforts, you could reasonably have called them a special-interest keiretsu. These days, that'd be like pinning a badge that says *lizard* on a T. Rex. Kind of misses the scale of the thing. If it has to do with the human footprint anywhere in the solar system or transplanetary haulage and trade between, then COLIN owns it, runs it, sponsors it, or will do soon. Their capital flow is the lifeblood of the expansion; their co-option of antique legal structure back on Earth is the overarching framework that holds it all up. And their supposed competitive market dynamics are no more real or significant than the posturing dance steps and face-offs of those svelte young things up on 'branegel display in the fun and friendly rain.

Meantime, the rain—the real rain, back here in the real world—stuttered abruptly out. It blew away to nothing, left a long pregnant pause, then started in again, weeping slow. Hard to know if the new code was working well; it could have been running that staggered feed as part of an energy-saving protocol, could have been teasing for effect, or could just be buggy as fuck. Eco-code geeks stood around all along the Strip, squinting up into the sky, arguing it back and forth.

"Toldya they'd get it sorted. Particle Slam are solid, soak. Whole other kind of outfit than those Ninth Street guys. Feel that on your face?"

"Yeah, just barely. Feels like some crap standard seepage to me."

"Oh, *fuck* off. Seepage wouldn't even make it down here. Look there— it's making *puddles* already."

I slipped past the debate, avoiding the puddles, filing the detail for later. Particle Slam—never heard of them. But I'm used to that kind of thing when I wake up. Eco-coding is a fast game even back on Earth, and out here with all the brakes off and gentle commerce smiling down, it's so fucking Darwinian you get tired just thinking about it. Out here a code house can go from next big thing to dinosaur bones in less time than it takes the shuttle to do the long season turnaround. Takeaway for down-at-heel ex-overriders scrabbling to make a living: when you've been dead to the world for the last four months, you can miss an awful lot.

But some things never change.

Every evening, the Strip flickers to languid life like some faulty neon tube given a kick. It blinks and fizzles and settles down, gleaming slant-wise and constant across the street grid of Bradbury's old quarter like a cryptic grin, like a signal for eager moths. Saw it once from LMO—I was drifting in decanted, mission's end on a mutinied belt freighter I'd sooner forget. Nothing better to do than prowl the silenced decks and stare out the window as Mars rolled by beneath. We chased the terminator in across Ganges and Eos, and as night fell I watched the Gash come up and around. Brooding rift valley walls sunk thousands of meters deep in the Martian crust, colossal piles and drifts of tectonic rubble across the vast open floor between. Here and there a dim, dotted crop of settlement lights, thickening and tangling together as they closed in on the big bright blotch of Bradbury itself, farther up the valley. And there, slapped right across the old city's heart, was that big, bent grin, 3,000 meters long.

Everywhere across town, corporate logos and COLIN promo panels sparkle the skyline with liquid crystal fire, doing their bit to hold back the encroaching alien dark. But there's only so much brand loyalty and be-longing you can buy against that darkness, and the forces inside you know it. Deep down where the human hardwiring runs, the clock is running, too—turning over its lurid numerals like the cards in an endless losing hand. Just a matter of time before you wake up to that fact. And when you do, the knowledge is chilly on the nape of your neck.

Sooner or later you're going to spiral on in and batter yourself against the lure of the Strip, like all the other moths.

Used to think I was different.

Didn't we all.

Filament-thin whine past my ear, and the inevitable needling sting. I slapped distractedly at my neck—pointless irritation reflex; the code-fly was there and gone, as designed. Even in Earth Standard gravity the little fuckers are way faster than the flesh-and-blood mosquitoes they get their basic chassis from; around here, tweaked for local conditions, they're like little stinging flecks of quicksilver in the wind. Touch, spike, payload delivered. You're bit.

Not that I'm bitching. I mean, you live out here, you *need* to get bitten. Can't live any other way. This is the High Frontier, soak, and you're just one small part of the giant rolling upgrade that is High Frontier Humanity.

Problem is, four months behind the hatch and you've missed so many upgrades every code-fly on the block has you in its evil little postorganic sights. Three days back out and you're a human fucking pincushion. Your skin itches in a dozen different places from the delivery punctures. Fresh gas exchange turbos for your lungs; melatonin reup version 8.11.4; booster patches for the latest—and shakiest—osteopenia inhibitors; corneal armoring 9.1. So forth.

Some of this shit you've paid to have inflicted whenever the new mods come in; some of it COLIN gifts you with out of the goodness of its efficiency-oriented little heart. But it all has to be balanced and bettered and optimized for performance and then bettered all over again, version by version, upgrade by upgrade, bite by bite.

And that makes it a dependency you'll never quit so long as you live anywhere other than Earth.

Not that I'm bitching.

.   .   .

VALLEZ GIRLZ WAS right where I'd left it four months back. Same tired old frontage, just past the escalator outflow point for Friedman Boulevard; still flashing the same old looped enticement footage from five-meter display panels either side of the door. Same sleazy Fuktronica backbeat and subsonics from speakers hidden away. The screen on the right was still cratered and cracked from where they'd smashed my head against it in the fight, and something looked to be wrong with the feed—footage of the dancers kept shredding to a confetti of airbrushed flesh and hair, laced through with bobbing, disembodied long-lashed eyes that floated like tears in zero G.

Or maybe it was supposed to look like that.

Moving too fast here, soak. Where's the pressure leak?

Running. Hot.

I forced my pace back down to a rubbernecker's amble. Slouched with hands in pockets, hood up against the intermittent rain. It gave me all the time I needed to scope out the front of the club. Loose crowd of hopefuls queuing to get in, milling about in the wash of Fuktronica heard and unheard. Two blunt guys on the door in time-honored fashion, headgear the usual wraparound shades thing. And the same old superannuated Port Authority scanner hanging spread-winged from the lintel like some prehistoric bat about to take flight. Skinflint Sal Quiroga, same as it ever was—he bought that scanner at a decommissioned tech clearance sale nine years ago, and even then they say he put the levers on someone in the Port Authority back office to get a chop on the price. *Leverage,* he told me once, *is the whole key to this place. You don't got leverage, you might as well go right back to Earth.*

Hollow laugh—for most long-term residents of the Gash, the only way you'll ever get back to Earth is via some pretty hefty leverage. Long Fall Lottery aside—*Fifty Fabulous Homebound Winners Every Single Year! It Could Be You This Time! But You Gotta Play to Win!*—it's not like they're giving the tickets away. No one on Mars is going home this side of insanely lucky or very wealthy or COLIN-contract engaged.

I should know. Been stuck here long enough trying.

I gave it another fifty meters in honor of those fabulous winners perhaps, then did an about-face and drifted back. Took down my hood as I went up the short run of steps to the door. No point trying to hide. When you work doors—and I've been driven to it myself once or twice over the years—nothing trips your internal alarms like a punter trying to shroud his features. *Uh-uh, pal, no you* don't. *Now you got me all woken up.*

I didn't want these guys waking up just yet, I needed to get in close. So I kept my expression dialed down to Fuktronica-induced consumer lust, met the right-hand doorman's blank shades gaze as he glanced my way. I didn't know him—and my memory's good for men who've handed me my ass in the past—so he couldn't know me either. But these days that doesn't count for much. Behind the headgear, he'd be checking his list. Face-recog systems—the bane of decent gate crashers everywhere on the ecliptic.

I spotted the tightening that went through his frame as the software flagged me up. Then the loosening that followed as he digested the data.

I saw his lip curl.

"Dom?" Attention wandering off to the side, where his colleague was busy scoping some barely clad curves that wanted entry. He touched his headgear at the ear, did something to the Fuktronica, pulled the ambient volume down. "Hoy, *Dom.* Remember that sad-case hib cunt you and Rico bounced a couple of months back?"

Dom glanced over at us, visibly irritated.

"Hib? What fucking hib? You mean that guy . . . ?" Voice fading out as he saw me. A wide grin came and lit his face. *"That* guy."

"Guess some people never learn, right?"

"I'm here to see Sal," I said mildly.

"Yeah?" Dom flexed his right hand idly, looked it over like it was some power tool he was thinking of buying. "Well, he don't want to see you. Didn't want to see you last time around, neither. Remember how that worked out?"

"He'll see me this time."

They swapped a glance—glitter of unkind mirth, back and forth, there and gone. Dom's companion sighed.

"Look, soak—it's a quiet night, all right? Do us all a favor. Fuck off before we have to do something structural to you."

I found myself grinning. *Running-hot.* "Can't do that, guys."

Dom snorted. Reached for me—

I snagged his hand at the wrist, *fast.* You've got to be fast—gravity at a shade under .4 Earth Standard, you're getting miserly returns on mass and momentum. Any impact you make is going to *have* to come from your speed. I snapped his little and ring fingers backward at the base, twisted them with savage force. He made a noise like rupturing, and I locked up the arm. Drove him to his knees on all the sudden shock and pain. Kicked him hard in the belly as he bowed.

Let go, let him sag and hit the floor.

You wouldn't usually get past doormen on the Strip like this. They're a hard-bitten lot, ex–Upland work gang enforcers mostly who can't hack the thin air anymore and can't afford the newer turbo add-ons to make up the difference. So they slide back down the Valley and into the stews of Bradbury and find what muscle work they can. As a man who's seen his own fair share of career slide, I don't hold it against them. They do a job that has to be done, a job I've had to do myself occasionally, and they mostly do it pretty well.

But these two were in my way. And everything their past experience and software said about me was wrong.

They didn't stand a chance.

The other guy went for his twitch-gun in the holster at the small of his back. Wrong move and too late—I was in too close, he was way too slow. Probably suffering a bit of shock; this wasn't supposed to be happening at all. I stepped in, blocked the draw before he could clear the gun, chopped him sharply in the throat. Tripped him as he staggered back, helped him on his way down with a hard palm heel to the chest. Even at .4 of a G, that'll do it. He hit the ground on his back, gagging and flapping.

I stooped and took the twitch-gun away from him.

Reversed it, shot him with it point blank.

Blunt crackle and hiss like a pan of heated oil poured out—I saw his shirt ripple where the splintered crystal load went through. His eyes rolled up in their sockets, his body arched up off the floor with the force of the spasm. Sudden earthen stench of bowels as they voided, a grinding, gagging sound from deep in his throat. Foaming spit on rictus-ripped lips.

One rigidly splayed hand flapped frantically at his chest, over and over, like a trapped bird's wing.

Off to one side, Dom lunged at me from the floor. I shot him, too.

Then I stepped delicately between the two spasm-locked bodies, under the batwing scanner, and through the door beyond.

TWO

INSIDE THE CLUB everything was dim and twilight blue by default. I slipped through a loose press of figures and ghostly faces, dodging the bright beams of follow-spot systems where they cut through the submarine gloom to irradiate the dancers. Here and there across the vaulted space, more subtle spots of radiance flared from firefly chassis ambient bugs, tuned up to swarm around the pheromone-drenched bodies of the Vallez girls, leaving the customers discreetly alone. Low-tempo beats and a swirling soundscape came welling from the walls—some archive chop of some remix of some cryopop hit I vaguely recalled from a couple of years back. "Sleeper's Long Fall" or some such mawkish shit. *But look on the bright side, soak*—no sirens, no alarms, and no break in the rhythms that the dancers wove. The twitch-gun in my pocket was house property, wouldn't set off any kind of weapons squawk as I carried it across the floor. And I was pretty sure I hadn't given either Dom or his pal time to flip any panic switches before they hit the ground.

Two minutes, three at most—that's what I reckoned I had before the mess I'd left at the door boiled over and followed me in. I forged on into the heart of the club, kept my motion smooth and unobtrusive. Nothing going on here, boys, keep your eyes on the goods on display if you will. Never mind the big guy with the spoil-your-night face, he's not your problem, and you don't want him to be.

I spotted Sal up at the big gallery table on the mezzanine, hosting some sober-looking Hellas types. No big surprise there, at least not for me. There's a notable absence of official cooperation going on between COLIN and the Crater Chinese, something both parties inherited whole from their respective parental power blocs back on Earth. But where long-standing Earth-based geopolitical animosity discourages fraternization, on Mars, gentle commerce will find a way. Crater money's been trickling into the Gash by the back door for decades now, and it looked like Salvador Quiroga was sipping from the supply just like everybody else.

I went unhurriedly up the broad spiral stair cut into the back wall of the club, made my way out onto the mezzanine level. The music was more muted up there, mingling with the surf of voices in loud conversation. I threaded my way between dance platforms, tacking for Sal at the gallery table. As I closed in, one of the suited Chinese got up and excused herself, turned, and headed for the restrooms. We passed each other close enough to touch. No way to know if she looked at me or not—in the low light the lenses on her headgear were impenetrable black.

At the table ahead I saw four more just like her, suits and headgear a uniform, obliterating individual differences. Three male, one female near as I could tell, all exuding the same quiet, impassive force. Deadpan audience, zeroed in on the rasping tones of Sal Quiroga in full flow. Fluent in both Spanish and Quechua, he was speaking English this evening in deference to his guests. But by the sound of it, that language switch was about as deferential as he was going to get.

". . . and if, my friends, you think I'll sit still for percentages like that, then you have come to the wrong fucking club. You don't have that kind of leverage with me. Don't forget who opened the door for you people down here. I'm not about to—"

I dropped into the vacated chair. "Hello, Sal."

Brief, panicky ripple of motion around the table. One of the Crater Critters reached for something beneath his jacket, let go again as a comrade put a soft hand on his arm. Behind Sal, the same twitch went through his security detail—two hard-faced locals in loose clothing that barely showed the bulk of their body armor beneath. I saw the one on the right subvocalize into her coms choker, guessed she was trying to talk to the door.

Good luck with that.

Quiroga took off his lenses, the better to glower across the table at me. "Who the fuck are you?"

"Now you're hurting my feelings."

"Yeah?" He glanced up at the body-armored muscle on his left. "Tupac here is going to hurt a lot more than your feelings if you don't tell me who the fuck you are and what you're doing at this table."

The woman leaned down and murmured in his ear. She'd have run the face recog, just like the guys out front. Pulled up a fast match and whatever else they had on me. At a minimum, my name and recent past.

Belated recognition dawned across Quiroga's face.

"You lost weight?" he asked me curiously.

"I'm three days out of the tank, Sal. Not got much small talk." Lifting the twitch-gun casually at Tupac as he yearned forward. "Don't."

He froze. Nonlethal is a just-about-fair descriptor for the standard twitch-gun, weak hearts and the elderly aside. But it leaves out the details of how much fun it isn't to be thrown through repeating epileptic seizures like so many plate glass windows; to feel acid-booted centipedes march up and down your nerve fibers and coil through your central nervous system; to shit and piss yourself on impact and lie there in helpless repeating spasm with the stench in your nostrils until the blast finally wears off.

You get shot once with one of those things, you try very hard to avoid it happening again.

I nodded at Tupac—*wise man, let's be smart*—lowered the twitch-gun back into my lap. On Sal's other flank, the woman never moved, but she watched me from behind her lenses with dead-eyed calm. Looking for an opening, the least little thing.

Sal, meantime, seemed to recall that he had guests.

"Look, I'm in a fucking meeting here," he snapped. "Whatever shit you want to talk about, Veil, it can—"

"Synthia."

"Syn—" He gaped. Made the connection. Barked out a startled little laugh. "No fucking way. Tell me, *please tell me* you didn't walk in here still chasing that. You fuckwit. Didn't you get the message last time around?"

"Yeah. Got the message you went back on our deal and iced her anyway."

"The fucking bitch stole from me!"

"She made a stupid mistake, and she knew it. That's why she came to me. She was sorry."

He smirked. "Certainly was at the end, yeah."

"We had a deal." I kept my tone cranked back to dispassionate. "You get your merchandise back, she walks away. You *got* your merchandise back."

He sighed. Playing, perhaps, to his guests—*look, we're all reasonable people here, it's all just business.* "You really think I could afford to have one of my dancers pull shit like that and *just walk away*? You think word doesn't get out?"

"I think we had a deal and you broke it."

"Look—"

"And when I tried to get in here and call you on it, you had your front-office goons beat the shit out of me, then kick me back out on the Strip."

"I told them not to break anything. I told them not to kill you."

"Yeah, that was your second mistake."

Like the click of ice melting in a glass. Under the soft insistence of the club's backbeat, a cold quiet, pressing down. Quiroga looked at me for a moment, and something twitched in his face. He put on a queasy smile.

"You were fucking her. Right?"

I said nothing.

"I mean—how else is she going to pay you for something like that? Got to be getting a loose slobber job or two at least."

"You're missing the point."

"You know she wasn't really a she at all, don't you? Our Synthia."

I leaned forward. "What she was, Sal—she was a *client*."

The flinch in his face again. The woman on his right was easing into a very small step sideways. I caught her eye, shook my head almost imperceptibly.

The Crater Critters watched it all play out without a word.

Quiroga snorted. "*Client.* You're not a fucking Black Hatch man anymore, Veil."

"It doesn't matter. She came to me for protection, that was the job I took." I met his eyes again. "You think word doesn't get out?"

This time the stillness held longer. Faintly through the backdrop of music and voices I heard it—the sound of panicked chatter from downstairs and back near the door. My grace period, burning down—time to get this done. I lifted my free hand, open and easy, like asking permission to speak.

"So we got this problem to resolve, you understand. And so we can do that, I've got something here you need to look at. Right here in my pocket." I patted my left breast. "Relax, Sal, I'm not going to shoot you. Give you my word on that."

Very slowly, gaze still on his security and their taut expressions, I dipped my hand inside my jacket, eased out the thing I was carrying. I saw a little of the tension go out of the woman's face as she saw it wasn't a weapon. Tupac just kept looking at me like he wanted to snap me in half for a bread stick and eat the pieces. But his gaze switched to the object in my hand as I put it down on the table. I saw him frown.

Clunky little ten-centimeter cylinder, like a slim drink canister; mottled gray alloy finish, connection vents in the base where it was supposed to fit into something else, a tiny blank touchscreen on the top. There's a good chance the guys on the door could have told Sal what he was looking at, but Tupac and the woman were altogether pricier items—pure city muscle, they'd probably come up via careers in corporate security or the Bradbury Police Department, never seen the inside of an Uplands work camp in their lives.

They'd be pulling a scan on their headgear, though . . .

"What the fuck is that supposed to be?" Audible relief coursing through Sal's tone. "I'm in no mood for jokes, Veil. You'd better—"

The distress flare cartridge blew up in his face.

.   .   .

SAVAGE WHITE FIRE, raging out across the mezzanine in all directions. It froze the dancers on their platforms, ripped their shadows from them like dark souls torn away. It wiped out everything. It bleached the room.

In the Uplands, you'd use a modified kite launcher to fire the whole package a thousand meters into the air, where it floods the surrounding landscape with abrupt radiance, pops a parachute, and drifts very gently back down, blazing like a miniature sun. Even that high up, your vision will blotch if you try to focus on the light. Sal Quiroga got the same blast from less than half a meter away, and it took out his vision on the spot. Don't know if there was enough UV in the mix to give him retinal burn as well, but he certainly screamed like it.

He clapped hands to his face, tried to rise, still screaming. Stumbled back against his chair and fell over.

In my own eyes, the BV-patented nictitating membranes slammed in sideways with the flare, blocked the white fire out. Through the hazed yellowish vision it gave me, I saw Sal's security, reeling flash-blind, groping for weapons, trying to cope. I shot them both with the twitch-gun— shredded crystal hail across the air between us, inaudible beneath the screaming panic and the backbeat in the club. The load went in through whatever armor they wore, through clothing and flesh alike, pulled out all their neural plugs, shorted them out head to foot. I saw them spasm and hit the floor.

The air filled up with discordant cries.

Up out of the chair now, over the table in a pounce, down on the other side. Sal Quiroga lay writhing on the floor before me, hands still clamped tight to his eyes, roaring obscenities and exhortations to kill me. Jarred by my passage, the flare canister toppled and rolled off the table still burning, dropped to the floor, and rolled again. Waves of crazed shadow chased across the walls and ceiling around me, made it seem as if the whole club were shuddering in the grip of a quake. The white-fire storm raged on, drenched us, buried us at its heart.

I dropped the twitch-gun to free my hands. Stomped Quiroga hard in the ribs. He convulsed and curled, clutching at himself with the pain. I straddled him and flipped him the rest of the way over, onto his belly. Crouched and got a barring arm across his throat, put a knee in his lower back.

"You'll like this one, Sal," I hissed in his ear. "It's all about the *leverage*."

THREE

BRADBURY PD FOUND me a couple of hours later in a diner called Uchu's up on Ferrite Drive. Pretty fast work, but then, I hadn't exactly been hiding from them. I had a window booth to myself, was sat there for all to see. Plate of food in front of me on the table, almost untouched—running-hot: you know you should eat, you just never feel like it—and an empty shot glass at my fingertips. Beside the glass, the bottle, a good few fingers down from where it had been when I came in. They know me in Uchu's. I did the owner a couple of favors a few years back, and now he keeps a liter of Mark on Mars behind the bar with my name on it. Must cost him a fair bit, keeping it topped up, but then the favors I did him weren't exactly cheap either.

A lean black BMW crawler drew up on the other side of the rain-beaded window glass. Unmarked car and no one who got out was in uniform, but they didn't need to be for you to recognize what they were. They hurried forward of the crawler, passed my portion of the window, heading for the door. I heard it slice open behind me. A blast of cold street air got in with the new arrivals, put a chilly hand on the back of my neck.

I sensed them come up on me, and a moment after that, she slid into the seat opposite.

"Hello, Veil."

"Nikki."

She looked good, but then she always did. Andean cheekbones, *café con leche* skin, eyes an improbable cobalt blue behind the clear lenses of her gear. Thick, shoulder-length cloud of mestiza hair to set it all off, jet-black tangled through with corkscrew strands of gray.

"Something I can do for you?" I asked.

She turned her head, brushed some of Particle Slam's rain out of her hair with the blade of her hand. It speckled across the tabletop and my plate of barely touched food. "Something you can do for me? Well, you could stop murdering minor OC guys in my jurisdiction, I guess."

"That was three years ago, Lieutenant. Ancient history. Since when do you hold a grudge that long?"

She gave me a fixed smile. Hacked me viciously in the shin under the table. Department-issue boots, steel-capped toes. I grunted, tried not to cringe forward on the pain.

"Don't fuck me around, Veil."

"Wouldn't dream of it," I managed tightly.

"Two hours forty-seven minutes ago you walk into Salvador Quiroga's club on the Strip. You disable his door guys, go straight to his table on the mez like you knew he'd be there. You sit down, you start talking. That's all a matter of monitored record, we got it filed. Two minutes later, Quiroga's dead of a snapped spine. So." She smeared some of the specks of water off the table between us with her fingertips. "Feel like telling me what happened?"

"What does the monitored record say?"

She nodded once, bleak-faced, and the cop behind me came down on my neck and shoulders like a rock slide. My plate and cutlery rattled with the impact, the shot glass jumped and fell over. Nikki Chakana caught the teetering bottle before it could follow. The cop pinned me to the table, twisted my head sideways to face his boss.

Chakana hefted the bottle, studied the label. "Surprised you can af-

ford this stuff. There is no fucking monitored record, Veil. The flare cartridge you dropped has the interior systems for the mezzanine whited out
for the duration. Surprise you?"

"Mhmf." Not the most comfortable way of holding a conversation, half
my face pressed into the tabletop. "Hadn't . . . thought of that."

"No, I'm sure you hadn't. Why did you go see Quiroga?"

"He owed me money."

The cop on my back made a noise in his throat. "So you fucking killed
him for it?"

I grinned into the table. "You must be new. Can't extort shit from a
dead man, soak. Graft basics—hasn't the lieutenant explained that to you
yet?"

The jacketed arm across my head ground down harder. Thin splinters
of pain spiking in my temples. I heaved and lunged back as best I could
with my left hand, grabbed for his balls. Bad estimate, I barely brushed his
leg—but he flinched back at the touch, and the pressure came off. I hooked
around in the gap it left, went after his eyes with the fingers of my other
hand. He yelped, and the rest of them piled on, two more at least. Someone got my arm and bent it a couple of millimeters short of breakage. I
snarled and lashed out with a foot. Someone else drew some kind of gun
and rammed the muzzle under my chin. Tight female voice in my ear.

"You kick again, man, I'll fuck you up!"

I bucked and managed to dislodge the gun. It gouged painfully up the
side of my head. "Come on, then, don't pussy around! *Do* it!"

I heard Chakana make a tutting sound, and just as suddenly, they were
off me.

Not far off, mind, and there were a lot of bared teeth in the faces that
ringed me. The cop with the gun was still pointing her weapon pretty
determinedly—nasty-looking Glock Sandman, standard departmental
issue. Would have taken my head right off if she'd pulled the trigger.

Pause for breath. We all straightened our clothes a bit.

Across the table, Nikki Chakana was peering at me with narrowed
eyes. "How long you been out of the tank, Veil?"

"Three days."

"Oh, for fuck's sake." She looked at the plate of untouched food, the bottle of Mark still in her hand. "How'd I miss that? All right, get him up. Get him in the crawler. We're going back to Police Plaza."

ON SOME AGREED signal I missed, they skipped the holding cage in the rear of the crawler and ushered me into a second-row seat instead, sandwiched between the cop who'd dropped his weight on me and the one who'd stuck her gun in my throat. Behind me, a faint mingled whiff of disinfectant and antiadrenals made it through the bulkhead grille anyway.

Chakana got in up front, next to the driver.

"Take Eighteenth and then Soyuz," she told him. "We're going to get tangled up a solid hour or more if we try to cut through the center now. Fucking rain parades."

Soft lights in the cozy dark as the instrument panels woke up. The BMW's magdrive cleared its throat, the crawler raised itself on alloy haunches, and we slunk out into traffic. I saw Chakana stifle a cavernous yawn.

"You could have told us you've only been up three days," she said without looking back at me.

"You could have asked."

She slumped in the seat, put one booted foot up on the dashboard. "Did ask. As I recall."

"Earlier. You could have asked earlier." I glanced at my flanking companions, got stonily ignored by both. "Might have saved us some trouble."

The driver sneered. "Still think you're something else, don't you, shithead?"

"He *is* something else," Chakana said wearily. "That's the problem. Like getting in the ring and trying to arrest Corky Svoboda at the second bell. My bad, people. My slippage. Shuttlefall blues. Been up nearly thirty fucking hours now, on Mulholland's clock."

"Would have thought that was Sakarian's job," I mused. "Getting everything shiny and colonial for the Earth folks. Keeping up appearances for when the new crop of qualpros go walkabout."

"You shut up. You don't get to talk about this stuff."

"Got the impression you wanted me to talk."

"Nope." Chakana arched her back against the confines of the seat. I could almost hear her spine crunch as it gave up the tension. "I wanted you to confess. But don't worry. We'll take care of that."

"Can hardly wait."

"You'll have to wait. You're going to sit in holding for a week or two, Veil. Got a lot of other shit to do right now, *important* shit, y'know. So until your body chemistry works its way down to something a bit more cooperative, I'm not wasting any more time on you. Oh, what the fuck is this?"

The crawler's halogens picked out a spill of figures across the street ahead. Surging tangle of braced forms back and forth along a battlefront, 'branegel placards tilting drunkenly in the rainy air as their backpack governors got jolted about in the fray. A fair few uniforms in the mix, Bradbury's finest and some others it took me a moment to place. A couple of bodies down on the nanocrete and getting trampled.

The driver grunted. "Pablito demo, looks like."

He braked us to a gentle halt twenty meters short of the heaving chaos blocking our path. The male cop on my right raised up and crowded forward, peering over Nikki Chakana's shoulder.

"Pablito again? I thought that shit died down months ago."

"They know the shuttle's just in." Chakana gestured forward. "Look at the 'gels. Red Planet, Red Hands. No Justice on Mars. Chance to make a big splash for the Earth folks. Jesus fuck, who did they put in charge of this?"

"It's not your people, Nikki. Those are MG4 uniforms at the back, it's a private gig. Your guys are just making up the dance card numbers."

"Thought I told you to shut up."

I shrugged. "Okay. Who's Pablito?"

No answer; they were all staring at the mess ahead. Chakana was getting twitchy, fighting the urge to get out and take charge herself. Sakarian had cleaner hands back when he was doing her job, but then he was never very hands-on in the first place. Heading up Metro Homicide was a stopover post for him, his elevator ride up off the shop floor, and he took it with careerist aplomb. He ran the department top-down and office-based, and he ran it by the book. The only time you saw him out on the street was to do terse damage-limitation stand-up for the feeds when something went awry. By way of contrast, Nikki Chakana stayed away from news crews on principle, let departmental PR bots handle that end of things. It's doubtful there's more than a hundred seconds public footage of her anywhere in the whole Mars archive. The public barely knows she exists. But whenever her officers found themselves up against it on the street, above board or not, you'd likely find her there in the thick of it, too.

"I could back up and take Eleventh," the driver offered reluctantly. "See if—"

"Fuck this shit. Stay here." Chakana dug in her jacket for a set of power knuckles, strapped them on her right hand. Rapid, escalating whine as the charge kicked in. She thumped the door release, twisted around in her seat as the door hinged up, pinned me with a stare. "You sit tight, Veil. And you two—*watch* him. He's running-hot; his whole metabolism is looking for an excuse to cut up rough. If he gives you any trouble, don't hold back. Break something."

Then she was gone, ducking out under the still-rising door, striding away through the rain and toward the fray. I saw her collar one of the MG4 uniforms on the fringes, none too amiably by the look of it. She started yelling at him, indistinct above the angry surf of the crowd. The driver did something to his dashboard panel, and the door came slicing back down again, shut out the rain and the noise.

"So who's Pablito?" I tried again.

On my left, the cop who'd stuffed her gun in my throat snorted. "Happened to your headgear, hotshot?"

"It's back home, gagging on upgrades." True enough—though a bigger factor in leaving it behind had been that its systems recall would have been admissible as evidence. "I've been in a hibernoid coma since end of Tauro, haven't had a lot of use for it in between."

"You really a hib, yeah?" the right-hand cop asked curiously. "That's got to be some sorry shit to live with. Didn't think they grew guys like you anymore."

"I'm a blast from the past. So—who's Pablito?"

"Some grunt fuckwit won the lottery back in Vrishika." Mr. Strongarm seemed to have forgiven me our tussle in Uchu's place. "Went off the grid right after, no one could find him, so he missed his trip home. Work gang unions were all screaming murder, corruption, and class war for weeks after. Sacranites got in on the act. Had us a couple of riots in the Uplands; marshals had to go in and break some heads. Static down here, too; in the end Sakarian stepped in. Got a big missing persons investigation fired up."

Vrishika—last full month of Martian winter, and the best part of seventeen months gone. I'd been bedded down at the time, my last but one hibernoid coma this Martian year, and evidently I missed the whole thing. You get used to that. Sleep four months out of every twelve while the rest of the world goes on turning, and along with the countless in-jokes and fashion trends, you're going to miss out on a whole lot of current affairs gossip.

I cranked an elaborate eyebrow. "Seventeen months, huh? And they still haven't found him? Not even pieces?"

A glum nod forward at the view through the BMW's windshield, the mounting chaos of the demonstration. "What do *you* think?"

"Maybe they *have* found him," offered the driver. "That'd kick it off all over again."

On my left, Gungirl shook her head. "We'd have heard. And anyway, Sakarian would have had this place locked down tight soon as the news broke."

This place—it dawned on me slowly that the frontage the demonstrators were faced off against had to be the new Horkan Kumba Ultra building. They'd been setting up the site when I went under back in Tauro, but there still wasn't much to see above the foundation level at the time. There rarely is with a nanotech build—nothing but prep layering for weeks, the quiet seething hiss of the protocol beds, and then you wake up one morning and there's a towering monument to corporate profit margins and colonial synergy. HKU's spaceflight subsidiary, Vector Red Haulage, won the renewed franchise on shuttle services back at the start of the year, so their license to print money was solid for another three decades, and, well, I guess you got to spend all that cash on something.

"So what's the leading theory?" I probed. "Accidental death or some jealous fuck?"

"Got to be the jealous fuck," Gungirl said darkly. "Accidental, they would have found him."

"Depends how hard they were looking. Who caught the case, old Tits-Up Tomayro?"

Sudden, frigid silence as everyone in the crawler found something of great interest to stare at outside.

"Fair enough. So how'd Pebble Rodriguez make out at Wall 101 this year?"

Some shifting about, some more silence, but a little less chill in the mix, I thought.

"Came in second," said the strong-arm cop grudgingly. "Still got that tendon problem dusting her in the long pitches."

"Really? Thought they fixed that back in the spring."

Gungirl snorted. "Got nothing to do with the tendon build, Frank. It was those fucking Osmotech turbos she's stuck with. She should never have signed with those assholes."

"Hey, it was a lot of money," said the driver.

"Yeah, and now watch them turn her into a test bed for every half-assed upcode coming down the pipe. Osmotech don't give a flying fuck about the sport, they just—"

"She's coming back."

"I don't see it, man. Not with the tendon failure and—"

"No, *she's* coming back." The driver pointed through the windshield at the approaching figure of Nikki Chakana. He hit the door release. "Looks like we're rolling."

"Yeah, or breaking heads," said Strongarm. "She looks pissed to me."

Silently, I agreed. Chakana was running a scowl to win medals with. She reached the crawler, ducked halfway in.

"Well, people, what can I tell you—it's a fucking mess. I got to stay here or these MG4 morons are going to mismanage it right into a full-scale riot. Fucking superintendent couldn't find Olympus Mons if it was a boil on his own ass. Frank, I could really use you for emphasis. You two going to be all right, bringing in our pal here on your own?"

"Just watch us," Gungirl said, and the driver gave her a laconic nod.

"Good." Chakana swung her scowl on me. "Veil, you know how this goes. You play nice, we'll park you in soft holding. Fuck us around, you can spend the next week in the coffins."

"Quality, Choice, Freedom," I riffed. "Good to see the Articles being honored."

It got me a thin smile. But she held my gaze while she made her real point. "I'm warning you, Veil—don't you even *dream* of making me come find you like this again."

I couldn't see the driver's face clearly, but I spotted the reaction on Gungirl easily enough. She was holding off a scowl of her own now. Couldn't blame her—Chakana's subtext was about as subtle as a Particle Slam promo.

Veil, she'd said, *I know the state you're in right now, you could probably take these two apart and skip easier than Pebble Rodriguez climbing a ladder. But if you do, then Pachamama and all her suffering saints help you when we bring you in again, because I'm going to make a fucking Christ out of your ass.*

"Lieutenant, we *got* this," Gungirl said sulkily.

Chakana was still watching me. I nodded at her. "They do, Nikki. They got me."

"All right, then. Naima, get him booked and locked down, then check back with me from the station. I'll tell you if we need more bodies. Frank, let's go."

Strongarm hit his own door release and bailed out. We watched the two of them stride off into the fray, Gungirl more than a little wistfully, it seemed to me. Then the driver hit the engines, and the crawler came to life. He looked over his shoulder at me as he backed the BMW up.

"Don't give us any trouble," he growled. "You know what's good for you."

I hack Naima in the face with an elbow and break her nose. Smash her down across the seat, take her Glock away. Jam it in under her ribs, pull the trigger—two shots in quick succession, making sure. I turn the gun on the driver before he can usefully react—see his mouth distort around a yell that never makes it out of his throat—blow his head apart, all over the rain-flecked windshield and the softly glowing dashboard display . . .

Running-hot.

I looked down at my hands where they rested motionless on my knees.

"No trouble," I said quietly. "Nothing farther from my mind."

FOUR

DIDN'T THINK THEY grew guys like you anymore.

Yeah? Then you're dumber than you look.

What, you think after Jacobsen, everybody just settled down and agreed to *play nice*? One mild-mannered, balding Swedish genentech specialist writes a report for the UN, wags his finger sternly around the room, and suddenly it's all over? Right across planet Earth, government agencies and superfunded corporate partners see the error of their ways, cast down their tools, and weep? Shit-poor women *don't* go on selling the future children spring-loaded into their ovaries so they can feed the actual here-and-now kids they've already got? Bright young things at cutting-edge gene labs *don't* go on buying the raw material by the kilo? Cash-strapped regional legislatures whose major remaining resource is remote and desolate real estate *don't* go on signing land deals to host evasively termed "research facilities" with no questions asked? Government spokesmen and corporate PR departments *don't* lie about it, and shadow enforcement agencies can't get any work covering it up?

What fucking planet are *you* from?

.   .   .

FOOTAGE OF THE shuttle was playing in continuous loop on screens all over Police Plaza when they booked me in. Half a hundred repeated angles on the moment of docking—the top of the Wells nanorack, center screen, like a vast, gunmetal dandelion sprouting up into low orbital space; the questing snout of the shuttle, angling in across the featureless black; the nuzzling for initial contact, the retrieval arm embrace, the kiss with tongue. Inside shots of the cockpit, underemployed human pilots grinning for the camera. Quarantine crews on their way up in the nanorack's personnel elevator, looking squat and half melted in their barrier suits. Mingled in with all this, a parade of still-shot images grabbed off the passenger manifest—new meat for the media feast. Qualpro hires starting their sky-high-paying three- or five-year gigs, ultratripper sports heroes and screen faces plus accompanying film crews and entourage, maybe the odd indie tourist or three.

Grunt convict labor sentenced to transportation would be on the manifest, too, but you weren't going to see *their* faces bannered across a screen anytime soon.

Welcome to Mars, soak.

Streamer text ran constantly along the bottom edge of the images, English, Spanish, and Quechua chasing each other across. The words carried other breaking stories, but most of them never made it to actual footage. Even Particle Slam's rainfall success couldn't jostle the shuttle coverage off the screen for more than a couple of ten-second segments here and there—rain-dampened nighttime streets, drizzle in the wind. Cheering crowds. Now back to our main story. *Shuttle's In!*

"You all still watching this shit?" I asked Naima as they checked us through to retinal and processing. "Fucking thing's been docked all day."

She shrugged. "Find a channel it isn't on, why don't you."

Later, in the cell, I tried. There was a scuffed and splintered plastic screen set in the wall across from the bunk. I powered it up and swiped through a dozen or more options before I gave up and let the incessant cascade of images and commentary run. The only other option was to turn it off and stare at the walls, which currently I was in no mood for.

When you're running-hot, you're painfully alive to environmental detail; your mind craves it, seizes on it like a starving man grabbing steak. I'm never very sure if that's a by-product of the cycles inherent in hibernoid physiology or a little bonus the designers threw in to fit mission specs. Either way, I'm stuck with it.

I sat and watched TV, casing the footage for every little clue and tell.

On screen, you had the usual library-standard shots from within the shuttle architecture—the long ranked march of cryocap pods in storage, cranked down to the deck now to allow for decanting, and strobed blue with scannerlight; the enigmatic stacked slab structures and blinking lights of the CPU room; crew quarters, messy with personal junk in zero G and the chaos of two days of coasting in; conduits and companionways and corridors and *there*—just for a couple of seconds, the camera glides by an innocuous, firmly closed hatch in the bowels of the ship. It's not black—mythology and movies to the contrary, they never are—but the decals and flashes over the pristine white surface are unmistakable. EMERGENCY SYSTEMS EXECUTIVE. ONBOARD CONTINGENCY RESPONSE. WARNING: HATCH IS ARMED AND ALARMED—DO NOT TAMPER. NO CREW ACCESS BEYOND THIS POINT.

You couldn't read all that, of course, not in the time it took the camera to pan past, but I didn't need to. I already knew what it said.

Top and center of the hatch, a slow-pulsing green bezel like a heartbeat. He was in there.

Or she was. Though that's a lot less common than the overwrought sex-n-slaughter-in-space immies like to paint it. Women do this work, sure, but not many of them, and generally not for anywhere near as long.

For me, it had been a dozen years, give or take, and I hadn't stopped out of any desire to start a family or reconsider my career path. Being an overrider doesn't work like that. When you've been groomed for the role since before you were born, there has to be something pretty tidal in your genes to make you want out, and nothing fitting that description had ever come calling for me. Blond Vaisutis TransSolar Enforcement and Security Logistics fitted me out for a purpose and set me in the heavens as their watchman nonpareil.

And when the end came, it was Blond Vaisutis that cast me down.

I lay back on the cell bunk and closed my eyes. Saw the green pulse of the bezel once more.

How long are you down for, my cold-dreaming brother?

Just the one trip, or did they have him on endless turnaround, the way Reuben Groell reckoned it was tilting these days?

Fucking treat us like pure freight, he grumbles over tumblers of Mark on Mars at Uchu's one night. There and back, there and back, there and fucking back. And get this—you don't sign the zero decant clause these days, you can kiss about half the decent-paying contracts good-bye. I'm telling you, brother, you're lucky you got out when you did.

That's one way of looking at it.

He catches my expression before I look down into my drink to hide it. Come on, Hak, that's not what I meant. Sure, Blond Vaisutis shafted you, I know that. They shafted a lot of people. They're a fucking transplanetary enforcement firm, it's what they do. But seriously? Would you really want to buy back in even if you could? Go back to the Big Cold all over again, always wondering if the next time you get decanted, you'll have a terminal case of Ganymede Freezerburn?

Come on, Rube. When d'you last hear of Ganny Rash killing anyone?

Doesn't mean it's not happening. You think they'd tell us?

I think the technology's moved on, brother. And frankly, I can think of a whole lot of other shit about the job that'd bother me more.

Yeah? Getting a little bleary and belligerent with the drink now. Like what?

Never mind.

The green bezel pulsed behind my eyes like a hangover, like old regret.

How do you fucking live with yourself, overrider?

Carla Wachowski, at bay in the corridor to the coms nest, droplets of Arko's blood in her close-cropped hair and hate in her shadowed eyes.

It's not a problem, I tell her, grinning. Mostly, I'm asleep.

That's the mission time talking, of course. Running-hot—I'm barely five hours awake, the cockpit fight's a scant ten minutes gone. Got what feels like copper cable spiking through my veins, and this crazy adrenaline smirk trying to split my face apart. We hang in zero G, Carla and I, faced off against each other, and she's better than seven meters away. I have the mission-standard Heckler & Koch deck broom with a cut-down barrel, she has a handheld monofil cutter and her hate. This is only going to end one way.

You fucking corporate cunt!! she screams.

Hurls herself at me, monofil cutter raised and shrilling.

I snapped my eyes open, sat up on the bunk. *Enough of that shit, Hak. Ancient fucking history.*

But I went on wondering about Reuben's zero decant clause just the same. How far various of the agencies and corporations under the COLIN umbrella might push it, given half a chance. And that's without taking into account the habitual abuses of the Beijing bloc.

Yeah, yeah, I know—old paranoia in big new boots. But the thing is, it's a big old solar system, with a lot of places to hide. Plenty of room for the odd cryocap facility on standby, rooted to some cataloged and forgotten asteroid or minor moon or just falling in endless cobwebbed silence along an orbit somewhere out past the belt. Cold and distant and lonely, but hey, you're asleep and getting paid for it, so what's not to like?

Didn't think they grew guys like you anymore.

Hey, they probably don't—got so many of us 'capped and stashed away in dark places they don't need to.

YOU CAN GET the wrong impression from a term like *soft holding.*

The cell they'd given me ran about four meters by five, including the wet niche with shower and latrine. No window or ornament anywhere, just the impact-plastic screen in the wall and a radiant tile ceiling. The bunk was a single piece of molded polymer welded to the wall and floor, topped off with an immovable memory-foam layer all of three fingers deep. A vented pipe at one end dispensed insulene mesh every evening ten minutes before lights-out—you got a couple of seconds of warning whine from the generator, then the stuff came slathering up out of the vents like gray-green cotton candy. You're supposed to wrap yourself in it for perfectly adjusted sleep, then flush it each morning after use. That's the theory, anyway. High-end insulenes will actually crawl around on your body looking for temperature differentials, fibers swelling or thinning down as appropriate, working to keep your whole body at the same level of warmth. But this stuff wasn't high end, and what it mostly did was cling stickily to your skin. By morning, it would already be starting to degrade.

I wasn't going to be doing any sleeping, but I knew the cell's ambient temperature would drop a few degrees once the lights went out, so when the mesh vent gave out its meager offering, I shawled the stuff around my shoulders and settled cross-legged on the bunk to wait. Wondering if anyone was watching me, wondering what they expected. It's a common misconception that guys like me can't stand inactivity at the wake-up end of the cycle, that confinement like this would be a kind of low-grade psyops torture for an overrider.

Yeah, right.

Waiting in confined spaces?

Try nineteen hours cramped into an EVA module disguised as a coms blister, waiting for one of the myriad glimmerings in the shingle of stars under you to finally resolve into what it was—a belt marauder come looking for its missile-smacked and immobilized prey.

Try a solid week barricaded in the cockpit of a short-hop shuttle while it falls to destination and its mutinous crew figures out there's no way around the booby traps you've built into the navigation system and the drives.

Try eleven hours of sneak combat alone in the tight corridors and companionways of an ore-processing barge, hiding and pouncing and hiding again, until you've whittled your opposition down to a remnant frayed and frightened enough to cave in and do what they're told.

Confined spaces are part of what we do—what I used to do, anyway—and any overrider that can't summon patience while confined isn't going to last very long.

The radiant tiles in the ceiling started to dim down—bedtime in holding. I grimaced and drew the sticky wrap of insulene a little closer around myself. Fixed my attention loosely on the screen—newly bright now by contrast with the darkened cell—and let the torrent of images wash over me like some endlessly unfolding visual koan. *Consider, o seeker, if you will, the smooth and soothing chaos of a myriad individual jagged significances, tumbled together until their edges wear smooth . . .*

Standard overrider tricks—I settled into it with something almost like comfort.

And then, *flicker-click,* just like that—on the screen, a change of pattern caught my eye. A reshuffle in the endless cycle of passenger images from the shuttle news segments. A new privileging of about a half dozen from the pack, sober-suited men and women wearing corporate promo smiles the way you'd wear a shoulder-holstered Glock. In the upper left corner of the screen, a new flashing red panel pulsed the promise—

BREAKING NEWS, BREAKING NEWS . . .

I hopped off the bunk in the gloom and swiped up the volume.

Just in time, too—the collage of news chop blanked out, replaced by artfully gloomed studio space and a sober-looking anchor spotlit in the foreground. Tailored jacket, casually sexual open-neck blouse, great hair and eyes. Behind her, a couple of prep-crew guys scurried rapidly out of shot. The hurrying every-hour-on-the-hour signature music swelled, then faded out. The anchor looked up to camera.

But under the armor of her on-screen composure, the strain seeped out visibly around her eyes. Her smile was dimmed way below normal wattage, and her hands fluttered about at her collar. Something *very* big must have come down the pipe to rattle her like this. She cleared her fucking throat before she spoke, for Pachamama's sake.

"Good evening, you're watching Valles Channel One. Tonight's big story comes to us from the newly docked Earth shuttle, where a recently decanted high-ranking Colony Initiative official has issued the following policy statement."

A 'branegel flared bright in the depths of the studio behind her. The camera angle swung, rushed obliquely past her at shoulder height, pulled the gel into full screen. Somewhere in a hotel lobby space, a briefing podium had been set up. A spokeswoman stood at it, someone entirely unlike the news anchor in dress and demeanor. Her hair was razored to stubble, she wore a plain shipboard coverall that wouldn't have looked amiss on a Sacranite apparatchik, and aside from the hollow-eyed look of recent decanting, her south Asian features held less emotion than a freshly rendered receptionist InterFace before the interactive protocols go in. News anchors habitually present as a classy and slightly flirtatious invitation to stick around and watch the news. This woman invited nothing and projected nothing beyond the simple message *Listen up, motherfuckers, I'm only going to say this once.*

And she wasn't high-ranking as Valles One had automatically supposed—for one thing, her face was as devoid of the rank tattoos so popular on Earth as it was of any eagerness to please. Whoever else was actually behind the announcement—and we'd likely see them soon enough—this was a soldier and a mouthpiece, conveying terms.

"On behalf of the Colony Initiative, Earth Oversight Committee, and General Secretary Ngoebi Karlssen, I hereby serve notice that the city of Bradbury and all outlying districts of the Valles Marineris Colony are now under extraordinary audit. Article Eighteen is invoked, with all legal and other enforcement provisionals live from this date. To all colonial citizens, I say this: remain calm and go about your business. These proceedings should not disrupt your lives in any way. The audit team expects to conduct its investigation with a minimum of disturbance and the full cooperation of existing Valley authorities."

By this point, I'd picked my chin up from the floor of the cell and started laughing. I really couldn't help it.

"Further statements and a fully detailed public briefing will follow."

FIVE

THE VALLEY WENT into spasm.

I sat out the rest of the night in holding watching it boil over. Ominous crowd scenes from around the city and in the larger towns up and down the Gash. Angry vox pop pulled off half a hundred street corners, factory floors, and work camp shift assemblies. No actual violence yet as far as I could see, but then, a lot of people were asleep right now. No telling where things would go when the rest of the Valley woke up. Meantime, the Earth shuttle sat docile in dock at the top of the Wells nanorack, still locked down under the last of the quarantine protocols, and despite constant revisiting of the footage from every conceivable angle throughout the night and on numerous different feeds, neither shuttle nor debarkation module showed any outward signs of change or activity at all. Whatever surprises were brewing within, they'd be a while coming out. Contrary to all the Mars First rhetoric you hear, COLIN isn't like a pack of hyenas or a feeding frenzy of sharks or whatever this month's highly colored predator analogy might be—it's more like a crown-of-thorns starfish, creeping up on its prey at glacial pace, then vomiting out its stomach to envelop and digest it entire. No less predatory in its way, but it moves *slow* and *steady*.

Perhaps with this fact in mind, Mulholland's people waited almost till dawn before they released an official statement. *Or*, I thought sourly, *perhaps it just took that long to spruce the fucker up for public consumption. Kick out whatever high-end working girls he'd had up to the governor's mansion that night, wipe their body fluids off his face and the SNDRI out of his eyes, slap some coherent sense into his scrambled brains.* Ah, *there* you go—

"Citizens of the Valley, my fellow pioneers." Solemn pause. "I know that some of you may have been alarmed by the COLIN announcement made earlier tonight. But there is no cause for concern . . ."

They'd dressed him down for the broadcast—coverall trousers with no sign of a brand name anywhere on them, a loose, dark work shirt with the sleeves rolled up. He'd even taken off his headgear, the better to look earnestly into the camera. Governor Boyd Mulholland—down-home man of the people, good-humored father surrogate for the frontier masses. Silver hair razored down a centimeter shy of military severity, features just that right blend of outdoor weathered and chocolate box handsome. Here was a man without the airs and graces of government or big business, a man who'd sit and take a beer with you come end of shift, whoever the hell you were, who'd wipe the sweat off his brow and curse good-naturedly at the itch of the unshielded Martian sun on your skin and his because, hell, these were the burdens of the frontier citizenship you both rejoiced in regardless of salary and station.

Here was a man *just like you*. Here was a man you could *trust*.

"In fact we welcome this audit, because it gives us the chance to show the folks back on Earth how much we have achieved." Lean cozily in to the camera. "My fellow pioneers, we have nothing to hide and everything to gain from a fresh assessment of our colony's strengths and weaknesses. That's what audits are for; it's why we have them. So I want to reassure everybody that there's nothing wrong here, nothing to worry about at all. It's Business as Usual on Mars, and Mars Is Open for Business. In fact, I want to welcome these Oversight officers, and I want you to welcome them, too. Let them see how we get things done out here on the frontier, let them experience being right out at the living edge of human expansion, because in the end . . ."

I grinned.

Look, you don't send a crash audit team across 200 million kilometers of interplanetary space because you think someone needs a few close tips on colonial management. Earth Oversight was COLIN's very own long arm of the law, with deep symbiotic bridges into government back home and an enforcement mandate that went way beyond the purely commercial. You didn't invoke them unless something out on the High Frontier was very seriously out of whack. This was a major crackdown in the making, and that knowledge was all over Mulholland's face. He looked like a man being forced to choke down spoiled oysters in zero G.

If Nikki Chakana had been clocking heavy overtime prettying up the meaner streets of Bradbury for this latest shuttle load of ultratrippers and new qualpro recruits, it was nothing compared with the work she'd have on her plate now. Earth Oversight banging on the door like the goons from Indenture Compliance rousting some base-camp brothel at dawn, Mulholland up out of bed and panicking, and every corporate scumbag from Eos to the Tharsis plateau scrambling to cover their unwiped ass. Someone had to fix this shit, and fast. Someone had to clean house. And my best guess was that our esteemed governor was going to get pretty short shrift from the upper levels of BPD if he went to them looking for help. You don't make commissioner in this town without being prepared to wink at a few irregularities, but Peter Sakarian was fundamentally straight. That had been his appeal, the reason he got parachuted into the post in the first place. He was a safe pair of hands so Mulholland wouldn't have to watch his back every hour of the day and night.

It was a tactic that had blown back spectacularly in the governor's face. Since Sakarian's promotion, the new commissioner had made no secret of his disdain for Mulholland's methods, and if my in-department sources were on the money, the two men had clashed more than once behind closed doors. Faced with *this* shit, Sakarian was going to take one huge step back, fold his arms, and watch as Earth Oversight hung Mulholland out to dry.

That left Nikki.

She'd be scurrying around like a ferrite bug in a mountain of rust, chewing up the governor's corroded mockery of colonial law enforcement particle by tarnished particle, transmuting it into the pure ore of correct procedure and blameless fresh air. Plugging leaks, disappearing inconvenient evidence and witnesses, getting stories straight. Terraforming local conditions, in other words, into some shiny simulacrum of what the good people back on Earth apparently expected things to be like out here.

Good luck with that, Lieutenant.

If my shin hadn't still been throbbing with stubborn pain, I might even have felt sorry for the bitch.

IT WAS A long night, but in the end, sure as a lobbyist gives blowjobs, morning rolled around, and the ceiling tiles flickered once more to life. The cell hatch cranked up a grudging forty centimeters, and a natty little drone on wheels barreled in through the gap, carrying an approximation of breakfast. It found me, by body heat I'd guess, rolled up to the bunk where I sat cross-legged, and stopped there like an eager puppy. The aroma of cheaply printed bacon and peppered rice wafted up at me from the plate.

I made myself eat—leaned down, took a rasher of the bacon between finger and thumb, and chewed it down. Then another. *Come on, over-rider, got to get the calories in.* I reached down for the waxy plastic canister that came with the meal, cracked the cap, and sipped at the watery caffeinated drink within. I don't think it was meant to be coffee.

On screen, I spotted Sakarian—caught by the cameras in a corridor at Police Plaza, ambushed between meetings and clearly holding back a desire to punch his interrogators in the face. He's a big guy, bulky by Martian standards, blunt features unmediated by any kind of gear frames or glass—he's kept the internal gear from his days as an Upland marshal—and he's still visibly dangerous if you know what to look for. But these days rank has put something of a leash on him.

"All right, I'm listening. Who's first?"

"Commissioner Sakarian—are you aware of the full extent of this COLIN audit? Are you aware that Article Eighteen has been invoked?"

Sakarian stared the speaker down, thin contempt in the set of his mouth, waiting for a question that merited an answer.

A second journalist jumped obligingly into the gap.

"Uh, Commissioner, will Bradbury PD be cooperating fully with the audit officers? And if so, how do you plan to enforce that?"

"In the usual fashion. Anyone who doesn't cooperate fully will be leaving their badge on my desk."

"How does Governor Mulholland feel about that?"

"Why don't you ask him?"

"But you've been in meetings with—"

"You saw the governor's statement this morning?"

"Uh, yes, but—"

"Then you know as much about the governor's state of mind as I do. I am not a politician; my role is law enforcement. And the law will be enforced."

"What about the Uplands, Commissioner?"

Just for a second, Sakarian wavered.

I saw it. Sat forward on the bunk, fascinated. The journalist who'd asked the question spotted it, too, went in for the kill.

"How will you handle the jurisdiction issue? Is Metro going to pull rank on the regional sheriffs? Will you have the marshals handle liaison?"

Sakarian got it together. "Go read the Charter, why don't you."

"The Charter states that—"

"That's all the Commissioner has time for," said a prissy-looking aide, cutting smoothly in from the side. "Sir, you are needed on the fifteenth floor."

Later on, pulling on that tiny loose thread, the same news team found themselves an Upland counterpoint—some hard-bitten sheriff's deputy up in Zubrin County, a sharp-end enforcer either dumb or don't-give-a-shit enough to speak his mind. He was pure media gold.

"No reason for those COLIN folks to come around here at all, far as I can see."

"By *here*, you're referring to the Upland zones?" There was a rich chocolate delight in the interviewing hack's voice as he realized what he'd reeled in. "Or do you mean *any* sheriff's department jurisdiction?"

The Uplander lawman shifted a wad of some stay-up-late weed he was chewing from one side of his mouth to the other. He sucked at his teeth and leaned into the screen.

"Talking about Mars," he enunciated carefully. "Talking about the whole goddamn planet. That clear enough for you?"

The interviewer let silence stretch out behind the words for effect. I rolled my eyes.

"So you're saying . . ." Let's have another histrionic pause here. "That COLIN has no place anywhere on Mars?"

"Nope. Not saying that. COLIN are welcome to come here and invest, just like anyone else. Mars is open for business. They can set up their holding companies, run their plants and their research projects, launch their outer system hulls from here if they want. But this ain't the Settlement years anymore. We're all squared away in the Valley now. We don't need Earth folk coming here and trying to tell us how to get things done."

"But the Mars Charter specifically—"

"Charter was written centuries ago. Written on Earth, for Earth's benefit. Why should something like that still be binding now?"

"The Charter guarantees our security." A prim note crept into the interviewer's voice now—he'd had his fun, he was heading back to safer ground. "Our safety at an interplanetary level and also in the event of any hostile incursions from Hellas."

The deputy grinned. "Think we can handle anything the Crater Critters throw at us. Don't need a fleet from Earth to sort that kind of static. Mars has got this; Valley hasn't needed Earth for more 'n a century now."

They pulled the plug on him then, killed the segment. Word likely came down from the control room sharpish—*the fuck are you playing at, you like your job or what? What's with this free-speech-for-assholes shit?*

Whether anyone had similar words for the deputy himself was a lot less easy to guess. Would depend on his immediate boss, his service record, what rep and relationships he'd forged along the way.

And how hard up they currently were for personnel.

Upland rules. Out there, beyond Bradbury city limits, it really is a whole other world.

SIX

"WE ARE NOT here in a punitive capacity," Audit Director Edward Tekele lied to the cameras with practiced COLIN aplomb. "The remit of Earth Oversight, both in this instance and more generally according to our charter, is to ensure the quality of systems and standards put in place for the good of all citizens both here on Mars and everywhere else in the Colony Initiative sphere. That is our sole mission."

He looked the part, too—kindly patrician features in weathered anthracite, close-cropped curly hair frosted with just enough gray to confer an elder statesman gravitas. They'd held off until well into the afternoon before they deployed this guy, and to judge by the way the media responded, he was worth the wait. Questions foamed up in the wake of his words like cracked champagne.

"How many auditors have you brought with you?"

"Has Earth Oversight issued arrest warrants for any ranking COLIN personnel?"

"—plan to cooperate with local authorities?"

"Is the governor under suspicion?"

"—long enough to get results?"

"What lines of inquiry do you—"

And a sudden wailing squall of feedback as whoever was running the sound feed decided the free press was getting a little too frisky for its own good. Edward Tekele frowned good-naturedly, waited it out.

The feedback shut down. He cleared his throat.

"If we could take the questions one at a time, please, and since my headgear is not yet synched with local dataflow, I'm afraid I will have to ask you for your names. Perhaps we could start with, yes—a gesture forward at the front rows—you, madame."

"How large—I'm sorry, Alex Rivera, *ValleyCat Vibe*—how large is the audit team you've brought with you?"

"We are 117 in total, including myself."

Low buzz of consternation in the pit among the journalists who were actually physically present for the briefing. And a ripple ran through the 'branegels floating at the back as those phoning in their presence tilted about to catch the response of the room.

Front and center, Rivera rallied, came back with most of her shock tamped down.

"That's, uh—that's a lot of people, Director Tekele. Are you really trying to tell us that with more than a hundred auditors ready to deploy, there's no punitive agenda here?"

"I certainly am, young lady. As you have already heard me promise, this—"

"Mr. Director!" The hectoring, overdramatic tone that cut across Tekele's was unmistakable by allegiance if not by actual voice. Male, midteens Mars-reckoned, and you could almost have lip-synched what was coming next. "Will you attempt to revoke the Valley Charter and Articles? Will you deploy armed agents on Martian soil?"

A long pause. Tekele peered out at his questioner as if the light in the briefing room had suddenly grown poor.

"And you are, sir?"

"My name is DeAres Contado, and we are legion. I stand witness for the *Mars First Intercept*, and I'm asking on behalf of the Provisional Citizens Council if this intrusion into Valley affairs is going to be imposed with armed force. How many of your personnel have military training?

How many of them will carry weapons? The people of Mars have a right to know."

An awkward silence settled in. Someone coughed. You could almost feel the other journalists rolling their eyes.

Perhaps Tekele picked up on it. He smiled a little.

"You mistake me for an admiral, Mr. . . . . Contado." Brief smattering of laughter from around the room. Tekele waited for it to wind down. "And I feel that even an admiral could hardly expect to take control of the Valles Marineris with a hundred men, armed or not. So—the answer to your question is *no, of course not.* We are not here to impose martial law. We are auditors, not marines; our concerns are not political. We are here in conjunction with the colony's own law enforcement mechanisms and will work in close cooperation with them." A measured pause. "Now, can I put anyone else's mind at rest about our lack of invasion plans?"

Another ripple of laughter, but like the first it was nervous, quick-drying—the forced laughs of an audience that wasn't comfortable with its entertainer, wasn't quite sure what the next joke might be or at whose expense.

"Any other questions, then?"

A hand went up in the pit. "Mike Tamang, *Bradbury City Prowl.* Do you currently hold any arrest warrants for Valley personnel?"

"No."

"When do you expect that to change?"

Tekele looked mildly put out. "I expect it to change, Mr. Tamang, at such time as we find evidence of individual malfeasance sufficient to justify issuing a warrant. We are here, initially at least, in a fact-finding capacity. The facts we find will inform how we proceed."

I snorted. *Yeah, and if you buy that, I've got a Martian ur-culture circuit board fossil out back I want to sell you cheap.*

On screen, Tekele was taking a question from the 'branegels.

"Elena Montalban, *Uplands Monitor,*" said the image of a shaven-headed woman with Andean lines to her face. "We were promised an extensive audit almost three years ago now, but it never materialized. And now you're here without any advance warning at all. Is this the same audit, running three years behind schedule?"

The measured COLIN smile again. "That's not something I can answer, I'm afraid. I was appointed to the post of audit director six months ago, and my time has been spent in marshaling the detail we need *this* time around. The '95 audit and its cancellation are beyond my remit. What I *can* tell you is that our concerns are all current."

"I'm sure they are. But even so, there must be ongoing issues that you've inherited from the shelved work. What about those?"

"I don't recall anything of that nature. Of course, all auditing draws on a continuity of data, but as to any specific holdover from three Mars years ago—that's a question you would need to put to my superiors back on Earth."

Pointed journalistic questions fired across a couple of hundred million kilometers of space for the attention of the most powerful corporate entity in the solar system. Good luck standing in that queue, Elena Montalban.

But Montalban either wasn't reading the signals or didn't care.

"Director Tekele, you cannot seriously ask us to believe that you're not conversant with the history of previous—"

"I think we'll take another question now. Yes, here in the front."

The camera, already tilting hastily away to find the new focus.

But not hastily enough to beat the sudden bright scribble of light as Montalban's 'branegel was summarily fried to a crisp.

AS A RULE and as a stubborn point of pride, I try not to be impressed by anything COLIN does. Usually it's not too hard. Fuck 'em and their midwives-to-mankind-in-space bullshit. Time served backstage with Blond Vaisutis took the sheen off that song pretty fast, and getting dumped on Mars corroded any residual sense of esteem I had left. The whole Valley is a fast lesson in what happens to corporate good intentions when the bottom line comes under stress.

Be that as it may—an audit crew 117 strong commanded an inevitable respect, even from me. They only sent 60-odd for the Titan Oligarch crisis, and that was reckoned a pretty big deal at the time. We had double that number right here in the beating heart of the Gash. Tekele could say what he liked; this was an invading army, and no one with behind-the-scenes levels of experience was going to believe anything different.

Certainly no one in Bradbury did. I spent the rest of the day watching a series of high-ranking city officials each do their own variation on one of two routines—either Mulholland's choking-down-rotten-oysters-with-the-dawn act or Sakarian's snappish business-as-usual shutdown.

And those were the high points.

The rest was an unending media drone of pretty infographics on how the audit might unfold, vacuous talking head commentary on what it all *meant*, and even more vacuous—when not summarily censored—street interviews with members of the public prejudged safe and stupid enough for screen exposure. Mingled in, you got the odd scene of actual street protest, there and gone too fast to catch more than a couple of 'branegel slogans and mixed about two to one with footage of excited crowds gathering for whatever ultratripper celebs the shuttle had brought this time. Some of the news carriers even threw in a rain parade or two from last night just to really confuse things. It was the Valley media's cocktail specialty—lazy-assed journalism stripped down to sound bites and sanitized dross, just enough to scratch the viewing public's itch for input. Raw spectacle shoved in a blender, shorn of all useful context or depth, then splattered across the audience's collective face like an endless series of cum shots.

Give Us a Minute, and We'll Give You . . . well, pretty much what you deserve, assholes.

And none of it could quite hide the colossal dearth of facts currently available to anyone in the media machine. More than anything, it reminded me of listening to the high, thin scream of air whistling out through a hull breach and into the vacuum beyond.

Eventually, I tuned it out. Went through some dissociative mind games out of the Blond Vaisutis training manual instead. I was a bit rusty at most of them; it had been a while since I'd needed the techniques. Tweaked opiates and Mark on Mars had been my dissociative tools of choice the last few years. But with a little effort the old ingrained habits came seeping back. I lost myself in the meditative sweet spot—and almost missed the rusty wheezing of the insulene dispenser as it prepared to cough up my covers for the night.

Looked like I'd managed to burn through the whole day already.

I reached down along the bunk one-handed and gathered in the wrapping as it cotton-candied up out of the vents. The psychosthenic trance dissipated as I pulled the insulene around me and let my attention drift back to the screen. Some lone reporter was pursuing a woman down the street at stiff marching pace, prodding at her with questions she showed no sign of wanting to stop and answer. Something familiar in the woman's stance, the set of her shoulders, or maybe just the cap of close-cropped iron gray hair. I'd muted the volume earlier—had to get off the bunk and kick it back up a couple of notches to hear what was being said.

". . . so presumably you'll welcome this audit?"

"Really?" Brusque impatience in her tone but room still for a rich layer of caustic irony on top. "Is that what you presume?"

"Well, uh, you have said, many times in fact, that, uh, *the Valley suffers under an ever-tightening yoke of corporate exploitation.*"

And so then, of course, I knew her. Click of recognition and a small, qualifying sadness. Like everybody does, she'd aged since I saw her last.

"Surely," the reporter pressed her, "You must be pleased that someone's finally come to rein that exploitation in?"

"Who says they've come here to rein anything in?"

"Audit Director Tekele just announced—"

"Tekele's a paid mouthpiece for the same interests that run the Valley. He's not going to change a single thing that matters."

Martina Sacran—the one-and-only, accept-no-imitations daughter of the Man Himself, for years heir apparent to the Struggle, and now Crowned Queen in Exile here on Mars, albeit queen of a shrunken and atomized realm whose savaged and defeated cohorts would have been a bitter disappointment to her father. I'd stood in her halls once or twice over the years and, my own bitterness aside, had not been overly impressed. There are places in the solar system where Mutualist political theory and Tech Socialism still draw a crowd, but the Gash isn't one of those places, and that was very likely Earth's purpose in dumping Sacran

fille here when her father died. She went through the motions, she organized and activized what followers and donors she could muster, but
mostly what she did was gather political dust. Quite enterprising of this
guy to track her down, really. It was certainly an angle no one else seemed
to have considered. Guaranteed that the segment would run, too, and
thus that our fearless freelance newshound would get paid, for scaring up
some harmless fun if nothing else. From what I'd heard, Sacran wasn't
even on a watch list these days.

"So you don't believe COLIN Earth cares about infringements of the
Valley Charter?" the reporter prodded.

Martina Sacran stalked on in silence. Quickened her pace a couple of
notches and took a corner into what I now recognized as Musk Plaza. A
sparse gathering of figures visible up ahead. It dawned on me she must be
on her way to a demonstration of her very own.

Not dissuaded, Mr. Fearless Freelance hurried to catch up.

"You're saying"—a little out of breath now—"that all the millions it
cost—to bring the auditors here—all the preparation—all that expense—
it's all a sham? All cosmetic?"

Something changed in the set of Sacran's shoulders. I don't know that
you could call it resolve; there was too much sag in it for that. But she
stopped and faced her tormentor. Handsome, narrow features under the
cap of close-cropped gray; her father lived on in the cheekbones and eyes,
the set of the jaw. But a lifetime of activism had put an edge on it all,
worked any excess flesh from the bone, given her in return the harsh lines
and crow's-feet, the gun-barrel stare.

"Look, fuckwit—I don't have the time to teach you the economics
you'd need to understand what's really going on here. But let's try a
primer. Do you have even the faintest fucking idea how much direct investment COLIN's corporate partners have sunk into the Valley just in
the last two years?"

"I, uh . . ." Of course he didn't.

"The disclosed figure is 128 trillion marins. Which, on past showing,
means you can put the actual figure somewhere close to 40 percent more.
Got that?"

You couldn't tell from the feed, but he must have nodded. Sacran nodded back, smeared a thin smile across her face. She knew she was the freak show, bait for a jaded audience appetite, just a tart little appetizer on the media buffet. She knew she was probably shouting into the void. But she took the shot anyway. A decade in exile and still she wasn't going to quit.

Maybe she didn't know how.

"Right. Let's take that famous handful of millions you were bleating about, the supposed cost of outfitting and deploying this audit. How do you think that stacks up against a couple of hundred trillion? The answer is *it doesn't*. It's a fistful of regolith thrown into the face of a Tharsis dust storm. Doesn't matter how hard you throw it, how high you aim—it isn't going to change a fucking thing."

Over my head, as if in emphasis, the ceiling tiles started dimming down. The rectangle of the screen was suddenly brighter again in the gloom, the grim handsome face staring out of it suddenly that much more isolated and intense. As if the phantoms of Sacran's past were gathering, squeezing the darkness in around her.

I felt an involuntary shiver of empathy. Bad politics isn't the only way to get yourself exiled out here.

"Now if you'll excuse me," she said with the same bleak lacing of irony she'd used before, "I've got a demonstration to address over there. See, even on Mars, some of us understand how deep these issues run. Even here, some of us are trying to change things at a level that matters. Come and listen; maybe you'll learn something."

No way to know if our intrepid reporter took up that invitation—the segment cut dead on a shot of Martina Sacran walking away, then we went to promos. I grunted, memories fluttering about in my head like spooked moths. I'd been up against quite a few Sacranites in my time, even before Carla Wachowski—back in the day, politically motivated piracy was an occupational hazard for any overrider on the outer system runs. Tougher to handle than the more casual profit-driven brands, but that wasn't the—

Soft clunk from the cell door.

Under the sticky wrap of the insulene shawl, I tightened up just a little. I didn't think anything was likely to happen to me in monitored custody, especially not now—with the storm boiling up around the audit, I was probably the last thing on BPD's mind. But the department has a long history of rendition to private law enforcement firms like MG4, where the Articles give convenient way to the rights of corporate bodies as citizens. You could fall a long way into the gray area that shit opened up and hurt yourself badly hitting the ground.

Pale light filtered in around the edges of the hatch. The ceiling tiles blazed back up into sudden life, the door grumbled away into its recess, sticking a bit. A uniformed cop I didn't know peered into the cell.

"You. Veil. Get your ass out here. You got a visitor."

SEVEN

THEY TOOK ME up to the interview rooms braced between two thickset zombie squad types while a third guy brought up the rear from six meters back, twitch-gun drawn. At some point during my incarceration, either someone had looked at my record or Nikki had passed the word back: *watch this fucker.*

"How's the audit looking?" I asked them brightly as we all got into the elevator.

The butt of the twitch-gun clocked me hard behind the ear, sent me stumbling into the closing doors. I had to brace against them with both hands not to go down. Dark tinsel pinpricks across my vision, the churn of my blood in my ears.

"He make a move for your riot stick there, Paco? Did I see that?"

The thickset cop on the left grunted. "Might have. Pretty fucking dumb if he did."

"That's right." The gun muzzle jabbed me sharply in the lower back. Its owner leaned in close. "Sort of thing could get a guy blood in his piss for a week."

"We'd need to check out the securicam," Paco said stolidly. "To know for sure, I mean."

"Yeah, afterward. But you know, those systems glitch out all the time. Seen it happen myself. You can lose *hours* of coverage." Snapped fingers next to my ear. "Just like that."

"It'd just be our word on it, then."

"Y'all think Nikki'd have a problem with that?"

"Can't see it myself."

Grim chuckles all around. I raised my head and looked at them, mirrored and distorted in the battered aluminum of the elevator doors, like creatures squeezing through from some other dimension. Or men twisted out of human shape by brutal alien forces.

"Got any other pressing questions, Veil?"

I said nothing. The elevator chimed and stopped. I got myself carefully out of my braced position, took my hands off the doors just as they split apart. The zombie twins ushered me out and into the corridor beyond.

Like most modern buildings in the Gash, Police Plaza was built soaring and tall, and the interview rooms were a fair way up. We stood facing stupendous floor-to-ceiling window views out over the twinkle and flare of Bradbury's lights. A quick grab after landmarks—the COLIN tower in all its coruscating nighttime glory, Hayek Boulevard lying straight as a broadsword across the downtown, the colossal slab of the Mineral Rights Building on Sixty-Second Street—I reckoned we were facing more or less south. Instinctively, my eyes sought the edge of the lights, the darkened plain beyond, and the vast loom of the valley wall beyond that. Hard to tell if you could make it out for real at that distance or if your eyes were just insinuating the detail.

"Come on, asshole. You've seen this before."

As if to prove him wrong, fitful purple aurorae flickered and smeared out across the sky—loose photons up near the UV end, spilling from some energy-rich adjustment between Lamina layers. For a couple of heartbeats, we all stood entranced.

"That's got to be from the rain, right?" Paco murmured.

The moment broke. The other zombie squad guy grunted. "Could be any fucking thing. Lamina tech, who knows what they're doing up there every goddamn hour of the day and night? Are we going to deliver this piece of hib shit or what?"

Along the curve of the corridor, picking up pace, away from the view and into a passageway of multiple facing doors. Next to each a softly glowing occupancy panel in red or blue. From the number of reds and the traffic stuffing up the corridor, it looked like a busy night. A pair of Indenture Compliance heavies stood around outside one door, chewing industrial quantities of stay-up-late weed and barking laughs at each other's bad jokes. I felt the twinge of memory, tight enough it was almost nostalgia. Farther on, an immaculately attired lawyer brushed past us trailing expensive perfume and talking rapidly to her headgear. The sheen on her suit and her perfect pale skin both screamed Marstech molecular systems, no doubt some colossally expensive recent-release suite. Another lawyer, not so well dressed or scented, sat on a bench outside another red door, headgear off, pinching the brow of his nose and blinking bruised-looking eyes that suggested he could have used some of what the IC guys were chewing.

Spot the public defender.

Nine doors up on the right, we stopped and Paco tagged the red panel with his signet ring. The door trundled back, and they shoved me through. Narrow window at the back, showing a slice of the same skyline I'd already seen. A battered alloy table took up the center of the room, a couple of cheap carbon-fiber chairs on either side. A suited Chinese woman sat with her back to the view, legs crossed, hands in her lap. Elegance to match the pricey lawyer we'd passed in the corridor and something on the table in front of her—a small, shallow dish filled with radial ribs and a blunt central nub like some upended mushroom in gunmetal and black. Resonance scrambler; looked like one of the new Sennheiser models. Pricey tech.

The twitch-gunner leaned in after me.

"Y'all got fifteen minutes," he drawled, and was gone.

The door sliced shut.

"This is unexpected," I said. "As I recall, you weren't supposed to be here until the day after tomorrow."

She gestured me to sit. Her headgear lenses were no less impenetrable than they had been the last time I saw her, in the blue gloom of the mezzanine level at Vallez Girlz. Her face was as impassive as when she walked away and left me her chair at Sal's table. Still, there was something in the way she sat now that trembled at the edges.

And she was two days early.

"What's going on?" I asked, not sitting down. "You clean up at Sal's okay?"

"It is in hand." The scrambler deadened the echo from both our voices, put an oddly muffled bluntness on everything, like talking to someone wrapped in cotton wool. "The police have taken witness statements from my people, all of whom corroborate the same story. A masked figure appeared out of nowhere; no one's very sure what he looked like. You shot at him with the twitch-gun but hit the others instead, you attempted to wrestle him to the ground but failed, he murdered Quiroga and was gone." She paused delicately. "If it even was a he. No one's very sure about that either. They were in a state of confusion, saved from blindness by their headgear but still very dazed and shaken by the violence."

"Shaken by the violence. Right. Nice touch." I pulled out the chair. "And what does Sal's security have to say about all that?"

"Nothing very much. They have been persuaded that aligning their statements with the new management is the wisest move." A negligent shrug. "They were in any case blinded by the flash."

I sat down. "All right, that should hold up. No one's going to buy it, but it'll wash. What about my money?"

"It will be drip-fed out to you over the next several months as we take over Quiroga's operation and secure his revenue streams."

"That wasn't the agreement."

"The agreement was necessarily elastic, Mr. Veil, as I'm sure you will recall. I'm afraid our cash flow is undergoing unforeseen scrutiny at the moment."

The audit, the fucking audit.

And suddenly I felt a lot less smug about Mulholland's gubernatorial discomfort. Fine that the asshole in chief and his cohorts were panicking, but it hadn't occurred to me that his problems might become mine. The joys of trickledown—I guess all those guys they name the boulevards for around here must have been on to something after all.

"Unforeseen scrutiny, eh?" Abruptly, stomach tightening, I saw where this was going. "Let me guess—this is going to put a dent in our schedule for getting me out of here."

She hesitated. "It's the opinion of the lawyer we have retained that any untoward haste in this matter can only attract attention we would rather avoid. He believes we should let matters sit, at least until due process begins to take its course."

"Due pro—" I leaned in. Hauled my voice down to a corrosive hiss. "We agreed three weeks, a month at most. Do you have any idea what due process looks like around here? For a Strip killing? And with everyone scrambling to cover their shit before Earth Oversight sniffs it out? I could be sitting in a cell until next fucking year before they get off their collective ass and decide to work the backlog."

"That is a risk, yes."

"Get me another lawyer. One with a work ethic."

"We only have the one lawyer. And contracting someone new would present the same problems of exposure."

"That's nothing to how exposed you're going to feel if I get sick of staring at the walls in here and start talking about our arrangement over Sal."

Short icy pause. As if I'd told some joke in very poor taste or spit on the table between us.

"I do not believe you'll do that," she said with poise that missed being steady by a micron. "You . . . have as much to lose as we do."

"Not really." I leaned in closer. "Remember how I told you, back when we put this together—with a piece of shit like Sal, BPD is just going to go through the motions? Well, that has a useful corollary here. See, they won't much care *who* blew him out the lock if they can shut down a Crater Critter operation for the price of letting me walk."

"We had an agreement, Mr. Veil."

"Yeah, and I'm not the one breaking it. Yet."

"We appreciate that the situation is . . . inconvenient."

I smiled thinly, nodded. "Inconvenient. Look . . . Hsu, right? Means 'Gradual'?"

"Yes." Guardedly.

"Well, right now I'd say it fucking suits you." I gestured out at the floor-to-ceiling slice of Bradbury skyline framed in the window. "Out there, I've got a mortgaged Dyson capsule with less than half the value paid off, and it's sitting in rented cradle space. It's not much, but it's home and I'm leveraged up the ass paying for it. In a little over eight months from now I have to crawl back inside that capsule and go to sleep. And I don't wake up again for four months."

"Your physiology is . . . we are aware of the constraints it places on you."

"Are you? Well, one of those constraints is *getting fucking paid.* The installments on the capsule, the rack rental, all that has to go on turning over while I'm down. I don't know how you manage that end of things over in Hellas, but around here? I miss a payment, I fall through the fucking cracks. So you tell me, *Gradual*—how the fuck am I supposed to earn the stored fat I need for those four months if I'm banged up in here on account of your cash-flow problems and your craven asshole lawyer?"

"We of course regret the—"

I got up abruptly. The cheap carbon chair went over with the force of it. She twitched back, hands rising, ready. Most of these Crater triad guys have some moves; their 489 wouldn't draft them in for duties in the Gash if he didn't think they could handle themselves. So I stood still long enough to let her realize there wasn't going to be a fight. I spaced my words evenly, reaching for a calm I didn't feel.

"Don't lie to me, Gradual. You don't regret shit right now." I leaned down on the table. "But you're going to if I'm not back on the streets forty days from now as per our agreement. I don't plan to sit on my hands in holding for the next eight months because you people have lost your balls in the face of a little operational complexity. Now you go back and tell that to your 489, because we're all done here."

I turned my back. Went to the door.

"Mr. Veil?"

I paused, one hand lifted to tap for exit. "What?"

"I *am* the 489 for this context."

I lowered my hand, turned back to face her. She looked back at me out of lenses gone suddenly transparent—almond-shaped eyes hard and watchful but offering no threat I could discern. 489—traditional triad notation—command enforcer. She'd been central to my dealings with the Crater crew when I set up Sal's death four months back, but it never occurred to me she might actually be heading up their soldiers. And now they'd sent her in to apologize. Her choice or someone else's back in Hellas and higher up—didn't really matter which. Either way, this was a bridge it might be better not to burn.

"All right," I said quietly.

"We are not . . . disrespecting you or your contribution. We will get you out. But you must allow us the flexibility to do so elegantly."

Like I have any fucking choice.

"Fine. You go ahead and get it done elegantly. Or you do it like a fuck in mud. I really don't care. Just get it done inside forty days."

I reached up and rapped at the door behind me. It slid back almost instantly, caught me off balance, and I half stumbled, half fell through the gap—

More or less into Nikki Chakana's arms.

EIGHT

"LOT OF EXOTIC new friends you've got all of a sudden, Veil. What's the matter, you developing a taste for Crater Critter pussy?"

I followed her into her office. Looked around for a chair. "You jealous?"

She slid behind her desk, got seated. Pulled a bottle of JD Red from amid the junk on the desktop and cracked it open. "Glasses in the cleanser. There, behind the—never mind, we'll use these. Sit."

I dragged my chair up to the desk and sat. Against the backdrop of another skyline view in the window behind her, Chakana poured into two grubby-looking shot glasses I hadn't spotted in the surrounding debris. She swept a tangle of harnessing and soft weblar armor patches off onto the floor, drove one of the glasses across the cleared space toward me.

"So."

"So," I agreed. "What are we drinking to?"

SOMEWHERE, IN ONE of those fuckwit lifestyle pieces foisted on you in places you find yourself having to wait, you'll doubtless have seen mention of the Ares Acantilado. *Seven Wonders of a Brave New World* was the tagline, maybe. *Eight Engineering Miracles You'll Barely Believe. Nine Most Luxurious Hotels in Human Space.* That kind of thing. And— implied but never actually stated in as many words—*Ten Places We'd Be Fucking Flabbergasted to See Your Shit-Poor Ass Ever Get Into.* Like the base concept of Marstech branding itself, exclusivity is key, and the Ares Acantilado delivers to the hilt. It sits fifty kilometers west of Wells and the nanorack ancillary settlement, fully pressurized and hanging off the top of the Valley's southern wall like a big bunch of mirror-skinned cubist grapes. From the windows underfoot as you walk the observation deck, not to mention the transparent bases of its three swimming pools, the hotel offers a gut-swooping uninterrupted view nine kilometers down to the valley floor. You can get a couple of inverted penthouse suites with the same effect if you're so minded, but most of the accommodation aims for slightly less menacing views—the standard is a picture window prospect out across the Gash at near Lamina height.

They say the trigger waves at sunrise and sunset are really something.

The vast majority of the Acantilado's paying guests come to it direct from Wells Terminal and the shuttle decant. They ride a pressurized out-door crawler with luxury fittings and display screen panels instead of portholes, from which they'll be delivered directly into the belly of a client experience probably not that much different from their day-to-day super-rich existence back home on Earth. Tastefully appointed interiors, solici-tous real-human attendants, a brisk sense of business being taken care of on your account. The warmth and security of total insulation from the real world outside never skips a beat.

We weren't guests. We came up the service elevator.

"Nice view." I leaned on the window guardrail, peering down at the grungy abyss below. Still a bit giddy from Chakana's whiskey. "You ever wonder what it'd be like to live up here, Nikki?"

"No. Why don't you sit down?"

We were alone in the elevator car—Chakana had flashed her palm at the queue of coveralls behind us as we got in, told them bluntly *police business,* and hit the doors-close panel. Now she had the rider's bench to herself. She sat sprawled in the center of its grimy exhausted nanofab surface, two meters away on the other side of the car from me, gritted around her tiredness, and glowering into the middle distance.

"All right." I faced her, my back to the drop and the view. Hitched myself up and into a precarious sitting position on the rail. "So you want to tell me a bit more about this auditor I'm supposed to baby-sit?"

Chakana rolled her eyes. "Like I told you, she's a little cog in the big Earth Oversight machine. Strictly second-team stuff. She's here to look into the lottery protocols and the link-up with Vector Red Haulage. And she wants to reopen the Pavel Torres inquiry."

"Is that independent of the main audit?"

"I don't *know*, Veil. It's a fucking audit. You think these Earth assholes are going to tell me anything they don't absolutely have to?"

Fair point. I shifted sideways a little on the rail, staring downward as morning moved in on the Valley. Gargantuan spills and tailings all along the wall we were crawling up, each turning slowly from silhouette to rouged and textured geo-mass as sunrise thrust its fingers down into the Gash. Out across the empty space beyond, dimly red-tinged mists and fledgling cloud from some inversion cap we'd come up through earlier were lit suddenly incandescent; below that, the slow retreat of darkness back along the rubbled Valley floor to the west, the distant glimmer of the lights from nameless towns still awaiting the broadsword sweep of the dawn.

Most of me was worrying about Gradual.

She'd seen me stumble into Chakana on my way out of the interview room. She'd be keeping tabs on me anyway, and in a matter of hours she'd know I was back on the streets. The way our conversation had gone, she probably was going to draw some ugly conclusions from that set of facts.

A situation like that doesn't have a good shelf life. I needed to make some calls and soon. But my headgear was still at home, and getting hold of a disposable set wasn't an option. And Chakana didn't look like she was going to let me out of her sight until this—whatever *this* turned out to be—was set up and running to her satisfaction.

"Something bugging you, overrider?"

"Not really." I tipped my head back against the glass and faked a yawn. Looked up to where the approaching cubist bulk of the hotel winked and shone in the full wash of the sun. I jabbed a thumb upward. "See, that's what I'm talking about. It's got to take what, thirty staff to run this place? Forty, maybe."

Chakana looked at me, red-rimmed eyes behind her gear lenses narrowed in what I had to hope was irritation and not suspicion. Back in the day, my Blond Vaisutis training had included some pretty tight gestalt cloaking techniques, but like everything else from that life, it had grown rusty over time. I didn't know what tells my body language and electrophysiology might be flagging up for Chakana's state-of-the-art BPD gear.

"Say thirty." I forged on, sowing what distraction I could. "And they're living canned the whole time—come end of shift, you just bus back to Wells and the personnel dorm, that's another tin can, with a little tin can on wheels to get you there. It's got to be like living right back in the Settlement era."

"Veil, I really don't fucking care."

"You might have to one day. I'm telling you, you spend too long canned, it starts to twist your head. Easy to end up psychotic."

She cranked a cavernous yawn of her own. "Well, you'd know, I guess."

"Back in the day, it wouldn't matter because the Settlement crews got rotated. But no one's rotating these poor bastards—they just got Quality, Choice, and Freedom to be out of work if they don't like the terms."

"You're breaking my heart. What are you, a Sacranite now?"

I grimaced. "I'm just saying, from an enforcement point of view, it's a bomb waiting to go off. One day the pressure is going to blow for someone up here, and you're going to find yourself dealing with a bunch of massacred ultratrippers or a hostage situation."

"I doubt that." The car slowed to a halt, juddered, and clanked as it locked in at the top of the track. Soft hiss of the pressure matching. Chakana got up and stretched. "Mostly, they just get wasted and cut each other up over in Wells on a Friday night. And that's not my problem, is it?"

The doors trundled back, revealed unsmiling faces and MG4 uniforms behind a security station. Chakana's grim face and curtly flashed palm holo got us through in short order. Then it was another elevator up a short hop to the hotel's main lobby and obs deck. Big, hushed spaces, decor in burnished bronze and oatmeal plush. Chakana crossed the lobby at an impatient lope, took the two steps down into the lounge, and stood looking around. There was subtle lighting in the corners, carefully designed not to interfere with the view down through the floor panels, around each of which were clustered big squashy sofas and armchairs. With ruddy early-morning light welling up through the glass, it looked at a glance as if the seating had been arranged around a series of barbecue pits just getting fired up.

"We in some kind of hurry?" I asked.

"Yeah. After I drop you, I'm going home to bed."

"Going to miss me?"

She curled her lip. Kept on scanning the lounge. "Getting tired of telling you this, Veil. I'll fuck you when you're the last man alive on Mars and I can't find a woman I like owns a strap-on. Ah."

Over toward one wall, a dark woman in a pale gray lounge suit was seated facing the room. She rose now, lifted a hand in greeting. Chakana led me over and made the introductions.

"Ms. Madekwe. Lieutenant Dominica Chakana, Bradbury Homicide. This is Hakan Veil, the specialist I told you about. Veil, this is Madison Madekwe from COLIN's Office of Internal Systems Compliance, Frontier Oversight Division."

We shook. Dry, faintly callused grip on the slim hand offered, some firm strength in the clasp she made. The face looking back at me was alert and intelligent, something faintly familiar in the features. Broadly African heritage—square jaw, long-lipped mouth, flare and lift in the cheekbones and nose. Inky skin, a little grayed out with decanting, and wide-set dark eyes, watchful behind her gear; something soundless and bright seemed to happen between us as I met her leveled gaze, something that spiked down hard toward my belly and balls. Madison Madekwe was tall, I realized, pretty much my height, full-figured and long-limbed to match, and with that subtle sense of bulk you get off anyone just in from Earth, all the muscle mass they're carrying that'll take months on Mars to slim down from, even with code-fly help. Wide shoulders and long slim hands, breasts and hips carrying pleasantly rounded weight. She lapped at my eyeballs like a tide, and all I wanted, there and then, was to taste her.

"Mr. Veil." Throaty roughness on her voice, but then everybody tends to come out of cryocap like that. She let go of my hand a little abruptly; she'd felt the sudden gut-deep spike as well. "It is, uh, very kind of you to make yourself available like this. I am sorry to bring you in at such an antisocial hour."

"No problem." I shot a glance at Chakana. "I was up anyway."

"Well, that's good. Myself, I'm afraid I have yet to adjust to local time. And I seem to have plenty of energy to spare, so . . ." She spread her hands. "Work is the obvious outlet, is it not?"

Her hair was long, dragged severely back in slim cornrows dusted Kandinsky purple, then coiled and wrapped tight to the back of her head in a ball. Against her brow, her headgear made a slim gull-wing swoop in gold, frosted beneath with an ultranarrow band of transparent glass so it looked like some kind of inverted low-slung diadem. Couple of COLIN rank tats on the right cheek like small dark tears down from that eye. Hard to tell her age; she had a forceful grown-young-woman allure that itched in the pit of my gut like tiny flickering flames, but it mapped onto the kind of upper-echelon good looks you can keep pretty much indefinitely if you have the money.

The faint familiarity clicked, popped into full focus, as I made her from the shuttle footage I'd watched in the cell last night. Her hair had been straightened out to a glossy stream, cascading to shoulder length, and there'd been a smile—your basic corporate promo shot. But the bones and the watchful dark eyes were the same. The leveled stare held you like a gun, like a question you couldn't easily answer. It was a pretty lush figure Madison Madekwe kept under her expensively tailored lounge suit while her eyes dared you to even think about dropping your gaze to look.

I held her stare. "Let's get to work, then."

"Yes, of course. The matter at hand. I understand Lieutenant Chakana has briefed you on our need to keep this low profile."

Lieutenant Chakana hadn't.

In fact, so far the full content of Chakana's instructions had been *look, just keep this Oversight bitch out of my hair for the next couple of weeks.*

Take her where she wants to go, show her what she wants to see, answer any questions she has, and make sure she doesn't get hurt.

"We've looked at the logistics of that," I said carefully.

"I'm glad to hear it. Shall we all sit down?"

WE GOT BREAKFAST off a 'branegel menu as it floated filmily past. An actual Islay single malt from actual Islay on actual Earth leaped off the display at me, but without my headgear I had no way to order it. Probably just as well, since I had no way to pay for it either—the price tag was higher than I've seen for some entire asteroids. So I nodded glum assent at Madison Madekwe's suggestion of a shared breakfast meze tray and coffees, and we all settled back in the big squashy loungers to talk about COLIN Oversight.

She wanted, she said, to be clear. Procedures at Vector Red Haulage were facing general audit along with everything else, and of course that included the lottery protocols. This was standard operating procedure, nothing more. However . . .

She had the good grace to look uncomfortable.

"Well, as I'm sure you're aware, the situation with Horkan Kumba Ultra is a delicate one at present."

"Yeah—be a shame if they lost their shuttle franchise less than a year after confirmation."

Chakana darted me a venomous shut-the-fuck-up look. Madekwe either didn't catch it or was being polite. She inclined her head.

"I'm glad you appreciate the implications. It is, of course, essential that HKU's portfolio on Mars be utterly beyond reproach. As with any other heritage corporation, the fallout from even minor operational impropriety can be severe. Thus the Torres case. What I am tasked to do, at least initially, is to examine Vector Red's general systems through the lens of this particular occurrence. It is an obvious anomaly, and to analyze it I shall need to form a clear picture of Pavel Torres. In short, I must answer the question—what kind of man doesn't show up for a ticket home?"

"A Man That's Happy on Mars," I said, deadpan.

"Yes, but surely . . ." The circuit closed—pretty sharp for someone only a handful of hours out of cryocap. "Oh, I see. Yes, I've seen the ads. Very droll, Mr. Veil."

I shrugged. "It's a gift."

"Moving *on*," Chakana said severely. "Ms. Madekwe would like to trace Torres's colleagues and known associates for interview."

"Shouldn't be too hard to do."

"Quite. I've explained you're the ideal man for this, given that so many of these people are likely to be out in the Uplands."

I blinked. "You're too kind."

"I understand you have worked extensively in Uplands contexts before, Mr. Veil."

Slow nod. "Among other places, yes."

The food arrived. Pan-fried bacon and chicken in marinated strips, miso bowls, black olives and cubed white cheese, freshly baked bread rolls with the steam still rising from them, French and Spanish omelets, a couple of dishes I didn't recognize. Coffee, richly fragrant, chilled fruit juices in carafes, a huge jug of water, and heavy cloth napkins. We waited in discreet silence while the well-groomed young server laid it all out, asked if there was anything else we needed, and then bowed away. Madison Madekwe gestured us at the spread, then plowed into the meat dishes with both hands and an abandon that made me like her a little bit more.

"This is really very good," she said when she came up for air.

I sipped at one of the miso bowls, dueling hard stares back and forth across the table with Chakana. Shame the running-hot end of the cycle wouldn't let me feel anything approaching actual hunger for a good few days yet. The lieutenant gave me a grim little smile, like a secret shared, and broke gaze. She picked at a plate of Spanish omelet, drank some juice. Then she slanted her eyes up and left as if catching an incoming call from her headgear. She dabbed at her mouth with her napkin and got up.

"I'm afraid I have to go. Thank you for the breakfast, Ms. Madekwe. Veil should be able to take it from here. But if you do need anything else, don't hesitate to get in touch."

"Of course." Madekwe stood and shook Chakana's hand. "A great pleasure to meet you."

"Likewise."

I went on feigning interest in my food long enough for Madekwe to get seated again and for Chakana to get as far as the edges of the lounge. Then I snapped my fingers, *hey, sudden thought,* and bounced to my feet.

"I'm sorry, would you excuse me a moment? There's something I need to clear up with the lieutenant."

Madison Madekwe nodded, still chewing, waved me off with every appearance of casual unconcern. But there was something odd in those hard dark eyes as she watched me get up. I filed it away for later, made long strides after Chakana, and caught up with her by the elevators, well out of sight of my brand-new client.

"*Just* a fucking minute."

She turned with elaborate poise, cocked an eyebrow at me. "Problems already?"

"You told me I was baby-sitting a procedural audit officer around town. What's this shit about the Uplands?"

Chakana shrugged. "Torres worked the Uplands mostly. It's where he went missing. Makes sense our illustrious auditor would want to go there, right? What's the matter, your lung turbos not up to scratch anymore?"

I glanced around. Lowered my voice. "You really want me to take her up there? Off the official tour route, no guardrail, no shiny brochure? You think Mulholland's going to like that?"

"Mulholland's up to his lip in shit right now. He's just going to have to let some things go. He asked for someone to ride shotgun on this one, to keep it low-key and off the books, and you're it. Now suppose you go back there and earn your get-out-of-jail-free privileges like we agreed."

The elevator arrived with a soft chime. I nodded curtly.

"All right, then. But you want to tell me why we're walking back through an investigation three months dead when by now Bradbury's finest should have the whole thing chopped and stored? I mean, once this blew up, Metro stepped in, right?"

"Like we always do." The weariness in Chakana's voice sounded bone deep.

"Right. Missing lottery winner—no one's going to leave something that explosive to the locals. You'd never hear the end of it. Got to be you or the Marshal Service, and the marshals aren't going to lift a finger for some low-rent scumbag like Torres. So Metro Missing Persons takes it, and they run their own case. Interviews, surveillance footage, background check—all written up and filed for the record. Even Missing Persons couldn't fuck that up, could they? Or did you guys not bother for an Upland work gang coolie?"

The elevator doors began to close. Chakana slapped a hand back against them without looking around, stilled the motion before it got properly started. She tried to look pissed off for a moment, then gave it up. Too tired to care.

She sighed. "I'm murder police, Veil. You know that. This was never mine. No body, no sus-circ worth a damn, and you know how often fuck-wits like Torres go extracurricular up there. Damn right, it got handed off to MMP. Tomayro took it, and he looked busy with it, made the right noises till the shouting died down, then dropped it like a puff-down pay-load. You want to go look at their files, be my guest."

"I don't get the impression Ms. Kandinsky Cornrow back there wants to sit and look at files."

Another patented Chakana shrug. "So find something else for her to do. Jesus, Veil, do I have to write you a manual? She's a concerned Earth bureaucrat slumming it on Mars. Show her around the Uplands, show her a slice of the lowlife. Show her a good time if she's up for it, I really don't care. Just keep her out of my hair for the duration."

She stepped into the elevator. The doors tried to close again. I thumped a fist sideways against one leading edge and stood in the gap.

"This is bugshit, Nikki. No one ships all the way from Earth for men like Pavel Torres. And *Mulholland* signed off on this investigation? Gubernatorial juice, direct from the Windward Office, all for some second-rate missing persons procedural?"

"No—all for the protection of Long Fall Lottery Holdings, Vector Red Haulage, and Horkan Kumba Ultra's good name. You heard Madekwe back there. Heritage corporation. They don't like to be embarrassed."

I shook my head, "That's not it. There's something else going on here, and you know it."

"So find out what it is, overrider." Chakana leaned in, took my lapels between fingers and thumbs, and gave them a tiny, straightening tug. "Find out what it is, bring it to me, and if it's anything halfway significant, maybe you'll get a cookie. Until then, you're on tour guide duties. And be grateful I'm shorthanded right now, because it's the only fucking reason you're not still locked down in holding. Now, get your hand off my elevator doors and go hold up your end of the deal."

She looked pointedly at my fist until I moved it. The elevator chimed its departure. The doors resumed motion, kissed together with soft precision. Left me staring at their burnished bronze facings, seeing myself reflected back.

Like something stupid and prehistoric, trapped in amber.

NINE

MS. KANDINSKY CORNROW didn't want to look at files.

"That's something we can come back to," she said with the small, tight grimace of someone enduring a sharp pain politely. "I already have a basic digest, for what that is worth. Which isn't very much, I'm afraid. I'd prefer not to point fingers this early, but it's clear that both the original investigation and the follow-up were handled badly. The last investigating officer, this"—shift of gaze under the diadem headgear, brief pause—"Borgia Tomayro. Do you know him?"

"Mostly by reputation." I lifted a fruit juice carafe from the table, found a glass. Still nowhere close to hungry. "But I've had dealings with him once or twice, yes."

"Your impressions?"

"Lives up to his reputation." Pouring judiciously. "Slack. Lazy. Mildly corrupt."

"Corrupt." Like she was tasting the word for the first time.

"Yeah, but nothing you wouldn't expect." I sat back and sipped my juice. Gestured with the glass. "Missing Persons is the parking orbit for guys like that. Not hardwired to the job enough to get rank anywhere useful, not incompetent enough to get fired."

"So corruption in itself wouldn't be enough?"

"I'm sorry?"

"Corrupt police officers don't get fired on Mars?"

I looked at her for a long moment to be sure she was serious. Then laughter bubbled up from my belly unbidden, split my mouth around a grin. Loose and easy, no mockery in it. It felt surprisingly good.

Her lips tightened. "I do not see the humor here, Mr. Veil."

"Welcome to the High Frontier." Ladling the bland tones of a quarantine AI into my voice. *"Please be aware that your body may be some time adjusting to local conditions.* Your expectations also, I'm afraid, Ms. Madekwe."

"I am here as part of an extraordinary audit for COLIN Earth Oversight," she said stiffly. "My expectations reflect the mission briefing I received on Earth, which, I have to say, did not paint a flattering picture. So I am not shocked or even very surprised. I just didn't expect you to admit these things so openly."

"I'm not admitting anything. I'm not a cop."

"Lieutenant Chakana said you were attached to the Bradbury Police Department."

"The lieutenant has a sense of humor. Any attachment I have to Bradbury PD is loose at best. And while we're on the subject, not by my choice."

There was a brief pause while Madison Madekwe digested that. Hard to tell, looking at her face, if the revelation pleased her.

"I see," she said finally. "Well, thank you for your candor, Mr. Veil. I'm sorry that your assignment is not to your liking."

"I've had worse."

"I cannot say I'm impressed, though. That the department can't—or perhaps can't be bothered to—find an actual police officer for the duty."

"Look on the bright side—if you'd had a real cop for an escort, he'd probably hate you."

"And you don't?"

Her gaze was a challenge across the table. I felt the little flickering flames in my gut again and smiled to mask the arousal.

"Hate's a luxury I don't often allow myself, Ms. Madekwe. It gets in the way."

More quiet while she poured herself another coffee, stirred in milk and sugar, gave herself time to regroup. I waited out the ritual. Caught myself wondering if there wasn't still some way to get that Islay single malt ordered on her tab before we left.

"All right, then, another question." Still idly stirring her coffee. "If the Bradbury Police Department habitually parks its worst officers in Missing Persons, how does anyone reported missing ever get found?"

I shrugged. "Anyone who matters isn't relying on the police. Government and senior corporate all have dedicated security teams. Most visiting qualpros get a cut-rate version of the same thing written into their contracts. Hard to persuade the talent you need to come out here otherwise. Plus, it's a productivity issue. Some qualified guy on a three-year turnaround disappears, COLIN's losing a substantial chunk of their investment for every week he's off the grid."

"Torres has been gone for the best part of three months. Isn't that a productivity issue for someone?"

"I doubt it. Depends what kind of work he was doing when he disappeared, of course. But from what I hear via the lieutenant, he was semi-skilled labor at best. Sometimes Indenture Compliance will track and trace those guys to make an example if there's a specific bounty in it. But if there isn't . . ." I spread my hands. "And that's if he was working at all."

"I thought everybody on Mars worked." Her mouth bent—not sure I'd call it a smile. A couple of millimeters of irony glinted in her eyes like a half-pulled blade. "We hear so much about it back on Earth. *Frontier necessity, the fully engaged society. The human spirit, rising to the challenges of a new world and the dawn of a new era.* Isn't that how it goes? I thought everybody out here *had* to work."

"Everybody out here has to make a living. It's not the same thing."

She drank from her coffee cup, held it in both hands, and looked at me over the rim. "And how do *you* make your living, Mr. Veil?"

"Right now, by keeping you out of trouble."

The moment stretched and held, and we matched stares in silence until it stopped being fun. Madison Madekwe set her coffee carefully aside. Her voice came out icy.

"I think, Mr. Veil, that you have misunderstood both your brief and mine. I requested a local police guide and adviser, nothing more. I don't foresee getting *into* any trouble, and I certainly don't need someone to protect me."

"You will if you plan to hit the Uplands asking questions about men who disappeared into thin air. That's a hazardous hobby. The locals aren't all that friendly up there at the best of times, and this is very far from the best of times. You're going to stick out like a club dancer's tits."

"Is that so?"

"I'm afraid it is. Your face is all over the feeds, Ms. Madekwe, along with everyone else in this little accounting hit squad COLIN has put together. And now every pair of eyes in the Gash is watching to see what you do next. I made you from the passenger manifest footage less than a minute after meeting you. There's no reason to think anyone else is going to find it more difficult." I leaned in, a little surprised to hear the urgency in my own voice. "Meantime, I can guarantee that the governor's people are out there already, stirring up some good old pioneer contempt for what you people are and where you're from. Probably have the Frockers marching on City Hall before you've been here a month."

"Frockers?" Sharp inquiry in her voice. "What are they?"

I sank back in my seat again. "Frockers, uhh . . . Independence hardliners. 4Rock4. Lunatic fringe of the Mars First movement. Mulholland's people are going to be cranking the Mars First line for all it's worth— *Entitled Bureaucratic Meddling from Old Earth; the Dead Hand of a Decadent World; the Tyranny of the Useless Billions.* I'm sure the rhetoric isn't new to you."

"Yes, well." She brushed something invisible from her lap. "That hasn't been the governor's line so far."

"He's making the right noises. But he's winking at his followers while he does it. He has them in the palm of his hand, Ms. Madekwe. You think you've come to save these people from the excesses of a corrupt administration, but for most of them, you're about as welcome as a curried fart in a pressure suit."

"So you're advising me not to go to the Uplands?" she asked coldly. "Is that it? I should give up the idea of investigating on the ground, should sit and read the files instead? Act just like one of the bureaucrats we're already despised for being?"

"Couldn't hurt."

"I see." Voice hardening toward real anger now. "You know, back on Earth, we're all familiar with this High Frontier Can-Do-ism you people shout so loudly about. I'm not seeing a whole lot of it in you."

"Well, I'm not from here."

"Where *are* you from, Mr. Veil? Who are you, *what* are you, that the police department brings you in, *loosely attached*, and pairs us in this way?"

Heads twitched up curiously at a couple of adjacent tables. Madekwe saw it and pressed her lips down tight on her anger. She looked down at the table as if trying to find a flaw in its surface.

"I am sorry," she said more quietly. She looked up again, met my eye. "I should not have spoken to you like that. I am—the decanting process, the adjustment, it is taking its toll. I have aches and tiredness, a lack of focus, I cannot sleep. I am *not* accustomed to feeling this way."

She coasted to a halt, perhaps uncomfortable at how much she'd unburdened herself. She pressed her lips together again.

"All I want, Mr. Veil, is to get on and do my job. Can you at least understand that much?"

I didn't just understand it, I'd spent a large portion of my life carrying it as a creed. I sighed.

"Look, Ms. Madekwe, let's not get off on the wrong foot. You want to chase Pablo Torres's ghost all over the Uplands, we can do that. But it's *the Uplands*, and you need to understand what that means. Don't expect things to go smoothly, because they won't. And when this shit blows up and hits us all in the face, don't expect to like the taste."

She set her jaw. "I have a pretty strong stomach, Mr. Veil."

"Good. You're going to need it."

. . .

SO WE WENT up to her suite on the thirty-second floor. Spacious beige rooms, inoffensive pixel-fog art in corners, framed Valley landscapes on the walls. Through a half-open door off the main living space, I glimpsed a huge unmade bed that looked like the scene of some fairly violent struggle. Tousled, torn back covers, pillows punched around and crushed, one that looked to have been hurled irritably to the floor.

I grinned. Cryocap dues—sooner or later, everybody pays. Sure, five-star decanting protocols will pamper you out of the nausea and most of the actual pain, but in the end you can only fool the cells of your body so far, only stave off their outrage for so long.

Then you wrestle with it like everybody else.

I put away a flash image of Madison Madekwe's long-legged ebony curves twisting restlessly around on the bedsheets. Looked back to the main room instead, and the picture-window views. I stood facing one of them, watching rapid, bruise-colored violences coil and uncoil across the invisible membrane expanse of the Lamina beyond and below. The windows would be void-standard pressure glass, impervious to vibration, and up here what passed for atmosphere would in any case be way too thin to carry decent sound. But some deeply rooted ancestor atavism insisted still; faintly, down near the limits of hearing, the vast spit-and-crackle rage of those particle exchanges came through.

"Thought you'd be used to that," she said, passing me on the way to a workstation by the far wall. "It's not unusual weather, is it?"

"No." I held down a sudden jagged longing for orbital views and distance. "Looks a little different from on top, though."

She prodded at things on the desk. "Well, I guess that makes me more curious to see it from below. Right, here we go."

A 'branegel peeled from the ceiling dispenser plate and wafted down into the air between us. Madekwe touched her gear, summoned her digest of the Torres case files, and flung it up on the 'gel. I circled around to get the distraction of the picture window behind me, peered intently at the display. Lots of text, not much in the way of visuals—always the way when you don't have an actual corpse or crime scene to work with.

"I had expected you to bring your own gear," Madekwe remarked. "Saw you weren't wearing any; I just assumed you had your lenses internally wired."

Not for a very long time, no. They rip that shit out when you get fired.

"Too expensive," I said truthfully enough. "Anything that touches mucous membrane tissue has to factor in the biocode upgrades, and out here that shit's getting rewritten all the time. You got human biological systems being pushed constantly, like racehorses. Complicated enough as it is, trying to make that work, without having to worry about wetware interference, too. It's a whole other level of immune system interfacing, side-code add-ons, preferential sequencing. Almost no one can afford those options, and most of the ones who can don't bother."

"Most." That keen edge of inquiry in her tone once again. "But not all?"

"Not all, no." I wasn't about to get into the truth of what had been done to me—what was gone, what was left. She hadn't earned that kind of confidence, and she probably never would. "Some of the very top echelon qualpros run it for status. And high-end law enforcement sometimes have it—the whole *Red Sands Warrior* thing."

"Red Sands Warrior?"

"It's an immie show. You don't have that back on Earth? *In the Uplands, one man has drawn a line in the sand. Cross it and you cross him, too.* Thought it would have had the audiences back on Earth creaming their knickers; all that High Frontier edge, all the Marstech porn."

Her mouth twitched. "Mars-made content is, uh . . . still pretty much a niche thing back home. Nobody really . . . uhm . . ." She cleared her throat. "I get the general idea."

"Yeah, well, like I said—*Red Sands Warrior*, that's not me. I'm just a guy Chakana calls sometimes. An outside contractor. And right now my gear's getting some heavy upgrades, so there really wasn't time to wait and collect it before we came out."

"You couldn't just pull down a gestalt iteration from the shed? Cram it into a pair of disposables?"

"You forget, I'm not part of Bradbury PD. Got nothing of mine *in* their shed."

"Well, then." She tossed me the controller she'd been fiddling with, harder than strictly necessary—postdecant irritation momentarily off the leash again. "Just have a good old-fashioned dip through that, why don't you. I'm going to change. I want to be down at Bradbury Central inside the next two hours. We'll do the Vector Red visit before anything else. Maybe we can pick up your heavily upgraded gear on the way."

She stalked off into the bedroom. I watched her go, then dropped into a crash bag by the window, reeled the 'gel after me, and brightened it a bit to cope with the light. Flecks of yellow highlighter showed up in the text—someone had been annotating. I hit pan and grab.

. . . investigative summary (background):

Pablo Karl Torres, born Adam Smith County 22/17/281 YC, age at death 19 Mars Standard (Earth comp 37). Family & educational records appended under separate file. Gene father absent from fourteen months; sporadic contact between ages 3 and 7, none thereafter. Failed basic diploma, enlisted private security cadet 9/14/288 YC Critical Infra Inc. Three-year tenure (detailed summary appended under separate file), no promotion, contract not renewed.

Which didn't mean very much either way. Outfits like Critical Infra hung around the county schools all the time, scooped out the low achievers en masse because they were cheap to train and use. Some stuck and stayed, but a lot didn't.

Subsequent employment record spotty, peripatetic; performance assessments habitually subpar, numerous disciplinaries, detail appended under separate . . .

Okay, so much for benefit of the doubt.

Some upskilling, largely virtual-format & sentence-mitigation mandatory (detail appended)—trace activity in: Zubrinville; Cradle City; Burroughs; Bradbury district 7, district 18; Citizen locational software habitually disabled/opted out.

Does not appear in supplementary tax base.

No surprises there. The Charter specifically guarantees citizens their right to privacy, to disappear from pervasively surveilled society, but your supplementary taxpayer types don't have much use for the privilege; you're lucky enough to make it into that income bracket, the system is working for you, so why'd you want to dodge it?

The millions the system doesn't work for have their reasons.

Previous form (combined jurisdictions)—assault, eleven counts; extorting sexual services, three counts; distribution unlicensed SNDRI substances, fifteen counts; trespass/b&e (corporate premises), five counts; t/b&e (private premises), nineteen counts; vehicular hack and theft, eight counts. All arrest and prosecution detail appended under . . .

"Model fucking citizen," I muttered. "And that's just the ones you got tagged for."

. . . last employment (rumored)—Ground Out Crew enforcer, Cradle City chapter (estimated dates mid-Rishabha—early Geminy). KAs—Zip Sanchez, Tenzin Tamang, Milton Decatur, Jeff Havel, Nina Ucharima . . .

Milton Decatur. Assuming it wasn't just a coincidence of names, I knew the guy. And come to think of it, Tenzin Tamang sounded vaguely familiar, too. But then, Tamang's a big clan name among the Nepalese contingent on Mars, and Tenzin's not exactly an uncommon given name either.

. . . last confirmed/monitored employment—work gang logistics for Sedge Systems Inc, deployed to the Morton Spread. Contract ran Dhanus 18th—Rishabha 11th, terminated b.m.a./waiver signed. Performance reviews appe—

"Do you want something to drink?" Madison Madekwe's voice floating in from the bedroom. I thought I read an oblique apology in the tone.

"Sure," I called back. "I'll take one of those Islay malts in the top shelf menu. Little water with it."

Long pause. She stuck her head and one naked ebony shoulder around the door. "It was a serious question, Mr. Veil."

"It was a serious answer."

She hesitated a moment. I waited.

"I'm not billing that to expenses," she said curtly, and disappeared again.

Oh, well. I went back to the file.

. . . last location and actions/datapool trace—night of Geminy 3rd/ early morning 4th: tracked on street securicam/overhead mobile Cradle City eastside, eighteen confirmed sightings (GPS/dp retrieval particulars

appended), i.c.o. Milton Decatur, Nina Ucharima, two others non-KA. Last confirmed trace 01:43, Payload and 10th, heading west toward mothballed hangar hub at Gingrich Field i.c.o. Ucharima. No orbital correlation, no further trace.

Cradle City. I grimaced. It was a bad place to be wandering round with your citizen's locational opted out. Without that, you're thrown back on happenstance and satellite cover, which the particle violences of the Lamina fuck with unmercifully. And as for Gingrich Field . . .

I poked around in the file a bit more. Found a holo ID of Torres, your basic top-to-toe walkaround. By the look of it, a mug shot—they had him stripped to his shorts, and he didn't look particularly clean or groomed. I pulled in head and shoulders detail, put it on slow twirl. Glowering macho good looks under hair grown unfashionably long; some impressive upper body muscle that looked lean enough to be speedy as well as powerful; a clutch of scars and injury flags in all the places fighters habitually get hurt.

Nothing the Uplands hasn't seen about a million times before.

There was an embedded interview with Nina Ucharima, plus summary transcript, in which she claimed to have ridden out to Gingrich Field with Torres in expectation of some hot sex up against a hangar wall. They were both TNC'd out of their heads at the time. Torres was rambling, some shit Ucharima had less than zero interest in, and she largely blanked it, she said. Players and schemes, some big score coming, the usual Cradle City strut. When they got pretty deep into the field, instead of hot sex, Torres decided he wanted to climb one of the hangars and get in through the roof. Ucharima hung around a while, zoned out on the drugs, woke up bored, and went home. Never saw him again.

Hmm.

It had the grubby feel of Uplands truth to it. But without watching the actual interview footage, reading the somatic scans, looking Nina Ucharima in the face as she talked . . .

Through the filmy veil of the 'branegel and what was projected onto it, I saw Madison Madekwe walk out into the room. She was wrapped in a high-collared gray coat that came snugly to midthigh, had a lightweight trail pack slung across one shoulder, and had tucked her hands into her pockets. Her legs were elegantly booted to midcalf, snugged into form-fitting black leggings above that. She looked like a fashion house asset, modeling this season's must-have Marstech trekking ensemble.

"We're set," she said. "I've organized a low-profile ride into town."

"Low profile? Out of this place?" I hit the *off* patch. Between us, the 'gel crisped and flared into brilliant airborne ash and then nothing at all. "You know, if you're thinking of taking the service elevators—"

"They will also be covered, if not by actual feed sharks, then at least by drone-cam. Yes, Mr. Veil, that had occurred to me, too. I have something a little more nuanced in mind."

I climbed to my feet. "Well, now I'm curious, Ms. Madekwe."

"Good." She tipped her head a fraction as if to see me better in the slanting light from the window. "Maybe we're getting somewhere then."

TEN

BY THE TIME we got back into town, I was really starting to miss my gear.

The trip down from the Acantilado was painless enough. The hotel ran helicopter shuttles into town for its guests every couple of hours, dropping off at Bradbury Central or elsewhere on demand. Most hotel clients used it for the simple reason it was free. The more publicity-conscious ultratrippers had an even better reason—it gave the paparazzi a nice big target to lock on to and lots of early warning.

Madison Madekwe's plan built directly off the latter tendency. We slipped aboard our flight in the wake of some doll-youthful ultratripper and his entourage and took quiet seats at the back. What abbreviated press presence had been permitted to hang around the hotel was so wholly blinded by the light of fame radiating from our principal passenger that no one gave Madekwe or myself a second glance.

Better yet, once the hatch closed and we lifted, I had just nine people to watch. No conceivable threat from the main attraction himself or the limp fistful of sycophants gathered around him, and the three minders they had along were more twitchy about me than I was about them. I traded a couple of professional courtesy nods with them, and that seemed to do the trick. We all relaxed and looked out the windows, and the whirl-igig spun us on down into the misty red-tinged depths of the Gash like a tiny steel spider falling on its thread.

But at Bradbury Central it was a whole different load-out. Abruptly, the vicinity was crowded thick with potential hazard—terminus staff, uniformed and not; errand runners in the livery of a dozen different franchises and firms from all over the city; a scattering of outward-bound Acantilado patrons, urbane and unmistakable in their Marstech fashion house finery and accompanied as often as not by their own personal fetchers and carriers; a thin crop of ValleyVac customers riding in or heading out to points east and west along the Gash. It was a human soup, rich with all sorts of risk, none of which I had any easy way to assess. No gear meant no systems—no clinical gestalt imaging to register elevated pulses or sweat-shiny skin, no sensors to spot out inappropriate hidden hardware, no predictive modeler to analyze motion and gesture.

No Osiris to pull it all together for me.

And still no chance to call Gradual.

"Are you angry about something, Mr. Veil?" Madison Madekwe wanted to know as we came through the vaulted, step-echoing space of the arrivals hall, a judicious distance back behind the untidy gaggle of the ultratripper's retinue.

"Just call me Veil." I watched a pair of ancillary workers go past, gawking at her looks. "We're not much for honorifics out here. You use 'Mister,' makes me feel like I'm applying for a crawler loan. And no, I'm not angry. Just trying to do my job."

Up ahead, at the far end of the hall, a thin scum of paparazzi was clotted along the security railings, waiting, no doubt, for our boyish ultra pal. Privileged-access fans surged and mobbed behind them, anxious for a look, maybe even a touch of the Flesh Itself. A loose chain of Port Authority security uniforms faced outward toward the crowd, their body-armored backs to us. I've worked a few low-rent celebrity minder gigs in my time, and it's a pretty straightforward set of dynamics if you know how to ride them. I mapped an exit strategy almost without thinking. Put out an arm to slow Madekwe's leggy, determined stride.

"Let's drop back a little here, shall we?"

We eased our pace, let the ultratripper party get farther ahead. The minders spread out as they neared the rail; the ultra kid stayed front and center, lifted his arms in greeting, like a priest inviting supplicants to rise. He wore no headgear—which probably meant he was lensed internally—and his hair was a voluptuous honey blond tangle to his shoulders. Loose black cotton jacket over a broad bared chest, slacks cut wide and high on the ankle, flapping and clinging around long muscular legs, naked feet thrust into espadrilles. A ripple went along the waiting fans and face hunters—shifting stances, a renewed surging for position, here and there hands rising to headgear for final fine adjustments on the camera systems they'd all be running. The Port Authority doesn't permit foreign drones anywhere in its environs, has in fact some natty countermeasures code that will summarily pull any drone right out of the air, then trace and fry its operator systems at the source. That throws intrusion specialists of all stripes back on more basic resources, and the paparazzi were no exception. They craned and jostled for shots, yelled for comments, elbowed fans out of the way, got cursed and jostled in return. The line of PA security stood immobile as steel dolls.

The ultra kid ate it up. He moved back and forth along the rail, struck poses, grinned.

"You got any idea who this fuckwit is?" I asked irritably.

Madekwe nodded. "Sundry Charms. He's a big name in Australia, most of the southern rim, too. Music, dance, and mindscape. He's here to do something on the Southern Wall."

Yeah, no shit, I didn't say. *Him and every other cut-rate brand face who makes it to Mars and doesn't have the balls to go Outdoors.* Someday they'll get the whole planetary atmosphere jacked up somewhere near Earth Standard, and we'll all crawl out from under the Lamina, and then maybe these idiots can go find some other Martian landmark to measure their egos against.

"SNDRI Charms," I said instead. "Very good. Never heard of him."

She hesitated a moment. "If you had a teenage daughter, you would have."

We edged past the media feeding frenzy along the railings, found our exit point between two of the Port Authority guys and through a staggered gap in the barriers beyond. I shouldered my way into the press, opening a path for us, striving for casual speed—*nothing to see here, folks, just a couple of white-collar nobodies in from Grokville, caught up in this mess and running on a clock, you know, so if you could just, thank you, thank you . . .*

We were almost through the loose crush of bodies when it all fell apart.

Some unusually bright spark—maybe one of the ones that used to be a real journalist back before that stopped paying—must have caught a glimpse of Madekwe. The pricey clothes, maybe, or the long-legged gait. Gaze snagged, lingering a fatal extra moment, and then, abruptly, he made her for who she was.

"Ms. Madekwe!" I tracked the voice, saw him snake around in the crowd, move to block her path. "Madison Madekwe, over here! Look at me! Is COLIN already—"

Took me that long to get over there. I grabbed him by the hand he was waving, yanked him around to face me like an overeager tango partner. Close enough to smell the stay-up on his breath, see the red-veined stare behind the lenses. I twitched his headgear off with my spare hand, thumbed him in one eye. He yelped and tried to recoil. I yanked him back in, planted a solid head butt in his face. Let go and uppercut him savagely under the ribs. He made a hollow whistling sound and went down, blood streaming from his nose.

I knelt quickly by his side. Felt a modest crowd massing at my back.

"Hoy, what's going . . . ?"

". . . didn't see . . ."

". . . just collapsed, I think . . ."

"Somebody call an ambulance," I snapped, surreptitiously folding up the headgear and slipping it into a pocket. "I think it's an upgrade failure; he's rejecting the new code."

The crowd thickened. This was interesting even against the ultra kid's antics on the other side of the rail. It was rare for code-fly-imparted biotech to mesh badly with someone's existing code, but when it did happen it could be dramatic and fun to watch. Rash, fever, spasms—no telling which way the conflicted systems might lurch. I eased back from the whooping, fetally curled paparazzo, let others take charge. Slipped away unnoticed in the gathering press.

I found Madison Madekwe standing much where I'd left her.

"Shall we?" I asked, and led her out.

OUTSIDE ON THE steps of the terminus, it was bright and sunny, which meant a sky like the world on fire as the Lamina caught high-energy particles for breakfast and ate them. Felt like some reasonable warmth in the air for the time of day, by Martian standards anyway. Nothing to peel your jacket off for, though. The breeze that came down the street was still keen and arid cold. I felt it sweep cool across the numb-hot patch on my forehead where I'd butted the paparazzo.

I fished his gear out of my pocket and tried it on for size. Probably user-locked but worth a try. Code fizzled and scrawled across my field of vision for a hopeful moment, then spluttered out. *Oh, well.* With time and help from Osiris, it would hack easily enough, but it was a lot of effort just to expedite the call to Gradual, and in any case this was hardly the moment. We needed to get out of the immediate vicinity. I went to take a step d—

Madekwe grabbed my arm, brought me up short.

"Just a moment, Mr. Veil." Voice low, taut, and angry.

I fought down an instinctive running-hot response—go with the grab, use the momentum, punch hard into the sternum—turned casually toward her instead. I freed my arm gently from her grip, slipped off the stolen headgear, and dropped it back in my pocket.

"I told you, it's just Veil," I said mildly.

Flickered glance around us, longing for my gear. A couple of meters on down the steps from where we'd stopped, another loose cordon of security was faced off against a big mob of young men and women, most of them in Sundry Charms T-shirts. A couple of 'branegel posters floated overhead, Charms's vaguely Asia-Pacific good looks etched across the air in Day-Glo lines. His features ran a stylized repeating sequence of facial expressions that seemed to include a violent yell, during which a tiny blue mandala emerged glowing from his mouth, grew to form a geometric web across his entire face, then burst and blew away.

For all that, the crowd mood looked orderly enough. And no one was paying us any attention as far as I could tell.

Under the gold gull-wing headgear, Madekwe's gaze was angry and intent. "I have heard stories about how policing is done on Mars, Mr. Veil—"

"Veil."

"—and I have no intention of countenancing that kind of behavior on my watch. Is that clear?"

I shrugged. "If you wanted to talk to the press, you should have told me."

"I did not *want*—"

"Well, it really was either talk to them or leave the way we did. There's this low profile you wanted."

She drew a deep breath. Held it a moment.

"Will he come after us?"

"Not in the state I left him, no. And I doubt he'll give up a scoop on you to any of his scavenger pals. We have a little time. But nothing you could stretch."

She thought it through, about three heartbeats by my count. Nodded.

"Very well. You had better get me out of here."

"Yes, ma'am."

I led her down past the waiting Charms fan base, around the corner, and up Harriman Boulevard toward the Vector Red Haulage block. On Mars, being able to go outside and walk around is still something the culture takes an inordinate amount of pride in, and you see that pride reflected as often as not in the architecture. Bradbury Central could have been a single overarching Port Authority monolith, and on Earth it probably would have been. Here in the Valley, it's a campus, strung out along spacious radial thoroughfares with the terminus building at its heart, sprinkled with sun-trap corners and plazas and engineered ironwood acacias casting dappled shade every twenty meters or so. We walked with the breeze at our backs and the quiet whisper of the trees overhead.

"It's . . . not the way I imagined," Madekwe said quietly. "Not at all."

It wasn't clear if she was talking about the sky, the architectural layout, or my hands-on approach with the local press. I rubbed at my forehead, gave her a noncommittal grunt.

"I thought I'd feel the gravity more, for one thing." Irritation rising in her voice again. "Well—*less,* I mean. I thought I'd feel lighter. Less anchored."

"That's the cryocap. They pump you full of shit en route to loosen up your muscle memory. Improve your body's adaptation speeds. Normal to feel like that." I paused. "You *are* bouncing a little bit, though, if it's any consolation."

"It is not. And I am *groggy*, Mr. Veil. Quite groggy."

"Veil. That's normal, too. It'll wear off."

We walked in silence for the best part of another minute before she got to her real point. "You know, on Earth you can't get away with assaulting a journalist in public like that."

"I know. Whole other world, isn't it?

"You don't have laws like that on Mars?"

"We barely have journalists on Mars, let alone laws to protect them." Stiletto-thin stab of a code-fly at my neck. I held down the urge to slap at it. *Jesus, how many fucking upgrades did I miss?* "This is the High Frontier, Ms. Madekwe. Not a lot of room for the niceties."

"Yes, that's becoming apparent to me."

We passed a maté stand set out beneath the spread of one of the acacias. Still a little early for custom—a forlorn scattering of skeletal carbon fiber chairs with nobody in them gathered loosely around empty tables. Above the serving barrow, a 'gel glimmered palely in the morning air— COLINAS DE CAPRI CHASMA: NUEVAS COSECHAS. As part of the new harvest promotion, they were hawking low-end disposable gear sets.

"Would you excuse me a moment, Ms. Madekwe?"

I would have just bought one of the disposables from the bored-looking Andino kid behind the barrow, but he wouldn't have it. Had to be free with any purchase over ten marins or nothing. All factored in and accounted for. More than my job's worth, señor, letting you have one any other way.

He was probably telling the truth about that.

Madison Madekwe came up tight on my flank. I turned to face her, and we were suddenly a lot closer than either of us had planned. Her eyes widened. I caught the faint tang of aniseed on her breath.

"Problem?" she asked a bit hurriedly.

"Not at all." I gestured at the hanging chain-linked triple-C logo over our heads. "You want to try this? Colinas de Capri Chasma. Best coca growers in the eastern Valley. Should take the edge right off your cryocap blues."

"Tea?" Her brows cranked. A grin flickered uncertainly around on her mouth. "You're asking me to . . . you're suggesting we *stop for tea*?"

"Sure. Why not?"

She looked elaborately around the plaza, used the motion to step back from me a little. The fun fell out of her tone. "You are not concerned that our journalist friend will catch up with us?"

"If he does, I think he'll keep his distance."

"Well. But I have no line of credit here as yet. I cannot—

I grinned back at her, a little too running-hot and wide. "My treat. I'll bill the department. Grab us a table."

She hesitated a moment longer, then shrugged in assent and went to take a seat. Watching her go, I caught myself staring. Felt the fading ghost of the grin, still not fully gone from my face.

I snapped out of it. Turned hastily away back to the barrow and the Andino kid.

ELEVEN

I ORDERED LARGE matés from the menu, added a plate of corn paste sweet cakes to get the total up past the magic ten-marin threshold, held out my hand for the complimentary gear set. The kid fished one out of the barrow and dumped it in my open palm, where it sat like a tiny dead octopus dyed the green and black of the Colinas de Capri Chasma livery, still slightly damp from the storage pod.

"I'll bring your drinks over," he said.

I held the limp plastiform drape of the set in my fist for a moment, watching as it reacted to my body heat and began to stiffen into shape. I was already regretting the impulse that made me acquire it. Not like I could run a call to the Hellas triads while the delectable Madison Madekwe watched me with who knew what level of subliminal perception tweaked into her own state-of-the-art COLIN gear.

I stuffed the half-congealed gear set into a pocket and went over to sit with her in the dapple of pale sun through the foliage overhead. I forced a smile.

"Be a couple of minutes."

"Yes." Not fooled. "Mr. Veil, if you need—"

"Veil."

"Veil. If you need to make some calls, Veil, then please don't hold back on my account."

"It's nothing that won't keep."

We sat quietly for a while. Hushing of the breeze through the acacia, the boiled water hiss and crockery clatter of the kid at work on the barrow. A handful of pedestrians passed us on a variety of vectors across the plaza. None of them even glanced our way.

"Do you miss Earth?"

I blinked. "What makes you think I'm from Earth?"

"The way you talk." A shrug. "The way you act in general. You told me you're not from here, you clearly have no liking for Mars, and your disdain for it would not fit if you were from the outer colonies or one of the O'Neills. How long have you been here?"

"Long enough to get used to it."

The matés came in big bowl cups printed out to look like hand-turned earthenware. The kid laid out the sweet cakes and a sugar bowl, left us alone again.

"You came here for work?"

I wasn't in the mood for confessionals. But I needed some way to distract Madison Madekwe from my tactical slip with the headgear, and it looked like this was it.

"On and off, yeah. I used to be an overrider for Blond Vaisutis." I saw the way she stiffened as I said it. "Outer system runs mostly. A lot of the time, you're dropped off here when the contract's done."

She covered for her first reaction with a concentrated frown. "Blond Vaisutis. I know the name. Though I can't say I'm familiar with—"

"No, you wouldn't be. They're not big on public profile. Enforcement biotech and postorganics, offworld plant management and logistics. Like that."

She nodded slowly. "Interesting employers."

"You got that right."

"And there was . . . a problem?"

"There's always a problem, Ms. Madekwe. They don't wake me up if things are running smoothly."

I caught the tense slip too late, cursed myself for a sad-case nostalgic motherfucker. Not sure if Madison Madekwe caught it, too.

"Of course," she said delicately. "I mean to say—you were let go. You lost your contract with them?"

"I lost a cargo and crew. Subsequently my contract and benefits, yes."

She stirred a sugar spoon gently in her maté cup. Still frowning. "You couldn't find another employer? Get back out there with someone else?"

"Blond Vaisutis revoked my operating license." I tried hard to keep the bitterness out of my voice. "All part of the process."

"How long had you worked for them?"

"Since conception." I considered for a moment. "Second trimester, anyway. My mother signed us both up for the Local Special Indenture Program pretty much as soon as she knew she was pregnant."

"You're a *variant*?" Eyes widening a little.

"Hibernoid. A lot of overriders are. Basic human code doesn't cope that well with the constant cryocapping. So yeah. Mother walks in the door at Blond Vaisutis provincial HQ, they needed hibernoids at the time, so that's the way I got tweaked. Hard to blame her, really. Where she was from, L-SIP was about all you had by way of prospects for a single mother. That or rent an upstairs room and tell the lads to form an orderly queue on the stairs."

"Christ Jesus," she breathed.

"Wasn't taking calls. And nor was whichever tumbleweed piece of shit supplied the other half of my start code, so—" I shrugged. "—what you gonna do?"

She was quiet for a while. We drank the matés slowly, picked at the sweet cakes without much interest.

"Tell me about your daughter."

"Hm?" She looked up. "Oh. Adanya. Yes—fifteen now. Making trouble for her father while I'm away, no doubt."

"Is that often?"

"This is my first interplanetary trip, though I'm away for business on Earth quite often as well. Adanya is accustomed by now."

"How come the shift? Did you volunteer?"

"I did. How did you know?"

Because everything you say marks you out a true believer in service cul-ture and the COLIN mission for mankind. I shook my head. "Lucky guess. Were you part of that mission COLIN pulled the plug on last time, too?"

"No. That was six years ago—Earth years, I mean. Adanya was so young. I, uhm, I was trying to travel as little as possible, you see. It was a different time for all of us."

Something about the way she said it. Absent Osiris to help me out, I took a random plunge in the direction the comment seemed to suggest. "You say Adanya's accustomed. How about her father?"

"He's fine with it." Tight-lipped.

"O-kay."

"We are divorced. For nine years now." She looked squarely at me, borrowed my tone of a couple of moments ago. "What you gonna do?"

The mimicry was sharp, well observed. I laughed. "All right."

"All right," she agreed.

VECTOR RED HAULAGE ran to five separate buildings grouped around a large ironwood-shaded quadrangle with a statue of Erica Horkan at the center, head tilted back and to one side in a posture I assumed was sup-posed to imply stargazing. Then again, executive administration was housed in the top segment of a soaring polished black tower directly facing her, and corporate legend had it she'd been the prime mover in securing the haulage monopoly, so maybe she was just looking up at the command levels and winking at them. We went up some modest steps from the basin of the quad and through tall doors that parted with less noise than the wind was making in the acacias. I ushered Madison Madekwe ahead of me, looked back once for certainty, then followed her in.

The interior was pretty much what you'd expect—self-conscious Settlement-era homage, but with all the rough edges gone. Reclaimed rock flooring, but polished to a high-gloss sheen by coded dust-mite ana-logues; brutally heavy vaulting overhead, but bearing the telltale wet gleam of active nanobuild; grainy deep space images of early colony shuttles playing in corners, but on 'branegels so state-of-the-art that they looked like empty air. Above it all, light from the fiery Lamina fell through angled skylights, made slim rosy columns in the hallowed quiet.

A receptionist 'gel drifted out toward us. Very beautiful, very high rez. Severe coverall couture to match the decor, Andean good looks. One groomed eyebrow raised.

"Do you have an appointment?" it asked us.

"No, we do not. I am Madison Madekwe of COLIN Earth Oversight. I'm here to see the lottery liaison director."

"I'm afraid," the image said smoothly, "that without an appointment, Mr. Deiss will . . . see you now. Please take the elevator at the rear of the lobby."

There was barely a blip as the subroutine kicked in, triggered either by Madekwe's name or simply the force in the words *COLIN Earth Oversight*. The 'gel drifted back a couple of paces; the woman painted on its monomolecular surface gave us a prim receptionist smile and gestured elegantly to one side. An elevator door opened in the gloom farther back, laid a soft tongue of light out onto the polished rock floor like a welcome carpet.

I fished the paparazzo's headgear from my pocket and held it up. "You people got a flash pan down here?"

"Is your gear irretrievably damaged?"

"Corrupted, yeah. Think it's a Crater Critter virus."

"Beside the elevator." The same elegant gesture, and a narrow horizontal vent dropped open at about waist height in the wall. Amber gobs of warning light tracked around the edges of the aperture as if sliding on oil. "Please mind your fingers."

I dropped the headgear into the gap, watched the flash pan snap shut, and then stood in the elevator waiting for Madison Madekwe to join me. The receptionist 'branegel drifted desultorily about in the space we'd just crossed for a few moments more, as if checking for further custom. Then it flared and shriveled out of existence.

"Crater Critter?" Madekwe asked as the doors closed.

"Chinese. They're over in the Hellas crater basin. Only other place on the planet where you can run Lamina systems to keep the air in—twenty-three hundred klicks across and seven deep. Doesn't work as well as the Valley from what I hear, but they're getting by."

"And are they in the habit of deploying hostile viruses against COLIN? I thought there was a peace treaty."

I grinned. "Let's just say it's a favorite paranoia in these parts. Good go-to if you want to be taken seriously."

"I see."

The elevator chimed gently and opened onto a bare minimum of waiting area, more a stylistic gesture at antique customs than an actual functional space. In this day and age, no corporation worth its share price would dream of letting anyone come upstairs to *wait.* The door to the office beyond was already open.

An expensively suited man stood there—Mars twenties, neatly coiffed graying hair, slightly haggard Caucasian features redone at a high-end chop shop to make him blandly corporate handsome. Martin Deiss—the Deiss Man, in the flesh. I knew him from the Ride4Free publicity footage, of course; those ads are fucking everywhere. *Ladies and Gentlemen, please welcome the Deiss Man. And let's roll!* But the big plastic company smile was nowhere to be seen today. Instead, he twitched in the doorway like a cornered rat, riding an obvious SNDRI habit and a bad case of come-down nerves.

"Madison Madekwe—this is, uh, an unexpected pleasure." You didn't need headgear gestalt systems to spot that lie—it was all over him like a ground fighter's endgame. His gaze skittered in my direction. "I hadn't, uh—"

"This is Veil," Madekwe said briskly. "Bradbury PD assigned him to me for protection."

"Right . . . Uh, well." He sniffed and just about held down the urge to rub at his nose. Mustered some executive hauteur instead. "Good day to you, Officer. Uhm, these are going to be clearance-privileged discussions, I'm not sure it's really appropriate for you to, uh . . . If you could perhaps wait . . . uhm, elsewhere, while we, uh . . ."

I took out the same grin I'd used in the elevator. "That's really up to Ms. Madekwe here."

"I'm sure that'll be fine," she said absently, barely glancing at me. "In fact, perhaps you could go and get your gear and then meet me back here later. Deiss and I will need the rest of the day, I expect. We can catch up at close of play. You have my number."

I held down a tiny, unexpected quiver of annoyance. "By heart. I'll call in as soon as I'm hooked up, and you can file the link."

"Excellent." She was looking expectantly at me now. "Thank you, Veil."

"All part of the service."

Truth was, it made a lot of sense. It was good use of the time, and it gave me the out I needed to call Gradual. Madison Madekwe didn't need me standing guard over her in a corporate tower you'd need military grade ordnance to get into uninvited. In fact—

In fact, there's no call for that annoyance at all, Hak. You're losing your touch. And whatever is going on between you and this Earthwoman, it's got nothing to do with your job or hers. If she can hold it down, so can you. Let's get a grip, shall we?

I stepped back into the elevator and hit the down stud. Saw the relief course over Martin Deiss's face like water from a warm shower. All alone with Madison, cozy and COLIN-cleared, the uncleared and unwashed summarily dispatched back to the levels at which they belonged. I nodded sourly at him, *see you soon, asshole,* and then the doors closed off my view. The car dropped away under my feet, bombing back toward the lobby. Subtle sense of wrongness about it all, but I couldn't pin it down. I felt a jumpy running-hot muscle twitch in my face.

I flashed on Chakana, stood in another downbound elevator, back at the hotel. The wary, sparring conversation we'd had.

This is bugshit, Nikki, and you know it. No one ships out all the way from Earth for men like Pavel Torres . . .

The small hard pebble of conviction.

There's something else going on here, and you know it.

Then find out what it is, overrider. Find out what it is, bring it to me, and if it's anything halfway significant, maybe you'll get a cookie.

Until then, you're on tour guide duties.

Tour guiding would keep. Fuck Chakana and her slipshod lack of interest. Fuck Earth Oversight and their elite technocrat airs and graces. Fuck the background noise.

Time to sort out your own life, overrider. Clock's ticking.

TWELVE

LIKE MOST OF its ilk, the disposable was worth about what I'd paid for it. Good for a couple of hours basic city-limits AR and a hundred calls anywhere in the Valley, but the AR field came clogged thick with nonessential locational markers for branded merchandise outlets and high-end service points, and for every call you made, you had to let ninety seconds of saccharine corporate advertising wash over you first.

Quality, Choice, Freedom, just like the Charter says. What you gonna do?

I hooked the damn thing over my face anyway and fired it up. No chance it'd have systems high-end enough to connect me with Osiris. I punched in Gradual's number manually and waited. I didn't wait long.

"TKS Holdings," said a careful male voice.

"This is Veil. Put Gradual on the line."

The voice went away, left me with silence and the almost imperceptible background warble of a scrambler algorithm. I stood in the plaza below Vector Red Executive Admin, glancing sourly up at the penthouse levels now and then.

Fifty Fabulous Homebound Winners Every Single Year!

But You Gotta Play to Win.

Same could be said for those of us who have to stay here, too.

"Mr. Veil." Gradual's even tones dropped into my ear. No image, audio only—content squeezed down for minimum detectable transmission. "What can I do for you?"

"I got out of jail without your help. You may have heard."

"Yes, our sources reported as much. We have been watching."

I ignored the veiled threat in that, held down the faint shiver it set on the nape of my neck. "It isn't what you think."

"Then what is it, Mr. Veil?"

"Not something I'll discuss over the phone. Let's just say the arrangements I've made have nothing to do with you or our shared business interests."

She let the silence drip in my ears for a few seconds before she responded.

"That is . . . remarkably convenient, Mr. Veil. And is the homicide lieutenant who came to collect you from the interview room similarly disinterested in our activities? Disinterested, too, in solving the homicide she arrested you for?"

"I told you—not over an open line."

"This line is not open, as I'm sure you must be aware."

"It is at this end, believe me. I'm using the cheapest piece-of-shit gear you've ever seen." Running-hot irritability rising in my voice. "Fucking thing was probably put together in a Hellas sweatshop."

"Why?"

"Nasty historical joke. You guys—"

"No, why are you using a substandard gear set?"

"Long story, and right now I don't really have the time. The longer I'm on, the better chance someone starts listening in."

"Then you had better come and see us."

Fuck.

"I really don't have time for that. I'm—"

"Now." The monosyllable had all the give of a depleted uranium slug. "You had better come and see us now. We will be waiting for you. Good day, Mr. Veil."

I took off the disposable gear set and looked at it, holding down an urge to crush it in my fist. Pretty pointless—you can't do any damage to plastiform with your bare hands no matter how pissed off you are. Fucking stuff is like Mulholland's standing with the voters—nothing makes a dent, nothing even scratches the cheap veneer, and whatever mangling it gets from misadventure, it always rebounds into shape.

Got to choose your battles.

Fuck.

A code-fly whined past my ear. Bit me on the cheek and was gone.

YOU TAKE THE Overground east, across the superdense tangle of Sparkville and into the Ventura Corridor beyond. You have to—back in the day, there was nothing out there but thin air and dirt, so they never extended the old metro-zone vac system to cover the ground. And by the time the sprawl of Bradbury finally did roll out that far, large-scale publicly-funded infrastructure projects had gone right out of style. Private contractors moved in instead, hungry for the soft meat of municipal finance. And on Mars, you can put up an Over line for about a hundredth the cost per kilometer of boring a vac tunnel. Overground was what the new districts got.

At least there's a view.

I got a window seat in the last carriage, sat staring out. Overhead, the Lamina had given up its fiery early-morning glare and settled to a transparency like grimy window glass. You could look up there and see the Martian sky above for what it really was—a washed-out saffron dome, studded here and there with forlorn squadrons of high-altitude TF cloud and poked through in the east with the pallid glare of a toy-sized sun.

High Frontier. Big whoop.

On the upside, I managed to get right across Sparkville and into Ventura without being bitten again. Felt like the onslaught was starting to ebb at last. Or maybe it's just that code-flies don't do as well aboard public transport—that slap impulse is hard to beat, most of us give in to it. And in an enclosed space, your chances of splatting the little fuckers improve massively.

A half dozen stations down and just into the Corridor, the train rolled past a garish LCLS panel hawking the services of some brothel out on the periphery. I gazed at it blankly for a couple of seconds, then fumbled out the disposable and hooked it over my face again. Punched in a number and waited out some interminable variation on the Particle Slam promo I'd seen in the sky the night before. Heard the phone at the other end finally ring.

Got the construct.

Hi—this is Ariana. I'm not taking calls right now. Girl needs her downtime, y'know. But leave me something anyway—sounds good, maybe I'll get back to you.

Great.

She couldn't still be working, not at this time in the morning—not unless she'd hooked some lucrative private dance at the dawn end of her shift at Maxine's and then it shaded into going home with the client. Then again, with all the excitement six doors down at Vallez Girlz, maybe she was still out somewhere on the Strip with some of the other dancers, sharing the gossip.

I crammed the disappointment out of my subbed voice, tried for upbeat.

Hey, Ari—it's your overrider pal next door. Been thinking about you. Give me a call when you get this.

I strained for something witty to sign off on. Failed. Dragged off the disposable and crammed it irritably back in my pocket. Went back to staring out the window.

The Ventura Corridor in all its dusty glory: endless cheap commercial units and easy-access street grids to service them, laid out southwestward like some huge mosaic tongue of circuitry lolling crossways from the city's mouth. No hint of the countless high-end young minds at work inside those units or the deep cabled flow of Deimos venture capital that keeps them fed. But somewhere inside that carpet of low-rise low-cost architecture, slowly but surely, the next generation of Marstech major players is being born.

Shame they can't trade on the statistical certainty of that and get the Overground line extended as the corridor expands. I got out at Viking's

Rest because you don't have any fucking choice, it's the end of the line. Still a couple of kilometers out from Gradual's place, but sending a reception committee to the station would be an obvious triad move. Meet and greet, at a minimum, if not slice and dice. It's certainly what I would have done in her place.

I took the steps down to street level with wary care.

But no one was waiting for me on the platform or at the bottom of the steps, and no one glided from the cover of the nanocrete stanchions that held the station up. If Gradual had eyes on me, they stayed hidden. The only visible human activity lay in full view ahead of me, under the station's raised bulk—here, in the slanting pale tresses of Martian sunlight falling through the gaps in the structure above, a group of lean-bodied pedicab drivers had improvised a card table from a discarded cable reel and ringed it with upturned packing cases for seats. They had a game of Jhyap going, five of them playing, a couple of others craning over their colleagues' shoulders and offering sage advice. Their rickshaws were parked up across the street in a short untidy line.

I flagged for attention, and one of the lean figures threw in his hand, climbed off his packing case seat, and jogged up to meet me. He was young, but there was a gritty rock-face certitude in his Himalayan features that belonged on an altogether older man.

"Where to, soak?"

"TKS Holdings: 11328 Doriot Broadway."

A brief shadow passed across his face, but he made no comment—just shrugged and gestured across the street at the parked pedicabs. I let it go, followed him to his vehicle, and ducked in under the canopy to my seat. Then, as he stood up on his pedals to get us under way, I asked him casually, "Been out there before?"

He grunted on the downstroke. "I know it. Crater Critter central, yah? You got friends there?"

"I wouldn't call them friends."

Another grunt. We picked up some speed, cornered onto the main Ventura spinal thoroughfare. Light traffic grew up around us, mostly other pedicabs. I watched the dip and flex of the cabbie's straining back for a while. Thought I detected a lack of conversation beyond the norm.

"Not a good fare for you, then?" I probed.

"Nah, take you anywhere, soak." He didn't look around. His voice took on the cadence of his pedaling. "But I hate those fuckers. My people, see—they're Bhotia from way back—came over to Nepal in the October Crossing. Had the PLA on their backs right to the border. Harassing, extorting—like that. We don't forget."

"No, I don't suppose you would."

My knowledge of Himalayan history was sketchy at best, but I'd rubbed shoulders with enough Nepalese and Tibetan colleagues in the Uplands to pick up the basics on the Crossing. Widespread social unrest across Tibet triggers a massive martial law crackdown to safeguard the smooth running of China's MarsPrep camps; lots of summary detentions, excessive-force police actions, and convenient accidental deaths both in custody and out; exodus ensues. Entire villages emptied out, the roads clogged up with people carrying their children and what few possessions they thought they could manage. Winter came early to the Himalayas that year, and it fell hard—even for a population bred to the conditions, it was brutally cold. Caught between the weather and the sharp end of a People's Liberation Army let off the leash, the refugees suffered the usual losses— the old and infirm, the newly born, and those hotheaded and angry enough to round snarling on their uniformed tormentors.

And the Sacranite bullhorn street infantry will tell you—if you stop walking long enough to give them the time—that the COLIN corporates are the root of all evil.

Go figure.

Perhaps running on ancestral rage, my driver got me the rest of the way out to TKS in record time and complete silence. He drew up at a curb corner and gestured.

"This good for you?"

I roused myself and looked around. We were down at the dreg end of the Corridor now—the cheapest, most recent rental spaces, basic nanofab structures sprouting on raw regolith plots either side of access routes that in some places still lacked the fundamentals of paving and illumination. In some cases the 'fabs were still devoid of features, with windows and doors to be sliced out later when the individual build requirements were known.

In others, the features were in but no one was home, and the chain-linked double O symbol was already spray-painted garishly across the curved walls. Option Open—signaling the early crash-and-burn casualties in the race for Marstech coded riches. Fresh space in the ranks for newcomers. *Barely used facilities! Reasonable rates! Call now!*

11328 Doriot blended right in. Modest two-story 'fab, nondescript muddied cream and red trim, fitted out with a handful of vertical strip windows in smoky reflective gray glass. TKS Holdings was lettered casually across the facing wall in red blaze paint characters the height of a man, looking like it had been done in a hurry by someone with better things to do. Marstech start-up standard, dull and innocuous to a fault—the perfect image of what it was supposed to be.

"This'll do me fine," I said.

"Fare's racked. No extras."

I looked at the meter epoxied to the rickshaw's canopy frame, nodded, and grabbed the smart carbon patch on the side strut, preparatory to hauling myself out. "Kick that up to a flat twenty, why don't you? Pretty fast trip."

He grunted his thanks, and the digits on the meter changed. I held on to the strut until the payment went through and the meter beeped.

"Watch yourself in there," he said gruffly as I got out. "These are not good people."

I suppose I could have clued him in, told him his race-based disapproval missed the mark by an astronomical unit or two. I could have explained that the People's Liberation Army, over in Hellas or back on Earth, would treat Gradual's crew with about as much love as they did this guy's own displaced ancestors way back when.

Come to that, I could have introduced myself and told him that a BV overrider wasn't very much different from a PLA thug—that you'd struggle to get a semantic quibble over economic systems into the gap between the two, that a fist is a fist, and in the end it doesn't much matter what uniform wraps the arm behind the punch.

Waste of time. Besides, the warning was heartfelt, and he wasn't wrong.

"Lot of bad people around," I agreed. "I'll be careful."

I watched him cut a broad U across the street and pedal off north at a leisurely, fareless pace. For the flicker of that moment I caught myself en-vying him—the muscular immediacy of the work, the quick-cash no-strings rewards it delivered. The simplicity of an existence that didn't include pissed off Hellas triad business partners, unhealthy relationships with Bradbury law enforcement, and a murder rap suspended low over-head, pending review.

Yeah—should have skipped out of BV indenture, become a rickshaw monkey instead.

Or a Reef Guardian. Like in that ad you saw when you were six.

Come on, overrider. Get a fucking grip.

The envy flickered out. I dumped my angst at the curb, walked up through the raggedly graded regolith verges to the front door of 11328, and hit the buzzer.

THEY WERE WAITING for me on the other side, in lobby space that still smelled faintly of nanofab resins and plastic. I guess they'd drone-cammed me on approach from the station, then prepped the reception committee accordingly. Beneath some generic brand icon formed out of Chinese characters I didn't have 'Ris to help me read, Gradual stood at apparent ease, flanked left and right by tall, impassive muscle in opaque-lensed gear to match her own—big guys, even slimmed down to Martian norms. They'd have pretty effective weapons scan built into those lenses, and Gradual probably did, too, but the muscle on the right stepped forward nonetheless with a handheld sweeper. I stood carefully still while he ran the little device up and down my body and glanced at the readout. He fell back, traded brief words with Gradual, back and forth in Chinese. No Osiris to translate in my ear, but the gist was pretty clear anyway.

Gradual turned to look fully at me, lenses fading slowly up from blank black reflective to politely transparent.

"You are unarmed, Mr. Veil."

"I'm here to talk."

She inclined her head. "That is also what we wish to do. Follow me, please."

Out of the lobby, then, and into the guts of the building, the muscle twins trailing after us at a discreet distance. Gradual led me through resin-scented corridors and crossways, past actual-hinge doors crudely labeled with Chinese characters in blaze paint scrawl. Some of it was common enough nomenclature for me to recognize the words all on my own—PERSONNEL, RESOURCE ALLOCATION, LEGAL; the standard portals of any Ventura start-up. We went up a short flight of stairs, structure fabbed to the wall so recently that I could feel the faint give in each step where the weld cultures at the edges still seethed and tightened toward their rest state. More doors on this level, more generic labeling—LAB 1, LAB 4, ANCILLARY TESTING. Something subtly off about it all, a lack of solidity in the texture of the place every bit as telling as the rubbery give in the stairs we'd just come up. There were no doors ajar, no voices from within the labs, no coming and going between. No abandoned coffee cups on the drinks machines, no crumbled traces of regolith tracked in on careless boots and crushed into the carpeting. No spillage, no buzz, no life. Everything around me felt perfunctory and fake.

"What is it you're pretending to make here?" I asked her.

"Skin creams," she said curtly.

"That's original."

Skin protector tech is the bargain-basement anyone-can-do-it starter pack option for just about every nascent coding effort on the planet. It's your biotech ante for a game whose ultimate jackpot is recognition back on Earth as a high-end Marstech brand and the thunderous cascade of revenue from credulous consumers that such elite exotic status will inevitably unlock. They say every seventh marin made on Mars is either directly or indirectly tied to human epidermal modding. Skin is one of the few basic aspects of human physiology that's an easy imaginative transfer for the mass consumer base back on Earth. *Yeah, Life on Mars—that's got to be pretty fucking rough on your skin, right?* goes the presumed internal narrative. *Guess I'd better go out and buy this insanely expensive cellular repair complex they tested right there, out on the Red Planet's surface! I know it's a lot to pay, but hey—it's Made on Mars!—it's High Frontier Tech!—it's the Best a Human Can Get.*

So forth.

Finally, we came to a door marked EXECUTIVE. Gradual hit the handle and opened it, nodded minimally at our escort, and left them outside. The room beyond was about what you'd expect—chairs scattered in a loose ring about an empty central space beneath a high-end 'branegel dispenser. Raw gray walls, no art.

"Have a seat," she told me, closing the door.

"After you."

I waited until she'd settled into one of the chairs, then hooked a seat of my own, set it down reversed, straddled it. I twitched a thin smile at her.

"Here we are, then."

"Yes. Thank you for coming."

"I didn't get the impression I had a lot of choice."

"We were concerned—"

"That I'd sold you out to Nikki Chakana for an early release. Yeah. Nasty suspicious minds you Crater Critters run on."

"It is more or less what you threatened to do."

"Yes, if you didn't get me out inside our agreed time frame. That was forty days, and we're still on day one. So you're a little premature. And if I *had* talked, believe me—you'd know all about it by now. Bradbury Homicide don't fuck around. Chakana would have used my statement for probable cause, staged a dawn raid, and burned this place to the ground. Probably with you guys still in it."

"And with Earth Oversight looking on?" Hard to tell, with Gradual's mannered voice, if I was being doubted, sneered at, or simply quizzed for local insight. I nodded sagely.

"*Especially* with Earth Oversight looking on. It's exactly the kind of distraction Mulholland's people would love to trot out right now—*How can you people come here worrying at legalistic shit no one cares about when we're under attack from the forces of evil in Hellas? This is the High Frontier; we're dealing with* real *problems here, we don't have time for all this bureaucratic shuffle you Earth dweebs think is so important.*" I spread my hands. "Gives Mulholland an instant stockade mentality to work with, and he'd milk it for all it's worth. Something like that, he could probably stall the whole audit, stop it dead in its tracks. Believe me—if I'd talked? You'd all be slammed up in the coffins by now or conveniently dead from resisting arrest."

"Hm." Behind the clear lenses, calm dark eyes watching me intently. And in her gear systems, in all probability, a gestalt scan program checking me for the telltale symptoms of a lie.

"So tell me, Mr. Veil," she said quietly. "If all this is as you say, then why *did* Lieutenant Chakana release you so fast? What have you agreed to do for her?"

"I'm not going to tell you that, Gradual. It's none of your business."

"We are making it our business." Her poise shifted subtly in the chair; her gaze hardened. "And I suggest you cooperate. Do you want to walk out of here?"

I snorted. "Do you want to make this the last place I was seen alive? You're not that stupid. Have you listened to anything I just said about Nikki Chakana and Bradbury Homicide?"

Silence—the brief beat of quiet while she recalibrated.

"You are working for her now."

"I'd say that much was obvious, wouldn't you?"

"Working on something to do with the Earth Oversight visit."

"Good—you're back to being smart again. Suits you a lot better."

She drew a breath, held it pinched for a moment. "You are a very rude man, Mr. Veil. You should not overestimate your value to us."

"We had a very limited business arrangement, and excluding the small matter of my fee, *which you still owe me*, that arrangement has come to fruition. Sal Quiroga is dead, you have your controlling interest in Vallez Girlz—and then some—and I'm out of jail. But you want to talk about rude—let's discuss how long you're going to keep me waiting for my money."

"You will be paid. I have already—"

"Yeah, I know. We agreed a fee on completion, but you can't pay it to me just yet. We agreed a schedule for getting me out of jail, but you couldn't deliver on it. We agreed to trust each other, but at the first sign of some operational complexity, you panic and haul me out here to make melodramatic threats. Tell me something, Gradual—back in Hellas, do they categorize the triads as *organized* crime?" I paused to let the insult sink in. "Because over here in the Gash, if someone inside the *familias andinas* was this fucking disorganized, they'd last about ten minutes. You want a little free advice to go with your extended payment schedule? You plan to stick around in these parts, *you're going to need to up your fucking game.*"

This time the silence lengthened.

"There is a problem," she said finally.

"I know there's a fucking problem. I'm standing at the sharp end, looking at it."

"Not the matter of your money. Something else." She shifted fractionally in her seat; the faintest hint of discomfort. "There is a problem we need your help with."

THIRTEEN

I WENT HOME.

Gradual had the good grace to call me another rickshaw and cover the fare back to Viking's Rest. With what she wanted done, it was pretty much the least she could offer by way of an olive branch. I told the rickshaw guy to step on it, got lucky with scheduling at the station, and caught the turn-around. I rode the train back up the Ventura Corridor and into Sparkville Central, where a nifty change I had to sprint for put me on a southbound metrozone vac ten minutes later. A fistful of fast dark stops after that, we bulleted into Ceres Arc station, one-time distribution hub heart for the fractal mess of southside streets they call the Swirl.

I got out into deserted nanocrete gloom, rode an empty escalator to the surface. Not much human traffic around here at the best of times; the Swirl is largely automated factory blocks and bulk storage of one sort or another. Its streets are weird and counterintuitively laid out, n-djinn de-signed back when everybody apparently thought that was a good idea. There's a slightly eerie feel in their endless curving away to something you can't quite see, and they're a nightmare to navigate on foot. No one lives here if they can afford anything else. And at this hour, even those who do call it home won't be out on the streets. They're either long gone across town to their shitty friction-free-economy jobs or home in their capsules and sleeping off the night shift.

I headed out along Ceres Arc to where it sprouted the first of its daughter avenues. The switch-head derelict at the branch point of Ceres Drive 4 was the only sign of life in any direction—though *sign of life* was really an overly generous term. He sat huddled in his niche as usual, glued to the paving in a small drying pool of his own piss and shit, leaning close to the factory wall whose power supply he'd managed to remote hack. There was a worn old plastiskin pilot's induction cap pinned on his head with snippets of duct tape, a brutally customized masterboard hanging loose in his slack hands and lap.

When winter comes in hard, you can just about spot the curl of frosted breath from his lips. In weather this mild you'd need your gear on to know he was alive.

They say he was a hotshot something or other back in the day.

But you hear that a lot in the Gash. Whole fucking valley's littered with the leavings of earlier endeavor and better days. At least it is if you believe the street poets and sacked historians tending bar or food barrows down in the Strip. *These days,* one of them told me one freezing slow-as-Sunday night, *we're all just feeding off the stored fat of a dream gone bad.*

You want soy sauce on that?

OVERRIDERS DON'T COME with much baggage.

Hard to know if that's the gene wiring or just the job. Spend large chunks of your life deep dreaming in a free-fall hull millions of kilometers beyond the reach of any human society, it's difficult to get attached to a favorite coffee mug. Artifacts take on a purely functional aspect—you wake up, see what's available, use it. Get the job done with the tools at hand. No other approach will work out there. Perhaps they saw that coming and tweaked accordingly at the embryo stage, or perhaps it just comes with the territory and you get used to it.

Either way, the habit spills over into life after demob. Guys like me don't need much space because we've got nothing much to put in it. The

Dyson/Santona capsule I sleep in measures 6 meters by 2.8, wet niche included, is just about tall enough to stand up in along the centerline, and from the outside resembles nothing so much as the no-frills deep space lifeboat on whose basic chassis it's built. It's a little bulkier than the standard-model living pods in the other cradles on the rack, but that's mostly the skin systems. You'd struggle to spot the difference if you weren't looking for it, and from about twenty meters down the street even those slight variations start to fade out, replaced by a lozenge uniformity. The whole rack looms at 1009 Ceres Drive 4.7 like some huge ornate stacking device for retired nuclear warheads. Dusty caged staircases and gantry walkways provide access, festooned with black-and-yellow power cabling the girth of giant pythons, draped about with careless loops of slim plastic piping, color-coded blue for water and red for sewage. The ass ends of the capsules in the first array all protrude out over the street a half meter or so like an apartment block of residents mooning the public in unison.

I let myself in at ground level with the residents' code, jogged rapidly up the eight flights to the fourth floor, pulse barely raised by the time I reached the top; the effort of the stairs felt like an appetizer for something altogether more violent to come. I shook my head at the sensation, but I couldn't really drive it away.

On the off chance she'd be in but not taking calls, I went down to the far end of the gantry walkway and hit the hatch buzzer on Ariana's capsule. I didn't hold out much hope—like a lot of dancers on the Strip, Ari habitually deep-dosed herself end of shift with whatever cut-rate sweet-dream biotech was changing hands at work. She could be down in the womb-soft depths of a melatonin cocktail dreamscape and not notice a nuclear blast on the gantry outside, let alone some sad-case hard-on banging on her front door.

I tried a couple more buzzes, then gave it up. Took my sad-case hard-on, went back along the gantry to the Dyson, and voiced myself inside. Sat slumped at the workstation for a minute. My gear lay glinting dully on the desktop next to the half-liter flask of Mark. Top right-hand corner of the left lens, a tiny green light winked the ALL DONE at me. I stared at it for a moment. Back at Vector Red, I'd promised Madison Madekwe I'd hook

up, so she had the number, but fuck it, that call would keep. And so would
Gradual's sudden errand. First things first—I wanted to stand under a
shower, wash the last twenty-four hours off me, and watch the residue
spiral away down the drain.

Someone had other ideas. Five minutes into my soak, an insistent
chiming rang through the capsule's inner space. I lifted my head in the
shower's drizzle, peered out through clouds of steam. *You've got to be fucking kidding me.* But sure enough, above the workstation, the screen was lit
in pale tones of gray and blue. Laconic ID from my contacts list pulsed on
and off—CHAKANA.

"Fuck's *sake*." I stepped out of the shower stream, raked water out of
my hair, and stomped in range of the phone. "Yeah, what do you want?"

On screen, she blinked at me, lost sleep smeared under her eyes like
last night's makeup. "A towel on you below the waist, maybe. That'd be a
start."

"I was in the shower, Nikki."

"Well now you're not. So put some fucking clothes on."

I cast about for a towel in the pile of crumpled laundry by the workstation. "I thought you were going to bed."

"I did, for about four hours. Things to do, Veil, things to do."

"So go do them." I tugged the towel loose of the pile, spilled everything else across the floor, wrapped myself tightly around the waist.
"Happy now?"

"Where's Madison Madekwe?"

"I left her at Vector Red Exec Admin, talking to the Deiss Man. Came
home to get my gear. Why?"

Chakana glowered at me out of the screen. "You're supposed to be
shadowing her, that's why. *Protecting* her. How you going to do that standing balls-nakèd in a shower halfway across town?"

"Well, let's see." I rubbed at my balls through the towel with malice
aforethought. "I'm pretty sure Martin Deiss isn't going to chop her up
and feed her to his flash pan. Not good for his profile at all, something like
that. And you'd need a tactical assault squad to get into that building
without clearance. So what does that leave?"

"It leaves, genius, her going walkabout while you're busy gussying yourself up over there in the Swirl. It leaves her asking the wrong people the wrong questions in the wrong part of town without you and getting a prospecting spike through her pretty little cranium."

"She could go walkabout while I'm asleep, too."

"You don't sleep, Veil. Not this end of the cycle. That was the whole point of putting you on this."

I grimaced. "Thanks. Nice to feel valued for something."

"I wouldn't call it valued. But just so we're clear—you want to stay out of holding, you don't let Madison Madekwe go *anywhere* without you from now on."

"Yeah, easy for you to say. Somehow I don't see Ms. Earth Oversight warming to the idea of a trip down here to Pod-Park Heaven just so I can collect my shades. And if you'd let me collect them this morning before the meeting like I asked, it wouldn't have been necessary in the first place. Oh, what's so fucking funny now?"

Her lips twitched again. "Pod-Park Heaven. Fits that fractal shithole you live in like a spray-on. What is that, Southside slang these days?"

"Earth usage. You'd know if you'd been."

"Fuck off." She leaned into the screen. "Get dressed, Veil, get your gear on, and get your skinny paroled ass back over to Vector Red before I start thinking about alternative arrangements. Don't make me call you again."

Her image fizzled irritably and went out—CONTACT ENDED printing out across the screen in apologetic pastel shades.

I looked thoughtfully at the lettering for a moment. I checked the time.

Couple of hours since I'd left the Vector Red block, three at most, and definitely less than ten minutes in the shower. And somehow, inside that time frame, Nikki Chakana already knew to call me at home and upbraid me for no longer being stapled to Madekwe.

It didn't make sense.

Back at the Acantilado she'd dismissed me like a minor task unloaded, had given the impression she was dismissing Madison Madekwe almost as fast. A secondary irritant in the mountain of woe the audit had brought to her door, neatly handed off to a has-been ex–corporate enforcer at no real cost to the department. Not her problem anymore.

Now suddenly it was more important than the sleep she craved—more important than any of the cover-your-ass countermeasures she was micro-managing for Mulholland—important enough to chase me up personally and see how I was getting on.

Fucking Mulholland.

He asked for someone to ride shotgun on this one, to keep it low-key and off the books, and you're it.

I toweled myself fully dry, found some fresh clothes from the pile on the floor. I dressed absently, chewing it over.

Assume someone somewhere in Mulholland's machine is keeping tabs. High-alt drone surveillance or—if that looks too risky, too hard to get clearance for in these paranoid days of audit—maybe just a bagful of aero-bugs. Stag beetle chassis with enhanced flight specs and twinned feedcam capacity in place of antlers; that'd work well enough. The Bradbury authorities have thousands of them deployed at any given hour of the day or night anyway, easy enough to shunt some over to the Port Authority campus. Of course, the tab keeper would need to know when Madekwe and I left the Acantilado and how. But that's what—a machine tap on shuttle departures, intercepted footage from hotel securicam systems? Maybe even something as Stone Age as a paid tip-off from someone on staff? No end of ways to do it if it matters enough.

Assume it matters enough. Assume this has been eyes-on from the start.

Why?

You don't go to that much trouble for a secondary irritant.

And speaking of secondary irritants—

Time to get Gradual's dirty work done.

I WENT TO the bed shelf and reached underneath. The cut-down tactical Heckler & Koch lives five centimeters in from the edge, webbed to the underside of the shelf like some field-effect catalyzer for nostalgic dreams. You could reach down and tear it loose in a heartbeat, clean out the whole capsule in a couple of blasts. But a deck broom's a bad choice of gun for concealment and street work, even chopped, and it wouldn't do for the errand Gradual wanted me to run. So I reached deeper under the shelf, hauled out the battered Blond Vaisutis tool case instead. Hit the thumbprint release catches and sat back on my heels as the lid hinged smoothly up.

The Dyson's ambient lighting glinted and glimmered across the smorgasbord within, left pockets of shadow between the padded flanges that held the weaponry in place. It wasn't all BV-approved gear—though what they approve officially and what they turn a blind eye to you carrying are always two different things—and some of it was technically illegal even on Mars. But from choke-film combat gloves and weaponized micromining render dust all the way up to the gleaming black carballoy bulk of the Cadogan-Izumi VacStar, there was something there for pretty much every occasion and taste.

I lifted the VacStar out and weighed it in my hand. It was a fucking cannon of a handgun, a ridiculously overstated piece of hardware built originally for navy EVC teams and good for killing men with a single shot in hard vacuum conditions or any number of other atmospheres, breathable or not. Utterly sealed system, damped recoil, suitbuster load as standard. Blond Vaisutis leased the patents from Cad-Iz as soon as the navy embargo clauses expired, and then, just for good measure, they bought the company, too. With it, they bought something of a vacuum combat legend. Strap on a Cad-Iz VacStar and you're not just arming yourself—you're making a statement to anyone who knows anything about combat hardware.

I dug out the gecko-grip shoulder holster and stowed the gun under my arm. Not exactly unobtrusive, but I wasn't trying for subtlety. The men I was going to meet were stupid and violent, and showing off was what they understood.

Still . . .

I sorted through the scatter of miscellaneous gear in the bottom of the case, came up with an old favorite—the ABdM morphalloy push knife, won at poker from a drunken Filipina Comando Vacio sergeant while we all hung around in the aftermath of the Aquino Dos mutiny, locked into our dead-engine cometary and waiting to see if anyone would bother coming out to retrieve us. In rest mode, the Manila-made weapon masquerades as four ugly iron skull rings, and nothing much short of full molecular analysis will tell you otherwise. But squeeze your fingers together and grind those rings tight—they'll melt and lock into a united knuckle duster and an eleven-centimeter double-edged blade that sprouts from your fist like magic. The morphalloy edge will slice through bone like it just isn't there.

I fitted the rings on my left hand, looked at my fingers, and flexed them a couple of times. Then I put the tool case away, went and picked up my headgear from the desk, settled it in place across my eyes. Sudden unaccustomed rush of upclosewrap as the systems kicked in—I relaxed into it, focused into the cool blue shifting fields beyond and what was waiting for me there.

Hello, said Osiris, like dark honey pouring over sandpaper in my head. *Miss me?*

"Stop that." My voice sounded overloud in the empty capsule. Four months in a hib coma, three days up and about largely without gear, I'd lost the habit of subvocalizing. I cleared my throat. *Stop that.*

The parameters are yours. Give me back the BV mission voice if you prefer.

I don't prefer.

Then don't complain.

Got a number I need you to call. I subbed through the digit chain Madison Madekwe had given me, waited while it dialed. The line picked up, audio only.

"Madekwe," she said crisply in my ear.

"This is Veil. Checking in as promised. You'll get me on this number from now on."

"Yes, thank you for that."

"No worries. Listen, I've got a couple of things I need to take care of across town. When do you plan on heading home?"

"You really needn't concern yourself, Veil. I am going to be occupied here until quite late tonight, and Martin Deiss has promised to have an HKU security detail escort me back to the hotel when we're done. You can meet me there tomorrow morning."

"Tomorrow?" Visions of Chakana's probable fury cascaded through my head. "Ms. Madekwe, I am your assigned security escort for the duration of any—"

"And I am well aware of that." She snapped abruptly into view on the overlay. Telltale generic pastel-shaded backdrop, it was a headgear image, synthed up from preheld and animated to fit voice and tone. "But I see no need for us to meet again today."

"Put Deiss on the line."

"I don't see how—"

"I don't plan to argue about this, Ms. Madekwe. Put Deiss on or I'm coming over there now." Crisis command subroutines shifted in my blood like prep for combat. Even across the facial simulator, she stiffened a little at the change in tone. The display jumped, then blurred out as she tuned Martin Deiss in.

He'd been at the sundries again or maybe some anticomedown chemical to damp out the need. The bland-handsome screen manner was solidly back in place, the smile an unbreakable ivory white shield and lure. Hands held low, well away from the tickle and temptation of his nose. When he opened his mouth to let the famous resonant voice out, I half expected him to start with *ladies and gentlemen, let's roll!*

But he didn't.

"Yes, hello, Officer," he began urbanely. "I think we can both agree—"

"I'm not a cop, Deiss. Don't make that mistake."

He stumbled fractionally. "Ah. Well—"

"I'm just a hired gun for Nikki Chakana. All the authority, none of the restraint."

He feigned an appreciative chuckle. "That's very g—"

"Yeah, laugh." I watched as the grin evaporated. "I'm coming to collect Madison Madekwe at end of play today. You send her back to the Acantilado before I show up, it's going to be a problem for you. Am I making myself clear?"

He cleared his throat. "Yes. Though Horkan Kumba Ultra's private security are platinum-rated, and—"

"Then you can send them along to keep us company. Let me talk to Madekwe again."

The image skipped again, came back with Madekwe's image, real-time actual now, tank-tired and scowling.

"This really isn't necessary, Veil."

"Perhaps not, but it's the way we're going to do it. I take it you prefer to be working in cooperation with BPD, not against them."

She gave me a thin smile. "That is our brief."

"Yeah, well take it from someone who knows—we'll all be a lot happier if you stick to Lieutenant Chakana's script."

"If you say so."

"I do say so. Long experience. Call me half an hour before you want to pack up for the day—I'll be there."

"Very well." Her image winked out.

She seems nice, said Osiris.

You shut up. I glanced up and left, saw nothing but an uninterrupted view of capsule wall. *Hoy—where'd the time go?*

Digits flared soft blue in my upper left field of vision. *There.*

You turn the display off? I subbed curiously.

It's an upgrade. They're phasing visuals out for circadian sense meld. Proprietary SomaSystems tech, on lease to the COLIN flow. You'll know the time instinctively, to the minute. Want it switched on?

No, fuck that shit. I want to be able to see the numbers.

Looking is slower than just knowing.

Yeah? What is that, SomaSys marketing copy?

It is a statement of physiological fact.

Leave the numbers where they are. And fire up the situational systems— we're going out.

FOURTEEN

"NOW WE SEE it clearly, brothers and sisters!! Now we see it whole and entire!!"

I'd been using 'Ris and a superannuated HappeningCity tracker routine to find these guys, but at two blocks out, I shut the trace down and stopped bothering. From here on in, all I needed were my ears. The hectoring male voice, taut with carefully rehearsed outrage, was unmistakable. Booming echoes chased one another out across the cold arid air of downtown, bouncing off the sleek reflective flanks of the skyscrapers, deformed at intervals by feedback squeal and some messy bass squelch from a squawk box system that hadn't had its preferences tweaked for current conditions. Fucking Frockers—never big on attention to detail even at the best of times.

"Now, brothers and sisters, now we witness the Mailed Fist of Overlordship, long hidden in the Velvet Glove of normalized asymetric power relations between two worlds!!"

They hadn't honed their rhetoric recently either by the sound of it. Like I told Gradual, this wasn't going to present much of a challenge.

I took a left turn between glass canyon walls, surfing a loose flow of rubberneckers attracted by the noise. A hundred meters beyond, we all spilled through into a broad plaza stacked on one side with low steps up to a secondary level and some kind of mall frontage. Halfway up the steps, a small group of shaven-headed young men and women were knotted up under a tatty 'branegel banner that read 4Rock4—Where Do YOU Stand?

Where most people stood was at a cautious spectator distance, so members of the demo went earnestly out to bridge the gap and mingle with the crowd. They zeroed in on likely targets, lectured animatedly, gestured at content summoned onto quicksplay minigels in their left hands. *Not convinced, eh? Let me just show you something here. I think it'll change your mind. You will not believe the data that's being hidden from you— from all of us. The lies they tell back on Earth, the agenda. Look—look here . . .*

Some of the summarily buttonholed beat a hasty retreat from this treatment, but most hung around, if only to stare at the bright scrolling images the outreach crew were conjuring to the 'branegel screens spread across their splayed fingers and palms like streamers of ethereal snot. It was garish in-your-face stuff if my previous experience was anything to go by, and it tended to compel your attention regardless of where you stood politically.

Made it pretty simple for me to get in among the crowd unnoticed and take position.

I was closing on an intense but slight young woman close to the rear fringes of the gathering—she looked like she'd be easy to manhandle and scare—when across the rubbernecker throng I spotted a face I knew. He was deep in the pitch when I saw him, attention darting between the bystander he was preaching to and the lit 'gel held out for her in the palm of his hand. But then, almost as if he felt the weight of my gaze, he glanced up in my direction and saw me, and the evangelical fervor on his face went out like someone had doused it with a bucket. He stumbled visibly in his rant. Behind his lenses, fear and anger tussled for position in his eyes. I sighed and moved in.

"Hello, Eddie."

"What do you . . . fucking . . ."

I snatched off his lenses. Shot the bystander a look. "Would you excuse us for a moment?"

Only too happy to, she slid away from us with the alacrity of someone being let off a BPD spot-search bust. I put out an arm and collared Eddie Valgart as he tried his best to follow her lead. I steered him back in, stepped close. Smiling amiably.

"Where you going, Eddie? Don't you want to lay it all on me, too, the iniquities of the Long Reach Tyranny from Earth? I'm all ears."

"You're fucking *from* Earth," he hissed at me. "And if you don't—"

I twitched my jacket aside, showed him the holstered VacStar.

"Let's not make a scene, shall we?"

He went pale. "Y—you wouldn't use that out here."

"You know that's not true, Eddie. Think back." I manhandled him around toward the rear of the crowd. "Now let's take a little walk, and I'll explain what I need you to do."

IN TWENTY-ODD YEARS as an overrider, I only ever had to deal with one Frocker-inspired crisis, and it was a farce from beginning to end. They sprang their hijack before the ship got out of Mars orbit, broadcast a set of incoherent demands on the general channel, and then sat back, apparently expecting applause. The end client promptly jettisoned the ship's drive segment remotely, sealed off the cargo decks, and killed the life support. Evidently, the Frockers hadn't planned for any of that. They didn't have an axman with the chops to reverse any of the—really quite predictable—system countermeasures, and they certainly weren't equipped to go EVA and get the drive segment back. Blond Vaisutis have a pretty straightforward playbook for situations like these—their crisis consultancy advice was *sit tight and wait*, and the end client concurred. By the time they woke me up, shipboard interior temperatures were down to minus ten or fifteen, oxygen content had dropped to 16 percent, and most of the separatists had had enough.

It made my job pretty much a formality. I had to shoot one of the more gung-ho types dead on the bridge—he started making speeches, had a Beretta riot gun it looked like he might still want to use—but that about wrapped it up for the separatists.

I'm not sure why they're so fucking useless. Reuben Groell once reckoned—grumpily, drunk—that it all came down to genetics, that anyone intellectually challenged enough to buy the hard-line separatist package was by definition lacking the candlepower to do any better. *You got the official Mars First party machine,* he argued, *scouting, siphoning off anybody with actual talent or intelligence, anyone that's not a total fuck-up. What's that gonna leave?*

Rhetorical question—it left 4Rock4 a dysfunctional rump, steeped in an underlying human slurry of tribalism and dumb incoherent rage. But then Reuben never had to live down here in the Gash. He saw it all from an orbital perspective and a handful of flying visits. And Rube's political opinions rarely ran any deeper than a cheap coat of paint slapped on over the raw metallic body of a hardwired commitment to his employers and their agenda, perhaps in an attempt to make it easier on the eye.

Living down here, a little closer to it all, I wonder if it's just that street-level political outfits like the Frockers have to appeal at exactly that level of dumb tribalism to stay afloat—they're competing for recruits and resources with the street gangs and low-end organized crime, after all; they have no access to respectable revenue streams. Perhaps no surprise, then, that they end up resembling the criminals they're competing with in real time and not the political movers and shakers they aspire to be.

Thus the chapter house on Schiaparelli Street, a protocol-expired four-story walk-up, long ago opted out of municipal maintenance and thus not even graced with spray-on repair cultures to take out the sour patina of graffiti on the nanocrete facings: 3z<4; FuckEarthGov; Kut the Kord; Remember Connaught; 0.4—Stand UP, Stand PROUD; Sanchez Lives . . . so forth. By the look of it, the layers went back decades unscrubbed. Antique storm shutters on the windows, most of them jammed partly closed or listing badly side to side, lending each aperture the look of a droopy, stun-blasted eye and the whole place an air of drooling insanity. The alloy plate door at the top of the stairs was scarred and dented; security ran to a single visible camera.

I'd seen Upland biker gang hangouts with more basic elan.

We stood for the camera in a simulacrum of comradeship that seemed to work. A bored voice crackled from the grille.

"Fuck are you doing back here, Eddie? Who's this?"

Eddie cleared his throat. "Gotta see Sempere. Guy here's got a deal he needs to hear about."

He gestured at me. I tipped the camera an ingratiating bob of the head. I'd damped my lenses down to almost complete transparency, was standing as unthreateningly as I knew how. The voice cleared its throat importantly.

"Sempere's what you call it, indisposed." Pause, chuckle. "Got Rosanna here at the moment. You know how that goes."

Valgart shot me a panicky look. I'd made it clear what would happen if he couldn't get me in. His voice went up a half tone.

"Are you fucking serious, man? I'm bringing in a major fucking revenue stream here, and Sempere can't wipe off his dick and get his pants on to hear about it?"

The speaker voice turned sulky. "Well, you go bang on his fucking door, then. Coz I'm not."

The scarred alloy plate split down the middle, and the two halves of the door grated noisily back on flooring that looked like it hadn't been swept clean of dust in months. Our boots crunched as we went inside.

The interior had owned some grandeur once—faint architectural gesture in the vaulted ceiling to the old hunker and bunker days, bas-relief renderings of early explorer camps on the walls, a floor in nanogrown marble-effect crystal whose surfaces had been generated specifically to imitate the ruddy swirl of Martian dust storms. A broad sweep of balustraded stairway in some bright alloy made grubby and smeared by time—it led up to a similarly appointed balcony level with big double doors visible at the top. Back when this style was popular, there would have been a slick nanotech sheen on everything, belying the rough and ready colonial origins it was all intended to pay homage to. Now there was real dust on the storm pattern flagstones, and the bas-relief explorer images were almost as graffiti-scarred as the outer facade. Gloom clung in corners like the raw material for a pixel fog artist who'd never shown up.

Muscle count—three bored-looking Frockers, all young enough to buy uncritically into the creed and, more important, to still enjoy the inherent thuggery of the movement for its own sake. One of them sprawled leggily on the lower steps of the stairway; the others leaned with elaborate indolence on the balustrade at points farther up. They were all clad in Uplands workwear or some cheaply printed fashion house approximation thereof; they all wore their hair chopped messily at jawline level; their eyes were hooded with identical razor thin deep-tint shades. They all had the DeAres Contado tat under the left eye. Osiris mapped their weaponry for me, based off body heat, flagged each item in cool blue glow-once-and-fade tags across my field of vision. Nothing much there to worry about.

"This your fucking revenue stream?" The seated one dealt me what she thought was a withering glance. "Doesn't look very high end."

The other two chuckled. One of them levered himself upright and came down the steps as if for a better look.

"Wouldn't trade him for a half hour with Rosanna," he remarked as he passed the seated woman.

"Right."

He skipped off the bottom step, did a half turn around me, surveying. Watchful eyes sunk behind the tinted lenses. He was bulky in that tight-muscled Martian way, a little taller than me, a lot younger, and there was a jerky chemical spring to him that I didn't much like. Possibly quite a handful if you let him get too close.

"Pack it in, Olivier," said the one who'd stayed up on the stairway. He yawned and stretched. "No call to be rude—yet. Eddie's never steered us wrong before. Right?"

Stifled laughter up and down the stairs. At my side, Valgart stiffened.

"Hoy, you got a fucking problem with me, you can—"

"'S a joke, Eddie," said the woman in a tone devoid of amusement. "Happened to your sense of humor?"

"This guy—"

"This guy can wait," said Olivier, tipping his head to one side, trying for eye-to-eye challenge.

"This guy can hand over that cannon he's wearing while he waits as well," said the one on the stairs. He seemed to be in charge. He shrugged, smeared me a smile he didn't mean. "House rules."

I gave him the smile back and a nod to go with it. I took out the Vac-Star and shot Olivier below the knee with it. Fat, echoing boom across the dusty lobby space. The suitbuster slug hit at midshin height, shattered Olivier's leg, and tore off his foot like a carelessly discarded boot. He collapsed sideways to the marble-effect floor and started screaming. I felt a couple of specks of blood from the splashback spot me across cheek and brow. The woman at the base of the stairs surged upright, cursing, fumbling her weapon from beneath her jacket. She fetched up with it less than halfway raised and the VacStar barrel a scant quarter meter from her face.

"You be smart," I told her. "Drop that. Don't move."

The weapon clattered to the floor. Olivier rolled fetally, shrieking gut-deep and clutching at the shattered stump of his leg. Blood spatter across the dusty floor and a couple of growing pools where he'd fallen—part of me always expects to see it bead and bubble and float around in a fine mist the way it does in shipboard contexts; by contrast, the effects of gravity always render spilled blood oddly tame. Off to the side, Olivier's booted foot lay on its side like some discarded piece of equipment, immobile and gore-pasted at the severed end.

Behind me, I heard Eddie Valgart throw up.

Most of my attention was on Mr. House Rules. He'd twitched with similar intent to his female companion, but he seemed less committed to the act. I made hard eye contact.

"Your friend here needs a tourniquet. You get rid of that shit in your belt, you can come down and help him."

He wet his lips. "Are you *fucking nuts*? You can't—"

"I'm fucking *bleeding out* here!" Olivier screamed. *"Help me, mother-fucker!"*

House Rules wobbled a second longer, then he sagged like a powered-down wireframe doll. He pulled the gun from his waistband and dropped it on the stairs. It bounced and tumbled a couple of steps downward, then stopped. He came after it, passed it one unwilling step at a time. His face said he couldn't quite believe what was happening.

I shifted sideways and kicked the woman's gun into a corner. It went like a puck on ice. House Rules reached Olivier's side, knelt there with his hands out trembling and not quite daring to touch the shredded mess below his friend's knee. I waggled the VacStar barrel at the woman.

"Looks like he could use some help."

She darted me a hating look, but she went to kneel beside Olivier. I saw her gag as she looked at the damage the VacStar slug had done. She reached tentatively to touch the knee, and Olivier shrieked and flinched away. She swore under her breath. At her side, House Rules was going into some species of shock—his face was gray, and he kept shaking his head minimally from side to side. He almost looked worse than Olivier.

Eddie was still retching, bent over on his knees and one braced arm.

"That's a Cadogan-Izumi EVC slug," I told them. "There are twenty-seven more where that came from. I'm going up to see Sempere now. Don't get stupid on me while I'm gone."

I left them trying to wrap some kind of fashion-statement bandolier around Olivier's upper thigh and went upstairs. I was almost at the top when Osiris flagged action at the lock on the double doors.

Heat trace, she murmured, tickling deep in the bone behind my ear. *One target. No weapons enabled, not many clothes either.*

I grinned. Skipped rapidly up the last couple of steps and held the VacStar leveled at head height as the doors parted, and Francisco Sempere came barging out in a thin gown he was still tying closed. Lenses off, hair a mess, a venomous rage on his slightly sweaty face, and a parade ground shout that died in his throat as he saw me.

"What the f—"

"My bad, Paco." I punched the VacStar muzzle forward and into his forehead. "I'm in a hurry."

The impact of the barrel knocked him backward, flailing to stay upright, gown billowing around him like useless wings. I followed him in over the threshold, a single long fast stride, pistol raised, and clubbed him hard in the nose with the butt. I felt the crunch as it connected, up through the weapon and into my hand. Blood spurted. Sempere yelped and went down in a heap.

Farther back in the room, someone screamed. I scoped the space around me faster than humanly useful. Overrider operational reflex. 'Ris picked up the pieces for me.

No combat threats. That, I would assume, is Rosanna.

Must be. I bent over Sempere, grabbed him by the throat, and dragged him sideways out of the doorway, propped him against a convenient piece of wall. Blood streamed from his broken nose, specked with snot and clogged in the stubble on his upper lip. I grabbed a handful of the robe, shoved it at him.

"Clean yourself up, Paco—we need to talk."

Another scream from the corner, more halfhearted this time— I glanced over and found the source, saw a cheap plastiframe camp bed with a young woman crouched on it in full working girl war paint and not much else. Her mouth was half open, but she shut it as our eyes met, so fast I almost heard the snap. I nodded acknowledgment, went back to Sempere, who was holding the bunched-up fabric of the robe pressed to his lower face. The eyes above it weren't beaten yet.

"You know who I am?" I asked him, half hopeful he might.

He shook his head numbly, wordless.

I sighed. "All right, doesn't matter. What matters is you sent your boys around to Vallez Girlz this morning and tried to collect Liberation tax from the new management. That's pretty fast work, Paco. I doubt Sal's corpse is fully cooled off yet. So what's the deal? Got overheads? Rosanna there more expensive than she looks?"

He wiped his face hard, spit out some blood. The faint spark of resistance kindling. "Fuck's it got to do with you?"

I hit him again with the pistol, hard into the side of the head. He fell sideways to the floor with a yelp.

"You're not paying attention, Paco. Now sit up and let's try again."

Slowly, unwillingly, he propped himself up. He clutched at his head where I'd hit him, looked at me wonderingly. But now there was fear in his eyes, and his voice came out a moan. "What the fuck is this, man?"

"I'm glad you asked, Paco. What this is—I'm a fortune-teller. Here to show you the future, free of charge. And it looks like this: you're not going to be collecting your Liberation tax at Vallez Girlz. Sal never paid you a bent marin, and nor will these guys. So don't bother going back there again."

"They're fucking Crater Critters!"

I tutted. Rammed the VacStar up into his throat so it lifted him a couple of centimeters against the wall. "What *would* Ares Sanchez think of that? *Mars Born Is Born Free*, right? Big picture, global struggle? Our Hellas brothers in bondage? Ring any bells?"

He gagged against the pressure of the gun barrel on his windpipe. "The struggle . . . has to be funded . . ."

"Yeah? Well, fund it someplace else. Our esteemed entertainment sector investors from Hellas aren't interested. They may look like a shoestring operation, Paco, but they've got more friends in the Gash than you'd think."

"Friends like you?" he spit.

"No. Most of them aren't this restrained." I held the VacStar up in front of him so he could focus on it properly. "You seen one of these before?"

It quietened him a little. Fucking gun's more famous than I'll ever be.

"You navy?" he asked. Then, when I didn't answer, "Ex-navy?"

"Never mind what I am. Just ask yourself if you ever want to see me again."

"You can't—"

"I can, and I just did. Go talk to your screaming minion downstairs. What happened to him can happen to you just as easily. You keep your little thug taxmen out of Vallez Girlz, and this is the last conversation we need to have. Otherwise I'll come back here and ram this gun so far up your ass it'll knock your fucking teeth out. Am I clear?"

He held my gaze for a commendable duration. Flinched finally away.

"Good." I tapped him firmly on the side of the skull with the VacStar barrel. "That's the spirit that conquered Mars."

I got up out of my crouch, cast a last glance around the room out of operational habit. Rosanna, still silent, had sunk back on the bed, waiting on some kind of cue. I made a careful display of putting the VacStar away.

"We're all done here," I told her. "As you were."

I headed out the door and back downstairs. Mission accomplished, favor done, and let's see if Gradual couldn't get her shit well and truly together now, get off my back, maybe even see her way to paying me what I was owed.

In the lobby below, they'd managed to get the tourniquet on Olivier, but he seemed to have passed out during the procedure. His severed foot still lay where the EVC slug had chopped and dropped it, his stump dripped blood onto the grit-strewn floor, and he twitched and moaned like someone in the throes of a nightmare. His companions stared at me like frightened children as I came down the stairs, like I'd come down to them on Pachamama's Own Ladder to the Firmament—some dark spirit too tarnished and twisted with sin to make it through, barred at the top by divine Inti's doormen, found corrupt and wanting, and thrown back down from paradise among the stars.

FIFTEEN

MARTIN DEISS'S PLATINUM-RATED HKU security team was five strong, dressed in identikit functional black, and looked every millimeter their rating. Their team leader did his best not to look down his nose at me.

"Used to be an overrider, huh? That's a tough gig."

"Only when they wake you up."

It got a couple of perfunctory, fast-fading smiles from other members of his crew. They were too wired for more, even here in the helicopter, and they didn't like the fact that I was armed one little bit. They'd made no comment on the VacStar when I showed up to collect Madison Madekwe, but I saw them tighten fractionally as they spotted it. They shepherded us across the Port Authority campus with immaculate care, spread out and casual in the encroaching dusk, operational poetry in motion. If you hadn't seen the start of it, you'd probably have only made two of them as connected with us at all. Pretty clear throughout that they were watching me, too, that I was a significant part of their risk assessment. They got us into a dedicated HKU whirligig at embarkation, made sure Madekwe and I sat separated. They lost none of their hardened watchfulness once the hatch was closed and we were in the air.

"Who'd you run for?" the woman seated on the other side of me asked. "One of the majors?"

"Most of them, one time or another. I was a plug-in contractor for Blond Vaisutis."

Maybe Madison Madekwe wasn't familar with the name, but these guys were. Someone whistled, low. I felt gazes shift behind the wrap-around lenses, a new focus.

"And now you're working BPD escort detail." The woman's tone said she didn't envisage any moves into the public sector anywhere in her own future. "Gotta feel weird. I guess they're pulling out all the stops for this audit shit. I reckon—"

The team leader tipped her a glance. Probably a quick squawk on her headgear as well—*want to remember who the client is here, soak?*—from the way she clammed up. If Madekwe noticed, she didn't show it. She'd spent the whole flight silent, staring out of the window as the Gash swung by below us. Once she glanced up and caught me watching her; we traded smiles, mine reflexive, hers twitchy and preoccupied, and she went back to looking out the window.

At the Acantilado, she tried to dismiss Deiss's team in the debarkation lounge. They were having none of it.

"We've been detailed to see you to your suite, Ms. Madekwe."

"But I am not *going* to my suite," she said, a rising edge of asperity in her voice. "I intend to dine in the lounge first. I have some agenda items for tomorrow to discuss with Mr. Veil."

First I'd heard of it, but I fielded the catch. I nodded affably at the team leader.

"We're good. You can take off."

"I need to call this in," the leader said grimly. "You wait."

Madison Madekwe flared up like a hard reentry. "No, we will *not* wait! Commander . . . Grant, is it? Martin Deiss placed *you* at *my* disposal, Commander Grant. Not the other way around. I am dismissing you now. Thank you for your service. You may *go*."

Grant stood locked for a long moment, impassive behind his lenses— for all I know, he did call it in and got a snappy response from the Deiss man—then he inclined his head. He turned to his expectant team.

"You heard the lady." The annoyance in his voice was damped down beyond human hearing, but Osiris tagged it for me. "Mission folded. Let's get out of here, people."

I followed Madekwe upstairs to the lounge. We got a table over by one of the huge picture windows, ordered cocktails and a hot meze tray from the evening menu. Outside, vast violet wave fronts tangled across the Lamina like mating snakes. The valley lay in soft gloom, ten thousand meters below.

"Thank you," she said into the contemplative quiet between us.

"For?"

"Following my lead back there. I really could not bear the idea of being escorted to my room like some scandal-locked Z-list celebrity."

"I don't think you needed me to send those guys away."

The pensive smile again. "Perhaps not. But it certainly made the process simpler. In my line of work, simplicity is something you can end up craving like a drug."

"Mine, it's usually the default setting."

"I can imagine." Abruptly, she took off her lenses and set them carefully on the table before her. She settled lower and deeper into her chair, studied me with frank interest. "Is that something you miss?"

Someone takes off their headgear in a context like this, it's considered rude not to follow suit. It's an invitation to intimacy, a stripping back of the day-to-day norms and stresses. I put my own lenses away in my jacket, put on a gentle smile. Again, the soft soundless explosion as our naked gazes crossed. This time I saw her mouth quirk with the impact.

"My work's much the same," I said, remembering Schiaparelli Street. "I just don't get paid as well for it."

She held the comment a moment, like the first mouthful of an interesting wine. "I see. There are no prospects of . . . career progression, then?"

"Not when you're asleep four months out of every twelve, no. I'm a niche operator that way. And frankly—I'm past my sell-by date."

"I'm sorry. It must be tough."

I shrugged. "You adjust. Did you really have some agenda items to discuss?"

"Hmm, not really." It was said almost sleepily, but then she seemed to focus again. "The truth is I'll need a few more days at Vector Red before we head out to do any actual investigative work on the ground. Plenty of time to discuss the security implications before then."

"I thought you didn't want to spend much time going over files."

"Yes." Her gaze grew evasive. "Well, some of the things that came up today suggest I may have been wrong about that. For one thing, Martin Deiss seems to concur with your assessment of the Uplands. Laying the groundwork here before we jump in does look like the smart move."

"What I said."

"Well . . . I am sorry, then, to have doubted you."

"I'll let it slide this time."

Her eyes darted back to mine, locked on. I smiled, more carnivorously than before.

A taut silence settled on us. There was a next step to take from here, but it wasn't conversational and we both knew it. We both looked around for the food, saw no imminent sign of rescue there. Madison Madekwe cleared her throat awkwardly.

"I have been thinking. About your situation vis-à-vis Blond Vaisutis."

The moment defused like a torpedo aborted on approach. I watched it coast demurely out of view, and sighed. "Try *not* to think about it too much, myself."

"Yes, but—look, it's not my area of expertise. But I'm fairly sure that your revoked license could be appealed."

"Are you a lawyer?"

She shifted uncomfortably. "No, not as such. But—"

"I hired a lawyer." There was an anger rising in me that I didn't want, that Madison Madekwe didn't deserve. I did my best to rein it in. "Pretty good one, I'd say, from what she cost me. She did a lot of expensive digging, and the news was all bad. See, it isn't just about getting fired. A lot of the residual wetware I'm carrying is BV proprietorial tech with no expiration clauses. Revoking my license protects their patents. Even if I could get the case ruling overturned, anyone wanting to hire me back as an overrider has to pay Blond Vaisutis a tech royalty every time I go out. That prices me right out of the market."

"Oh."

"Yeah."

We both stared at the table for a bit.

"I'm going to go."

"No." She reached out, palm spread as if to press me back into my seat. "Please. At least stay for the drinks. We can find something else to talk about."

I gestured around at the loose gathering of hotel guests in the lounge. "I'm sure you have colleagues here who'd be happy to dine with you. Got one hundred seventeen of you in residence, after all."

"Yes." She met my eyes. "But I'm asking you."

I felt the torpedo turn, banking back around. Too far out to know yet if it was rearming for another shot. I caught a flicker of movement out of the corner of my eye, spotted the drinks inbound on a natty little silver tray held spritely aloft by a svelte young thing all smiles and tightly clad musculature. I shrugged.

"Okay, then. Something else. You can tell me why COLIN Oversight would be so concerned about some born-to-lose pod-park fuck-up who managed to get himself killed right after the biggest stroke of luck he'd ever had in his life."

"Isn't it obvious?"

Young Svelte laid out the drinks—classic Mojito for Madekwe, North Wall Banger for me. Food, he told us, would be right out. I took my glass, lifted it at Madekwe, and knocked back the top half. Long sweet burn of the blended liquors down my throat and into my belly. I settled back into my seat, loosened and musing.

"Obvious? Well, let's see. At a guess, I'd say you're worried that some-one found a way to crack the lottery protocols and Torres got bumped to make way for another name with hacker friends in high places. You don't care about Torres as such; you just care whether Vector Red's systems have been compromised, how deep the crack goes, and if it's an ongoing issue."

"Does that offend you?"

"It doesn't surprise me all that much. Guys like Torres are never going to be the main issue for anybody, on Mars or anywhere else. They're only ever a symptom."

"A symptom of what, exactly?"

"Doesn't matter what. For the Sacranites, they're emblems of class dysfunction and heroic ghosts of the struggle when they're dead; Mulholland and his asshole PR crew turn them into mythic fuel for the High Frontier narrative. Cops log them as statistics, powers that be plot them against public policy and law enforcement spending. Feeds use them for scapegoats or object lessons or just generalized tearjerker stock. And now you guys are going to use this one as a localizer for glitches in the corporate governance mainframe."

"I see." She sat up a little in her chair. "Am I sensing some sort of solidarity here, Mr. Veil? Abandoned mother, no functional father. Hardscrabble origins. Do you . . . identify with Torres?"

I snorted. "Ms. Madekwe, I was born into a Blond Vaisutis crèche on Earth, already tweaked for elite functionality. I spent my entire childhood swimming in corporate-funded largesse. Torres and me—we're barely the same species."

She made an elegant gesture with one hand. "Then?"

"Then nothing. I'm just pointing out the obvious, like you asked."

"You object to me using Torres as nothing but a starting point for a broader investigation?"

"Hell, no—knock yourself out. But I think you should prepare for the possibility that there is nothing very much to find. Guys like Torres burn up on reentry ten a fortnight out here. The Gash is littered with their corpses."

"But this body was never found."

"That's not so unusual either. In fact, if Torres hadn't been a lottery winner in the first place, it's doubtful anybody would have even bothered looking for him. Certainly wouldn't have had Metro Missing Persons on the case."

"For all the good that did."

"Well, it's the thought that counts. Fact remains—launch determines orbit, and Torres got a launch in life that put him low and in decay from the start. You just give it time and watch the sky." I lifted an index finger and drew a slanting trajectory across the air between us. I made a noise like oil in a pan. "Bye-bye, Torres."

"Even with a lottery win under his belt?"

"That's just fuel for the vector. Good luck won't save these guys any better than bad. Bad's the air they breathe. If good comes along, it just fucks with the mix. Get some big payoff or other, they'll most likely go out ODed or smashed up in some high-spec crawler they blew all the money on." I thought about it. "Or they maybe just swagger in the wrong direction, piss off the wrong OC asshole, end up buried in the regolith."

"You think that's what happened?"

I spread my hands. "Hey—I'm not a detective. You do the investigating, I'll just stand around and make sure no one tries to stop you."

"But you know the Uplands. This . . . Cradle City. You've been there?"

"Yeah, I know the Cradle. It's an entertainment hub for the West End Shelf Counties. See, you work Indenture Compliance, you spend a lot of time in places like that. Every other Grokville Greg that goes off roster, you just know you're going to end up rousting him out of some working girl's bed he thinks he fell in love in. Lot of working girls in the Cradle. Entertainment hub, like I said."

"I see. And do you still have contacts there—in Cradle City?"

"Remains to be seen. But we might be in luck—that Metro Missing Persons report you showed me named one of Torres's KAs in the Cradle as Milton Decatur. A few years back, I worked IC with a guy had the same name. Decatur's not a common surname, only time I ever ran across it in the Gash, so it's likely the same soak."

She made to reach for her headgear, evidently thought better of it. She sat back again and sipped her drink instead. "That's very interesting. Could be useful."

"Yeah, well, don't build up your hopes just yet. Might be the same guy, might not. And like I said, it was a few years back."

Young Svelte came back balancing another tray, this one roughly the size and shape of an elliptical orbit around Jupiter. He set it down with a flourish, and the aromas that billowed up from its arrival put a kick through even my running-hot shriveled stomach. Behind Svelte, another waiter dealt out a pair of small plates and associated cutlery with the speed and precision of a high-end blackjack croupier. Then the two of them backed off with expectant smiles and left us to it. I picked up a dainty little skewer of something dark and nibbled at it. Watched, a little envious, as Madekwe loaded up her plate.

"Assuming, then," she said absently, eyes more on the food than on me, "that this Decatur is the same man, were the two of you on good terms?"

"Saved him from getting his skull caved in one time, took a bullet for him on another occasion." That got her attention back, sharpish. I gestured with the skewer. "It's a rough gig, Indenture Compliance. Parting desperate men from their fantasies of escape. No one's ever very pleased to see you."

Someone loomed over us. Proximity sense had flagged the approach, but I'd written it off to Young Svelte or one of his helpers, back with more food. Now I glanced up and saw I was wrong. Same handsomely muscled dancer's frame, whole other face at the top.

"I know you. Both of you."

Sundry Charms—in the youthful and apparently not very sober flesh. He swayed a little over the table, switched a red-eyed gaze back and forth between us.

"You're eating."

I nodded. "Well spotted. Try not to fall in it."

He held himself up a bit tighter. Wagged a finger at me. "You were both in my copter this afternoon. I saw you."

"Belongs to the hotel."

"Wha?" He blinked, soggy with cryocap dues and whatever he'd ingested to make the evening more interesting. "Whaddya say?"

"It isn't your copter. It belongs to the hotel. That's why we were in it."

It seemed to cause a reset. Charms looked me over with a little more attention. He treated me to a slow smile, a worldly one that was supposed to show how *old soul* he was behind the youthful features and the hair.

"You know who I am?"

I shrugged. "Dunno. Some Earth has-been trying to quick-fire his dying career with a gritty-on-Mars reputational reup, maybe? We get a lot like that."

"Veil . . ."

I shook my head at her. "It's fine. We're fine here."

Not strictly speaking true. Running-hot is an unavoidable feature of turbocharged cryocap decanting, and it comes bristling with downsides. You want your overriders out of the packaging fast, ready to fix a nasty shipboard crisis from the off? You want snake-swift situational reflexes, amped-up risk assessment intelligence, full-on fight/flight biochemistry? Fine—but for those options, you're going to pay a stiff price in antisocial tendency. You're not exactly building model citizens, and I was still way too twitchy from the Frocker showdown and the restraint it had demanded. All I needed from Charms was the thin end of an excuse.

Madison Madekwe flashed him a diplomatic smile. "We're, uhm, a little busy right now."

"That's right." Charms either missed the hint or filed it under *don't give a fuck.* "Busy with all your colleagues putting the boot to these poor colonial fuckers. How's that working out for you so far? I heard a lot of angry speeches today in town. Wouldn't want to swap fan bases with you, that's for sure. Don't know why you COLIN people don't just go the whole trajectory and call yourselves a solar fucking empire. In the end, it's what you are. Slavers on the ecliptic."

Madekwe kept her smile. "Just like the song, right?"

"Just like the song. Wrote it for a reason, y'know."

"Really? And there was I thinking you wrote it to cash in on that big wave of anti-COLIN fashion coming out of the Chilean coastal clubs."

"Hey—that many people listen to me, I gotta be saying something true."

I burst out laughing, louder than I'd intended in the urbane low conversational buzz of the lounge. People at nearby tables looked up. Charms swung on me with an ugly intent that in other circumstances would have gotten him a deck broom blast in the chest.

"Something's fucking funny?" he grated.

"Yeah, almost everything that comes out of your mouth." I looked intently at him. "That going to be a problem?"

"Veil, I think I'm going up to my room now."

It was said rapidly, and Madison Madekwe was already rising to her feet as she spoke, swiping her headgear from the table in the same smooth motion. I watched her come elegantly upright and felt a sudden carnivore itch in the angle of my jaw.

She looked significantly at me. "Are you coming?"

I dropped the confrontation with Charms like a used towel.

Perhaps he spotted the shift. Internal lenses, if that's what he had, would read out the telltales—warming skin as the blood just dumped off into major muscle groups came seeping back to the surface; pupils settling down from crisis dilation to a more general-purpose width; body posture no longer defined by preparation to fight. Any halfway decent gestalt software would process the data, tell him what it meant. He gave me just enough space as I stood up. Gave me a sneer.

"Going already? Feels like I'm just getting to know you."

"You watch yourself on that wall," I said mildly. "Don't let the low gravity go to your head. You'd be surprised how badly you can get hurt on Mars."

Then I walked out at Madison Madekwe's side.

SIXTEEN

IT GOT IN the elevator with us like a third person. We stood apart to give it room, but it wasn't fooled. It coiled restlessly in the confined space, wreathed us like smoke, prickled where it touched. Madison Madekwe stared pointedly into an upper corner of the elevator car as if deeply engrossed in the hotel's choice of decor.

The silence stretched to snapping point.

"I did this to get you out of there," she said.

"I know."

"A major brawl in public with an incoming Earth celebrity is not the kind of profile I want for this job. In case you wondered."

"Wouldn't have been major."

She wrenched around to stare at me. "You—what *is* it with you, Veil? You have an *appetite* for this kind of violence?"

"Yes. Hardwired in at third trimester, they tell me."

"Well, right now your appetites are not . . ." She looked blankly at the elevator display. "Why is this taking so long?"

"I hit the stop button."

Her eyes widened. I smiled. She stepped in sharply, a closing move that could have been combat but wasn't. Something lighting her eyes from within. The blade of one hand came up, index finger flexed separate from the others, like admonition, like the bare bones of restraint. I saw the tremor at the rigid edge of the gesture. Her voice came out a low growl, not necessarily friendly.

"What do you want from me, Veil?"

"Isn't it obvious?"

She growled again, wordless now, deep in her throat. She moved up against me hard, mouth on mouth, her tongue hot and spice-tasting from the food she'd eaten. We shuddered back a pair of steps and hit the wall. Soft mass of her chest pressing into mine, grind of hips. I dropped one hand to the curve of her ass where the leggings molded to it, cupped it, pulled her harder against me. Pressed her into the swelling at my groin. She made a warm, appreciative noise, tilted her hips upward. Arched her neck back, took her mouth off mine, and looked me in the eyes.

Abruptly, something came down in her gaze like blast shutters.

"No," she said.

Nothing playful in the tone at all; it had all the erotic charge of a gunshot. I nodded slowly, lifted my hands off her, held them upward, palms out. She cleared her throat, stepped quickly back out of range. Shook her head.

"No. We are not doing this."

I looked pointedly down—at her breasts, the tight cinch inward to her waist, and the flare of her hips below. The territory we would not be prospecting after all. I drew a deep, stabilizing breath.

"Fair enough."

I found the flashing red lock decal on the elevator control panel, touched it, and sent us on our way again. Seconds of stiff silence while Madison Madekwe rearranged her clothing by minute fractions it didn't need and avoided my eyes at all costs. The elevator bumped almost imperceptibly to its halt, opened its doors onto the dense, carpeted quiet of the corridor beyond. You could see the door to Madekwe's suite just past the right turn at the end. No one in sight and no sound from behind the other doors that lined the passage.

We both stood for a long moment, looking out into the potential of that secluded twenty-meter walk. Then Madekwe stepped firmly out into the corridor and turned to face me from a safe distance. She was still breathing a little fast.

"Thank you, Veil," she said formally. "It has been . . . a good first day. I will see you tomorrow morning in the lobby at six."

I nodded. Watched her turn away. Held the elevator on open and watched her walk all the way to her door, too. Probably not smart—it certainly didn't do anything to ease the pressure in either my groin or my head.

But Madison Madekwe of Earth Oversight was proving a hard woman to look away from.

I THOUGHT BRIEFLY about going back to the lounge and picking up my quarrel with Sundry Charms where we'd left off. Discarded it as a bad idea by the time the elevator hit bottom. *Yeah, admirable restraint, Hak.* I slipped my lenses back on, checked the lobby for copter departures, and saw nothing was leaving for an hour. That left the service elevators I'd come up in with Chakana. I headed down to the service level, blagged my way past the MG4 security station—not difficult; they were there to check people coming in, didn't much care about traffic the other way—and shared a car ride down with a crew of dataflow liaison engineers who'd evidently spent the day trying to harmonize the Valley's local systems with Earth Oversight's audit deployment pile. I asked them casually how it was going and got a set of bruised looks back. One of them shook her head.

"Some real aggressive code, I can tell you that for nothing." She frowned and flexed her shoulders, cranked her arms up over her head, putting a trim young body into sharp relief beside me. She rubbed vigorously at her stubbled skullcap hair with one hand. "Mistah Earthman is *not* messing about. Got drill-head protocols in there like you wouldn't believe."

"Yeah," one of her male companions agreed darkly. "That blond COLIN bitch in the presentation—keeps banging on about the handshake systems, looks more like fucking crucifixion to me. Give me your hand right now or I'll drill a big fucking hole in it for you. They take that shit for a serious walk around here, and half the systems in Bradbury are going to be bleeding before the end of the week." ·

Someone else sniffed. "Fucking invasion, whatever they say."

I stared down at the darkened rift we were lowering into. Nighttime towns and transit stations glimmered across the valley floor like phosphorescent deep-sea life-forms, bulking corpuscular, trailing the whip-thin antenna appendages of roads before they faded to dark where the traffic petered out and the lighting systems went to sleep in response. Four hundred kilometers beyond it all, Bradbury was a lurid monster medusa oozing up over the line of the horizon.

"You guys heading back into town?" I wondered idly.

"Nah, they got us bunked at Luthra Cross. Cuts the commute." I heard a grin of invitation curl in her voice. "Plus, y'know—group accommodation, easier to pull us all in after hours if something breaks loose. You?"

"Me?" I turned away from the view, returned the grin. "Drifting back that way, but I got all night."

"Oh, really. You wanna eat?"

"Sounds good."

But of course it didn't, not really. Hunger was an appetite the running-hot still wouldn't let me have, and the appetites I did own were either out of bounds or channel-jammed with the taste of Madison Madekwe on my tongue, the sense impression of her body pressed up against mine in the elevator, and the swing of her unattainable ass as she walked away from me down the hotel corridor. Added to which, Luthra Cross is a miserable little spiderweb of hostels and service outlets, swept like the glitter of cheap broken glass into the interstices around the crux where two major ValleyVac lines meet. It's a place whose name might as well be Passing Through, and nothing you do there is ever going to feel like it happened in the real world or mattered very much to you or anyone else.

I tried for a while to drown all that out in the horseplay and tight-crew camaraderie of my newfound companions, but it wouldn't take. I wasn't part of their crew, didn't get most of the in-jokes, and my heart wasn't in the work of pretending. In slow but inevitable stages, their hilarity began to blur into white noise around me, blending with the restaurant's rowdy music—some Mars Metal band out of Eos, apparently—to form a soundscape devoid of meaning. It felt like a perfect fit for my mood. In front of me, the food on my plate cooled off uneaten, and across the table the grin of the female coder who'd invited me aboard was starting to congeal. Finally, she got up, came around to my side of the table, and crouched at my side.

"Not hungry, huh?" she shouted over the noise.

"Tell the truth, I ate earlier."

"You wanna dance instead?" She inclined her head. "Place across the street. Got good ambients, better than this thrash shit."

I forced a smile, let myself be tugged away from the table and out the door. We crossed the street on a diagonal, chased by a cold Valley wind, and scooted in under the portico of a place called—no kidding—The Dome. Heavy thudding beats came through the wall at us, light leaked around the edges of the entry. There was no queue to get in.

In we went.

She danced well, and generously with it, cut long sinuous moves around me that made my own efforts look better than they were. She got up close a few times, and I reciprocated as best I could. But ten minutes in she met my eyes on her latest passing glide, and we both admitted defeat. She tipped her head, let her gaze slide off mine. I reached in and caught her around that trim waist with one arm, put my mouth close to her ear to make myself heard over the obliterating beat.

"I'm sorry. Got some bad timing here. It's not you."

"Shit, I know that," she shouted back. "Don't worry about it, you didn't break anything. Just do me a favor."

"Sure."

"Don't come back over the road for a while. Going to cramp my style."

I nodded, relieved. "You got it."

I dropped my arm from her waist, watched her slide off through the loose press of bodies, arms held high, hands sculpting the laser-lit air above her head. She danced herself right to the door and out. Left me standing there immobile, wondering what my fucking problem was.

You know what your fucking problem is, Veil. It walked away from you down a hotel corridor a couple of hours back.

Eventually I got bumped enough times by the dancers around me to take the hint. I headed out into the street, stood there in the chilly wind for a while. Looked up at a largely quiescent Lamina and the stars beyond. To the south, a towering blackness cut off the sky like Pachamama's End of All Things running ahead of schedule. This close to the Wall, the human eye loses interpretive competence, refuses the task of understanding what it can see. All you get for your trouble is an impending sense of doom. I shivered a little and turned up the collar of my jacket.

See if you can get me Ariana, I subbed.

The log says you already left a message from the disposable headgear you were wearing earlier today. She will know you tried to contact her.

Maybe she didn't recognize the number and scrubbed the message.

You do not believe that.

No point in arguing with Osiris; she runs continuous brain MEG and hormonal load profiling as standard. She knows my biochemistry and synaptic map like a mother knows her own child's face. *Yeah, well. Call her anyway.*

We got the machine.

I FOUND A bar a prudent distance down the street from the restaurant the coders were partying in. Ordered myself a North Wall Banger and nearly choked on what they served up. We were a long way below Ares Acantilado levels now.

She seems to have gotten under your skin.

Ariana? I sipped more carefully at the cocktail. *Nah. Just being neighborly.*

We both know I am not talking about Ariana.

I said nothing. Above the bar, the digits turned over on an antique clock that looked like it might have arrived on Mars with Luthra's original crew. I watched the day reach midnight and zero out. *A good first day, Veil.* Yeah, right.

There is a VV departure for Bradbury in thirty-seven minutes, Osiris said helpfully. *You would be back in town before one in the morning.*

Yeah, and back to the Acantilado again for six. I don't see the point.

Sitting here drunk is not an optimal strategy for you in terms of biochemical well-being and gestalt function.

I sank another chunk of the cocktail and grimaced. *Nor is riding the Valley Vac for all of ten minutes and then wandering the streets of Bradbury until it gets light.*

At this stage of the hibernoid cycle, you need tasks and goals. The sense of transit may help. And Bradbury provides more opportunity for meaningful task completion than . . . this place.

My lips twitched again, this time in a grin. I've lived for decades with 'Ris in my head, but it's not often you hear quite that level of disdain in her voice.

Task completion, huh? Okay, how about we file a progress report? Call Chakana. Use the line she called the capsule on.

If you insist.

Oh, I insist.

The phone rang a while before it picked up. Whatever Chakana was doing, it was more important than me. I found an odd kind of comfort in that. Despite every itching instinct I had to the contrary, I still wanted to believe that this was exactly the low-level shit-work caretaker gig it purported to be.

"Yeah, what?" Audio only—her voice came through sluggish with sleep, lack of focus burning off like morning mist as she saw the number and realized who it was. "Jesus fucking Christ, Veil. Doesn't that overrider wiring of yours run to a time chip?"

"Sure it does. I just don't sleep this end of the cycle, remember? Thought you weren't sleeping much either these days."

"I'm fucking not—look at me. I'm talking to washed-up psycho hard men who ring me in the middle of the fucking night for no good reason. What do you want?"

"We're not going to the Uplands just yet."

Soft grunt as, presumably, she sat up in bed. "What?"

"Thought you'd like a progress report. Our illustrious second-rank

Oversight investigator has decided she'd like a few days in town before she ventures out into the vicinity of the actual crime scene."

"Seen no good evidence yet there ever *was* a crime," Chakana grumbled.

"Scene of the incident," I amended. "Seems a little odd, though. This morning Madekwe was all fired up to head out into the Uplands *cuanto antes*; she comes back from one meeting at Vector Red totally laid back about doing file work here in Bradbury first. I mean, Deiss comes across well enough in the ads, he's pretty and all, but he never struck me as the kind of guy could get intelligent people to change their minds about anything."

Chakana grunted again. "Don't fall for the surface. You know he built that whole *Let's Roll* thing up from nothing as an outside concept on his own? Then sold it to Vector Red with himself as showrunner. Walked in the door one day five years ago with the pitch, some nobody copy scribe out of nowhere, and carved himself a whole little subempire around the show."

"Been keeping tabs on him, huh?"

She left that one alone. "You back in town?"

"Luthra Cross." In case she had some easy way to check and could be bothered. Lies are a precious currency—you have to be careful how and where you spend them. "I'm due back at the Acantilado by six, going to hang here until then."

I heard the smirk in her voice. "Luthra Cross, huh? Enjoy."

"Yeah, thanks." The barman came over and gestured the offer of another drink. He went away rapidly at the look I gave him. "Listen, Nikki—before you sign off, scratch an itch for me, will you?"

"Can't imagine why I would. Not my fault you've ended up in the ass end of Mid-Gash for the night, is it? You want phone sex, you're going to have to pay for it like everybody else."

"Doubt I could afford your prices. Meantime, back to what I really meant—just answer me a question."

"What question?" Suddenly guarded.

"Earlier today—when you got me out of the shower, how did you know I'd gone back to the Swirl without Madekwe?"

"I have magical powers," she said shortly, and cut the line.

. . .

I LEFT THE bar and the dregs of my poorly built cocktail. Wandered out into the Luthra Cross night and eventually found what I was looking for—a squalid, pointless brawl on a street dealers' corner. Easy enough to make it happen. The local chemistry set looked to have been sipping from their own supply, and the resulting blur had about the side effects you'd expect. They took one look at me and read me as out-of-town talent trying to muscle in.

I didn't do anything much to dissuade them.

When the fight was done, I stood panting between the downed bodies, watching incuriously as the bloodied ABdM push knife on my fist melted back down from erect to its dormant form.

Happy now? Osiris wanted to know

I touched blood from a long shallow graze on my forehead, looked at my wet fingertips. *About the same, actually. Any sign of the cops?*

There's nothing on any of the standard channels. Why, do you want a fight with local law enforcement as well?

I shrugged. *Might be good practice for Cradle City.*

Might also make you late for your appointment with Madison Madekwe. Before which, by the way, I think you need to visit a dispensary. You will not get past hotel security at the Ares Acantilado looking like this.

True that. I looked around. *All right, I think we're done here.*

That one's still moving.

I tracked groans and soft curses to a body trying to brace itself up on hands and knees from the gritty, detritus-strewn paving. As I stepped closer, his face swung my way—teeth bared, eyes full of rage still undoused. Spirit that conquered Mars. You could see from the flex in his shoulders that he was going to make it back to his feet.

"You stay down, pal." I bleached the admiration carefully from my voice, kept it flat and cold. "Fight's over."

He snarled a kind of grin at me, blood in his teeth. I lined up for a stomp kick to his head, then changed my mind.

Not like any of this was the chemistry set's fault. They were just selling their substandard shit to the general population at hoisted prices, and if that's morally wrong, then every motherfucker in business on Mars is likely going to hell. At worst, these guys were guilty of youth and poor judgment. Time would fix at least half of that for them, and if they paid attention along the way, they might do something about the other half, too. You could see a brighter future for them if you squinted hard. You could call this a learning curve.

I settled for a couple of brutal kicks under the ribs to give me walking-away time, dropped the dealer winded and choking to the pavement again.

Then I went to find a dispensing booth to cure my more physical wounds.

SEVENTEEN

"WHAT HAPPENED TO your hand?" she asked me as the copter spun us down into the Valley's predawn gloom.

I glanced at the knuckles of my right hand. The tissue weld shots I'd gotten for it were low-end—it'd be a while before the torn flesh was completely healed. I'd paid a little more for the gash in my temple, mindful of 'Ris's warning about hotel security, and it seemed to pass muster.

"Long story," I said. "Not very interesting."

"I see."

Neither of us had much to say to each other after that. At Bradbury Central, I walked her through a largely deserted arrivals hall and out across the Port Authority campus; conversation never got beyond monosyllabic platitudes. She walked with her arms wrapped around her upper body as if she were cold, which in the chill of the early-morning wind she very well might have been. We passed the Colinas de Capri Chasma tea stand, still folded down and unmanned at this early hour. I thought her gaze tugged briefly sideways at it as we passed, but she made no comment, and she looked away swiftly when she saw I was watching her.

I saw her into the elevator at Vector Red. As I turned to leave, she twitched fractionally forward in the car. I stopped.

"Yeah?"

"Veil, I, uh . . . We're both professionals, right?"

"I used to be."

"Right." Lips tightening again. "Look, about tonight. I really don't think there's any need for you to—"

"Talk to Chakana," I said flatly. "If you can get her to take me off the detail, hey—I'm gone. No one going to be happier about that than me. Otherwise, Ms. Madekwe, I'm afraid you're stuck with me, and I'll see you at close of play, same as yesterday."

If I'd been hoping for some kind of wince at any of that, I was out of luck. Her face stayed impassive, and the elevator took her away.

I turned on my heel and headed for the doors.

Talk to Chakana—last night's conversation with the lieutenant spun briefly through my head, the smooth evasion, the lack of purchase—*yeah, good luck with that.*

Still . . .

And there it was. Spurred on by some churned cocktail of emotions, caught up and carried on the chilly wind in my face as I walked outside. Decision.

Time to change some operational parameters.

Time to see the goat god.

IN THE HARSH light of day, the Mariner Strip resembles nothing quite so much as a sour and stony critique of its nighttime self.

I picked my way between stains on the scuffed and cracking thoroughfare, stepping wide to avoid the more colorful spatters where someone's overloaded stomach had let go in the whirling neon-shot dark, dumping recently ingested contents for later passersby to smear and track through repeatedly. Elsewhere, I spotted chunks of food that had never even made it into a digestive tract before their owner lost interest and dropped them. And seasoning it all, the ever-present tiny vials, alternately crushed to shards and powder or rolling tiny and lethally unbreakable underfoot. I saw a couple of municipal cleaning bots sniffing at the debris here and there like small oblong dogs, and once, on the edge of a pool of vomit, I spotted the telltale glimmer of a nanobe sanitation colony getting to work. But it'd be a good while before those systems made a dent in the sheer volume of this mess.

A few hard-core merrymakers were still awake and on their feet, too cranked or lost in it all to go home. They shambled aimlessly up and down the Strip like survivors of some colossal bomb blast nearby or else stood around in knots at closing food barrows, faces slapped numb and stupid in the comedown and the cold. I sidestepped a couple of the most environmentally challenged and crossed to where the Dozen Up Club hugs an unremarkable block corner directly underneath one of the Strip's giant escalator belts, almost like it's hiding.

Which it might as well be. There's certainly nothing resembling advertising anywhere outside the blank black double doors that hint at entry—*provide* would be too generous a word—along the Stripside frontage. There's a sign over the entrance, but you can't even see it without a dedicated decrypt routine running on your gear. And the story goes that on Fridays and Saturdays they sometimes light up crowd-control subsonics from hidden speakers just to keep the passing nightlife at a distance. There is no queueing for the Dozen Up. If you're not inside seconds after you present at the club doors, you're not getting in at all.

"Morning, Veil," the doors said sardonically as I reached them. "You're up early."

"Haven't been to bed yet. You going to let me in?"

The matte black surfacing splintered jaggedly along lines designed to suggest a smashed pane of glass. The pieces separated smoothly from one another, withdrew on all sides into the surrounding wall. I hear they can reverse that trick very fast indeed if they want, and did once, years ago, leaving a would-be hi-tech gate crasher impaled from six different angles on his way through the gap. Happened before my time if it happened at all, but as with so much else about this place, the legend lives on.

I stepped deftly through and headed down a long, low-lit corridor toward a kinder brightness than the morning outside had to offer. Heard the *snick-hiss-clunk* of the doors locking behind me like a well-bred sigh of relief. I followed the light out into the main dance floor space, tipped a glance up at the glittering insane chandeliers they have suspended up there in the ten-meter vaulted ceiling. It misses my own tastes by a couple of astronomical units, but you can see what they're trying for—the myriad stars! the vaulted canopy of space!—and they sort of manage it. If you've never seen the real thing, it must seem pretty impressive.

Even at closing time.

Behind the long polished sweep of the bar on the right, a handsome ebony-skinned woman held glasses up to the light one by one, subjecting them to mistrustful scrutiny, then stacking them away. Muted going-home music waltzed the room, soft and mildly upbeat, loud enough to dance to, quiet enough to talk over if you wanted. Old-school cleaning robots bumped around between the vacated tables; tiny luminous moisture bugs clustered on tabletops and fed at spillage. At the center of it all, near enough directly under one of the chandeliers, a single glamorous-looking couple danced in a slow clinch, she with her face buried in his shoulder, he with his cheek laid against the top of her head, eyes fixed pensively on the middle distance.

I went to the bar. The woman stacking glasses nodded absently at me, went on with what she was doing.

"Hannu?"

She shrugged. "He let you in, I guess he'll be down. Can I get you something?"

"Mark on Mars, some ice?"

"You got it."

She spun me up the drink, set it in front of me, and went back to work. I turned and leaned back against the bar, watched the dancers for a while.

"Well, would you look at this, Tess," said a deep, melodic voice from down the bar. "The overrider himself, in the flesh. Thought you'd still be safely in custody, Veil."

"So did I." I sipped my drink. "Why'd you think I let them take me in?"

"Yes, that did seem unlike you." I heard the delicate metallic scrape of his footfalls drawing close along the bar. Felt him loom up at my side, hang over me like a cliff. "But it makes all kinds of sense, I suppose. Stay off the streets until Sal's various friends and enemies thrash out an accord, everybody calms their little selves down. So how come you're out?"

"It's complicated." I examined my drink. Steadfastly ignored the blood-deep ape instincts screaming at me to turn and face him. "I don't want to bore you."

"Well, that would be awful, yes. How are you?"

I gave up, turned to face him. "You tell me, Hannu. You're running gestalt, right? You never turn that shit off."

He grinned down at me—an alarming experience in itself if you're not used to it. "All right, then, let's see. I'm getting slightly elevated pulse, trace fight/flight pheromone, and a bunch of *very* weird-ass MEGs. But you know what, I'm going to call that Black Hatch normal at three days awake."

"Five days," I said absently. "Normal, huh? That's good, coming from you."

I don't know how tall Hannu Holmstrom was before he plowed the private-hire dreadnought *Weightless Ecstatic II* into the Ophir Chasma, but I think it's safe to say he's taller now. The prosthetic choices he made have seen to that. Consciously antique alloy running blades and combat armor midcasings lift his solidly worked out body a good half meter higher than the legs they replaced ever would have. They also make him look like a mechanized incarnation of some ancient goat deity out of legend—an impression that's pretty solidly reinforced by the eerie green slit-iris eyes he opted for and the LED-festooned piercings in nose, ears, and lips that paint cryptic-blinking sequences of light across his elf-pale features and thickly rooted iron-beaded dreads.

He dropped a heavy hand on my shoulder. Licked his lips—flicker and glint of the triple-studded tongue—and grinned again.

"You know, I reckon that's why I like you, Veil."

"Because I'm abnormal?"

"Because you're the only soak I know who has no problem standing there insulting me to my face."

I knocked another chunk off my drink. "Happy to help."

"The obvious ones are just scared of me, of course," he mused, gaze drifting outward to the dancers in the center of the floor. "And that's just fine and dandy. A little fear doesn't hurt, running a place like this. But the others, the ones who know the story, who look at my legs, and then the pity crawls out all over their faces like they've got a bad case of gas . . ." Something happened in the fine lines at the corners of his eyes. He sniffed. "Well, no matter. I take it this isn't a social call. What can I do for you?"

"Couple of things. If I give you some names in Cradle City, strictly street-level stuff, can you run me a scan and scoop?"

"Simple enough. What's the other thing?"

I hesitated. "Other thing's tougher, Hannu. I need you to get into the COLIN datastacks back on Earth."

He pursed his lips in a soundless whistle. "COLIN Earth."

"Yeah. COLIN Earth."

"Don't want much, do you, darling?"

"Hey, if my credit's bottoming out here, go right ahead and tell me."

Short, stinging silence. Holmstrom gave me a reproachful look. We don't talk about that shit, we *never* talk about that shit. And I shouldn't have snapped.

Running-hot, Hak. Take it down.

I softened my tone. "I don't ask often, Hannu."

"No, that much is true. All right, how deep you need me to go?"

"Not deep. Just a personnel profile from the Oversight division, anything else tied to it. Internal memo levels at worst. Most of what I want is probably going to be somewhere in the public domain anyway. It's a parking orbit, Hannu. A shallow dive. You could do it standing on your head."

"Hmm." His gaze grew remote. "Shallow dive or not, I'm going to need some time to put it together. Hacking anything COLIN-level is work, even here on Mars. Doing it on Earth, though, across a quarter-hour coms lag, well—that's a lot more work. Take a couple of days at least to put all the intrusion virals in place. And I'll need to take the whole night off to make the run. Can't do that until after the weekend. You stand to wait that long?"

"Sure. What about the Cradle City stuff?"

The slit-irised eyes seemed to burn a slightly deeper green. He dipped his head a little closer to mine.

"Get that for you right now if you want to freshen your drink and stick around."

SO TESS BUILT me another drink, and I gave Holmstrom my list of names and the background, and he went away. Which is to say, he stayed there looming at my side and chatted absently with me about the recent fortunes of the Dozen Up Club, the COLIN audit, and the shit Mulholland must be in now it was coming down, about Pebble Rodriguez and the difference between a genuine wall rat and someone faking it for the feeds, and a few other news items I hadn't had time to register since I woke up. If you didn't know him, you'd think he was giving you his full attention.

I knew him. Knew the fractionally dulled look in his eyes for what it was. Knew I was talking to a subroutine.

Back on Earth, he'd probably be illegal. They don't take kindly to demobbed navy personnel walking out the door with their battle AI still hooked up, and there are some pretty stringent separation protocols in place to stop it from happening. Out here on the High Frontier, though, there's a bit more slack in the system—along with your rugged corporate dynamism, you get a kind of monkey-curious laissez-faire that's far less interested in enforcing protocols and far more into watching to see what happens in the raw hinterlands beyond regulation. Given the right circumstances—and Pachamama knows I worked hard and shed blood to create those circumstances for him—guys like Hannu Holmstrom get winked at, nodded through the gate, and largely left alone. If they end up pissing off the wrong corporate body, there are ample means of street-level redress said corporate can take.

If they cause some damage to more ordinary citizens, well, that's life on Mars. Get over it.

"Yeah, looks like the usual Grokville mess to me," he said when he surfaced. "Behold, a bunch of half-smart Shelf County thugs running things via the local city hall and their very own pet mayor. Who could credit such a thing out here on the cutting edge of the High Frontier?"

I repressed a grin. "Hey—Mars Is Open for Business, right?"

"It certainly is. And your Cradle City mob are no exception. Got some half-assed arrangements with the *familias andinas*, kickbacks to local PD to keep things sweet, like that. Your Pablito Torres swings by unemployed to catch up with an old flame, see if he can't get laid for old time's sake—"

"This is Nina Ucharima?"

"The very same. She and Torres have history all over the place. Stuck together in the data like tissues on a lap dance cabin floor. But it looks to me like Torres was cruising for a bit more than a nostalgia fuck. Reading the patterns, I'd say he managed to leverage his thing with our Nina into a full-dress introduction to her OC pals higher up the chain. Tracking with them postdates his involvement with her. Might even have been what he was trying for all along. Oh, and you were right about this Decatur, you do know him. Same soak you worked Indenture Compliance with all those years ago."

I grimaced at the memory. "He still with IC?"

"Not as far as I can tell. In fact, he seems to have done rather well for himself in the interim. I'm seeing a lot of luxury item purchases in his wake, even some last-season Marstech. He's living out of a hotel on the main drag these days. The Crocus Lux." Holmstrom blinked his slit-iris eyes solemnly. "*Very* classy."

"And Tenzin Tamang?"

He shook his head. "No, I looked for any links to you in the general flow, backed up, and took it from your end, too. I'm pretty sure the Tenzin you're talking about got stabbed to death a couple of years ago over in Burroughs. You don't know this one."

"Makes sense, I guess. He had family there, was always talking about going back." I felt a qualified sense of relief. The less previous history hanging around this, the better it would play. "What about the others? You think Ucharima's story holds water?"

"Cabbed out into the Field with him for hot sex, lost him there in a TNC haze, went home? It does sound like a pretty standard Grokville Saturday night, doesn't it?"

"Doesn't it just."

Across the floor, the dancing couple stirred as if they'd heard us. They split apart and held each other at arm's length for a moment. Then they both laughed—rueful, mannered mirth out of down-curved mouths.

"Oh dear," I thought I heard him say. "Oh dear, oh dear . . ."

She turned our way. Heart-stopping natural beauty or a very good imitation thereof, blurred a little with chemicals and no sleep. She couldn't have been much over thirteen or fourteen years old, Mars reckoned. She smiled, not at me.

"Hey, Hannu," she said vaguely.

Holmstrom flexed himself fully upright, hitting two and a half meters plus. "Hey, yourself, darlin'. Time to go home?"

"Oh." She pouted. "Have we outstayed our welcome, then?"

"You, my dear? Never. The Dozen Up will always be here for you." Holmstrom coughed delicately. "But it has been light out now for several hours. I don't like to think about who you might run into at this time of day, tripping down the Strip with your illicit beau in tow."

The pout melted into an angelic smile. Down at her side, she squeezed her partner's hand.

"We'll call the car," she said. "Can you let us out the side door?"

"The *side* door—what a delightfully louche end to the night." Holmstrom gestured down the bar and into the shadows at the back of the club. "You'll remember the way, no doubt."

"No doubt," she agreed, and raised her free hand languidly. "Thanks, Hannu. You're a doll."

She wiggled her fingers in farewell, murmured something to her date, and tugged him away into the gloom. We stood and watched them go.

"Good customers?" I asked.

Holmstrom looked genuinely taken aback. "You don't *know* who that was?"

"Evidently not. Who was that?"

"Ohhhh, no. If you didn't make her, I'm certainly not telling tales out of school. Actually, you probably wouldn't even know the name. You're *such* a little iconoclast when it comes to the social whirl."

"Hey—you're talking to the man who shared a whirligig ride with Sundry Charms yesterday morning. And nearly punched him out over dinner last night. Know who Sundry Charms is, Mr. Whirling Socialite?"

"Of course I do. He came in on the shuttle last week, bless his rigid little abs. The Pacific Rim's very own chemically assisted Loverman Non-

Plus-Ultra. Last Man Standing of the ill-fated Star-Crossed Crew—even you will have heard of them, right?"

In fact, I had—some natty superlean bunch of bright young things, known and loved for doing vaguely rhythmic and/or risky things with their bodies against a variety of backdrops, real and virtual. Some noises, too, stuff you could charitably call melodic, I guess, though I didn't recall ever seeing any of them standing anywhere near an actual musical instrument at any point. Strictly an Earth-based phenomenon, anyway, but with that saccharine life-is-a-club whole-ecliptic human appeal. A couple of Ariana's dancer pals had been fans a few years back. I nodded sagely.

"Star-Crossed Crew, right."

"Yes, well, our boy Sundry—now he's very much a star in his own right. So much so, they say, he's eclipsed pretty much everything they ever did as a group act, up to and including all their youthful chemically assisted sulks and near-death experiences, apparently." Holmstrom gave me a beatific smile. "Here to do Wall 101, isn't he? Realign his profile in time-honored ultratripper fashion?"

"You skimmed all that, didn't you? Just now."

"Look in my eyes, overrider. I'm right here."

I stared up into the slit-eyed pupils and had to concede the point. Holmstrom settled a little on his machine haunches, came closer to my height again. He gave me an amiable grin.

"What you don't get, Veil—with me it's not just the wiring and the attention to detail. I'm *interested* in people. I *like* them as a species."

"Lucky you."

"There you go. And that right there is the big difference between us, not those fifty-seven kilos of AI core I keep upstairs. That's just *capacity*, that's the means to an end."

"Felt like a lot more than fifty-seven kilos at the time."

"I'm sure."

We were both silent for a couple of seconds, remembering. The navy had come looking for their hardware, of course; they always do. Not much Hannu could do about that, fresh out of the crash in Eos, hospitalized and half dead in a Bradbury ICU. But the core was still active, running on backup power from the same hardened crash capsule that had saved

Holmstrom's life, and at semiconscious levels beneath his radiation-induced delirium, they were still talking to each other. I never was very sure if it was the core itself that found and hired me, or Hannu, or some mangled gestalt combination of the two. At the time, I didn't much care. It was work, it got me paid.

No easy gig, though—those navy retrieval agents are a tough proposition. They don't mind getting bloody, and they go down hard.

I picked up my glass and peered into it. The last of the melted ice and about a finger of dilute Mark looked back up at me. If I wanted another, I'd have to make my own—Tess had gone home a while back, wandered out with a brief nod of farewell and a hard-copy book clipped in her long slim fingers. Just me and the cyborg goat god left now, hanging out under the chandeliers.

I cleared my throat. "So what do you reckon, Hannu? Torres wins the lottery—like the ad says, *someone's* got to—then he goes out jacked up and swaggering to celebrate, upsets the wrong Cradle City shark, and gets eaten?"

The goat god nodded, gaze diffuse across the club's dance floor. "All right. And then?"

"Shark stashes the body or renders it down because, hey, they know how it works—no body, no murder; no murder, no murder police. Handed off to Metro Missing Persons, some useless lazy fuck of an IO rides the ValleyVac out for a look, pokes about a bit, goes home, and parks it. End of story. Sound about right?"

"Hmm."

"You don't like it? Where are the obvious holes? Because I'm not seeing them."

Holmstrom shrugged. "Only the employee files. Torres quit a perfectly good job at least two months before he could have known he'd won the lottery. Seems odd."

"Not if you look at his employment record. Guy was a perennial fuckup. Probably got it in his head the supervisor was looking at him funny and cut up rough. Or they busted him out for something else as stupid."

"After the best part of ten months toeing the line? Come on, Veil. He'd been there since early spring. That's a long time for an Upland casual.

Even got a couple of minor promotions, and he had more in the pipeline if I'm reading between the lines right. Look, I'll send it all over to your cache, you can see for yourself. But this Sedge Systems—they're a good outfit to sign on with—they stick to the Charter, got a humane approach to medical care and downtime, solid core business in dermal modding, limited R&D exposure to anything too edgy, good balance sheet. Old school. Torres looks smart enough in the record to have known a good thing when he saw it. So why skip when he did?"

"And it was definitely before the lottery call? You're sure of that?"

He gave me the look. "He quits his job with nothing else to go to, he wins the big ride home, he disappears without a trace. In naval dataflow terms, we call that anomaly clustering. It doesn't *have* to mean anything— sometimes it's just the universe fucking with you, just sheer dumb coinci- dence. But any navigational analyst worth her gear sees an anomaly cluster slide up on screen, she hits the siren. Because nine times out of ten it *does* mean something, and what it generally means is *bad shit inbound.* It means that somewhere out there in the Big Black, *something's coming.*"

Despite myself, I felt the faintest of chills slide down my back. I drained my glass to hide the shiver, set it down carefully on the bar.

"Maybe."

"Yeah, maybe. You going to tell me what all this is about?"

"They're reopening the Torres investigation," I said economically. "To do with the audit."

"Seems an odd order of priorities. What with Mulholland's balls hanging all the way out and his dick buried deep in the Charter's peachy ass."

"It's not a priority thing. I just got stuck with escort duties for the second-team suit they handed it to."

"Whose profile you want me to dig out Earthside and shake to see what falls out." The slit-irised glow-green eyes nailed me. "Good guess?"

"Good guess."

"So that's why Chakana dragged you out to play early. She's subcon- tracting out the shit she doesn't think matters."

"Something like that."

"And you think it does matter. Otherwise, why the Earthside poke?"

I studied the empty dance floor, the space the beautiful people had just vacated, as if I might find some useful answers drifting in their wake. But the memory of Madison Madekwe stood there instead—long-legged and poised in my memory, hands tucked away in the wrap of her midthigh coat, shrewd dark gaze, quizzical stare. The taste of her mouth on mine, the press of all that warm Earth-metabolism flesh up against me. The spiking force of the clinch, down into belly and groin . . .

"I don't know what I think," I said irritably. "Got a shit job to do, I'm just trying to cover all the angles."

EIGHTEEN

I LEFT HOLMSTROM with the details for the Earthside run, got a promise out of him that he'd call it in as soon as it was done, and then I headed home. Shower, change of clothes, make some calls from the privacy of the capsule. Check in with Gradual, check that Sempere's Frockers had backed off their revolutionary tax collecting at Vallez Girlz as advised. Maybe have another go at bracing Chakana for some answers that made sense of what was really going on.

Maybe call on Ariana.

I was still walking the last half klick from Ceres Arc station when Osiris flagged me an incoming call. A tiny grinning skull and crossbones floated up into my left field of vision, impaled top to bottom with a red question mark. *Unknown contact.* I blinked it open anyway. Yeah, nine times out of ten it's an algorithm, trying to sell you expensive workplace comp or some new gear upgrade you don't really need. But that tenth call will turn out to be a twitchy would-be client trying to stay anonymous. And clients weren't something I could afford to pass up this early in the lean season. I triggered a stock conversational avatar of myself, watched the line open.

"Mr. Veil?"

It was a personal assistant interface, one of the rougher ones where you can see the better-than-real rez issues around the eyes and the corners of the mouth. Sexual appeal amped up way past subtle—deep, shaded cleavage, predator makeup, fine dark just-out-of-the-shower hair, cut to jawline length. You can rent them by the minute from most Bradbury AI providers. Cheap, anonymous, effective. I suppressed the renewed hot squirt of hormonal need it triggered in me.

"Yeah, I'm Veil," I said curtly. "Something I can help you with?"

"My employer would like to know if you are available for a consultation this afternoon."

"Over the link?"

The perfectly sculpted lips met in a smile. "A meeting in person. Do you know the Plurry Slunge on Sixty-Seventh Street?"

"The slush-rider bar? Sure, but it won't be open until at least—"

"My employer will meet you *outside* the Plurry Slunge at two o'clock. Please be punctual."

"There's the small matter of my fee. I usually charge—"

"An initial payment has been deposited. Please check your accounts. If you do not wish to retain the remuneration, failure to make the meeting will cause the payment to revert. Do you have any questions?"

Got nothing *but* questions, I carefully didn't say. "No, that's fine. I'll be there."

"Excellent. Thank you for your attention." She inked out on a seductive smile.

I stopped for a moment on the endless desolate curve of Ceres Arc Drive, blinked up the general screen. 'Ris ghosted into my head.

You called?

Get into the main account, would you? Check for any recent action.

A brief security-sequence pause, almost like Osiris clearing her throat. *Yes, there has been. One new payment, as of seven minutes ago. Discreetly routed funds out of a numbered Deimos account—six hundred marins, clean. No transaction fee, no deductions for tax.*

Moonbeam money.

It's what they call it on the street out here, neatly reflecting origin, transfer method, and maybe the covert nighttime allure it owns as well. But whenever I hear the phrase, I remember the gleaming silver coins in that kid's fairy tale that the crèche AI used to tell us. Coins that chime and jingle down from the moon—the real moon, the big bright one, not something that looks like a chunk of fossilized turd in orbit—in a magical silver stream. That land at the foot of the child's bed in the still of the small hours and wake him up. That know no owner, leave no trace behind, and bring the kid an inescapable adventure somewhere out in the fragrant desert night.

I stared at the pulsing figures for a long moment.

Six hundred slash.

Pretty steep for standing on a street corner and hearing a pitch.

On the other hand, if this was a trap, six hundred slash for bait was straight up insane. I would have cheerfully gone over to Sixty-Seventh Street for a retainer a fifth that size. Anyone who knew me would probably know that, too.

I sighed.

Okay, thanks, 'Ris. You can lock it up again. The account screen vanished. *Pull me some street maps on the capsule console. Plurry Slunge, Sixty-Seventh Street, surrounding three klicks. Surface and sub, infrastructure systems, population flows for this afternoon. And run me a weapons advisory for the meet. So far, I trust these mystery money fuckers about as far as Mulholland with a teen intern.*

BACK IN THE Dyson, showered and changed, I sat at the desk console and walked the meeting through in my head. I recalled what I could about that stretch of Sixty-Seventh Street cold, then pulled up the maps 'Ris had grabbed for me and refreshed my memory. I imagined distances and angles, the exposure I was likely to run.

You can let the machines do this shit for you entirely if you like. But like anything else, if you want to really own it, you've got to put in a little synaptic time of your own. And owning the game plan can sometimes be the difference between making it home in one piece and a slow cold cometary drift out into the void.

"Here is your weapons advisory," said Osiris, patching through into the Dyson's internal speaker system.

Listening. I cleared my throat—subbing is all very well, but it's nice to actually use your voice from time to time. "Listening."

"The Cadogan-Izumi VacStar will serve acceptably as your principal equip. It is covert enough to pass muster in a daytime street context."

"Yeah, what I thought. Beats the HK."

"It is also easily detected by weapons scan hardware at a distance. It will thus draw their attention and make an impression. It gives you ranged capacity to eighty meters and will take down any human targets, armored or not, with single shots. However, it is not ideal for close-in work if you are outnumbered. Suggest—"

"The Balustraad, right?"

"—the Balustraad Shredder, with standard thirty-centimeter proximity-fused load-out. Plus two packets of Webb M-Systems antipersonnel towels for emergency withdrawal."

"And keep the push knife?"

"And keep the push knife."

I went to the bed and dragged out the BV tool case again. Ferreted out the Balustraad from under a wad of other junk and blew the dust off its minimalist frame. It's a surprisingly slim gun for the damage it can do; you can wear it in the small of your back and pretty much forget it's there, though you pay for that with a severely limited nine-shell magazine. Hopefully, you don't need all that many shots. It's a tooth-and-nail firefight weapon, after all, a reflex pull-point-and-plug gun, good up to about twenty meters, after which the heavily packaged slugs start to tumble. But get within that magical thirty-centimeter radius of your target, and the patented Balustraad cluster munition will tear anything human to bloody shreds. You can buy specialized rounds with a broader proximity fusing range, but I tend to stick with the standard 300 mill because honestly, if I can't hit that close to what I'm shooting at, what's the fucking point? I'm probably already dead.

The Webb towels are a more subtle thing altogether—peel them from the pack, press them harmlessly and invisibly onto clothing almost anywhere you care to choose, and they'll go to sleep more or less indefinitely.

You can grab them loose and fling them in an opponent's face at a moment's notice, and their superacid surfacing triggers in microseconds. Webb Tech was designed for zero-G combat contexts and much bigger membrane sizes, but the small ones work okay in a gravity well, too, and on Mars they'll hang in the air like thistledown for upward of a couple of minutes before they hit the ground. Even in broad daylight, they present as little more than a soap bubble gleam until it's too late, and they'll sear pretty much anything they drift into contact with. They cover a hasty retreat like nothing else I know.

I looked from the Webb packs in my palm to the swarm gun in my other hand. The push knife rings on my fingers, the VacStar holstered under my left arm. It was all starting to feel a bit like overkill.

But that was the running-hot talking.

And biochemical overconfidence has killed more men like me than explosive decompression ever did.

TO KILL SOME time, I sorted through Holmstrom's Cradle City data digest and pulled up the detail on Milton Decatur. The goat god was right: he'd come a long way since our rousting days with Indenture Compliance.

. . . founder/executive director/majority shareholder Tharsis Gate Security Solutions (inc. 294 YC).

. . . retained security adviser Cradle City PD & Adam Smith County Sheriffs'

. . . assistant treasurer, Cradle City Chamber of Commerce

. . . honorary secretary, CCPD Benevolent Fund

. . . security coordinator for Cradle City mayoral election campaign of Raquel Allauca, Prosperity Party candidate 293 YC; subsequently Allauca's Head of Security for two terms of office '93–'95, '95–'97 . . . video attached . . .

I skimmed the footage, thought some of the '95 stuff looked vaguely familiar. A while back now, but I remembered following Allauca's reelection in the feeds at the time. Casual interest sparked, a brief flicker of nostalgia at the Cradle City establishing shots. I couldn't recall much about the story itself except that it was a messy, mean-fought campaign. Lots of rancor and recrimination about the previous term, a lot of accusations flying. She still got in. Mulholland was Prosperity, too, so there would have been some serious pushback from the party machine right across the valley. Party largesse and large boots deployed; accusations staunched, rancor soothed, rumors choked off. That same old fucking song.

The rest of Decatur's résumé was stuff I mostly already knew—IC service record, a run of low-end enforcement gigs before that; some of them I remembered Decatur rapping about between yawns on stakeout or in the comradely comedown blear as we closed out bars or rowdy parties to celebrate a lucrative bust.

I skipped through it.

Stapled to the general records, though, was a subdigest from a law enforcement tracker AI. Made interesting reading.

No criminal record at this time. (see below)

Reputed capo for Ground Out Crew (West End chapters). Criminal investigations into Charter Rights abuse, extortion, Restricted Biotech forgery and human trafficking instructed by Uplands Marshal Anil Lamichhane 28/15/295. Multiple lines of inquiry opened.

Case pursuit put on hold following Marshal Lamichhane's death in the line of duty 19/16/295. Successor Marshal Sixto Maura chose not to reactivate the inquiry, citing lack of material evidence and reliable witnesses.

All further conjecture based upon circumstantial or anecdotal evidence, remapped with data-state extrapolation tools (CrimKit 9.4; Diamond Inference 14.1; 4th Degree Systems, Amber Suite) and thus subject to usual limited liability parameters in the event of legal proceedings; specific algorithm operating legalities and restrictions also apply (see appended)

. . . suspected involvement in Marstech chop shop supply chains throughout the West End and Tharsis corridor . . .

. . . implicated in disappearance of known Adam Smith County crime boss Jackson Gurung . . .

. . . connection posited with biocode hacking and license theft activities at Subeti Resistant Strains Biotech, leading to bankruptcy proceedings and hostile takeover . . .

. . . believed responsible for . . .

. . . alleged . . .

It was all colorful stuff, and a lot of different verbs got used, but *arrested* and *charged* were both notable by their absence. Milton Decatur was nothing if not shrewd, and he always did have the luck of an Eos Chasma saint.

Veil, man, I'm telling you—the whole West End, right up to Tharsis Gate, it's wide fucking open. Oddly enthused about it one night as we wait outside a Burroughs dance bar for a trio of midlist bountied Grokville Gregs. Guys like us, we should be seizing the fucking moment, building ourselves an empire out here, 'stead of doing this tired shit.

This tired shit is paying the rent. And it's easy.

Yeah, but just think it through for a minute. Building intensity in his voice. I glance sideways at him, curious. See the light of something like inspiration in his eyes. Or maybe that's just the street halogens. Why's it so fucking easy? Because these guys are born-to-lose fuckwits, just like all the others. And so are 90 percent of the population up here. That leaves the other 10 percent, the ones who have to ride herd on it all, and they don't give a shit so long as the machine ticks over and they can get comfortable for the duration. Look at Allauca—she don't care how we bring these three in or what shape they're in when she gets them back. She just wants the problem solved, the file work straight, and no late-night calls.

Raquel Allauca's a fucking venom sac on legs.

Name me a Compliance regional that isn't. That's my point, Veil. The way they look at things up here, so long as it doesn't hurt the bottom line, criminal's just another word for cheaper, faster, and makes less noise.

That's Compliance. You go up against the marshals—the way Carvalho did, remember?—that's going to be a different story.

Ahh, the fucking marshals. A broad slinging gesture with one arm. His coffee dregs slop up out of the cup, liquid black under the halogen glare and splattering wide across the cracked nanocrete paving. He pitches the cup after it. They're spread thin, soak. What have they got, five dozen of them to cover the whole West End?

They still killed the fuck out of Carvalho.

He got careless. Got greedy, got too fucking impressed with himself. Decatur's tone eases, grows patient and musing. Thing is, Veil, the marshals only show up when there's already a mess in progress. You don't make that fucking mess in the first place, they're going to be someplace else, killing some other motherfucker.

Yeah—pretty sure I heard Allauca say that in briefing a couple of months ago.

He shrugs. Well, she's a smart little algo.

She's a cunt.

That, too. But you just watch. She's going to be mayor of one of these shithole towns one of these days.

Well, well.

I'd left the Uplands the following year, chasing some higher-end work back in Bradbury. Never went back. Decatur and I kept up a sporadic flow-based contact for a while, not much beyond Christmas or Martes Challa salutations and the odd *look at this sorry shit* video grab. Once he showed up in Bradbury, hiding out from some heat he'd generated in the West End. I was hitting end of cycle pretty hard at the time, groggy and vague with the coma-onset chemicals, short on funds, and only a couple of weeks left to secure myself a safe four-month haven for the crash. I had memories of going drinking with him a few times, talking, but I had absolutely no recall of what we talked about. If he was already on his way to better things riding Allauca's jets by then, either he never saw fit to mention it or he did and I wasn't paying attention. He was still in town when I went down into hibernoid sleep, but when I surfaced four months later, he was gone, and I never saw or heard from him again after that.

I grimaced. Maybe it was something I said.

I HAD OSIRIS put in the call, waited while it rang long enough to prove there wasn't a machine at the other end.

"Crocus Lux Hotel," said an actual human brightly as they picked up. "How may I help you?"

"I'd like to talk to one of your guests."

"Certainly, sir. I'll see if I can connect you. What name?"

"Milton Decatur. Tell him it's Veil."

He glitched. "I, uh . . . Milton Decatur, yes. Uhm. Mr. Decatur doesn't actually . . . well, uh . . . Just one moment, please. Mister . . . ?"

"Veil."

"Yes, of course. Mister Veil. One moment, please."

I grinned. It's the standard mark of high-end hotels to use human staff where the rest of the human world would use a construct. But you have to be *really* high end for those humans to run as smoothly as the machine they're so ostentatiously replacing. So far, the Cradle City Crocus Lux looked to be floating a little adrift of its aspirations.

The receptionist came back, more composed this time. "I'm afraid Mr. Decatur is currently unavailable. I have passed on your message, and—"

"That's fine. He can call me back. This number, when he gets the time."

I dropped the connection.

Sat staring pensively into the weaving rest patterns of the screen for a while, not entirely sure what I'd just done or why.

NINETEEN

SLUSH RIDERS—THE REAL ones, not the brand-name imitators that fuck it up for everybody else—are a recalcitrant bunch by and large. I guess riding down waste outflow waterfall systems up to six and seven kilometers tall for fun and not much profit must do something to any natural inclination to deference you might once have owned. The Bradbury Slushers clubhouse stood on a street thick with mineral rights brokerage firms and high-end property lawyers, crowned with a pixel-fog image of the thundering brown slurry grandeur that is Fonseca Efflux Head Ten. It looks like nothing so much as a solid stream of liquid shit emptying itself endlessly from the twentieth floor to the pavement. It makes a thick gurgling noise to match, triggers subliminal odor responses so you'd swear you can smell the effluent, and if you want to get into the club, you have to step right through it.

As does anyone walking up or down Sixty-Seventh Street on that side.

I got there a few minutes before two o'clock, parked myself in front of an adjacent frontage, and spent a while watching the local legal talent mostly step off and cross the street rather than go near the slurry effect. It was childish and it got old fast, but it took my mind off feeling like I was standing there with a target decal painted across my chest.

Down to my left and five streets over, the COLIN Mineral Rights Building loomed up behind the intervening architecture like some fallen god's gravestone. The gargantuan shadow it cast put an angled block of gloom right across Sixty-Seventh Street, and as I waited, the edge of that gloom walked right up the avenue toward me like some inescapable rising tide.

What do you reckon? I subbed casually. *Stick around or walk?*

They are not that late by human standards. Remember, you are running-hot. Impatience is a standard symptom.

Fair point.

14:22 by the clock in the corner of my eye, and a steely gray-green limo crawler with opaqued windows slunk around the corner two blocks down. It stayed in the creep lane, prowled up the street in my direction, ghosted to a halt in front of me. 'Ris ran the specs without being asked— armored Bugatti Mariner 420 or a very good chop shop copy thereof. All the tension in my muscles puddled out—fake or not, the crawler was a pricey ride. Whoever this was, if they'd wanted to ice me, they could have hired it done from a window ninety stories up on the MRB's facing slab side. These people really had come to talk.

The limo hatch cracked and cranked down a handbreadth. A worried clerkish face peered out at me. Chin a couple of days unshaven, ugly-functional gearframes dumped across insomnia eyes. Seemed like nobody was getting much sleep these days. "Hakan Veil?"

"In the flesh. You didn't scan me on approach?"

"What was your fee?"

"I don't believe we've discussed it yet."

His voice turned snappish. "What did we pay you to come here?"

"Six hundred, local."

The hatch rolled smoothly down to floor level. "All right, get in."

I ducked and stepped into a plush interior. The clerkish type gestured at me to seat myself beside him, facing the rear.

"He is armed," he said colorlessly.

Someone snorted like they'd just been told a joke in poor taste. I got myself seated, took in the other two occupants—skimmed the woman, masked the sudden uptick in my pulse as I made the lean, hard-featured man at her side. But I nodded amiably enough at him and settled deeper into the limo's smart cushioning. Did the polite thing and disabled the opaque on my gear lenses so I could meet their eyes. The hatch rolled back up, and we pulled away from the curb so smoothly I barely felt it.

"I could have come all the way downtown just as easily," I said. "Commissioner."

He looked grimly across the plush space between us. "So you're Veil. Nice rings you've got there."

It didn't seem to warrant a reply. I waited in silence as Peter Sakarian exchanged a glance with the woman seated beside him. The silence stretched.

"Veil," the woman said finally. "That's not your real name, though, is it?"

"It is on this planet."

She was pretty clearly Earth business—the same muscle bulk in limbs and frame that I'd spotted on Madison Madekwe, a couple of the same COLIN facial tats, starker here against pale Caucasian skin. Elegantly hard-boned features that could have been chop shop or real, watchful dark eyes behind nondescript alloy-framed gear. She wore her hair short and combed across—what they used to call a pilot wrap back in the day— severe streaked tones of blond with sharply differentiated spikes tipped in purple radiating along her left cheekbone and out over her brow. That Kandinsky thing was starting to look like fashion. I put her at about fifty, Earth Standard.

Sakarian saw me looking. Grunted.

"This is Audit Security Superintendent Astrid Gaskell of COLIN Earth Oversight. And you know who I am, so I guess we can get started. How much is Mulholland paying you?"

I buried reaction beneath an uncivil grin. "I can't discuss my clients with you, Peter. You know that."

"So you admit you're working for him?" Gaskell put in.

"That's not what I said."

"*Are* you working for him?"

I smiled faintly at her.

"You've been paid," Sakarian said sharply. "Rather well for a flushed-out over-the-hill ex–corporate enforcer, I'd say. You want to keep that money, you'd better start answering our questions."

"You paid me to show up—which I did—and to listen, which I'm still doing. Nobody said anything about my client list. That's data I don't share." I paused, looked from one to the other of them. "Just as I won't be sharing *this* cozy little chat with anyone else. That's what your six hundred slash has bought you so far. Now what else can I do for you?"

The commissioner bristled. He's not a small guy; there's a lot of tight-wired muscle in that big lean frame, and he hasn't let it sag with age and seniority the way Mulholland has. Sakarian made his bones the hard way—multiple stints as an Uplands marshal, decorated half a dozen times, and wounded in the line of duty at least as often before the winds of popular acclaim blew him back down the Gash to head up Metro Homicide. The dark gaze had seen it all, the hard-boned features were seamed and creased with the memory. When he was angry, you knew it.

"You're a fool, Veil. You think Chakana's going to shield you when this storm breaks? You think she'll even try?"

"Hard rain going to fall, is it? You sound like those assholes over at Particle Slam."

Sakarian made a noise in his throat. Astrid Gaskell raised a forestalling hand. "Let's . . . not get off on the wrong foot, Mr. Veil. The aim of Oversight is to track institutional malfeasance and punish it; we have no interest in by-catch. But if you get in our way, you will end up gutted and thrown overboard just the same."

Sense memories of the ocean blew through my mind behind all that metaphor—the Caribbean turned a sudden sullen gray under the rapidly darkening sky, the cold papery taste of rain already in the air. Local Dominican fishing skiffs out on all that gunmetal chop like toys, heeling in the harsh scuffle of the wind. Behind me on the beach, a hastily extinguished and abandoned barbecue trailing the thick mingled scent of fish oil and smoke, my fingers still faintly scorched and greasy from the food. Blond Vaisutis kept a trauma recuperation complex just back beyond the palm line and up a shallow sloping path; a short enough walk even in my state, but something kept me there on the beach, waiting for the storm to break.

"Nice to know nothing's changed back on Earth," I said mildly. "All still runs on cheap threats and collateral damage, does it?"

Not much reaction; she had it tamped down pretty tight. But I saw the way her eyes flared. She tried to hide it, turning elaborately aside to Sakarian.

"You didn't tell me we were dealing with a . . . a *Frocker*, are they called?"

Sakarian was staring at me like something he'd just coughed up. "Who knew?"

The limo went over a bump, took a corner a little tighter than you'd expect with upholstery this plush. I factored in a human driver beyond the panel at my back. Which meant this was an off-the-books car—in Bradbury, the official staff limos all run on city-sanctioned AI. Seemed our esteemed commissioner was playing this one very tight to the chest.

For the first time, I wondered just how clean Sakarian really was, how long in bed with COLIN Earth Oversight he might be.

And where this ride might be going if I didn't shape up the way they wanted.

Almost absently, a cold, dark part of me walked the logistics through. Simple enough to kill the three people seated here, I was wearing three different options for that, not including my bare hands. But there was no easy way through that panel to the driver's compartment.

I breathed out slowly.

"I didn't say I thought things were better here. Mars is a shithole, we all know that. But I got no illusions about things back home either."

Twitch of anger across Sakarian's stony face. He might not be a paid-up Mars First nut, but he was local born, and the comment would have stung. At his side, Astrid Gaskell just nodded absently, as if conceding the point. Behind her gear, her eyes were busy—sketching up and right, up and right, scrolling something down.

"That's very interesting, Mr. Veil." Her tone said it really wasn't. "I find it rather poignant that you talk of *back home* given how long you've been here on Mars. And your file says that you find yourself here under, shall we say, forced circumstances. Overrider contract terminated, summary discharge, blacklisted, and, ah, more or less *dumped* here. In practical terms, exiled. Would you care to comment on that?"

"Not really." If she could get through those firewalls, she didn't need my commentary. "It is what it is."

"Indeed." Her gaze quit the scroll, switched back to front and center, nailed me. "Well then, Mr. Veil—how would you like to go home?"

YOU DON'T KEEP track.

I mean, sure—seven years and change, Mars Standard. That's easy enough, just count the seasons around. But then you have to multiply your figure by not quite two to get the Earth equivalent I still count my age in. And then, technically, you should factor in some fairly high proportion of the four months out of every twelve I spend dreaming deep, with all the cranked-back cellular processes that involves. Dialing back my biosystems that way twice each Martian year shaves about 20 to 30 percent off the lived total. Work through all of that if you can be bothered—there's an end figure in there somewhere.

I stopped giving it space in my head a long time ago.

"Did you hear what I said, Mr. Veil?"

I kept my face carefully impassive. "I'm listening."

"In the course of this audit, we will be making arrests and seeking material witnesses. When we're done, those detainees and material witnesses will be returned on the shuttle to Earth." Astrid Gaskell smiled thinly at me. "It's a wide-ranging mandate. We've got plenty of cryocap space set aside."

"Glad to hear it. You plan on crating the scum out of the Gash, you're going to need an icebox the size of the Mineral Rights Building back there."

Sakarian sneered. "Says the Black Hatch murder op."

"I didn't say I stood out from the crowd." I shrugged. "But then, you're the people trying to hire me."

"Yes." Gaskell was watching me keenly. "We are. My question is whether we're succeeding."

She had me at *go home,* and she probably knew it via her headgear's gestalt scanners if not through simple observation and smarts. I built another shrug, tried to make it casual.

"It's an attractive package. I'd usually charge operating expenses on top."

"That seems reasonable."

"You're six hundred slash up already," Sakarian growled. "Don't push your luck. You want a place on that shuttle, you'll start cooperating right now."

"Cooperation runs both ways, Commissioner. I'm going to need some guarantees in place before we sign off on any of this." I treated the two of them to an amiable smile. "I don't trust COLIN or the BPD any farther than I could throw you both."

Sakarian leaned in, eyes hard as antipersonnel shot behind his gear. "You have me confused with some other motherfucker, Veil. I *am* Bradbury PD. If I say you're getting cryocapped back to Earth, you will *be* cryocapped back to Earth if I have to pack the ice myself."

"On departmental funding, you might have to." I turned to look at Astrid Gaskell. "I'd rather hear what the Earth money has to say."

She nodded. "What . . . other guarantees would you accept, Mr. Veil?"

"The obvious. Initialization data for a cryocapsule locked to my gene code and filed at Vector Red as a matter of public record. After that, I figure it's going to cost you more to stand the cap down than to keep your word. And one thing I do trust is your dedication to the bottom line."

A small, tight silence. Sakarian snorted again.

"Moral little fucker, isn't he?"

"I wonder." The look in Gaskell's eyes was speculative. "Moral or not, Mr. Veil, you'd perhaps do better not to judge us all by the standards of your former employers."

"Why not? Blond Vaisutis was still a fully paid-up COLIN member last time I checked. *The Colony Initiative Hereby Pledges All Means at Its Disposal to Fund and Secure Humankind's Place among the Stars.* And we won't look too hard at our contributors, their means, or where the money comes from, because in the end it all spends the same."

"Hard to explain what we're doing here as auditors, then."

"Paying lip service, Ms. Gaskell. *Tooth whitening on a Komodo dragon*, like Sacran says. But if you want to believe something more mission statement–based, go right ahead. You wouldn't be the first."

"My entire team believes the mission statement, Mr. Veil. Oversight recruits for a service-oriented culture. It is the basis on which we work."

"Sure. Me, too, once upon a time. These days I'm down in the Swirl, no mission statement, just trying to make the rent."

A querying look at Sakarian. "Swirl?"

"It's a shithole part of town. Took Veil a few years to find his level, but he managed it."

I thought bleakly about killing him then. In a pinch, it was always going to be him first anyway; he was by far the most dangerous part of the equation. But that was logistics. Now I let the insistent running-hot thrum come up through my eyes and the palms of my hands, I let myself want it with unguarded hunger. I smiled at him.

"Well, we can't all finesse our way into high-ranking enforcement roles on the strength of kill scores racked up in Grokville, now can we, Commissioner?"

He tautened. "Shut your fucking mouth."

"Sherpa's Gap? Sanguinello? Shooting born-to-lose fuck-ups off the wire in Uplandia, I mean, how hard can that be?"

It was a complex insult and mostly unfair—Sakarian had been exonerated of all blame in the Sherpa's Gap massacre, and he hadn't been anywhere near Sanguinello—but there was a harsh Uplands truth at the heart of it. The marshals were a force to be reckoned with, and sometimes that force got out of hand. I guess it was that truth that got to him. He twitched forward in his seat.

"This is going *nowhere,* gentlemen." Sharp note of reproach in Astrid Gaskell's voice, a command call with it. The fledgling confrontation collapsed. "Mr. Veil, I am sorry your levels of trust for COLIN and local law enforcement are so low. But I'm afraid that for the time being you're going to have to take my word. You do at least have a gear grab of this conversation, and I would hope that can serve as interim collateral. In the meantime, I will set the cryocap encoding in motion. I understand BPD has your gene record on file—"

"This piece of shit? Oh, yes."

She shot Sakarian a weary glance. He shut up, but his gaze stayed on me.

"Well, that should expedite matters, then. But it will still take some time to secure the cap against your codes."

I spread my hands. "Take all the time you like. I'm not going anywhere."

She gave me a thin smile. "In point of fact, you're going to Cradle City within the next few days, in the company of my colleague Madison Madekwe. We're less sure why *you're* being sent, why this Lieutenant . . . Chakana chose you for the assignment. Perhaps you'd care to enlighten us."

"Because she doesn't think it warrants using a real cop, maybe?"

Astrid Gaskell's eyes narrowed. "She told you that?"

"She didn't tell me a thing, Ms. Gaskell. She hired the work done, and I didn't ask any questions. Like I said, I'm trying to make the rent."

"Logbook for Police Plaza says you were in holding night before last." Sakarian, still hard-eyed and unforgiving. "Prime suspect in an OC Strip hit. Two days later, here you are, back on the streets again. Been trading favors with Our Lady of Eternal Graft, have we?"

"I believe it was a case of mistaken identity," I said evenly. "Lieutenant Chakana was good enough to shake out the kinks and expedite my release."

"She's heading for a fall, Veil. You do know that, don't you?"

"What, like Mulholland was back in '95, you mean? I'll bet she's trembling in her boots."

I saw Gaskell doing quick mental math, matching Martian years with the Earth calendar or maybe just pulling up the reference on her gear. She grimaced when she got it.

"That was . . . unfortunate," she said. "There was a lack of political will at the time and way too much going on elsewhere."

I'd had a couple of Bradbury acquaintances who were quietly disappeared because they'd turned whistle-blower in the run-up to the supposed audit of '95 and their witness protection collapsed in the aftermath of the COLIN mission abort. Informed rumor says they both ended up a meter down in the Upland regolith somewhere outside Keplerville, wrists wired together behind their backs, buried alive. From what I hear, they're probably not short of company.

Unfortunate. Yeah, you could call it that.

Maybe Astrid Gaskell saw some of this in my eyes. She cleared her throat.

"As I understand it, the audit prep was in any case a rush job and, frankly, pretty shoddy work. Hurried, full of holes and flawed premises, wild accusations, and crusader zeal. I'm told it never would have stood up. Had COLIN not aborted when they did, we would have had a public relations catastrophe on our hands. Holding off like this until we were ready for the fight, we've saved ourselves a very real credibility gap."

"Good for you."

She leaned forward, voice tightening with true-believer intensity. "It's for real this time, Mr. Veil. Make no mistake. We are here to take Mulholland down once and for all, and anyone we can prove was complicit under his patronage is going down with him." Deep breath—she visibly forced herself to sit back again, to put a studied calm back into her tone. "Which is why I will not tolerate any local interference in my agents' fieldwork. I won't ask you again about Lieutenant Chakana's instructions because, frankly, I no longer care. You have a new brief now, from me, from COLIN Earth Oversight, from the top. You are to protect Madison Madekwe's life as if it were your own—"

That wouldn't keep her very safe, I thought sourly.

"—and provide Commissioner Sakarian here with regular updates on her progress once you reach Cradle City. You will follow any instructions we give you during this time, up to and including bringing Ms. Madekwe back to Bradbury whether she herself deems it appropriate or not. That's how you get your ticket home. Am I clear?"

"Very. Is Ms. Madekwe aware of this touching concern for her safety? Or does she not need to know about this conversation?"

It got me a slightly more generous COLIN-vetted smile. "Madison Madekwe is a courageous and talented investigator, but her courage has been known to tip over into inappropriate risk taking. And she is not very amenable to compromise or operational restraint. So yes, we are asking for discretion on your part."

"Tell her and your ticket home is fucked," Sakarian supplied in case I had any lingering doubts.

I ignored him. "Why don't you just tell her to stay put? Conduct her investigation from Bradbury, stay out of the Uplands altogether? You're the security executive. She'd have to follow your orders, wouldn't she?"

"You think the Uplands are the only place she won't be safe?"

I traded glances with Sakarian, felt a sudden, unlooked for fellowship in the exchange. We'd both spent enough time up there to know.

"Not the only place, no, but they're a very good start. You haven't answered my question, Ms. Gaskell. Why not order Madekwe to sit tight?"

She hesitated—whatever answer she was building still not quite assembled. I waited for her to put it together.

"You were an overrider once," she said. "An interplanetary op. In Madekwe's position, would you follow an order like that, an order to *sit tight*?"

"If it served mission-critical objectives, yes."

"And if—in your on-site opinion—it didn't?"

I nodded slowly. "All right."

"Payload *costs,* Mr. Veil. I'm sure you don't need me to tell you that. As with the corporate bodies we oversee, we are not in the habit of hauling dead weight. To be deployed at the interplanetary level, our auditors must, by definition, be high-value operatives. Every member of the audit team is seasoned, resilient, resourceful, tenacious . . . and self-reliant. None of them will play safe in the face of challenges or follow orders that tell her she should. And despite anything you'll see or hear me say for public consumption over the next several weeks, I really wouldn't want it any other way."

"Right." I judged the moment well and truly defused. "You mind answering me a question, Ms. Gaskell?"

"If I can."

"What's so fucking important about Pavel Torres?"

. . .

IT WAS ONLY a heartbeat hesitation, but it was there. I saw the strain it put on Gaskell and Sakarian as they struggled not to glance at each other. I felt the clerkish guy at my side stiffen in a very unclerkish fashion.

Opposite me, Gaskell was suddenly elaborately casual.

"As far as I'm aware, there's nothing very important about Torres himself. He's really only an indicator, a sign that something may be wrong somewhere in the lottery system's security protocols." She used the urbane smile on me again. "But really, I don't have much detail on the matter. Auditors are largely autonomous in the cases they're assigned, and the lottery review isn't mine. You'd do better to ask Madison Madekwe herself about it."

She was good. Might have beaten a run-of-the-mill gestalt warning package, maybe even some of the stuff at the pricier end of the market. Most of those systems can be fooled if you know what you're doing and have enough hard-drilled discipline to deploy that knowledge. But even the best-of-breed premier-brand gestalt software suites are a pale imitation of the off-limits military tech they're derived from. And Osiris runs most of that tech as standard.

I looked through my lenses at Astrid Gaskell of COLIN Earth Oversight as she smiled at me, and she might as well have had the word *LIAR* stenciled across her forehead in centimeter-thick crimson marker.

TWENTY

THEY LET ME out on a corner somewhere south of Charter Row—it wasn't quite the Swirl, but I guess you had to give them points for coming close. I'd done some work in the area a couple of years back and recognized the unlovely streets—automated guesthouse facades, work apparel dispensaries, and a scattering of cheap glass-fronted restaurants long emptied of lunchtime trade, not yet gearing up for dinner. One of them was so cheap they were paying a human to mop the floor.

Aside from the cleaner, I saw no other signs of life. No vehicle traffic, no passersby—all told, a pretty good place for a drop-off. The insomniac clerk stepped out with me and pointed up the street.

"It's that way," he said not very companionably. "You can walk from here."

"Yeah, I know."

I watched him climb back aboard the limo, watched it pull away and corner sharply north at the next intersection as if anxious to get back to a better class of neighborhood. I turned to face the other way and started walking.

Incoming call, said Osiris in my ear. *It's the girl next door.*

All right.

"Hey, overrider." Voice almost as throaty as the one I'd given Osiris and twice as inviting—I felt a twinge go through ancient protocols in my groin. "Where you at? Been trying to get you for a solid hour."

"Yeah, sorry—locked out calls for a meeting. Been busy. What can I do you for, Ari?"

"Hey, *you* called *me*, remember?" she growled. "You want me or not? I'm just off the cheap shift here, killing time. How's it hanging?"

"Pretty shriveled and unimpressive, since you ask."

"You want me to come over and fix that for you?"

"That a trick question?"

She laughed. I thought of her head tipped back, that long tanned throat. "How come I can't see you, soak?"

Because 'Ris keeps me stripped back to bare audio feed whenever I'm on the move. Black Hatch operational habit, improves focus, cuts out any backdrop clues to your location. Stay cautious, stay alive. And like so much from those long-gone days, I've never gotten around to disabling the preference.

"You *can* see me," I said, pace quickening of its own accord. "Be there in half an hour."

"I'll be waiting."

"You do that."

I made Ceres Drive 4 in seventeen minutes and change. Forced pace, blood pumping, running a light sweat by the time the capsule rack came in sight. Makes all the difference when you've got something to run toward. I punched in the access code, eased up on the stairs, took my hurry down to something a little more deliberate, trying to arrive with a modicum of the killer poise she liked.

She was waiting propped against the flank of the Dyson, wrapped in an Uplands greatcoat with the storm collar closed. Headgear off, Medusa clasp still in her hair from work—thick, dark tresses weaving slowly around her face as if in eerie obeisance to her sculpted cheekbones and lips. One booted heel up and pressed back against the curve of the capsule surface. She pretended not to notice me as I came along the gantry, studied her nails intently instead. I got up close, put a thumb into the static seam that held the greatcoat closed. Took off my gear with my other hand, stashed it in my jacket, tried to meet her eyes. She tilted her head away, went on admiring her nails like I wasn't there. Humming a little tune now, infectious grin starting to split her mouth. The coat opened under my hand, hung aside, revealed the worked-out, worked-on dancer's body beneath.

She wasn't wearing a lot more under there than she would have on stage at Maxine's. My eyes grabbed after detail like a poor man stumbling to gather up a spill of high-end groceries—the tat-delineated cleavage, the subcute support web lifting the full breasts high and wide, the taut tanned midriff below, and the long, muscled thighs. I breathed in hard, got the waft of stale perfume and sweat rising from her skin. I pressed one palm flat to her belly, fingertips touching the joint of her thigh and the thin strip of black mesh cloth that spanned it. A poorly suppressed chuckle welled up in her chest, broke loose low and dirty. Her flesh felt fractionally sticky to the touch with dance sweat and the pheromone aerosols they sprayed at Maxine's. She tilted her hips up against the pressure of my hand, turning, grinning, laughing mint breath into my face. Pupils still a little blown with the last of the cheap sindree she wrapped herself in to get through work. I closed up the final gap between us, put my other hand on a breast. It felt a little like falling.

"Ask me how it's hanging now," I said tightly.

She pushed one thigh in hard between my legs. Put her mouth over my ear. "Rhetorical, darlin'," she murmured. "You going to invite me in or what?"

I voiced the Dyson unlocked, had to do it twice to beat the shiver and gasp in my voice as she bit at my neck. The hatch cranked, we fell in through it, nearly fell over. Made it stumbling, tangling limbs and clothing, about halfway to the bed before she shoved me in the chest to hold me off, shrugged the greatcoat off one shoulder at a time, and let it slide to the floor. She stood hipshot, boots and black mesh thong, restless dark Medusa hair to her naked shoulders. She lifted her chin at me.

"This what you want?"

"Is that a tri—"

She slammed up against me, fingers across my mouth. "You shut up. You shut up, overrider. You use that mouth for something else now."

And she pressed me down slowly, past the jutting wet-dream breasts, the faint gathered scent of her body in the tat-tracked hollow between, the tensed muscle wall of her dancer's belly, and then into the tight black mesh cloth at the juncture of her thighs, already damp with arousal. I rubbed the bridge of my nose hard in the crease, got her scent for real, got hands on the thong, pulled it aside.

Sank my tongue in deep.

She shuddered, dug nails into my scalp, pulled me tighter in. I worked the parted flesh insistently for a while, urged back and forth by her cradling hands, moved up at last and found her clit, sucked it in, teased around it with my tongue the way I knew she liked. She gusted a single filthy choked curse, and I felt her knees unlock. Her rigid dominatrix stance gave way, she crumpled giggling to the floor, curling where the greatcoat lay, thighs flexing gently open and shut like the jaws of some undecided mantrap. I dropped to my knees beside her.

"C'mere, you." She reached for my loosened trousers, tugging them down.

I wagged out and free, pulsing hard as a clenched fist—four months dreaming deep will do that to you—and she grabbed hold of me like a cop pulling a billy club. She rubbed the head of my cock back and forth over her breasts, grinning, watching me watch, pulled me closer, rubbed the glans across her face, around and around her parted lips, finally pressed it into her mouth and sucked hard.

The force of the sensation nearly bent me double. She took my prick back out of her mouth, raised her brows at me comically.

"No? Too much?"

I made a soft snarling noise, pushed my hips at her. She nudged my cock with her nose, darted her tongue out and licked at it.

"Say please."

"Fucking please."

"Well, why didn't you say so?" She plunged her mouth back over the glans, cupped my balls in her free hand. We settled in against each other, comfortable with custom. I reached and levered her thighs apart. She squirmed closer, breasts pressing and rubbing flat against my belly, nipples like softly prodding little fingertips. She flexed her lower body at me.

"Race you," I said, and lowered my face back into all the wet creases and her languidly urgent heat.

AFTERWARD, EMPTIED OUT, we lay there top to tail across the folds of her coat without speaking, and she hummed a sated little tune to herself to fill the quiet. As neighbors go, Ari's pretty hard to fault, but she really can't handle silence in any quantity.

"Took you some time," I said for something to say.

Legacy of four months in a hib coma, I'd blown apart in her mouth long before I managed to get her off. And I like to think I'm not unskilled in these things. She chuckled.

"Yeah, you were *real* excited back there. Been a while, huh?"

"Been since the last time we hooked up. You?"

"Well, yeah, a while, too. But—you know." She lifted a shoulder against my hip. "Creeps at the club. Takes some time to let go of it all sometimes. Daylight crowd don't tip for shit, either, get some real assholes in. Fucking shitty day all around. Where'd you get those rings?"

"Won them at poker. Why, you like them?"

She pulled a face at the ceiling. "About as much as that cannon you got slung under your arm. Which has sharp edges, by the way. You plan on showing up to all our playdates strapped like that, we should maybe get out of our clothes properly next time."

"Slipped my mind. You hear what happened at Vallez Girlz?"

"Uh huh."

"Anybody talking about it?"

"Are you fucking kidding me?" She propped herself up on one elbow to meet my eye. Her hair hung flat and immobile around her face now that the Medusa clip was off—it made her look oddly vulnerable. "It's *all* any- one's talking about, Hak. Girls are running their mouths backstage like their opinion suddenly started paying better than blowjobs."

"That'll be the day."

"Yeah, well." She lifted one leg, flexed her foot, and peered critically at the scuffed toe of her boot. "You ask me, they better tamp it down. Talk like that with Sal Quiroga's guys cruising the Strip for answers, you got a good shot at ending up like Synthia did."

I said nothing. She caught the silence, looked at me, and abruptly dropped her leg back where it had been.

"I didn't mean nothing by that, Hak. I know you did your best for Syn; I never would have brought her to you if I'd thought Quiroga was going to go fucking nuts like that. You being late in the cycle and all, it wasn't—"

I reached out and touched her face very gently. "Skip it. She was your friend, Ari, she needed your help. You knew I did that kind of work. You didn't do anything wrong."

"But she . . ." Mouth clamped tight, the sindree-blasted pupils staring and lost, facing the desolate truth of where she lived her life. "They fucking . . . what they *did* to her . . ."

It flashed through my head, lurid with imagined detail. I never saw the body. BPD bagged it as a standard Mariner Strip fuck-up fatality, and I had no official business going anywhere near it. But Sal made a point of letting a couple of Vallez Girlz dancers catch a glimpse of what had gone on in the back office that night, and they didn't dump the remains very far up the Strip either. The word went out—duly aided and abetted by a restless media maw, hungrier, as ever, for impact and sensation than for anything resembling actual journalism. *Dancer found violently raped and mutilated, we have footage from the scene, right after these messages from our sponsors.*

"I'm *glad*," Ariana said vehemently. It squeezed out tears in the corners of her eyes, it made her look suddenly very young. "I'm fucking *glad* Sal Quiroga's dead, he was a piece of shit. I only wish . . ."

Looking at her, I felt something melt a little behind my own eyes. Coming that hard had kicked the thrum of running-hot right out of me. Sure, it'd be back, but not for a while. I hinged myself into a sitting position, gathered her into my arms.

"Hey, Ari. Let it go."

She looked up into my face, must have seen something there that I'd let slip. "Hak . . ."

"Yeah?"

"Wasn't *you*, was it? That shit last night? Fucking Quiroga up like that?"

"Oh, come on. I've been out of the tank what, two days?" Not entirely sure why I was lying, except it felt like protective measures for one of us or maybe both. "This is some turf thing, Ari. It's just a falling out between the *familias andinas*. Or it's some other crowd trying to move in on Sal's action. Just keep out of it, keep your head down, you'll see. It'll blow over."

She sniffed a little. "Yeah, I guess."

"You still lighting those candles for Syn?"

"I don't know—sometimes, yeah."

She sniffed again, harder now, like snorting something down. She swiped impatiently at her tears. The old guardedness crept through her once more, a progressive tightening up that was almost visible. She elbowed herself firmly up and out of my embrace, sat away from me a little, hugging her knees to her chest. Body language unequivocal—she just got a little too naked with me for her own peace of mind.

"Couple of the girls at Vallez said there were Crater Critters in the club that night." Her tone settled back toward conversational detached. "Said they'd been in a lot the last couple of months, not as customers neither. Meetings and shit."

"There you go, then." *Let's get off this vector, Veil. Change the subject.* "Hey, you see who blew into town off the shuttle?"

"Yeah, sure." Riding a sudden jag of sindree-crash irritability. "Bunch of interfering fuckwit Earth superclerks trying to tell us how to run things."

"Apart from that."

She shook her head *no, and I don't give a shit.*

"Sundry Charms." No reaction—just the beginnings of a distant comedown stare setting in. I cranked up my efforts. "You know, the guy from Star-Crossed Crew. You were into their stuff, right? That summer I was working doors for Maxine?"

"Not really. That's Chami you're thinking of." She levered herself abruptly to her feet, tugged at her greatcoat by one sleeve. "You're sitting on my coat."

I rolled aside, wordless, propped myself back on my elbows. She fished the coat up, shrugged herself back into it.

"Gotta go, Hak."

"Hey, no you don't. Stay, have a drink. I want a rematch."

She fixed a small bright smile on her mouth. Scooped up Medusa clip and thong from the capsule floor, stuffed them both in a coat pocket.

"Nah, we both got what we wanted here. I'll see you around."

"Well," I groped around for some way to fix the sudden chill. "You tell Chami when you run into her, I rode down from the Ares Acantilado yesterday, sitting right opposite her pal Charms."

"She won't care, Hak. She's right off him ever since he split from Star-Crossed."

"Oh."

"Yeah. Told me when she saw the feeds on him coming out, he's a cheap fucking fake—had so much work done, it barely looks like the same human being anymore. That's Earth for you, right? All that fucking gravity dragging at everything, all the vanity trying to fix it. Decadent fucking deadweights. Why'nt they just leave us alone?"

She went to the hatch. I voiced it open for her, watched her blow me a halfhearted kiss and duck out. I lay back on the hard capsule floor with a sigh, pressed the heels of my palms into my eyes, and arched myself rigid for what seemed like quite a while.

Decadent fucking deadweights from Earth. Right.

Madison Madekwe—the aniseed-flavored heat of her mouth on mine, the press of her body up against me in the elevator . . .

Yeah, yeah—all right, enough of that.

And deep in the fibers of my hibernoid makeup, the first creeping trickle of running-hot, already making its way back.

YOU'RE A FOOL, *Veil.*

Sakarian's words floating back through my head. I grimaced, trying hard to believe he was wrong. I got my trousers back up from around my ankles. Got to my feet. Nearly clouted my head on the low curve of the capsule roof on my way up. Come *on,* overrider. Enough of this postcoital shit—get it together. I reached under my arm, tugged the Cadogan-Izumi and the gecko-grip holster loose. Fucking thing had been digging painfully into my side as well all through the festivities. I tossed it onto my desk and pulled the rest of my disarrayed clothing irritably back together. Went to wash Ari's juices off my face.

You think Chakana's going to shield you when this storm breaks? You think she'll even try?

I lifted my face from the basin. Wiped water off my face and met my own eyes in the mirror.

What storm?

The audit? That storm had already broken as far as I could see. Mulholland was running for cover, Chakana was running damage limitation for him, and the COLIN Earth Oversight team was unfolding out of Wells and the Ares Acantilado like some sleepy but *very* hungry octopus, tentacles coiling and prodding, searching for felony prey . . .

What storm was Sakarian talking about, then?

He thought I knew about it, that much was obvious. But then, he and Astrid Gaskell clearly thought I knew all sorts of things I didn't.

I went and sat on the floor with my back to the bed shelf, arms draped loose on my knees, staring into the pastel-shaded geometric weave of screen art above the desk opposite.

Chakana hires you to protect Madison Madekwe like it's no big deal, Madekwe can't get rid of you fast enough, Chakana finds out in no time flat. Madekwe wants to head out to the Uplands as soon as possible, then, suddenly, she doesn't. Meantime, COLIN Earth Oversight hires you secretly all over again to do the job Chakana already gave you.

Hannu Holmstrom's anomaly clustering was starting to build up around me exactly the way it built up around Pablito Torres right before he disappeared into Upland thin air.

It was all starting to feel very—

A sudden sharp chiming took down my musings like crashed navigation. The pastel shades on the workstation screen blew out, replaced by rapid schematic traceries in black and harsh orange. Lines met and matched, lozenge decals lit up.

"External threat detected," the Dyson's skin systems said in cool, motherly tones. "External threat detected."

TWENTY-ONE

WHEN I WASHED up on Mars fourteen years back, things were pretty hand to mouth for a while. There'd been some kind of systemic cash-flow choke back on Earth, and the Marstech markets were in spin along with just about everything else. No one in the Gash had money for anything, least of all hiring me. Safe hibernation for my first couple of seasons as a Martian hinged on cobbling together favors from the overseers of moth-balled research facilities, watchmen at bulk storage parks, and managers of bottom-end capsule hostels up and down the Valley. Every eight months, Earth reckoned, I went down to sleep knowing I was vulnerable to spec break-ins and ram raids, vandalism, flash asset sales, staff restruc-turing, and, of course, simple changes of heart on the part of men and women I mostly had very limited reasons to trust.

Something had to change.

I bought the Dyson capsule out of bankrupt stock from a bunch of second-tier asset strippers on Reagan Boulevard. Like most of their spe-cies, they didn't have a clue what the gear that passed through their hands was really worth. The company logo embossed on the hatch—cogs and stars, generic and dull, perfectly forgettable—meant nothing to them, and they'd probably never heard of the Lagrange Point tax haven the company was registered out of either. All they knew in their feral market innocence was what their primaries told them—some transworld corporate had to get out of the shipping business in a hurry, was off-loading its long-haul hardware to shore up a rapidly crumbling balance sheet, and did they want a piece of this fucking action or not? It never occurred to them to wonder why an operation like that would need to wind up quite so fast or why its hardware assets should need to be broken up and scattered to the winds of commerce quite so completely.

Or what those assets might really be worth.

I never saw any good reason to bring them up to speed.

I called in some favors, agreed to a couple of pieces of work I'd rather not have done, got some credit leverage from dubious sources to cover the rest. I took the Dyson out of there on a flatbed crawler, found a place to hook it up in the Swirl the very same day. I cleaned it up, plugged it in, got the lights back on and the sleep-state batteries back up to charged. The sense of kinship I felt for the thing was dizzying.

I had a home at last.

And with it about 50 million slash of hardened military-grade skin systems.

I slept a lot better after that.

"THREE SUBJECTS, ARMED," those very expensive skin systems told me now. "Variable distances. Mapped and scanned."

I was already on my feet. "Let's see it."

The screen's alarm display blew apart in black and orange fragments, settled back into a grayscale wireframe map of the Dyson's immediate surroundings. Three floors below us, a blue wireframe human climbed the caged staircase, touched with red at the right hand. The skin systems spun in tighter, grabbed the red-effect blotch, unpacked it into a verification cube, and flung it to an upper corner of the screen. Specs welled up around the weapon it showed.

"Glock Sandman, second generation," the Dyson reckoned. "Spectra-bounce indicates local alloy manufacture under Mars license."

"Well, he's not getting in here if that's all he's got, doesn't matter where it was made. What about the others?"

The screen view pulled back, gave me a broader context. Two more wireframe humans coming up the street at a fast lope. Red in the lead figure's cradling arms, under the second's armpit. And a big crimson blotch on number two's shoulders, backpack size.

"What the fuck is that?" I snapped, pointing.

"Ng Systems Void Anti-Hull Missile submunition, stripped and timer-equipped for clandestine deployment." The screen grabbed the toasty glow of the backpack, spun it up, and laid it on its back for me in another cube. Dense spider-thin specs text sprouted all over. The other two weapons followed. "Smith & Wesson full-auto riot carbine, spectra-bounce indicates—"

"Never mind the fucking finger food! What can you do about the VAHM?"

"Countermeasures running."

I leaned into the screen, pulse ticking upward a notch. Looked like about three hundred meters down the street, and the lead scout had breached the gate security for them already. They could be all the way up here and setting the charge in less than five minutes. Anybody's guess what capacity the subwarhead might retain, severed from its delivery system like that, but at even single-figure percentages of optimum yield, it'd be enough. In fully fledged form, a VAHM is a fire-and-forget ship killer. They can launch from anything up to a hundred thousand kilometers out, chase down their quarry, and turn it into so much shredded space junk in the blink of an eye. Dumped against the Dyson's skin by hand, at a bare minimum, the submunition would punch right through the hull and turn the interior into a superheated blizzard of shrapnel spalling. Anyone inside was going to get simultaneously cooked and shredded like pulled pork shoulder.

No sitting tight, then. If the countermeasures didn't work, if the Dyson's antique hackitecture couldn't get into the warhead's predator brain, I was going to have to go out and meet these motherfuckers hand to hand.

I glared at the little wireframe procession. They were moving at covert recon pace, hugging the fractal-curved side of Ceres Drive, checking corners as they went. Suggested they were strangers in this part of town. Even if there had been anybody on the streets, the locals in the Swirl aren't big on community action.

These guys didn't seem to know that, and it was slowing them down.

Yeah, but slow or not, they're getting there, Hak.

It was a couple of minutes or less. And about thirty seconds before the advance scout reached my door with his Glock and had me blocked in.

Decision time.

I shot a glance at the bed, the edge the Heckler & Koch sat webbed beneath.

Shit, shit, shit . . .

"Where are those fucking countermeasur—"

On screen—a sudden soft-blooming vermilion flower.

The two wireframe humans in the street inked out at the heart of the bloom, gone forever. A split second later, the shock wave rolled in and slapped the capsule lightly across the side. I felt it through the soles of my feet. Below the gantry level, I saw the wireframe of the advance scout stagger slightly on the stairs.

"Countermeasures effected," said the Dyson serenely.

I was already moving, tearing the HK loose, darting for the hatch.

"Door!"

The hatch cycled across—I toothpasted through soon as the gap stood wide enough. Heard boots clatter on the staircase below, heading away. *Rabbit motherfucker.* I sprinted for the top of the stairs. Caught a glimpse of dark clothing below as the figure made the corner and the next flight downward. I plowed down the stairs, hurled myself into the angle of the caged stairwell, another flash glimpse, threw up the HK, and fired.

Hollow boom. Antipersonnel shredder load pinged and splintered off metalwork everywhere. I thought I heard a yelp. Maybe tagged him, maybe not. I leaped after him, three steps at a time now. Came around the next angled turn, leaned for the shot—

Something cracked sharply at my feet.

Thick white boil of smoke; it came up fast around my legs, wrapped me like sudden fog. The nictitating membranes slammed across in my eyes faster than conscious thought. But I drew breath before I could lock the impulse up. Felt the ragged tearing edge of the gas in my throat and started choking. I fired through the smoke on general principles, got the same hollow boom again, the same musical peppering of the load off metal. Couldn't see a *fucking thing,* murky yellow membraned vision, but I already knew. Target lost. You can feel these things. Tagged or not, this particular rabbit motherfucker was gone.

I hung my head, wagged it side to side, squeezed my eyelids shut. No dice. The gas seeped right through anyway, put tiny razors in my eyes.

And in a minute I was going to need to breathe.

I made a ragged snarling noise in my throat. Staggered back up the stairs and out of the worst of the smoke. *Keep moving, Hak, get clear of this shit.* Two more flights up, bracing each step on the railing, and my lungs bottomed out. I let myself draw breath, gagging and coughing violently, turned and collapsed sitting at the top. Pulse in my temples like fists, chest heaving. Coughing, fucking *coughing* until the tears were starting from my eyes and my rib cage ached as if from a beating.

Finally, the spasm wound down. I sat wheezing hoarsely with the HK laid across my knees, chopped barrel still warm. Below me, the slowly coiling smoke thinned and blew away, gave me a view down through the gantry grating of the pod rack's levels. Hard to be sure with the membranes, streaming eyes, and all, but I didn't think anyone was hanging around down there.

I kept a finger on the HK's trigger guard anyway.

Paco Sempere, I'm going to take your fucking guts out hand over hand for this.

I canned the thought, satisfying though it was, almost as soon as it surfaced. Sempere's Frocker crew couldn't have put this together if their collective lives and separatist dreams depended on it. They were barely up to—

Footfalls on the gantry behind me.

I whipped around, HK rising in my hands.

"Christ, Hak! It's *me!*" Ariana was a dozen meters away in cheaply printed pajamas, half her smeared war paint still on, frozen into a flinch as she saw the shotgun raised against her. "What the *fuck?* What's going on?"

I put down the HK. Gestured vaguely at the street below. "Had some visitors, but they blew themselves up. Listen, the cops are going to be here. You holding Mellow?"

She blinked. "Yeah, scored some Pillow Bomb from Pete couple of nights back. Why, you want?"

"Not for me." I pressed thumb and finger into my streaming eyes, wiped away some of the copious tears. "But if I were you, I'd get right back inside and dose yourself up. Save you getting cold-called and marched down to Sojourner Street for one of those extensive witness de-brief numbers."

Her shoulders slumped. "They can just kick the door in, Hak."

"Not without probable cause and not without some decent intrusion tech. Neither of which they'll be bringing right now. Probably get around to bracing you at some point, but it could be days. Maybe more with this Earth Oversight shit going on."

"But . . ." She hesitated, halfway to turning and going. "You okay? You going to be—"

I waved her off. "Go on. My party, I'll clean up."

She went.

She looked back twice on the way, though. That made me smile.

MY EYES WERE still burning when Chakana showed up.

I leaned on the end gantry rail and squinted my blurred vision down to something approaching focus as she swung out of the crawler in the street below. Laconic greetings back and forth to the holding team they had down there in the gathering dusk. Heads bent together for a moment, then someone gestured upward at the rack and she tipped her head back to look. She seemed to be staring right up into my swimming, stinging gaze.

I raised one slow arm in salute.

No wave back. She headed briskly for the stairs. I thumbed some of the thinning crop of tears out of my eyes in preparation.

"Popular guy, huh?" she offered when she got to me, only mildly out of breath from jogging up the eight flights. "You think you could have left *something* for forensics? They're having a hard time finding six organic molecules still stuck together down there."

"Talk to the Dyson."

"What for? We can't touch it." She got back the last of her wind with a single hard breath. "Fucking home defense ordnances. If I ever get to be commissioner, that shit is going out the lock."

"Hey, you got my vote."

"Don't be an asshole, Veil. What really happened here?"

I shrugged. "Like I told your Response sergeant. Three guys, one Void Anti-Hull Missile warhead. One advance scout and a carry crew of two. Dyson hacked the VAHM, took care of the crew, and I let the scout get away."

"That's not like you."

"What can I tell you? I'm mellowing with age."

Sudden twinge through my left eye, and it started streaming again. I grunted, cursed, pressed a palm heel hard into the pain.

"Oh, yeah—they said." Something crept into Chakana's voice that might just about have been sympathy. "You got hit with a weepy, right?"

I grunted again, tipped my head back in an attempt to stave off the pain.

"Here—come here—let me see that." She cupped my head firmly between both hands and tilted it down again. "No, not like—"

"I'm fine, Chakana."

"Fucking take your *hand* away for a minute, will you—just let me—"

"I *said* I'm fine."

"Yeah, yeah. Sure you are." She took my wrist, levered my hand gently away from my face. For some reason, I let her. "You can get corneal scorch from that shit, you don't clean it out. What fucking use you going to be to me if I let you go blind?"

She peered narrowly into my face, eyes intent behind her gear lenses. She pressed the edge of my lower eyelid down with a fingertip.

"Crime scene guys already gave me a rinse kit," I told her. "I'm good. This is just trace, probably caught some under the nictitating layer."

"Yeah, well." She shifted her attention to my other eye. "Best to be sure. You get any kind of look at this scout you let go?"

"Dark clothes. Fast moving."

"Good, succinct. We'll put that out there, probably have him in custody by nightfall. All right, you're not showing any damage my gear can find." She let go of my head, gave it a slight shove. "You stink of pussy, though. Fast work even for a slut like you if that's our Madison."

"It isn't."

She gave me a speculative look. "If you say so. Where is she?"

"Where do you think? She's at Vector Red, just like yesterday."

"I thought I told you to—"

"Give me a motherfucking break, Nikki!"

That seemed to get through. She nodded grimly. "All right, we'll come to that. Meanwhile, suppose you give me a name for that pussy you've spent the afternoon with your nose in."

"What for?"

"What for? That's a good one. How about *because we're investigating your attempted fucking murder and this is how it's done?* That work for you?"

"You're wasting your time. Working girl, she's got nothing to do with this."

"Classy." Chakana's face said she didn't believe a word of it. "Well, whoever it was, did you consider she might be why you were so, uh, *mellow* about this scout guy you didn't manage to catch?"

I'd been thinking the same thing myself for the last hour. I covered for it with a sour grin. "You really have to get that jealousy looked at, Nikki."

"My violent impulses, too, so I'd shut the fuck up if I were you." She leaned on the rail at my side, stared past me into the street below. Silence sat between us, almost companionable. I waited. Finally she shifted. "So. Other than angry husbands, can you think of anyone might have this much of a grudge against you?"

"Off the top of my head? Can't be more than a couple of dozen guys up and down the Valley. Not really the point, though, is it?"

"No? What's the point?"

"Point is, I don't know anyone who has this *capability*. A tactical naval warhead? Most of the people that want to kill me barely have the budget for a nice knife. This isn't street, this is something handed down from on high."

Chakana snorted. "On high where? Everybody up the chain's too busy running for cover at the moment to worry about guys like you."

"I don't think this is about me."

"Not about you? You really are mellowing with age."

"Come on, Nikki—this is about Madekwe's Pablito crusade coming to bite us in the ass. I already told you there's something else going on there, and you didn't want to hear it."

"Still don't now. You think I haven't got enough else to do?" She shot me a sidelong glance. "And anyway, I don't see how killing you scuttles anything Madekwe's doing. She can always get another tour guide. Why would they come after you?"

"Thanks."

"No one's irreplaceable, Veil." Levering herself off the rail with a sigh. "You know that. Now come on. You're going to let me look at the Dyson's memory, right? Not going to force me to get a warrant?"

"Sundry Charms."

She was already on her way back along the gantry. She stopped and turned. "Sun-dried what?"

"*Sundry*. Charms. Ultratripper off the shuttle, big cross-media star back in the Pacific Rim on Earth. I rode in with him. He's irreplaceable."

She stood looking at me warily. "What's he got to do with this?"

"Nothing. I'm making a point. Charms *is* irreplaceable. He's . . ." I gestured with both hands. "A living brand. He's like human Marstech. His job is *being* Sundry Charms. No one else can do that. Ergo—he's irreplaceable."

"Yeah. Fascinating. Veil, what exactly the *fuck* are you gibbering about?"

I hesitated. "I don't know. But early yesterday morning you haul me out of jail and give me a job looking after Madison Madekwe. Now here we are, not forty-eight hours later, and someone *very* well equipped is trying to kill me. You really think that's coincidence?"

"Doesn't have to be. Could just be circumstance. You were in jail for a reason. Maybe this is the fallout. Maybe it's your Crater Critter pals tidy-ing up loose ends. Ever think of that?"

"Why—" I stopped myself. Started again more carefully. "Why would anyone out of Hellas want me dead?"

"Well, let's see." She paced back toward me until we were punching distance apart. Close enough that I could smell the coffee on her breath. "Because you killed Sal Quiroga for them, maybe, and now you might talk? Because you're out of jail without their help, and maybe they figure you spilled your guts to cut a deal? Because in the end they could give a shit about the life of some Gash ghost stupid enough to hire on as a tool for triad leverage in the Valley, and now that tool is surplus to require-ments? Come to that, could be Quiroga's own connections after you. I mean, word is the high-end *familias* soured on Sal years back, but still—they can't be very happy about this little power shift you've midwifed for Hellas."

I said nothing. I knew I wasn't currently surplus to requirements where the Crater Critters were concerned because I'd been out yesterday sorting their tax affairs for them. And I seriously doubted the *familias andinas* would lift a finger to avenge Sal Quiroga. I'd done my homework on that angle back when I was putting his death together with Gradual.

Chakana gestured impatiently. "Any of this making shapes you recog-nize? Or do I have it all wrong?"

"No, you might have something there—if I'd actually killed Quiroga, that is."

She rolled her eyes. "I'm trying to help you out here, Veil."

"Are you? Got anyone in particular assigned?"

"What's that supposed to mean?"

"You want to know what hardware that advance scout was packing?" I'd toyed with not telling her, but she'd pull it off the Dyson's memory now anyway. Might as well see her face as she found out. "A Glock Sand-man."

She went still. The shrug came late, way too late for my liking. "So? Popular gun last I checked."

"Yeah, standard police issue last I checked as well."

"Oh, *what,* Veil? *What?* You think *I* put out a contract on you? You think *I* had eyes on you all this time?"

"I think someone did."

"Anyone in this fucking city could own a Sandman, and you know it. Anyone who—"

She went abruptly silent, raised one hand to silence me, too. Her gaze flickered behind her gear. Call incoming.

I sighed, turned back to the rail, and leaned there while she took the call.

Down in the street, forensics appeared to be done. They were packing their scanners and samplers back onto the truck they'd come in, folding down the situational Dorn lamps, shouting irritably back and forth to one another, gesturing at the places they'd flagged with soft-blinking pixel-fog crime scene markers. I wondered if they'd shut those down, too, or leave them in place until some local gang graffitist came along, hacked the resolution codes, and turned each marker into something more street-approved—a giant sculpted turd in BPD uniform or the corpse of a gruesomely butchered patrol officer were the usual poetic fare. And around here, it wouldn't take—

Abruptly, I felt Chakana's stare, hard on my back like the force of a hot summer sun back on Earth.

Whatever they'd phoned her with, it wasn't good, and somehow I was involved. I got up off the rail with exaggerated care, feeling the world tilt infinitesimally under me as I moved. Intimations rising like detritus dust devils off the machine shop floor of my mind, the shape of something almost formed. Sudden lightness in my belly. *Here it comes, Hak.* Hannu Holmstrom's bad shit inbound.

I turned to face her. Met the red-rimmed sleepless glare, the pressed-thin lips. Saw the muscle of her jaw knotted up with rage.

"What?"

But truth was, I already knew.

TWENTY-TWO

THEY TOOK HER at the terminal, using the loose crowds in the concourse for camouflage until they could get up close and knock down her security detail point-blank. They made it look easy.

She'd cut out on me, left Vector Red early, with Grant and his platinum crew as escort. And it hadn't been enough. The assault team, whoever they were, used twitch-guns and close-combat brute force, moved in so hard, so fast, Grant's guys never knew what hit them. They never even cleared their weapons. Most of the bystanders in the terminal didn't realize anything was happening until it was already almost over. And a quintet of strategically placed pixel fog bombs triggered across the concourse had rendered individual headgear recall next to useless.

Building surveillance was root compromised beforehand; some cheap and nasty nonspecific virus tipped into the feed protocols six minutes ahead of the grab. By the time Grant's guys got hit, the intrusion spike was cresting and every camera in the terminus was fried. The garbled images that remained were like shadows from some brutalized hostage's PTSD nightmares—bulky indistinct masked figures, ghost image overlaid and heavily snowed with static, bent and wrenched repeatedly out of shape by tightly spaced induced hiccups in the feed.

"Could be anyone, could be fucking *aliens* for all the use this is," Chakana said disgustedly. She stood icily erect before the broad horseshoe of display screens up in the PA security eyrie, watching the whole mess on loop. "These fuckers knew exactly what they were doing. We won't even get a kinetic signature off this shit."

The terminal duty chief and his assistant exchanged glances, but neither of them wanted to risk venturing an opinion. They both had a slim and youthful back-office look that spoke volumes about how often the Port Authority had to worry about violent criminal incursion, and the sudden shift in the status quo looked to have shaken them badly. The duty chief reached gingerly past Chakana and gestured in the pickup field, swept the images off the screens in favor of a new set.

"There is, uh, this—from their exit route . . ."

Long panning shots along tunnel walkways, the phalanx of attackers frog-march Madekwe rapidly away down the angle of perspective. But it was as hopelessly corrupted as the rest, detail eclipsed and continually shivered apart. I thought I counted six figures including Madekwe but couldn't swear to it. And you'd only know it was Madekwe in the middle by sheer logic. For all the visible detail, it could have been pretty much anyone tall and dark. Even sex characteristics barely showed up in the fried and fractured images. For the others—

"This is useless, too," Chakana snapped. "Could *still* be fucking anyone."

I nodded. "Sure. Anyone who already knew Madekwe was at Vector Red, could turn on a pebble the moment she left, and just happened to have a half dozen spec ops thugs on hand with the meter running."

That got me a guarded look. The question sat there in the air between us, unasked and not really needing an answer—*Who has that kind of manpower? Who has that kind of surveillance capacity?*

Who carries the Glock Sandman as standard issue?

The terminal security chief cleared his throat. "They used the evacuation tunnels, you can see that much. Got out onto the ValleyVac platforms for eastbound traffic. The Dawnfinder was in lock and boarding. We still can't tell for certain from what we've recovered, but, well . . ." His shrug was closer to a wince. "Looks like that's how they got out."

Chakana said nothing, seething. I looked at the time stamps on the mangled footage, checked them against the time in the corner of my eye. Same time within minutes to when my naval warhead pals had come calling in the Swirl. Simultaneous strikes. And now here we stood, better than ninety minutes into the aftermath, watching them get away with it.

"They're long gone, Nikki," I said quietly.

"Oh, you think?"

ValleyVac transit—the jewel in the crown of COLIN infrastructure on Mars. Run at *real* speed, the ads like to say, and for once they're telling you the truth. The Valles Marineris is over 4,000 kilometers long, and the ValleyVac can do the whole trip in a theoretical hour and change. That *theoretical* gets some serious crimps put in it by the inconvenient fact that there are stations along the route and people aboard who want to get out at them, but still—even allowing for safe deceleration, station lockdown, embarkation times, lock release, and respeed—ninety minutes out of Bradbury Central, the Dawnfinder would ordinarily be halfway to Eos Gate.

"You talked to VV command," Chakana prompted. "Please tell me that much. You got them to stop the train."

"Yes, of course. They locked it down at Rand Junction." The duty chief raked a nervous hand through a fringe that really needed cutting back to keep it from falling forward over his gear lenses. "It, uh, they tell me it took that long to override the AI without an onboard threat-to-life protocol."

"And?"

He spread his hands. "No trace. They've got a forensics team going over the compartments now, and they're backing up through the onboard surveillance. But it's fried like this stuff. And everyone they took off at Rand checks out. Whoever these people are, they got off somewhere sooner."

"We've got local PD checking the other stations," volunteered the assistant.

Chakana grunted. *Lot of fucking good that'll do,* said the look on her face.

Rand Junction—seven major stations out on the eastward line, not counting a couple of in-town courtesy stops before the train got properly clear of Bradbury's metro sprawl. Probably a few shithole dormitory towns in between that I'd forgotten about, too. Lots of options however you sliced it and no way to know which stop they'd used, what kind of onward transportation they'd had waiting for them, which direction they'd choose to shake pursuit.

They'd just given us the whole mideastern tranche of the Gash as a search zone.

"You talk to any of the escort crew yet?" I asked.

The duty chief shook his head. "They all caught multiple twitch blasts, couple of them got hit in the head pretty hard as well. Crash team took them to Santa Yemaya."

"Anyone else said anything useful?"

"We got some early witness statements. Nothing concrete so far; these are civilians, and they're mostly too dazed to have coherent recall right now." He looked like a civilian himself as he said it, eyes still slightly wide around his own shocked disbelief. "Couple of people said they were masked in black, someone else said faces like water, got one woman says she recognized two of them from TV, but *with the exact same face on each one.* Got another statement says they all looked like *demons.*"

I nodded. "Iterative masks on fast cycle. Makes a lot of sense—freak out Deiss's security, give them a split-second advantage in the shoot-out, cover themselves at the same time in case the logic bomb in the surveillance system didn't take."

The duty chief looked at me numbly, like I'd crashed through the ceiling wearing an iterative mask myself. He went on talking, I think, almost on autopilot. "All we really know is it was total chaos down there. Insane. Someone told us the shooters were running around screaming some pistaco shit about tearing out people's livers."

"Livers?" asked Chakana, deadpan.

"Yes, ma'am. Got corroboration from three different bystanders, and we've pulled, uhm, this off the audio feed." He gestured again in the field—a couple of the screen images gave ground to mixing board schematics—cool blue lines tangled across graph space, wavering multi-colored meter displays. A sound track slithered hissing and crackling into the air around us—squashed noise that sounded like thunder and under-water screams, and in the middle of this, a single string of phrasing plucked out.

"...*anc*...*eh*...*a*...*o*..."

It was no clearer than the mangled images the screens had held earlier. At best, you could make out the cadences as Spanish.

"It's a mess at the moment," admitted the duty chief. "But the predictive software writes it like this."

The background noise erased. An accentless male voice spoke into freshly minted quiet.

"Arráncales el hígado."

Chakana shot me a glance. I shrugged.

"It fits the witness statements," the chief said stubbornly. "'Tear out their livers.' We're still working to clean out the intrusion code, get the voice closer to real."

I picked up the faint beat of enthusiasm in his voice—this was work he knew, was good at, felt useful doing. I guess you couldn't blame him for clinging to it.

"Yes," Chakana said with dangerously sweetened calm. "And—tell me—were any of the injured actually missing liver tissue?"

The duty chief pressed his lips together a moment. "No, of course not, but—"

"Then what the fuck are you doing wasting machine time on this?" It wasn't quite a shout, more of a compressed snarl, but she turned on him like a gun turret. "We've got a VIP abduction here, a fucking COLIN-ranked ultratripper snatched right out from under Port Authority's nose, gone clean, nothing but shredded garbage from the security systems, and you want to chase *this* voodoo bugshit?"

"I—we thought—"

"No, I doubt that very fucking much actually." Chakana made a visible effort to hold on to her temper. She gestured, chopping with one loose hand. "Kill it. Right now. We don't have the time or the processors to waste on whatever cheap Andino scare tactics these clowns were throwing around down there. I want their *faces*. I want *names*. I want to know *where the fuck they are right now*! That's what you spend your machine time on here, that's what you spend the next ten hours doing, and you don't sleep until it's done. Am I clear?"

The chief nodded, swallowed. His eyes were already flinching around behind his gear, firing off the orders. Chakana stared at him a moment longer, wordless, then turned away. Stiff silence took the room.

"Anyone else get hurt down there?" she asked finally. "Any civilians?"

"Yes." A dull anger crimping the chief's diffidence now. "They shot up about two dozen nonspecifics on their way out. No reason to it, no pattern; they hit everything from kids under five to some old guy in a mobility suit. We talked to witnesses, they said it looked random."

"Then it probably was." I peered at a repeating loop of the masked phalanx in retreat down the evac tunnel. "It's a good exit strategy—widespread panic and bodies down. Smart."

No response—I glanced back from the screens, found duty chief and assistant both staring at me resentfully.

"Two of those kids died," the chief said tightly. "Two-year-old's heart stopped when the load hit her CNS. Another one went into shock and choked. They've got the old guy at Yemaya now; they don't think he'll make it either."

The quiet stiffened again, like a wound in cold weather. Chakana seemed to shake herself out of a trance.

"You two, get out. I want to talk to Veil."

They went with alacrity, glad to be gone from the eye of whatever storm was building behind the lieutenant's impassive calm. Chakana waited carefully until the eyrie door slid shut. Prickling pregnant pause, and then she swung on me.

"I ought to dump you right back in holding," she said tightly. "You *stupid* motherfucker! I *told* you not to leave her on her own."

"Oh, you think I could have stopped this?" I gestured impatiently at the looping, torn-up images on the screens. "Your faith in my hard-man prowess is making me all warm inside. I'm a retired fucking overrider, Nikki, not the Red Sands Warrior made flesh."

"You were supposed *to protect her*."

"Yeah, so was a platinum-rated security team. I met those guys last night. If five of them couldn't stop whoever did this, what difference do you think I would have made? As it is, they came this close to killing me down in the Swirl. Or do you still want to claim that's some Crater Critter action out on my darkside flank?"

Chakana glared at me. Said nothing.

"Who is she, Nikki?"

"What the fuck are you talking about?"

"Madison Madekwe. Who is she really?"

"I told you who she was when I briefed you."

"Yeah, a second-team suit with an overactive work ethic. You *still* trying to sell me that shit? *No one* puts together this much effort to take out the second team. And Mulholland doesn't come down out of his eyrie to detail special bodyguard privileges for minor league players."

"Special bodyguard? You?"

"We're getting played here, Nikki, and you know it!"

"*We?*" She coughed up a disbelieving laugh. "There is no fucking *we*, Veil. I gave you a simple task, and you fucked it up. *We* are done here."

I waited a couple of beats to see where she'd take it, if I was headed back to holding. She just turned away. Stared at the churn of torn-up images across the screens before her. I hovered for a moment on the brink of telling her about Astrid Gaskell and Sakarian, as much to yank her back around, to see the look on her face, as for any practical purpose.

Perhaps not. With Gaskell's going home for good behavior plan, I still had far too much to lose.

I cleared my throat.

"Look—Madekwe's not dead yet. They used twitch-guns for a reason. That's nonlethal force. She catches a stray blast in the melee, it's no big deal. They wanted her alive. Ransom, maybe, or something else, something more political—hammer a recantation out of her for broadcast, sharpen the contradictions, provoke a reaction from Earth Oversight."

No response. Chakana never turned, her eyes never left the displays. I grimaced and plunged on.

"Whatever their game plan is, Nikki, it's going to take them some time to set in motion. So you put out a standard press release—terrorist attack, no leads at present, BPD pursuing all lines of inquiry. You keep Madekwe's abduction out of it, don't mention her at all, force them to act first if publicity's what they want. Meantime, we—"

She swung to face me, abrupt as combat, biting as a wind out of Tharsis.

"Are you about done explaining to me how to do my job?"

"That's not—"

"Because I'm about done listening to you." Voice rising now, taking on heat. "In case you hadn't fucking noticed, I've got a Valley-wide manhunt to organize here. So why don't you just fuck off and let me work?"

"You're making a mistake, Nikki. I can still—"

She shot me a look so red-rimmed savage that I shut up.

"You're done, Veil," she said flatly. "Now get the fuck out of here before I decide I can spare the time to lock you up again."

I held her gaze for a moment, but there was no defeating those murderous sleep-deprived eyes. I shrugged, headed for the door.

Paused on the threshold one more time.

"You know, Nikki—maybe I did fuck up here. But it's not that simple. Earth Oversight are running some kind of game with Madekwe, and you know it. You can't trust them."

"I don't trust them. I never did. I trusted *you*, Veil."

She turned away from me and stood there, staring at the screens and the fucked-up images they ran over and over again.

I walked out with her last four words looping in my head the exact same way.

TWENTY-THREE

I GOT OUT of the terminus building through the same exit I'd used with Madison Madekwe the day before. Stood a quiet moment alone on the steps, feeling weightless and cold. Over my head, the Lamina soaked the sky with heat-exchange auroras in soft blues and greens, dimming out the stars beyond. Nightfall frosted the air around me, whetted the edge on the wind. I twitched up my collar and stared grimly out across the dotted lights of the Port Authority campus, trying to make sense of the last thirty-six hours and what they contained. What I'd missed, what mistakes I'd made, where I'd fucked up.

I trusted you, Veil.

I grimaced. *Yeah, well—your mistake, Lieutenant. Blackmail a better class of over-the-hill enforcer next time.*

There was a certain bitter satisfaction in the words, like biting down on a bruised gum. But it didn't really help. At the end of the day, I'd slipped, badly, and I was short one COLIN auditor, therefore one cryocap ticket home. And thanks to the showdown with Chakana, I was now locked out of any helpful resource BPD might have afforded me in getting her back.

Not to mention having no remote clue what the fuck was going on.

And standing here moping isn't going to fix any of it.

I let the chill wind chase me off the terminus steps. Went down them heedlessly fast, three and four at a time. Martian gravity's good for stunts like that, but there's precious little satisfaction in the jolt each time you land—it feels too much like floating. When I hit bottom, the restless anger was still in me, a palpable iron lump in my chest, not helped by the running-hot backbeat it had found there to feed on.

I tried to walk some of it off—put the lit-crystal luminescent bulk of the terminus at my back, took long, hard, impatient strides down random thoroughfares across the campus, and then, when that didn't work, headed out into the shimmer-bright nighttime whirl of the downtown beyond.

No call from Gaskell or Sakarian yet. That was odd.

No odder than any other fucking thing in this mess.

Rip out their livers, boys.

I heard the machine-made voice again, the flat, affectless exhortation—*arrancales el higado!* It wasn't an unheard-of threat, but it rang weird and out of context. Chakana's *voodoo bugshit* call was dead on. The Andean grunt labor that formed so much of COLIN's early spearhead efforts on Mars had brought with them their own myths, faith, and legends, increasingly retrofitted as time went on to suit their new home. And preeminent among these is the pistaco, a tall, pale-faced humanoid creature with a dreadful knife who comes at night to drag away sleeping Andinos and butcher them in lonely places for their fat deposits and organs.

Back when I worked the Uplands, those tales were still common currency among the descendants of that same grunt labor force. There's a tweaked species of steppe fox that runs loose up there, introduced as part of the Foundational Fauna Program, back when anybody was still paying attention to that kind of thing. The noise those things make in mating season will put a guaranteed chill on your spine the first time you hear it—sounds like small children being tortured. But you'll find plenty of Uplanders who'll say it's not the foxes you can hear out there at all, it's the ghosts of the pistaco's victims reliving their final agonies under the knife, every night the same, until Pachamama in her mercy brings on the end of time.

More than a few of the enforcer types I moved with in the Upland camps used to trade off the cultural shudder you could get out of referencing the pistaco. Threats to *cut the fat right off your bones if you don't cough up, slice the liver right out your back* had a grim ring and rhythm to them that carried well by word of mouth. In most cases, actual punishments tended to the more prosaic—who has time for shit *that* elaborate, after all?—but I'd heard of one or two object lessons that went the whole gory distance when the offense was deemed serious enough.

But it's not the kind of thing you yell randomly in the middle of a fire-fight.

Not, at any rate, when you've already tricked out the Port Authority security systems slicker than fucking in a tub of nanolube. Not when you've taken out a dedicated security detail without a single return shot fired. Not when you apparently can lay your hands on tweaked naval ordnance pretty much on demand for no better reason than to obliterate some over-the-hill minder five entire city districts away from the woman he's supposed to be looking after.

Guys that thorough and well equipped don't beat their chests, they don't *trade off cultural shudder.* They don't need to.

A fucking VAHM warhead, for Pachamama's sake. Just on the off chance that . . .

I ground to an abrupt halt in a neon-blasted plaza somewhere south of Hayek and Tenth. Cast about the plaza for street signage, got my bearings. Let my thoughts and furies catch me up.

The off chance that . . . what?

They knew where I was relative to Madekwe. They knew I was too far off to possibly intervene when they made their grab at the station. They knew they'd be long gone before I could get there.

So what the hell was so scary about this over-the-hill minder that they felt the pressing need to vaporize me anyway?

I FOUND AN Al Packers outlet in a side alley off Hayek—it was doing brisk business when I got there, and I had to queue. The prospective diners ahead of me waited mostly in silence, hunched against the cold. Cheap bulky clothing, the telltale poverty indicator, and clouds of frosted breath. What few mumbled shreds of conversation I caught were all about the shuttle and its newly revealed passengers. *Fucking Earth Overlordsight. What do those assholes think they're doing here? This ain't the fucking Settlement years no more.* So forth. There were a few jokes, crude and cruel, the hate-driven hallmark of the dispossessed. Most of them I'd heard a hundred times before. *What do you call an Earthwoman with good tits? An Earthman steps off the shuttle and sees a garbage bug looking at him. Three Earthers go into a brothel and ask for the best . . .*

When it was my turn at the hatch, I punched up the Lean'n'Mean combo and ate it standing, straight out of the wrapper. Steam rising off the cheaply coded meat, hot sauce burning my mouth. Still not feeling hungry, but that wasn't the point. I was going to need the fuel. The chili stung my taste buds dead about three bites in anyway, which was a blessing in no great disguise—those things taste about as close to real alpaca steak as mouthwash does to whiskey. Worse than shipboard food, and that's saying something.

I'm glad to see you overriding your sensory impulses for a change, 'Ris said out of nowhere. *Are we mission-bound?*

I stopped chewing for a moment. It was a good question.

I just got fired, I subbed through the cheap food still in my mouth. *Didn't you hear? And Madison Madekwe is long gone, dragged off someplace east and good luck finding out where. No, we are not mission-bound.*

Then why are you eating?

I chewed through the rest of my mouthful, swallowed it down.

Dunno, I admitted. *Something's not right.*

Without applying rationale as a mediator, select your first impulse. What would it be?

Talk to Holmstrom.

Why?

He was chasing data for me on Madekwe. No, hold on—he's not going to have that stuff till after the weekend.

Then why talk to him? What else was he doing for you?

I wolfed down the last of the Lean'n'Mean combo to give myself some respite. Strip-mining your subconscious for operational benefit is a standard feature of Osiris protocols, but that doesn't leave it feeling any less irritatingly intrusive.

He pulled up some detail for me on Cradle City, I subbed finally. *Known associates of Pavel Torres. Turns out . . .*

And I felt the click long before it made any actual sense. Knew I had an answer before I knew exactly what the answer was.

Words with Chakana on the gantry outside my capsule home:

I don't see how killing you scuttles anything Madekwe's doing. She can always get another tour guide.

No one's irreplaceable.

And my instinctive, unexamined comeback.

Sundry Charms.

His job is being Sundry Charms. No one else can do that. Ergo—he's irreplaceable.

No one else can do that.

My own previous modesty came back at me: *I don't think this is about me.*

But it was.

Fragments of the conversation with Hannu Holmstrom bouncing back through my head, squash-ball loud off the walls of memory with the sudden significance they'd gained.

Oh, and you were right about this Decatur, you do know him. Same soak you worked Indenture Compliance with all those years ago.

He still with IC?

Not as far as I can tell. In fact, he seems to have done rather well for himself in the interim. I'm seeing a lot of luxury item purchases in his wake, even some last-season Marstech. He's living out of a hotel on the main drag these days.

Running the MEG and hormonal load monitor, Osiris spotted the breakthrough pretty much the instant it bloomed in my head.

Without applying rationale as a mediator, she said serenely, *select your first impulse.*

I balled up the combo wrapping and dropped it to the floor, brushed my fingers together to get the worst of the grease off them.

Get me a seat on the next westbound ValleyVac out of Bradbury tonight, ride as far as Cradle City. Light stowage space, boarding somewhere that's not Central. Use one of the Western Spread courtesy stops. No-name pay-

ment, and I want it routed discreetly, somewhere it'll be hard to find. Oh, and find me somewhere cheap to stay once we get there—capsule cheap and not too far from the downtown.

Done. Booking references crawled wormlike across my vision for a moment, then shriveled up and disappeared. *Departure in two hours and thirty-seven minutes. You are booked into the Mansions of Luthra, Musk Plaza branch. Are you going to Cradle City to look for Madison Madekwe? Might I remind you that the train her captors took out of Bradbury was eastbound?*

I grinned mirthlessly. *Yeah, wasn't it just.*

You assume this was an attempt at misdirection. But there is no statistical reason to—

Pavel Torres disappeared in Cradle City. Madison Madekwe disappears because she's going to Cradle City to poke around after him. And wouldn't you know it, I have a unique connection to the Cradle myself—I used to be IC stakeout buddies with one of the guys that's running the place now. That's my Sundry Charms brand value, that's what makes me irreplaceable. They didn't come after me tonight to keep me from protecting Madekwe; it was to stop me going after her and stirring up trouble with the Cradle City mob.

It took 'Ris a beat or two to digest the stream of consciousness she'd triggered from me, to leaven it down as data and then apply her own inexorable analysis.

This does not mean that Madekwe's abductors will take her to Cradle City—or indeed anywhere else in the Shelf Counties—right now.

Doesn't matter, I subbed grimly. *Whether she's up there now or not, Cradle City is the key. It's where I start kicking things loose.*

And are you carrying sufficient firepower for the Uplands?

She's a Blond Vaisutis crisis management system; you can't really blame her. OSIRIS—Onboard Situational Insight and Resource Interface Support. It's her whole designed purpose to plan and oversee critical conflict situations, and with that comes a tacit enthusiasm for the fight. I say tacit, because somewhere in the 11,000 meters of tightly wound and bunched postorganic processor filament threaded so thoroughly into my nervous system and brain that taking it out would turn me into mincemeat, there actually are a few protocols associated with minimizing loss of life. Where possible, an Osiris will prefer to avoid damage to high-value personnel—they *are* company assets after all—and sometimes even to human beings in general, because it understands that large numbers of casualties can be a public relations nightmare.

But the parameters of *where possible* are orbital around a central mass of *mission-critical objectives,* and there is no escape velocity worth mentioning from those concerns. Come the crunch, Osiris will always prefer murder and mayhem to failure.

I'd like to think I'm made a little differently, but deep down I suspect it isn't true.

Firepower I've got will be fine. I'm going up there to ask questions, not start a war.

You are not convinced of this, she pointed out unhelpfully. *Will you be informing Lieutenant Chakana of your plans?*

Why would I do that?

It might be useful to have some backup from Valley law enforcement if your questions are not as well received as you inexplicably seem to think they will be.

I considered. Backup isn't really a concept overriders have much use for—99 percent of the time you won't have it as an option; it's just you and the problem they woke you up to solve, falling endlessly upward together through cold hard vacuum black. There's an icy and isolating math to contexts like that, and the conditioning they give you reflects it. You fix things alone or you fail.

And besides—there was still that Glock-bearing motherfucker outside my capsule door to think about. Didn't *have* to be a cop; Chakana was right about that much. But I hadn't much liked the look on her face when I told her about it.

No backup, I decided. *We go in dark. The fewer people know where I am right now, the better it's going to be.*

But you might be right about the firepower.

.   .   .

CERES ARC AND its daughter avenues by night—machine-dreamed architectural outcrops and loomings, hard edges softened by the darkness they were sunk in, and endless curving paths into the eerie gloom beyond. The Swirl runs minimal neighborhood lighting, a scheme tailored for the machine systems that take up the bulk of the rental space. You can reckon on a sparse crop of low-key maintenance markers, blaze-painted on surfaces next to the access ladders and hatches they announce, staining the surrounding structure with their dull red glow. And here and there, you'll maybe spot the brilliance of a rooftop corporate display high overhead, climb-proofed and armored, spilling miserly glinting fractions of trickle-down radiance into the streets below.

Aside from that, you're on your own.

The Swirl's human residents suck it up. They're smart enough to know the city won't do anything to improve the situation—headgear *comes* with night-sight options, doesn't it, what *are* these people whining about?—and they console themselves with the old hymn about Rugged Frontier Humanity Making Do. They tag the buildings with cheap blaze paint of their own in blue-white or hazard yellow, arrows and address markers and graffiti that is, frankly, rather mild, all things considered. They hustle or beg or steal the necessary software and extra battery capacity demanded by the really rather power-thirsty night-sight add-ons for their bottom-end gear. A lot of them figure it's the smartest short-term move—after all, they're not going to be down and out in the Swirl forever, are they? Something's going to come up, something's got to give. Like they say, *the High Frontier is a constantly shifting matrix of opportunity for motivated humans to get ahead.* Work hard, work smart, the rewards are almost guaranteed. And everyone out here is descended from someone who came to Mars by choice instead of languishing in bureaucratic lockdown back on Earth. That pioneer spirit is in their genes; how can they fail?

A few less starry-eyed types head down to the Strip to mortgage themselves for a longer-term solution—rapid-growth retinal mods, supposedly from cultured owl- or shark-gene stock but more likely—given the price—taken from the endless supply of stray cat genes the city streets offer up. Takes a couple of weeks for the tapetum lucidum crystals to grow in fully behind the retina—that can be painful and prone to complications, but hey, they say the tweaked rod-and-cone arrays kick in almost the next day.

I got my shark-mod eyes courtesy of Blond Vaisutis at a candidate enhancement clinic in Exmouth when I was about six weeks old, back when my infant brain was still working out how to use the vision I'd popped out of the womb with. Apparently, it's the ideal time for the add-ons to bed in. I don't imagine it was much of a fun procedure to go through for a nearly newborn, but the upside is I've been using the resulting vision all my life. I slipped through the darkened Swirl streets with no more at-tention than if I was wandering down Hayek Boulevard in broad daylight. Faint blue-limned shark-mod sheen on everything, perfect operational clarity.

The pixel fog crime scene markers were still in place outside 1009 Ceres Drive 4, unvandalized so far, and there was a lonely little CSI sentry drone spidering around in the dark. It scanned me with strobing red light as I approached, decided to let me pass. I resisted the urge to give it a kick as it scuttled aside. Those things are better armed every time I come up out of a coma, and BPD operating parameters have grown pretty unfor-giving since the last round of 4Rock4 riots. If it no longer pays to antago-nize the city's police—and to be honest, it never really did—then that goes double for their AI.

I went up the caged stairwell and found Ariana waiting at the top. The same cheap pajamas, face fully stripped of war paint now and blurry with undispersed sleep. An uncertain smile slipped out onto my mouth.

"Change your mind about that rematch, then?"

"Don't *joke*, Hak. I was fucking worried about you. Only popped a quarter cap, enough for trace if they grill me about not answering the door."

"Smart."

She gave me a sour look that said *don't you fucking patronize me, you prick.* I cleared my throat.

"Look, Ari, why don't you at least come in for a nightcap? I could—"

"Someone was here," she said impatiently. "Looking for you."

. . .

I MADE HER the drink anyway, a long, sweet rum-heavy cocktail I knew she liked. She sat on the edge of the bed shelf and held the glass in her lap untouched while I played back the Dyson's external surveillance footage for the last few hours. The abortive chase on the gantry stairs, the sudden white bloom of the tear gas grenade, and me staggering up out of it like a twat; me seated coughing and wheezing, wiping at my eyes; me and Ariana, then me alone; then me and the cops; then me and Chakana.

Then: exeunt omnes.

"Woke up about an hour ago," Ariana said to break the quiet. "There was a BPD flag in my mailbox, jeeping on and fucking on. Contact Sojourner Street station if you noticed anything unusual between the hours of yadda yadda yadda. Doesn't look like they bothered doing the door to door after all."

"No," I said absently, eyes on the flickering surveillance images. "They got pulled for something bigger."

"Assholes." It was said without much venom. Like all Swirl residents, Ariana understands only too well her relative importance in the grand scheme of urban policing. "Yeah, so anyway, I get up and kick on the doorcam, y'know, pull a scan, just to check they've really all gone. And there's this guy hanging about on the gantry right outside your place, just creeping around."

"Yup, and there he *is*," I muttered. The screen gave me a nondescript figure, medium bulky clothes, the inevitable hood and opaque lenses. I thought there might be something familiar in the lower half of the face, but not enough to trigger actual recognition. And the furtive darting looks he kept casting around didn't help. "Fucker knows his surveillance basics."

Ariana yawned, fighting the melatonin. "You think he's with the guys who blew themselves up? Or a cop that came back for something, maybe?"

I put the captured figure on loop, punched up some infrared and spectrabounce. No sign of a weapon. And the body language wasn't profession-of-violence either. Whatever this guy had come for, it didn't look like another attempted hit.

Maybe someone was reconsidering their strategy.

I felt a muscle twitch under my eye. I stowed the anger carefully away for when it might be useful.

"Listen, Ari—I'm heading out of town for a while. You see anyone else messing around near my front door while I'm gone, you stay well out of their way. These are not people you want to get tangled up with."

"Sure." Dancer in a skin joint—she handled people she didn't want to tangle with every day of her working life. She took a pull on the drink I'd made her. "You going anywhere nice?"

She's Mars-born; she didn't mean it as a joke.

"Couple of weeks by the ocean," I deadpanned, still staring at the figure on the screen. "Catch up on my surfing."

"What?"

"Doesn't matter." Suddenly, I felt mean-spirited and grubby. "Just—like I said, you watch yourself. You watch your back, Ari. Bad enough this shit is breaking loose around me. I don't need you taking collateral damage, too."

She grinned and leaned back on her elbows on the bed. "You're cute sometimes, Hak. You know that?"

"I'll put it on my résumé."

Beneath the cheaply printed pajamas, she tilted her hips, moved her thighs languidly together. "You need to do a little more than that."

I drew a deep breath, looking down on her. "Is that right?"

"That's right, overrider."

"You all finished with that drink?"

She looked quizzically at the tall glass in her hand, the ice and bright cocktail mix still filling it to the halfway mark. She lifted it as if for a toast, raised an eyebrow at me. Then, slowly and deliberately, she poured the contents out over her pajama top. It drenched her breasts, molded the cheap printout cloth to their form, plucked the nipples erect with the chill. She let the emptied glass roll out of her open hand and onto the floor. Tucked her chin into her chest to examine her handiwork, seemed to consider it gravely for a couple of beats, then looked up and grinned at me again.

"All finished," she said throatily. "All wet and sticky, too."

TWENTY-FOUR

SAKARIAN CALLED ME on my way to the ValleyVac. I was propped in the corner of an Overground carriage, idly watching the Bradbury night skyline slide by and feeling way happier than I had any right to. Lurid action replays of my rematch with Ariana holding court in my head, packed bag at my feet, sense of running-hot momentum through my veins. The joyous pulse of motion and mission time.

"Veil, where the fuck are you?"

"Riding the Over. Why?"

"I'm going to assume you know what went down at Bradbury Central this afternoon."

"I'm aware."

"You were supposed to be protecting her, Veil."

"Yeah, instead of which I was busy cruising around in a limo talking to you and Astrid Gaskell. Hard to be in two places at once, Commissioner, even for me."

The line was audio only, but I heard the way he bit back his first comment. Breathed hard while he thought about it.

"Gaskell isn't happy," he said finally. "If Madekwe comes back on a slab, you can kiss that cryocap berth good-bye."

"Sakarian, please tell me you were better at motivational menace back in the Uplands. You're ruining my image of the marshals."

"Want me to ruin your open-air privileges, too? I checked the book on your arrest, asshole. Chakana is getting sloppy. I lift a finger to Internal Affairs right now and you'll be back in holding so fast it'll give you whiplash when you hit."

"Gaskell might have something to say about that. I'm going to have a hard fucking time finding Madison Madekwe from inside a cell."

Another hesitation. "You've got leads?"

"There are some people I need to talk to. Where it goes after that remains to be seen. But this much I know: Madison Madekwe was chasing a hell of a lot more than some suspected cracks in the lottery protocol. And my bet is that Astrid Gaskell knows a lot more about it than she's telling you."

Sakarian snorted. "What is that, Frocker paranoia? Listen to yourself, Veil. You sound just like one of those DeAres Contado clones. Big bad bureaucratic Earth Oversight, coming to steal our souls. Probably the selfsame victimhood shit that set off whichever fuckwits it was snatched Madekwe in the first place."

"I wouldn't write them off as fuckwits till you've read the report, Sakarian. It was a pretty slick run. They took out a dedicated HKU security detail, wiped out the surveillance systems at Central, and got clean away. They tried for me, too, over on the Southside at about the same time, and with tactical naval hardware. That sound like a victimhood grudge crew to you?"

He was silent. You could almost hear the overclocked whine of his thinking as he ran to catch up.

"That was you? That bomb blast thing?"

"It was nearly me. And it wasn't a bomb, it was a modified shipkiller warhead. Like I said, don't underestimate these guys."

"And the people you're going to see?"

"I won't be underestimating them either."

"That's not what I meant. Who are you seeing? Which part of town?"

A sudden thought seemed to strike him. "Is your citizens locational opted out?"

"I don't have one. I'm not from here, remember?"

"Pachamama and all her suffering fucking saints. *They let you through naturalization without the implants?*"

"It happens." Particularly when you dedicate a substantial portion of your meager severance package to making sure it does.

"I don't like this, Veil."

"Quality, Choice, and Freedom, Commissioner. Just exercising my rights under Charter like everybody else."

"Yeah, well, while you're busy doing that, you might want to consider what happens if these people you're going to see don't like the questions you have for them." Abruptly, the sneer leached out of his voice, left something that might have been genuine concern. "You want to tell me where you'll be? Let me put some eyes on your shoulder, maybe a tac squad to come pull you out if things go sour."

See, 'Ris put in. *It's not just me.*

"I don't think that's going to work, Sakarian. I'll be trading off a pretty delicate relationship. Lot of trust issues, lot of insecurity. You put a phalanx of your best hard-faced door kickers into the vicinity, someone's apt to notice. It's going to fuck up any goodwill I've got."

"At least you'd be alive."

I thought about some of the things I'd been witness to in the Uplands. "Maybe not. Depends how fast your hard-man contingent can kick the door in and get to me."

"BPD rapid response teams are—"

"Yeah, spare me the promo. Just let it go, all right? I'll get back to you and Gaskell as soon as I have something worth sharing. And meantime, Sakarian—watch your back with Earth Oversight. Whatever the real game is here, neither you nor I have been properly dealt in yet."

I cut the line over his protests.

VALLEYVAC TRANSIT—it never gets old.

You'd think falling through interplanetary space at barely conceivable speeds for a living would have cured me of any wonder at high-velocity travel. But space is a different gig—you can't see your motion in any meaningful fashion out there, and the places you're going are generally a very long way off. Initial acceleration, the odd overly sharp course correction or high-impact tactical maneuver—these are the only times you're likely to register that there's anything happening to the hull around you at all, and even then it tends to feel less like motion than it does random physical abuse to no good purpose. The rest of the time, dense, unending quiet pervades everything around you, and it doesn't feel like you're going anywhere at all.

Filing into the grubby, electrostatic-smelling double-stacked carriages of a VV transport canister at rest is the polar opposite—it feels like you're climbing into the chamber of some colossal soon-to-be-fired gun.

Which, to some extent, you are.

The decor may be tired and dated, the seats may be puffy and slow to respond, but you're still about to be hurled down the barrel of the Valles Marineris vacuum transit system at speeds approaching a thousand meters per second, and even allowing for stopping stations in between, you can be at Tharsis Gate in less time than it takes to cross the whole of Bradbury by Overground. Stay on for the whole ride, you're going to step out at the dreg end of human habitation on Mars, and all you'll have done to earn the change is doze in your seat for a couple of hours.

Dozing wasn't really an option for me—despite Ari's determined efforts to dump a surfeit of endorphins into my system, the running-hot came trickling back well before we got out of Bradbury's city limits—and staring at the viewport masquerading as a window beside my seat just felt fake. The only thing beyond the carriage skin and outer canister hull of a VV train in motion is a protocol-active glossed nanocrete tunnel wall, whipping past in total darkness at hundreds of meters a second—not something guaranteed to relax your passengers, so the Transit Authority opts for screens showing generic Martian landscape portraiture instead, animated to roll by at a soothing 6 percent of real-time speeds, and interspersed with frequent product promo breaks. The chosen images bear no geographical relation to anything you'd actually see if you went up on the surface above the line of the Valley Vac tunnels, but then the promos aren't exactly tightly bound to reality either. Like so much of what goes on in the Gash, the overall aim is consumer tranquillity, not truth.

Within the carriage, my fellow passengers offered little in the way of distraction. This late at night, there weren't many of them, and I'd done a basic head-count-and-file check when I got on board, as much out of habit as from any real fear I was being tailed. I could close my eyes behind my gear, bring to mind faces and seat locations for all twenty-seven without much effort. I even did it for a while as an abstract exercise, playing the old game with 'Ris.

Big grizzled guy by the door—retired slush rider, scraping a living from promo stand-up and tissue weld endorsements.

I don't think any slush rider, retired or otherwise, would be seen dead in headgear like that.

Fair point. Okay, woman six rows back from us—qualpro busted for noncompliance, fine paid out of earnings, rehired at half her original fee, looking at life on Mars or a decade of poverty before she can go home.

That is plausible. Though she may simply have a headache.

And so forth.

In the end, for something more meaningful to do, I called Holmstrom. Got a natty little surrealist avatar made of beads and cabling and a snappish tone to go with it.

"Veil. I already told you I couldn't make this dive of yours until after the weekend. So don't try charming it out of me sooner, because I won't do it."

"Wasn't calling about that. Did you happen to notice an explosion over on the Southside earlier this evening?"

"Noticing it now," he said grumpily. "Let's see, 1009 Ceres Drive 4—that's right outside your place, isn't it?"

"Yes."

"I suppose it's foolish to wonder if it had anything to do with you."

"Best guess is they were trying to kill me on account of my new Earth Oversight friend. Who they managed to abduct from Bradbury Central around the same time they were trying for me. The feeds probably don't have that yet. I'm guessing BPD put out a fuzzy press release about a terrorist incident instead."

"Yes, I'm just looking. No names as yet—*a violent terrorist assault whose purposes are as yet unclear*, quote unquote. No mention of Madekwe or COLIN at all. So they did all that to take this woman out of the picture? How very embarrassing for all concerned. Weren't you supposed to be with her?"

"She wasn't *supposed* to be wandering about in the first place," I gritted. "She ducked out of a meeting early, didn't call me, and went home with a borrowed security squad instead. Platinum rated."

"I see. No expense spared."

"Yeah, for all the fucking good it did. These guys went through them like Supay's prick through sinners. Fried the surveillance systems at Central to cover their escape. Oh, yeah—and the team that tried for me used a modified Ng Systems VAHM warhead to do it."

He was silent for a beat. "That's . . . flattering."

"Isn't it just. You think you could spare a subroutine or two to chase up navy surplus sales of shit like that over the last couple of months? See if anything obvious spikes in the data?"

"Are you sure this ties to Earth Oversight, Veil? That isn't the sort of hardware you pick up on a whim. If they sourced it specifically for the hit, then it's someone who knew they were coming for you long before our auditor friends made their dramatic entrance."

I grimaced. It was a fair point. "Just have a look, would you? See where it leads."

"Your wish is my command, overrider. I am already about your bidding." Sepulchral echo spliced onto the voice with malice aforethought, then fading slowly out. "Initial pass shows nothing of note—no navy surplus munitions changing hands in places they should not be. In fact, no such items changing hands at all on Mars in the last couple of weeks as far as I can see. It looks very much as if the local squadrons are all stocked up."

"What, *all* of them?"

Mars is lousy with private naval contractors. Back in the early days of the Gash, they clustered around the big navy yards out at Wells, sucking up what grudging secondary contracts Fleet would give them. But after the Gingrich Trust stormed local legislatures back on Earth and brought the deregulating scythe, the private hire tendency spread like unchecked bathroom mold. Out beyond the Lamina-protected verges of the Valley, the planet's Upland surfaces are honeycombed with dreadnought launch silos and covert refitting stations.

"Yes, all of them," said the goat god succinctly.

"What about over in Hellas? You check there as well?"

"That would require a hack. *Another* hack. Do you want me to queue it behind the one you've already scrounged?"

I grimaced. "Uh, no. Guess not."

"You guess correctly." Pause. His voice softened a little. "Look, Veil, do the math—better than 30 percent of anything man-made in space is Chinese-built these days. Ng Systems ship to clients all over the ecliptic. Half the ordnance aboard *Weightless Ecstatic* had their stamp on it. I don't even think they're majority Chinese owned anymore; Vietnamese management buyout at the end of the last decade, if I recall correctly. And anyway, even if some corrupt PLA naval commander *did* hand a detached warhead over to some grubby little private hit squad or their intermediaries, they'd still have to get it from Hellas to the Gash, and that'd show up in the dataflow at this end like a hard-on in a thong."

"You're sure of that?"

An elaborate sigh. "It's *me*, Veil."

"All right." Despite my best efforts, it came out grudging. "Thanks anyway."

"You're welcome. I'll call you early next week. Should have something for you on your Earth Oversight playmate by then."

"Yep."

I stared out at the fabricated Martian landscape, lost myself in it for a while. I'd had numerous demonstrations of Holmstrom's acuity with dataflow assessment. There really was no good reason to second-guess him.

That said . . .

Get me Gradual, I subbed.

The telltale, hearing's-edge warble of the scrambler at work. The tamped down audio-only line and Gradual's measured tones.

"Mr. Veil?"

"Progress report—your tax affairs have been settled, at least for the time being."

I thought her voice eased the faintest fraction. "Thank you, Mr. Veil. We will not forget your support in this."

"That's good, because I could use a favor in return. Someone tried to kill me earlier today. Came right to my door to do it."

"That is . . . troubling."

"It's certainly troubling me. These guys were high-end. They came after me with a stripped-down VAHM warhead. Do you know what that is?"

She was quiet for a moment.

"I have heard the terminology before," she said finally. "It's a naval weapon, is it not?"

"Yeah. This one was Ng Systems–built."

"You're implying a connection to us? Half of all spacegoing hardware is Chinese in this day and age. Given your employment history, you cannot be unaware of this."

"I'm not implying anything. But I'd be very keen to know if anyone in Hellas has shipped a detached Ng Systems VAHM warhead to any below-the-line clients recently. You think you could check that out for me?"

Another long pause. "We could . . . look into this. It will take time."

"Yeah, well, don't take too long about it—these guys are likely going to try again. I'd rather not be a corpse by the time you call me back." A soft chime rang through the VV carriage. "Got to go, Gradual. You let me know."

The chime rang again, this time with a soft male-voice chaser.

"Ladies and gentlemen, citizens and visitors, we will shortly be arriving at Cradle City. Please return to your seats for docking. Cradle City, next stop."

Beyond the carriage skin, the smooth, low whine of the canister braking systems kicking in. On the viewscreen, the passing Marscape slowed down in deference to the ongoing illusion, eventually reaching a complete standstill on some conveniently pretty view of low rock outcrops under a tranquil night sky. I felt the barely perceptible shunt as the VV canister came to a final halt in the tunnel. A sequence of distant-sounding clanks marched down the carriage from end to end as we locked into place on the station's breech segment. Then, finally, we got the hard, inertia-breaking lurch underfoot as the outer canister was rolled summarily into the dock and the twin-decked carriage rotated in turn inside its greased collar to stay on an even keel. The lights brightened overhead, and the debarkation hatches sliced open at either end of the carriage.

"Cradle City, ladies and gentlemen, citizens and visitors," said the soft male AI voice. "This is Cradle City. The time is now eleven minutes after one a.m., current temperature on the surface is minus three degrees, expected to fall to minus seventeen before sunrise. Light winds from the west, humidity at 9 percent. Please take all of your belongings with you on exiting the carriage and mind your step down onto the platform."

People were already standing up in their seats along the carriage, twisting themselves awkwardly out into the aisle, drifting eagerly for the exits. I stayed seated and watched them go, running-hot irritable, the smooth sense of momentum I'd owned since Bradbury abruptly and oddly stalled out.

Look at these fucking mugs, it's like they got tickets for an amusement park out there or something. Like they won the Ride Home Lottery and this is Earth. I mean—it's Cradle City, people, it's the fucking Shelf Counties. What's your rush?

Perhaps they have family waiting for them.

You shut up.

I grabbed my bag from the overhead rack and slung it across one shoulder, followed the last of the happy homecomers to the nearest door and down the debarkation tube. Casually on the way down, I checked position on the VacStar under my arm and the Balustraad in the small of my back. Strictly operational reflex—outside of the usual taxi touts and hostel pimps, I didn't expect there to be anyone out there waiting for me at all. Certainly no one who'd offer any kind of threat.

But you can always hope.

TWO MINUTES LATER, I got my wish. Standing on the underground platform, bag at my feet, stretching expansively to work some of the journey's kinks out of my lower back, I caught a flicker in the corner of my eye. I carefully avoided reacting, eased down slowly from the stretch without turning my head.

You get that, 'Ris?

If you are referring to the iris-response and grab focus in your extreme left field of vision, then yes, I got that.

I reached down and picked up my bag, slung it casually across my shoulder again. *Good. Split field, play back and track. Let's see what we've got.*

Sequestered in my upper left field of vision, a slowed replay of the glimpse I'd caught. The debarkation tubes from the upper and lower carriages of a VV canister complement each other in orderly swooping elegance, the lower disgorging at either end, the upper from a broader hatch in the middle. It was in the slow dribble of passengers from the upper deck tube that I spotted him. Average height, wiry, nondescript clothing and hood, but he went and spoiled it all with the way he froze as he entered my field of vision. Hadn't been for that sudden immobility, I'd probably have missed him altogether.

I made my way briskly down the platform to the mountainous escalator stack at the end, stepped on for the long ride to the surface. A few seconds into the ride, I turned casually around, as if admiring the vast vaulted architecture of the tunnel and the view back down. Osiris scanned and grabbed the nondescript guy out of the crowd as he followed me, limned him in yellow, mapped his kinetics, and flung them up into the corner display for analysis. If my tail was fazed by me turning, he gave admirably little sign. He did his shadowing by the book, took a parallel escalator so as not to follow me directly up. But by then it was too late. He was made.

Same guy from outside the Dyson, right?

To a high degree of probability, yes. His motion range here is too dissimilar from that in the Dyson's footage to deliver a certain match, but it is reasonable to assume this is the same subject.

Salients?

Male, early forties, Earth Standard, no apparent combat functionality—

Good to know.

I'm not finished. I said apparent. *Spectrabounce indicates a recent facial injury and some use of tissue weld, so perhaps the combat competence is of an unfamiliar kinetic style or simply well hidden.*

Or just not that competent. He's the one with the injury.

Competence is not the same as invulnerability—you are being childish. There is no way at present to assess this contact's threat level.

I turned around on the escalator treads again, back to face my direction of travel. The first gust of frigid nighttime air blew down from the tunnel exit above, brushed over my face, and wrapped my neck like an undead tentacle feeling me out for prey. I held down an unpleasant grin.

Oh, yes, there is, I subbed. *Threat assessment coming right up.*

And we rode smoothly on up the cavernous escalator tunnel into the cold unforgiving embrace of the Uplands.

PART II

SHELF
LIFE

Until you have actually experienced the so-called High Frontier, seen at first hand its innumerable costs and miseries, spoken in person to its worn-down, struggling inhabitants, do not presume to tell me how it ennobles our species. In my experience, the forces unleashed on a frontier—any frontier—are anything but noble. In eleven years of governorship on Mars, what I have seen is not nobility but a voracious masturbation fantasy of territorial and technological gain, underwritten by working practices little better than slavery, enforced by violence in a semilegal or wholly criminal mode, and infused with rampant corruption at every level.

Let the record show, then, that my only crime has been to deny that fantasy; let the record show that I was not removed from office by men with guns for any refusal to carry out my official duties or obey legal instruction from Earth; let the record show that I was usurped instead for a refusal to endorse the pernicious, politically useful myth of what is supposed to be happening here and for speaking the truth of what this fresh colonial reality entails.

—Ex–Governor General Kathleen Okombi
Opening Statement to the COLIN Court of Inquiry
(unredacted edition—not for public broadcast)

TWENTY-FIVE

THE CRADLE CITY Crocus Lux might not have offered swimming pool floors and underfoot panels with views to a 10,000-meter drop below, but it did have some nice-smelling flower arrangements in the vases along the reception counter. I stood next to one and breathed in the mingled scents of lilac, sandstar, and Upland rose.

"I'm here to see Milton Decatur," I told the receptionist. "My name's Veil."

He made a small noise in his throat, gave me a smile that was a little too wide. "Oh, yes—you are expected, Mr. Veil. One of our, uh, concierges will take you up to the Olympus Lounge."

"Don't put yourselves out on my account. I can probably find it myself."

"No, no—it's . . . no trouble." He put a brake on his hasty delivery. Behind politely transparent lenses, his eyes darted around. He cleared his throat, pulled one from the manual. "At the Crocus Lux, we pride ourselves on individual human service to all our clients."

"I'm not actually staying with you."

"No, but, uh . . . as a visitor, you, uhm . . . Ah, Gustavo." Palpable relief coursing into his voice now as someone bulky loomed up at my side. "Thank you. Would you convey Mr. Veil here to the Olympus Lounge?"

Gustavo grunted. He topped two meters and wore the Crocus Lux's livery the way a snake wears a skin it's not far off shedding. His lenses were impenetrable black. I grinned into them and lifted my arms loosely out from my sides.

"I'm not armed, Gus."

He checked me out behind the lenses anyway, then jerked his head wordlessly to the right. I followed him in that direction, across the vaulted and sparsely populated lobby space, through double doors that swung back utterly silently for us to pass, down an empty marble-walled corridor, then up a tight spiral stairway that, it struck me, would be very easy to defend against unwanted interlopers.

At the top was a water garden.

Not as much of a big deal as it doubtless was back when the Crocus Lux chain first went from flowers to *water* flowers as its signature luxury touch, but still—the aura of outrageous indulgence clung. We walked among broad ornamental ponds beneath a dusty glass containing dome overhead, ridiculously gratuitous expanses of open water turned gunmetal dark by the filtering light, engineered at a variety of heights so the brooks and rills that ran between them made a constant babbling backdrop and put faint ripples on the surface. Lotus and water hyacinth clogged together at strategic intervals, but never enough to interfere with flow. Some kind of tweaked willow/mangrove variant was planted around the edges and across the higher slopes of the garden, casting artful shade. A high, sweet rinse of birdsong counterpointed the sounds of the water, and as I glanced up, I saw a couple of actual birds fly from side to side of the containing dome overhead. We must have spooked them coming up the stairs.

"Veil? That you, motherfucker?"

I grinned. Couldn't help it. "Who wants to know? You got a *warrant,* motherfucker?"

Laughter, belly-deep from the shaded rocks and ponds on the upper level, like some debauched shrine god rejoicing in a new batch of temple virgins. A figure loomed above us, darkened to silhouette in the fractured light through the trees. He paused a moment, then vaulted down from between a couple of serene stone placements some Zen gardener had probably spent months brooding on, knocked one of them out of alignment as he passed, put the stone clumsily back about where it had been. He came fully into the light.

The intervening years hadn't hurt him much—he was darker than I was now, legacy of sticking with the Uplands while I hid and paled in the deeper canyon streets of Bradbury. The muscled bulk in the body and the unstooped height were both still there; he never had fixed his broken nose—*dunno, Hak, sends a message, don't it?*—and he came at me now with arms up in a loose boxing guard. He feinted a right jab, grinned as I stepped inside it, caught me up and crushed me in a bear hug that hadn't lost much of the force I remembered. I did my best to crush back.

When we were all done, he stood back at arm's length and looked at me. Clapped me on the shoulders with both hands and nodded approvingly.

"Pretty good shape—for a Bradbury sellout, that is. You lost some weight?"

"Just woke up."

"Ah, right—that sorry shit." He plucked off his lenses, grinning. "Still, you're not looking bad on it. Man, how you *been*? Fuck are you doing back in this shithole?"

I shrugged. "Looking for a woman."

"A woman? What, you gotta come all the way up here to get laid these days?"

"It's a little more complicated than that."

WHEN I'D LAID it out for him, he sobered. We sat together, lenses off, on broad flat stones in a tacky meditation arbor beneath one of the willows. He stared pensively into the lotus-dotted waters of the pond before us.

"You really think she's still alive?" he said.

"If they wanted her dead, they could have put a suitbuster slug in her head at Bradbury Central and saved themselves a lot of trouble."

"Yeah, they wanted her alive *then*. Could be they've gouged everything they need to know out of her by now and she's already facedown in the regolith."

"Doesn't feel that way."

He gave me a narrow look. "Or you don't want it to."

"I don't think they took her for interrogation, Milt. She doesn't *know* anything. That's the whole point; she's here trying to find out what happened to Torres. From other people. She only got out of cryocap three days ago. Couple of months before that, she was still back on Earth. What possible intelligence could she have?"

"Okay, so they don't want her for interrogation, they don't want to kill her. What's left—ransom? Try to drive off the audit, maybe? You think the Frockers got her?"

I snorted. "Those assholes? They couldn't abduct a finger full of snot from their own noses. No, I don't think the Frockers got her. I think some highly organized motherfuckers with a very specific local agenda got her and Pablito Torres is their ground zero."

Decatur shook his head. He darted me a perplexed sideways glance.

"It's still a stretch thinking they'd have brought her *here,* Hak. I mean, if this really is ground zero for them, they'd take her pretty much *any-where* else instead. And you did say they headed out *east* on the VV."

"That could just be tinsel for the cops. Or staging post convenience."

"Or not."

I nodded. "Or not. At VV speeds, they could be anywhere in the Gash by now."

"Right."

"But this is still where I pick up the trail. Torres disappeared here, and if I dig back far enough into that, I'm going to find out why Madison Madekwe disappeared, too. Plus, there's you."

He looked around again, harder this time. "Me?"

"Yeah. You. Two days ago someone tried to kill me, Milt, and the only plausible reason I can come up with is that it's because we're friends. That call I put in to you here at the Lux couple of days back? The one you never came back on? Hit came down the very same day. Matter of hours."

I was watching him closely as I spoke—albeit with lenses off—and his shock seemed genuine. He came fully around to face me, features taut with anger.

"Someone I know *put out a fucking hit on you*? Someone *I* fucking know?"

"Might just be someone who knows *about* you," I conceded. "They tried to take me out at the same time they were snatching Madekwe, and they went to a lot of trouble to do it. I was halfway across the city at the time, light-years off the action, no threat to their snatch or their exit route. The only way that makes sense is if they thought I *would* be a threat to them up here afterward. And the only thing this place and I have in common apart from Madekwe and Torres is you."

"Ahh . . ." Decatur spread his hands. "Jesus, Inti, and Supay, Hak. *That's* your fucking reasoning? Maybe they just scoped you out in the flow, made you for a stubborn mission-headed motherfucker—which you are—and figured you wouldn't let it go. Not wrong, were they?"

"Milt, they came at me with a fucking decommissioned naval warhead. No one's that scared of me, not even people who know me well." I eased up a little, loosened my tone. "But for what it's worth, yeah, I think you're right—they did scope me out in the dataflow, they did their due diligence. And they weren't worried about me coming up here after Madekwe, because hell, that's an easy fix. Twice as easy to vanish me here as in Bradbury. No. I think they were worried about me coming up here and *you* getting in the way if they tried to take me out."

Silence drifted in around us like the scent from the lotus blooms in the pond. We sat in it for what seemed like quite a while. Down on the lower slopes of the garden, Gustavo picked up on the stillness and twitched in our direction. I saw Decatur just barely shake his head, and Gus veered off like a shark smacked on the nose. Decatur cleared his throat.

"That a request, then, Hak? You asking for my help?"

"Don't know if I'm going to need it yet. But if I did, I hear you'd be the man to come to. You run this town now, right?"

He laughed, less mirth in it than earlier. "I don't run this town, Hak. Raquel Allauca does that. Didn't you see the 'gels?"

"Yeah, all over town. Third term, unbroken run. Guess the locals must really love her."

Decatur grunted. "If they know what's good for them, they do."

"She hasn't changed, then."

"Have you?" His tone sharpened. "It's a pretty sweet machine we've got running up here, Hak. You're not going throw grit in it for me, are you?"

"Hey, I just want to ask some questions. You know someone's going to get upset about it, just point them out to me. Save me a lot of time."

I got the mirthless grin again. "Okay, I'll save you a lot of time. Pavel Torres was a dust devil fuck-up from the day he dropped out of his mommy's crotch. He died the same way he lived—fucked up and not paying attention. Don't matter who you ask, that's all anyone's going to tell you around here."

"Even Nina Ucharima?"

He looked at me. "Been doing some due diligence yourself, huh? Yeah, even Needles Nina. She'll tell you the exact same thing. I mean, they were fucking and all, but she's a smart girl. She could see it just like everybody else. Might as well have had it tattooed across his forehead. Born to fucking lose."

"Did she know Torres won the Ride Home?" I tightened in on him, wishing there was a polite way to put my lenses on. "Did *you* know?"

"Not till Metro Missing Persons came up here and started shaking the sheets. And if Torres said anything to Nina, she never passed it on to me."

"Was she supposed to?"

He coughed a laugh. "You've never met Nina Ucharima, have you?"

"I read the file."

"You read the file." He sighed. "Look—you remember that deputized marshal we ran into up in Hayek County? Double bust at Babyglow's House of Lights, the Synacralon deserter thing?"

"What—stiletto restraint girl?" Even now, the memory brought a faint smile to my lips. "*You just stay there and bleed, motherfucker. Don't ruin my mood. That's* Ucharima?"

"No. That's how Ucharima would have ended up if she'd ever been dumb enough to take on a law enforcement job. So you want to imagine a woman like that, but even sharper, even tighter-wired. That sound like someone who'd keep tabs on an old flame for me?"

"Doesn't sound like she'd be interested in a dust devil fuck-up like Torres in the first place. But apparently she was."

Decatur shrugged. "You'd have to talk to her about that."

"Yeah. I plan to." I stared down at the water for a couple of quiet moments. Looked up abruptly and caught his eye. "Come on, Milt—old time's sake. Kick me up a flare on this. What the fuck was Torres doing hanging around Cradle City with a Ride Home ticket in his back pocket? He could have caught the VV down to Bradbury, snagged a suite in a big hotel at Vector Red's expense while they did the press, then probably held court there until loading time. From the look of the file, he's the sort that would have lapped it up. What went wrong?"

"You're asking me? He wasn't *my* pal."

"You gave him a job, though."

Decatur shook his head sagely. "Nope. Jeff Havel gave him a job, and even that was only because Nina asked him to. You'd have to talk to them. I don't run with the Ground Out Crew, never did. Wrong side of the fence."

"Right. And I suppose Havel isn't your pal, either."

A small smile. "Been known to drink with him on occasion. Hunting trips up the Valley, that kind of thing."

"Yeah. Been known to fix elections with him on occasion as well?"

The smile flickered on and off his lips like an indecisive butterfly. "That is a *wild* accusation, Mr. Veil."

"Milt—I don't care, all right? I'm not a fucking crusader, you know that. But they took Madekwe on my watch. I want to know why, and I want to know who, and I want to meet them in person."

He gestured. "So you can kill them."

"Doesn't have to come to that."

"*Don't Wake the Overrider*, huh?"

"Ah, come on—that was a fucking immie. Piss-poor production values, too. I sat through a couple of eps once just to see. Hours of my waking life I'm not getting back. I just want some straight answers and Madekwe back in one piece. That happens, there's no reason for anyone to get killed."

"And if Madekwe isn't in one piece anymore? What are you going to do then?"

I looked down at the surface of the pond, found a dark and faintly distorted reflection of myself peering back at me from the rippled water. I said nothing. Decatur sighed.

"Yeah, that's what I thought," he said.

GUSTAVO WALKED ME out, not trying very hard to hide a cordial professional mistrust. As I crossed the lobby, I caught the flicker of triggered recognition routines in my lenses. My sticky fellow traveler friend from the station, huddled over at the reception counter, talking earnestly to one of the staff. He avoided looking in my direction with such casual aplomb that I wanted to applaud as we passed.

"So does Milt have you guys here around the clock?" I wondered to my escort.

Gustavo shot me a narrow look without breaking stride. "I guess he'll tell you shit like that if he wants you to know it."

"I guess."

"You need a cab?"

I shook my head. "Staying at the Mansions of Luthra, just across town. I'll walk it."

"Mansions of Luthra. Right." His lip didn't quite curl as he said it, but you could see the seep of disdain across his face.

We reached the broad lobby doors—cascading crocus patch motifs in stained glass—and stepped through them into the pale strained-through-parchment light of the Martian day outside. Quiet midday on main street, quiet sky overhead. Traffic scudded by in the street at small town density; a scattering of pedestrians hurried past on the sidewalk with the feeble noon sun on their faces. Over the door, the hotel's courtesy humidifiers poured warm clouds of water vapor languidly down onto us, took the sting out of the arid Uplands air. A patient code-fly hanging around in the muggy cloud saw its chance and swooped, whined by my ear, and got me on the cheek.

I slapped at the site of the sting, felt the tiny satisfying crunch of the little fucker's exoskeleton as it crushed into my palm. Humidity must have slowed it down. Gustavo, meantime, recoiled a solid meter from the motion, hands flying up to guard, an outraged look on his face. I peeled him a weary look.

"Code-fly." I showed him my hand, the black, blood-specked smear across the skin of my palm. "I was going to hit you, there's no way you'd see it coming."

He dropped the guard, embarrassed. He snorted. "Hard man, huh?"

"Hardwired," I said absently, wiping the traces of postorganic carnage off my hand against the door pillar. "You're a big man, Gus, and you're in pretty good shape. But with me it's a helix-level job."

I shot him an amiable nod, stepped out of the humidifier's reach and onto the street. Cradle City's bonsai downtown rose around me, small crop of towers to modest heights, a lot of them recent add-ons to the original huddled Settlement-era stock. Couple of 'branegel tether blimps hovering but no other visible air traffic. Raquel Allauca's features painted a hundred meters high above the street to the west, maternal-severe and full war-paint garish. Red-lettered legend floated over her discreetly displayed cleavage—WHAT'S MADE IN THE SHELF COUNTIES BELONGS TO THE SHELF COUNTIES. The red-lipped smile bade you welcome to partake at the table, the hard eyes told you to keep your hands where she could see them.

A gust of wind whipped by, left me with a patina of fine grit on my teeth.

I checked once to see if I was being followed—if I was, it didn't show up either to my senses or to Osiris—then I turned and slipped into the steady flow of pedestrians, heading uptown under Allauca's watchful gaze.

TWENTY-SIX

NINA UCHARIMA LIVED in a newly sprouted apartment block on the western edges of town, but she didn't want to meet me there. We settled instead on a Lamina-geek pipe house she knew locally, a seedy low-lit place in the observation levels of a reconditioned storm-monitoring tower. Get wasted, gawp up at the big old light show in the sky. I got there half an hour ahead of time, cased the floor plan and thin early-evening crowd, saw nothing much to worry about. I found myself a balcony table and settled in with a cherry-flavor tweaked THC pipe. Ucharima showed about twenty minutes late and lied to me from the off.

"That ID shot Deck sent me—it's out of date," she said brusquely as she peeled out of a battered-looking high-altitude jacket, dumped it on the table, and dropped into the seat opposite me. "Lot more meat on your face whenever they took it, and, y'know, the hair—less gray."

"Thanks."

"Why I'm late." She gestured for me to hand the pipe mouthpiece across. "Been around the whole place twice looking at faces before I finally made you. Veil, right?"

I nodded, ignored the lie—I'd been keeping watch, knew she hadn't been past the balcony windows until now—and handed her the pipe. I watched as she drew on it while in the left field of my lenses 'Ris brought up a confirming snapshot of our own and ran gestalt. Like Pavel Torres himself, Nina Ucharima was a variation on an Uplands classic—young, leggy, and lean, dressing to show it in workshorts hacked off just below the crotch, sheer black tights, and chunky flat heel boots. Beneath a loose silver-toned T-shirt her shoulders were wide, and hard, slim-muscled arms showed below the high-cut sleeves. Her hair was chemically jet, shot through with colors borrowed from some violent energy-exchange event in the Lamina, and the tangled mass of it clouded around her face in a way that was supposed to defuse the impact of hard Andean cheekbones, slash mouth, and jutting chin. Behind big pirate-patch lenses, her eyes were irised a vivid watchful green, creased permanently in the corners from staring down life in the Uplands. Across the front of her T-shirt, tight, high, and probably augmented breasts made promising mounds under a logo I didn't know, a tall grim figure trailing dust clouds like a cloak, and the scrawled legend GASH HELL CONDEMNED—STORM'S COMING.

"So," she said tightly, and gusted up a long plume of smoke. "Deck says you wanna talk about Torres. What you wanna know? If I was fucking him?"

"We could start with why. You seem pretty tight-wired, and from the police report, he comes across as a complete asshole."

"A complete asshole." She gazed into the remains of the pipe smoke between us as if she could see her ex-lover projected there. "Yeah, I'd say that's accurate. Kinda cute with it, though. *Very* large cock, too, very . . . talkative. You'd be surprised what a girl can put up with in other departments when that works out right."

"Good to know. Did he ever get around to telling you what he was doing back here?"

She cut me a grin, hiked one thigh over the arm of her chair, and settled lower in the seat. "You're taking *talkative* the wrong way there. We didn't actually talk all that much."

"Did he come to Cradle City specifically looking for you?"

"Said he did." She shrugged. "He was a lying sack of shit most of the time, though, so who knows, right? I wasn't the only one he knew here; he had a whole bunch of . . . friends."

"Any that he saw a lot of?"

The shrug again. "Jeff Havel gave him a job, so he had to see him. They had meetings, went downtown together, shit like that. Don't know about the others."

The purpose of her initial lie became apparent. Nina Ucharima was going to be evasive as fuck on just about everything, and lying to me right at the start had set up her gestalt so deception was the default. Whatever else she outright lied about, it was going to be hard for 'Ris to spot amid the general somatic noise.

"You said in the police report that he was going on about some big score he'd dreamed up. That accurate as well?"

She sipped at the pipe again. Looked at me over it. "You're not from here, are you?"

"Depends what you mean. I used to work IC this end of the valley with Decatur."

"Yeah, he said that. But you're from Earth originally, right?"

"By way of a few other places."

"Yeah, well, if you *were* from here, you'd know that the next big score"—brief sketch of Taiko drumming with her hands—"is all anybody in this town talks about, ever. Whether they've got one in the chamber or not."

"So it was just talk?"

"Fuck would I know? Like I said, I wasn't with him for the conversation."

"He didn't tell you he had the Ride Home in his pocket?"

She shook her head—a little vehemently, I thought. I prodded harder.

"Seems odd, though, doesn't it? As big scores go, that'd wipe the board. Gash-wide celebrity in less than a month, Earthbound before the summer's out. You think maybe he didn't want to let on he was leaving? Didn't want to hurt your finer feelings, maybe?"

She gave me a pitying look, a bent grin. Bizarre, defiant pride rising in her voice as she shot me down.

"What planet are you *on,* soak? You think guys like Torres give a flying fuck about a girl's *finer feelings?* You think you hang on to a guy like that by, like, whining about your *relationship* and shit? He'd had the Ride Home in his pocket, I would have known. *Everybody* would have known—he'd have been yelling it from the rooftops."

"Or the roof of a hangar out at Gingrich Field?"

The grin faded out. "Look, I don't know why he went up there. Like I told that dick from Metro Missing Persons, we were both pretty baked at the time."

"And you never saw him again after that?"

She heaved an exaggerated sigh. "That's right. Just like I told MMP."

"You're sure about that?"

"Oh, you think it would have slipped my mind?" She drew on the pipe mouthpiece again, breathed clouds of smoke out at me. "Look, is this really it? Walk back through everything I told the cops in case I decide to tell it different this time? Getting kind of bored, y'know."

She is deflecting, 'Ris said in my ear. *Has been since she walked in, but this appears to be the crux. Suggest—*

Yeah, I know.

I loosened off, held out my hand for the pipe. "Okay, Nina, wouldn't want you to be bored. So answer me this instead—you say Torres never mentioned the Ride Home to you or to anyone else in Cradle City, and you reckon that means he never had the ticket. You're saying Vector Red lied? It was, what, some kind of fix? Torres never won the lottery?"

She leaned in as she handed me the mouthpiece, closer than she needed to. She flashed the hard little grin again.

"What I'm saying, soak, is Pablito Torres never once in his life even fucking *played* the Ride Home Lottery."

OVERHEAD, A JAGGED green wavefront ripped across the Lamina east to west. Aftershock discharges rippled out in its wake, gold and silver gray. Murmurs rose like startled birds from the tables around us on the balcony. The sky had been putting out similar stuff all evening, but this dwarfed the previous displays. A few of the smokers stood and gestured, somebody even whooped. Ucharima didn't even glance up. Behind her lenses, the green-irised eyes were fixed on me, watching my reaction. I held her gaze while faintly, faintly, the sound of the discharge rolled down on us like the whisper of nighttime rain.

"You going to smoke that or what?"

I blinked, looked down at the pipe mouthpiece, forgotten in my hand. "I'll pass right now. Look, if that's true—"

"Why didn't I tell the cops?" She crooked her fingers at me for the pipe. I handed it over and watched her draw deep, let her have the moment. She mouthed a couple of perfect little smoke rings at me, cranked her eyebrows up and down twice for comic effect, then plumed the rest of the smoke out across the table.

"Never told the local cops *or* MMP," she said, slurring a little, "coz, fuck them, right? Corrupt motherfuckers, always with a hand out to the mayor, or Deck, or Havel and the Crew. Just going through the fucking motions. And that glimmery fucking streak of piss up from Bradbury, Tomatin, Tamora, whatever the fuck he was called . . ."

"Tomayro."

"Yeah, that's it. Tomayro." She sipped again at the pipe, gestured broadly with the mouthpiece. "Fucking Suit Central asshole. Spent the whole interview checking out my legs, he didn't give a shit about Pablo or anything else going on up here. Could smell his expense account bacon *bocadillo* coming out the printer, that one."

"Sounds about right. In Bradbury, they call him Tits-Up Tomayro."

She blinked back at me, leaking a slow grin. "Tits . . . Up . . ."

"It's how most of his cases end up." I grinned back, pointed twin index fingers at the ceiling. "Really. He's known for it."

She sniggered, and it blew into a full fit of the THC giggles. It made her look suddenly young. I'd been smoking a lot less, and I had 'Ris at work shutting down the effects of what I did inhale, but I put together a loose laugh of my own to keep Ucharima company. It wasn't hard. I took the pipe from her and waited her giggles out.

Maybe she spotted it. She sat up straighter in her armchair, suddenly serious.

"All right, look," she said. "I knew Pablo Torres since we were both kids growing up hardscrabble in Sombra. I got memories of him going back to three years old and younger. Back before he started with that bugshit of calling himself Pavel like it made him different from all the other Pablos. I fucked *Pablo* Torres when we were both still in high school, couldn't have been more than seven or eight years old, either of us. We worked reclamation together for EduKredits till we quit, then we got indentured together, pulling vertical crops along the Tith Chasma for AresAg and the Forge Group. Went our separate ways after that, but we'd catch up, y'know. Every few years, fall into bed together if we had nothing heavier going on. And I'm telling you he never played the Ride Home. He wasn't interested. Thought it was for mugs and morons. *What they think they're going to find on Earth apart from more fucking gravity dragging your prick to the floor?* he used to say. *We're Martians for fuck's sake, it ain't a ride home, it's a fucking trip to Shitsville.*"

"Was he political?"

"You mean the Frockers?" She snorted. "Gotta be fucking joking, right? I remember one time they came up here shouting about Cutting the Chains of Old Earth, Pablo asked one of them for his hand. Twat thought he wanted to shake, he put it right out there, but Pablo grabbed his hand and turned it over, kind of *stroked* it." She lifted one slim fingered hand of her own toward me, palm upward, and demonstrated. Her eyes sparkled at me in the low light from the table lamp. "It was soft as shit, right. Fucking Bradbury creep. So Pablo, he grabs the fingers, bends them right back till the creep yelps and falls on the ground. Pablo leans over him, says *you ain't paid the dues to come up here lecturing us, asshole. You take your soft pamphlet-scrawling hands and your wannabe scrabble-class-hero lectures and you fuck off back to the big city where they'll put up with your bugshit, coz up here we won't.* Then he drags him back to his feet, dusts him down, and pats him on the head like he was a fucking dog. Yeah." Nodding along with her own story, chuckling now as she told it. "Fucker just stood there blinking, didn't know whether to say thank you or cry, and Pablo, right, he gives him this *huge* kick in the ass, nearly puts him on the floor, barks out *we're done here, asshole!* Goes to kick him again, you know, to help him on up the street. And that city-bred soft-hand asshole—he ran like he had the fucking pistaco on his heels."

She wound down, laughter gone a little hard and shrill as it outlasted the tale. I thought I caught the trace of tear sheen in her eyes.

"Gimme that pipe, willya?"

I handed it over. Brooding a little on Torres's apparent political sophistication. It wasn't something you'd expect from reading the police file—a lot of hardscrabble Uplanders are dyed in the blood separatists, and even among the ones who aren't, there's a casual contempt for more joined-up political thinking.

But then that's humans for you—never can trust the stroppy fuckers to live up to the stereotypes you assign.

"So he didn't like the Frockers. What about the Sacranites? They're still active here, right?"

She sniffed. "Yeah, they got that place up over the lip, the old observatory. He used to go up there sometimes, back when he was younger. More for the pussy than the politics, you ask me. He was always getting laid, bringing stories back about it. Those social justice bitches do just about anything for a taste of hardscrabble cock."

"What about more recently? Before he disappeared."

"That too." I saw the quiet hurt in her face as she said it. "Went a bunch of times, said he wanted to hear some lectures they were giving, but hey"—a tight shrug—"it was what it was. *He* was what he was. Not like I didn't know him, didn't know what I was getting in the bundle. He even went up there when that whasserface, y'know, the daughter, was there. Always said she was kind of hot, if you believe that."

"Martina Sacran?"

"Yeah, that's it, Martina." She exhaled, pulled a face. "I mean— seriously? Sometimes I think he was just trying to wind me up with that shit."

"Maybe he just liked a challenge. He'd be waiting a long time for Martina Sacran to jump on his dick, that's for sure."

"Oh, yeah?" Some residual loyalty to Torres edged her tone, put it a finger's width away from hostile. "You like, *know* her or something?"

I shook my head. "Knew one of her girlfriends."

"Oh." Ucharima blinked muzzily through her THC buzz. "Like that?"

"Yeah. Like that."

"Tried yourself and got knocked back, huh?" She leaned in, grinned lewdly. "Poor you—all steamed up and no one to rub you down. You hard men don't take well to that state of affairs, do you?"

"I don't recall saying I was a hard man."

"Deck tells me you were an overrider back in the day." She leaned in again, close enough to touch this time. "Don't get much harder than that, right?"

I sketched a smile, tried to ignore the abrupt trickle of blood to my prick. "You don't want to believe everything you see in the immies."

"Waking up in agony from the decant, no painkillers coz they need you functional and paying attention fast." Her lips stayed parted as she paused. Her tongue tip flickered in the gap, touched her upper lip. "Fight/ flight all ramped up from the off, blood to major muscle groups as standard, task focus hardwired in . . ."

"Sounds like you been reading my operating instructions."

What are you doing?

Following a lead, what does it look like?

Frankly? It looks like you're trying to cop off with this skank because she's got good legs and an attitude and she'll fuck anything she thinks might be dangerous.

Right now, this skank is the only lead we've got and we know she's holding out. What do you suggest?

"Hey, overrider—I'm right here." Ucharima snapped her fingers at me over the table. "You feeling okay?"

I nodded at the pipe. "Strong shit, this. Yeah, I'm good."

What I suggest is that you lay off the psychotropics until I can get your levels of functionality back to something approaching sensible and then we assess this move with a clear head.

No time for that, 'Ris. I could feel an impending smirk in the muscles under my face. I worked at holding it down. *Mission clock is ticking. Got to call this in the here and now.*

You do not believe that.

"You know," I said a little too loudly. I stopped, dropped my voice. Made a framing motion with both hands before me. "This table. Feels like it's . . . in the way."

Nina Ucharima tilted her head. Licked her upper lip again, a whole lot more obviously. "Yeah, it kind of is. You want to get someplace with less furniture?"

"Sounds . . . workable."

We both stood up jerkily, in eerie unison, as if pulled there by the same urgent puppet string. Ucharima swayed a bit with the surplus momentum. I put out a hand on reflex, wrapped it on the taut muscle in her upper arm. She grinned, flexed the arm a little, and leaned into my grip. I moved around the table and gathered her in from behind. She folded her arms low on her belly and clasped both of my arms in place, leaned back into me, ground her ass against my groin.

Suit yourself, then, 'Ris told me sniffily. But don't blame me when she starts asking you to pull her hair at critical junctures and says you don't measure up to Pablo Torres in the only way that counts.

TWENTY-SEVEN

WHATEVER THE THC was tweaked with, it had my BV-patented onboard filters beaten hollow. I guess the technology moves on. We seemed to reach Ucharima's apartment like wisps of brightly colored silk tangled together and blown in gusts along a series of dull, dark alleyways by a rising wind. In the doorway of her block, we blew to a halt, hands on each other, tongues in each other's mouths, scintillating schools of silvery fry scattering away as our faces came close. I looked up once along the darkened planes of the architecture above and would have sworn I could see its edges seethe with protocols still not settled, or reacting, hypersensitive, to the Tharsis Gate wind. Ucharima twisted around in my arms and hit a handprint panel, let us inside, led me up what seemed like endless darkened stairs, through another door that seemed to dissolve for us more than open, and into a broad, dimly lit living space beyond.

She turned to me, got up close again, and slid off my lenses. I heard them skitter away somewhere across the floor. She melted out of her clothes, boots kicked off, jacket shed onto the floor like an old skin, T-shirt up over her head and gone. High breasts and hardened nipples beneath. Eyes defocused with want now, restless hands reaching for my waist.

"Okay, *hard* man—let's see what you got for me here . . ."

If she was comparatively disappointed, she didn't let it show. We got across the room, through a doorway, and onto a bed somewhere beyond, but even under the soft blurring of the THC, it was already starting to feel a bit like wrestling—two bodies not really wanting the same things, two ill-matched scripts vying for system dominance. I struggled awkwardly to get the tights off her while she laughed excitedly into my teeth, scraped her nails over my back and shoulders, and hissed at me to rip them. I did in the end, tore them apart with both hands to get access, went with it and flipped her bodily onto all fours in front of me. Ucharima panting excitedly now, face down in the sheets, lifting her ass in offering . . .

She stopped, looked back. "What are you doing?"

"I, uh—pulling your hair . . ."

"Well—fucking *don't*! Just—just *fuck* me, overrider. Fuck me with that big cock, make me fucking come!"

And so on.

We got through it in the end, the drugs smoothing out what under other circumstances might have been a pretty irritable encounter but also adding a duration neither of us really wanted. We finally rolled apart on the bed, unplugged and panting, eyes on the ceiling, not touching. Barely a quarter meter of space between us, but the ebbing THC made it feel like a gulf, and the air was ringing and angry. Ucharima's house AI had started piping some violent Mars Metal ambients into the room while we tangled, then took a while to notice we'd stopped and to fade the noise back down. For which I was grateful; quiet right now would have been worse.

Was worse as it started to creep in.

"Thanks," she said finally, maybe by way of reassurance.

"My pleasure." I reached for conversation, schooled by Ariana's habitual postcoital needs. *Pachamama and all her little fucking saints, wish you were here now, girl.* "What was that we were listening to?"

"Gash Hell Condemned—*Live at Wall 101*. Not keen, huh?" She chuckled without much humor. "Yeah, Hidalgo hated that shit, too. Acquired local taste, I reckon."

I sat up on the edge of the bed, looked back at her where she lay. "You mind if I ask you something personal?"

She laughed, out loud and hard this time. Cranked herself up on her elbows and raised an eyebrow at me. "You've just had my tongue up your ass and your cock in my mouth. I'd say we're a little beyond *personal* by now, wouldn't you?"

I forced a small smile. "Since you mention it."

"So ask away." She slumped down again on her back, staring upward. Her breasts sat mounded up on her ribs with resilient augmented appeal, but the nipples had already softened back from any arousal she might recently have owned. "It's what you're here for, right? Task focus? *Don't Wake the Overrider.* Deck said you were a mission-headed motherfucker, and I guess that's what you are."

"I, uh—I had a good time here, Nina." *Just about.*

"Yeah, me, too." Eyes still fixed on the ceiling. "Scratched an itch. Go on—ask your personal shit. This is getting boring again."

"You reckon Pablo Torres is still alive somewhere?"

Sudden stiffness in the supine body before me. I wished I'd gotten my lenses back on, but the signals were pretty clear anyway. I was watching for the tear sheen, caught the tiny gleam of it in the low light.

"No," she said flatly. "Pablo is dead."

"And you know that how?"

She sat up again, face a hardening mask. "Because I'm a fucking street logistics wrangler for Deck and Havel both, and I know how things work up here. Pablo Torres went mouthing off about his big score to the wrong people like the big swinging dick asshole he thought he was, and it backed up on him. End of the sad, sad story. Now I think maybe you'd better go."

"His big score that didn't involve the Ride Home."

"I already said that."

"And you don't know who these wrong people are, and you don't care about finding out. You, a street logistics wrangler for the Ground Out Crew, with, I would guess, the resources to bury Pablo's killers facedown in a regolith grave still screaming if you can get to them before the cops do. That why you didn't cooperate with MMP?"

She summoned a raw smile. "You don't want to believe everything you see in the immies."

"Something's eating at you, Nina. You can't hide it, and you don't strike me as someone who scares easily. So you should know I'm here with some heavy backing. Earthside backing. Whatever this is, it can be handled."

She sneered. "Black Hatch Earthman gonna save the Poor Little Good Girl Gone Bad from the Big Evil, huh? Seen that saccharine immie shit a whole bunch too many times, Earthman, and I don't like happy endings."

"Just thought you might want to pick the winning side," I said mildly. "While you still can. I am going to find out why Torres was killed, and I am going to find whoever did it. And things are going to get bloody in the process. There's no reason you should get caught in the cross fire when that happens."

We stared at each other for a couple of seconds. Then she rolled off the bed away from me, came lithely to her feet.

"Get dressed and get out, overrider. You're done."

"You're making a mistake."

"Mistake was bringing you up here in the first place." She put her hands on her hips, the brash confidence of someone fully dressed in the stance, tilted her head as if to see me better in the low light. "You know, you don't fuck half as good as Pablo did, but you are like him in a couple of other ways."

Abandoned mother, no functional father. Hardscrabble origins. In the back of my head, I heard Madison Madekwe's voice reeling off the list. *Do you . . . identify with Torres?*

"I'm nothing like Pablo Torres, Nina. You're going to find that out soon, and so is whoever iced him."

She shook her head. "No, you are like him. You got the same swagger, for a start. And the same bugshit belief there's a happy ending waiting for you around the next bend. You want to talk about winning sides? This is Cradle City, Black Hatch man, this is the Uplands. There is no winning side up here, there's just staying alive and staying ahead. Torres didn't—" Abruptly, her voice caught on something jagged. She ducked her face away, blinking rapidly. Came back fast, though, raw-toned and glitter-eyed. "Just *get the fuck out,* all right? Just *go.* You got your questions answered, you got laid. What else you fucking want? Go home! Tell Deck I cooperated—whoo-hoo, did I fucking cooperate!—and just leave me the fuck alone!"

It took an awkward while to find my scattered clothes and put them on.

When standing and watching me do it got ridiculous, Ucharima folded herself back onto one side of the bed, sorted through an adjacent cabinet and found herself a box of Air Rated. She shook out one of the yellow-papered spliffs, sucked it to life, and smoked in gloomy silence as I dressed. She was still, sat there in the cloud of sweet-smelling smoke when I finished, one knee up, chin sunk on it, staring into the corner of the room, the Air Rated forgotten between the fingers of one trailing hand, burning steadily down to a stub. I slid on my lenses, hesitated. Something incomplete, something I'd missed, nagging at me . . .

She caught the hesitation even through her fresh numbing buzz and vision that had to be peripheral at best. She didn't look at me, didn't look up at all. But she brought up the spliff and drew hard on it. Tiny crackle in the big silence that held the room, the brightening glow of the embered end. The voice that followed was almost as small and dry.

"Which part of *get the fuck out* didn't you understand, hard man?"

I got the fuck out.

SO HOW DID you measure up?

You shut up.

I stood for a moment in the cramped lobby space at the bottom of Ucharima's building, feeling the gloom. Low light from high-set panels spilled down, showed me raw nanocrete walls still stippled with the micro-porous fresh-gray-meringue look of recent build. Partway back up the stairs, a scribble of brighter yellow caught my eye, like piss in fume-stained snow—I'd missed it on the way down while the lights were scrambling to catch up with my irritable-speedy descent. There, a scant meter up off the stair treads, someone had crouched and scarred indenture-lament poetry into the surface with a counterculture spray:

> *The High Frontier can kiss my ass*
> *I never swam, nor fucked in grass*
> *Grown green from summer rain, nor will before I die*

The dues I paid, the blood I gave
From Cradle City to the grave
Fed pale pistacos under some other fucker's sky

The script was ragged around the edges where the build protocols had tried to eat it away, but so far the yellowish countercultures were holding their ground.

"Not our pal Pablo's work," I muttered. "He fucking loved it here, apparently."

That is not exactly what she said.

Near enough, it is.

He was not interested in Earth as a destination. You should not assume all disadvantaged Martians crave the same escape as you.

I ain't a fucking Martian.

I went to kick at the door to let myself out, but it whipped slyly back before I could make contact. I went out into the street—icy-arid air scouring my nostrils on contact—and set to work retracing my steps from the pipe house. It took longer than it should have. Navigational instinct is one of the capacities overrider programs test for at third trimester and then tweak upward at various stages during the conditioning. Make a living finding your way around the labyrinthine architecture of spacecraft inside and out, orienting yourself in the weightless black void the vessel swims in, and getting lost isn't something you often worry about. But the pipe house product had given those routines a pretty severe kicking; it was a while before I spotted the storm-monitoring tower in a gap between blocks and was able to tack my way to it.

From there, I walked back to my capsule at the Mansions of Luthra. There was a rudimentary underground system in Cradle City, but it ran infrequently and none of its limited array of stations came up close to Musk Plaza. The surface public crawler network was even worse—sketchy routes with few official stops and a service worse than skeletal once night fell. Whatever platform Raquel Allauca got herself regularly reelected on around here, it didn't seem to include infrastructure investment.

I shrugged it off—the walk would do me good. Clear my head, let me think. Digest this shit about Torres not playing the lottery.

In many ways, said 'Ris chattily, *the whole concept of the Ride Home is an anachronism. It is a throwback to a time when only a tiny handful of citizens were born on Mars and settlement was largely a process carried out by reluctant volunteers, misfits, and exiled criminals, all overseen by a caste of fixed-term visiting qualified professionals and administrators. Desperation, escape, and extreme financial reward were the primary drivers of the migration, and offering a possible escape hatch of free return with attached glitter and fame played to those same incentives. Like all lotteries, it was an attempt to distract and dilute labor force discontent with irrational hope.*

I grunted. The slow-gathering pressure of a comedown was starting to make itself felt somewhere up behind my left eye. Over the tops of the tower blocks I passed, the Lamina made blood-red and violet counterpoint. 'Ris warbled on.

Return itself was also far more of a media event during that era for the winners themselves and for audiences on both Earth and Mars. Now, with multiple generations born and raised here, the assumption of a population longing to return to the bosom of Earth is outmoded at best, at worst counterproductive in understanding the sociopolitical dynamics of the Valley.

People still buy the tickets by the dumb-fuck million.

In fact, current sales totals are lower than you might imagine. At the last count, some 17,400,000 tickets per available berth, far fewer than other comparable lottery operations with more conventional prizes.

That's still a billion tickets a year!

Slightly less—but yes, the gamble is still a popular one. Though you should remember that for the last thirty-nine years, winning has been a round-trip offer, with the return ticket available should the winner not wish to remain on Earth after all. Many Valley citizens are playing not to escape their home permanently but for the chance to become an ultratripper in reverse.

Yeah—if they keep their wits about them.

I'd heard Martina Sacran lecture on the subject once, *cold-blooded corporate manipulation of low educational norms and proletarian failure at deferred gratification, yadda yadda moan, moan.* There was a sunset clause on the return trips; activation was required within a limited period or you were cashed out for a—reputedly low—percentage payment against the actual cost of the cryocap berth. Sacran's complaint was, near as I recalled, that the activation date was calculated and set to fall well before the average die-off of the media orgy with which Ride Home winners were habitually feted. And even a low percentage of the cost of a cryocap berth to Mars looked like a lot of money when it was stacked up in cash and offered with no strings attached. By all accounts, most winners never got around to activation, took the cash instead, and Vector Red quietly charged the subsidized cryocap at full fare for some outward bound qual-pro or similar. It was, as Sal Quiroga might have said if I hadn't broken his spine last week, *one sweet little mechanism.*

That being said, 'Ris hesitated a beat, *there are still a number of problems with the idea that Pavel Torres did not play the Ride Home Lottery.*

Oh, you reckon?

Yes—

What, like how the fuck did he end up with his DNA coded to the winning ticket? Or if he didn't, who lied to put it there?

These, yes. Patiently. *But also—what was the big score he claimed to have lined up, if not the lottery win?*

Thug fucker back there says it was all swagger, nothing solid. Says all the local toughs pillow brag that way, and I get the distinct impression she knows what she's talking about.

You are unconvinced of this. And I detect some additional recent rancor. Did you not, then, measure up to Torres in some important aspects?

I grinned sourly to myself. *You shut up. I'm a lot like him, apparently.*

I repeat—you are unconvinced.

I walked in silence for a few moments. Glanced up at the Lamina, which seemed to have settled down to transparency for the time being. My eyes pulled involuntarily to a dim speck high up in the starfield; no need to search it out, the yearning that had it mapped for me was old and bone deep.

Without applying rationale as a mediator, select your—

Yeah, yeah. I'm on it. I thought about Ucharima, the final spiky minutes in her apartment, the bitter dregs of failed connection beneath our face-off, the deeper currents beneath that. Looking for the glitch, the piece that didn't fit. Something was—

Tear sheen.

I stopped.

You reckon Pablo Torres is still alive somewhere.

No. Pablo is dead.

The stony flat tone of certain loss.

Pablo Torres went mouthing off about his big score to the wrong people like the big swinging dick asshole he thought he was, and that shit backed up on him.

"He did have a big score." I said it slowly out loud, tasting the new insight, mystifying a couple of passersby on the almost empty street in the process. "She knew it, and she knew it killed him. That *everyone-has-the-swagger* shit was pure smoke screen. He had a score lined up. Good chance she knew what it was as well."

Why would she hide this knowledge from the police?

I started walking again, fresh energy in my pace. *Who knows? Could be she's looking for some private payback on her own time, could be she's too scared to move on it, could be she's been cut in on the deal in return for shutting up. No way to know right now.*

Further and more forceful interrogation might—

No.

'Ris paused for a long moment, infrequently needed subroutines waking to unaccustomed life. *That seems . . . uncharacteristically squeamish of you.*

Yeah, it is. I'm uncharacteristically squeamish about shitting on Milton Decatur's doorstep without a very good reason. He was a good friend once, and he might turn out that way again if I play this right. Whoever tried to kill me was worried Milt and I would end up cooperating, worried maybe that we'd be on the same side of whatever this is. And maybe we are. That's not something to squander just yet.

Is this really your only reason for—

Oh, look—here we are. The Mansions of Luthra, twinkling at us in all their tacky, minareted glory at the far side of the sparsely trafficked plaza we'd just entered. The trademark life-size Mars lander model sat stolidly between the four minarets, framed on either side by pressure-suited figures in unlikely symmetrical positions. One of them was missing a triumphantly raised arm, snapped off below the elbow, and another had lost most of one leg to cheap printer stock and storm-wind erosion or maybe to crowbars wielded by the same bored vandals who'd scrawled lurid cartoon features on the blank surfacing of the pressure suit face masks.

First Humans on Mars—the Glory Lives On.

A solitary figure loitered near the entrance, trying to look casual and unoccupied. I snorted back laughter and altered my course, heading for a covered service alley on an adjacent side of the plaza. A few dozen other people were milling around the square, mostly strolling couples. A loudly clowning kid gang hung around the abstract sculpture in the center, annoying everyone, and a couple of shuffling switch-heads worked their way along the walls in search of an easily hacked power source. According to 'Ris's kinetic analysis, no one was paying close attention to either me or my sticky friend.

I wove through the loose churn of night owls at a leisurely pace and slipped into the alley. I'd cased it the day before, designated it ideal as both bolt-hole and private arena—open-ended, giving out into another, smaller square a couple of blocks away, roofing proof against any but the most high-end aerial surveillance. Stern warning decals along the alley proclaimed high-voltage antiloitering charges in the walls at ankle height, which would keep the space clear of derelicts, switch-heads, or hard-up couples wanting to fuck. I headed past a short row of parked autobins, ducked into a suitably shadowed gap between two of them.

I didn't have to wait long.

He came hurrying past the bins, hood still up, anxiety written into every line of his moves. The tissue weld trace 'Ris had picked up at the station was still there, still detectable on heat sig, though fading as the wound healed beneath the weld. I let him get level with my hiding place, then stepped out hard and grabbed him. He yelped and put up fending hands. I let go, stepped back, stood grinning.

"Jesus fuck, Veil," he snarled. "Is that supposed to be funny? Where the fuck have you *been*?"

TWENTY-EIGHT

HIS NAME WAS Seb Luppi and, for his sins, he still fondly imagined himself a journalist. I didn't have the heart to point out the obvious; that covering ultratripper antics for a drooling fandom or who's fucking who among the Bradbury glitterati might deserve a variety of job titles—dung beetle, maybe, or public pacification op—but *journalist* was not one of them. That'd be like calling the dancers offering three-minute handjobs out the back of Vallez Girlz *nirvana dispensers.*

But let it go—I didn't have any operational incentive to upset Luppi. When your job involves waking up aboard a hurtling canister full of spilled shit in deep space, you learn to case the environment at speed and then work with what you have at hand. That includes the people around you. Luppi had parachuted himself into the middle of this mess—which showed some grit, given the head butt I'd stuck on him at Bradbury Central—and I figured he could be useful. Tempting to crack the lid on his obvious self-loathing, throw him down the well of his own existential remorse, and watch him drown, but that got me nothing useful in the end.

Far better to use that same self-loathing as leverage and put him to work.

. . .

I TOOK HIM in the freeze-dried darkness of the station landing zone a couple of minutes after we emerged under the cowl of the escalators up out of the VV platform depths. It was intentional procedure—'Ris had him flagged as combat-injured and possibly dangerous, I figured the edge I'd have in the Uplands open air might help offset any skills he might own. I checked on peripheral vision to see that he was still on my tail, looked for other ways to tip the odds.

Air transport had been sent to collect some of the new arrivals, and it settled now in a cluster of blazing lights and screaming turbines, kicking up a small storm of dust from the center of the field—most likely a local corporate picking up indentured labor back from furlough, saving them the temptations of the taxi-and-capsule-whore operators that plied the routes into town. I cut wide of the lights and noise, headed for a darkened corner of the field, now sunk even darker in gloom by contrast with the transport's lights. My eyes brought up the soft blue shark-mod glow. Luppi followed me at a prudent distance until it dawned on him belatedly that there was no exit on this side, only a writhing barrier of activated livewire a meter tall and three meters wide.

I felt his pace ebb behind me and spun around. He was about twenty meters off, flagging to a halt, and nothing much of combat awareness in his stance or any weapon in sight. I ran straight at him, left fist clenched, summoning the morphalloy blade. He flinched, stumbled, turned to run. Made a dozen paces before I cannoned into him from behind, knocked him flat in the frigid dust, and rolled him over. In the glow from the transport's landing lights, his face was a regolith-smeared, gibbering mask of terror, lenses gone. The tissue weld was clearly visible across his nose and cheek—very cheap work, done in a hurry. His breath steamed in the cold, as he drew big panting, panicked breaths. I rammed the ABdM knife up under his chin, but with less force than I'd originally intended. I think I was already starting to recognize him.

"Now who the *fuck* are you?"

"I—I—I, Luppi—Sebastian Luppi, I—I—was following you."

"Yeah, no shit." I went over him brusquely for any trace of weapons, found nothing. Had to raise my voice over the turbine whine from the transport. "Following me *why*?"

"You . . ." A hint of self-righteousness crept into his voice, gave him an odd air of wiry resolve that hadn't been there before. "You broke my fucking face, you Earth asshole. And you stole my lenses. You're deep cover for COLIN and the audit, cozied up to Madison Madekwe, plugged in with Dominica Chakana and BPD. You think I'm so far gone I can't smell a story like that when it rubs its filthy unwashed cunt in my face?"

The air transport lifted shrieking in a fresh cloud of dust and then tilted away westward. I took the blade out from under his chin.

"I know you, don't I?"

"You were fucking fast enough to take me out when you thought I'd rumbled you, yeah." He struggled to prop himself up, still trembling with reaction. The noise of the transport's engines faded out. In the settling quiet that followed, his voice came out as a half laugh, shaky and bitter. "What's the matter, COLIN looking to cut a side deal with Mulholland? Or maybe our sainted-to-Pachamama oh-so-clean-hands commissioner?"

I wiggled the knuckle rings, shut down the morphalloy blade. "How the fuck would I know? You got dirt on these people, why you following me?"

"You're going to tell me you're not deep-cover Earth?"

"*Deep-cover Earth*—what are you, some kind of Frocker conspiracy nut? I've been here fourteen fucking years. That's not deep cover, that's fucking *buried*."

"You've been here eight," he said defiantly. "I ran a trace on you."

"Yeah—fourteen *Earth* years. Seven and a half local. You really think COLIN plans that far ahead?"

"They use deep-cover agents—COLIN and the navy both. We saw that on Titan."

"You saw it in some bugshit immie about the Titan Oligarchs, you mean. When were you ever offworld?"

"Not talking about offworld," he said sulkily. "Talking about right here in the Gash. Ten years ago, I had sources, man, real sources, and they—"

"Oh, *shut up*. Sources." I stood up, preparatory to leaving him there in the cold and dust. "You know what you stupid fucking conspiracy ass-holes just don't get? *No one is that well organized.* There *is* no big Deep State evil, no Corporate Earth Plot to Enslave Humanity. It's just a bunch of conflicting interests making a fucking mess wherever they go. No different on Mars than anywhere else."

"If that's true, what are you doing out here?"

I leaned in closer over him, watched him trying not to flinch. "What's it to you, glamfly? Why aren't you back covering the Gorgeous Goings-On of Sundry Charms and Friends? That's your job, isn't it?" I gestured at him. "Or are you a *deep-cover* journalist, just posing as a paparazzo? How long's that mission been running?"

He looked away, something jarred loose behind his face. I grinned fiercely. "Yeah. Now fuck off back to your tinselly little glamfly world and don't try creeping up on me again, because the next time I may not be in such a good fucking mood."

I turned to go. He just lay there, covered in Martian dust, made no move to get up or even wipe his face. I hesitated.

"You used to be a journalist?" I turned back. Pitched my voice less harsh. "A real one?"

He nodded jerkily, looking away at things I couldn't see.

"Here." I put out my hand. He blinked up at it from where he was sprawled. "Get up, come on. I'll buy you a drink."

WE RODE ONE of the AI crawler cabs into town, shut down its pimping routines as soon as they started, and sat in silence until we hit the downtown.

Find me a halfway decent all-night bar, walking distance from Musk Plaza, I subbed 'Ris in the meantime. *Flag it to the cab. And if the AI tries to derail us to some sponsor-recommended flesh joint, sting the fucker so it hurts, then steal the fare.*

The Mansions of Luthra itself has a bar that might fit the description halfway decent.

No, I need the disconnect. Find somewhere else.

We came in through the low-rise suburban ring, huddled and hump-roofed dwellings converted from storage sheds and hangars on all sides, a sparse low-intensity scatter of municipal lighting like the embers of a fire almost out. It was a skyline barely changed since Cradle City's origin as a pre-Lamina catch-point for hazardous bulk cargo fired into puff-down from orbit. When all that ended and the catch-point camps had to relocate up out of the Gash, hungry new subcorporate players moved in behind experimental Marstech cultivation and human genotype upgrade trials. Brash and hyperleveraged, they'd seen no reason to waste time or initial capital on rebuilding. *High Frontier Humanity Makes Do!* Got a whole new sky over your head now, people, and air to breathe! Rejoice in your newfound freedoms! *Let's Go to Work!*

So forth.

Ahead, the lights of the bonsai downtown blazed like a recently landed alien vessel bent on conquest.

The cab vacillated at an intersection—sponsor protocols in the navigational AI maybe struggling against Osiris's BV battle tech for a couple of vain seconds—then it grumbled on and dropped us at a grubby-looking corner establishment called Payload Blue. Confirming my suspicions, the fare counter had zeroed out—'Ris had gone in and fucked the taxi up. I saw Luppi notice it, too, put it together with what he had on my past, and come to a journalistically astute conclusion. Hard to tell from his face, but I hoped he was impressed.

We went in, ignored stares from locals in various states of retreat from reality, took a table in the cozy gloom at the back. I ordered a couple of shots of JD Red and a jug of local-brewed *chicha* from the wan and weary-looking late-shift waitress.

"Been to Cradle City before?" I asked Luppi while we waited.

"No. Places like it, though."

The drinks came. I took my shot and drained it, put it down on the table, and looked Luppi in the eye.

"So," I said.

"SO YOU WERE right about your pal Decatur," he said, glancing nervously up and down in the tight confines of the alley. "Less than an hour after you left the Crocus Lux, Raquel Allauca shows up in slop-wear and hoodie. No big hair, no heels, no suit. And no entourage, just a couple of low-key minders. She goes right through the lobby, never breaks stride. I doubt anyone in there but me even realized it was her. But man, if looks could kill, Decatur's a fucking corpse by now."

"Not really. She came to him, remember. How long was she in there for?"

"No idea—I cleared out about forty minutes after that. Hotel security got fed up with me buttonholing the customers with that bugshit questionnaire."

"*On a scale of 1 to 10, how do you view the recent Earth audit? Will it affect your attitude to Martian independence?* Come on, it's not bad cover for spur of the moment, even you said so. Closest thing to journalism *you've* done in the last ten years, anyway."

I saw the anger rise in his eyes, but it wasn't the flinch of our first meeting. Something had kindled in Seb Luppi since our last encounter, either the rhythms of the work itself or a sudden conviction that what he was doing might matter. He jerked his chin at me.

"What about you? Ever going to stop using *Earth years* like some sad case qualpro moping up at the stars and counting off the days till contract's end?"

"Five years," I amended. "Five long cold fucking Martian years. Happy now? What else you got for me?"

"Not much. I prodded the local cops about jurisdiction and how they felt about the idea of oversight from Earth, how it compared with oversight from, say, Bradbury. That's about as close as I could ease up to the Torres case without making it fucking obvious. They mentioned it in passing, but there wasn't any kind of reaction you'd call significant. Not twitchy about discussing it, not really bothered about it one way or the other."

"Well, what *did* they say?"

Luppi shrugged. "That no one's going to miss this Torres guy, he was a fatherless fuck-up walking around way past his expiration date; that he probably just wandered off somewhere bombed, fell in an uncovered slurry culvert, drowned in corrosive industrial effluent. Also said that

Metro Missing Persons did fuck-all to find him, and wasn't that always the way? They pretty much hate BPD on reflex around here—they especially hate Metro Missing Persons—but they'd take both with open arms over an Earth Oversight team. I don't envy whoever eventually comes here to clean this mess up."

I grimaced. "You're looking at him."

"I meant whoever COLIN send, your new pal Madekwe or someone else. That can't be far off happening, right? Edward Tekele's got a system-wide reputation for getting shit done; I checked. I don't see him leaving you and the locals on point."

I thought about that, brooded on Astrid Gaskell and her cozy relationship with Sakarian, and wondered just how much of that particular subroutine Edward Tekele was or was not party to. Like most modern dynamic systems, COLIN was thoroughly decentralized and modular to a fault—you really can't get things done on an interplanetary scale any other way. Regulatory bodies like Earth Oversight served at best as a tightly stretched containment membrane to bag up the modules and prevent undue spillage; at worst, well—give it to Sacran senior again, he called it about right: *tooth whitening on a Komodo dragon.* Corporate PR and damage limitation. And with all that modularity jostling in the bag, it'd be naive to expect too much unity of purpose.

"Don't you worry about Tekele or Madekwe," I said. "Let's just stick to the matter in hand."

I'd been deftly economical with what I told Luppi—he thought I was undercover for BPD, he'd seen me around with Chakana, put two and two together and made three and a half. I let him run with that. Here to find out the truth about Torres, because COLIN was curiously obsessive about it, no idea why, and Chakana wanted answers. End of story, byline—a Seb Luppi exclusive, he hoped. As long as BPD and COLIN kept a lid on Madekwe's abduction—and the nonspecific terrorist assault line looked to be holding in the feeds—Luppi should stay satisfied with what I'd fed him. He'd chase the Torres angle exclusively for whatever it might yield.

But beyond that was the truth I hadn't told him, that I had at least as many unanswered questions upstream of Madekwe—who she was really, why Astrid Gaskell was keeping tabs on her, what made Mulholland so keen for her to be bodyguarded—as I did in the case she'd been bearing down on when she vanished.

"I am sticking to the matter in hand," Luppi said, his newly rediscovered journalistic integrity aggrieved. "And I'm telling you, whatever this is, local PD isn't in on it. One of the gals I spoke to—detective sergeant with six years in. That's six *Mars* years to you. Pretty senior. I doubt there's much going on around the station she doesn't know about—she could have been discussing shift rotations for all the interest she showed in Torres when he came up. You know, they might be on to something with this slurry culvert thing, right? It is where a lot of Upland missing persons show up eventually."

"Yeah, so do murder victims shoved there to take the heat off. Even if that is where Torres ended up, it doesn't get us any closer to knowing why. And there's a big fucking *why* behind this, believe me."

"If you say so. You going to tell me where you've been all night?"

I looked at him. "What are we, married?"

"I was hanging around out there for the best part of four hours like a fucking idiot. That's not good investigative procedure. I don't want to get noticed and tagged in your vicinity."

"I've been busy," I told him. "That's all you need to know. You talked to anyone up at Sedge Systems yet?"

"Got an appointment with their local PR manager day after tomorrow. I had to line them up as part of a sequence. Got some cutting-edge outfit called Shelf County Dawn tomorrow morning, they're falling over themselves for anything that looks like publicity, and then Allauca's old company, Khadka Sanchez Labor Logistics, in the afternoon. Same basic question set for everyone, uh, lessee"—he was reading them off his lenses—"indenture dos and don'ts, possible abuses, is the system fit for purpose? Are they worried about any potentially aggrieved employees who might go running to Earth Oversight and telling tales out of school? That lets me segue into Torres in the case of Sedge Systems—famous case, Ride Home winner who missed his ride, Pablito riots back in Bradbury, we're all very curious, he seems to have left Sedge mysteriously *be-*

fore he knew he'd won the Ride Home, any comment? That's about as close as I dare push it."

I nodded. "Fair enough. Let me know if anything surfaces out of all that. Anything really urgent comes up, you can come and punch in a message to my capsule at the hotel. I'll pick those up at least once a day. Otherwise I'll meet you day after tomorrow, late, some time after midnight. Use the bar this time—Payload Blue. Back table."

"Right." I could almost hear the nervous click in his throat as he swallowed. "You think they're watching us? Right now, I mean?"

"You mean Decatur's crew? Or Allauca?"

"Either/or." He attempted a nonchalant shrug, failed badly to hide the underlying tremor. "Both, maybe?"

"In here, none of them are." I gestured at the alley's roof, poured a reassurance I didn't feel into my tone. "Not with anything basic, anyway. And I've got systems that'll spot near-vicinity surveillance bugs or targeted beam sweep; it's showing nothing so far. I don't think they're tracking me very hard, because right now I'm not hiding from them. They might have a high-alt drone or some rented satellite time on the hotel." I shrugged. "Risk you take. If someone's looking for a connection between us, they're going to find it. We're banking on them not looking for it in the first place."

Luppi swallowed again. "Right."

"What's the matter, you getting chilly fingers?"

"I'm just . . . if they come after me . . ."

"Then you run," I said sharply. "The minute you think this thing is starting to tip and slide, you put in a screech call to Nikki Chakana at BPD and then you grab the next VV right the fuck back to Bradbury."

Despite his best efforts, he shivered. "I have done this sort of thing before, you kn—"

"Yeah, a decade ago at least, by your own admission. Ten years peek-and-tell nightclubbing around corporate hotshots and founder clan princesses in the meantime doesn't count."

The barb went home. My lenses picked up the way he flushed in the gloom. "Look, I could—if they took me—I've got a cover. I could say I was shadowing you, that you didn't know anything about it. Footage from the VV would bear that out, and I could—"

"You're too kind." I put my hands on his shoulders. "Now forget it. You don't fuck around with these people, Luppi. This isn't like creeping backstage on the Sundry Charms entourage. They won't just rough you up a bit for this, they'll cut your fucking face off and bury you. If you're lucky, they might shoot you first."

I stared at him until he broke. He nodded convulsively, looked away, and I took my hands off him. He drew a hard, steadying breath. "Okay. So what now?"

"Now? I'm headed out the back way. Give me a chance to get out in the open, let anyone who's been tracking me pick me up again, then you go back the way you came. You got a good excuse for why you came in here?"

Luppi's Adam's apple bobbing visibly in the low light. "Yeah. Bad food, too much booze. Had to find somewhere to puke." He held up a couple of fingers. "Going to leave a trace."

"Old school. Good for you." I clapped him briskly on the shoulder. "See you in a couple of days."

As I walked away, I heard him get started at my back, retching repeatedly in the narrow confines of the alley, fingers gouging down his throat until his stomach finally gave in and vomited up what it held.

I hoped it wasn't an omen.

TWENTY-NINE

THE STREETS AT the other end of the alley were an unprepossessing utilitarian warren not dissimilar to the one I'd navigated back from Ucharima's apartment block. No surprises there—shiny new downtown notwithstanding, Cradle City is a pretty unprepossessing place all around. I messed around a bit at intersections, head tilted back to watch the violent sky, went to a couple of bars, and sat in front of drinks I didn't want, waiting for any tracking Decatur or Allauca might have on me to catch up. Mission-time memories from my years at IC with Decatur kept popping up in the back of my head like targets in a training virtual—some of them obvious, expected, easy to nail and put away; others elusive, playing tag through the fading fumes of the pipe house THC; and some completely out of nowhere, with the shock impact of a fright mask clown around a corner.

How'd that happen, then?

Decatur, nodding at the Heckler & Koch as it lies on the pool table between us, along with all the other mission hardware we've prepped.

How'd what happen?

The damage, man! He points, index and ring finger together like a gun, at the scarred metal across the HK's lower rail and breech. In the glow from the low-hanging overhead lights, the damage he's talking about is bright and obvious across the weapon's dull alloy lines. Looks like a pretty full-on bang.

Monofil cutter. I shrug. Let someone get too close.

He cranks a brow at me, loading up his own Remington Red riot gun with nonlethals, one regolith-dry click at a time. He's the first-choice shooter tonight and the voice of IC reason; I'm the pistaco backup, the silent grim-faced threat if things go bad. It's early days for the partnership, we're still sounding each other out. Testing boundaries, learning the terrain.

Not very fucking Black Hatch of you, soak. Don't let that sort of thing happen often, I hope.

I shake my head. Just the once.

Whyn't you get it fixed? Alloy culture up at the shop, couple of hours, you're good as new. Cost you next to nothing and you can forget all about it.

Yeah—it would save me getting grilled on the subject by nosy mother-fuckers like you all the time.

He grins, wide and tight with the adrenal trickle of go-time just around the corner. Got that right.

Might think about it, then.

No, you won't. His gaze is turned down to the Remington's open slug feed, but his focus hasn't gone away. You can feel the force of it, floating there. Want to tell me why?

It takes me a moment to decide, to let it go. I pick up the HK one-handed, touch the scarred metal with the other hand. Some mistakes, you need to remember. This is definitely one of them.

I picked up my current unwanted drink and sipped at it, brows raised at the unlooked-for tide of recall I was suddenly surfing here. Chalk it up to pipe house THC. I glanced up and down the bar, saw nothing with potential to distract me from the haunt of memory and mistakes past. Around me, the customer rhythms of the place I was in had slowed to predawn sluggish. A diffuse sense of slippage coated everything, like slow-acting toxic dust settling on the shoulders of the remaining patrons. Nothing going on but the dying of Martian hours.

Incoming from the goat god, said 'Ris brightly.

Well, okay. Grabbing at it. *Put him on.*

"You're not going to like this, Veil." Something odd in Holmstrom's voice as it came through, a tone I wasn't used to. I frowned.

"Yeah, well, why should you be any different from anyone else I talked to today? What you got?"

"What I've got, darling, is next to nothing. I ran your little Earthside dig about an hour ago, and let me tell you, it did not go well."

The odd tone in his voice fell into place—it was chagrin. Holmstrom doesn't like to fail at anything.

"I thought you said it was a parking orbit?"

"No, *you* said that. I said nothing's easy over a quarter-hour coms lag, and I was right. But that isn't the point. See, I got my intrusion spike settled into Oversight's personnel stack chummily enough, got whole gigs of general crap on the whole audit crew from Edward Tekele on down—he seems like a nice man, incidentally—but the minute I hit your playmate Madekwe, it rang bells from here to Pachamama's throne and back. I am talking *major* countermeasures, Veil. I barely got out ahead of a return spike the size of Supay's dick on Judgment Day."

I sat in the dying bar and stared at myself in the mirror behind the bottles. Let it sink in. Like I told Chakana at the elevator, like I'd known all along. Anomaly clustering, bad news inbound.

"You sure it wasn't just time spent?" I tried reflexively. "Took that long for the CM systems to notice you'd broken in?"

"It's *me,* Veil."

I rubbed a hand across my face. "All right. So she's definitely not a second-team suit."

"I would say not."

"Did you get anything on her at all? Before you had to get out?"

"Fragments." The chagrin was back in his voice. "And even those don't add up. You said she had a family?"

"Yeah. Teen daughter and a husband, divorced."

"Not according to what I have here. The header file I managed to pull has her down as single, no dependents."

"Well . . ." I groped around in the dregs of the THC comedown for some kind of sense. "That's got to be a cover, right? Some kind of security measure?"

"Sure. Or her telling you she had a family was. Either way works."

"How does her inventing a daughter and a divorced husband for me work as security, Hannu? I'm 50 million klicks off ever meeting either of them. What's the point of lying about it? What's the fucking point of mentioning it in the first place?"

"Perhaps she didn't trust you and decided to play it safe. Perhaps she enjoys lying to men for its own sake. Perhaps she was laying down the lies on spec so you can't read her. I have no idea. But she's some kind of undercover operative—the countermeasures all over her data suggest that—so spinning cover probably comes as second nature. Perhaps she thought portraying herself as a divorced mother would make her softer in your eyes, more vulnerable. It might let her get under your defenses."

Do you think she got under your defenses, Veil?

You shut up.

I cleared my throat. "That's all you got? Madison Madekwe—single, no kids, tells lies?"

"And she's thirty-seven years old, Earth reckoned."

"Oh—good to know!"

There was a long pause, long enough that I thought Holmstrom might have hung up. "Do you mind if I ask where you are, Veil?"

"In a cheap bar."

"That much I could have guessed. A cheap bar where?"

"Does it matter?"

"Looking at the variance in this signal, I'm going to hazard a guess and say you have already left town for the Uplands. You're hunting Madison Madekwe and her abductors?"

I glowered down into my unfinished drink. "Something like that."

Another pause. This time Holmstrom's voice sounded strained. "Are you committed to any immediate course of action?"

"No. Just poking around."

"Then please don't go beyond that for the moment. Intrusion countermeasures like this, you have definitely stumbled into something serious. I have cleared my diary at the Dozen Up. I intend to make a second intrusion run on Madekwe's data tomorrow—"

"Thanks, Hannu, but you don't have to—"

"I *do* have to. I will not allow myself to be locked out of some bloody *civilian* datastack just because it happens to be a quarter-hour coms lag away. When I had the helm of *Weightless Ecstatic*, I fought and won data engagements at double that distance without breaking a sweat!" His voice softened. "And I am not going to leave you wandering around the Uplands without mission-critical data that could keep you in one breathing piece. You stand by, Veil. I'll be in touch."

He went away, left me looking at myself in the bar mirror.

I told you, Nikki. I fucking told you. Second-team suit, my ass.

You're not talking to me?

Are you called Nikki?

No. But Lieutenant Chakana is not here physically or electronically, however much you might miss her—

Very fucking funny.

—and it is part of my remit to monitor and where possible enhance your levels of mental stability, so—

My levels of mental stability are just fine.

Yes—now you are talking to me, not people who are not here.

Yeah? I stood up, knocked back the remainder of my drink. *Well, now you can shut up and get me a cab out to Gingrich Field. Sandeko Hangar complex.*

You think revisiting the site of Pablo Torres's disappearance is going to be productive in your current state?

I think it's what I've got left. Just get the cab.

Done. Incoming, three minutes.

I grabbed the payment rail under the bar top and settled my tab, put a modest tip on it. At the other end of the bar, the gray-bearded barkeep blinked away whatever he'd been staring at in his lenses, looked up at me, and nodded acknowledgment. Behind the blacked-out gear, he looked like some blind old oracle, studied and wise in the ways of Pachamama and the world, sagely encouraging me further on my path of enlightenment.

Fucking tweaked THC.

.   .   .

BACK WHEN I still worked Indenture Compliance across the Shelf Counties, the five thousand–plus hectares of abandoned hangars and silos and heavy plant build at Gingrich Field were the closest thing secular locals had to an urban legend storehouse. I doubted things had changed a whole lot since I left. Living offworld seems to trigger some stubborn aspect of our capacity for superstition; it's like we need our monsters and our hero saviors a lot more when we're under alien skies. A BV psychotech specialist I had a fling with back in Exmouth during induction reckoned it was the difference in gravity, felt at a cellular level, around the clock without respite, triggering deep anxieties that the rhythms and rigors of Earth would ordinarily damp out. *And that old offworld angst,* she'd say, slapping me emphatically on my naked teenage rump, *is like me, Hak, it has to be fed.* If your education or your common sense wouldn't let you believe in the pistaco, the Tharsis Prowler, or Inti's Recording Angels Made Flesh, not to worry—you could still thrill to the horror stories they told about Gingrich.

We picked it up on the horizon as the crawler cab pulled out of Cradle City's low-rise eastern periphery in the predawn glow—skeletal crane assemblies against the sky, frozen like dinosaurs caught in the distant flash from ground zero at Chicxulub, whaleback-humped storage structures huddled against the encroaching light, corroded silos stabbing skyward like the fingers of some buried-alive prophet of doom. *This is where they landed and stored the Great Old Ones,* go the whispers. *They found them drifting and frozen out there in the Oort cloud, tethered and towed them back in for who knows what insane purposes. Couldn't risk taking them all the way to Earth, see, but they wanted to study them, and this was the closest they dared come.*

Too esoteric, too atavistic for you? Try the shambling misshapen figures of the Toxin Zombies from Cradle Seventeen—the remnants of a work gang hideously scarred and mutated when a lethal biohazard load left unlabeled in error was carelessly dropped from its crane and cracked open, spilling out, seething, and steaming all over the hapless workers in the vicinity of the cradle. Corporate kill squads moved in, massacred the ones they could find, but in the dark and the screaming chaos, many fled, escaped among the storage sheds and covered ways of the site, stayed hidden as scavengers and *cannibals,* and, so it was whispered, eventually *bred their own awful progeny.*

Too Grand Guignol? What about the mournful ghost intelligences of an eons-lost Martian ur-culture? Unwittingly released by Earth's archaeologists when a top-secret dig program uncovered ancient machines in the caves under the Southern Wall and realized too late that the creatures who had built those machines lingered on attached to them in some attenuated spectral form, who knows, perhaps as guardians against some awful misuse. Only go among the hangars of Gingrich Field on certain nights sacred to the ur-culture's calendars, and though few had ever caught a glimpse, you'd hear them, moaning and weeping in the alleyways and cradle spaces for all that had passed away a billion years before.

The cab sped in among the first outcrops of structure on the field, rows of hangars and cradles still vague in the thinning gloom—up above the Lamina and the Southern Wall, the Martian day would already be dawning. Down here, things took a while longer, but I was hopeful the dark would be pretty much done by the time we got on site. Bad enough poking around a decayed hangar complex on spec without having to run on shark mod vision while I did it.

Maybe I'd get mistaken for a ghost.

Or a member of—one of my favorite Gingrich horror tales, this—the fabled *Lost Black Hatch Platoon.*

Yeah, them.

Barely human postorganic cyborg overriders, vat-grown for deployment in the event of an attempt by the Free Peoples of Mars to throw off the chains of Earth oppression, stored against that day in serried ranks of cryocapsules out on the field. Versions vary after that; in one, the locational codes for their pods were lost—sure, I mean, who *hasn't* put down a consignment of cryocapped supersoldiers for a moment and then forgotten where you left them?—and they stayed hidden until some kids stumbled on them and accidentally triggered the wake protocols; they woke up, they killed the kids, they stalk the field by night, and so forth.

Or—take your choice—they woke up, felt indebted to the kids, and did their bidding for a while, then eventually wandered off—stumble on them yourself and you can ask them for Knightly Favors. Because there's nothing in the world us overriders like better than that unpaid hero shit.

Better yet—the whole Lost Black Hatch Platoon is in fact not lost at all, has instead been safely stored away out among Gingrich's endless abandoned hangar rows. They're still sleeping there, all of them, and, relic of some mistaken subroutine in their gene code, they've become unbending Warriors of Honor Who Will Ride Out in Humanity's Greatest Hour of Need.

Oh, yes!

I've yet to hear the one where they're sleeping one step ahead of rough in a capsule down in the Swirl, taking any grubby local enforcement gig to get by.

The cab took a sharp left, abrupt enough that you'd suspect it of having a human driver. I looked out the side window, pulse quickening.

Fuck was that, 'Ris?

We have been hacked. The instability was a result of my pushback. Attempting to regain helm protocols now.

Motherfuckers. Can you see where we're headed?

Eight point seven kilometers southeast. Nineteen hundred meters north of the Sandeko Hangar complex. Mapping cross-reference suggests close proximity to a landing site. Our new friends probably arrived here by air.

Yeah, and that's most likely how they plan to take us out. Looks like someone wants to talk to us pretty fucking badly. The cab showed no signs of slowing or wavering in its course. *You going to be able to debug this, 'Ris?*

In all probability, no. The rerouting was generated in the core protocols—the hack was effected at owner/operator source. Very high level. However, I can short out and destroy the entire navigational intelligence, in which instance the vehicle will return blind and at a safe crawl to its point of origin garage for repairs.

No. I sat up, feeling the full surge of the running-hot now. *Don't do that. They're at a landing site, then they've got a whirligig, and they'll come after us in it. Nail us before we get halfway back out of the field. What about full burnout—can you crash-stop us before we reach them?*

It will require a total teardown of the systems. No possibility of navigational control once that happens, impact will be unmediated. And we are moving quite fast.

I glanced out the window again. The low-rise storage units and hangars snapped by—we seemed, if anything, to be picking up speed. *Any way to make sure we can get out of this thing after we hit?*

I can force the door locks to open, but—

Do it, I snapped. *Total teardown. Do it now!*

Executing.

The crawler juddered along its length, wavered on the road—sudden stench of flash-fried electronics in the cabin confines. Weird machine gibbering from the datahead behind the dash. An inspection panel blew out over my head, hung by thread-thin cables, spitting blue fire like something alive. The crawler slewed, violently this time. The datahead screamed.

Brace for impact, said 'Ris serenely.

I felt the crawler's brakes lock on. We staggered, blew sideways off the roadway, and tumbled like an angry gambler's dice. Another panel blew out in the roof, hit me in the head. Looming darkness in one window—I jerked around and saw a hangar wall coming at us like the grille of an autohauler a hundred meters high . . .

Lights out.

THIRTY

I FLAILED AWAKE in dust and dull red gloom. Mouth full of regolith—you never forget *that* fucking taste—head ringing, right eye gummed shut.

"Statu—" I coughed, and spit out some of the dirt. *Status. Tell me we're not dead, 'Ris. Tell me I didn't break anything.*

We are both functional. The crawler AI is dead.

Pretty sure I heard the tint of satisfaction in 'Ris's voice. I peered groggily around in the gloom with my working eye. Didn't need the shark mod or enhancement from my lenses, which were—just about—still on my head. A red pulsing glow diffused from six identical emergency lighting lozenges around the cabin, clogged dim in a still-drifting soup of ultrafine dust. We were, I realized, upended, and I was crumpled on top of the cabin's forward panel amid what felt like a lot of dirt. The windows on one side were smashed in—we must have plowed along on that side and dug a furrow in the regolith—but the other side of the cab seemed intact. I lifted my lenses, rubbed at my right eye, got some vision back. My fingers came away sticky wet. Looked like blood, but anything would in this light. *What's this shit?*

You sustained a superficial cut to the scalp just prior to the crash, another on impact, and the blood has run into your eye. It's not important.

They coming for us?

Yes. I have suppressed the cab's SOS beacon, so they will have to search for us blind. But they are coming.

Right. I settled my lenses back in place, tried to sit up. It took a couple of attempts, hurt dully in a couple of places. I grunted and checked my weapons—the VacStar was still in its holster, but the Balustraad had gone missing in action. I groped around for it on the paneling under me. *Can you blow the emergency locks?*

No, the systems damage is too thorough. There was that battle satisfaction again. *But the doors are unlocked. You should be able to force one of them up.*

I found the Balustraad, tucked it away in the small of my back again, then shoved hard with both hands on the nearest door's emergency escape rung. The weight of the thing pushed back at me for a moment, then it lifted to tipping point, and the door hinged smoothly up—for me, in effect, sideways—revealing a clearer predawn gloom beyond. I dragged myself up out of the gap, balanced precariously a moment on the sill, and jumped down.

Dry crunch of my boots in the dust, a catalog of flaring pains reporting in from rapidly bruising sites all over my body. I scowled and looked around.

The wall of the hangar we'd hit ran at an angle away from us, showing the dents and scrapes we'd put on its antique alloy hide. The crawler had bounced off, tumbled across a narrow loading yard, and ended with its ass in the sky against a neighboring crane platform. The skeletal structure loomed multiarmed above me like some rigid iron kraken out of a retrotech geek's worst nightmares, like a shrine to some tentacular robot god.

Like it was about to voice a colossal, grinding shriek of rage, reach stiffly down to human heights with its hinged arms, and set about tearing apart anything that lived.

"All right, then," I muttered to it like some surreptitious worshipper. "Let's go kill these Grokville motherfuckers, shall we."

. . .

THEY CAME IN a loose pack on foot, with vehicle support rolling far enough behind them not to get tangled if things got messy. I counted six operatives, casually dressed, no obvious armor or tactical optics. A couple of them had long-gun firepower, looked like either mag-fed tactical shotguns or assault rifles. The rest were either handgunners or unarmed. It brought a bleak smile to my lips. Obvious corollary—they hadn't expected to be hunting me like this. This was a scratch abduction squad, scrambled on very short notice—the only real question was who'd scrambled them and why.

Osiris dropped me right into their coms channel.

"—is how the *fuck* this guy managed to fry an autocrawler's systems. Thought he was supposed to be some retired IC thug."

"He *worked* IC," said another, more patient voice. "But back before that he was from Earth. Some kind of vacuum assault ninja, like those guys the navy used at Hab Nine. Probably got tech skills up the ass."

"Bugshit, Sammy. Vacuum assault, my balls—guy was an overrider."

Laughter, tinny over the coms hack.

"You don't have any balls, Jesika."

"Figure of speech. Now stow the chatter and scope up. I'm getting a heat signature and weak electricals from down by that hangar at eleven o'clock. Looks like he pulled off the road there."

Silence tautened between them. Someone kicked on a roof-mounted flood-lamp array on the support crawler. The beam snapped an oblong of hard blue light into the predawn. One of the foot patrol whistled low.

"Pulled off is right, Jesika. Look at those fucking furrows! Some speed he was doing; must have flipped that mother right over."

"Glass fragments, too," someone else reported. They'd all have their lenses cranked up and portioned for close focus and analysis by now. "All over the road, tracking that way. Maybe this fucker saved us some trouble and snapped his neck in the crash."

"You'd better hope not," Jesika told them grimly. "Chand's going to be pissed enough this mess happened in the first place. He wanted a stealth swoop, not a manhunt in broad fucking daylight. We don't bring this soak in alive, you can kiss any bonus you've stacked up this year good-bye."

"Hey, forget bonus." It was Sammy, the patient one. "I know Chand, I came up with him back in Louros. We fuck this up, we're all gonna be guarding sealed silos up at Morton for the duration. Pack your fucking face shield and some footage of your kids. You'll be lucky you see them twice a year for Christmas and Martes Challa. Holy fucking Christ, will you look at this."

They'd found the upended crawler.

"Hold off!" Jesika snapped. "Sammy, Zhang, stay back. Spread out, give us some cover in case he's still in there. Valdivia, Chetry—you go check it out on my call. Ericsson, where are those fucking floods? Back up and paint this mess for me!"

Sammy and Zhang—the long gun contingent. They spaced themselves wide, a broad bracket for anyone who might try to emerge from the wrecked crawler shooting. I shifted my own position in response as rapidly as I dared. Face and fingers chilled almost numb, starting to shiver with the cold. This needed to happen soon.

Soft growl of their crawler maneuvering to get the flood-lamp glare fully on the crash site, though it was making less and less difference in the strengthening dawn light. Valdivia and Chetry moved up cautiously on the door I'd come out of and then slammed shut. Chetry was the bigger of the two; he got some purchase on the door's bent and torn edges, braced himself to lift it open again.

Now!

I let go of the icy alloy frame of the crane arm I was crouched on, vaulted out, and dropped, teeth bared in a silent snarl. Cold rush of air, giddy moments of free fall, mission time running-hot pulse. Twenty-plus meters, as high as I'd dared go and still reckon on walking away from the impact. Mars gravity is forgiving, especially under the Lamina, where there's air resistance worth talking about—but it isn't that forgiving. I hit Sammy in the head and nape with both heels, probably snapped his neck on impact. He went down with no more than a soft grunt; I don't think the others even noticed at first. I hit and rolled in approved fashion beside him, came up crouched around a dozen meters off Zhang's left flank.

Ignoring the fallen long gun—shiny new AK variant, almost certainly user-locked—I pulled the VacStar and leveled it. Zhang was just waking to the fact that something had happened; I caught a flash glimpse of his shocked young face as he pivoted toward me.

Hollow boom, echoing off the hangar walls, shattering the quiet of the ambush.

The suitbuster slug tore into Zhang at chest height, punched a hole in him I could see right through, dropped him where he stood. I was already swinging the VacStar on the next nearest target. This time I snapped the shot off in haste, took him left of center. He spun violently around, collapsed to the ground in a puff of dust, as if turning away in sudden disgust and tripping in the act. Running-hot nerves—*get a fucking grip, Veil!*

"Sammy—Zha—" Jesika's voice, high-pitched in shock, catching up late. "He's fucking *here*, he's—"

Enough of the two-handed marksman shit—I pulled the Balustraad from the small of my back, stalked wide around the angle of the wrecked crawler, got eyes on Valdivia and Chetry. Both were turning, weapons out—both were too slow. I pumped three Balustraad slugs at them, left-handed, still moving and a little long on range. Blood splatter across the carapace of the crawler behind them, broad painted streaks of it and chunks of gore small enough to stick. They both went down, ruined and screaming.

A single shot snapped through the air by my head, close enough to scorch my scalp.

I whipped around and saw Jesika in her own two-handed marksman's stance, not much more than eight meters away. She wasn't going to miss again. I shot reflexively from the hip with the VacStar, got her somewhere low in one thigh, enough to knock her off her feet and give her other things to worry about.

Predictably, Ericsson tried to run me down.

I heard the crawler engine crank up to a roar, sprinted across the loading yard and toward the hangar on the other side. The vehicle came plowing across the regolith-strewn ground at me, slithering badly. It hadn't been built for this kind of thing, and in all probability neither had Ericsson. I put my back to the hangar, dropped the Balustraad, and brought the VacStar up in both hands.

Eight shots, evenly spaced across the reflective windshield. Whatever it was made of, it didn't stop EVC munitions. Splinter and crack, holes the size of fists. Booming echoes. The crawler slewed wildly, plowed past me a couple of meters off my right hip, smashed headfirst into the long-suffering hangar wall. The impact hinged it right off the ground on its front tires for a moment, then it crunched back down, drive turbine still whining high. I scooted up close to the side window, thought I caught a hint of movement within, and pumped another two suitbusters through the glass for good measure. Tight shriek, a thump against the door panel, and the movement stopped. The turbine quit and ran down to a low mur-mur, then died altogether, probably killed by some safety subroutine wak-ing up to the fact there'd been an accident.

Quiet drifted across the yard like smoke.

I lowered the VacStar by fractions, did a vicinity check. The quiet wasn't as complete as I'd thought—behind me, someone was still scream-ing, but weakly now, almost done. I glanced around, pinned the noise to one of the shredded Balustraad casualties, and zoomed in with my lenses. One forearm flopping and wagging brokenly from the ground, a half-flayed, bloodied head trying to turn in my direction. Both eyes were gore-glutted holes; whoever it was must have been working on sound alone. And no motion from Jesika—switching focus to her crumpled form, I realized Ericsson had inadvertently driven over her in the attempt to get to me. I breathed out hard, clearing adrenaline.

Jesus, what a fucking mess.

I tried the crawler door. It was locked.

Can you hack this?

On it.

The door hinged up, and what was left of Ericsson tumbled out. He hung there like a discarded rag doll trapped halfway out of a toy box, legs still caught up inside the crawler. He was young and looked very scared, huge dark eyes in a Himalayan complexion gone parchment sallow with shock. He was bleeding profusely from a shattered right hand, now torn and bisected like some alien claw, and a big hole in his rib cage on the right. When he tried to speak, he bubbled like a blocked drain.

"Ho-hosp . . . Hospital . . ."

"You're joking, right?"

"Wasn't . . . wasn't meant to—" He coughed up blood, mouth filling with it, voice drowning. Had to swallow it again. "To *be* like . . . this . . ."

"It never is at your age." An obscure anger flared through me. "You kids always die so fucking surprised."

"Not trying . . . to kill you . . ."

"Yeah?" I put the VacStar away. "You could have fooled me."

"Orders . . . orders were . . ." Voice drowning in blood again. This time he didn't have the strength to clear it from his throat. He gagged and gurgled. The eyes pleaded. I grimaced, reached in, and lifted him, tipped his head to one side. Thick red gore ran out of his mouth and puddled in the dust at my feet.

"Come on, then. Orders."

"Orders," he murmured faintly. "Bring you in . . . alive . . ."

"Yeah, I can imagine how much fun it would have been after that. You want to tell me who sent you?"

"Can't . . ." It whispered sadly up out of him. "Co . . . vert . . . op . . ."

"Suit yourself." I dropped his head and straightened up. "Enjoy the sunrise."

I cast around and found the Balustraad where I'd dropped it. Dusted it off and stowed it in place again. The feeble screaming from over by the autocrawler had damped down to moans; no motion from that quarter now.

". . . please . . ."

Barely audible, like bubbles bursting in a slurry runoff puddle. I looked back at him, saw the eyes again, the desperate pleading disbelief. His lips were cherry red with blood splatter. He looked about fucking twelve.

Oh, for Pachamama's sake . . .

I went back to him, lifted his head again, tried to clear the blood from his throat. It wasn't making much difference anymore. I propped him back up in his seat inside the crawler, was turning to leave, when he pawed convulsively at my arm with his undamaged hand. He didn't look at me, was staring straight ahead through the bullet-starred windshield, and for a moment I wondered if he knew I was there anymore. But then his eyes slid sideways at me, terror-filled gaze, as if he barely dared look to see what had crept up beside him. His hand pawed again, insistent, like the pleading of a hungry dog.

I sighed and took it in my own. He said nothing, just nodded minutely, jerkily, sat there panting delicately, staring at what was coming. I leaned against the edge of the door hatch, staring out at the carnage I'd wrought, and waited with him as his breathing slowed and his sweaty attempt at a grip started to loosen, then tightened, panic-stricken again, then loosened . . .

Pale shadows slid down the hangar wall behind us. The toy-sized sun came up, washed out and distant. I began to worry about a follow-up crew.

". . . algo . . ."

I looked in at him, not sure why the utterance had snatched at my attention so hard. I squeezed his hand.

"Hoy-hoy, Ericsson—say again?"

He shot me another sideways look. His windpipe made a rusty scraping sound as he tried to summon breath for some vital last message.

"Tell Mom," he managed. "Hidalgo. We gotta . . . stop him. For *Mars*!"

"Hidalgo?"

One more tiny, jerky nod. His fingers were suddenly loose in my grip.

"Tell . . . Mom . . ." he bubbled, and stopped for good.

I CHECKED THE other bodies, found that Sammy wasn't dead after all despite the interesting angle our encounter had left his neck at. Hard to tell if he was conscious, but there was a pulse and the whisper of breath from his open mouth. Wary of more gunshots now the sun was up, I used the ABdM knife to cut his throat.

The others were all long gone.

Predictably, no one had ID. Whoever had put this together was half smart at least.

Hidalgo.

It nagged at me, some tiny familiarity I couldn't lock down. I gave myself a final minute among the corpses and the wrecks, but it wouldn't come. In the end, I shrugged it off. Surveyed the surroundings one more time.

I miss anything, 'Ris?

You have been admirably thorough. With time, we could perhaps hack one of the user-locked weapons and learn something. But taking one with us risks the possibility that it is also satellite-tracked.

Yup. Not taking those odds.

DNA samples run a similar risk. We have no secure facility in which to test and trace unless you feel you can completely trust your friend Milton Decatur.

I coughed a laugh. It was a little early to start getting paranoid, but on the other hand this was Decatur's turf, and he was one of a very limited number of people who knew I was in town.

Completely, no.

As I imagined. Then no secure facility.

Yeah, and run that shit through an unsecured lab, it's going to ring every security bell from here to Tharsis Gate and back. I sighed. *All right, we're out of here—*

Low, insistent queeping from somewhere. I cast around, realized it was coming from Ericsson's crawler. I jogged over and leaned in past his corpse. The dashboard coms panel showed a single pulsing light. I hit accept. An angry male voice crashed into the cabin.

"About fucking time! Ericsson, the fuck is going on out there?"

"Ericsson's dead."

Hissing silence over the channel.

"They're all dead," I said. "Valdivia, Chetry, and Jesika, some of them in easy-to-carry pieces. You send anyone else after me, they're going to end up the same way."

"Who is this?"

"You know who this is. You had questions for me, you should have come yourself and asked them politely. You're Chand, right?"

More silence. I felt the corners of my mouth twitch.

"If I were you, motherfucker," I told him, "I'd start looking over my shoulder in public places."

I left the coms channel squawking in the cold morning air, picked a direction that looked like it might offer some decent cover from air pursuit, and set off at a brisk adrenalized trot. I didn't know how many more they might send after me, what level of kit and expertise they might bring with them, but none of that seemed to matter very much right now. The appetizers were off the table, the dish was served, and down in the deep fibers of my muscle memory, down in the pit of my belly, the running-hot was whispering joyous preneolithic anthems to a blood-splattered rave that my pulse liked way too much. Chand could send whatever backup he liked out to Gingrich Field now; it wouldn't make any fucking difference.

When they wake you as an overrider, your main job is to save the ship. How you get that done can end up being a delicate, lengthy, and complicated process.

Staying alive and killing people is the easy part.

THIRTY-ONE

"JESUS, HAK—did you have to kill them *all*?"

I flicked a shoreline pebble into the lotus-dotted pond. Tiny brown torpedo shapes scattered from the splash. "Technically, I didn't. Their team leader died when the driver ran her over with their crawler."

"Oh, good," Decatur growled. "That makes all the fucking difference!"

"She probably would have bled out anyway. To be honest, Milt, even if she hadn't, I'd have had to kill her. She seemed pretty competent. Couldn't very well risk leaving her alive for debrief and then maybe have her come back at me grudge-supercharged."

"Ahh, *Pachamama's fucking tits!*"

Decatur got up and stormed away from me, fists clenched at his sides, looking for something safe to punch. Flicker of motion at the lower level of the garden—Gustavo ducked his head in from the exit where he stood guard but evidently saw nothing to worry about and ducked back out again. Either Decatur had talked to him or he was just getting used to the dynamic. I wondered idly whether his boss was like this a lot or it was just me bringing out the old hard-boiled IC ghost in him.

I glanced back to see what the ghost was doing.

Decatur stood in front of the nearest willow mangrove variant. Good luck punching that. But the tree's hard-to-reach slender central trunk seemed to have calmed him down somewhat with its inaccessibility. I saw him make an exasperated throwaway gesture with one loosening fist. He looked back and met my eye. His voice lowered back near normal levels.

"Hak, I thought we agreed you weren't going to shovel grit into my machine up here."

I shrugged. "Talk to the dead guys who tried to take me out. All I've done so far is wander around town and spend some quality time with Nina Ucharima."

"Yeah, heard about that." He came back to the water's edge, seated himself again. A grin quirked in the corner of his mouth. "Gave you a rough ride, eh?"

"Had worse."

He grunted. "I don't doubt that, brother. That mad slush-rider bitch over in Keelsville for starters. Remember her?"

"Trying to forget."

A grin surfaced on his clouded face. "Still got that image of you in my head, man. The way you dragged yourself out of that trailer the next morning."

I felt a reflexive grin slip across my own features, but it was short-lived. I still had the tattooed ache of playtime with Jesika's crew across my ribs and limbs and two taped cuts on my scalp. I'd spent the best part of five hours skulking around across Gingrich Field before 'Ris reckoned there was no pursuit and it was safe to call another cab to bring me back into town. And even then I'd ridden the whole way back taut and running-hot wired, waiting for another less fucked-up intrusion attempt that never came. None of that had gone away since. I wasn't in the mood for a walk down Decatur's memory lane.

"You know there's a good chance Ucharima put them on to me, don't you?"

He shook his head. "No, that's not Nina. She wouldn't cross me like that. And she'd go to a shallow grave in the regolith sooner than sell out to the corporates, especially one that had anything to do with Torres disappearing. Whatever hard-ass Uplands psycho-bitch face she puts on, she's still grieving. There was something special there with Torres."

"Certainly was—she told me all about it. Hung like Supay on the rampage, apparently."

"That's not what I meant."

"She also told me—I don't think she meant to—that Torres was working on some big score that *didn't* involve taking the Ride Home. You wouldn't know anything about that, would you?"

Pointedly, I had not removed my lenses for this visit. Decatur, face already naked, had said nothing, just looked hurt. 'Ris clocked the telltales for me, logged them as my old partner looked for a way to lie to me convincingly.

But he didn't. He gave it up, sat, and stared glumly into the pond instead.

"Wouldn't be on speaking terms with someone called Sandor Chand either, would you?" It had been surprisingly easy for 'Ris to find the guy for me. She only had to shred a couple of underpowered corporate firewalls to get to him. "Listed as a consulting security executive up at Sedge Systems. The same Sedge Systems that employed Pablo Torres until he suddenly decided he didn't want to work for them anymore and walked two months before he got his supposed lottery win."

"All right."

"Chand, who sent a grab squad to lift me for interrogation and then presumably a quick disappearing act into a slurry culvert—"

"Yeah, all right—"

"—on *your fucking turf, Milton.* I mean, what the fuck kind of crime boss are you? Does your word count for anything up here, or is it all that cunt Allauca now?"

"I said all right!"

On his feet again, fists knotted—he wasn't looking for trees to hit this time. I stayed cross-legged on the bank where I was. It seemed like the safest thing to do. I tossed another pebble into the pond, scattered the same fish again. You'd think they'd learn.

"Punching me out isn't going to solve this, Milt," I said quietly.

"*I know that!*" He slumped back to his seat on the flat-topped stone cairn beside me. Looked at his still knotted fists like they were tools that had inexplicably stopped working. "You think I don't know that?"

"I think you're conflicted. And I'd like to know what about before the fallout sends any more corporate hit squads my way."

He shot me a glance. "You think Chand tried for you in Bradbury?"

"No. His lot wanted to turn me inside out and find out what I know. The Bradbury crew just wanted me vaporized. And I get the feeling that if it had been the Bradbury crew trying to lift me out at Gingrich this morning, you wouldn't be talking to me now. This is two separate houses, two different agendas, and two *very* different levels of competence."

"Nice to be wanted, huh?"

It was an old line from the partnership days, something we used to quip to our IC quarry when we bagged them. I sketched another brief smile in acknowledgment, took off my lenses, and laid them carefully in the manicured grass beside me. I rubbed at my eyes.

"Could live without it, to be honest. So come on—did you know about this big score Torres had or not?"

He nodded. "Yeah, I knew. Jeff Havel told me he'd gotten something, wanted a direct meet with Allauca to pitch it. Wouldn't crack on what it was till he saw her, but he swore it'd make us all rich."

I gestured at the surroundings. "Looks to me like you're already rich."

"Richer than this, he told Havel. A lot richer."

"Really? Hard to imagine anyone like Torres could count that high."

Decatur gave me a look I couldn't read. "He could count pretty much as good as the rest of us, Hak. Point was, he said this was ultratripper-level wealth. No limits."

"And you never thought it was worth listening to him? Come on!"

"I told you—he'd only talk to Allauca. So I set it up, and Allauca passed on it. I figured it was the same old Shelf Life swagger, never gave it much more thought. I was kind of busy at the time, you know? City doesn't run itself."

"Your newfound public service ethic humbles me. And what about when Torres disappeared? Didn't give it any thought then either? Or when the Pablito riots kicked off and Metro Missing Persons came fumbling around here? Or when I showed up yesterday? You could have told me all this shit then, you know."

"You want to know why I didn't lay all this out for you? Because it's not your fucking business, all right? I work with Allauca. We're partners in shit that goes way back, got Ireni to thi—" He stopped, started again. "There's history, Hak, and it means something. I'm not going to put Allauca in the firing line just because you're sniffing around after some dust devil fuck-up like Torres who should have known when to back off."

"You're saying Allauca had him iced?"

"She says she didn't."

"Oh, and of course Raquel Allauca would never lie about anything! What is she, a Jesus-of-the-Valley freak these days?"

"I was wearing lenses when I talked to her, Hak. How stupid do you think I am?" Decatur lowered his voice with a visible effort. "I asked her point-blank, back when MMP were poking around, and I was wearing lenses with a high-end gestalt scan package. She told me she didn't know what happened to Torres, last time she saw him he was alive, the deal he brought her was bugshit, exposure to no benefit, so she'd told him to fuck off. I got no reason not to believe any of that."

"Except for maybe a fistful of ultratripper-level wealth she didn't want to share."

"Then where is it? I run security for all the mayoral accounts, I sign off on any expenses above day-to-day basic. Nothing moved out of the ordinary, then or any time since. And I'll tell you something else, Hak. You don't like Allauca, but she is AI-smart and she can smell a sweet deal a hundred klicks off in a Tharsis grit storm. If Torres had had something—*anything*, anything at all—worth even a tenth that kind of payoff, she would have been all over it. I'm telling you, I talked to her lensed up, and I saw—she was pissed off with Torres, but she wasn't lying."

I looked at him, watched his eyes. I didn't need lenses.

"All right." I sighed. "What about this fucker Chand? You know him?"

"Heard of him. Background in IC same as us, but I think he mostly worked the Eos end. He blew into town back when Jeff and I were setting up for Allauca's first candidacy, wanted to come aboard on contract. She liked him, we didn't, so we passed. I hear he's made himself useful around the place since."

"In the flow, he's down as a consulting contractor for Sedge. That them covering their ass?"

"Might be. More likely, they just got no taste for that covert ops shit, so they hire it in on temp whenever the weather gets heavy enough to force their hand. Tell you, Hak—Sedge are a real fucking bunch of throwbacks." He shook his head wearily. "Fucking heritage outfit. Gilt-edged stock, Settlement-era roots, old school. Can't do anything with them. They don't approve of just about anything that's happened since fucking Kathleen Okombi went home."

"That's a century ago, Milt. I mean fifty years Martian, at least."

"More than that. Like I said—fucking heritage outfit. They don't do all this corporate espionage and share leverage shit. Fuckers act like they're just so above it all."

"They weren't so above it all when they tried to lift me for interrogation this morning out at the field. Or are you saying you think Chand could be off contract? Using their resources to get his own shit done?"

"It's the Uplands, Hak. He could be doing pretty much anything so long as it turns a profit and doesn't upset any of the established players. For himself, for Sedge, for anyone else with the cash. But I had some of my guys do a flyby of the coordinates you sent me, and there's nothing there. No bodies, no crashed crawlers, no blood, nothing. If it happened like you say—"

"*If?* Fucking *if?*"

"All right, keep your dick in your suit. I'm just saying—whoever's clock Chand did this on, Sedge or someone else, they're resourced enough to send in a cleanup crew within hours of it happening and high-profile enough to give a shit about keeping it quiet."

I sat for a moment, digesting that. Remembering myself crouched under the grating of a disused culvert in some nameless decaying payload processing plant out on the field for three shivering hours while Osiris searched the airwaves for any sign of us being hunted and came up empty.

Then where the motherfuck are they? had been my elegant rejoinder at the time.

Perhaps it is more important to them to retrieve their fallen comrades and cover their traces than to extend the operation at this time.

That mean we can go now?

Not just yet, no.

"You know I'm not going to let this stand, don't you, Milt?"

"Yeah, surprise me, why don't you." He brooded for a while, a demeanor I knew not to stampede. "Look, Hak—at least give me some time to get into it. Last thing I need is you going full overrider in the streets of Cradle City. You say I'm conflicted, you're not wrong. This is heat nobody needs. *No*body. Jeff Havel and I got Allauca up there, and she has delivered, Hak, for the city and for the Shelf. She believes in this place, and she's not afraid to twist Mulholland's arm to get a better deal for people up this end of the Gash."

I rolled my eyes. He saw it, flushed.

"Oh, fuck you, Hak! Look around! Go on! You've been here long enough now. You tell me the Cradle hasn't moved on since you and I were eating its dust eighty hours a week for IC. You tell me it's not better."

I looked elaborately around me. "Crocus Lux certainly seems to be flourishing, I'll give you that. Got to have your high-end hotels, right? Where else people like you going to live? Havel got a suite as well?"

"Oh, fuck off." But he said it without heat, suddenly listless. "No one made you leave. You could have stayed and had a piece of this action. I practically begged you to at the time."

I smiled faintly. It was true enough.

"Didn't I?"

I clapped him on the shoulder, hooked my lenses with the other hand, and got up. "Certainly did, Milt. You certainly did."

"Then what's your problem? Oh, you *going* now? You a fucking *Sacranite* all of a sudden, Hak—is that it? Found a cause, have you? Fuck's sake don't just *walk out.*"

"I'm not walking out," I said mildly. "I'm giving in. You got it. I'll sit tight, give you some time. You get me Chand and a basement somewhere remote to get some answers. But it needs to happen soon, Milt. Very soon. Everything I've tripped over so far tells me this thing is going to blow up. The Earth audit, Torres disappearing, Madekwe getting snatched—

somebody, maybe more than one somebody, is scrambling to keep wraps on something that wants to explode. And when that happens, I want to be well out of range with Madison Madekwe already in my back pocket."

"And fuck the rest of us, huh?"

"Little help from you and maybe it doesn't have to be that way. Maybe you and I can defuse this thing together before it blows. Save everybody a lot of pain."

Decatur grinned mirthlessly. "Everybody except Chand, right?"

"Fuck Chand. He's a dead man walking."

Stiff quiet. Decatur got up. He went to hold me by the shoulders, but it was tentative. The bear hug of the day before was gone, for now at least.

"Look, man," he said awkwardly. "I am sorry about this shit. You're right, it should never have happened on my patch. But we're going to get it sorted, we'll find out what the fuck is going on. You got my word on that."

"Sure." I patted him back, grinned. Slipped my lenses on and turned to go.

Then I paused, snapped my fingers, turned back.

"Oh, yeah, Milt—one last thing," I said lightly. "You know anything about someone called Hidalgo?"

THIRTY-TWO

DECATUR WAS GOOD. At a human level, he had it covered. But the poly readout from 'Ris was merciless, and he must have known. He didn't speak, he didn't move. He just looked at me like I'd sprouted Tharsis Prowler fangs in midconversation.

"Want to tell me about him?"

"Where'd you get that name?" he asked harshly.

"From a dying kid out at Gingrich Field. Seemed pretty important to him, too; it was the last thing he said before he died. Who is he, Milt?"

Decatur swallowed hard. "He's a fucking ghost is what he is."

WE RODE UP the levels of the Crocus Lux in a private elevator. Views across the bonsai downtown, the dusty retrofitted low-rise beyond. I narrowed my eyes, spotted the endless receding sprawl of Gingrich Field beyond the eastern periphery. Elsewhere, from the fringes of the city on out, the Shelf Counties lay in multicolored pastel shades, the gay patchwork carve-up of crop sectors, eco-coding pastures, and experimental nanogrowth farms as far as the unaided eye could see. And southward, the thick crayon line of the Wall, whole kilometers stubbier than its mid-Valley tranche, still looming up like a gargantuan wave poised to break and fall and crush everything beneath it. Ride all the fucking elevators you like in the Gash, climb all the towers to the top, you're still trapped down here like a bug under glass.

"This Hidalgo shit started about three years back," Decatur said, staring south. "We had this sweet deal over in Sombra—postorganics research into aerobug design. You know, build a better code-fly, get the minimum weight of surveillance beetles down, like that. Solid revenue stream, COLIN secondaries with a good sucking grip on Fleet local funds, and Earth backing; 'course, there's fuck-all research going on in those labs."

"I am shocked."

He grinned, not much humor in it. "Bet you are. Here, this is us."

The elevator slowed to a flawless halt, and the doors parted silently on a split-level lounge space about five times larger than anywhere I'd ever lived. Big desk on the upper split, facing inward from windows to the west, a couple of loungers around an empty circular space below a 'brane-gel dispenser in the ceiling took up the lower section. In one corner, a high-rez life-size pixel fog portrait showed a woman I took for a moment for Raquel Allauca, crouched with her arms around two small children, a girl and a boy, both of them stamped with a mediated borrowing of Decatur's features and skin tone. I saw the way his eyes flickered to the image, then abruptly away again as he crossed the room, gesturing me to take one of the loungers. I lowered myself into the luxurious pushback yield of high-end response upholstery, nodded at the portrait.

"Didn't know you had kids."

"Barely do." He went to a cabinet, brought out bottle and tumblers with his back to me, set them out on the desk. "Ireni split last year, took them to Bradbury to be with some uncle she's got in the *familias*. I send money, I get pictures back. She brings them up here every couple of months if I behave."

"Tough break. Is it just me or does she look a lot like Allauca?"

"Yeah." He cracked the bottle, poured into the tumblers. "Younger sister. They don't get on. Which is fucking weird, because they're really

not that different when it comes down to it. Should have had my fucking
head examined, right? Knowing Raquel the way I did, then getting in that
deep with anyone got her blood running in their veins."

I said nothing. He brought the tumblers over. Rich, smoky whiff as he
handed one to me. "Earth single malt all right? That Islay shit you used to
wank off about? Le Frog? Le Fraig?"

I shook my head. "Jesus fucking Christ, Milt."

"Cheers."

I lifted my tumbler, touched it to his. Sipped and felt the Laphroaig
sear a couple of cuts in my mouth I hadn't realized I owned. I savored it
anyway, set the glass down carefully beside the lounge bag. "Kids look
great, though. Gotta be worth it, right?"

He looked at me. "You got kids?"

"Uh—no."

"Then shut the fuck up, you don't know what you're talking about."
He dropped into the lounger opposite, slopped his whiskey a little as he
landed, cursed, changed hands, and sucked his fingers clean. "So—where
were we?"

"Sweet little deal over in Sombra, labs that don't do any research."

"Yeah, that. We got a few tame qualpros, guys that look good on paper,
but really they're all burnouts, defaulters that never made contract's end,
up to their eyes in debt trying to pay back their fines from IC court. You
can pick them up all over the Gash for not much more than a couple of
installments in hand and a promise of rescheduling."

"Nothing ever changes, huh?"

In the immies, when a qualpro runs, it's pretty much always some
noble innocent who's somehow been tricked into defaulting on their contract, would never otherwise have been so stupid or weak; those flaws are
reserved for the grunt-level thugs and disposable bad guy stock. In reality,
of course, it's a little different—what looks like a great little earner from
back on Earth can get pretty fierce a couple of years in, and a lot of qualpros crack. And when that happens, they're often a much easier mark for
the Uplands vultures than any seasoned local indentured grunt or trans-
ported convict would be. They show up on the scope of every working
girl with an angle, barfly vampire gigolo, and straight-up con artist, all the

usual denizens of the Valley's rat runs—meat to the feast. By the time IC catches up with a qualpro runner, they're usually not just AWOL and Earthsick, they're broke and broken down; asset-stripped, plucked, and picked clean; busted way below zero, even before the fines and restitution get totted up and added to the bill. You look in their eyes when you catch them, and it's not just desperation, it's full-blown horror, the slow dawning realization of the ten-klick fall and a life without remission at the bottom of the Gash.

"You listening to me, Hak?"

I blinked. "Yeah, sure. Pick 'em up all over for pennies. Go."

"Yeah." A bit disgruntled. "So—we have these guys and gals fly existing bugs around in a couple of sterile sim chambers; whole operation's cheap as last year's chips to run, like about a tenth what the R&D's getting written up for. They fake test data for us, make it look good—and then every eighteen months or so they run supposed outdoor trials, crash and burn them every time. Insoluble aerodynamic issues; back to the drawing board." Decatur gestured. "Money keeps rolling in. No big deal, we're not talking millions. Not like Fleet and COLIN Earth are going to miss it, right?"

"Very nice. So what happened?"

"Hidalgo happened." It was like a shadow across his face, like it hurt him to say the name. "He burned it down. Torched it."

"What—literally?"

"Yup. First thing I know, I get a call from an underboss over in Sombra, says there's fire in the sky over at the lab. I grab a whirligig, blow over there to see what's gone wrong, and by then it isn't gone wrong, it's fucking *gone*, all of it. Wreckage and charred bodies, whole place blown apart. Looks like some kind of mining charge in the power plant, then accelerant cultures sprayed on everything else."

"Pretty thorough." I tipped an imaginary hat. "What about the virtuals?"

Decatur nodded grimly. "Gone too. Firewalls all torn down, some kind of viral deconstruct raging through the finance stack. Confessional note from the lab senior floating on top of it all, begging forgiveness for the con. We had to close the whole thing down, get behind our own firewalls, and leave the COLIN secondaries to pick the bones out of it. We've got limited exposure, all set up that way, but I still lost four good junior guys who took heavy jail time to cover for us. Fucking COLIN-convened court down in Bradbury, *examples to be made*. Two of my people are still serving the time that fucking judge handed down."

"Could your lab guy really have cracked like that? Had a late-breaking qualpro attack of conscience?"

"What, coz the noble blood of Earth runs in his veins?" A derisive snort. "Guy was a fucking switch-head waste, he'd have turned his own baby sister over for another three months off his debt schedule. No. Someone stood over that fucker with a gun, made him give them his account codes, and then had him sign that note. Probably broke his fingers to get it done, but there's not enough left of the body to know. Meanwhile, we paid a very expensive axman to back up through the viral damage in the financials, and guess what?"

"Cash diverted."

Decatur snapped his fingers, mimed a pistol at me. "There you go. Strike went down less than three hours after that quarter's funds transferred in. And less than three minutes before the charge blew in the power plant, someone funneled the whole lot back out into a Deimos account."

"Smooth."

"Yeah, you think you could try to sound a little less impressed? We lost the best part of eight hundred thousand marins that night."

"And the name? Hidalgo? Where'd that come from?"

He shrugged. "It filtered out over the next few months. We were pushing hard, trying to dig up someone who'd talk. Getting nothing but fragments, and most of that was useless, didn't check out. Someone knew someone who heard someone was looking for an inside man in the Sombra lab. Somebody told somebody else they saw some guys break into a mining storehouse near Tharsis Gate. Someone's looking to buy black market access codes, ahh—" He gestured, throwaway, disgusted. "You know how this shit goes, Hak. People will say any fucking thing if they think it'll get them favors with the mayor or some juice with the Ground Out Crew. And they spill even more useless bugshit if they're scared someone's going to hurt them."

"Yeah, the Ground Outs never were very subtle, were they?"

"Oh, and we were, Mister Fucking Overrider? Like you never worked Indenture Compliance in your life."

I didn't tell him that he had it backward—that the things I'd done as an overrider would have put everything he'd ever seen me do for IC in shade so deep that you'd freeze to death trying to find out where it had gone.

He took another pull at his drink. Grimaced it down. "*Any*how—the whispers start to come in. There's this badass heavy heist guy out there somewhere on the Shelf. Hidalgo. He comes and goes in the night, he takes down major corporate warehousing and cutting-edge Marstech IP, he's nine kinds of fucking lethal if you get in his way."

"Heard that song before. You got any actual scores you can set against all that rep?"

"Oh, yeah." Decatur nodded grimly. "Three or four IP breaches that we know about, Marstech labs across the Shelf Counties and back down in Louros. Rumor puts Hidalgo behind all of them. Even got matching gene trace off a couple of places, guess he got careless."

I frowned. "So who's he selling the tech to?"

"You tell me. We've run the gene swab, there's nothing in the Valley records. Wiped clean. We've locked up every receiver our end of the valley, made it very clear what'll happen if they take delivery of any of this stuff without notifying us. We got feelers out farther east, some favors in Bradbury and beyond." He spread his hands. "We got nothing."

"Nothing? On cutting-edge Marstech? You can't track that shit back down? Come on, Milt. You're losing your touch!"

"It's a big fucking valley, Hak."

"Yeah, and you're a big fucking crime boss with Bradbury *familias andinas* for in-laws."

"Who hate my guts."

I bit back another retort. In all the grubby years I'd worked IC with Decatur, I'd only ever seen him vulnerable a handful of times. Back then he was loudly childless and fancy free, but once in a while someone got under his skin. Most of his damage came from trying to live the illusion that they hadn't.

The mess it made on his face wasn't pretty to look at, then or now.

"The *familias* hate *anyone* who doesn't own a name that came here on a work barge two hundred years ago," I tried lightly. "Come on, it's who they are, it's a point of fucking pride with those assholes. What'd you expect?"

He grunted. Glowered into the pale gold depths of his drink and said nothing. I sipped my own liquid fraction of superlux Earth indulgence and gestured.

"You ever think this Hidalgo might be sitting on the hauls? Your Sombra operation must have netted him enough operating capital to run silent for a while. Not like he'd need a top-up anytime soon, right?"

"In that case, what the fuck's he doing it for?"

I nodded reluctantly. "Yeah, there's that."

"These are tough heists we're talking about. Expensive to set up, lots of exposure. Why go through all that and then sit on the shit you've stolen? It's *Marstech*, Hak. Loses market value with every passing season; some of it's going to be broke code inside a year. Wait too long on that shit, you'll barely be able to hand it off to the peddlers on the Strip for cost."

"You think it's a grudge? Someone you or Allauca pissed off maybe? She can't be short of enemies. Nobody liked her much even back in the day."

He shook his head. "There are smarter ways to hit us than this. Most of those heists didn't cost us anything outside some local loss of face. If it's a grudge, it isn't against us. Or at least it's not just against us. But it is hurting our profile. Hidalgo makes us look weak. Guy's turning into a fucking legend out there on the Shelf."

"You put out a bounty on him?"

"Yeah, for a while now. Used that gene trace we got." He met my eyes, and abruptly the old Decatur was back. "Why, you want the work?"

I smiled. "Got a few things of my own to sort out first, Milt. Besides, I just got here. Where would I even start?"

"Wouldn't put you far behind the rest of us," he said gloomily. "Been after this guy for nearly three years now and we're no closer than we ever were. We've lost a half dozen good enforcers to him in that time. Double that in independent contractors who came in after the bounty. They all come back the same way"—he sketched a gesture at his own face—"dead as Luthra, with a big fucking H gouged into their forehead."

I sipped my drink. "Novel."

"Isn't it."

"You try going official with it yet? Get the marshals involved?"

"Oh, they're involved. I guaran-fucking-tee you that much. Those players who had their Marstech broken into didn't make a big public noise about it; that wouldn't be good for market share. But they've lodged it covertly with the Marshal Service, and it is Being Looked Into."

"You know that for certain?" I watched a sour grin broaden on his face. "You got a pipeline into the UMS now?"

At some obscure level, I was disappointed. My ragging on Sakarian notwithstanding, the levels of incorruptibility and dedication among the Upland marshals were legendary and, in my experience, deserved. You could buy up most local PD out here for the price of a Strip dancer's blowjob and a couple of lines of whatever tweaked SNDRI cocktail was topping the chemical recreation charts that week. But the marshals had always been another matter.

Decatur rubbed at his stubbled chin. "Wouldn't say a pipeline exactly, no. But put it this way—latest batch of those independent contractors I mentioned? Two of them were ex-marshals; they had a lot to tell us about what's going down inside the service. No one's talking about it, but Hidalgo's on their most wanted board, too." He gestured carelessly with his drink, slopped it a little again. "Hasn't made any fucking difference."

"He can't be operating on his own. You offer a backstabber bonus yet?"

Decatur nodded. "Thirty K for information leading to his where-abouts, payable when he's taken down. That's up on the twenty K we were offering last year. Shifts no dust, Hak. Whatever backing Hidalgo's got, it's air-lock tight, and everyone else is too fucking scared to turn. Like I said, he's dealt himself into Uplands mythology. Talk to people out there, he's Inti's Black Henchman, the Tharsis Prowler in the Shroud of Human Flesh. He's the fucking pistaco walking, Hak."

He saw my face. Saw it change.

"What?"

"Hmm?" I shook my head. "Nah, nothing. Just—y'know. All that bug-shit we used to spout in IC about being the pistaco. Kind of ironic when it comes back to bite you in the ass, right?"

"Glad it keeps you entertained." Decatur puffed out his cheeks, leaned in at me. "Look, you sure you don't want to run with this? It's a good purse, Hak. Hundred fifty K—dead or alive. I could probably get Allauca to sweeten it a little on top for you."

I raised an eyebrow. "That's a lot of money."

"Isn't it."

"What makes you think I could pull it off when two ex-marshals couldn't?"

"Honestly? I don't know if you can. But right now, I'm willing to throw anything that might even halfway work at this fucker. And tell you what—you bring him down for us—" He lifted his glass. "—I'll throw in a crate of this Le Frog shit right on top of the one-fifty."

I put on another smile. Raised my own glass in echo.

"Now you're talking."

HE'S THE FUCKING *pistaco walking, Hak.*

Walking away from the Crocus Lux an hour later, I gave myself a couple of hundred meters on general principles before my running-hot eagerness got the better of me.

'Ris. You got coverage from the Port Authority control room, right?

Of course.

Pull that pistaco shit they were trying to make out in the audio feed. Play back at the best definition you can manage.

A discrete window unfolded and pasted itself into my top left field of vision. Frenetic wriggling blue lines modeled the audio signature. Hiss in my ears of the cranked-up repro fighting the squall of intrusion virals:

. . . anc . . . eh . . . a . . . o . . .

Do you want to hear the presumed model as well?

Sure.

The hiss abated, the audio ran out clean—*Arrancales el higado!* The affectless nominal male voice. The old pistaco threat.

All right. I drew a deep breath. *Now let's back it up and assume that the last word is in fact the name Hidalgo—*

The cadence pattern is not the same.

No, but the witnesses might not speak Spanish as a first language. And they would have been pretty shaken up. Factor in the name, run your own predictive.

The clean audio ran again.

Arrancate, Hidalgo!

Move it, Hidalgo!

I nodded slowly.

"Gotta be." I whispered to myself. "That's got to be it."

Hidalgo had come looking for Madison Madekwe, all the way from the Shelf to Bradbury. Had hacked his way through a platinum-rated security detail to do it and sent me a gift-wrapped naval warhead in passing, just in case.

Hidalgo had taken her.

THIRTY-THREE

I FOUND A cheap basement maté house on the fringes of the downtown, took a secluded corner booth, and sat wreathed in the damp-green aroma of coca leaf tea. On the tables, low reddish flames guttered from the cactus-spine wicks of locally grown candles, casting fitful light over retro 'branegels hung in corners to ape public information posters from the bad old air-lock days—HEAR HISSING? REPORT IT! LEAKAGE CAN KILL; OUT-SIDE IS NO PICNIC—GO PREPARED; APPRECIATE THE GRAVITY OF THE SITUATION—DON'T SKIP YOUR OSTEO REUP. So forth. I sat in the gloom beneath them and watched steam rise off my tea like sluggish summoned sprites. Soporific cryopop remixes moped and moaned from the sound system. The air around me smelled Earthen and warm.

Counterpoint—the wounds in my scalp itched with the rapid repair eco-code I'd applied, my other aches provided a more somber throb. The urge to *do something* pulsed in my head and the palms of my hands.

I called the goat god.

"Hello, overrider," he said. "You are a little premature. I haven't—"

"Not calling for that. You want to run a Valley-wide on the name Hidalgo for me?"

"Just that, the *name* Hidalgo? Do you have any *fucking* idea how many—?"

"Midlevel covert push, Hannu. My guess is you'll see where it goes pretty much immediately."

"I'm assuming this has to do with the current matter in hand?"

"I'm assuming that, too. But hard data would help."

"I'll call you back."

I tried the maté. It wasn't Colinas de Capri, but I'd had worse.

Flicker-flash of Madison Madekwe's grin over the top of the fake earthenware mug back in Bradbury. That thing in the pit of my stomach, the spark across the space between us. The carnal weight of Earth still on her bones, the casual talk of life back there, like it was a place you could just reach out and touch if you felt like it.

A shadow fell across the table.

"Well, well—Veil. It has been a long time."

Familiar female voice. I looked up bleakly. "Not long enough, Madame Mayor."

She was hooded up for anonymity, just the way Luppi had described her, looking almost slight without her heels and the big hair. She'd either taken off her lenses for the occasion or she no longer needed externals. Something faintly mother superior in the severity of her barely made-up features beneath the hood. Bulkier shadows stood at her back, big in the shoulders and chest, faces impassive as the stone saints in Bradbury's Mother-of-All-Souls Cathedral.

"And you remain as charming as ever." She made a face, mock-wounded. "Milton said you hadn't mellowed much."

She took the other side of the booth. One of the shadows she'd brought along took it upon himself to loom at my side. I glanced up at him, looked back at Raquel Allauca.

"That's not a good start," I said mildly.

She nodded at the shadow, and he receded.

"I don't want to get off on the wrong foot here, Veil. There's really no need for friction between us at this stage."

"That's coming later, is it?"

"That depends on you."

I nodded. "Does Decatur know you're here?"

"I haven't told him, no." She pushed back her hood, tossed her hair a little looser. "But feel free to go running back to him if I scare you."

"You don't scare me yet. Maybe when I know the stakes, that'll change. You want to tell me what Pablo Torres's big score was? The one he pitched to you just before he disappeared?"

She smiled. "It wasn't us, Veil. People disappear in the Uplands all the time, you know that."

"I do know that. Helped you arrange it more than once."

Her face clouded. "That's ancient history. For both of us."

"People don't change."

"Perhaps not. But sometimes their incentives do." She got her smile back. "Did Milton not tell you? We have a good thing going here. Status, control, money coming in. You really think I'd risk all that? Get out of IC management, become mayor of the biggest city on the Shelf just so I could go on wading knee-deep in the same kind of slurry as before?"

"I think, Raquel, you'd cut the laugh out of a toddler's throat with a blunt scalpel if you thought you could sell it for cab fare."

Her smile flickered and went out. "You're a fucking asshole, Veil. I got children of my own now, you know?"

"Sorry to hear that. But I guess they'll survive you."

Fury lit in her eyes, and for just a moment her gaze flickered sideways to the muscle she'd brought along. I smiled over the table at her invitingly. Brought the ringed fingers of my left hand into a loose preparatory clench. The running-hot surged and pulsed inside me. I wanted the fight as badly as I'd wanted Madekwe in the elevator, as badly as I'd wanted anything since Sal Quiroga's death.

The moment stretched and held like a strip dancer's finale pose on the pole.

You have an incoming call.

Park it.

Allauca broke the tension with her dry precision laugh. It wasn't a sound I'd missed in the intervening years.

"Something amusing you?"

"No." An airy dismissive gesture. "I'd just forgotten all that brooding rage you like to carry around. You never forgave any of us for your getting stuck here on Mars, did you? What is that now, eight years and counting? It's got to really burn. I mean—eight *years*, Veil. Looks to me like you're never going home."

I focused on the red pulsing pinpoint of light in the corner of my vision, the call waiting. I breathed.

"You going to tell me what you want, Allauca?"

She opened her hands. "What any good mayor wants. For things in my city to stay civilized. For instance, I hear you had some trouble out at the Field this morning. I'm here to tell you that'll be taken care of."

"News travels fast around here."

"It does to my desk. You'll want to remember that." She leaned back in her seat, gestured casually again. "We're all grown up now, Veil. You want to poke around Gingrich Field again, just let me know. I can have some of my people run you out there, provide an escort while you work."

"An escort? In this grown-up civilized town you've got going on?"

She smiled again, thinly. "I'm making a point here, Veil."

"I know you are. I'm just not sure what it is."

"Perhaps I should spell it out, then." Leaning in now, eyes intent in the guttering candle glow. "You're out of date, Veil. Out of step. And I won't have you bring your superannuated Black Hatch manners onto my streets just because you haven't moved on like the rest of us. I don't suffer from the same romantic attachments to the past that Milton has, and I was never as impressed with your overrider rep as he was, even back in the day. So." She got to her feet, settled her hood back in place. "I'll be in touch. Your maté's on me. Meantime, you're welcome in Cradle City for exactly as long as you don't stir up any trouble here. The moment that ceases to be the case, you'll be on the next ValleyVac back to Bradbury in whatever state it takes my management team to put you there."

I nodded equably. "That or vanished into thin air like Torres. Right?"

"Oh, Veil." She sighed theatrically. "I just told you I had nothing to do with that. You're wearing your lenses. Tell me I'm lying."

She wasn't.

"You still haven't told me what his big pitch was."

"No. Because his much-vaunted big idea wasn't viable, which is why

I turned him down. I don't know who'd been filling his head with pseudo-political fantasies, but . . ." She shook her head. Sighed again, less theater this time, more genuine weariness. "Look, Pablo Torres was like a whole lot of these people—he dreamed big and dumb against all the available evidence, and he had no fucking idea what structural realities he was up against. Sad case, but there you go."

"Yeah, you look pretty broken up about it," I agreed. "So which *structural reality* in particular do you reckon took him down?"

"I really don't think it would be appropriate for me to speculate. Torres's past was . . . variegated. I imagine he was trailing minor enemies like a comet tail on approach. As to which of them caught up with him—well, perhaps you should ask your Earth Oversight friend when you finally catch up with her."

I grimaced. "Milton's getting chatty in his old age."

"You've been gone a long time, Veil. Friendship's like that dicey purple binding weed they're trying to grow on the Wall down at Louros. You've got to tend it if you want it to take the weight. Decatur's moved on, that's all—just like the rest of us."

"Good to know."

"Well, then." She made an entirely superfluous minor adjustment to the hang of her hood. "I believe we're done here."

"I know I am."

She treated me to one more of her *really-growing-tired-of-this* smiles, then turned from the booth and slipped out amid the murky loom of her escort. I watched them all to the spiral staircase, waited until they'd disappeared up it. I pushed the maté cup carefully across the table and left it there.

Get me that call back?

Dialing.

"Hey, Hannu—that was fast."

"You are mistaken," Gradual's careful tones informed me. "Is this a bad time to speak with you?"

"Not if you found something on that Ng warhead, no."

"That would be . . . overstating the case. However, I do have information that may be of interest to you. Our military contacts in Hellas can confirm that there has been zero black market trade in PLA naval ordnance for at least the last four months."

"That's . . ." I caught up with what she'd actually said. "Hold on—zero? You're saying nothing moved at all?"

"That is correct."

Quiet on the line. I listened absently to the barely audible scrambler warble behind her silence, thinking it through. The PLA at Hellas was as generously resourced a military complex as any I'd ever run up against, stockpiled up the ass and out both nostrils. And party-led cronyism in the ranks made the whole place a byword for corrupt practice and low-level profiteering. Add in an insatiable systemwide hunger for cheap and serviceable matériel, and there you have it. Nature abhors a vacuum, they say, and maybe they're right—what I know for certain is that *human* nature abhors a gap in the market, especially one you can fill at a fat margin without breaking a sweat.

"I don't see how you could know something that absolute, Gradual. I mean, not unless you guys have sources at theater command level, and that I *seriously* doubt."

I felt her hesitation over the line. Triad culture isn't big on external trust.

"The rank our contacts hold has not been important in this context," she said finally. "There is a top-down temporary directive in place for all PLA forces in the Crater zone. A standing order to root out all black market activity by any means necessary, immediate court-martial and summary execution of all participants upon detection."

My lips formed a brief silent whistle. "That's a war footing measure, isn't it?"

"It is . . . crisis-level management, at a minimum. Not necessarily war, but something of a similar gravity, yes."

"Like *what*? What the fuck are they expecting over there?" The realization dawning like sunrise on Mercury. "Christ, is this about the audit?"

"It may be." Reluctance in her voice—no one wants to wake up and find her newly sprouted business venture dumped in the path of an oncoming geopolitical sandstorm. "We do not have specifics, only the general directive. But you can at least rest assured that your would-be assassins were not supplied by Hellas."

"Understood," I said mechanically. "Thanks."

Hellas Crater is a long way off—better than ten thousand kilometers straight-line distance from the eastern end of the Valley, impossible to reach overland without sealed rough-transit vehicles, pressure suits for backup, and a shitload of supplies. Access at either end is fenced off by the intensive security cordons both sides maintain, air traffic between the two blocs is sparse and tightly regulated, data coms are heavily monitored and constrained. Might as well be talking about two different worlds. By rights, nothing much going on in Hellas need concern me out here.

But it didn't feel that way.

It felt instead like some more of Hannu Holmstrom's anomaly clustering, piling up with malicious intent.

I LEFT THE maté Allauca had paid for cooling where it stood, and I headed out. I'd stopped taking her money six years back when I quit IC. I wasn't about to pick up the habit again.

Outside, over the skyline of the bonsai downtown to the west, a suitably bonsai sun was dipping toward the level of the Lamina, blurring and melting against their discharge, its own feeble glare put to shame by the lurid display. Plenty of daylight left—even up here on the Shelf, the Lamina layer is several solid kilometers overhead, and Cradle City sits far enough out from either Wall not to get shadowed early on. But the cold comes in harder and faster at evening in the Uplands, and I could feel the early promise of its bite. I turned up my collar, blew on my hands.

Better get me another cab, 'Ris. If we're not blacklisted after what we did to the last one.

I used covert measures coding, she said evenly, somehow still managing to sound like a tutor lecturing a not very bright child. *Scorpion protocols, which—*

Overwrite themselves sixty seconds after trip completion, I recited drably. *Remove the data and replace it with randomly sourced local noise,*

making any trace illegible. Right. Let's just hope cab company countermea-
sures haven't upped their game recently.

To the level of Blond Vaisutis intrusion tech? You do not believe this, you
are allowing mood to influence your—

Just get me a cab. And call this number while you're at it. Keep it ring-
ing, ice out any cutoff protocols you find at the other end. I want an answer.

And where are we going this time?

To see some pseudo-political fantasists.

THIRTY-FOUR

THE SEARCH FOR extraterrestrial intelligence was an early export to Mars. It had just the right blend of hard science and nutcase appeal to get taken seriously at all the best budget meetings. While the early settlers were still living under COLIN-funded glass in what would eventually become the Strip, plans to build a SETI observatory somewhere on the lip of the Valley were gathering stealthy back-burner force. Actual construction began within the decade.

Of course, once they'd actually *found* the alien signals—four of them, undeniable, entirely unrelated to one another, too far off to do anything about or even ascertain whether the civilizations that had sent them still existed—all that enthusiasm for SETI began to wane. Search for extraterrestrial intelligence, right—been there, done that. Box ticked. Funding sputtered, dried to a trickle, finally choked off altogether. A couple of attempts were made to repurpose the observatory, but its distance from the heart of the burgeoning new colonial culture at Bradbury worked against those good intentions. Architectural nanotech, test-driven and proven on Mars at speeds and scales that would never have been permitted anywhere on Earth, meant that whatever your project requirements, it was always cheaper and simpler to build from scratch closer to the action. Eventually, the observatory fell derelict and was left that way.

It took the Lamina deployment and the best part of another century before Valley population reached densities and dispersal sufficient to change things again. But change they did, and when the new owners finally showed up, they found the observatory's mothballed systems in perfect working order.

How do I know all this? Yeah, well . . .

IT TOOK MARTINA SACRAN a long time to answer, but I'd expected the wait. Having the heir apparent to Tech Mutualism on speed dial doesn't guarantee that she'll ever be keen to take your calls. Or that she'll be in a particularly good mood when she does.

"I'm busy, Black Hatch. What do you want?"

"How about a triple A pass to that teaching retreat you keep up at the old SETI base on the South Wall?"

"The observatory?" Hard to know whether the avatar in my upper left field of vision was real time or stock, but it went on scowling at me anyway. "Fuck do you want up there?"

"Not what I want, Tina—it's what a guy called Pablo Torres wanted eighteen months back. Trying to track him for a client."

"Pablo Torres?" Sacran frowned, derailed from whatever sneer she'd been shaping to unload on me. "You talking about that lottery soak Vector Red fucked so one of their oligarch pals could take the Ride Home instead?"

I nodded. "Turns out it's a little more complicated than your class analysis there, but yeah, that's the one. Sources tell me he was up there a lot, mostly getting laid but maybe looking for some kind of political leverage, too. It'd make my life a lot easier if you could tell your people to let me in and help me ask around."

"Access all areas, huh? Just let you in like you were a fully paid up comrade?"

"How is Carla Wachowski these days?" I asked pointedly.

"Fuck should I know?" She reached back on her head, rubbed at the bristle of her cropped iron-gray hair, eyes hollow with lack of rest and maybe something else. "Went back to Ganymede on an ore contract, haven't spoken to the bitch in better than three years. But thanks for bringing it up."

I hesitated. "Sorry to hear that."

"Yeah, aren't we all." I saw her put the memory away. "All right, Veil. I haven't forgotten what I owe. When are you heading up to the Shelf?"

"Already up here. I'm on my way out of Cradle City to the Wall now."

"*Now?* Pachamama's pussy, you don't hang around, do you?"

"Black Hatch decision making." I let my voice harden a little. "It's why Wachowski's still alive."

She sighed. "Fine. I'll speak to whoever's on security at the observatory right now. How far out are you?"

"Just left town." I glanced out of the cab window. The last of the city's peripheral low-rises had fallen behind, replaced by fields of coding pasture turned iridescent by the setting sun, dotted here and there with the metallic glint of silo towers. "I'm overground in a crawler cab. Be there in a couple of hours."

"Okay, I can make that work. Convenor's name is Tomas Rivero—he'll be apprised by the time you show up. Shouldn't give you any trouble. But do me a favor, Veil—next time you want something like this, try and give me some fucking notice."

THE CAB LEFT me at the base station.

There was an obvious retrofitted feel to the facilities; the massive airlock doors that once fronted the garage area had been torn off and replaced with natty black nanofiber storm drapes that the cab brushed through without appreciable effort. The interior was bathed in cool bluish light from the huge swipes of white blaze paint that the Sacranites had put up and whose protocols were nearing the end of their useful life. I climbed out and made my way up a short stack of steps to the main elevator gate. I nodded at the securicam array mounted above.

"Evening."

"You're Veil?" A doubtful female voice from hidden speakers. "Thought you'd be older."

"I get that a lot." True enough—say what you like about hibernoid biorhythms, but four months in the coma every year does wonders for your skin tone. I struck a marketing doll pose. *"Work or Play—Life Is Hard on Mars! But Six Layer Solution from Suchet Ghosh keeps my Essential Cellular Oils in Harmony, No Matter What! Now I Can Work and Play as Hard as the Planet!"*

"Suchet Ghosh went bust," the voice said drily. The elevator gate cranked back, revealed a grimy, poorly lit interior. "Better get in, then."

It was a long, dull ride up. Less than half the height of the Ares Acantilado's service elevators to cover, but the engines were ancient and slow, and there were no windows for a view. Like all pre-Lamina builds, pressure safety had been the paramount consideration, so they'd tunneled up through the rock and sealed everything tight. There were hard plastic seats around the sides of the car and display screens on the walls, the latter clearly intended to relieve the boredom of passengers in transit. It didn't look like they'd been lit in decades.

I sat in one of the unyielding seats and shuffled through the catalog of aches and bruises still reporting in from my crash out at Gingrich Field, the faint heat and tingle of healing in my scalp wounds. Call it a winning hand if you like—I guess Jesika and her slaughtered abduction crew would have to agree from whatever shadows they now inhabited beyond Inti's veil.

Rolled eyes at my own introspection—*get a fucking grip, overrider.* I mapped dents and scrapes on the alloy paneling for something to do, stared at the grilled flooring under my feet until it blurred. Fell back eventually on reliving my THC-fogged conversations with Nina Ucharima.

Yeah, they got that place up over the lip, the old observatory. He used to go up there sometimes, back when he was younger . . .

What about more recently? Before he disappeared?

That too. Went a bunch of times, said he wanted to hear some lectures they were giving . . .

It was pretty thin stuff, but it was all I had.

What are you doing?

I, uh—pulling your hair . . .

Well—fucking don't! *Just—just* fuck *me, overrider. Fuck me with that big cock, make me fucking come!*

I smiled sourly and tried to put that one away. The deep routines were having none of it. Ucharima's long slender back and uplifted ass, weaving in my face.

Her restless tongue and fingers . . .

Her insatiable Uplands hunger and drive.

You know, you don't fuck half as good as Pablo did, but you are like him in a couple of other ways.

I'm nothing like Pablo Torres, Nina.

Apart from a shared distaste for the music of the Gash Hell Condemned, apparently.

The elevator wheezed and jolted to a halt. I shrugged off my recall and stood up. The gate clashed back. A severe-looking young woman stood just outside, peering in as if I might be an exemplar of some species that bites. She wore tinted lenses to shroud her eyes, and she held herself with a poise that looked to me like combat training. Her right hand was folded loosely closed over something small and smoothly metallic—my money was on a one-shot sticky-bond twitch-bomb.

I tried to take it as a compliment.

"Mr. Veil." She gestured with her other hand. "Welcome to the Sacran Teaching Retreat. Convenor Rivero will see you directly. If you'd like to follow me."

We went along gloomy abandoned corridors where the silence pressed down like dust. Old-school pressure doors stood at intervals on either side, cycled permanently to open, giving onto rooms that didn't seem to have much of anything going on in them. The architecture screamed Settlement-era safety first—reinforced bracing on ceilings, heavy sectioning to the corridor walls, the grim hint of compartmentalizing breach barriers suspended in the channels overhead, ready to crash down and seal off in ways no one down in the Valley had needed for over a century. The original human response systems made sporadic contributions to lighting our way, recessed lamps in the grimy alloy panels flickering feebly here and there as we went by. It had all been superseded a while back with broad horizontal swatches of blaze paint that someone had daubed on the floor and dragged along each wall at roughly shoulder height.

It felt like no one had been back since.

"Keeping busy?" I asked as we passed the third empty room.

She shot me a glance. "We don't use these levels much."

The corridor ended at another pressure door, a broad double this time with interlocking teeth at the edges. Both sides were jammed halfway open, the one on the left leaning badly in its slot. Beyond was a shallow spiral walkway rising to the level above. We walked around and up, into what I guessed had to be the main supervisory chamber for the landing field.

After the gloom of the corridors below, it was like someone taking a lid off your field of vision. Ten-meter-high ceilings, big open command space, and a broad viewport that ran almost floor to ceiling and took up most of the facing wall. You looked down from a height of fifty meters across what once would have been a pristine nanocrete expanse, precisely etched with markings for orbital landers and bull's-eyes for one-way payload puff-down.

Now a thin Martian surface wind blew boiling clouds of finest-grade regolith across the view, dimming down the weak evening light even further, driving restless snakes of sand across what exposed nanocrete there still was, adding to the dunes that had already buried the rest.

A slim solitary figure stood in front of the viewport, arms folded as if against cold. He didn't turn as we approached.

"This is the overrider," said my escort.

"Thank you, Serena. You can leave us. I'm reliably informed Mr. Veil does not pose a threat. Apparently he's retired." Rivero came around to face us now—dark hawkish features, neatly bearded face, ostentatiously heavy steel-framed lenses, hard dark eyes behind. "Isn't that right, Mr. Veil?"

"Just here to ask some questions," I agreed. "Nothing that's going to get in the way of the revolution."

That got me a sharp look from Serena as she was turning to leave. Rivero caught it, shook his head dismissively. He watched her descend the spiral walkway all the way out of sight, then turned back to the window, stared out at the boiling dust storm again.

"I'll confess I'm a little surprised you've been permitted to come here," he said quietly. "And make no mistake, I argued quite strongly against it."

"Lucky for me no one listens to you, then."

He swung on me. "Retired or not, you were once an overrider. Do you know what Enrique Sacran said about men like you?"

"That we were cutting into his piracy revenue?"

"Oh, yes, you'll call it piracy, as your corporate masters always did. Hijacking. Economic terrorism." Fervor building in his voice now—we had a true believer here. "We were *at war,* Mr. Veil. We are *still* at war—for the greater good of the human race, against the corrupt metastasis of oligarchic power that stomps on humanity's neck everywhere in this solar system. Sacran said that in end-stage capitalism, as systems of human efficiency reach their event horizon, the ruling class reaches an ultimate logic; they no longer recruit foot soldiers to their cause, they manufacture them instead. Why expend revenue and effort on indoctrination when you can bypass inconvenient human impulse at the source, abolish social and political consciousness, build running dog loyalty from the genetic ground up? I look at you, and I see he was right. Corporate utility given flesh, that's all you are, overrider—a commodity algorithm masquerading as a man."

"Sounds dangerous to me. I reckon I'd try to stay the right side of polite if I were talking to something like that."

He bared his teeth at me, more snarl than grin. "You don't scare me, Veil. You're just part of the detritus the winds of Mutualist change are going to sweep away. Sacran would have put a bullet through the back of your head as soon as look at you."

"Yeah, well, his daughter seems to have a more nuanced approach. She wants you to answer my questions about Pavel Torres."

"Martina is a . . ." He drew a deep breath. "She has an overly romantic view of indebtedness and personal favors. There is no room in the march of history for such baggage."

"Easy for you to say. It's not your hijacker girlfriend still walking around in one piece because some 'corporate utility' given flesh chose not to blow her away. Oh, and lost his fucking job and got dumped in exile on Mars as a result. How's that for baggage, asshole?"

It grew very quiet in the viewing chamber. There was a brief, joyous moment when I thought Rivero might actually try for me. He wanted to, I could see it rising in his eyes—the righteous anger of the professional crusader provoked—and there was something reasonably combat-competent to the way he sized me up. He'd likely seen his share of street brawls against police and low-grade corporate muscle over the years, might well have taken fight biochem upgrades in service to the cause. But whatever fight the convenor had in him, natural or trained or just tampered in, the Sacranites are not the Frockers, and their cadres aren't stupid. Rivero had a higher purpose to steep his violent impulses in, a broader vision and a patience that would wait for the day of reckoning and the firing squad wall.

That, plus you don't pick fights out of dented pride with an overrider, even a retired one, and expect to still be standing when it's over.

Rivero stood down.

"I am not unaware of what you did for Carla Wachowski," he said stiffly. "I merely—"

"You'll merely do as you're fucking told. Sacran's given this her blessing, and you're going to get in line behind it. Now, tell me about Torres. Did you meet him personally?"

He hesitated a moment longer. Nodded. "Yes, I remember him. He came to some seminars. We got used to seeing him around. Not as stupid as he liked to pretend. He sat in and listened mostly, hung around afterward. Sometimes he'd have a question."

"Such as?"

"You're asking me to recall questions from the audience of a seminar I attended more than eighteen months ago?"

"All right, then—what was the subject?"

He gave me a sour smile. "The inherent instability of interplanetary capitalist systems. We don't talk about much else up here. That and the preparations for what we must do when those systems inevitably fail. I don't recall which seminars Torres attended, and quite honestly, I doubt he would either—he seemed far more interested in scoring with some of our more impressionable female comrades. I understand he even made some overtures to Martina once when she came up from Bradbury for a guest lecture."

"Got to admire his ambition. Martina aside, was he successful with any of these women?"

"More often than not, yes." Abruptly, Rivero's tone turned prissy. "Torres presented as the fallen underclass hero, damaged goods in need of redemption. A sex object they could unload all their yearning for social justice onto."

"Any of them still around?"

"I, uh—yes, I imagine so. Most were on staff here. One or two may have moved on since, but—"

"Good. I'd like to talk to as many of them as possible."

"That is . . ." His mouth tightened on whatever he wanted to say next, personal antipathy struggling with cadre discipline and the orders he'd been given. The discipline won. "That . . . will take some considerable time to organize."

I shrugged. "Better get on with it, then."

A RELIC OF its days as an operational command point, the viewing chamber had been fitted with various suites of retracting furniture and equipment that could be made to emerge from or sink back into the floor at need. Rivero summoned a low table and two long sofas somewhere well back from the windows and off to one side. They rose out of the polished flooring like an omen of some congeniality the Sacranites had yet to show me.

"Wait here," Rivero told me, and summoned Serena to make sure I did while he was gone.

I sat on the sofa and watched the storm developing outside. Serena stood a dozen meters off, open disdain in her expression, arms folded across her chest, one hand still loosely cupped around whatever glinting metallic thing she'd held as a talisman against me on the way in. She stared past me at the windows.

"You want to sit down?" I tried, gesturing to the sofa opposite.

"I'm fine here."

"I don't bite."

She peeled me a glance. "I'm not afraid of you, Veil. I just don't like you."

Out beyond the big viewing port, night had almost fallen. On some trigger or other, flood lamps along the roof kicked in, blasting out a fierce bluish radiance that collapsed the darkness and seemed to light the raging storm from within.

"Scouring winds of history, eh?" I said. "Not all they're cracked up to be."

Another sliced glance. "What?"

I nodded at the glass. "That storm out there. Looks like it could really do some damage. *Blast away the trappings of societal oppression, scour down the surface of quotidian things so raw truth is revealed.*"

The quote got me her full attention. "You've read Sacran?"

"I've had him quoted at me a fair few times. Guess some of it stuck."

"Is that why you didn't murder Carla Wachowski?"

I said nothing, just stared out at the wind in the darkness, caught in memories I'd rather not have. *Screams and the flat-crack echo of gunfire in the red-lit zero-G corridors of* Sunrise in Sapphire *as the BV boarding party cleans out the crew section. Rage pulsing in my temples and throat with the way this has all gone sideways so fucking fast. And minute telltale droplets of Wachowski's blood pearling in our wake as I shepherd her aft toward the cargo lock. It's not a bad gash I gave her with the butt end of the HK, and she's tough, she's bearing up. But the human scalp bleeds like a motherfucker on very little provocation, there's no time to staunch and clean up properly, and now she's dripping a trail in the chilly shipboard air that the boarding party commandos could probably follow blindfolded. Only a matter of time till they track us down.*

Why are you doing this? she keeps mumbling as I tug her along. Why didn't you kill me?

I grimace and listen and scan channels for sounds of pursuit and wish I had an answer that makes any fucking sense.

"Someday," Serena began, and drew a deep, preparatory breath. Mutualist speech incoming. Not having that.

"It's all an illusion," I said harshly.

"What is?"

"That scouring wind you're looking at, this coming storm you're all dreaming of so hard. It looks ferocious, but it's not. Even with all the terraform eco-magic they tried back in the day, atmospheric conditions out there are still pretty close to Old Mars pressures. Last I heard, it's less than 4 percent Earth sea level standard. Put on a suit, you could go out and stand in the middle of all that, you'd barely feel the breeze. All it's doing is blowing the dust around."

She flushed. "Is that how you see us?"

"Not really about you, it's about local conditions. You talk up a storm in your retreats and your universities, but go outside and you don't have the critical density. This valley is filled with people who don't give a shit about your theories of history and economics, and the people they listen to have already sold them a shinier dream."

"Which is what?"

"Lifetime membership in Humanity's Rugged High Frontier Elite, with a side order of aspirational consumer tech product for the masses. Exceptionalism, a sense of belonging, and shiny toys to play with along the way. What have you got that's going to compete with that?"

"It can't last," she snapped. "It's a bubble, a fantasy. When it all falls apart—"

"Yeah—if and when that happens, sister, you'd better fucking pray you're not standing anywhere close to ground zero." Some jagged shard of old anger spiking in my voice now. "I've seen what happens to humans when *it all falls apart*. Believe me, it isn't pretty."

She opened her mouth to retort, then changed her mind.

We went back to ignoring each other and staring at the storm outside.

THIRTY-FIVE

RIVERO CAME BACK with six names. One had left the Sacran Retreat some time ago, was rumored to be down in Bradbury and working back office for a celebrity affairs feed. *She's dead to us,* Rivero didn't actually say, but you got the general idea anyway from his tone and the look on his face.

The other five were all either still around at the observatory or doing outreach somewhere contactable. With varying degrees of enthusiasm, they'd all agreed to talk to me.

What Martina Sacran asks of her father's faithful, they willingly give.

NISHA KHARKI.

"Fucking asshole."

I blinked. "Sorry?"

She twitched forward impatiently on the sofa, delicate Himalayan looks rucked up in an indelicate scowl. Her silky dark hair was cropped short, something like Martina Sacran's but without the gray. Perhaps it was aspirational.

"Wanna talk about Torres, right?" she said. "He was a fucking asshole. Typical Uplands prick, all mouth and schemes and busted promises. Thought I'd left that shit behind when I joined the Movement, but they get in here just like everywhere else."

"Did he tell you what he was doing up here?"

"Chasing pussy was what he was doing."

"He told you that?"

The corner of her mouth tugged upward in a sneer. "No, I worked that one out all by myself."

"How many times you two get together?"

"Oh, just the once. I like to learn from my mistakes. Not like that stupid fucking bitch Guzman."

DEVU GUZMAN.

"It's just he—he was so lost." She smiled as if the memory pained her. She wore her hair long and rainbow tinted, let it hang forward in her face as she talked. "There was so much swagger in him, but it was all covering up, substituting for who he really was."

I raised an eyebrow. "Who was he really?"

"Just this—this . . . damaged child. A child trying to live up to stories of a father he barely remembered, trying on manhood like a necktie he wasn't sure how to knot. In the end, all he was doing was choking himself with it."

"I understand you saw him a few times."

"Yes, he came to most of the COLIN Mythos lectures. Sometimes we'd go back to my rooms afterward."

"Despite the fact he was seeing some of the other women, too? That didn't bother you?"

"Oh, no. No." She shook her head a little too vigorously. Her rainbow hair swung and obscured her face. "Not really. Of course, you feel a— a twinge. But sexual jealousy is false consciousness just as much as coveting the latest Marstech. It's the same destructive need to possess something. You have to shed it to grow."

"Did you get the impression at any point that Torres was . . . growing? What did you talk about when you were together?"

The pained smile again. "He tried. He really did. He understood how illusory everything they sell is, how it can all come tumbling down. We talked about that—he totally got it. But—he lived this life like it was a storm."

We both looked out the viewport, the boiling nighttime fury of wind and dust beyond. Her smile faded out as if scoured away by the same forces.

"Poor Pavel. What chance did he have?"

"He moved on after you," I said with experimental brutality. "Why was that?"

"Oh—appetites." Still staring out at the storm, seemingly lost in it. "Pavel wanted things I didn't. Wanted me to do things I wouldn't."

"Such as?"

She looked back at me, put her sad smile back together. "Things with other women, mostly. I'm sure you get the picture. There's still this persistent meme in the Movement—that freeing your mind from societal constraints has to mean catering to the appetites of any comrade who comes along with some transgressive fantasy or other. Maybe Pavel thought that kind of thing would be easier to find up here. The Shelf Counties are strange about sexual stuff, it's in your face on every 'branegel you see, but when it comes to actually *doing* it, there's this sudden prudish economy going on. Doesn't really fit with all those outlaw pretensions they have, now, does it?"

"And did Pavel find what he was looking for up here?"

"Oh, yes. It wouldn't have been hard. Some of my female comrades are quite . . . flexible that way." Her smile gained force. "And he had such a lovely cock."

INEZ THAPA.

The 'branegel framed her in a brightly lit meeting hall somewhere. Cheap carbon fiber chairs and tables scattered around, a display screen on the wall cycling news feed segments in silence. Beside it, a big poster of Sacran Senior, airbrushed up from one of the stock shots of the Address on Ganymede. Inaccurate dawn skyline behind him, rosy-cheeked followers on all sides.

The hall itself looked pretty empty.

In the middle of all the abandoned furniture, Inez Thapa perched elegantly on the edge of a table, smoking a lung turbo snout and looking vaguely displeased through the ribbons of vapor it gave off.

"You should understand I'm not very comfortable talking about this." The reek of a wealthy background smoldered from her in gesture and word—well-bred disdain in the voice, smooth brow and delicate falcon nose wrinkling as if somewhere beyond the edges of the 'branegel, someone was cooking something noxious. "I get that Martina's sanctioned it, that it's important for some reason. But I'd just as soon not go into all the sordid little details."

"We don't have to. I'd just like to confirm that you had, uh, sexual relations with Pavel Torres and Julia Farrant."

"Yes, I did."

"At the same time?"

She sighed. "Yes. At the same time. Look, I'm not proud of it, all right? It isn't something I . . . habitually do. But Julia was a friend and it was what she needed at the time, so I went along. It was . . . theater, nothing more. A tacky little show for her grotty little boyfriend."

"They had previous history, then?"

"Oh, yes, I think so. They had stories in common, in-jokes, Uplands attitude about everything. There was a . . . rapport, I suppose you could call it." She pulled a face. "Though, honestly—if you want my impression?"

"Please."

"I think he would have dropped her off a cliff as soon as it suited him. He struck me as that sort. But something else as well—when we were . . . in the act, as it were, I caught him looking at her scars. Staring at them in a way that was . . . odd." She gestured, gave me a sardonic smile. "Given that there was so much else on offer to goggle at in those moments."

I frowned. "Farrant was scarred?"

"Not especially badly, but it was there. Patches on her body, one on her face here—" She made a motion with an opened palm, cupping the left side of her jaw, the cheekbone above. "—some kind of chemical burn, I understand. I did wonder if that was the point of our little threesome. Something to entice him back if the scarring had put him off."

"And she left after that? Quit the cause, went to Bradbury, and got a job?"

"Yes, it wasn't long after, now you come to mention it. Perhaps she caught him looking, too. Or maybe . . . I don't get the impression Jules was ever very committed to the cause; seemed like she was just using it to hide out from something else. But yeah, she's gone. She dropped by here at the outreach station to see me on her way down-Valley. Told me she was going to get her skin fixed, whatever it cost. I gave her some Bradbury addresses, people in the trade I knew back when I . . . before."

"Before what?"

Something changed in her face—a conviction, a kind of peace. She gestured, perhaps at the poster on the wall behind her, perhaps just at the place she was in.

"Before I chose this, Mr. Veil. Before I found a way to live that wasn't just grubbing by day to day on the stored fat my family laid down generations ago."

LIZ BASPINEIRO.

Long tousled blond hair, steady blue eyes, relatively pale skin for the Uplands. She had the 'gel focus reeled in tight, no clues to her location other than it was somewhere outdoors—you could make out the soft orange fabric of the toss-tent in whose unsealed mouth she sat cross-legged, reflected firelight in her eyes and the ruffle of wind through her hair. Her accent was deep Valley, Bradbury or somewhere not far outlying.

"Sure, Torres. Did him one on one a couple of times, and then with Karishma one night after this seminar we had on Marstech markets." A lewd, knowing grin. "Just about blew his brains out, that did—he loved that girl-on-girl shit."

"And you didn't mind it?"

She kept the grin. "Well, not *really* my thing. But y'know—kicks the intensity up a few bars. Kari's got a great body, certainly didn't mind playing around with that. And Torres—what can I tell you?—he was a great fuck. Would have been anyway, with or without the added extras. Had a cock on him like you wouldn't believe."

I gave her a pained smile that would have made Devu Guzman proud. "So I've been hearing."

KARISHMA ADIKHARI.

"Yeah, I like girls. What about it?" Amused challenge in the down-curved smile, the thick raised brows. "They don't allow that sort of thing on Earth? Got to get some big government bureaucrat to sign off on it first? Form 21-B Eat-Pussy?"

She sprawled at ease across the sofa opposite me. Messy black hair, laughing dark eyes, and Liz Baspineiro's assessment of her body was, to my way of thinking, pretty accurate. The whole way she held herself was a *you-wish* flaunt.

"Someone told you I was from Earth?" I asked.

She waved a hand. "We don't get that many visitors up here even with the outreach stuff. Same two hundred-odd faces rattling around the same old tin can corridors—you can get pretty bored. You're quite the topic of conversation this evening. Earthman Overrider with the Heart of Gold. The Man who Let Carla Wachowski Walk Away."

"It was a little more complicated than that."

"Usually is. Like Sacran says—*depend upon simple solutions with humans and you will simply fail.* Still, I know Martina. Pretty rare for her to feel she owes anybody anything—especially anyone from That Mother Earth."

It was an old joke, but I sketched a smile for it anyway.

"It's been a while since I was from That Mother," I said. "And yeah, they got girls that like girls back on Earth. I'm just trying to make sense here. You went to bed with Liz Baspineiro and Julia Farrant, but in both cases you took Pavel Torres along for the ride. You like girls, but you like boys, too?"

A shrug. "On occasion. Depends on the boy, I'd say. I can live without them." She gave me an *out-of-your-league-sonny* smile to go with her posture. "The girls, not so much."

"So you went with Torres because it got you Baspineiro?"

"Yeah. Price worth paying, y'know. That blonde is dirty through and through. Not much she won't do given the right incentives."

"What about Farrant? She fit that description, too?"

"Julia? No, that was . . ." For the first time, I thought I saw a crack in the gorgeous composure. The laughing eyes hooded briefly. She sighed. "Yeah, Julia was probably a mistake. She wasn't really into it, y'know. Whole thing felt . . . awkward. Reckon she was just doing it because he wanted the thrill. They used to be an item, her and Torres."

"Yeah, I heard that. *Uplands True Romance*, huh?"

Her lip curled. "Soak, don't even talk to me about that show—fucking low-grade immie wank fantasy shit. And no, that wasn't them, not even close."

"Okay, but whatever they had—it was Uplands-based, right?"

"Oh, sure, yeah—they had this whole colorful Shelf Counties past they talked up whenever anyone would listen. Lot of stories. Think that was what pulled me after Julia in the first place, that whole outlaw waif thing she had going on. Running with the gangs out on the Shelf, cutting cordons and corners everywhere they could, sharing pipe and pistol with guys like Hidalgo and Saville Jeff Havel. All that good transgressive shit."

"Right." I hung lightly in the moment, pulse thundering at running-hot tempo. I willed my tone down to casual passing interest. "You think that was real, though—hanging with Hidalgo, with Havel? Or just talk?"

Adikhari thought about it. Made a wavering horizontal blade with one hand. "Could have been exaggerating. Julia could talk a Wall-beating line of shit when she was hitting the SNDRI."

"So she probably never even met, like, Havel, right?"

"Been in a room with him, maybe—I know Torres was supposed to be doing stuff for the Ground Out Crew down in Cradle City. So." Another shrug, more generous this time. We were on ground Karishma Adikhari wanted to explore. Abruptly, she swung her legs off the sofa, leaned forward with arms on knees, all trace of posturing gone. "Look, I always figured he was blowing that shit up way bigger than it was. But the Hidalgo stories—they rang true. Little details, just the way they used to tell it, the way they both chimed on the same things."

"Things like what?"

"That he was from Earth." She saw my reaction. "No, really—they both swore it was true. I think it *was* true, not just ultratripper hype. Julia said he could never get with the local music or the food. Bitched about it all the time, apparently."

I grunted. "Some of the music I've heard recently, that wouldn't—"

I stopped dead as it dropped on me.

Like the sky falling in on the Valley in violent-colored splintering shards. Like Particle Slam's much-vaunted downpour promises finally brought home.

What was that we were listening to?

Gash Hell Condemned—Live at Wall 101. *Not keen, huh?*

Lying with Nina Ucharima in the semisatisfactory aftermath of our coupling. Violent musical insistence raging from the apartment's speakers like a maniac's endless head butting into steel plate.

Yeah, Hidalgo hated that shit, too. Acquired local taste, I reckon.

Tweaked THC, postcoital discomfort, general over-the-hill incompetence—call it any way you like. I'd had my lenses off, and I hadn't been paying attention. I'd heard *Torres*, not *Hidalgo*, because Torres— and his big fucking cock—was on my mind, and Hidalgo was still three meaningless syllables I'd hear later from a dying corporate man-boy thug out at Gingrich Field.

I WENT THROUGH the rest of the interview pretty much on autopilot. Learned nothing else from Karishma Adikhari that I hadn't already heard from the others. Torres was an asshole; big cock, though.

I tried not to let it grate.

When we were done and Adikhari had sauntered off across the viewing chamber's airy storm-gloomed expanse, I sat slumped and staring across the table to the empty space where they'd all been and the glass shielding beyond. Outside, the sandstorm raged on, tall dancing plumes of fine-grade regolith driven past like the lost souls of some massive alien race in exodus. Streamers of dust flung themselves soundlessly against the towering windows, imploring entry. Inside felt cozy and remote from it all, a haven from a world where we didn't belong. It wasn't hard to see what huddling instincts might have helped trigger Torres's run of carnal success among the retreat's personnel.

Are we leaving?

Yeah, we're leaving, I subbed reluctantly.

I couldn't help it. I wasn't looking forward to what I had to do next. And it didn't help that I appeared to be doing it in the cause of justice for a dick-driven minor league thug whose best claim to fame was that he could have had a promising career in immie porn.

Footfalls across the chamber space: Convenor Rivero returning. He was wearing the same pinched and puritanical expression he'd had on when we talked before. He stopped a few paces off and stood with his arms clasped tightly behind him, as if holding himself back from some violently retributive political act. Perhaps he'd been talking to Serena.

"So. Was that . . . fruitful?"

"You could say that. Everyone was very cooperative."

"Yes, well." He hesitated, mouth pursed. The words came out like pulled teeth. "As it's getting late, I . . . am instructed . . . to invite you to stay for the night. Here. At the retreat."

I shook my head. "I have what I came for; I'm going to head out."

"You're quite sure?" he evidently felt compelled to ask. "We do have guest rooms below."

"I'm certain," I told him, and grinned. "Us corporate commodity algorithms don't need sleep. But let Martina know this one said thanks."

THIRTY-SIX

'RIS GOT ME another cab, and I rode it back from the Wall toward Cradle City. The Martian night pressed in on the windows like ink, relieved by occasional restive purple lightning flickers from the Lamina above. I tilted my head beside the glass and watched the charge differentials fire like gigantic short circuits through the system of the world.

That's some fucking score Torres made up here. How long was he coming to these seminars?

Correlating what we know—a little under three months. 'Ris paused. *Approximately the same amount of time he spent in Cradle City before his disappearance.*

So that's all these space cadets and Nina Ucharima, too. Christ! Got to wonder if he didn't just get offed and buried by some jealous boyfriend.

Or girlfriend. Or, for that matter, a lover he slighted or discarded too abruptly for her liking. Nina Ucharima for example.

Yeah.

Perhaps you should have pressed her harder when you had the chance.

I twitched restlessly on the cab seat. *Get me the goat god again.*

Dialing.

"Veil. I was just going to call you."

"That's good timing, then. This Hidalgo thing is taking off—what have you got for me?"

"Not much. I mean, he's front and center in the West End flow, sure. Didn't take more than ten seconds to see who you were talking about. But there's no deep trace. I can't track any date or place of birth, any medical records or education—"

"No, you won't. Motherfucker's from Earth."

"Is he now? How very interesting. You wouldn't happen to know when he arrived?"

"No, but he's not recent." I thought back to my conversation with Decatur. "Been here at least six years—Earth years, that is, three Martian. Probably a bit more."

"That would make sense, it's about the time the trace shows up. It is also, interestingly enough, about the same time that the most brutal reprisals against whistle-blowers began in the wake of the canceled '95 audit."

I blinked. The correlation had never occurred to me. "You think he was tied into that somehow?"

"There's nothing in the data to suggest it. But perhaps that in itself might point a rather rigid finger. If you were a wanted whistle-blower needing to disappear before the Prosperity Party sicced its thugs on you, it would make sense to originate a whole new identity. Allowing that you had access to the funds and expertise, of course. Maybe our friend Hidalgo isn't from Earth at all, he just wanted people to think he was."

"Kind of high-profile way to disappear, isn't it?"

"Hide in plain sight, maybe." I could hear in Holmstrom's voice how he dropped the idea like a cat killing prey it's grown bored with. "Look, I'm not trying to sell it to you, Veil. And wherever this Hidalgo is from, whoever he was before this, he certainly doesn't seem to have wasted any time drawing attention to himself again. He's made quite a few enemies up there in the West End. There's a bounty out on him with the local OC syndicates, and the Marshal Service have him on their most wanted board—though they aren't making that public."

"Any obvious reason for that?"

"Nothing that shows up. It's not unheard of procedure, to be honest, but it is unusual. Suggests they know something about him they don't want to become common knowledge. And keeping it quiet is evidently more important than bringing him in."

I thought of Sakarian, the iron dislike in his stare. "Doesn't sound like the marshals."

"Well, quite. Of course"—reluctance surfacing in the goat god's tone—"I *could* go back and dig deeper, see if they've committed anything to deep covert files anywhere, but that's just going to get in the way of the Earth run. Which I would have to totally dismantle and prep again from scratch. Your call, Veil."

"No. Nothing that detracts from getting through on Madekwe. She's the key to this whole fucking thing however it boils down. I find her, everything else is going to fall into place."

"Glad to hear it." The relief in his voice put a grin on my face. Holmstrom was itching to get back into the datastack that had kicked him out so summarily. It was a point of pride now. "By the way, I did some ancillary digging elsewhere on our Madison—basic dataflow stuff to get a better fix on who she actually is. You want the detail?"

I looked out at the speeding darkness around the cab. Off to the right, dawn was starting to show like a bleach line on the black. "Sure, why not? Hit me."

"So there's a fair bit on the parents—mother comes from California tech money, one of the old Rim States aristo clans. Father's from Lagos originally, distinguished career in the Nigerian military, then globally via Addis Ababa, Johannesburg, and New York. He made colonel in the Pan African Rapid Deployment Force, got promoted to tactical adviser at AU General Assembly, then private consultant to a bunch of COLIN primaries with interests in the Sahara Regeneration Zone. Met the mother while she was on a fact finder to Chad, followed her right back to the Rim. There's some suggestion she might have gone home pregnant. Anyway, they did the nomad seclusion thing with little Madison—she was born and brought up as part of a Midwestern horse tribe construct in the annexed ranges."

"That's the Dakotas, right?"

"More like Montana and Wyoming. I think it takes in some of northern Colorado, too. Mother's clan have had people out there for going on a century by the look of it. Mother was raised nomad as well. Looks like she rated the experience pretty highly; she and Madekwe's father both went full abdicate to raise Madison."

I grunted. There's something ironic about the fact that on Earth the truly wealthy get to divest themselves of modernity and live simple reverted lives as hunter-gatherers while the rest of us scurry around fixing and fine-tuning the myriad complexities of the modern world that lets them do it.

"How long she stay out there?"

"Quite a long time, considering. I mean, general record says she started taking trips out with Mum and Dad age seven or eight, did the Vandever Critical Gestalt Assessment back in the Rim States at eleven. Signs of leadership potential, general resilience, high scores in a bunch of other stuff. They flagged her for early entry to some cadre schools in the Rim, a couple of prestige universities in West Africa, but she sidelined all of it indefinitely. Chose to stay in-country right through her teens and out the other side, long after her parents headed back to the real world. She made tribal council by nineteen, which I understand is pretty exceptional. Doesn't seem to have wanted a life in the outside world at all— there's no trace there until she starts to show up in junior COLIN Oversight roles in her late twenties, mostly training camp stuff and back-office support."

"Sounds a bit low-key."

"Was my thought as well. Maybe she fell out with her parents, went the whole make-it-on-my-own route. Happens sometimes with these rich kid types. Very high levels of wastage with that background. Or hey, maybe just hitting the real world after so long was a wrench, and she didn't wear it well. One day you're chasing antelope for dinner on horseback, telling tall tales about it around the campfire afterward, the next you've got a stack of files for action piling up behind your eyes, 'gel presence conferences on three continents, and a deadline at the end of the week."

"Do they have antelope in the annexed ranges?"

"Antelope, bison, what's the fucking difference, darling? I like my meat delivered on a plate, not walking around still shitting and bellowing.

My point is, I imagine not everyone can pull off a smooth transition be-tween two worlds like that."

I thought back to the Madekwe I'd spent time with in Bradbury. She'd managed the immediate transition to Mars pretty well for a civilian.

"Fair enough," I said dubiously. "Can you send me the files?"

"Already done. And by tonight, my friend," his tone grew predatory, "I'll have that COLIN datastack cracked wide and sucked dry for you. Depend on it. Oh, yes, one more thing before I go—it's only in the num-bers, might not mean anything, but I have another minor anomaly flag around Hidalgo."

"Which is?"

"That his depredations in the Shelf Counties began at approximately the same time Vector Red undertook their revamp of the lottery interface and instituted the so-called Deiss Man Show. There is no actual link in the data, only the coincidence of timing. But given the connection to Tor-res, I have to wonder."

I remembered Deiss and his SNDRI comedown, the twitchy nervous bustle as he got rid of me, the relief in his face as I left. Didn't have to mean anything other than a badly managed drug habit in a show-biz 'gelface terrified that Earth Oversight had just shown up on his doorstep and might scalp him.

Didn't *have* to mean anything at all . . .

But.

"I'll keep it in mind," I said.

"You do that. Meantime, I'm shutting down all incoming until noon tomorrow, so don't be surprised if you call and I don't pick up."

"I thought you were doing this tonight."

"I am. But this is heavy intrusion work across a quarter-hour coms lag. It's not a picnic. Even if I get done by dawn—which I doubt—I'm still going to be synapse-crashed and wobbly for six to eight hours after. You'll get your answers, Veil, don't worry. But there's a price to be paid for everything. You'll have to be patient."

"Right." I hesitated. "Listen, you stay sharp out there, Hannu. You watch that code."

"It's *me*, Veil." I thought I heard him yawn. "I'll be in touch."

. . .

I WENT BACK to the Mansions of Luthra. In a fluid situation, you need to keep track of all actors, and I wanted to know if Seb Luppi had dropped me an interim note. Our meeting at Payload Blue was still the best part of twenty-four hours off, and there was no telling what he might have stumbled on in the meantime. And somewhere in my belly, amid the general itch of the running-hot, was a colder, creeping intimation that whatever canister this was I'd woken up to find myself riding, it was tipping close to critical.

Seeing Gustavo's grinning face as I got out of the cab did nothing to change my mind. Lensed up and restless, he hulked about in the paling neons beneath the hotel's portico like something haunting the place that must be gone by break of day. He'd swapped out his Crocus Lux livery for nondescript black workwear. Colored to match, a chunky little jeep crawler sat idling a dozen meters ahead of where the cab had pulled in. Gull-wing doors angled up, waiting.

"Looking for me?" I asked.

He snorted. "Genius detective, huh? C'mon, got something Decatur wants you to see."

Inside the crawler, the fittings were high end and smelled new, but there wasn't a lot of space. I squeezed up to allow Gustavo in beside me, and the door hinged down. We coasted gently away from the hotel, out across the plaza, and merged with machine precision into thin traffic heading east to greet the dawn. A few minutes in, I started to recognize landmarks I'd passed before.

"So what's out at Gingrich Field that won't keep till morning?" I wondered aloud.

I saw in my lenses how he twitched, how his pulse jumped at the guess I'd made. But he kept it tamped down too low for unaugmented vision to spot.

"That is where we're going, right?"

He gave me an unpleasant smile. "Just sit back and enjoy the ride, Veil. Not where we're going that matters, it's what you're going to see when we get there."

We raised the field on the horizon and split from the main traffic flow soon after. Eerie sense of déjà vu as the early-morning light grew up around us. The jeep ran in among the outermost of the disused units, dipped into an underpass that shut out the morning behind us, and then took a branching tunnel that curved steadily north-northeast.

Not heading to the same place Torres vanished, are we?

No. We are already a significant distance north of that location. Unless the tunnel structure is exceedingly unorthodox, we are unlikely to return to that part of the Field.

The crawler came to a gentle halt in a brightly lit segment of tunnel, opposite a set of pressure doors that someone had obligingly cranked back.

"This is us," Gustavo said superfluously, and popped the hatch.

Beyond the doors, we took a big bulk-load elevator upward a couple of floors. Gusty gloom and the faint medicinal odor of use-exhausted sanitation bug corpses rotting in the dim spaces at each level we passed. Whatever this place was, it had been mothballed for generations. The elevator platform juddered to a halt in a similarly empty space, this one harshly lit at center by four big, spider-legged Dorn lamps.

At their point of focus, a single human form was lashed into a wheelchair.

Faint chill on my spine at the sight. And when figures emerged from the surrounding gloom as we approached, it felt like a rising premonition of doom. I counted them off. Five in all, visible to standard human eyes; four more lurking farther back in the darkness, tagged and limned in faint hazard orange on my lenses by 'Ris and the threat assessment software.

No surprise to see Raquel Allauca leading the party.

Critical systems, I subbed very gently.

Running.

We met in the broad puddle of Dorn radiance, a couple of meters from the slumped and bound figure in the wheelchair. It was hard to make out his features given the way he'd been worked over—flesh around the left eye swollen to the size of a weather blimp run aground on the gouged and splintered ledge of the cheekbone, nose broken and mashed almost flat into the face behind it, teeth missing in the loose drooling gape of the mouth. Beneath a work shirt liberally daubed with blood, the right shoulder looked to be dislocated, and at the end of that wrenched arm someone had snapped back three of the fingers, left them so they stood up at jagged obscene angles from the binding that held the rest of the hand in place.

Still, through the blood and damage and slackness of features, I recognized him. I kept my face stony, turned to face Allauca.

"Been busy, I see."

"Veil." She didn't offer her hand. "Thank you for coming. This is Sandor Chand, independent security consultant at large and the man whose team tried to disappear you from Gingrich Field last night."

"I know who he is." I looked elaborately around. "What happened to Decatur? Thought he was supposed to be here. Has he not got the stomach for this shit anymore?"

"Milton has been unavoidably detained. Municipal matters. The audit is generating some . . . business complications for us. Now—" She placed a proprietary hand on her captive's sagging shoulder. "—I told you yesterday evening that I have no intention of allowing matters in my town to become unruly. And I said that there would be redress for the assault you suffered out at the Field. I am, as I'm sure you recall, a woman of my word. Would you care to do the honors?"

"I'd prefer to ask him some questions—if you left a tongue in his mouth and enough functioning brain mass to talk with, that is."

Allauca rose back to her full height. She gave me a mannered shrug, for all the world like a classy head chef offering someone her signature dessert dish on the house only to have it brusquely turned down. Her eyes glittered at me behind her lenses.

"You didn't always have these scruples, overrider."

"I still don't. I just don't want to see him dead before he's use-exhausted. Seems to me you used to be a bit more considered about shit like this, Raquel. What's going on? Someone got you rattled?"

She gave me a fixed little smile. "Fine. Let's have your questions, then. What do you want to know?"

"Primarily, why this piece of shit was so keen to bring me in for questioning. And how his people tracked me down so fast."

"Oh, that much he has already told us. You shouldn't take it personally, Veil. You're just a blip on the scope. He had feelers out for anyone asking questions about our lucky lottery winner and a monitoring algorithm strapped to the traffic systems, something that'd track anyone routing out to where Torres disappeared. As soon as you requested the cab, it rang the bell and he scrambled his team. All of which makes me think you should go check out the place again."

"How do you know I haven't?'"

She peeled me a weary look. "I'm trying to help you here, Veil. You really shouldn't let your personal animosities get in the way."

"Did he give you any kind of why on any of this? All that effort—is he doing it for Sedge or someone else?"

"Yes, on that he's been rather more reticent, I'm afraid. I think there may be some deep conditioning involved. But if there's something you think you know about interrogation that my people don't, I'm sure they'd be eager to learn." Allauca stepped back from Chand, nodded at one of her entourage. "Wake him up."

The muscle stepped forward and produced a chiller spray can, the sort you use to freeze wire fencing so you can snap it apart with your hands. I made him for the overzealous one who'd tried to crowd me in the maté house the night before, but now he looked slightly bored. He held the can a judicious end-of-effect distance out from Chand's sagging head, displaying a casual competence in estimates that said he'd done this a lot. He triggered the can, played the visible white aerosol cone casually across the security consultant's neck and the side of his face. Standing to the side, I still felt the chill from the blast like a cool wind across my skin. Directly in the line of fire, Chand jerked convulsively and came conscious with a yelping cry. Overzealot sniffed and shut off the can, stowed it back in his jacket.

Allauca crouched to eye level with her captive, peering intently. Then she got up again, shot me a strange conspiratorial smile, and nodded me forward.

"There you go, overrider—be my guest."

I moved up close to Chand and gripped his jaw in my hand, tilted it gently up until I could look into his face. His undamaged right eye flickered. On the other side of his face, a thin line of blood ran out from the swollen, clogged-up slit where his left eye socket had been. It painted a single red tear streak down his bruised cheek.

"Do you know who I am?" I asked him.

"Veil . . ." The voice came gusting like a surface breeze whispering over the regolith at canyon's edge. The torn-up mouth twisted into what could almost have been a grin. "The overrider. You're a dead man walking."

"Well, at least I'm still standing up. You want to tell me who you work for?"

He bared what teeth he had left. This time there was no mistaking the grin. "I'm going to fucking kill you now, Veil."

I coughed a laugh, involuntary. "All right."

"You ready to die, overrider?"

"That a religious question? You a 'mama freak, Chand?"

He seemed to gather himself, to steel himself against something I couldn't see. He jerked his jaw free of my grip, drew a hard breath in. I stared down at him, fascinated at the force of will on display.

"Sedge Systems." He spit it out. "Chasma Corriente Nineteen. And *fuck* you on your way down, motherfucker!"

His head sagged again, his breath came hoarsely. Blood dripped from somewhere on his face into his lap. I frowned, glanced at Raquel Allauca.

"You get any of that?"

"Well, Sedge. Obviously. But the rest of it?" She shook her head. "You know, I wonder if we should run this by Decatur."

"Decatur?" It sounded strange the way she'd said it. "Why, what's it going to mean to him?"

"Indulge me, Veil." She looked past my shoulder. "Gustavo, you want to—"

And something electric grabbed me, slammed through me, took my systems down like careless demolition. Snatched out my limbs and kicked them into spastic autonomy, snapped my jaw shut on my tongue, voided my bladder and bowels.

Dropped me twitching and shuddering to the floor.

. . .

THE FIRST HANDFUL of times they hit you with a twitch-gun, you go right out.

But the brain's a tough piece of engineering, just like the rest of you, and it learns. Repeated exposure brings change. Get hit a couple of dozen times with a stun charge—as part of your childhood indentured training, say—and you start to build resistance.

I lay on the floor, roaring nighttime surf dumping out on the sand in my head. I heard the gargantuan scrape of footfalls and, impossibly distant above me, the cardboard-crumpling sound of bass-voiced gods in conversation.

"Get his lenses."

"He doesn't got internals?"

"No, they ripped them out when he got axed from the program." It was Allauca—her trademark somber satisfaction came through loud and clear. "Still got the onboard, but it's blind, deaf, and dumb without an access path."

"Man, if I'd known that . . ."

Rough hand across my face, swiping the lenses away. Twitch reflex of a block down my arm—not even the ghost of actual response in the muscle and bone. Too late, I subbed for 'Ris. Got nothing back.

"Looks like he shit himself."

"Yeah, they always do. What, you think an overrider's going to be different, got no working asshole or something? C'mon, give me a hand here."

Laughter, bass-inflected and racing away from me now. I felt myself lifted brokenly up, then tipped headfirst over the edge of a well.

I fell hurtling into dark.

She calls him Milton, I worked out for myself on the way down. *Never Decatur. Decatur was prearranged, the signal for Gustavo to take me down.*

"Get him cleaned up," was the last thing I heard Allauca say. "Can't have him dying in this state. It's got to look right."

Still falling. And then—

Black water at the bottom, icy cold and deep. I hit like a bomb with its fuse system shorted out, went under, and didn't come back up.

THIRTY-SEVEN

WEIGHTLESS, SHUDDERING COLD, and pain—and something else. *Takes me a moment to get a lock on it, understand what it is.*

Fear.

Hakan?

Memory comes back in unwelcome chunks. The firefight across the hull of Shuriken Gaze. *The mistimed move. The exposure.*

The hammer-blow sniper kill shot out of nowhere. Losing my grip on the hull.

Spinning, tumbling—head over boots over head over boots over head over boots over head over . . .

Red lights across on the heads-up display. My suit, shrilling in my ear— Breach! Breach! Breach! *Violent, ear-stabbing pain as the decompression hits.*

Europa, ghost-lit, striated, and crystalline, whipping up and past, up and past, like something I'm supposed to grab.

I think I even tried.

Sinking into darkness, sinking into shock . . .

Can you hear me, Hakan?

'Ris? Subbing is hard with a throatful of blood. I croak instead. "That you?"

Yes. Her voice is curiously diffident. Were you . . . expecting someone else?

"Out here?" Terror rises winged and screaming with the recollection, the sharp understanding of where I've ended up. Muzzily, I get a choke hold on the fucker's throat, hold him down, and force some calm. "Who the fuck else would be out here with us? It's just you and me, right?"

That is . . . materially so.

"Materially?" I chuckle—try to anyway; it sounds like drains clogging. "You're a fucking battle AI, 'Ris. Get your shit together. This is no time for finding religion, it doesn't help us get out of . . . oh . . ."

There's a silence broken only by the faintest hissing of star static in the coms. Then 'Ris begins again, each word a step through a minefield.

Sometimes, according to research, near-death circumstances can trigger latent religious impulses even in the most hardened materialist mindset.

"That's what this is?" I whisper the question aloud. "It's that bad, is it?"

It has been argued that servicing these impulses may provide some last comfort to the dying despite any previous beliefs held. Some claim to see loved ones who have died before them, some speak with a deity or spirit guide drawn from familiar cultural stock or—

"Yeah. Well, we won't be doing that."

That was my working assessment—that you would prefer—

"No bugshit last-minute plea bargaining for exemption from the drop. Good call." I renew my choke hold on Terror's wiry, slimy writhing neck. I smother his wings. "So what else you got for me in there?"

The NDC protocols specify emotionally supportive companionship to the moment of your death, but within those parameters I have wide latitudes of discretion. I can imitate loved ones from filed recall or spirit guide figures and deities from a wide variety of cultural stock in the general cache, but you have rejected these options explicitly. I can also retrigger and enhance favored childhood memories—

I grimace. "If you can find any."

—or review life milestones and achievement and provide philosophical or metaphysical counterpoint. I can sing lullabies or—

"How about you just lay out the damage for me?"

Brief, almost human hesitation. Then, gently, she tells me:

You are bleeding out. Your suit has self-sealed and repressurized, and I have applied vasoconstrictor nanochemistry where possible, but the damage sustained from the autosniper round is too severe and widespread to staunch without surgical intervention. You have already lost 44.1 percent of your blood, and that figure continues to rise, albeit slowly. We are on a decaying orbital trajectory, which will impact with the surface of Europa in 97.8 hours. But by then you will be dead.

"Yeah, no shit." I try to blink my eyes—the lids are leaden, they feel gummed shut. "Why can't I see anything?"

I have sedated you to manage the pain from your wounds and to prevent excessive levels of unproductive panic. You are functionally comatose at this point.

"But I'm talking to you."

No, you are not. We are communicating through a limited bandwidth internal synaptic link designed specifically for NDC palliative support. You are hallucinating the physical act of speech due to the load levels of neoendorphin in your blood.

"Then I . . . I . . ."

Veil?

Veil!

VEIL!

TINY INSISTENT SCRATCHING at my inner ear. I snapped awake.

'Ris?

Yes. Do not attempt to subvocalize. It is unnecessary and may draw attention.

You came in on the NDC channel? Bad-dream cold sweat falling away as I caught up, remembered the Europa debacle was in my past, remembered I didn't die. *I thought you couldn't do that unless—*

In a very real sense, these are near-death circumstances. Raquel Allau-

ca's associates have twitch-gunned you, and strategic extrapolation suggests they intend to set you up as Sandor Chand's murderer, then kill you as well. Given this, there is enough leeway in my programming to force the protocols.

Right. But . . . is there anything you can do to get us out of this?

Not at present, no. The covered levels they brought you to are transmission-shielded, I have no dataflow access beyond some very antiquated local maintenance systems in the walls. I am working to restore your consciousness and muscular function ahead of their expectations. I may be able to do more later, but as Allauca correctly deduced, I am blind, deaf, and dumb without an access path. Once you come back to full consciousness, even this channel will be swamped with real-world interference. I need your eyes and ears, your explicit instructions.

"Hoy, Gus—look at this shit!" A vast blurry voice crashing across the clarity of the synaptic channel. "Go get Allauca. I think this asshole's coming around already."

"Motherfucker!"

Footfalls, hurriedly receding.

Exaggerate how scrambled you are. Her voice was fading out as gross organic signals from my wake-up came storming aboard, shouting down and squashing out the synaptic channel. *Their ingrained expectations will do the rest. I will try for performance spike capacity. And remember— I am blind. Anything you want me to know, you must subvocalize . . .*

I let my head loll backward. Cracked my eyelids a millimeter and took stock.

Lower. We'd gone lower. There was a low-ceiling loom to the space we were in and dim yellowish light from antique recessed lozenge lamps in the walls. Pump and gauge machinery on one wall and a long meter-width pipe crossing two-thirds of the room on waist-height mountings, dividing the chamber neatly in two, then taking a right angle down into a thick locking collar and the floor. Hinges and secondary locking mechanisms along the middle of the raised section, big splatter tray welded to the floor beneath—looked like some kind of sampling station for exotic effluent. The faint but ever-present background whiff of corrosive chemicals in the blood-warm air.

On the opposite side of the pipe sat Chand, still in his wheelchair. They'd parked me facing him, and by the feel of it I was similarly trussed up. The lack of stench or dampness from my nether regions confirmed my last few memories from before I went out with the twitch-gun blast— they'd stripped me, cleaned me up, put me in fresh trousers before they locked me down. Appearances, it seemed, were important in whatever came next.

A meter off to my left stood Overzealot, looking me over warily. His lenses were going to tell him everything he needed to know about my wakefulness, so I let my eyes slide halfway open and faked a choking cough. He sprang in and shoved a gloved finger brusquely into my mouth, checked on my tongue. I rolled with it, maxed up the cough into a full-body shudder. The chair I was in rocked with the force of it.

"What the fuck are you doing to him?" Allauca in full offended-authority mode. "I told you not to—"

"Looked like he was choking, Ms. Allauca. I'm . . . that's it. We're good." Overzealot braced one hand on my forehead to hold me still, took his fingers out of my mouth. He shook his head. "Never seen anyone come back from the twitch that fast before."

"Yes, well." She pursed her lips. Evidently this was messing up her plans. "Welcome back, Veil."

I made soft, incoherent noises, kept my face slack. Let my head fall forward as if exhausted. They had me in a simple carbon fiber frame seat, flimsy by contrast to Chand's wheelchair but pretty much unbreakable. My bonds were plastic cabling—I tested them gingerly, found very little give. Watching at Allauca's shoulder, Gustavo snorted.

"Yeah, some comeback. Helix-level, huh, Veil? Fucking Black Hatch shit. Look at you now."

I stared down into my lap. I'd read Seb Luppi's data wrong. Allauca hadn't rushed to the Crocus Lux because Decatur had summoned her— she'd come because she had a bug in Decatur's inner sanctum, and that little bug had reported in as soon as I'd shown up.

And I'd missed it.

I'd gone with Gustavo when he came calling, trusting as the next fucking Mars moron voting the straight Mulholland ticket. I'd read him as

Decatur's man, the same way the fuckwit voters somehow always seemed to think Mulholland was theirs. And I'd turned my back on him in Allauca's presence without a second thought. Overrider nothing—I'd fucked up. I *belonged* here, marooned on this shitty buying-its-own-inflated-bugshit planet, drowning in this mess, *tied to this motherfucking chair.*

Rage at my own incompetence sheeted through me, lit the embers of the running-hot within.

"I'm going to fucking kill you, Gus," I slurred, head still down. "That's if Milt doesn't sniff you out first and do it for me."

Gustavo guffawed. "Hear that, Zac? Overrider's going to get me."

Echoed laughter from Overzealot.

"Let's not get too impressed with ourselves just yet," Allauca said sharply. "I want this done right. Milton Decatur thinks Veil's here with Bradbury backing, and I have no reason to think he's wrong. If and when they come sniffing around, this has to look good."

"It's no problem, Ms. Allauca." Overzealot sniffed. "Pressure overload, innit? Wants to torture Mr. Chand, doesn't know how to work the system, screws up the dumping protocol while he's trying to shut it down. Blows the whole place apart, him still in it. That's twenty thousand tons of nanocrete, a hundred thousand liters of slurry, all falling in on itself. Going to take them a week just to dig down and find what's left. By that time, what with the chemicals and the cleanup bugs, all they'll get are dregs."

Allauca sighed. "Well, it's not elegant, but it'll have to do."

I stopped my hasty subvocalizing to 'Ris. Lifted my head with a grogginess that wasn't all that hard to fake.

"Come on, Allauca," I said blurrily. "Wake up and smell the reentry. This isn't going to work, and you know it."

Quick steps across the dark metal floor. Her shadow fell over me. I got my head fully up, met her eyes, bared my teeth at her.

"You might sell this shit to MMP like you did when they came to look for Torres, but I'm Nikki Chakana's spearhead. You got friends in the city; you know all about Chakana. You really think you're going to *brush off* BPD Homicide?"

"Chakana, eh?" Allauca looked thoughtful. "News from the city is that Chakana's got her hands full right now. She's spread thin with the audit. I think it'll be a while before you're missed."

I held down a spasm of panic. "I'm here on audit business, Raquel. You kill me, it's going to make a very big splash, and sooner or later they'll come for you. Local yokels like you don't get to take down a Bradbury homicide detective and walk away. They send out kill squads to settle that shit."

She smiled at me, almost maternal. "Hmm—they do, don't they? And if I'm honest, this would have been a lot better for all concerned if you'd obliged me upstairs and put a bullet in Chand's face. You could have walked away, at least for the time being. This is messier, but you know what? You're *not* a BPD homicide detective, and I think it'll wash."

"Keep telling yourself that." Trying to keep the edge of desperation out of my voice, the suspicion that she was right. "Earth Oversight is driving things now. This whole bury-the-bodies-and-fake-the-files shit is over."

"Somehow I doubt that. See, this is what Torres never understood—the basic mechanics of power on this planet. It's like Russian dolls, Veil, all lined up behind each other. Behind Jeff Havel, Milton; behind Milton, me; Torres wasn't totally stupid, he worked that out. But behind me, there's the regional governor, and behind him, Mulholland. And behind Mulholland, the whole piled-high corporate edifice of Mars. You deal with the doll whose face you can look into. But you never, ever forget that behind that doll is another one, taller and heavier and looking way beyond you to a horizon you haven't even thought about. And if what you bring to the table fogs up that view, then those dolls are going to fall on you hard."

"Like you fell on Torres?"

"Veil, Veil." She spread her hands in good-natured exasperation. "Are you *still* running on that rage and bitterness mix? Still looking for targets? You used to be smarter than this, I swear. I told you to your lenses that I didn't raise a hand against Pavel Torres. Why is that so hard for you to accept?"

I stared back at her, and, oddly, there in her casual lack of animosity I felt the cold dispassionate breath of my own certain death whispering at the nape of my neck. For Raquel Allauca and the Cradle City machine, this wasn't personal or anything close. This was business, this was just safety. Allauca was taking a troublesome piece off the board early, just to be sure.

Wouldn't be the first time for either of us. Back in the bad old IC days, I'd done the same thing for her myself on a few occasions.

I held down a shiver that was equal parts recollection and rage. I buried it. *Hold back the moment, Veil, any way you can.* I jutted my chin at Allauca, stared her down. "If you didn't touch Torres, then tell me what his fucking deal was. What's Chasma Corriente Nineteen? Go on! What difference does it make to you now?"

She paused for a moment. Evidently saw something in my eyes that needed answering. She sighed again.

"You want a bedtime story, do you? You want it to mean something? Fine." She nodded at Gustavo. "Get me a chair. Then go get his guns, they'll have to be found with him. And tell Havel to get the others packing up. Full wipe on everything—like none of us were ever here."

There were more of the skeletal carbon fiber frame chairs like the one I was roped to, gathered in the corner of the chamber like a group of diffident witnesses awaiting a summons. Gustavo hooked one in one hand, brought it over, and set it down facing me a couple of meters away. He gave me a pitying look and headed for the door. Fading footfalls down an iron corridor

I nodded after him. "Havel, eh? Got the whole Ground Out Crew along for the ride, did you?"

She shrugged. "They make useful foot soldiers. I try to keep these things in-house as much as possible."

"You're really not worried he'll spill to Decatur?"

"Not really, no. Havel knows where his best interests lie."

"And Gustavo? What about him? Muscle like that, they're no good for the long game. He'll give something away sooner or later, and when he does, Decatur's going to work out what really happened here. And hang you out to dry."

"You really think so?" Mild inquiry in her voice, as if she were considering it. "I think you're wrong. Jeff Havel and Gustavo both have their limits, but in the end that won't matter. What counts is Milton."

She didn't sit down in the chair. Instead, she went to the big pipe that divided the room, talking to me as she moved.

"You see, Milton Decatur isn't the man he used to be. He's just not that hard-boiled Uplands soak you used to run with anymore. Success and easy living softened him up a while back. And then Ireni took the kids and pretty much broke what was left. These days, he lives the penthouse dream and goes with the flow. He'll be upset you got killed, he might even suspect there's more to it than the cops turn up. But that's as far as he'll chase it, and in the end he will take instructions from me."

She lifted something from the curved surface of the pipe. I felt a chill blow through me as I saw what it was.

"It was the same with Torres," she said, drawing on the heavy black hazmat gloves, carefully tightening each one on up to the elbow. "Milton knew Torres was pitching me a deal, he knew it was supposed to be big. But I told him there was nothing to it, and he let it go."

"You told *me* there was nothing to it, too."

"Not quite." Allauca walked around the end of the pipe where it plunged to the floor, moved up on Chand's slumped and motionless form. "I told you it wasn't viable. There's a difference. Zac, you'd better get this fired up."

Wordless, Overzealot went to the wall and punched instructions into a series of instruments paneled there. Faint tremor and rumbling through the chamber—I thought I saw the raised pipe vibrate.

Allauca raised her voice slightly over the noise. "See, Pavel Torres had the genius idea to try to blackmail Mulholland and the interests he represents. And in his idiot innocence, he thought I'd come in with him on it."

I took another break from subbing into 'Ris's silence. "Blackmail Mulholland? With what?"

"With Chasma Corriente Nineteen. Just like Chand said."

She nodded again at Overzealot, and he worked a new sequence on the controls. The secondary locks on the middle section of the raised pipe hissed and cracked open. The top half of the pipe hinged up, and an eye-watering chemical stink rushed the room. The hinges dropped the raised section to their fullest extent and left a trough of roiling brown fluid on view. Chand twitched in his bindings, started to stir back to consciousness.

Allauca grimaced. "Excuse me a moment."

She got behind the wheelchair, rolled it right up to the pipe, and jammed it there. Chand made moaning noises, tried to raise his head away from the chemical reek. Hard to tell if he'd made it back to fully conscious. Allauca stood at his side, voice pinched hoarse from having to breathe through her mouth.

"How anybody ever thought it was cool to ride down waterfalls of this shit, I'll really never know. Some dumb male thing, I guess."

She grabbed Chand by the back of the head with one gloved hand, forced his upper body forward from the waist, pushed his face down into the slurry.

And Chand was awake after all.

The noise he made going under was animal, all conscious self gone, sheer peeled-back bawling terror and despair in its place. He spasmed violently back against Allauca's grip, came up streaming slurry and smolder from rapidly melting features and eyes already poached blind. Somehow, he seemed to be staring right at me. He howled, just once, from a mouth melting back to teeth and bone as I watched, then Allauca had him with both hands and forced his smoking face back down again. Big greasy bubbles burst around his submerged head as the breath came out of him. I guess he must have breathed the slurry in reflexively, sucked it down in a last agony of confusion and the struggle to live. A massive spasm went through his upper body, a shudder so violent that it nearly shook Allauca loose.

Then, abruptly, Chand was gone.

Allauca held him under a few seconds longer, maybe making sure, maybe just frozen in the grip of what she'd done. It's not easy, whoever you think you are. She met my eyes across the chamber, and I thought something passed between us in the stare, some coded transmission. She raised her eyebrows at me like a confession, like some conspiracy we'd just shared. Slowly, she loosened off. Hauled what was left of the front of Chand's head back up and into the dim dungeon light for inspection.

"There," she said, still a little out of breath. "Look what you did. Revenge of the overrider. Who's not going to believe that?"

THIRTY-EIGHT

ALLAUCA DROPPED THE smoldering ruins of Chand's head and let the rest of his body sag forward against the bindings that held it in the wheelchair. I was glad—it wasn't a vision I was going to forget anytime soon. I coughed on the raw fumes emanating from the slurry pipe trough, tried to blink the tears out of my eyes. Allauca came around the down-pipe end of the assembly and back toward me, unsteady steps, gloved arms at her side. Her voice came squeezed tight in her throat.

"Close it up, Zac."

At the wall, Overzealot hit the control panels again. The hinged section of the pipe wheezed up and over, clanked solidly closed. The knifing reek of the slurry retreated to bearable proportions. Allauca stood in front of me, her eyes marbled wet.

"Feel good?" I asked her quietly.

"Sure." She drew a deep, shaky breath. "You, uh . . . you ever see anything like that before, overrider?"

Through the raised thunder of my pulse, I held her gaze and steadied my voice. "Things like it. Hull breach, explosive decompression. Chemical cargo leaks. Fuel splash."

"But you ever *cause* any of that?"

"Couple of times. What are you trying to prove here, Raquel?"

She gave me an odd smile. Dropped into the chair before me as if the joints in her legs had abruptly failed on her.

"I . . . uh, I could let you go, couldn't I?" The breath gusted out of her as if in a hurry to be gone. "I mean—you give me . . . guarantees. Your much-vaunted word. You walk away from Torres, Sedge, this little Earth Oversight playmate you've lost."

"I don't think that's going to work."

She looked into her lap at the long black hazmat gloves she still wore. "No," she whispered. "Perhaps not."

"It's the adrenaline drop," I told her. "Funny things happen to your feelings on the ride down. Looks to me like Decatur's not the only one who's lost his taste for this shit."

Her gaze snapped up to meet mine. Like she was the one strapped into a chair and sentenced.

"So I really have to fucking do this, do I? Just like the bad old days? You're going to make me kill you? That fucked-up mission-headed hard-wiring they gave you, that thing you try and pacify with your insane levels of client loyalty and personal commitment—you're really going to let it take you to the fucking edge and push you off?"

"It's your decision, Madame Mayor. Don't dress it up like it isn't. We both know what we are, and you can't fight that any better than I can."

"Speak for yourself, Black Hatch man. I haven't—"

"Oh, *give me a fucking break!*" Glad of the chance to let my temper scale and rage, to let go of all the tamped-down tension and calculation. "*What is this?* This bugshit lie you're suddenly spouting about redemption and wisdom and better selves? Take a look at Chand's face, why don't you? *There's* your better self, Madame Mayor, *there's* your fucking redemption. Nobody's changed here—no*body*! Power never changes in the Gash, and that's the face it wears."

Silence. Something cold seemed to settle over her like gossamer transparent 'branegel stock, floating softly down to stick and then tighten over face and form.

"Very poetic," she whispered.

Every spare second I could buy for 'Ris would count. I poured the full force of BV's command psychotechnics into my face and voice. "Why don't you tell me about Chasma Corriente Nineteen."

She coughed up a shaky little laugh. "Really? Now?"

"Burn your bridges, Raquel. Do it. You want to know how being an overrider is? How it works out there? I'll tell you—we do the things we do out in the Big Black because *there is no other way.* There's no way back. There's just the situation you wake up to and what you do to resolve it. So do yourself a favor and tell me too much to let me live. Because from where I'm sitting it looks to me like you don't have the—"

"All right!" A ragged shout in the oppressive low-ceilinged gloom. Abruptly, she was on her feet. Glaring down at me, trembling. "It's Marstech! It's a fucking skin fix! All right? That what you want to die over, Veil? Skintech gone wrong?"

"I don't want to die at all. But I came here to get Madison Madekwe back, and finding her means finding out what happened to Pavel Torres."

"I don't *have* your little Oversight fuck buddy, Veil!" Just as suddenly, her voice dropped. She gestured disgustedly. "And I'm getting tired of telling you I don't know what happened to Torres."

"But he came to you with a blackmail plan, and that was Chasma Corriente."

"Yes." She tugged irritably at one of her gloved hands with the other, working the heavy hazmat material off her fingers. Talking like it could keep her from thinking about what she had to do next. "Iteration Nineteen. Chasma Corriente's a Marstech dermal repair brand back on Earth, has been for a couple of decades now. Major league shit. Coded and tested here, sold at top-rank Marstech brand prices there. It's marketed out of a calistech house called Acropolis Solar, but that's basically just an Earth distribution subsidiary for Sedge. *Skin Solutions Built on Mars.* Except Iteration Nineteen wasn't."

"Wasn't what?"

"Wasn't built on Mars, genius. Wasn't Marstech at all in any real sense."

She finally managed to tug the left glove off and dropped it to the dark alloy floor. Flexed her freed fingers a little, stared morosely at her still-gloved right hand.

"And Torres had proof of that?" I asked.

"Said he did." She gestured again, tiredly now. "He and some of his asshole pals broke into a Sedge Systems storage archive out here on the Field and they stole some samples. Seems someone at Sedge screwed up their lead time for the new iteration, or their budgets maybe. Either way, there wasn't time or money to go through the full dev cycle here on Mars before they went to market back on Earth. So they cut corners. They used code developed on Earth for an early iteration, sent it here, and mocked up some stock in isolation chambers. Stuck the Sedge stamp on it, then shipped it back masquerading as the core samples for the Earth product."

I nodded very slowly, letting it sink it. "Smart. No development run at this end and no remodding expenses to tailor it for Earth when it gets back. Marstech markup at generic cost. Makes you wonder why no one thought of it before."

"Maybe they did, Veil. Isn't that the whole fucking point?" She started the process of working off her other glove. "Brand placement, illusory added value. Isn't that what this whole place has been built on ever since Luthra touched down? The lie that there's something better here, something *beyond*—a place, a way of life, a feeling, a name? Mars! Marstech! A way to scratch the itch that modern life denies."

I took another break from subbing 'Ris. Skinned a fierce grin. "Now who's getting poetic? You missed your calling, Raquel. You should be writing copy for some big-name corporate somewhere."

"You think I'm not? What do you think being mayor of this place is? What do you think Mulholland's real job is? We sell the lie, Veil. We soothe the crowd with what they want to hear, with what it takes to get them back in line and doing what they're told. Prosperity Party? We're a brand like any other. We're the glue that holds the Valley together."

"And there I was thinking you were just a bunch of semicompetent crooks milking the High Frontier for all it's worth."

She smeared me a smile. It made her look oddly hunted. "Laugh all you want, Veil. This whole place is built on myths, and that's what Torres was threatening. Pay up or he brings the whole Mars skintech myth tumbling down."

I nodded, seeing the sense. Every seventh marin made on Mars. And beyond that, maybe shockwaves broad enough to pull down the whole mythic edifice of Marstech and Mars itself

"Did his research, huh?" I said. "Talked to people who knew."

Allauca sneered, suddenly jagged. "What, you mean those posturing Sacranite twats up at the observatory?"

"Tracked me there, did you?"

She dropped the other glove next to its mate. Stared down at it, ignoring me as if I weren't there, talking almost to herself. "He thought Sedge would pay to keep it quiet. Pay to keep their reputation intact. He . . . he fucking thought *Mulholland* would pay."

Mulholland, I reflected, would likely have gifted anyone who even heard about this shit with an AP slug through the back of the head and a shallow grave somewhere up over the Lip.

"You really didn't kill him, Raquel?" Because somehow that seemed to matter to her. And if I was going to get out of this, I needed every millimeter of leverage I could gain.

She shook her head. "I sent him away, told him never to come near me with that shit ever again. And I guess it's probably why someone else killed him. But it wasn't me."

The footfall clatter of Gustavo returning. Overzealot turned toward the sound. Allauca looked up at me, met my gaze almost unwillingly. Hollow stare.

"Time, then," I said softly.

She got up hurriedly, face changing as she turned on the new arrival. Wrapping herself back up in the bleak robes and mask of power, hiding who she'd been with me. "You took your sweet fucking time!"

"Yeah, talking to Havel. He wants to know if—" Gustavo saw the sagging remains of Chand by the pipe. "Oh. You're done already?"

"We had to do something to stave off the boredom! Did you get the hardware?"

"Sure." Gustavo strode toward us, brandishing the VacStar in one fist, the Balustraad in the other. He sniffed and glanced at me. "So, we offing this piece of shit now?"

"No, you are not. I want to be a minimum of two hours gone from here before his vitals go flat. I have an alibi to get up and running at City Hall. And anyway, I'm not—"

There was never going to be a better moment.

Trigger, I subbed.

Sirens erupted from speakers mounted in the roof. Across the wall of instrument paneling, red and amber lights flared and stuttered like machine insanity. My heart leaped at the caged doors of my chest. Somewhere beyond the chamber came the leaden thunder of some system of locks and bolts shifting configuration. Gustavo and Allauca both gaped at the flashing displays, then turned their stares on Overzealot.

"What the fuck did you do?" Gustavo yelled, and Overzealot shook his head, pawed helplessly at the instruments in response.

Spike, I subbed, and came snarling up out of the chair.

Nothing was promised, nothing was sure—but in Blond Vaisutis and the indentured specialism gene labs we trust. There are things patented gene-tweaked flesh and bone will do in an extremity if you treat them right—if you treat them *wrong*—and you can always pay the price later, if later is in the cards. I braced my back and my legs, and I *stood up*. I tore through the plastic wrist bindings like they were licorice lace. I felt the savagery of the move lacerate my flesh down to the bone, flaying off skin and subcute tissue in bloody skeins and a fine red spray until at last—it seemed like forever—the plastic *snapped across*. Blood everywhere now, but the bone beneath the flayed skin held out, and the carbon-reinforced tendons stayed at their posts.

And I was upright and *loose*.

Hard thunder of the pulse in my ears in the wake of the cellular spike. The running-hot raged in me like some blood-deep counterpoint to the sirens' scream. The scene around me seemed to slow down, then jam to a halt and shatter apart in iridescent snapshot collage.

Raquel Allauca, swinging around to face me, mouth distorted around a shocked yell she never got to utter. Gustavo at her side, head turning too late. My left fist, already clenched, already in motion, blood ribboning hot and wet down my wrist and arm. The rings melding, the morphalloy blade sprouting from the line of my knuckles, edges still rippling like heat haze with the molecular shift, like some geometric black demon summoned to my hand. I stabbed upward, in under Allauca's jaw, drove the blade right through tongue and palate and on into the volume of her skull.

"*Boss!*"

Overzealot, voice twisted to a scream. Allauca made a choked gagging sound, maybe in response. Her eyes rolled up in her head, her lips peeled back from gritted teeth, and blood exploded through the gap. Beside her, in the siren-screaming chaos of the room, Gustavo stood rooted in shock, gaping at my rise like I was the pistaco summoned to carry him away.

Still roped to the chair at both shins, still holding Allauca up on the ABdM blade, I hurled myself and the dying woman bodily at him. The three of us went down in a tangle; he lost his hold on the guns. The Balustraad—my ideal choice—skittered away out of easy reach, but the VacStar was too heavy to go far. I eeled desperately across Allauca's still-twitching body—dragging the chair like some triggered mod hound with its jaws sunk in my leg—grabbed the gun. Squirmed around . . .

There!

Overzealot stood at the wall, a weapon pulled, trying for a shot that wouldn't hit Allauca instead of me. His hesitation killed him. I threw out my arm, fired. The VacStar boomed once, deep throated in the high-pitched cacophony of the sirens, and the EVC slug took off his head, shattered the instrument panel behind him, slapped it with a thick wrap of blood and pale-flecked gore. His body fell back against the wall still standing—thin arterial spurt from the ruined neck, it hit the ceiling like a high-pressure hose and rained back down around him. I was already rolling frantically back, looking for Gustavo.

Too late—he landed on me hard, batted my gun hand away with shattering force, punched me in the face. The VacStar went flying. I slashed at him with the push-knife blade, and he scrambled backward to avoid the stroke. Savage grin—he got up in a crouch. I flexed my whole lower body, jackknifed the chair up into his face, and he staggered back screaming, one hand to an eye. I jerked my legs in tight, got the morphalloy blade to my bindings, and sliced myself free. I kicked the chair away in Gustavo's direction, rolled to my feet. Being bound had put some numbness into my limbs, but 'Ris's cellular spike drove it back out, left the muscles fizzing but functional. I charged Gustavo, took him back to the floor.

Give him his due, he dropped the hand that was cupped to his damaged eye—blood welling up in the socket where the end of the chair-leg had gouged him—and tried to fight. I blocked it all, smashed down his guard, chopped him savagely in the throat. He gagged and flopped.

"Did warn you," I heard myself growl—voice grating deep and ugly like some last-legs unoiled machine thrashing its gears. Panting on the words. "Helix level. When Blond Vaisutis builds something, motherfucker, they build it to *win*."

I brought up my left fist, punched the morphalloy blade through his damaged eye and into the brain behind. Blood spritzed out, splattered my hand and face.

I twisted the blade 180 degrees just to be sure.

RUNNING-HOT IS A deep code process, and it takes weeks to ebb, but the cellular spike 'Ris had given me would burn down inside a couple of hundred seconds. At best, I had maybe two minutes of that left.

I got up off Gustavo's corpse, wriggled my fingers in the shutdown configuration for the ABdM knife, and watched the blade melt away, shedding a fine sprinkling of gore across my knuckles as it went. I scooped up my guns, stood blood-streaked and silent a moment in the thunder of my own pulse. Hard to hear anything less local through the endless shriek of the sirens in the roof, but I was loath to have 'Ris shut them off. Wherever Jeff Havel and his cohort were in this warren, any brief, shocked paralysis of purpose they might have suffered would be over by now, and they'd be coming to find out what had happened. The screaming of the maintenance system's alarms was the closest thing to cover I had.

Better go and meet them, then.

I tried on Gustavo's and Allauca's lenses, but both were owner-coded. I dumped them and edged cautiously up to the chamber's exit, VacStar in my right hand, Balustraad in my left. There'd been a heavy security hatch on the doorway once upon a time, but now it lay dehinged and dumped flat in the corridor beyond. I walked over it, saw some kind of tiny scavenger bugs scurry away from its edges in the low light. Two dozen meters beyond, the passage took its first turn. I was about halfway there when the first of Havel's thugs came around the corner at a brisk pace, hands free and any weapons he might own stowed. He saw me in the siren-screaming gloom, nodded and opened his mouth to call out—grasped belatedly that something was wrong and scrabbled for something in his jacket. I sprinted the gap and cannoned into him, hit him in the side of the head with the butt of the VacStar, knocked him into the wall. Flash glance around the corner showed an empty corridor beyond. Overrider snap assessment: this was strictly a messenger boy—*find out what the fuck Allauca is playing at, get this racket shut down!*—and that meant Havel was still unaware.

I crouched where the thug was trying muzzily to get up, dropped the Balustraad to free my left hand, and grabbed him by the throat. Sank fingers in deep enough to tear flesh. I plucked off his lenses with the fingers I could spare from the VacStar in my other hand and stared into the suddenly naked gaze behind. Raised my voice above the screaming alarms.

"What's your name, motherfucker?"

He croaked and flailed, eyes bulging, tried with both hands to unlatch my hold. The cellular spike made welded iron of my arm and grasp. He might as well have tried to break fingers off the statue of Luthra in Landfall Square.

"Last chance," I told him bleakly.

"C-Carlos." Barely audible in the noise from the sirens.

I eased up rather than choke him. "You want to live, Carlos?"

He nodded vigorously, wheezing. Stubble rasping in the raw flesh on my wrist, not yet felt as pain. He was young, barely into Martian teens by the look of it. Terror in his eyes.

"How many of you?" I snapped. "How many did Havel bring?"

"Not—not many. I think—nine . . ."

"Weapons?"

Another jerky nod. "Just—just handguns 'n' shit. Reggie got an AK riot, Havel got that Saville Seeker he always hauls. That's it, man. We didn't come for no war."

"Good."

I hit him repeatedly in the side of the head with the VacStar butt while the sirens screamed. I felt the bone cave in. Dumped him beside the wall, scooped up his lenses from the floor, and crammed them on. They were a poor fit across the bridge of my nose, tight against the sides of my head, and pretty low-end, but they'd do. I blinked up a couple of basic screens. Picked up the Balustraad again and ghosted around the corner in a wary crouch. I'd never had dealings with Havel or the Ground Out Crew before, but if they were all this slack, there was a good chance I was getting out of here in one piece.

'Ris? You getting this?

Loud and clear. It is not a quality portal set, but it is adequate.

Any chance you can call out?

Still not. Schematics attached to the maintenance systems indicate we are nine levels below the surface, and the shielding is extensive, consistent with pre-Lamina-era blackout tech. Clumsy and outdated but still very effective.

Great.

On through the siren-screaming passages. Cozy gold cubist filigree unfolding in my upper left field of vision as 'Ris painted the area schematics across the lenses for me. Exit via a stairwell, not too far off. Two more turns, two more lengths of dimly lit corridor past closed-hatch doorways with nothing going on behind them, but by now the spike was almost done. Nagging fingers of weariness crept in all over my body, harbingers of the coming cellular-level exhaustion. The gouge wounds on my wrists were starting to hurt. My vision fogged briefly at the edges, and I had to stop and lean against the wall, get myself back fully on line.

Even the running-hot was going to struggle with this.

I took a third corner and saw the stairs—a steel frame staircase. Bright well of light filtering down from above and the shifting of shadows.

Kill the sirens a moment, 'Ris.

The screaming in the ceiling evaporated abruptly. Brief, staggering silence, and then sardonic cheers rolled out from above. Voices back and forth, some laughter.

Can you amp that up?

Enhancing.

The soft mumbling flexed in my ears, rinsed through a couple of filter protocols, and came back crystal clear.

". . . 'bout time. How fucking hard can it be to hack a century-old sewage system?'"

"Older'n that. You see that graffiti back in the garage?"

"Guys, don't you know anything? This isn't a fucking waste processor anymore. Got repurposed for Fleet black-site operations back in that mess after Okombi stepped down. They did all that abduction, torture, and shit—grab 'em, fly 'em in, and go to work. Dump the bodies out in the regolith after. No telling what those navy assholes did to the systems back then."

"Still doesn't mean—"

"Hoy!" I hoarsened up my voice to mask it, stepped onto the first of the stairs, looked directly upward. "Little help down here?"

Three or four heads appeared, craning over the railings two floors above. I saw grins below their lenses.

"That you, Carlos? You been *running* or something?"

"Happened, soak? Tell me these City Hall assholes are done and we can—"

I filled the stairwell air with slugs from the Balustraad. Flat whip-crack reports of the shredder load shells, echoing in the tight confines of the well, and screams as they burst on detection of life-sign human warmth. I sprinted up the steel grille stairs in their wake, squeezing the last dregs of the cellular spike for all it was worth.

I reached the top, panting hard, quartering left and right with both guns, trying desperately to cover everything at once.

Saw what the Balustraad shells had done and sagged with relief.

There had been three of Havel's Ground Out Crew waiting on the upper level—or maybe four; it was hard to tell at a glance. Most had been close to the railing when the antipersonnel load erupted, and the damage it had done was massive. Butchered chunks of human being lay in broad pools of blood everywhere, limbs torn off or gone to trailing tasseled ropes of tissue, bone flecks and chunks of gore spilled and splattered like vomit on a Strip Friday night. Amid it all, I saw a skull fragment lying cup-upward like a red-daubed archaeological find dropped by some criminally careless dig team.

Soft sobbing, somewhere close in the quiet. A frantic shuffling.

I cast around, realized abruptly that I'd slumped to sitting on the top step as the relief and the spike crash washed simultaneously through me. *Get up, Hak—this is no fucking time. We're not done here. Still got three or four of these motherfuckers between you and the door.* I puffed out hard, breathed in the musty iron-tanged air, and held it for a moment. Drew thin rags of strength around me, got back on my feet.

The upper level was a higher-ceilinged airy space bearing all the hallmarks of a former storage bay. It was better lit than the corridors below, but not by much. A sparse leaving of crates hulked in gloomy corners, stacked six or seven high, residual trace of some vagary in market trends past or a long-forgotten corporate restructuring that couldn't be bothered with full stock clear-out. Crane cables and hooks dangled from the roof here and there like invitations to suicide or other, less clean-cut torment.

I picked my way past the carnage, following the small human sounds. A little way off, a bloodied female figure was dragging herself painfully toward the shadow and shelter of a crate stack. Whoever she was, she must have caught cover from someone else's body in the blast. She had wounds to body and limbs and a clotted patch of gore seeping through her hair at the top of her head, but most of it looked superficial.

She must have heard the crunch of my footsteps behind her, because she froze for an instant, then frantically redoubled her efforts to crawl away.

I stood over her and tried to summon some focus, tried not to sway. The spike crash tugged insistently in my blood, put veils of dimness over my eyes. It felt like toppling; it felt like sleep. It would have been the easiest thing in the world to sit down beside this woman, pat her on one bloodstained haunch for reassurance, then lie down on the scarred alloy flooring and just . . .

Get your shit together, overrider.

I stowed the Balustraad gun carefully in the small of my back. It seemed to take a long, fumbling time to do it. I drew a deep breath, ground the ABdM rings together on my left hand, and summoned the blade.

'Ris, how about you get the sirens back o—

"Veil!!" Not a voice I knew, but hey, I'm good at making enemies. Assume the worst. "Veil! *You murderous piece of shit!!*"

I swung, stupidly slow with the crash, saw a crouched figure twenty meters back along the line of the crates, a sawn-off-looking weapon leveled. Sinking, sickening plummet in my stomach—he had the drop on me, and I'd spun the wrong way, my head not yet caught up with what I'd just done with my guns. The Balustraad was an itching *lack* in the palm of my curled up left fist, supplanted by a *useless fucking knife blade* I couldn't even throw, and the VacStar was hopelessly far off line, tracking around in my right hand slower than spit falling on Ganymede—

Weird high shriek in the warehouse gloom, the unmistakable cry of a Saville Seeker shell in flight, swerving and homing in on its prelocked target. The slug kicked me in the shoulder as I turned—a miracle; I hung on to the VacStar—spun me staggering around, and I fell over from lack of better options. Some honed instinct made me flatten out on my back next to the injured Ground Out girl. Another whooping cry from the Saville, and she jerked with the impact, started screaming. Jeff Havel had his fancy heritage weapon set to basic heat seek, the stupid fuck.

"Safira!" Panic stricken with realization at what he'd done. *"Safira!!"*

I loosed a couple of shots over the woman's thrashing body, firing blind, rolled clumsily to my feet, and found my target properly. No time to get the Balustraad, which would have wrapped this up *very nicely, thank you.* I leveled the VacStar on Havel's form, fired. Seeping numbness up that arm, and my aim sagged on the shot, missed Havel by meters. He flinched, fiddled with the Seeker, trying, at a guess, to shut down that expensive heat seek option. He'd be done any instant, and at this range . . .

I ran in, shooting wildly.

Missed with every single shot.

Threw up my right arm with the VacStar for a club as I reached him. Havel swung the carbine length of the Saville up to block. Pretentious fucking look-at-me custom-grown walnut stock and all. I let him have the block, lost my gun with the force of it. Punched him savagely in the belly with the ABdM push knife on my left fist. He yelled hoarsely, hurt and outrage in equal measure, and head butted me. I saw it coming, dropped my chin, and took it mostly on the brow. Twisted the knife in his belly, gouged it upward toward his ribs. He screamed. Dropped the barrel end of the Saville and triggered it—I felt the shot tear through my shin and foot, collapsed instantly sideways with the damage it did.

The ABdM blade tugged free of Havel's lacerated guts as I went down. He seemed to feel it, stared grimly at the blood leaking from his belly, and grimaced.

Then, swaying, he lifted the Saville and sighted carefully down it at me where I lay on the ground.

"This is—" He coughed and spit out some blood. "—for Safira, you cunt."

I snarled and tried to get up on my shattered leg.

"Valley marshals! Lay down your weapon!"

This time I knew the voice even through the ampbox distortion. I blinked in disbelief as I heard it and everything seemed to freeze. I stared into Havel's contorted face as he tried, still swaying, fighting the pain in his guts, to work out the new logistics.

"Do it now, motherfucker!"

I husked out a laugh. "I think he means it, Jeff."

Havel's face hardened, and he spun soggily to face the new arrival. He got about halfway around, and harsh staccato gunfire broke across the warehouse gloom. Some magical wind seemed to sweep in and pluck at Havel's clothing, then pick him up and hurl him sideways, drop him in a tangled heap of limbs close enough to me to touch. Eyes nailed wide, Jeff Havel was all checked out and gone.

"Target down! Deploy! Check the stairs!"

They came hurrying past me in the awkward bent-knee shuffle of tactical advance, assault rifles lifted high to the shoulder and canted slightly down. Grim, black-visored faces, slim, jointed carapace armoring that made them look like impossibly svelte ferrite bugs up on hind legs. I counted four, then six, then seven. They moved up on my handiwork by the staircase, poked rifle muzzles and glances cautiously over the railing, then started down.

I rolled my head weakly back the way they'd come.

Saw Sakarian, visored and combat suited, poised there with the Glock Sandman now lowered but still cupped warily in both hands.

He looked so much like his legend, like the whole long line of marshal legends the Uplands are built on, that I started laughing, and then, for all it hurt me everywhere to do it, found with some surprise that I couldn't actually stop.

THIRTY-NINE

THEY WRAPPED MY gun-shot foot and lower leg in a spray-on cast, shot me full of neo-endorphin and service-grade crank, then asked me if I thought I could walk out.

"Out of this busted-ass party?" I cackled, unsteady with the new chemical cocktail coursing through my blood. "Just stand the fuck back and watch me fly."

That got some grins, but nobody liked it enough to let me keep my guns, and they took away my ABdM rings under the polite pretense of crime scene inventory. They left me in the charge of a wiry, leather-faced marshal called Tamang whose avuncular cool wasn't fooling anyone. His hands were empty but they were never very far from one of the weapons stowed in his dusty black combat suit.

No one actually said the words *under arrest* to me; they didn't need to.

Meantime, seemed it'd be a while longer before they'd let me put my banged-up, wrung-out physique where my mouth was and see if I could indeed walk out on my damaged leg. Sakarian was busy downstairs looking at the corpses I'd made, makeshift forensics were being deployed everywhere there was blood, and the tech end of the intrusion squad wanted to jump-start one of the old bulk elevator banks to save us all a long zigzagging climb back to the surface the way they'd come in. Marshal Tamang and I sat on a convenient crate to wait and watched as forensics bagged the last bits and pieces by the stairwell.

"You did all of this yourself?" Tamang was clearly struggling to believe. "From a captive start?"

I shrugged. "Got lucky. Got some pretty serious onboard systems, too. That helped."

Your newfound appreciation humbles me.

You shut up.

"Guess Chand wasn't so lucky."

I saw it again, flash glimpse—the screaming, melting, blinded face in the last breath it grabbed at before Allauca shoved it back down into the slurry and held it there.

"No," I said quietly. "He wasn't."

We sat for a little while in silence. Forensics finished up, ambled off talking among themselves. Tamang made no move to follow them.

"They say you were an overrider once."

"Yeah."

"What made you quit?"

"Long hours, too much overtime. You know how it is."

"Fucking tell me about it," he said feelingly.

Sakarian came back up the stairs, and he didn't look happy. He nodded curtly at Tamang, who scooted down off the crate without comment and headed across the storage bay to where the tech crew was gathered. Sakarian watched him go, let him get well out of earshot before he turned back to me.

"You and I need to talk," he said grimly.

"Sure. Thanks for the intervention, by the way—don't think I said that earlier. How'd you find me so fast?"

He stared at me. "That's not what we've got to talk about, Veil. You killed the mayor of Cradle City down there. Not to mention the rest of your body count. This has got to go to the regional governor at least. You want to tell me what the fuck is going on?"

"I don't know yet."

"You *don't know*?" He jabbed a finger angrily back at the stairs. "Raquel Allauca hasn't been within shooting distance of a provable criminal offense in five years. By Valley standards, she's a model fucking politician. Now suddenly she's dead in the middle of a torture-murder gone wrong and you just happen to be there. That's a big fat fucking coincidence, isn't it?"

"You tell me, Commissioner. You're the cop. I'm just here looking for Madison Madekwe."

"And how's *that* going?" Voice rising now. "Made any progress apart from pissing off the local municipal machine and nearly getting yourself killed? You have even the faintest idea where Madekwe is? If she's alive or dead?"

"No. But I will do soon."

That brought him up short. He glanced around, brought his voice under control again. "You do know you're under arrest, don't you? You noticed that?"

"Yeah. But you're going to let me go."

"Am I? Am I really? What gives you that idea?"

"Oh, I don't know—the fact that about a week ago you and Astrid Gaskell wanted Madekwe protected badly enough to offer me a cryocap ride home to Earth for the service. I don't pretend to know why, but I doubt the situation's changed much in the last few days."

Sakarian sneered. "You were hired to protect her, and look how that turned out."

I said nothing, just looked at him.

"All right," he said finally. "Spill."

"Oh, no. That's not how this works." I banged a hand off the freshly hardened cast on my leg. "I didn't go through all this so I can watch from the sidelines while you and your marshal pals wrap this up and take the credit. I am going *home* on this shit, Sakarian. I am taking that fucking cryocap ride."

He leaned in close, nailed me with a cold-eyed law enforcement stare. "Well, we'd be glad to see the back of you. But right now all I hear is a lot of aging Black Hatch bluster from a recent cripple whose life I just saved. You're not filling me with hope for a happy ending, Veil."

I grinned back at him, fortified with the neo-endorphins and the crank. "Here's what's going to happen, Commissioner. You're going to patch me up with whatever late-code curatives the Marshal Service sick bays are running these days. You're going to give me back my guns and get me some high-spec lenses. And then you're going to put me back in the field, stand back, and let this play out."

I paused for effect.

"And in return, I will get you Madison Madekwe. And Hidalgo."

Something twitched in his face. Too clear a reaction for him not to own it. He backed off, stood a fighting distance back from where I sat.

"Hidalgo?" he asked tightly. "What do you know about that mother-fucker?"

THE NEAREST FULLY staffed Marshals' Office was 300 kilometers south of Cradle City, just outside a slowly dying agri-code town called Shade's Edge. It was a legacy location, predating the Lamina and harking back to a time when experimental coding for a global Martian atmosphere was still something people got paid to do. Back then, Shade's Edge, with its extensively funded R&D parks and eco-code farming, had looked like the strongest contender for a regional capital, and the Marshal Service built accordingly. Nor were they much missed up at Cradle City, whose grubby spaceport environs had already formed a perfect petri dish for contraband supply chaining, semilegal recreational commerce, and low-grade criminality in general.

That differentiation proved crucial.

By the time it dawned on everyone that the Great Global Terraforming Dream was over and all the money gone to chase faster, sexier projects, it was too late for Shade's Edge and for the Marshal Service, too. Cradle City's business model had quietly made it the de facto economic hub for the Shelf Counties—complete with a broadly compromised police department that had about as much intention of hosting the famously incorruptible marshals within the city limits as it did of building a statue to the pistaco outside the station house. Attempts by the service to relocate were vigorously rebuffed. Shade's Edge was home, and that was the way it was going to stay.

"Nice and quiet, though," Tamang mused, perhaps trying to wrap up the history lesson on a positive note. He nodded downward as the Service whirligig banked in the sky over the stark, denuded lines of the town's urban grid. "Show up anywhere in this shithole with an unfamiliar face, the whole town knows it inside ten minutes. Makes it real easy to keep tabs and maintain a perimeter. You can stash protected witnesses here for weeks at a time during testimony and never worry about getting blind-sided."

"Even easier with dead men," Sakarian said sourly, and the others laughed.

We dropped in among dusty nanofab blocks whose spacing spoke volumes about the plans for expansion their architects had once had in place. There was a raw, unfinished look to their lines, basic starter towers denied the later flourishes of the expansion build. The vacant lots between were cultivated in a few places, but most looked like dumping grounds. We soared over a couple of the latter, and I saw reclamation crews look up from behind their dust masks.

The Marshals' Office was distinguished from the surrounding blocks by a completed build that gave it the look of a short, fat half-opened crocus bloom in purplish black. We wafted in over the top of the loosely whorled petal segments and dropped down the space in the center to a pair of broad landing platforms set atop the central structure. Encompassing sense of protection and graceful sheltering power from the petal architecture as it rose up around us; through the cunningly angled gaps between came long bright slices of outside light. I climbed down out of the whirligig onto the landing deck, and it felt like I'd stepped into the throne hall of some mildly agoraphobic god.

Down steel frame steps off the platform and into the upper levels of the central block—here the scale was a lot more human, but the corridors and elevators were sparsely trafficked, and a lot of the office space seemed mothballed. Serious-faced men and women came and went, occasionally in conversation with one another, but the overwhelming sensation was of quiet and space. Once or twice somebody traded laconic greetings or a fist bump with members of Sakarian's incoming team, but mostly we were ignored.

"Kind of quiet around here," I said to Tamang. "Where is everybody?"

He shrugged. "Cuts. Bad all over, what are you going to do?"

They'd thrown together a situation room for Sakarian down on the fifth floor, and by the look of it we had the entire level to ourselves. Most of the insertion team had peeled off and gone their separate ways by the time we got there. In their place, I found a medical team waiting for me with handy scanning equipment and toothy grins.

"This is the guy," Sakarian told them brusquely, slinging his jacket over a chair. "He's banged up, but not too bad. We need him back in circulation soon as. Fix the leg, fix the foot, clean up the wrist damage. Let me know if there's anything else."

"There is something else," I said.

He looked bleakly over at me, *don't push your fucking luck* written all over his face. "And what would that be?"

I'd thought it through on the flight down, figured it was the best chance I was going to get. I didn't like the idea of surgical intervention on the Commissioner's tab; he was for certain going to find some way to include a locational implant in the work. But given that the surgery was going to happen anyway . . .

"I want internal lenses," I told them. "Wetware multichannel coms and full compatibility with my onboard systems. Whatever you guys are fitting as infield standard these days."

The senior medic suddenly looked interested. "What onboard are you running?"

"Osiris System 186.1, tailored suite for Blond Vaisutis Earth."

She nodded. "We got some of the older guys in the field still run Osiris 180s. I'm familiar with the protocols. Earth code usage that old might be a bit arcane, but still. What's the operational tag?"

"All right, *wait*." Sakarian took a couple of steps into the space between the team and me. "I agreed to get you your gear back, Veil, or replace it. No one said anything about internals. We don't have a lot of time to play with here."

"Oh, it wouldn't take long," the medic said blithely. "It's a standard upgrade procedure, really. Got precoded stock for it right here, in store on site. And it's not like we've got anything else much on the slate right now."

We all looked expectantly at Sakarian.

LATER, I SAT in a wheelchair in prep-op, watching news of my own death in amid all the other morsels of random stimulus that pass for journalism in the Gash. It was local coverage, upgraded to the Valley-wide channels, and not on my account.

". . . demise of Mayor Raquel Allauca under undisclosed circumstances comes as a violent shock for the Prosperity Party, whose most senior figure, Valley Governor Boyd Mulholland, is already embroiled in rumors of corruption and recent deadlock with the staff of the visiting Earth Oversight audit committee . . ."

Hopelessly vague aerial footage of Gingrich Field. Cut to shots of a Marshal Service whirligig landing somewhere dusty and irrelevant.

"Marshal Service spokeswoman Indira Khasa would not reveal details of the ongoing investigation but said that Mayor Allauca's remains had been recovered intact, along with several other bodies; among the dead are known local capo Jeffrey Havel, senior gang enforcers Isaac Rosado and Gustavo Bhandari, and a Bradbury-based former overrider named as one Hakan Veil. What part these men played in the mayor's presence at a decommissioned navy black site has yet to be ascertained, but the motive of abduction with a view to political extortion cannot be ruled out."

Cut to a podium fronting the Marshal Service emblem—an improbably noble-looking tiger staring out from a stylized cliff edge across a valley floor dotted with the lights of human habitation. Marshal spokeswoman Indira Khasa stepped up, hard-eyed and straight-backed, looking like she'd rather be almost anywhere else, including a moderate firefight with no backup. Raised journalistic voices chopped at her for attention.

"Can you tell us if Mayor Allauca died accidentally or was murdered?"

"No, I cannot."

"Was this part of an existing investigation into the Prosperity Party's finances?"

"Are you cooperating with Earth Oversight?"

"The Marshal Service exists to enforce the law in all areas of the Valley regardless of terrain or jurisdiction and without prejudice or favor. To the extent that Earth Oversight asks us to fulfill that commitment, we are of course in full cooperation."

"But are you investigating the PP?"

"That's outside the scope of this briefing."

"What about this overrider? Was he accredited to Earth Oversight?"

"Have the Charter terms been breached? Is Earth deploying shock troops now?"

"Did he come here on the shuttle?"

"No." Sharply dismissive. "Hakan Veil was a Valley citizen for seven years. He was a Martian like anyone else."

"*Residency* doesn't make him a Martian! I am DeAres Contado, we are legion, and we demand to know if this overrider—"

"Former overrider."

"—if he has provable ties to Earth interests. Have the marshals considered the possibility that Veil was in fact a deep-cover Earth agent?"

Khasa's lip curled derisively. "We are considering all *reasonable* avenues of investigation."

"Is there any indication—"

The sound dropped out, the screen blanked. I looked across to the doorway and saw Sakarian standing there.

"You all right?" he asked gruffly.

"Not bad for a dead man." I lifted my tissue-welded wrists for inspection, flexed my newly reencased leg, straightening it out from the chair. Faint twinges under the cast amid all the quiet, hot seething. "Cleanup surgery's all done. Bone regrowth protocols went in an hour ago, everybody's very happy, apparently. They tell me I'll be up and about in three days or less. Back from the dead, just like Pachamama's favored son."

"He was nailed to a cross, speared in the side, and had both his legs broken."

I shrugged. "Needed to work on his dodge reflex, then. What do you want, Commissioner?"

"How about a game plan? Okay, you're listed as dead, which gives you some capacity to blindside Hidalgo and whoever else is in the mix. You got this Ucharima woman to chase down and interrogate. Now what about some backup? You turned it down last time, and look how that nearly came out."

I rubbed one itchy, rapidly healing wrist against the other. "Could have been worse."

"Not by much. I don't think you realize how lucky you've been, Veil. Lucky I had juice with the marshals, lucky I put in the call when I figured out where you'd be going. Lucky they picked up rumors about that firefight fuck-up you stumbled into, lucky they were all over Allauca when she made her move. Luck like that doesn't line up twice for anybody."

He didn't know the half of it.

Lucky 'Ris had the operational creativity to use the near-death protocols when she did; lucky she mentioned the maintenance systems in passing and could hack them. Lucky Allauca's goons chose to truss me up only with standard-issue law enforcement plastic, lucky they missed the ABdM knife rings, lucky there weren't more of them in the chamber when the moment came. Lucky Allauca's scheme required me to be found with my guns, lucky Gus brought them right back to us ahead of killing me, lucky Cradle City's organized crime gangs were so fucking amateur-hour slack . . .

Lucky, lucky, lucky.

Just thinking about it still brought me out in a cold sweat.

You can't rely on luck in a crisis, went the veteran comments in BV induction, *but you sure as shit can leverage it when it shows up.*

I cuffed each healing wrist by turn in the opposite hand and rotated it gently, massaging at the itch, trying vainly to stifle the memory of those final gut-sick moments when I stalled Allauca for time, got ready to call on 'Ris and the spike and the maintenance system sirens, and didn't know if any of it would actually work.

"Well, you're lucky or you're dead, Commissioner," I said mildly. "That's how it works."

"You can still give yourself a better edge."

"Let you tag me?" I smiled at him. "Come on, you've had the medics do it already. Tell me you haven't."

In a handful of hours, I'd have the gift of internal, eternal lenses once more, just like back in the day. But right now my gaze was naked, and Sakarian was too seasoned to give much away even to trained eyes. I gave up trying to guess. Even if he hadn't tagged me internally, there were a couple of centuries' worth of other surveillance tech options at his disposal if he wanted them. Truth was, one way or the other, Sakarian already was my backup whether I liked it or not.

"I don't believe in going against the Charter, Veil," he said stiffly. "We're building something here in the Valley, and if we don't honor our founding principles, it all falls apart."

"Sounds like a pretty accurate situation report to me. That last bit, I mean."

As if a pervasive bad smell had just drifted in from the corridor outside. "I don't expect someone like you to understand."

"Someone like me? Sakarian—you work for *Mulholland.*"

"I serve the office, not the man."

"Yeah, well—in case you hadn't noticed, it's been the same man in that office for the last eighteen years."

"Don't be absurd, it's barely been eight."

"Eight Martian. I was talking about *real* years, Sakarian, real *human* years skipping by, not this drawn-out fucking colonial crawl."

We glared at each other for a while. Then he leaned in a fraction, spaced his words hard and slow.

"I have not had you tagged internally without your consent because it is against the law. But we are spending a lot of money and effort on you here, and I want results. Letting you fuck up again and get yourself killed might make me smile, but it isn't going to get me Hidalgo. Or Madekwe. So you bet your balls we're going to be shadowing you, Veil, whether you like it or not. Get used to the idea. You won't see us, and nor will anyone else. But we'll be there. And if you want that cryocap back to Earth—in fact, Veil, if you want *anything* other than a very long stay in pressurized penal containment—then you had better stay focused and deliver."

I nodded. "Good luck."

"What?"

"I thought one of us should say it. Didn't look like it was going to be you."

Silent beat. Then he coughed out the edge of a grudging laugh.

"All right," he said. "Enjoy your surgery, Veil. Enjoy your upgrade. But keep in mind—none of this is free, and the tab is coming."

He walked out, and I watched him go, thoughtful. No surprise that Hidalgo had supplanted Madekwe in Sakarian's concerns; his name was what had really unlocked this deal. Without that magic, I estimated there was a very good chance I'd still be in Marshal Service holding right now. Or worse.

But I would have given a lot to know where Astrid Gaskell and Earth Oversight stood in this. How many other interested parties there might be lurking in the shadows around Nina Ucharima when I got to her. And how safe my Ride Home promise was even if I did somehow manage to pull off this awkwardly long shot.

Someone, I remembered grimly, had promised a Ride Home to Pavel Torres as well.

And look how that came out.

FORTY

SOMEWHERE, AN EIGHT-YEAR-OLD slum kid is screaming, summoning in vain the strongest word magic he knows how to wield against this rising agony he's drenched in.

That hurts, that fucking hurts, no, stop it, STOP IT, you cunts you MOTHERFUCKERS, fuck you, FUCK YOU STOP STOP . . . Strength draining, resistance fading, violence into tears, Stop, that fucking hurts, stop, stop STOP please stop, please, no, no, please, please stop . . . I want my mum, I want my mum, I want . . .

Hush, Hakan. Breathe. Breathe the pain out.

Mum?

I am not your mother. But I can help you more than she can now. Breathe and let the pain go. It will recede, your body will know how to cope.

But it hurts . . . Whimpering, final reserves guttering down to a faint candle-stub glow.

Yes, it hurts. That's because the installation you are currently receiving includes raw neural interface with your hypothalamus and somatosensory cortex. This interferes with your body's ability to interpret pain and renders outside analgesic measures ineffective. But your body and the patented

Blond Vaisutis systems it now connects to are relearning their relationship as we speak. Breathing helps.

Mum, Mum, Mum, Mumumumum—

No. Stop that. She is not here, she cannot help. Listen to me.

Who . . .

The rising question gleams, half mudded over in the pain and confusion like a coin in seabed silt, like the splash of sunlight on the rippling surface of water far, far above. Half asked, awaiting completion, it's the slow unsheathing of a glimmering blade, an edge, a purpose, a path back to self.

Who . . . are you?

I am Osiris. I am here to help.

And, like the magic the taboo words could not ignite, the voice brings a tiny, tiny ebbing in the pain.

I am Osiris, and from now on and forever, I will be with you. I will see through your eyes, I will hear through your ears, I will never sleep. You may call on me at any time, and I will respond and help you in any way I can. For the rest of your life, we will grow together, our survival and purposes will be shared, and we will never be apart.

And now—breathe, breathe, little Hakan, breathe—your pain is fading . . . fading—*is gone.*

And, like the wiping away of fog on a pane of glass, it's done.

THE L-SIP NOKDORM sprawls inland from the curve of Coral Bay, modest duplex units set up in radial ranks around a small central complex. It's a poster-child build for Blond Vaisutis—underclass unfortunates plucked from poverty all over the Australasia catchment, children raised up as valued corporate exponents at the Exmouth facility, next of kin housed here, in state-of-the-art homes, walking distance from one of the finest beaches the coast of Western Australia has to offer; white sand, blue skies, and limpid, protected waters. L-SIP family credits cover living expenses, high-performing children at the facility can earn bonus payments, and there are opportunities for next of kin to take on supplementary work in the environmental monitoring and high-end tourism industries nearby. It's close enough to Exmouth to defeat any accusations of wrenching the indentured young from the embrace of family, far enough away to neatly eliminate any familial influence beyond the symbolic. The buses run twice a month for two-day sleepover visits, if they've been earned, and for extended family bonding time—usually a week or two—every four months.

I step down from the bus into glaring blue brilliance and the pale dust churned up by the younger kids as they charge off into the complex in search of mothers, grandparents, less-well-defined primary carers, even, in the oddest of odd cases, a father. My eyes shade up automatically against the glare. I walk the rows between the duplex units with a loose feeling in my guts, a premonition of what I'm going to find this time.

Still, the sight of the vacant unit hits like a jab punch to the chest.

The plastic easy chairs have been taken in, the barbecue unit is scraped back to shiny clean and tidied away against one off-white wall. Even the stained-glass wind chimes she made are gone. There's a faint remaining whiff of chemical cleanser hanging in the air instead, the last trace of the removal team when they hosed everything down. They'd likely have some-one new moved in by the end of the week.

She fucking did it, I sub numbly. She really fucking walked.

I tried to prepare you for this. The pattern has been emerging for some time now; it is not an uncommon dynamic.

You . . . I swallow hard. Shut up.

I stand there in that synthetic scent of leaving, and the door to the neigh-boring unit cracks open, then swings wide. Lottie comes hesitantly out, stocky, stable grandmotherly Lottie with her weathered ebony features and bleached blond cloud of hair and her deep-set horizon-seeking eyes. Every-thing I have locked down behind a mask of stone I see slosh out onto that face instead. Her mouth tightens up, her nostrils flare, her eyes well up.

"Oh, Hak," she says, wiping her hands on her potter's apron. "Hak, I'm so sorry."

"Hey, Lottie," I say distantly.

"They fought about it, they did. She was yelling at him all week before they left."

"But she left anyway."

Lottie says nothing. She comes and takes my hands in hers. They're cool and slightly damp from the clay she's been working.

"Where'd they go?"

"I don't know, Hak, she wouldn't say. Perth, maybe. It's where he's from. Said he's got work lined up down there."

"Doesn't sound very likely," I say from what still feels like a very long way off. "She's on full credit for at least another three years. They dock her emotional support bonus if she walks, but they can't cut the basic. It's contractual. Even when I qualify and deploy, she gets a Q&D operational pension. Can't see that cunt Dougie working while he's got a revenue stream like that to live off." I reel myself back in a bit, disengage gently from her hands. "How's Max going?"

"He's good. Still got another three days before he has to go back. Arthur's hired a boat, taken him out to the reef."

"Great."

"You could swim out, meet up with them if you like. Arthur'd be happy to see you."

You could certainly use the physical exertion, 'Ris says intimately in my ear. *You are carrying a lot of anger, and if you take it back to the facility undischarged, it'll affect your performance for days.*

"Think I'll pass, thanks, Lottie."

"You want to come in? I was just going to put a brew on."

"Did she say anything?" I ask abruptly, hating how it sounds even as the words fall out of my mouth. "Leave a message?"

Lottie shakes her head. "Your mum and I didn't talk so much since Dougie moved in. She knew I never liked him, never approved. Hard enough to watch the way he treated her, just too much like my Ellie and that fucking bastard Quinn before he . . ." She chugs to a slow halt, hitched up abruptly on the store of her own long-held grief. She looks down, away, blinking. "I mean Dougie never actually hit your mum, you know, but . . ."

I nod. "But he was going to, sooner or later."

"He knew the dorm wardens here wouldn't wear it. And he was scared of you, too, Hak. Especially after that last time."

"You think—if I jumped fence, went after them . . ."

"You can't do that, Hak. You know you can't."

You certainly can't. They'll track you and bring you back before you've gotten halfway to Carnarvon.

Not if you fucking helped me, they wouldn't! Through gritted teeth now, almost actually vocalizing. Deep down in the well of conditioned control, I can feel a pair of tears squeezing free. Not if you were really on my side like you always say you are.

"Hak . . ." Lottie isn't quite backing away from me, but there's clearly something in my face that makes her want to.

Hakan, I am on your side. That is my whole purpose. But at the moment I am also hardwired to turn you in as soon as you run, because that's what anyone on your side right now would do. It's two months' solitary for jumping fence and a year's canceled privileges.

I don't fucking care!

Your mother has made her choice and left you behind. There's an urgency in 'Ris's voice I haven't heard before. What exactly do you think you could do to help her now?

I could fucking kill Dougie!

Silence. For a moment, I think she's stopped talking to me.

That is true, she says finally. And it would address the immediate issue. But not the underlying problem.

"Hak, what are you . . . ?" And finally, there's a harsh snap in Lottie's voice. "Is that your Osiris? What's it telling you?"

The change in her tone brings me back. In all the years I've known Lottie, I can count on one hand the times she's raised her voice to me. I look in her face, and the fear I see there hurts me deeper and keener than any aspect of the tidily emptied unit that used to contain my mother.

"Telling me not to do anything stupid," I say gently. "It's okay, Lottie. I'm not going to jump fence. But I'll take that tea you were going to make."

She comes back to me very slowly, eyes narrowed. She wipes her already mostly clean hands repeatedly on her apron.

"Hate those fuckin things," she says with uncharacteristic venom. "Max hasn't been the same since he got his either."

Max is a few years behind me at the facility—he likely only had the surgery eighteen months or so back. I remember my mother taking it hard the first year or so after mine.

"Lottie, come on. It's just—it's like a PocketPal or a ByteMate. Just—

y'know, internal. We don't have to carry ours around with us. No gear, no devices. It's just better tech."

"Well, it makes me feel like Max doesn't need us anymore. And I think it made your mother feel the same." She sighs. "There, I've said it."

"Lottie . . ."

"Come on, I'll make that brew."

She goes to turn, and I catch her arm. She stops, reluctant, not looking at me. "I shouldn't have said that, Hak. I'm sorry."

"Lottie, you got to tell me. That's not why she left, is it?" My fingers tighten on her arm. "Is it?"

Another sigh, this one soft and edged with pain. She unpins my grip firmly and turns back to look me in the eye.

"No, Hak. That's not why she left. But it didn't help matters."

"What's that mean, Lottie? Didn't help."

"It means that Dougie was saying, over and again, how you didn't need her anymore, you didn't need a mother now you had that fuckin thing in your head. And you didn't give her a lot of ammunition to argue back with."

She pushes through the doorway into the unit she and Arthur have made home. I hear her banging around in the kitchenette.

I stand outside for a long time before I follow her in.

THE BLOND VAISUTIS *lawyer sits a safe distance away from me in the holding cell, lenses on and blacked out, projecting panels of light into the air between us by remote link. It's not much of a barrier, the 'branegel he's writing on, but the cascading filled-form pages and the luminous authorization stamps paint a separation as final as any docking release that ever clanked through the hull of a ship I was on. I crouch coiled on the bunk and watch in silence as it plays out, the air-lock seals already engaged and my BV-assured future falling swiftly away into black.*

"So it's clear to you what compromise has been reached with regard to your installed Osiris capacity?"

It isn't really a question, so I don't bother with an answer. That seems to make him uncomfortable.

"I need you to actively participate in this interview," he reminds me sharply. "We are being recorded, and this needs to look professional on both sides. And frankly, in view of your conduct, I think you have absolutely nothing to be sullen about."

"Is that what you think?" I work hard at not coming off the bunk to chop him repeatedly in the throat just to watch him fall and writhe and strangle to death on the cold cell floor. Whatever subroutines he has running in those expensive black lenses, he ought to ask for his money back. Under any other circumstances, reading my gestalt as sullen *right now would count as a pretty lethal error.*

He scrolls back on the 'gel, highlights a couple of paragraphs for me.

"The terms of your severance are, to say the least, remarkably lenient."

"I keep quiet about your death squad policy aboard Sunrise *in Sapphire, you pay me severance and don't quite throw me to the wolves."*

"Other men and women in your position have faced the death penalty."

"Yeah, but not with a major PR disaster waiting in the wings for Blond Vaisutis and their clients and a propaganda coup for the Sacranites hard on its heels."

He sets his jaw. "That is cheap surmise at best, arrant fantasy at worst, and it is in any case not material to the matter in hand. Do you or do you not understand what will happen to your Osiris capacity?"

"You're going to rip it out," I say tonelessly. "Primary lens function alignment, bone-based cell resonance audio, broad channel connectivity, intuitive interface function, all gone."

"That's right." He seems encouraged by my recital. "Contractually, we cannot permit your continued existence as a fully functional overrider agent following your exit from dedicated Blond Vaisutis service. At the same time, extensive research by our psychology wing has determined that total separation from an Osiris after many years of connection may induce unacceptable levels of psychosis, and we would not want that on our conscience."

I feel myself grin. "On your what?"

His tone sharpens again. "You will still be able to access the bulk of the Osiris systems through appropriately equipped external pickup devices. I hope you realize that."

"Sure." I nod at the ring on his finger. "Like you being allowed to fuck your wife through a shower curtain."

You exaggerate; the loss of fidelity need not be so bad.

You shut up.

"Of course, I haven't met your wife—for all I know, you'd consider that a plus. Maybe she would, too."

"What did you say?"

I can feel the itch to violence in the palms of my hands now. Summary contract termination, exile on Mars, separation from 'Ris. Someone's going to pay for all this, and it might as well be this guy—the urbane corporate face of Blond Vaisutis, bland and dispassionate and utterly unstained by the blood that bubbled and floated in the zero-G corridors of Sunrise in Sapphire like bright red playthings abandoned by thoughtless children.

"What are you, fucking deaf or something?" I lean forward a little. "I said that I can't imagine any halfway decent female wanting you to put your sweaty little paws or your limp skinny dick anywhere near her. Come on, man, she's with you for the paycheck—admit it, why d—"

He lunges at me through the 'branegel and the glowing legal spells he's magicked onto it. The 'gel pops and vanishes, the cell glooms down as the legal magic goes out, and I rise to meet him in the space it leaves, grinning like a skull.

BRIGHT WHITE LIGHT from radiant bars set low in the wall beside the bed. Traces of sticky pain, stabbing with every waking blink, fading rapidly out.

I snapped upright. Awake like sun glare on steel.

Flurries of multicolored light across my vision, diadems and scopes, zooming in and out. I put my hand to my face, looking for the lenses.

Found only my naked, newly open eyes.

I blinked again, snatched a quick thermal map of the room for the sheer unleashed joy of doing it. I felt a tiny butterfly laugh lodge in my throat, had to cough it up. I got out of bed, nearly fell on my face.

You are still suffering poor coordinated motor function from the neural interface surgery. You should avoid gross physical motion for the moment.

'Ris? Jesus fucking Christ, 'Ris, you sound . . .

She sounded crisp and close, the throatiness in her voice raising hairs on the back of my neck for the first time I could remember in years. She sounded like sex for its own heated sake, like death in a good cause, like clarity of purpose without the dragging, piled-up weight of a million dirty little compromises along the way . . .

Yes, I imagine I do. The technology has moved on rather a lot in the last fourteen years. Adjusting your neural responses now.

Like all the broken promises of youth, now mended and renewed; like the dapple of late afternoon sun on Indian Ocean waves.

Like the keen, cold glint of light off a killing blade.

PART III

UNDER PRESSURE

If the situation seems complex, confusing, or conditional, rest assured that really it is not. Your imperative is simple—Save the Ship, at whatever cost. The rest is logistics.

—Blond Vaisutis
Overrider Induction Manual

Which bit's the Ship again?

—Bulkhead graffito

FORTY-ONE

A FULL WEEK and the news of Allauca's violent death had rung the changes at Nina Ucharima's place. There was a hefty new high-security lock on the entry to the block and a burly street escort hanging around in the lobby. He was lensed up and carrying something bulky under his jacket, and he pivoted around like he meant it as I came briskly in through the 'Ris-hacked door without really breaking stride.

"Want to die?" I asked him brightly.

He gaped at the leveled HK, perhaps also at the ghost in the long marshal's duster who held it. I jerked the barrel of the shotgun at him. He shook his head numbly.

"You—but—you're fucking . . . you're *dead*, man!"

"I got better. Lose the lenses."

He twitched them off, held them out to me. I gave him an acid smile. "Listen, it'd be a lot easier to just kill you—don't make that any more attractive than it already is. Drop those, turn around, put your hands on the wall, and lean, *hard*."

Faint scratch-clatter as the lenses fell. He moved slowly, assumed the position.

"Look, man—"

"Harder than that. Touch the wall with your forehead. Good. Now, who's Nina got up there with her? If you lie to me, I will know."

"Nobody." He scrambled to clarify. "I mean, it's just some guy. Don't know him. Greg something."

I snorted. "Grokville Greg?"

"I don't know his fucking name, man." Edge of desperation in his voice that I judged sincere. 'Ris put a gestalt mesh over him, drew the same conclusion. I pushed the muzzle of the deck broom up against his kidney, saw a tremor go through him at the touch.

"Easy. I wanted you dead, you already would be."

I let go of the HK barrel with my left hand, reached inside the borrowed duster for the borrowed twitch-gun, and shot him with it. He went spasming to the floor, bashed his forehead on the wall hard enough to draw blood on the way down. It left a smear. I stowed the twitch-gun, skirted his crumpled form, and went up the stairs at speed. They'd seemed endless in the THC haze of my last visit but turned out to be only ten flights once you were grounded in the here and now. Still—twinges in my recently repaired left shin and ankle by the time I got to the top. Up on the landing outside Nina Ucharima's front door, I paused to get my breath back and listened for activity within.

Two human heat signatures, at least two meters' separation. Room on the left.

That was the living room, right?

Difficult to know, I have limited footage to recall. Nina Ucharima removed your lenses on entry last time you were here, and in the moments before that, you were not visually focused on architectural features.

I suppose you think that's funny.

I think it's accurate.

Just hack this door, will you?

The lock caved to 'Ris's assault, and the door slid noiselessly out of my way. Low lights in the apartment beyond. I slipped inside, amped up the shark mod vision a touch, heard voices ahead of me.

". . . isn't the point, Nina."

"Then what is the point? Easy enough for him to say *hold out here* like nothing's going on—Jeff Havel is *dead* in case you hadn't noticed. The mayor's dead, that asshole overrider is dead, it's starting to look fucking contagious."

"We don't know if that's—"

"Oh, *come on*, Greg!"

I stepped out into the broad living space beyond the entryway. Found the two human heat signatures as promised. Ucharima stood by the window, glowering out, and a slim, pale character sat at a dining table about three meters from her, his discarded lenses and an innocuous gray handgun set out before him in place of crockery. Slim Pale saw me first, long before Ucharima started to turn my way, and maybe I didn't make the HK as obvious as I should have. He surged to his feet, grabbed the gun off the table in a single smooth motion.

"Who the fuck are you? You'd better—"

The HK boomed, echoes off the low ceiling like snappish, short-tempered thunder. The antipersonnel charge caught Slim Pale approximately at chest height, stopped him like a slap, dumped him to the floor behind the table. He didn't move again, and I didn't need to check—the load I was using would have shredded everything in his chest cavity to Bolognese sludge. I was already retargeting, had the deck broom leveled at Nina Ucharima before she could rush me, which, from the look on her face, she was giving some serious thought to doing.

"Just don't, Nina. One fucking moron's enough for today."

She froze in midstep. Looked wide-eyed sideways a moment at the remains of Slim Pale, then got herself back together with remarkable speed.

"Hey, overrider," she said flatly. "Looking good for a dead man."

I nodded. "I bounce back. So Greg there—I'm guessing he's one of Hidalgo's?"

"Pachamama's tits, Veil! Was I really that bad a lay? Most guys would just trash me on GashNet and move on. You know, when I said—"

"Hidalgo," I said evenly. "Don't try to tinsel me on this, Nina, I'm in no fucking mood. Hidalgo—everything you know. I'm already halfway there, so don't fuck me around, just fill in the gaps."

Her mannered, steel calm never cracked, but one of 'Ris's brand-new scope subroutines limned her, ran diagnostics, and flung them up into my top left field of vision to read. Pre-lie tension, physical readiness for violence held on the margins of release, nothing much you could call fear anywhere in the mix.

"Sure," she said. "Ask away."

I tipped the barrel of the deck broom a little, indicating. "Back where you were—over there by the window. Sit down with your back to the glass. Knees up, hands around your legs, and clasp."

She complied slowly, glint-eyed.

"You're not wearing your lenses," she noticed, apparently for the first time. "Nice coat, too. You a marshal now?"

"Not so's you'd notice." I hefted the HK again. "This is what you got to pay attention to, Nina. Heckler & Koch Navy Autoloader, shipboard AP load. I see you unlace those fingers before I tell you to, you're going to lose both legs below the knee. Now—you tell me about Hidalgo. He's from Earth, that much I know. Profession of violence, been here a while, doesn't much like the Gash Hell Condemned. What else?"

She snorted and rolled her eyes as I named the band. Memory flooding back, I guessed. I jiggled the barrel of the deck broom encouragingly.

"What else, Nina?"

She shrugged. "What else? Not a bad fuck, I suppose, when he could keep his mind on the job. Think most of him just wanted to be back on Earth. I really slipped up there, huh? Named him for you, right there in the postcoital."

"Don't beat yourself up, neither of us covered ourselves in glory that night. You dropped the name, and I nearly missed it. That pipe house THC is something else."

"Isn't it."

I tried for brutal. "So were you fucking him before Torres went missing in action or only after?"

She stared me down. "Couple of times before. Not like I was going to wait on Pablo every time he went off to his fucking Sacranite harem. Not that kind of girl, y'know. Hidalgo showed up chasing Pablo, so . . ." Another shrug. "Supposed to be all concerned about him not wanting the

Ride Home, this big fucking mistake he was making, wanted to know if I could talk him around. But in the end he was no different than any other guy. Pinch back your shoulders, cross, uncross your legs a couple of times, they all come around."

Certainly true in your case.

You shut up.

"You know about Chasma Corriente?" I asked her. "Iteration Nineteen?"

"That shit he uncovered out at Gingrich? Yeah, he talked it up some—big fucking scandal, bring down the Marstech corporates. Or blackmail them into making him rich, anyway. Him and that vacuumhead bitch he used to hang with, Tarrant or something."

"Farrant. Julia Farrant."

"Whatever. Dumb cunt was just along for the ride anyhow. I mean, Hidalgo hired them both out of Sedge grunt staff, but it was Pablo he trusted to pull it off."

"Pull what off?"

She rolled her eyes. "What do you think? He had them crack some archive warehouse out on the Field, looking for this Chasma Nineteen shit. I guess he already knew it was there, just needed their personnel codes to make getting in easier."

I thought about what Decatur had told me. Multiple raids on Marstech hot properties, no sign that any of it was getting sold on. Hidalgo either sitting on the proceeds or . . .

Or throwing them away because he didn't give a shit. Because he was looking for something, and that wasn't it. Nothing, maybe, was it, until this—Sedge Systems and the ruin of the Marstech dermals market.

All I lacked now was any understanding of why.

"All right," I said. "So they get into the warehouse, and then what?"

Ucharima snorted. "Then what? Then Pablo and Farrant, fucking idiots, both actually dosed themselves with some of that shit. They thought they were getting a jump on some high-end Marstech skin therapy. Beat the Earth folks to the cookie jar. Of course, then they both came down bad with some reaction or other. Looks like this stuff didn't play too well with whatever the code-flies were spiking us all with that month."

"Did he burn?"

"No. I hear she did." Gloomy satisfaction in Ucharima's tone. "But all Pablo got was a bad fever and some shitty all-over rash for a couple of days. That's what he told me, anyway. All happened a while before he blew into town and looked me up."

"You knew he went to Allauca with this?"

"Yeah. He kept back a sample, something he didn't hand over to Hidalgo when they got out. Took it to Allauca to offer as leverage against Sedge and COLIN."

"He didn't tell her he'd used it on himself?"

She looked at me like I was insane. "Would you? We're talking about Raquel fucking Allauca here."

"And how did your new fuck buddy Hidalgo feel about all this?"

"How do you think? He blew a fucking circuit. He'd promised Pablo he'd rig the Ride Home for him, get him right up there with the Deiss Man, face on all the feeds, reserved cryocap berth, the whole fucking sky. Typical Earth asshole, couldn't believe anyone on Mars wouldn't love a free ticket back to the Mother World."

"Typical," I echoed tonelessly.

"You people, you don't get it, you never did. It may not look like much to you, the Gash and everything in it, not if you've seen oceans and shit, air pressure everywhere, rain whenever you want it." She hugged her knees tighter to her chest. "But it's *ours*. We *belong* to it, like we're never going to belong back on Rock Three. Pablo knew that, knew it in his bones, like the rest of us know it. You can't just step up into another world, one that doesn't know you, doesn't fucking want to know you except as some noble savage or some borderland scum they saw in an immie once. You think Pablo ever would have *belonged* back on Earth? You think any of those sad case lottery-zombie wannabes could ever make a place for themselves back there like the one they already have here in the Valley?"

"I have no idea. So Hidalgo—somehow—has the means to magic a lottery ticket out of thin air, and he was sending Torres home as proof of this fake Marstech processing up at Sedge?"

She nodded, staring over her knees into nothing I could see. "That's the way Pablo told it, yeah."

"And did he ever tell you how Hidalgo managed that? Hack the lottery, drop a particular gene code into the slot?"

"No."

"What about Hidalgo? He ever talk about it?"

She peeled me a sneer. "You think he'd explain that shit to me? I was pure tits and ass, man—bit of Uplands rough for Our Hero from Earth Central."

"Yeah, you certainly seem to pick them."

Her lip curled. "Picked you, didn't I?"

"Prove my point for me, why don't you? So what really happened that night out on the Field? You and Pablo certainly didn't go out there to fuck. Was it the same warehouse he and Farrant cracked for Hidalgo?"

Another nod, short and tight. We were getting close to the core.

"What was the plan?"

"What do you think the fucking plan was?" she asked bitterly. "Allauca kicked him back, told him to drop it or get out of town. But she kept the sample. He was going back for another one, ship out down the Valley and see if he couldn't pull the same thing off somewhere else."

And Hidalgo showed up.

"And Hidalgo showed up?"

She flinched. "How did you know that?"

How 'Ris knew that, I wasn't entirely sure—something out of the gestalt scan and predictive subroutines. Gotta love BV tech. I took it and ran with it.

"It's written all over your face, Nina. Were you the one that called him in?"

"I . . . no. No." Shaking her head minutely, repeatedly. "He came to me. Said he was worried about Pablo, needed one last chance to talk to him again. So . . ."

"You set it up."

"Hidalgo just wanted to talk." There was a quiet desperation in the way she said it. "Pablo wanted to climb up and crack one of the roof hatches, get in that way. He got some tools from Havel, said it would be easy. Hidalgo got there late; Pablo had already gone up. So he went up after him."

"And killed him."

"It was an accident. He said it was an accident. Pablo slipped—I heard voices, they were arguing up there—he went over the edge."

She stared away into the memory again. I let her live with it for a few seconds while I processed the possibilities. It felt grubby and stupid enough to be the Uplands truth, and that's a feeling I've learned the intimate heft of in my fourteen years of exile. Getting so it feels almost normal.

"Must have been awkward," I said casually. "Hidalgo's living organic code evidence, not living anymore, and splattered across Gingrich Field into the bargain."

"Fuck you, Earthman."

"We already did that. So where's the body now? Hidalgo's got it stashed somewhere, right?"

She shook her head, swallowed visibly. "They flushed it into a slurry vent. Didn't want anyone local finding it."

"You really expect me to believe that? Pablo's body has the truth about Chasma Corriente Nineteen written into it at the cellular level, and Hidalgo just *dissolves* the fucking thing? Nina, you're not trying. Where'd they stash him?"

"It's the *truth*, you asshole!" Blinking rapidly. "He said it was no use. I don't know why. Dead was no good; he needed Pablo breathing." She looked up at me, tear sheen in her eyes. "That's what he said. Go ahead and shoot me if you don't believe me, you piece of shit, it won't change what happened. Pablo's fucking *gone*."

I said nothing. Nina Ucharima sniffed hard and wiped the back of her hand across her face twice. She thumbed the underside of both eyes, met my gaze again.

"It's what happened," she said quietly.

I sighed. "All right. So Hidalgo's crew cleaned up the mess, disposed of the body, then you topped up on TNC and went home with your bug-shit cover story? Because otherwise Havel, then Decatur, and then Allauca were all going to find out you'd been in bed with Hidalgo. And getting squeezed to give him up wouldn't be good for your health, now, would it?"

She said nothing.

"Okay, Nina—here's the good news. I don't care. None of that shit matters to me. I'm not working for Decatur or anybody else that matters up this end of the Gash. I just want Hidalgo. You give him to me, I'm gone without a whisper."

She chinned her knees. Teeth lightly gritted; the bitten sound of it came through in her voice. "And if I don't?"

"Then I'm going to tell Decatur he's got a rat in the house and it's you. I do that, I figure he'll save me some trouble and get the same information out of you the hard way."

She looked up at me quickly. "Deck wouldn't do that."

"He wouldn't have much choice, Nina. Allauca and Havel may be down, but that machine they built up at City Hall isn't going to skip a beat. What I hear, Ireni Allauca's coming back up from Bradbury to take the reins now her sister's gone. Bringing the reset and probably some old-school *familia andina* muscle to sort this shit out. Everyone's going to be looking hard for answers and someone to blame."

She turned her gaze away, stared past the table to where Pale Slim's remains lay collapsed and leaking onto her apartment floor.

"Mama Pachamama," she gusted. "What a fucking mess."

"Tell me about it."

Something seemed to kindle in her then, something close enough to anger that 'Ris flagged it for attention in the corner of my eye.

"Men like you," she said slowly. "Men from Earth. You come here, you bitch and moan about what a shithole the Valley is, you act like you're so fucking above it. You move us around like pieces in a game, you fucking *play* us. And then, when the piece doesn't jump the way it should and something goes wrong, people like Pablo die in the mess you make. And for what? The bottom line on some fucking COLIN balance sheet? Marstech added value?"

"Hidalgo didn't tell you, then?"

"Didn't tell me what?"

I put up the barrel of the HK, knew I wouldn't need it now. I slung the shotgun over my shoulder, gestured at her to get up. She got warily to her feet, eyes still on the weapon.

"Didn't tell me what?" she repeated.

"What he's really here for," I said.

FORTY-TWO

IT WAS JUST one link in the chain of bad news and damage I'd been pull-ing on since I got out of surgery back in Shade's Edge, but as links go, it was a big one.

And now it looked like it might cost Hannu Holmstrom his life.

I'd checked the call log for incoming as soon as I woke from surgery, got nothing from the goat god or anyone else. At the time, I thought noth-ing of it. The marshal station was sealed up tight for coms, and before that I'd been buried beneath layers of shielding at Allauca's ex-black-site tor-ture chamber. Even in the unlikely event that Holmstrom had woken early from his exertions on the Earth run, he couldn't have found me if he'd tried. Added to which, down in the deep cellular levels of my condition-ing, the running-hot had been feuding with whatever anesthesia suite Sa-karian's medical crew was using these days, and the resulting clash had left me with a screaming head.

Later on in the day they cracked the cast on my newly healed leg and gave me some pain relief, and I managed to scare up a trip into town. Sa-karian didn't like it, but our uneasy truce was holding and he wasn't pre-

pared to fight about something this minor. He settled for sending me out
with an escort.

"You wear a service duster," he said, throwing the coat at me. "Keep
the collar turned up and stick close to Tamang. Number of marshals
hanging around this town, most likely no one's going to give the pair of
you a second look. If for some reason they do, Tamang, you get him right
back here before it takes."

Tamang nodded equably. "No worries, boss. They see the coat, no
lenses—only one way to read that in Shade's Edge. And it's not like Black
Hatch here is famous anymore. He's had his ninety seconds."

That much was true. Raquel Allauca being dead was still top of the
local newspile, but my own moment in the spotlight had come and gone
like that of any other second-rate Valley thug caught up in heat he couldn't
handle. Brief flash in the public attention–span pan, a nondescript impassive mug shot for a couple of days, degrading rapidly into name-only
mentions on the fringes of the real action. And that was the local level—on
the Valley-wide feeds, the whole Allauca story had already been relegated
to a decaying tail position behind the latest pieces on the Earth audit, the
Bradbury coding scene, and some puff piece about Sundry Charms being
too decant-fried, poor dear, to make his attempt on Wall 101 as planned.

No one gave a shit about me.

We took a marked crawler the five blocks into the Shade's Edge town
center and wandered around the flaky half-tenanted environs of an en-
gagement mall, ostensibly to road test my repaired bones and the internals.

"Take your time," Tamang suggested, and wandered off to look at
some temporarily sponsored art tech exhibit sandwiched between blank-
windowed empty units. "Be right over there."

We're still clean, I take it, I subbed as he walked away.

*According to the reflexive self-assessment routines in my security baf-
fling, yes. And those are deep-wired protocols. If the marshals have tagged
me, it has been done at a systems base level, and given the surgery time involved, I think that unlikely.*

Good enough. Check the call log again.

Three logged calls within the last seventy-two hours, each with a mes-

sage: the Girl Next Door, someone called Tessa Arcane, and Sebastian Luppi.

I frowned. *Nothing from Holmstrom?*

Did you hear me name him in the list?

All right, all right. Maybe he'd ghosted me while I was off-grid in Allauca's dungeon or the marshal station, found no trace, and professional caution had backed him off until such time as I surfaced properly. *Park the messages, find Holmstrom for me, wake him up. Must have been a busy couple of nights at the Dozen Up.*

I waited the habitual few beats, got nothing but deadened silence down the line. I felt the frown ease unhurriedly off my face, felt the settling in its place of an impassive combat mask to cover a rising disquiet.

Grid request returned. It's flagged as an empty line.

That's not possible. Hack a way through.

It took less than a second. A high-pitched screaming came across the connection, barely discernible transmission packets drowning in an ocean of siren intensity to match the shriek the hacked slurry systems had made when I murdered Allauca and her men. The volume and pitch scaled rapidly toward eardrum-shattering proportions, then vanished off a cliff as Osiris pulled the plug.

That, she said redundantly, *was a contamination alert.*

Yes it was.

I stared out across the mall space, gaze defocused on the sparse scattering of figures it held. A ghostly patina of augmentation tools dancing across it all as the new systems tried to work out what I was looking at and why. My eyes ached with lack of custom, and now there was a slow, cold subsidence in the pit of my stomach. Holmstrom's words came back at me—*the minute I hit your playmate Madekwe, it rang bells from here to Pachamama's throne and back. I am talking* major *countermeasures here, Veil. I barely got out ahead of a return spike the size of Supay's dick on Judgment Day.*

And then he'd gone back in.

On my account.

Well, would you look at this, Tess. The overrider himself, in the flesh.

I snapped back to sudden focus.

Tess.

'Ris, give me the playback on Tessa Arcane.

At the Dozen Up Club, her voice had been smoothly textured and urbane. Here it hissed and crackled with anger.

Listen, asshole, I don't know what you asked Hannu to do for you, but he's upstairs in a fucking coma now as a result. You fucking call me as soon as you get this.

Dated three days ago. I gritted my teeth and made the call. The line rang for quite a while before anyone picked up. Tessa Arcane came through hesitant and throaty. If I'd had to guess, I'd say she'd been crying a lot.

"You?" she whispered down the line. "You're dead."

"I got better. Tell me about Hannu."

"He's—I don't fucking *know*, all right? I came in Tuesday morning, found him still upstairs, crashed on the floor. Comatose. Systems peeled back to nothing."

"But he's still alive?"

"Yes, but . . ." The edge of a sob. She started again, calmer. "I called some guys, this cleanup crew Hannu uses sometimes; they got some fluids into him, they got him on a drip. But they said his processing capacity is shut down and baffled at every iterative level—said it's like he's a ship with a hull breach and the systems have locked down all the bulkhead hatches. And there's something in there that's burning him up."

"Tess, that's a viral countermeasures fever. They've got to keep him—"

"I *know* that. Think this is my first fucking time out? Hannu and I go back." She sniffed hard, snorting back tears. "We've got him packed in ice in that coffin capsule he kept from the *Weightless Ecstatic* wreck. But it's not helping. He's stabilized, but he's not improving. He just lies there, and . . . and—it's been three fucking days, and *he's not coming back.*"

The sudden savagery in her voice peaked, choked off. I heard her hitch her breath in.

"What the fuck did you ask him to do?" she husked.

"Tess, listen—"

"No, you listen to me, Mister Earth Motherfucker." Voice not quite steady yet but getting back there. "He was doing you a favor, and I have to believe you're his best chance of coming out of this alive. Where I found him, on the floor upstairs—he'd gashed his scalp open with a circuit stripper, pulled the whole workbench over to get to it. He used the blood to write something on the floor. Just two words. Makes no sense to me, so I figure either it's a message for you or it's some synapse-fried gibberish and we're all shit out of luck."

I pressed my mouth tight. The running-hot surged and splashed inside me, hungry for targets, hungry for release.

"What did it say?"

"It said 'Navy Code,'" she told me flatly. "Mean anything to you?"

I WENT MECHANICALLY through the other two messages, barely half of me listening to what they said. The rest of me was locked onto those two words.

Navy Code.

Hey, overrider—your girl next door here. Missing you, y'know. Get the chance, give me a call back some time—wherever you are. Oh, yeah, and just to tell you—fucking cops came back, made me give a statement about that blowup in the street. Some murder police lieutenant sniffing around, real hard-ass bitch, did not like her at all. I'm telling you, either she's got a thing for you or you did something very bad and she's tracking it. Either way, I think you'd better tread soft for a while when you blow back into town, just in case. 'Kay, that's it. Like the song says—thinking soft suction thoughts of you, overrider. Get back to me soon.

Navy. Code.

Veil? This is Luppi—obviously. Where the fuck were you? I waited all fucking night in that bar. I know we said no electronic contact, but this won't wait. I've been up to Sedge Systems, and you are not going to believe what I dug up. There this enforcer guy they use, name of Chand . . .

Fading out before the full force of what I now knew.

Navy Code.

And if anyone would know Navy Code when it came and bit him in the ass, that someone was Hannu Holmstrom, private hire dreadnought pilot and seasoned long-range code warrior from way back. When he was helming *Weightless Ecstatic II*, he swam in the stuff every waking hour. Half his job was wrangling weaponized protocols and their countermeasure shadows.

Navy fucking Code.

Who'd have the muscle and know-how to swing a VAHM warhead on short notice just to make absolutely sure a troublesome variable got taken off the board?

Who'd have an even chance of taking down a platinum-rated security escort in a public space and getting away clean?

Who could go deep cover for years down in the Valley and not get caught? Fund themselves out of smash and grab on local covert revenue streams, run silent, run deep for as long as the mission required, and meantime set up an exit strategy that short-circuited the lottery system to make space for an emergency ride home?

Fleet Special Operations Command—the navy's hidden hand.

No wonder Hidalgo had run rings around Decatur and his pals. No wonder he took down their kiddy-level fake research scam and walked away with the proceeds. No wonder he broke into Sedge Systems' private stash with impunity. Fleet fought wars and policing actions everywhere across the ecliptic, toppled awkward local governments for a living. Special Operations was its monofil cutting edge, the blade that sliced deep and left you dying before you even saw the blood.

There is a top-down temporary directive in place for all PLA forces in the Crater zone. Gradual's arid voice floated back through my mind. *A standing order to root out all black market activity by any means necessary, immediate court-martial and summary execution of all participants to follow upon detection.*

That's a war footing measure, isn't it?

It is . . . crisis-level management, at a minimum. Not necessarily war but something of a similar gravity, yes.

Hellas knew—maybe not yet as actual fact, but they'd seen the shape of it in their espionage data, and their predictive analysis tech would have laid it out for them, instructed the appropriate local response.

Not a war, no. But for the citizens of the Valley, something almost as much fun.

Fucking navy. They were really going to do it.

Like some bugshit Frocker conspiracy wet dream. Like going back in time to some fuckwit rerun of all the old bad choices ever made.

Kathleen Okombi's nightmare, rising once again in gory grinning splendor from the grave.

UCHARIMA GAPED AT me in the shadowed room. More shock on her face now than when I'd walked through her door unchecked and undead half an hour ago and blew her companion away with the deck broom.

"A *coup*?"

"Yeah, it looks that way. Like I said, you certainly know how to pick 'em."

"But . . ." She'd taken a seat at the table while I talked, put her back to Greg's remains. Now she rested her elbows on the tabletop, pushed the heels of her hands into her eyes as if trying to ram the concept home. "Earth Oversight. They're fucking *auditing*, Veil. They don't need the navy to step in; local law enforcement are cooperating. It's all over the feeds."

"I don't think this has anything to do with COLIN or Earth Oversight. I don't think they know."

"How can they *not know*? It's . . . they—they *own everything*, they run *everything*!"

"Not that simple, Nina. COLIN is commercial—they stick pretty much to what they know and like, which is opening interplanetary markets, making money, and spearheading continued human expansion into space. They're not a government and they mostly don't try to be one, because they know it's something they won't be good at and it doesn't pay. They work *with* government to sustain the model, and Earth Oversight is the bridge, the sheepdog that keeps the flock together."

"Sheepdog?" She blinked. "Isn't that one of those fucking hybrid things they got up at Ares Animalia?"

I sighed. "Doesn't matter. The point is, Earth government owns a lot of different dogs. And they don't all get on or even come to heel that easily when they're called. There are a lot of ways Fleet could get off the leash out here and not much the powers that be back on Earth could or would even want to do about it in the short term. Something like that has a momentum all its own—I've seen it happen before."

"So that's it?" Anger kindling in her eyes. "We sit still and let fucking Earth roll right over us?"

"I hope not." Studiously ignoring that sudden and unwanted *we*. "Fleet taking control of the Gash doesn't get COLIN and the corporates anything but a headache. You can't build long-term markets when the streets are on fire; the money gets too scared. That's why there might be a way to slam the brakes on this before it happens. But you have to give me Hidalgo, and you have to do it now. Where is he?"

She sneered. "You think I'd know? You think I've got a cable tied to his dick or something? Tug on it and he's here? I've seen Hidalgo precisely twice since Pablo died, both times for less than an hour. I've talked to his crew maybe a couple of times more than that. Rest of the last eighteen months—I just sit tight hoping he doesn't run out of luck, get caught, and spill his guts to Allauca's interview boys." She jerked a thumb over her shoulder to where the body of Slim Pale lay. "You want Hidalgo? Nice going—you just shot the only person in the room who might know where he is."

I stared at the corpse I'd made. The glimmerings of an idea like a freshly lit candle in the low-lit room.

"Yeah. On the other hand . . ."

FORTY-THREE

"HOW DO YOU know he'll come?" Sakarian still wanted to know once we'd all set up and sunk back into the shadows.

"I don't," I said patiently. It was ground we'd covered before. "Do you have a better idea?"

Silence on the coms while he chewed that over. A knife-cold wind gusted down the alley outside Ucharima's place. I turned up the collar on my coat, moved closer to the shelter in the angle of the balcony wall. My hands and face felt icy smooth from the weather and the antiscan masking we'd all greased up with before deployment. Overhead in the slice of sky between buildings, the Lamina went through a green and gold coruscation like sparks showering off a dark exotic alloy mass under attack with abrasive tools. It made a faint, pervasive hissing to counterpoint the ghost moan of the wind. Sakarian cleared his throat.

"I just wish we didn't have to trust this skank," he muttered.

"Sakarian, I wish I didn't have to trust *you*. But here we are. She made the call, she'll be fine."

"She flipped that easily, huh?"

"She's got no other choice. It's either play ball with us or I throw her to Decatur and the *familias*. In her place, what would you do?"

He grunted. "Still feels pretty fucking shaky to me."

If that had been the whole truth, he would have had a point. But Sakarian was operating on partial intelligence. He didn't know—because I'd carefully failed to mention it—what had really flipped Nina Ucharima for me: Hidalgo's Earth Navy connection and his plans for the impending coup. Of all the betrayals Ucharima had endured in her Uplands life, evidently that was the one that really stung.

You find patriotism in the strangest places.

And there was a lot I didn't feel the need to share with our esteemed commissioner right now.

"Tell me something, Sakarian," I prodded him. "Since we're waiting. You know if Sedge Systems have prior form with this fake Marstech scam? Did the marshals have any open files on them when you were still working up here?"

"Not as far as I'm aware, no. Why?"

I thought back to the excited message from Luppi, the conversation I'd had with him later the same day. Somehow, he'd managed to stay safe when the wrath of the Cradle City machine descended. Ten years out of the game or not, he was still afloat and undetected, and now was not the time to be blowing his cover. I chose my words with care.

"I'm just wondering about Chand, is all."

"Wondering what?" he asked sharply.

"How well connected he really was, who he knew. See, Sedge kept him on retainer as a corporate security exec, but he wasn't on staff. He was an independent contractor. And according to Decatur, he had prior links to Allauca and the Cradle City machine. All very cozy, and that's probably why Allauca could get hold of him so fast once she knew I was on his trail. She calls him in, he thinks it's for some kind of debrief, turns out she's just welding down the bulkheads, trying to isolate this breach on Chasma Corriente. She knew I'd get to him sooner or later, she knew I'd probably get it out of him."

"She could have just killed you instead."

"Harder to do."

He snorted. "Right—*Don't Wake the Overrider.* I'd completely forgotten how you fought your own way out of that dungeon all alone and then just dropped by to see us at Shade's Edge in your own good time."

"The difference," I said evenly, "is that I was the *unknown* variable. Allauca couldn't get to me as easily as she could to Chand, didn't know whether I'd take a bribe or what it would cost her, and bigger than all of that, she didn't know what backing I might or might not have brought with me from Bradbury. Staunching the leak with Chand was simpler, and the way she played it I was either going to be complicit in his death and in her pocket or dead myself right on top of him. Truth is, she'd probably have killed me later anyway just to be sure. And anyone else standing too close to the proceedings."

"That's a pretty extreme reaction for someone who's spent the last five years trying to sanitize her past."

"She panicked."

"Have that effect on people, do you, Veil?"

I ignored him. "Truth is, I don't really blame her. There's a good chance Sedge will go belly up if this comes out—faking Marstech isn't the sort of thing you want on your investor relations prospectus. They're a gilt-edged heritage outfit, a pillar of everything this place is supposed to stand for. And we're talking about a product type that accounts for a double-figure percentage of all Martian revenue. The fallout doesn't bear thinking about. COLIN investor confidence drops through the floor, the marin crashes, the whole Valley economy goes into a tailspin. That's just for starters. There's no telling what the powers that be might do to keep a lid on this. Mulholland—"

"Incoming." Tamang's voice, laconic across the link. "Late-model crawler, rolling up the frontal approach. Looks like a Tesla or a Gurung-Mithra. Two blocks out."

"All right," Sakarian snapped. "Sniper units, acquire and stand by. The rest of you, silence on coms, stay tight to cover, don't breathe unless you have to. Let's wrap this up clean."

Relief in his tone from dropping the conversation and something concrete to deal with instead. I felt myself grin, not really surprised. Mission flow—wipes everything else out like a drug. I listened to the sniper team sound off with *vehicle acquired*, and for all it was happening around on the far side of the building, my pulse ticked upward with anticipation.

"Crawler stopped," Tamang commented. Sounded like he was chewing gum. "Not our block, boss."

"Stay on them."

"Two targets," said one of the snipers. "One male, one female. Acquired."

Echoes from his colleagues.

"They're propping each other up," said Tamang, and snorted a laugh. "Both fucking faceless on something by the look of it."

The tension on the coms net took a palpable turn downward. I flashed back on my first visit to the neighborhood, stumbling and cooked on THC, arm in arm with Ucharima. Less than two weeks gone, and it felt like a different lifetime. Like things had shaken up inside me, broken apart, and settled into some fresh configuration.

"They're going inside." Tamang again. "Crawler's backing up. Leaving."

Get to Hidalgo, I reminded myself. *Make him give Madekwe up; bring her in for Gaskell. Sideline the static, get it done.*

Go home.

It was suddenly close enough that I could taste it.

"And clear," said Tamang. "That's it, folks; show's over."

Grumbling across the coms. I couldn't blame them—felt my own elevated pulse rate decay and the slow plunge of disappointed combat expectations. The complaints tapered off as Sakarian told his team to shut up and stand down. Things went quiet for a couple of minutes. Moan of the wind, hiss of the Lamina's light show overhead.

I prodded coms again. "Sakarian?"

"Yeah, here. What is it now?"

"Like I was saying about Chand . . ."

He sighed. "Thought we were talking about Mulholland."

"Mulholland's a factor, yes. But our esteemed governor gives the regions a lot of rope; he doesn't much care what they do so long as the tribute rolls in. You know that. Something this big, though? I can see him coming all the way up-Valley like Supay Himself awakened. I can see the

Prosperity Party's goons doing a bit of breach isolation themselves, cleaning house the way they did when COLIN pulled the plug on the last audit back in '95—arrests and disappearances, show trials and shallow graves, all that good shit."

"Those accusations were never proved, Veil. They never found a single solid link back to any official Prosperity Party channel. It was local OC action all the way."

"Sure. And that's a genuine Martian ur-culture circuit board fossil you want to sell me—worth millions. Give me a fucking break, Sakarian. We all know what went down back then, and Allauca was probably standing closer to the action than most. She knew what this Sedge blowout could trigger. She thought Torres had gone away, and then suddenly I show up chasing his ghost. She must have nearly shit herself. And she moved to lock it down any way she could."

He was silent a while.

"Fine. But I don't see why you're still worrying at Chand. If you're right about all this, then it looks to me like he was strictly collateral damage."

"He probably was. But that independent contractor thing is still bugging me. It won't go away. Chand worked a lot of other places in the Gash. If he was any good at what he did, he'd have to have a whole network of connections outside of Sedge and Allauca. I have to wonder what they were." I paused, then dropped the carefully crafted question I'd been working toward. "Is there an angle we've missed here, some fallout coming we still haven't seen? You ever have sight of any open case files on him?"

"No. I told you, I never dealt with Sedge Systems."

I nodded grimly to myself. "Not talking about Sedge. Talking about any other files you might have seen up here. Unrelated shit."

"That either, near as I recall." Another sigh—the weariness behind it came clearly over the coms channel. "I was a marshal for eight years, Veil. That's a lot of files. Lot of individual scumbags to remember."

I stared out across the alley to the dark loom of the opposite block, scanning for movement. I couldn't see any of the marshals deployed there, but we were as strong back here as Tamang's squad out front. Sakarian had come as mob-handed as he could manage without waking CCPD to the intrusion on their turf.

"Lot of scumbags everywhere," I said quietly.

I've been up to Sedge Systems, and you are not going to believe what I dug up. There's this enforcer guy they use, name of Chand . . .

I shivered a little, checked my weapons.

"You flag Astrid Gaskell about any of this yet?" I queried.

"No. Like you were so keen on telling me last week, Earth Oversight are playing out their own hand here and keeping it pretty tight to the chest. No reason we have to hand them every little thing as soon as we dig it up."

"That's very 4Rock4 of you all of a sudden. Liaison not going as smoothly as you'd hoped?"

"It's Earth, Veil. We can all pretend to hold hands and get along, but in the end they're a bunch of ignorant entitled assholes just like anyone else who pitches up from That Mother."

A couple of suppressed sniggers on the line. I glowered out at the other balconies.

"No offense," Sakarian added.

"Oh, don't worry, I wouldn't—"

Tight hiss from someone on the link. "Back alley. Car coming. Looks like an all-terrain."

"Okay, then—this is mine. Right, Commissioner?"

Pause, then his voice came through, reluctant as a dragged corpse. "That is correct. Veil has the con. Go on his command."

"Thank you. Sniper units, sound off."

We went through the power-up as before. The crawler came rumbling up the alley—one of the trad models, built for hard duty, clear lineage back to the Settlement years and the reason ground cars on Mars are called crawlers even when they aren't. My new internals yanked in my view of the vehicle for close assessment, dusted it with readout data like a Luthra's Eve fireworks display.

Land Rover Viking, third generation, 'Ris summarized for me. *Seal-certified status, platinum-level build, surface ready. Optioned for armor, looks like a security forces surplus model. Twenty years old at least. Searching vehicle registry now.*

Skip it. Just find me the weak points in the wear and tear.

Scanning.

"That one of ours?" queried a sniper, evidently reaching similar conclusions.

"Not with that paint job," someone else said.

The crawler came to a halt, and the hatch cracked. Figures spilled out—a telltale economy of motion to the way they deployed. I felt the tension go crawling on my nerves, fizzing for relief. *Navy action,* it said. *Here we go.*

"This is it," I murmured into the coms. "This time for real."

"Three targets," one of the snipers said crisply. "Two male, one female. Spectrabounce indicates concealed weapons. Looks like they're heading in."

I tipped my head around the angle of the balcony wall and reeled in the view. All three figures were clad in nondescript dark gear loose enough to cover a multitude of hardware sins. They faced the back access to Ucharima's building like they expected the Tharsis Prowler on the other side. Kill mode deployed.

The two flanking players were geared up, impassive lower features twinned to anonymity below their lenses. The naked-faced woman between them . . .

—in my head, something cold went *click*—

. . . was Madison Madekwe.

FORTY-FOUR

THE SHOCK HELD me weightless, locked up. Sudden icy grip of shrink wrap around my heart and guts. It took a conscious effort to break free.

Move, overrider!

Duck away and off the balcony, back into the main space of Ucharima's apartment. Check the HK—safety off, load engaged. No clear understanding yet of what I was going to do. Ucharima sat slumped on a lounger bag in the center of the room, cuffed wrists held before her, mouth tabbed neatly shut with an enzyme-locked gag plaster. A marshal sat on a straight-backed chair in front of her, three meters distance, twitch-gun held loosely in his hand. They both looked up.

Nod brusquely, don't stop, just get past them. I slipped out of the apartment door and onto the landing beyond. Cranked my hearing—the faint scuff of careful footfalls ten flights below, starting the climb.

I headed down, made no attempt to shroud the sound of my steps. Just your average apartment dweller, heading out for the evening.

Critical systems, I subbed.

Already running. But your strategy is not clear to m—

Just keep up.

Two flights down and the doors cracked on the commandeered lower-level apartments to my left and right. Hunched black-clad figures peered out behind lenses and the dark glint of their readied weapons. I made a lip-swiping gesture for silence, waved them back inside as I passed.

The footfalls below had paused. They'd heard me coming down, weren't sure what to do, were working out how to play it. They were off balance.

They had the panic-stricken call-in from Ucharima, babbling about a door-down lightning-strike hit on Slim Pale aka Greg by masked figures unknown and a cryptic warning to stay out of Blond Vaisutis affairs. They had a dead channel back from any calls they'd made to Slim Pale for confirmation. And if his gear had any decent high-end medical monitoring options, it would have recorded his death when I put the AP load through his chest. *Something* was wrong, they knew for sure. And stirring Blond Vaisutis into the mix would just add to the confusion. They knew—thought they knew—I was dead, but they'd also know who I used to work for. Allow a leavening of covert ops paranoia in Hidalgo—and if he hadn't owned any of that when he started out, six years of deep cover alone on Mars was pretty fertile soil in which to grow some—and there was no telling what tense conjectures he and his little gang might have arrived at by now. Long story short, Ucharima at risk equaled exposure, and that made it a risk Hidalgo couldn't take.

It was the best I could do for a misdirectional mind fuck on short notice. Felt like a pretty solid example of the form. Just a shame Madison Madekwe had to show up and wreck all my working assumptions.

I came around the angle of the landing to the first-floor stairs, saw them there, paused and listening. I came down toward them without breaking stride.

"Evening, gents. Ma'am."

Wide, disarming grin plastered on, countering the starkly obvious black swipes of the antiscan grease across the rest of my face, the HK held low and back in the folds of my Marshal Service duster.

It'd buy me a heartbeat or two at best . . .

Madekwe made me through the grease. Gaped in disbelief. She hadn't drawn a weapon, and now she wasn't going to have time. The other two were ahead of her, nasty-looking folded-stock FN Herstal carbines already out from under their coats, held low in both hands. Not a weapon you want to see anywhere near the horizontal. Running-hot cranked, I swung the HK up from the folds of my duster, put an AP shell through both men in quick succession. Gruff boom of the shots, blending almost to a single sound in the stairwell. I got them chest height, more or less—they sagged like things abruptly unplugged, tumbled backward down the stairs, lit by the muzzle flash of the deck broom as it tore into them. They hit the halfway landing in a messy tangle of limbs and red leaking bodies. Dull clatter of their dropped weapons, making the trip with them.

The moment stretched to breaking.

"Shots fired," hissed someone over coms.

"Under control," I snapped back. "Hold where you are."

"*Veil?*" Madekwe, looking at me like I'd punched her under the ribs. She'd hacked her hair, I noticed vaguely, taken it back to a tight cornrow helmet with nothing much left over. That and the absence of the gull-wing gear she'd worn for show in Bradbury gave her face a broader, stronger look.

I chinned my throat mike off, cut the marshals out of the loop. "Is there anyone in the car?"

"You're—they killed y—" She flailed around, gaped down at the corpses I'd just made. "You just—"

"*Is there anybody in the fucking car?*"

She shook her head numbly.

"Then let's go." I wagged the shotgun muzzle at her. "We got a minute or less. This place is stacked with Marshal Service door crews. Want to meet them?"

"But . . . you—"

"Jesus fucking Christ, you want to *die*? Got no time to explain. Let's *go!*"

Back down the stairs, past the fallen bodies and the spreading pools of blood—my boots picked it up in passing, left it again in sticky prints on the next flight down. I blipped coms back on.

"This is Veil. I'm coming out the back—one prisoner. Hold fire, scan the periphery for incoming."

"Veil?" Sakarian. "What happened in there, what—"

I killed the link.

We hit the basement level, found the door out into the alley. The Land Rover's armored bulk stood in Lamina flash-lit gloom like something prehistoric about to wake.

Hack this piece of shit, will you?

Done.

The engine rumbled to life; the hatch on our side cracked and sprang open. For appearances, I shoved Madekwe ahead of me with the shotgun. Ushered her into the vehicle, piled in after.

Get us the fuck out of here, 'Ris. Evasive routing, stay speed legal if you can.

I can.

The Land Rover took off backward with a jolt, accelerating on a high turbine whine. Hung a perfectly calibrated braked turn at the next intersection, darted left and away. I picked myself out of the corner it had thrown me into. The marshals woke up in our wake, broke into confused chatter over coms. A lot of shouted questions, none of them very polite.

"Veil? *Veil?!*" Sakarian's furious tones cutting across it all. *"What the red sand fuck are you playing at?"*

I chinned the link again. Feeling the shaky adrenaline grin all over my face like the grease from a cheap printed kebab. "Sorry, Commissioner. Taking the prisoner into temporary protective custody. Can't trust *you* to keep her safe, can I?"

Stillness. From the way the background chatter inked out, I knew he'd cut the general channel. It was all the confirmation I needed.

"Veil?"

"Come *on*, Sakarian—give it up, why don't you?"

I glanced sideways at Madison Madekwe, the ebony sheen of her face in the backwash glow from the instrument panels. Christ and Pachamama, she was gorgeous even in postcombat comedown. I made a gesture at her for quiet, and she nodded tensely. I hit *link* on my internals, saw the Land Rover's coms board light up. Sakarian's voice crashed into the cabin.

"I don't know what the fuck you're talking about, Veil. But you'd better get back here before—"

I cut him off. "Sure. Let me walk you through it, Commissioner. Showing up out at Gingrich Field like that? Big Marshal Service rescue? You covered for it pretty well at the time, but it never did make any sense. You weren't there to rescue me—you were tracking Chand."

"You're paranoid delusional, Veil. That overrider conditioning BV gave you has terminally fucked you up."

"Really? You want to explain this to me, then?" I blinked up the message from Seb Luppi, patched it across, and let it run. *"I've been up to Sedge Systems, and you are not going to believe what I dug up. There's this enforcer guy they use, name of Chand, Sandor Chand. His name crops up all over their area security footprint, so he was an obvious go-to. Couldn't get to see him, of course, they fobbed me off with some low-end PR liaison. But I was sitting there a couple of hours in the visitors' corral while they waited to see if I'd get bored and go away. And you want to know who showed up to see him and got shown through with all due ceremony? Only Commissioner Peter fucking Sakarian in all his ex-marshal glory. You'd have thought he was an ultratripper the way they treated the fucker. I don't kn—"*

Silence opened up like a chasm as I cut the playback. Across the Land Rover cabin in the other seat, Madekwe was still watching me with eyes I couldn't read.

"I don't know who that was talking," Sakarian tried finally. "But—"

"Doesn't matter who was talking. Forget him." An unlooked-for splinter of anger broke my tone. "And I'll fucking kill you if you go near him, that's a promise."

"Veil, I didn't go up to Sedge Systems to see Chand, I—"

"Nice try, Commissioner. But lying's really not your thing. Not twenty minutes ago you said you have no links with Sedge. Now suddenly you do?"

"Right, I lied about that." Urgently now. "Sure. Can you blame me? You think I'm going to share field intelli—"

"Oh, just fucking stop!" The yell was out of my mouth before I realized it. Madekwe shot me a curious look. I cranked my voice back down. "I am so fucking sick of you people and your High Frontier bugshit! You are

corrupt, Sakarian; you're in bed with them all! You and Sedge, you and Chand. You and fucking Mulholland, too, for all I know. You know, Tamang blew you out of the water while we were waiting on your forensics crew, only I didn't make the connection at the time. He *named* Chand, he already knew he was down there. But he hadn't been downstairs with you, so how's that work?"

"I—"

"It works because like everyone else on your team, he'd been briefed. And that brief was to track Sandor Chand and bring him in. Because you were working with Chand to get to Hidalgo. To shut him down, rescue Sedge and salvage the grand fucking myth of Marstech that props up this whole sad little wank fantasy of a world."

Another silence, ugly this time. I could feel his rage on the line.

"That's my home you're talking about, Veil."

"Yeah? Well, enjoy. Meantime, I'm taking Madekwe here back to Gaskell as promised, and then I'm waving the lot of you a fond fucking farewell. See you in the feeds."

I killed the connection with a grimace. At my side, Madekwe stirred. I shot her a raw sideways look. "You stay put, Navy Girl. Don't even think about it. I *will* fucking shoot you."

Tiny quirk at the corner of her mouth. She nodded. "When did you work it out?"

"About three fucking minutes ago when I saw you show up with your hit squad friends. But I should have seen it a long time ago."

"Don't get upset. I do this for a living."

"You shut up."

I slumped in the Land Rover's bucket seat. Stared out over the controls at the sleeping city as 'Ris threaded us nimbly through it. Tall darkened buildings on all sides, stamped with the irregular patterning of the few windows still lit, and between them an oncoming highway I didn't recognize at all.

"Where are we going?" Madekwe asked quietly.

"You want to give me a fucking minute here? I don't know where we're going. I just burned most of my fuel for you back there."

"I did not ask you for that."

"Yeah, well, I didn't ask for armed assholes to show up at my place with a naval warhead. But they did."

This time, I thought she might have flinched. "That wasn't my call."

"Didn't warn me about it either, though, did you?"

"I did not *know*. Hidalgo is—" She cut herself short as the name passed her lips.

"—a deep-cover navy psychopath just like you. Yeah, I got the memo. Killing your way up and down the Gash like back in the Okombi day."

For a split second she looked like I'd slapped her. Then her face hardened, fast as triggered nanocrete surfacing, and she leaned back in the chair, nailed me with a dead-eyed silent stare. I pushed on, chasing the residual itch of rage that the combat on the stairs had left sloshing inside me.

"When did the recruiters show up for you, Madison? Late teens out on the range, was it? When you made tribal council? Or was it right after your Vandever CGA results?"

The gorgeous long-lipped mouth unfastened for a moment. "Been digging, I see."

"Had a friend do it for me. He's dying now, fried with a navy countermeasures viral."

"You blame me for that?"

"Don't change the fucking subject. No, I don't blame you. You weren't the one that asked him to go digging."

Tight silence between us. We seemed somehow to have moved closer to each other across the Land Rover's seats.

"It was the Vandever results," she said.

I nodded. "Right. So you get headhunted by Fleet for their SOC teams, head out for training while everyone thinks you're doing the rich-kid hunter-gatherer jig in the Annexed Ranges. And somewhere along the line, someone over at Fleet High Command decides what the navy could really use is some deep-cover ops in the COLIN Oversight infrastructure. Not quite as glamorous as armored vacuum suits and EVC somewhere out beyond the belt, but hey, you guys go where you're needed, right?"

She leaned in, challenge in her eyes. "You tell me, Veil. You seem to have all the answers."

"If I had all the answers, I'd know why you lied to me about having a teenage daughter. I'd know why you rubbed yourself all over me in that elevator, then ran like some simpering forty-year-old virgin—"

"Dented your overrider ego, did I?"

"Your fucking loss."

"Is that right?"

Abruptly, we were less than arm's length apart across the space between the seats. I could feel her breath on my face, see the gathered weight of her breasts where she leaned forward, the lines of her thighs and hips where she twisted toward me. I felt my own arousal shift treacherously beneath me, combat rush and rage morphing seamlessly into desire held back for far too long. Throat tight, pulse pounding.

Madekwe, breathing hard now. "You aren't going to shoot me, Veil. That's not what you're going to do."

"Come here and say that," I growled.

She lunged across the last of the gap, eyes gone unfocused and liquid dark with the same rising tide of need, hands reaching for me like talons.

Her mouth fastened on mine.

THE LAND ROVER was fitted with two facing benches in the rear of the compartment, and there was a surprising breadth of space on the floor between. Our hunger got us there in fumbling, panting disorder—my right hand forced up under her clothing and trapped there, cupped around one swollen breast, pressing hard so the nipple thrust into my palm. Her hands busy at my waist. Bitelike kisses down my neck. The sway of the Land Rover on a bend toppled us sideways from kneeling, and we collapsed against the benches. I got upright again, shrugged awkwardly out of the big marshal's coat. Dragged my hand free of her clothing again to shake off the right sleeve, spread the folds of the garment hastily across the metal floor.

This is . . . unwise . . .

You shut up!

I got hands on the heavy-weather leggings Madekwe wore, found the seal patch at the crotch, and felt the fabric loosen as it fired. I tugged the leggings down to knee height, exposed hard ebony thighs. Her scent billowed out, washed over me. I let go of the leggings, grasped each thigh, and ran my tongue up the inside of one after the other. It triggered a soft, wanting moan. I crooked her knees and opened her legs as wide as the clothing would allow, sank my face into the heat between. Scrap of soft white cloth blocking my way; I tongued it impatiently aside. Found the coarse tight hair and slippery slick flesh beyond, took it gently into my mouth and sucked.

Madison Madekwe moaned again and redoubled her efforts to get me naked below the waist. My trousers peeled, folded down over my boots. My prick came out in her hand; she worked the shaft up and down, up and down with one tight, callus-roughened hand, all the time jerking at her tunic with the other, trying to get it up and over her head. I slipped my tongue inside her, flickered deep, brought it back out and up, broad and flattened, to the budding nub of her clit. She made a choking sound, floundered, voice softened and throaty.

"No, wait—wait, stop, stop . . ."

Then her back arched, and the words soaked away in groaning like water into arid sand. Her hands abandoned my prick and her recalcitrant clothing, grabbed the back of my head instead. She ground herself hard against my mouth, breath coming tighter and hoarser, gripping my head in both hands as if she could pull me inside herself by sheer force. The tight breaths became hissed words, *yes, yes, like that, yes, oh, yes,* her hands made fists in my hair, and, abruptly, shuddering violently like some engine shaking itself apart, she came.

You are aware that covert ops training includes the use of sex as a tactical option? Madison Madekwe has—

No, really, 'Ris—shut the fuck up now! I mean it! Get lost!

I lifted my face from her thighs, looked along the collapsed sine-curve architecture of her resting body at her face. Eyes hooded almost shut, mouth split and grinning, chest still rising and falling as her panting ebbed. She sensed me watching, roused herself, and lifted everything she was wearing above the waist in one violent cross-armed over-the-head tug. She got about halfway there; the tangled layers of clothing jammed at shoulder height, her profiler cups stayed molded to her breasts, still in function mode. She struggled for a moment, head totally obscured.

"You want to help out a little here?" she asked, muffled.

I got the profiler cups, pressed them into detach mode, and they fell away. Her breasts swung free, hung full and rounded below the broad swimmer's shoulders. I cleared the rest of her clothing from her head, skinned it down her arms as she lowered them. Threw them aside. Madison Madekwe put one long-fingered hand flat on my chest, turned her head like a sniper loosening her neck before she settles. I saw the chopped cornrow ends kissing at her nape like tiny tousle-headed snakes. It's always the little things—I felt a spasm in my aching prick at the sight, and maybe she saw the twitch run through me, too. She reached out and grabbed me, pulled on me hand over hand, as if tugging on a rope.

"I want you inside me," she said shakily. Cupped her cunt in one hand, slid fingers inside herself. "I want you here, Veil. *Right* now. I want to feel you come in me."

I wiped my mouth, grabbed hold of her by the hips, and hauled her in. She parted her cunt for me, leaned back. I slipped inside her, gasping at all the slippery ease and heat, and she thrust up against the bar of my erection, grinning fiercely. I slid one hand under her ass, sense memory of the elevator crashing back in, thrust back at her hard. She cupped an arm under her breasts, gathering them together in the crook, and I came down on them like a starving man, sucked one nipple up into the roof of my mouth.

And down the length of our tight-pressed bodies, I felt her skin burn against mine like the warmth of an Earthside summer sun.

FORTY-FIVE

AND STILL . . .

It took me a full woozy postcoital minute to register that it wasn't just us; the Land Rover had stopped moving, too. I lifted my head from where it was pillowed on Madekwe's chest, raised up, and my deflating cock slipped slickly out of her with the shift. She made a soft regretful sound.

"'Kay, bye-bye."

I sat up in the welter of discarded clothing, listening.

"We're parked," I said.

"Yeah, I noticed." She propped herself up on one elbow beside me. "Thought that was you and your BV-patented battle AI."

"Now who's been doing some digging?"

I tried, too late, to put a grin on it, but it slipped and hung unconvincingly. Her answering smile flickered and went out fast. I sighed.

Put yourself on speaker for a moment.

If you insist.

"Where are we, 'Ris?" Feeling self-conscious speaking to her out loud.

"Currently, we are stationary in the lower levels of a mothballed crawler storage facility on the Cradle City west side." Her voice rinsed through the Land Rover's cabin speakers, a bit low-rez and distant-sounding by comparison to the new internals. "I have engine coolant systems ramped to maximum, bringing down our heat signature to negligible levels. To casual subgeo scans, should anyone attempt them, we will be largely indistinguishable from surrounding vehicles."

Madekwe sat up with a grunt, propped herself casually against one of the benches in a way that made me ache. "Good call. Did you give it that voice?"

"For the time being it is a good call, yes. However, following the interface surgery Veil recently received from Marshal Service medics, it is likely that the marshals can now run predictive modeling of my systems and form a functional map of the evasion strategies I have used. Remaining stationary at a nonterminal destination is the easiest way to short-circuit a predictive routing program. But it is in itself a choice that can in time be predicted. We should not linger here too long." 'Ris paused, picked up again without a change of tone. "Yes, he gave me this voice. Downloaded from Persona Grata Custom, Western Australia franchise. All rights reserved to the estate and descendants of Asia Badawi."

"Never heard of her."

I cleared my throat. "Me either—it was off the rack. Didn't have the money for anything else back then, I was still in training." Abruptly aware of how defensive I sounded. "So—you and Hidalgo. That was a thing, was it?"

"Not anymore."

"But back on Earth, right?"

She nodded. "A long time ago, in training—yes. It's an intense environment, SOC basic. You can end up . . . close. Of course, he wasn't called Hidalgo back then."

"That why they sent you? Close connection?"

"I don't know why they sent me," she said, irritably enough for it to ring true. "When you work long-term covert, you don't get to query your orders. There's no frame for it and usually no time. Maybe it was that, maybe I was the only agent they had who could fit into the audit crew. Does it matter?"

"Was he pleased to see you?"

She gave me a hard look. "You have a problem with what we just did, Veil?"

"No, Madison, I got a problem with what you're planning to do next. Tell me, does Fleet *really* think another navy coup is what this planet needs right now? I mean—regime change? It went *so* fucking well last time, didn't it?"

"If you're talking about Kathleen Okombi, that was a century ago, and this isn't the same thing. It won't b—"

"I'm not just talking about Okombi, I'm talking about Nielsen on Ganymede, Ngata-Maclean in the Bauble Swarm, Chang on Titan. *It is the same thing every fucking time.* Navy covert ops. You storm in, kill anyone who doesn't get on the floor fast enough, then vanish everyone else for black-site holding until they tell you what you want to hear or die refusing. I saw some of your handiwork in the Swarm, Navy Girl, and I met some of the men who did it. I know how it works."

"And what you do is *better?*" Tiny incredulous cough—I tried not to notice the way the ample Earth-born weight of her breasts moved with it. "Slaughter among the stars for the bottom line on some corporate balance sheet? I'm talking to the man who just shot two total strangers dead in cold blood on the stairs of that apartment block back there."

"Friends of yours?"

"No, but—"

"You know your disappearing act at Bradbury Central cost at least three lives, don't you? Two small children and an old man."

She looked away. "I saw the reports. It wasn't planned that way, it— Deiss said . . ." She sighed, still wouldn't look at me. I found myself staring again at the chopped cornrow ends where they kissed at her nape. She shook her head. "These . . . people that Hidalgo works with, the local talent . . . he's making do. They're not much better than some Dakota steppe thugs. He was as shocked as I was when they started shooting into the crowd. I saw his face."

Arrancate, Hidalgo!

The sound bite ghosted through my head. I saw him, too, frozen there, locked in place by what his fuckwit Upland recruits were doing.

"That may be the case. But I don't think you're in any position to lecture me on moral behavior, so how about you don't do it?"

"Oh, what the fuck was I *supposed* to do, Veil?" The sudden spike of exasperation in her voice twitched something in me, in throat and guts and groin. "I was sent here to find Hidalgo and bring him back in. How—"

"You're not working *with* Hidalgo?"

It was an angle that hadn't occurred to me. Mingled anger and fuck lust had me derailed, and that, along with a historic dislike for the navy, had stopped me from considering much beyond immediate appearances.

She sketched me a weary smile. "Not really, no. I mean—yes; at the moment I am cooperating with him, but . . ." Another sigh, heavier this time. "Look, Veil—it's complicated. And I've had very little room for maneuver since I got here. As soon as I arrived, local law enforcement had me handcuffed to *you*—on your own admission, a burned-out Black Hatch killer. Local ties to organized crime and the Crater Chinese. I read the files on you, Veil. You ever seen those? You know what they say about you? How was I going to execute my orders cleanly with you hanging over me at all hours like—like . . . some . . . sleepless fucking corporate *ogbanje*? I had to get rid of you and run dark because how else was I going to do my job?"

"That doesn't explain the elevator."

"You need the elevator *explained* to you?" Whiplash swift, she grabbed my arm. Split her thighs apart and sat back farther against the bench, pulled my hand in and pressed it tight against the damp heated mound of her cunt. "You need *this* explained? *I wanted to fuck you, Veil.* I *still* want to fuck you, and we only just got done. Feel—"

She gasped as I slipped fingers inside her. She pulled harder on my arm, got me close, made an urgent noise in my ear. In my lap, my prick heard it and responded as if trained to the sound. I tightened stealthily but steadily back toward erect. Our mingled fluids had left Madekwe slick and open; it was easy to work my fingers deeper in, rubbing soft circles with the tips. I felt the muscles inside her clench and flutter involuntarily. She put down one hand, palm tensed flat, and by accident or design it brushed my cock, found it taut and yearning upward. She laughed against the soft skin of my neck, wrapped her hand around my shaft, pistoned it gently up and down. Then she slid gracefully sideways and back down into the folds of my coat, hooked my hips with her hands, and pulled my cock into her mouth, shoved her cunt back into my face.

I breathed her in, mingled raw scent of our juices and behind that something at a pheromonal level that would not be denied.

IT TOOK LONGER this time, much longer. The edge was off for both of us, and the confined space between the benches made for some painful barking of legs and arms as the passion built. I got her off eventually with tongue and fingers, but my own end lingered stubbornly out of reach. Operational detail worrying at me, the sudden agenda gap between Hidalgo and Madekwe, what might be built in the space it left . . .

In the end, she gave up, got up in the narrow space, and grinned down at me.

"Marathon man, huh?"

I wiped my mouth, propped myself up. "Hey, I'm getting there."

"You lie down," she said, and helped me comply by straddling me, facing away and sitting on my chest. Neck tilted forward, head tilted fractionally to one side, as if she were making a close study of the cock she had in her hands. Curving spread of her ass and hips over me, a tantalizing distance in front of my face. I craned forward to lick at her, to bite at all the taut dark flesh, and as soon as I moved, so did she. She slid forward with hands on my ankles, wagged her ass at me as if in admonition. Paused and raised up briefly to fit me inside her like a chambered HK round.

And then, without another word, she rode me fast and hard into a climax that lifted my arched back off the floor of the Land Rover as if she'd hit me with a twitch-gun.

"AND NOW WHAT?"

We lay tangled together in the folds of my borrowed Marshal Service coat once more, her broad swimmer's back pressed into my chest, my arms folded loosely across the cushioned swell of her breasts. Her head leaned back into the hollow under my jaw, our legs crooked and tangled up together, feet in a loose clasp.

"Now?" I echoed.

She tilted her head up a fraction against my jaw. "Now that we have thoroughly scratched this itch, Veil. Now that we can focus once more on . . . operational matters."

"That's what this was about?"

"Well, you know." A small shrug. "They teach you two solutions to this kind of problem in basic. One is to blind it away, to make it not matter, to bury it deep under your training and stay mission-focused."

I smiled a little to myself. "Get out of the elevator.

"Exactly. Get out of the elevator while you can still easily do it."

"And the other choice?"

"Higher risk. But it can give you better clarity."

"Okay, let's shoot for that." I shifted our position a little, cupped one dark Earthborn breast with my hand while I could still count on access. "Let's shoot for clarity. You want to tell me where Hidalgo is?"

Another shrug. "Moving around."

"Getting ready to move, you mean. That's why he sent you to deal with Nina, didn't come himself. What's it going to be, storm the governor's mansion like they did with Okombi, put a gun in Mulholland's face?"

"We don't need to do that," she said quietly. "Mulholland called this one down all on his own. Why do you think he had BPD put a minder on me the minute I arrived? We're his escape hatch. If he doesn't deal with us, he's going to drown in all the shit COLIN has on him. He's looking at impeachment proceedings before the month is out, extraordinary judicial review, and then probably the rest of his life up over the Lip in one of his own PPC units."

The irony was manifest. Pressurized penal containment had been a mainstay of Mulholland's administration and reelection campaign— *Harsh Conditions for Bad Hombres,* ran the marketing at the time. *Remove—Isolate—Contain. Clean Up the Valley—Shovel Out the Scum.* Tightened sentencing and a new puritanism in the political discourse provided grist. MG4 and a loose association of investment partners built eight surface-level prisons in a matter of months, a regulation hundred kilometers out from the Lip like a rash of blisters around an infected mouth.

"So he cut a deal," I said tonelessly. "Hang Sedge Systems out to dry over Chasma Nineteen, precipitate a Marstech crisis and a crash, usher in emergency powers, and hand the keys of the kingdom to Fleet. That's his contingency plan. That's what Hidalgo's been working toward all this time?"

She shook her head. "It's not like that. Fleet wants a velvet transition. But this whole thing is on the fly; it always has been."

"That'd explain why it's such a fucking mess, I suppose."

She breathed out hard, like letting something go. Stared away into a corner of the car in silence. I waited.

Finally she twisted around in my arms, pushed herself a little way free, and met my gaze. Trace memory of her breast in the palm of my hand, the loosening of our tangled legs. Serious dark eyes a half meter away. Her breath dusted softly over my face.

"Listen to me, Veil. You're right, it is a mess. It's a fluid situation and very volatile. But I am trying to finesse it. I'm not a commando op, I'm strategic. I don't want a bloodbath any more than you do. If we can hold Sedge over COLIN's head behind the scenes, then they will cave in and Fleet can take over without a fuss." She hesitated, hung from the moment, and then she jumped. "That's what I'm working toward, and I could use at least one person less to worry about at my back right now. Can we call this a truce?"

I shrugged. "I'd call it afterglow, but okay, yeah—truce." *Until I can figure out how to get you back to Astrid Gaskell in one piece, anyway.* "You want to lay it out for me, then? How we ended up here? Words of one syllable?"

She closed her eyes briefly. Opened them wide again like someone shattered trying to stay awake.

"Words of one syllable, right. You remember the aborted COLIN audit in '95?"

"Everyone here does."

She nodded. "Yes, well, Hidalgo was on loan to COLIN back then, along with Deiss and eight others. Two SOC teams seconded for covert insertion ahead of the audit date. Their orders were to bed in and dig for actionable evidence against the regime. Then someone back on Earth leaked the audit plan to Mulholland, he called in some long-standing favors, and before you know it, COLIN axed the whole thing. Maybe that was Mulholland's influence, too, maybe Earth Oversight just decided to cut their losses and put it all on hold. Either way, Hidalgo and Deiss lost half their team overnight when Mulholland's goons brought the crackdown. The rest of them went to ground, ran silent, refused to come in even when Fleet finally got a recovery mandate and came looking for them."

"You can see their point."

"Yes, I can. It was a fatal breach of trust. Hidalgo and what was left of the team recoiled. They went looking for a safer way home. They backed up through their evidence list, found an easy mark—some fake research scam or other; he didn't tell me much—and they looted it for a war chest. Then Deiss took what he needed and infiltrated Vector Red. He sold himself to them as a walking, talking paradigm shift, New Code, New Face, regenerate the Ride Home as a brand. He used that as a platform, and he built an emergency exit for his team in the new protocols, buried backdoor codes to get everybody back to Earth as lottery winners and still undercover."

"Built himself quite a little career in the process, too."

"It's what he was trained for. Deep-cover foreign market intrusion, parasitic takeover, and protocol subversion. Learn the local culture, map the social dynamics, apply templates for maximal effect. It's what SOC used on Titan. We hollowed out three of the five principal investor keiretsus and then just pushed the whole thing over. This would have been much smaller, much easier."

"I'm sure. If a venal piece of shit like Mulholland can surf the wave, keep the frontier dancing to his tune, how hard can it be? But since Hidalgo and Deiss are still here, I have to assume something went wrong."

She smiled. "No, Veil. Something—finally—went *right*."

"Sedge Systems and their dirty laundry."

"That's right. Hidalgo cracked the Marstech facade, found his leverage and the perfect means to get the evidence home. Only he wasn't doing it for COLIN anymore. They burned that bridge when they left him high and dry back in '95. He wanted payback, and payback was handing the evidence to Fleet instead."

"Who then use it to blackmail COLIN into compliance and engineer a seamless transition to a soft martial law dictatorship." I grunted. "That's payback, all right. Tear down the temple, kick out the moneylenders, fuck 'em all up. Very Pachamama's End of Days, that. Very Sacranite Winds of Change, too, come to think of it. I guess everybody loves a seismic shift—until it's *your* kids getting shot down in the street for breaking curfew, of course."

She blinked at me. "What?"

"Doesn't matter. Just something I saw happen in the Swarm. So now that Hidalgo's lost his living evidence leverage over COLIN, what's he planning to do instead? What are *you* planning to do?"

She stared off into the corner of the crawler, maybe looking at the soft glow of the dashboard displays.

"I don't know," she said simply. "Something's snapped in Hidalgo. I don't know him anymore. Maybe it was the betrayal, maybe just too long undercover with a price on his head. I've watched him these last few days, I've seen what he's become. He's . . . clenched. He's hanging on to operational matters like some kind of comfort blanket, and only by his fingernails. This fucking valley has set its teeth in him."

"Stay here long enough, it'll do that to you."

"Six years, Veil." The way she said it sounded almost like a plea. "Six years hiding out, ducking and running, shifting operations, just *staying alive* out here. And digging, all the time digging for something to bring the house down on Mulholland and COLIN both. I think it's all he's got left."

"Try fourteen years and change," I said quietly.

"I don't—" She shook her head. "I've tried to talk him down. He just wants the Valley to burn, he doesn't care how. He's talking full navy crackdown, troops deployed, and blood in the streets. Chasma Corriente is exactly the detonator he's been looking for all this time, and he'll use it any way he can."

"Skin systems." I nodded drearily. "Every seventh marin made on Mars. And Sedge Systems is an old-school heritage outfit, synonymous with Marstech glam, repository of High Frontier ideals, so beyond reproach it brings tears to your fucking eyes. Except suddenly they're not. Suddenly they're exposed as lying, faking fucks, and for who knows how long. Sedge goes down, most likely the whole skin-tech sector goes down with them."

"Yes. Not to mention the share value of every company associated with Sedge and probably every other heritage company operating in the Valley. You begin to see what a bargaining chip the proof of this would be."

"I begin to see why COLIN shot over here with a second audit like their collective ass was on fire. They want to shut this down before it gets started."

"Of course. The audit is damage control, nothing more. Word must have gotten out, most likely a distress flare of some sort from Sedge after the break-in. COLIN will seek to institute proceedings against the regime, indict Mulholland and some few dozen others, frame everything as a political issue, and hide the economics of it behind a curtain of prosecutions for corruption. They put in a caretaker governor general pending new elections once the show trials are done and the sentences handed down. That's probably why Tekele's here at the helm; he's got the profile for it."

"And the Marstech industry never skips a beat."

"Right."

"But that's not what Fleet wants."

She hesitated. "What Fleet wants—it's pretty inappropriate me having that conversation with you, Veil."

"Inappropriate?" I gestured lavishly at our stained and languid bodies, the lovers' tangle our feet and lower legs were still wrapped in. "Right."

She barked a laugh, involuntary. Grew instantly solemn again, like a child called out on dizzy behavior. "I don't know what the game plan is, Veil, because right now there isn't one. Like I told you, my brief was find Hidalgo quietly and bring him in. I thought that would include the Sedge evidence and we'd have the bargaining power to face COLIN down. They'd give us control, and we wouldn't crash their markets. Nobody gets hurt."

"That'd be a first."

She stared at me. "I already told you, Veil, I don't want this turning bloody any more than you. It's not in anyone's interests. We're not the fucking Chinese, you know."

"But you are in direct competition with them. That's what this is about for Fleet, isn't it? Navy moves down from the Wells garrison in force, installs a military governor and enacts martial law, and ramps up the barriers between Hellas and here. Crank up a bit of brinkmanship, draw some lines in the sand."

"That is above my pay grade. I simply do not know what Fleet will do. But you know, Veil, we're not the ones throwing strategic nukes around out beyond the belt. It's not us talking like an empire on the make, telling the Ceres Mining Collective *We Are a Big Power and You Are Small.* And last time I checked, it wasn't us that dropped a full military deployment on Io and called it *an internal matter.*"

"After what your people did in the Swarm, you'll forgive me if I struggle to see a lot of difference in the operational approach."

Her legs withdrew abruptly from the clasp with mine. She folded them sideways under her, shins like a sudden barrier against me. Her stare grew narrow and evaluative. I felt the last of the afterglow shrivel and die.

"I thought we had a truce," she said coldly.

"We do. But it's a decaying orbit, Ms. Madekwe, and you know it. Sooner or later, circumstance is going to force this one, and our truce is going to burn up on reentry."

"So. You plan to bring me back to Astrid Gaskell after all."

I cursed my own loose tongue, my loss of cool with Sakarian over coms. "That was the plan, yes. I do that, I get to go home. Now?" I spread my hands. "Like you said, it's a fluid situation. If Fleet want to spot me a cryocap back to Earth, I got no problem switching sides."

Her posture eased the barest fraction. "That's something we could deal on, I think."

If she was lying, it didn't show up in gestalt.

"And you're authorized to offer that?"

"I'm deployed. That comes with extraordinary logistics authorization." She shrugged. "Anyway, Fleet have dreadnoughts docking in geosynch over Wells all the time. Warships that big run surplus cryocap capacity in case of evacuation duties. No big deal to fire up an extra freezer when one of them rotates home."

"Good to know. Then I think we have a working arrangement."

"Thank you." It came across surprisingly solemn. But she'd folded her arms across her breasts as she faced me, and whatever we'd had in that narrow space was clearly back on ice. She avoided my gaze, peered elaborately around. "First steps, then. How exactly do we get out of here? Please tell me you had some longer-range extraction plan in mind than this."

I reached for my clothes, started pulling them on.

"Hey—fluid situation, remember? Why should I know what I'm doing any more than anyone else around here?"

FORTY-SIX

IT WASN'T QUITE the view from Decatur's penthouse, but the overall effect was much the same. Floor-to-ceiling windows commanding views out across a nighttime carpet of lights. The distant, brooding bulk of the Wall just visible against the paler dark, like a storm front brewing, like a bad dream inbound.

The windows ran high-end augmented; you could prod them and call up notable local features, real-time mapping overlay, and weather digests. The rest of the suite was a match—slightly loud, slightly overstated luxury fittings and a decor that constantly reminded you what a high-end establishment you'd booked into, how very, very important you were.

It was so Cradle City it should have won some kind of mayor's pride local business award.

"Honeymoon suite," Decatur said with a sour grin. He'd bounced back pretty fast from the shock of me not being dead. "That all right with you guys?"

I hadn't washed my face, so maybe he could smell Madekwe on me.

Or maybe everything about how we looked just screamed it.

. . .

DECATUR LEFT US alone, I got in the shower for a long soak, and about five minutes later, Madison Madekwe climbed in with me.

Things weren't getting any less complicated.

"YOU REALLY TRUST this man?" she asked later, lying sprawled top to tail with me on the vast honeymoon bed.

I hinged myself up into a sitting position and looked down at her. Smooth anthracite slices of Earthborn flesh cocooned in the bright white cover of a big fluffy Crocus Lux bathrobe. I rubbed hard at my face with both hands.

"I trust Decatur to keep Sakarian and the Marshal Service off our backs. Cradle City PD eats out of his hand, and they never liked the marshals much anyway—got jurisdictional grudge shit going back a hundred years. Even if Sakarian does work out where we are, CCPD is never going to give us up without a fight—and our beloved, beyond-reproach commissioner is in no position to be making that much public noise right now. We're safe here for the time being."

"You told me Decatur's tied in with the *familias andinas*."

"Yeah—married to one, in fact. Ireni Decatur, née Allauca—little sister to the mayor of this shithole town, who was also Decatur's unofficial boss."

"The mayor you supposedly died in combat with."

I grinned lopsidedly at her. "That's the one. And from what I hear, Ireni is stepping in now for the *familias* up at City Hall. Where they've also got a price out on Hidalgo's head. I wouldn't worry about it. We're a bit beyond the secondary concerns now."

"Secondary concerns? These people are gangsters, Veil! This is organized crime we're talking about!"

"Not very well organized from what I've seen. And you might not like it any more than they do, but right now these people are our natural allies. The *familias andinas* are Valley democracy's biggest fans. Due process and elected officials—all for sale to the highest bidder; free market capital flows, light-touch regulation, corporate ascendancy as a result. They love that shit—they can buy it and sell it and subvert it at every turn. Hard-core military governance and troops on the streets, not so much. Last thing they want is the navy coming here and putting the boot in."

"You know that I can't guarantee how Fleet will handle this."

"Don't worry, I'll do it for you. I'm telling you, faced with the straight choice between a velvet top-down takeover and a crackdown, the *familias* will do anything they can to secure option A. That's the angle we work with Decatur. Now, are you going to let me talk to Hidalgo or not?"

We'd swapped true connector codes earlier in the shower. Clinched from the waist down, water streaming down her breasts and my chest to pool and runnel off where our bellies pressed together. Gazes locked on hard in the steamy air—we'd opened our internals to each other and poured the handshake protocols across. No external gear to mediate this time, something gut-deep and discomforting in the new levels of naked it implied. Arms wrapped around each other in the moment, oddly tight, as if to stop one or the other of us falling.

And the feeling of a sudden drop anyway—a fall into her dark-eyed stare like it was the ocean at night.

For a moment, I'd nearly slipped and stumbled against her in the stall.

'Ris hadn't quit scolding me for it since. She made me a neat little list of all the counterintrusion extras she was now running just to be safe, pegged it high in my left eye for the next twenty minutes.

Now Madison Madekwe sat up a little on the bed and met my gaze again. Alphanumerics flared in my lower right field of vision, shunted across to the left, and winked out.

"That's him," she said quietly. "You had better not fuck this up, Veil. If you do, you're beyond any help I can give."

"YOU REALLY TRUST this woman?"

I sat back in Decatur's lux response upholstery and stared into the pale gold otherworldly depths of my Laphroaig. I felt a slow grin leaking out across my face.

"Something funny?" he growled.

"Yeah—she asked me the exact same thing about you."

"Well, that's pretty fucking ungracious, now, isn't it?" He crossed the room again, restlessly, drink in hand. Stood staring down out of the window as if looking for enemies in the streets laid out below. "Considering I'm all that stands between her and a cuffed ride back to Bradbury or a shallow grave out beyond city limits."

I shrugged. "She's Navy SOC. What'd you expect, flowers?"

"I don't know what to expect, Hak, because until you blew into town last week, Earth military ops weren't playing in our sandpit, were they?"

"Yeah, they were. You just didn't know it. Hidalgo's SOC covert as well; that's why he's been pissing all over you for the last five years."

That brought him around from the window, eyes wide.

"Hidalgo's fucking *navy*?"

"Should make you feel a lot better about not catching him, right?"

Decatur came back to the lounge space, stood over me like a teacher with a failing student. "You're dance-carding with fucking Fleet SOC? You do know what'll happen if that goes bad, right?"

I sipped at the Laphroaig. "I've had navy dances before."

"Oh, listen to the fucking overrider. Any of those dances involve a full-blown coup waiting in orbit?"

"Not as such."

"Not as such." He nodded grimly. "All right, let's talk about another minor issue—do you have any idea what it's going to take to stop Ireni and her big city friends from icing you on the spot soon as they find out you're still alive?"

"How about the threat of a full navy crackdown? That do? Because that's what's coming, Milt, if we can't finesse this thing."

"You're going to *finesse* a navy coup? *Are you fucking listening to the words coming out of your mouth, Hak?*"

I saw the faint trembling in his frame and around the eyes. I guessed neither Raquel Allauca's death nor Ireni's return were making it any easier for him to sleep at night.

"How are the kids?" I asked quietly.

He took a chunk off his drink. "She didn't bring them. They're still in

Bradbury with some fucking *familia* ninja nursemaid looking out for them."

"Maybe for the best if she's expecting things to get bloody up here."

"What, bloodier than her sister getting slaughtered along with her whole entourage by persons unknown at an ex-navy black site, you mean?" He glowered down at me. "What the fuck really happened out there, Hak? What did you do?"

I looked back at him steadily. "You don't want to know."

"I'm fucking asking you, aren't I?"

"Yeah, and if I tell you, then it's going to be all over your face when you talk to your ex-wife. Who doubtless wears lenses every time you meet her these days. You always were a shit liar, Milt. I doubt you've improved with age."

For a stretched second the rage clung to him—upper lip lifted in a snarl, jaw knotted tight. Then, abruptly, it was gone. His expression sagged.

"You're such an asshole," he said wearily.

I spread my hands. "It's hardwired in. What are you going to do?"

He snorted, something that might have been a laugh, drained the rest of his drink, and cupped the empty tumbler into his palm as if he were thinking of glassing me with it. Instead, he dropped heavily into the lounger opposite. Landed there like a puff-down payload someone hadn't bothered to tie up properly.

"Yeah, all right," he said.

"What you *can* tell your ex is that your business model up here is going to take a pretty savage knock if Fleet decide to come heavy. Not to mention her *familia* connections down in Bradbury. This is a game changer, Milt—we're none of us going to be able to stand up in this wind once it starts blowing."

"And you can stop it?"

"I'm not promising anything. But yeah—I think so."

"That mean you have something resembling a plan? Because I don't want another set of broken ribs like at Ciudad Hayek."

"Never going to let that go, are you?"

"Do you have a fucking plan, Hak?"

I grimaced. "Right now what I've got is a window of opportunity and a list of calls to make. The plan part's going to have to come later."

"Heard that before. And now tell me the truth—how far do you really think you can trust Navy Girl with this?"

I shrugged. "Probably not very far. But she'll ride along for now."

"Got the impression she'd been doing some riding recently, yeah. Please tell me you're not letting that get to you. You and women, Hak, you've never been exactly—"

"Hey, I'm not the one with the fucking divorce!"

He nodded sagely. "So she is getting to you. They train for that shit, you know."

"What, women? All of them?"

He made as if to pitch his tumbler at me. "Undercover ops, you fucking twat. You do know any gestalt read you get from Navy Girl on those pricey new internals you're wearing is going to be fucked up beyond recognition by all the sex chemistry she's running, right? Pre- and postcoital. Generalized arousal signature—it's the classic masking move, Hak, every working girl and hire-out stud in the Uplands knows it."

"Yeah. So do overriders."

That stopped him.

"You're—"

"We're both doing it," I said harshly. "We're playing the same game, using the same base attraction resource, running the same interference on each other's systems, because it's what people like us do, all right? And we both know it. Just a question of how far we can ride it before it burns up on reentry."

He grunted. "Sounds like my divorce."

"If you say so. I'm hoping for a slightly better outcome."

He looked at me strangely then, as if seeing some facial feature he'd never noticed before. I gave him a tight, repelling smile, there and gone.

"Don't wake the overrider, huh?" he said softly.

I drained the dregs of the Laphroaig. "Fucking right."

He nodded at the empty glass. "You want another?"

You do not.

"Not what I need right now," I admitted, and held out the tumbler. "Hit me again anyway. Then I'm going up on the roof and make those calls."

THE WHISKEY AND the running-hot fought it out for a while in my belly and my head, finally settled on a just-short-of-nausea armistice. It came with a murderously slow-thudding pulse rate that, for lack of alternatives, I borrowed in place of conviction. The retinal display screen painted on my vision juddered slightly in time, put a tiny migraine crimp in the sound of the line ringing incessantly out.

"You're looking well," Martina Sacran said sardonically when I finally got through. At a guess, she'd been checking the line to see if the call was genuine, not some mocked-up simulation subroutine playing entrapment for the marshals or worse. "Not nearly as dead as our hungry-for-truth media would have us believe, I see."

"You could try and sound happy about it."

"You could save us both some time and tell me what the fuck is going on."

"Got a proposition for you."

She hesitated, just a beat. "This is starting to be a bad habit, Veil. I'm not your fairy fucking godmother."

I waited. Around me, the arctic cactus in the Crocus Lux roof garden stood stiffly, like sentinels awaiting command. Hardscrabble winter blooms raised tiny luminous petals toward the crackle and glow of the Lamina sky, as if in chromatic echo. A cold wind out of the west, same as it ever was.

Martina Sacran cleared her throat.

"All right. That I apologize for," she amended. "I'm not sleeping much right now. But frankly, it's starting to feel like this debt we have is pretty much paid."

"You've heard from me twice before in the space of fourteen years," I said evenly.

"Yes, and now twice in as many weeks. What do you want this time?"

"Wanted to discuss a scheme of mutual benefit, actually. How'd you like to stop being a political irrelevance. Swing some negotiating weight at COLIN levels for a change? Make Daddy proud?"

She stared at me. "Little late for that, wouldn't you say? My father is dead and gone. Or have the last seven years out here rotted your brain enough that you're turning into a 'mama freak?"

"Figure of speech. You want in or not?"

Long pause. Her hand went to her cropped hair, the old tic, hesitant this time. I waited for the answer I'd banked on.

Saw it in the hollow, needing eyes long before it came out of her mouth.

THIS IS NOT *a stable model.*

Oh, you think?

There are too many moving parts we cannot control, and we are likely to find ourselves outgunned at the mission crux.

I'm working on that.

CHAKANA PICKED UP almost instantly—taken as read, BPD had a lot better coms security than the Sacranites. Her stare into the lens wasn't friendly.

"You're supposed to be dead, Veil."

"Shed a tear, did you?"

She cut me a razor smile. "I spit in the gutter on my way up Hayek Boulevard when I heard—that do you?"

"From you, Nikki, I'll take what I can get. You talk to Sakarian recently?"

"I try not to do that unless I absolutely have to. You mind telling me what exactly the fuck you two are playing at up there?"

"Too soon, it's already old news anyway, and I'm kind of busy. But I do have something else you might want to hear. You never much liked Sakarian for commissioner, did you?"

"Get to the point."

"I'm sending you someone. Guy called Seb Luppi, he's a journalist." I saw the sneer on her face, guessed she was probably already pulling up Luppi's details on a side screen. "Ignore his résumé for the last five years, he's a tougher soak than he looks. And he has a story to tell. You need to get him into a WP safe house somewhere deep inside the city, some place the Marshal Service don't know about and can't get to."

"The fucking Marshal Service?"

"What I said. And you'd better put a half dozen of your best inner circle thugs on baby-sitting. I think Luppi's got enough to pretty much neutralize Sakarian for good."

A long silence. "What exactly do you expect me to do with this, Veil?"

"You do what you want with it, Nikki. That's your call, not mine. Just don't tell me I never did anything for you."

HIDALGO, AT LEAST, wasn't what I'd worried he'd be.

There's a particular kind of enforcer Fleet likes to deploy when things get serious—I'd run up against them a few times, most recently when they came after Holmstrom and the AI core for *Weightless Ecstatic II*. Dead eyed, incurious, functional at seemingly inhuman levels and depths, they seem less like people and more like some variation on the pistaco or maybe Madekwe's *ogbanje*. You look into the face of one of these guys and you find yourself wondering if maybe, just *maybe*, some military lab somewhere really did hit the future warrior jackpot and come up with something truly posthuman.

There was, at least, none of that machine-eyed dead-soul threat in Hidalgo's face. Thrown up onto a big display 'branegel in the suite's lounge, he wore the scars of how far he'd come, sure enough—there was a gaunt hollowness, a grim force of will applied in the weatherbeaten Caucasian features and the way he spoke over the link, and he had an actual physical scar knifing bone white through the dark stubble on his shaven skull to the left. But his gestalt was lit from within by shrewd intelligence and even the odd gusty candle glint of humor.

Under different circumstances, I might have liked him.

"Hakan Veil," he said. "This is a surprise. You do know you're supposed to lie down when you're dead, right?"

"I heard that, yeah."

"So I'm guessing the Blond Vaisutis shit you got Ucharima to spout is just tinsel. And you're coming in on this line, which means Madekwe gave it to you. You got to her in the end, too, huh?"

I shrugged. "Or she got to me. Does it matter which?"

"I take it my men are dead."

"Yeah. Temperature got dialed up fast, there wasn't time to finesse it. Sorry about that."

"Don't be. They weren't anybody's idea of upstanding citizens even for this end of the Gash." He held his palms upward to me. "Local fucking talent, what are you going to do?"

I thought of Torres and Ucharima, the local forces that had shaped them, and I found a small, unlooked-for measure of anger seeping into me.

"Been here a little too long, have we?" I asked coldly.

"Don't ask. What do you want, Veil?"

"What does any overrider want? Save the ship. I was in the Swarm for Ngata-Maclean, I've seen what a full force Fleet deployment looks like from close up. I don't want that happening here."

"Then you're shit out of luck, overrider. Torres is dead and gone, Sedge cleared out the warehouse right after the first break-in; whatever remaining samples there were most likely went into an industrial capacity flash pan somewhere. I've got no evidence to hold over COLIN's head anymore. We're going to have to force the issue. Take Mulholland into protective military custody and have him invoke Article Twenty-Seven with immediate effect. After that, well—all bets are off."

"You activate Twenty-Seven, you're going to have a fully armed insurrection on your hands inside two days, and you know it. It'll bring the Frockers and the moderates together like nothing else could, probably rope in the Sacranites as well before you're done. They'll storm the governor's mansion to get Mulholland back."

He snorted. "They'll try."

"How many people you plan on killing for this coup, Hidalgo?"

"Veil, I don't fucking care. These idiots want to fight tooth and nail for their shithole valley and their asshole overlord in chief, they're welcome to it. We've got no choice anymore."

"You want to tell me why you didn't keep Torres's body after you pushed him off the roof for talking back?"

His eyes narrowed. "That's not what happened. He slipped. Cranked to the eyes on SNDRI, throwing his arms around, and yelling like a maniac, no fucking surprise really, if you knew him."

"I didn't."

"Yeah, well—take it from me. Pavel Torres's worst enemy was always Pavel Torres. Upland fuckwit, he was an accident waiting to happen."

"I still don't get why you wouldn't stash his corpse somewhere, keep it on ice. I mean, sure, no one's going to ship a dead body home as a lottery winner. But if Torres went down with a mismatch reaction to a codefly bite and some skintech supposedly built on Mars, that'd still show up in the cells, alive or dead."

"And who on Mars could I trust with that? You know Torres went to the local mafia with his code mismatch? Tried to cut a deal with Raquel Allauca to blackmail Mulholland with the evidence of what Sedge has been doing?"

Faint shiver as I remembered my last minutes down in the black-site dungeon with Raquel Allauca—I held the grimace off my face with an effort.

"Yeah, I heard. Can't blame him for trying to pull the same shit you were lining up for Fleet to pull on COLIN, though, can you?"

"I can blame him for being dumb enough to think he'd get away with it."

"Hey, what are you going to do? High Frontier Humanity—just can't help it, we're always looking for the angle."

He blinked. "We?"

"Figure of speech," I said curtly.

He seemed to consider that for a moment.

"Yeah, well—if Torres hadn't fallen off the roof out at Gingrich Field, he most likely would have wound up dead at the hands of some enforcer for Allauca not long after. He blew up his own exit about as solidly as I've ever seen anyone do anything. Maybe at some born-to-lose fuck-up level, that's what he wanted. Couldn't stand to leave, so he sabotaged any chance of it happening. Point is—local OC were scrambled, they were sniffing around. We had to clean up and leave no trace."

"So—scrub down the nanocrete and stuff what was left of Torres in a slurry culvert?"

A shrug. "I like to think it was a bit more thorough than that. But near enough, yes."

"And you didn't even keep cell samples?"

"Cell samples?" He made a derisive noise—it was too harsh and bitter to call a laugh. "Don't you get what's going on here, Black Hatch man? How *big* this is? Cell samples won't cut it. You can discredit them at a dozen different levels. Same with recorded witness testimony—easy to tweak, easy to fake from scratch, no one buys it anymore. Best score you could hope for with *cell samples* is some minor league conspiracy nut noise, a few token questions asked, then we all go back to business as usual. People don't *want* to believe shit like this, they'll shrug it off if they can. Marstech, the *idea* of Marstech—hell, even the idea of *Mars*—makes them feel good, and that's all that counts. It's thin air, all of it. But back on Earth people breathe it like it was real, and they won't let you take that away from them. To really blow this up, you need a living breathing witness statement giving living human samples—not some fucking cells scalpeled off a dead man no one remembers. Cells just paint a big fucking blaze paint arrow for the cops and the *familias andinas* right back to the raid on Sedge, the break-in, and then on to . . . my whole operation."

I picked up on the faint hesitation. Saw the fracture point I'd been waiting for. I grinned, tried to tamp it down, keep it friendly.

"Hidalgo, come on. Give it up."

Slow moment. I saw it then, a flicker in his eyes that brought back memory of the men I'd had to kill over the *Weightless Ecstatic* gig. And I think I knew then how it would go, how no amount of finessing had any hope of rendering this one bloodless.

"What"—bitten-off enunciation—"are you talking about?"

"Talking about Julia Farrant, Navy Man. Pablito's pal, the other Upland fuckwit you sent in there who was stupid enough to sample the goods. I know all about her. *That's* who you were terrified they'd track back to if you left any trace of Torres. Farrant was your other shot at shut-tling home the evidence, if you could find her. How's that going, by the way?"

He said nothing, looked back at me, stony-faced.

"Sacranites turned out too tough to crack, eh? What happened, they smell navy on you? My guess is one whiff of that good shit and they'd close up on you like a bulkhead hatch in a blowout."

Still nothing. Just the eyes, the thwarted rage in exile behind them, the narrowed gaze pinned on me like ranged targeting. I smiled back amiably.

"What if I said I could broker you a deal?"

FORTY-SEVEN

UNDER THE NANOCRETE bones of Viking's Rest station, the rickshaw drivers' Jhyap game was still going strong.

The players were bundled up warmer at this hour, quilted jackets in reds and purples with collars turned up against the nighttime chill. They'd moved the cable reel that served as their table, dragged it directly beneath one of the recessed Dorn lamps set into the nanocrete structure overhead. In the bright cone of radiance blasting down from the lamp, seven players hunched intently over their cards. Around them, a larger group crowded in with commentary, loud enough that we got pretty close before anyone noticed us. Their vehicles were drawn up in two nose-to-nose ranks under the lights farther down.

My driver from the last visit was in the crowd. He spotted me and shouldered his way out, grin fading as he cast a dubious glance over the company I was in.

"Going to need three cabs to carry you," he said. "Three each in the first two, and then *that* guy goes in the third. Big soak like that, he rides alone."

Hidalgo glanced at the largest of his enforcers, a taciturn two-meter tall Tharsis Prowler try-out, name of Badarou, who hadn't said ten words since we were introduced.

"Hear that, Baddy? They want you to ride alone."

The giant snorted. "Fuckin' Bradslurry bugshit."

"See, where we're from," Hidalgo drawled, eyes back on the driver, "pedicab seats up to five, and I never heard anyone complain about it. Not like you're hauling in Earth gravity, is it? Now go get me *one* more driver and let's get on with this."

The young-old Himalayan face never changed.

"Where you're from, soak, I don't know it." A gesture back at the crowd around the Jhyap game. "But you won't get anybody around here to carry more than three of you at a time."

Hidalgo's stare hardened. "What are you, fucking unionized now?"

He'd been in a shitty mood since we met him on the platform at Sparkville. At a guess, running covert through the stews of Bradbury was a level of operational stress he hadn't had to deal with in a while.

"That'd be illegal," the rickshaw driver said mildly. "Just telling you how the guys around here work. Where you going anyway?"

I shot Hidalgo a warning look. "447 Fairchild Loop. And three cabs is fine."

"Fairchild, hah? You guys a start-up?"

"Something like that," said Madekwe, and as I met her eyes, I was surprised at the depths of weariness I saw there.

THREE DAYS, CLOSING on four, since she'd walked out of the Crocus Lux without looking back.

I'd wanted to go with her, at least partway to the city limits, but she'd spiked that one before the words got fully out of my mouth. No way was I meeting Hidalgo before she'd prepared the ground, and if I was so concerned about her having an escort, I shouldn't have killed the last two she brought with her. No, she didn't need these soft-play OC types to help out either. She'd be *fine*.

This is what I do for a living, Veil. Try to remember that.

Spent the last forty-eight hours trying not to, I tell her. But the smile it gets me barely twitches her long mobile mouth. We stand a few centimeters apart in the hotel lobby, face to face, not quite touching. Behind our eyes, the constant flicker and sweep of systems deployed, but under that filigree veil there's something else building, and neither of us wants to look too hard at it for fear of rupture and what might spill out of the wound.

Just keep up your end of this bargain, she says curtly. I'm trusting you on this.

I shrug. Trust gig, right? Cuts both ways.

And then she's gone, through the parting Crocus motif doors, under the humidifier spritz beyond, and out into the arid cold of the Uplands night. Back to Hidalgo and her navy concerns.

The tracker micro I snagged into the hem of her coat upstairs goes dark before she's even halfway out of the downtown.

I can't help smiling when it does.

The days after that were too busy to dwell on peripherals. Locational logistics to nail down, transport to coordinate, fine detail to negotiate with actors who were reluctant at best. Contingency planning, risk assessment. Bradbury was upside down and buzzing like a cracked code-fly containment vessel—fresh hints of corruption and abuse of office blown in on the media breeze every day like the waft of a hidden corpse rotting. And behind that, the tightening certainty everywhere that something massive would have to be done about this soon. I'd seen the same dynamics at play in the Swarm, just before the crackdown. Demonstrations and minor riots, the fuckwit instinctive demagogues picking up the scent and coming out to play. Armored cops deployed. No one quite ready to show their hand just yet but a general will to violence in the streets, vitriolic hate across the dataflow, and increasingly stupid brinkmanship on all sides.

They tell you to save the ship at all costs.

No one ever talks about whether the passengers and crew deserve all that effort.

With thoughts such as these, I stood on the Over platform at Sparkville and noticed belatedly that the running-hot was gone.

As always, I couldn't tell if I was glad or I was going to miss it.

Chanting farther up the platform—a loose tangle of Frockers marching my way, fists pumping in the air, belting out a hoarsely passionate rendering of "The Battle Hymn of DeAres Contado." They were all young and mostly male, deploying baleful stares at the passersby, and you could smell the itch for violence on them like it was something they'd rolled in. No faces I recognized or—'Ris briskly mapping and indexing them against visual recall—that would recognize me.

I slid back a couple of steps to give them ground anyway.

The next train rolled in, and the Frockers got on, shoving people out of their way with calculated nonchalant brutality. A couple of doors down, I saw Madekwe and Hidalgo emerge, closely followed by five lean and leather-faced Uplanders whose casual demeanor wasn't fooling anyone. They wore big loose coats, and a couple of them were carrying a backpack across one shoulder. Madekwe spotted me and led them over. We nodded our hellos. Back in the train carriages, the "DeAres Contado" started up again.

"Fucking clowns," Hidalgo muttered.

"Don't worry," I told him. "If this goes bad, you'll get the chance to shoot a whole lot like that. Be mowing them down in the street like a slaughtermatic chasing fattened roos."

That earned me a funny look and some bristling from a couple of the Uplander phalanx, Badarou included. Interesting to wonder how much of the deep game Hidalgo had chosen to share with his local recruits.

Then again, looking at their faces, I guessed he wouldn't have to. There was a blunt, incurious look to them that I'd seen enough times before in and around the work camps, cut-rate brothels, and indenture training colleges that stitched together what passed for Uplands society. They were hardscrabble Mars to the bone, sandblasted from birth into conformity with the Valley's brutal expectations and predator norms. These men and women knew the Gash for what it was—an ocean of treacherous economic weather and pitiless food-chain dynamics just waiting to bite. On one piece of raw navigational luck or another, they'd thrashed their way to the profession of violence that would serve them as a halfway decent raft in these waters, and they'd dragged themselves aboard. But they knew, because they'd seen from scanning the horizon as younger men and women, that the ocean was endless and offered no havens and all that really mattered was staying afloat.

High Frontier Humanity—Whatever It Takes.

All down the departing train, the doors sliced shut and the Frocker hymnal was abruptly silenced. Hidalgo seemed to shake himself out of a trance. He ran a hand over his stubbled skull, looked me up and down.

"Good—I see you're not armed."

I shrugged. "What we agreed, right?"

Like most weapons check software, his had missed the ABdM knife, but that didn't leave me feeling any less naked. I didn't recognize the version of Bradbury that had woken to life in my absence. It felt like some cheap Virthalla imitation, same buildings, same skyline, but with all the civilizational norms dialed down to facilitate maximal gaming savagery; it felt like the fucking Uplands brought suddenly home to roost. You wanted instinctively to check the caliber of your load-out, make sure it was something massive.

Perhaps seeing some of this in my gestalt, perhaps reassured by it, Hidalgo grunted.

"Let's get this done, then, shall we? Where to now?"

"Ventura Corridor line," I said, forcing a grin for Madekwe. "Westside platforms. Ladies and gentlemen, step this way."

THEY WERE STILL planting the Fairchild Loop out—recently dug regolith everywhere in low dark mounds and cleared spaces pegged out with solemnly blinking cherry-top survey markers. Tiny, fringe-of-hearing susurrus from the ferrite bugs and all their terraforming chemical cousins still at work, chewing up the soil so you'd be able to grow something pleasing to the eye a few months hence. Here and there, some of the lots were already sold and the nanobuild was going up, but even they ran mostly to skeletal framework and rudimentary foundation roots still growing in. About one in ten had walls and a roof. Less than that were lit. Jeweled and bright in the desolate darkness between, mobile adgels drifted like hyperanorexic sentinels, offering slices of animated virtuality on the site, as if you were peering through some kind of time portal into a future version of the neighborhood. *Buy now,* they murmured repeatedly to themselves. *Buy now, why* not *buy now?*

Lot 447 was one of the few completed structures, casting low ambient glow from the windows like the candles for homecoming in some kids' fairy tale. I'd picked the place for its isolation, and it delivered to a fault. We had to leave the rickshaws a good fifty meters out and pick our way up a darkened raw dirt track toward the lights. Overhead, the Lamina rolled bilious green and bruise-blue across the sky, put a grudging, fitful glimmer on everything.

"Let's take it slow," I suggested, spotting an unruly eagerness in Hidalgo's escort. "We don't want the same psychopathic mess you guys made at Bradbury Central."

Badarou and one of the women shot me angry looks, but they said nothing. And they did slow down, glancing toward Hidalgo for guidance. He nodded and gestured for them to spread out. Drew a compact twitch-gun from under his coat and watched as his crew produced their own variations on the theme. He smeared me a smile, wolf flash of teeth in the dark.

"Right. In fact, I think you'd better take point, Veil. Show us how it's done."

Grins from the crew. I felt a cold tightening in my belly, maybe at the words, maybe at the gestalt. So many, many ways this could go bad. Behind my eyes, 'Ris was all over Hidalgo with readout, but all she could tell me was that he was at high operational pitch and trusted me about as far as you would a Kirk Market fossil trader.

Yeah, no shit, I subbed back tensely, and glanced across at Madekwe. *What about her?*

Not much better, I'm afraid.

"Come on, Black Hatch." Hidalgo wagged his twitch-gun ahead at the lights. "What are you waiting for?"

I grimaced and strode past them all, took up the lead on the darkened approach. I felt Madison Madekwe's eyes on me as I moved, and a small, glinting sadness welled up somewhere deep inside me at the blank functionality of that stare. I put it away, *time for that shit in the aftermath, overrider,* kept my posture loose and relaxed as I walked. Enough heat in the equation without me adding to it. Eyes on the door ahead, and the long dark path to going home.

When we got about halfway there, an adgel crossed our path, slanted to show me a neatly paved path between manicured lawns, completed builds in bright pastel shades, plenty of early-evening light still in the sky, and out on the lawns in unlikely social gatherings a judicious scattering of pretty-looking tech types you just *knew* would be aces to work with.

With options like these, the 'gel wanted me to know, *you'd be Earth-bound dumb not to get in on the ground floor. Buy now. Why not buy now?*

Some amused grunts from Hidalgo's crew. I waited for the 'gel to get out of my way, then picked up the pace again. Up ahead, the door cracked open and put a thin triangular slice of radiance across the regolith. I saw the minute scrambling away of TF bugs, some nighttime variant that evidently didn't like the light. Then a slim female figure moved into view, silhouetted against the light, casting a long black shadow out toward us.

One of Hidalgo's enforcers grunted. "That Farrant?"

"No," I shot back over my shoulder. "That's Martina fucking Sacran. Don't you guys watch the feeds?"

The speaker shook his head. "Fuck that political shit. Not interested."

"Don't let her hear you say that."

Sacran came out to greet us. She was muffled up in a cheap, bulky surveyor's coat, collar wrapped loosely closed across the lower half of her face, cheap gear with transparent lenses over her eyes. Her breath steamed in the cold. Her gaze slanted warily at us.

"You're Hidalgo?" she asked.

He nodded. "What they call me on this shithole world, yeah."

"I suppose I should congratulate you, then. Not easy staying ahead of the corporate bloc *and* our *familia andina* brethren for as long as you have."

A shrug. "It's a discipline. You train for it."

"Yes. I can't say I'm so enamored of what else your people use that training for."

"I'm not here for a political debate, Ms. Sacran. Did you bring Julia Farrant with you?"

"As agreed. She's inside." Sacran's lip curled. "You won't need the twitch-guns. She's nervous, but I think the promise of a spotlight moment on Earth has her convinced."

A couple of the crew twitched forward, but Hidalgo stayed where he was.

"You're nervous, too," he said. "In fact, you're trembling, Ms. Sacran."

For one lightning strike instant, everything stopped. As if the Lamina had frozen in mid-discharge over our heads. I felt it spike down the inside of my arms, wrap chilly fingers around my heart. Watched 'Ris's displays systems ink over into crisis colors.

"It's cold," Sacran said evenly. "In case you hadn't noticed. So how about we get inside and handle this at a decent temperature?"

"Sounds good to me." Glancing back over my shoulder. "We haven't got all night."

"No."

The twitch-gun was up, leveled past me at Martina Sacran. Hidalgo's gaunt features tight with a whole new level of operational intensity. I saw the five Uplanders pick up the beat, bring their own weapons to bear. Felt the start of the cold slide in my guts.

"Stay where you are, Ms. Sacran," Hidalgo snapped. "No fun getting shot with one of these. Don't make me do something you'll regret."

I rolled my eyes. "Fuck's sake, Hidalgo."

"I've been twitch-gunned before," Sacran said with activist hauteur. "Probably more times than you've pulled a trigger on one, Navy Man. But if you want to blow up any chance of Julia Farrant trusting you, go right ahead."

Madekwe surged up beside Hidalgo. "What's going on, Nate?"

I held down an inappropriate, high-tension smirk. "Yeah, *Nate*— what's the deal? You want to fuck this up the way Torres did the last time around? We don't have an unending supply of Chasma Corriente misfires to play with, you know."

Madekwe shot me a violent shut-the-fuck-up look.

"Nate, listen—"

"Something's *wrong*, Maddy." He spared her a tight sideways glance. "Can't you fucking feel it?"

"I'm going back inside," Martina Sacran announced. "You amateurs get your shit together, come in when you're—"

"Don't you fucking move!" Hidalgo's arm, higher and straighter by taut fractions. "You stand where you are, bitch!"

"All right, that's fucking enough!"

Pitching my voice hard in the frigid air for command—it got everyone's eyes on me, at least. I held my hands open, arms wide, as if bracing the empty space between me and Hidalgo's crew. I saw them react, let 'Ris map the risk. Apparently, it was worth taking.

"Fucking morons. Enough of this shit," I barked at them. "Lower your weapons."

They did, sort of—an uneven line of halfheartedly drooping muzzles. Best I was going to get.

Madison Madekwe, staring at me, trying to fathom what this was . . .

Out across the chilly cleared space of Lot 448, the bright turn of an adgel toward us, like the one friendly card in a losing hand. And a shadow, stepping out from behind the glow.

"It's a setup," Madekwe screamed, eyes wide on me.

I dived past Hidalgo, tackled her to the ground.

And the night shredded apart around us, gunfire and muzzle flash on all sides.

FORTY-EIGHT

IT WAS OVER in moments—combat chemicals stretched time on the rack for me, made it last longer. Shark mod vision gave me daylight clarity, and 'Ris mapped the detail, filed it away for recall at a later date. Stuttering muzzle flash lit the night like some belligerent shouting match conducted on the electromagnetic spectrum. Hidalgo's crew got off a few panicked return shots, but most of them were hopelessly wrong-handed—twitch-guns are short-range weapons, pretty much useless in a firefight, and the shadows rising across Lot 448 didn't give anyone much chance to change up for something more effective. I saw Badarou grabbing a backpack from one of his comrades, reaching desperately inside for something . . .

An AP round came out of the night and took off most of his face.

He stood a defiant second with the damage, chin jutted out as if show-ing off all the shattered, blood-drenched mess above it, as if he were some-how proud. Then he crumpled like a tower coming down. The woman with the pack collapsed on top of him, eyes shocked wide in death, star-ing, it seemed, right at me.

Beneath my smother, Madekwe eeled like a minor earthquake, threw short, brutal ground fighter techniques at me in an attempt to wrestle free. Her strategic op status saved me—it was trained technique, not the lethal custom of experience. I rode the blows as best I could, got nose to nose with her in the dirt.

"Stay. Fucking. Down," I gritted.

"You *piece* of *shit!*" A jabbing thumb, almost in my eye. I fended it off.

Hidalgo—my major concern—was down, still moving but not in any way that looked like it could last. Martina Sacran huddled back in a corner of the build doorway, looking admirably self-possessed. She'd been tagged as a friendly back at the setup, and I guess she'd taken her fair share of fire in the streets over the years, but still—none of that makes you bulletproof, and mistakes get made.

More muzzle flash and boom. The last of Hidalgo's goons was giving trouble—somehow he'd made it to cover in a shoveled-out declivity beside one of the regolith piles, had a nasty-looking spray gun out and spitting at the shadows. I grimaced, groped over Madekwe's body, found the handgun I'd clocked earlier, and yanked it loose. She registered the move too late to stop me, kneed at my groin instead. I missed the block, caught enough of the blow to really hurt. I snarled and rolled away from her, threw out my arm, and pointed the gun. The trigger clicked, dry and impotent. User-coded.

Hack this fucking thing, will you?

Done.

Shut out the cramping pain in guts and groin just long enough to steady the weapon again and shoot. Deep, throaty boom across the chilly air. Our last-stand hero wannabe jerked with the impact, scrabbled desperately around looking for the source of the fire. I emptied the rest of the clip—hard, rapid reports like a stubborn fit of coughing. Last Stand pawed around at the air like a man trying to swat code-flies, then slumped over slowly in the small storm of regolith dust he'd raised.

A smattering of further shots out of the dark, like late applause.

"Done!" I husked, as loud as the black pain drenching my guts and balls would let me. "We're fucking *done!* Stand down!"

Voices yelled back and forth in Chinese, too fast and dialect-inflected for me to catch meaning. The gunfire shut down.

Behind Martina Sacran's hunched form in the doorway, another slim female figure stepped out into the light.

Gradual.

HIDALGO WAS NEARLY gone by the time I got across to him. The regolith where he'd fallen was blotched dark and wide with blood; hard to be sure in the queasy greenish Lamina light, but he looked to have taken multiple hits in the chest and guts. Damage way beyond the remit of any SOC custom internals he might or might not have been fitted with.

I crouched beside him.

"Veil," he rasped, gaze slippery on me with his fading. "Ah—you . . . *cunt.*"

I tipped my head in admission, maybe apology, too. "Only way I could see to stop you, Navy."

Naming the service seemed to stiffen something in him. A thin smile smeared across his mouth. His voice blew a little stronger. "No way you'll stop it now, overrider. Fleet gonna move on this whatever."

I shook my head. "Can't see it myself. You're down, Madekwe's neutralized, Earth SOC is an astronomical unit off the action, and no way to call the play. Who else is there? Fleet at Wells is a garrison, not a Special Ops outpost. Jarheads and deckmen and officers of the line—they're all here under oath to protect the Valley from Crater Critters and pirates, not overthrow the local government. It takes some big fucking chain of command to swing something like that. So you tell me—who's going to call down the thunder now?"

He groped for breath, found some fresh pain with it. Bared his teeth in defiance. "You—you going to—kill her, too?"

"I didn't want to kill *you*, Hidalgo. Just the way it came out."

"Ah. Feel—better now."

I smiled, I couldn't help it. Adrenal backwash still sloshing around in my guts from the firefight, twitching hard at the corners of my mouth. I felt someone come up behind me, snapped around, and saw Martina Sacran. She raised her hands in a hasty placatory gesture, so I don't know what she saw on my face. She cleared her throat.

"I think you're wa . . ." Voice fading away as she saw.

"Give us a minute," I said gently.

"Ah, yeah—Farrant." Deep groan, chopping into Hidalgo's voice like an ax into a tree trunk. He grinned savagely up at us both. "She's not even fucking here, is she?"

Sacran looked away, maybe embarrassed. I shrugged. "Yeah, 'fraid not."

"Should have known better. Should have *fucking* known—" He coughed on the sudden, flaring anger. Had to wait it out. His hand fluttered up a bare fraction from the dirt where it lay. "Just fucking wanted it to *be*, y'know. Wrap this shit up, go home. This ass-crack excuse for a world. Been out here . . . so fucking long . . ."

"Yeah."

His hand moved again, more determined this time. He grabbed my arm, surprising force still in his grip, but it emptied his voice of any strength it had had.

"Fourteen years," he gusted. "How the fuck did you do it?"

I shrugged again. "Day at a time. It soon stacks up."

"Yeh." Panting softly now. "Time we both went home, huh?"

"I'd say."

His eyes left my face, wandered upward. Like he suddenly lost interest in it all. "Yeah, I think . . . going home . . ."

His hand slipped off my arm. His eyes hooded briefly. But then he started coughing weakly, splattering fresh blood up onto his lips. His eyes glared open again, rimmed with tear sheen, fixed on mine.

"This shithole," he creaked.

I waited for more, but it was all he had. Sacran had gone, had bowed out at some point in Hidalgo's last guttering moments and left me alone with him. So I crouched alone at his side, watched as the focus in his eyes dulled out, and he went on staring up right through me like I was the one who'd just left the scene.

"Mr. Veil?"

I sighed. "Hey, Gradual. How we doing?"

"Very well. There have been no injuries on our side, and Ms. Madekwe is . . . suitably detained. We have her inside. She has offered no resistance so far."

"Good to know."

Gradual stepped past me, hands dipped elegantly in the pockets of a long dark storm-collared coat by some Crater label or other—three tiny red Chinese characters stitched down the lapel, vaguely familiar. Like her hair and makeup and the blank black lenses she wore, the sheen on the garment was immaculate. She looked down intently at Hidalgo's corpse.

"I thought he'd be bigger. He doesn't look like an Earthman."

"Hasn't been for the last six years." I gestured. "Three, I mean. Three years, Martian. He was deep cover all that time."

"Impressive."

"Well, they train for it." I sighed again, more heavily. I pressed thumb and forefinger to Hidalgo's eyelids, pushed them closed. Stood up. "Good work, anyway. Nice and clean. You didn't bring Gaskell here, I take it?"

"No, she is waiting for you at the TKS site. I thought it better not to expose her to the . . . operational complexities."

I grimaced down at Hidalgo and the pool of blood he lay in. "Looking pretty simplified now. You'd better bag him."

"And you are quite sure this will be well received by the *familias andinas*?"

"Here in the city, they're not going to care that much. But the West End chapters will, and that counts at Commission level. They've had a bounty out on this guy almost as long as he's been here—hundred and fifty K, dead or alive. If you're smart, you'll waive the reward and call this a gesture of goodwill."

"Yes. In Hellas, we are . . . accustomed to such gestures."

"Good. Then you've just bought yourselves some very handy *familias andinas* juice. Welcome to the neighborhood."

WE LEFT GRADUAL'S team clearing away the corpses and took a nondescript Naspac utility crawler down the darkened highways of Ventura toward TKS Holdings. Gradual rode up front with the driver; the rest of us got the rear cabin. Fair enough; it was her ride, and in her place I wouldn't have wanted to sit out the atmosphere in the back. The rear seats were set in facing benches the way the Land Rover had been, and I ended up sitting opposite a cuffed and stony-faced Madison Madekwe. Jubilant-looking Crater Critter muscle flanked us both on either side, tooled up with the chopped-barrel Norinco assault rifles they'd just done their killing with. Faint reek of propellant in the air and nothing on the floor between Madekwe and me now but raw welded steel.

"Proud of yourself?" she asked me as we all settled into our seats.

"Not often," I admitted. "But I'm going to let myself have this one. Rolling you people back has to be the best result I can remember getting since I crashed here."

She sneered. "Yeah, and I suppose cashing me in to Gaskell for your ride home has nothing to do with it."

"If you're asking do I trust Gaskell to get me a cryocap more than you and your navy pals, then yeah, sure, that was a factor. But taking Hidalgo out was a favor to everybody in this Valley. You said it yourself, Madison—"

"Don't you use my fucking name!"

I sighed. "Fine. I don't know your rank. Captain, is it? You said it yourself, Captain Madekwe—Hidalgo was fucked up, burned down, nothing left but the mission and some paranoid hate. That's nobody's idea of a safe package."

"He just wanted to go home."

"Don't we all."

Martina Sacran squeezed in at the end of my bench and hit the door stud. The crawler's rear hatch cranked down, and under our feet a world-weary magdrive wheezed to life. Madekwe switched her gaze like a gun turret.

"And you, crusader. Happy with your new organized crime associates?"

Sacran traded her stare for stare. "I won't take lectures from a state terrorist. My father told me what you people did on Ganymede. It haunted him to the end of his life. So fuck you, Navy. I'll take what allies I can find."

The Naspac bumped over torn-up regolith, found the highway's edge, and dipped down onto it. We took a tight U-turn, and then, abruptly, it was all smooth running. The crawler picked up some speed.

"Ganymede was unavoidable," Madekwe said quietly.

Sacran's turn to sneer. "Sure it was—just like the rest of SOC's greatest hits. Unavoidable consequence of people wanting to decide their own destinies. I'm sure they're all happier dead and frozen."

"I would have thought if anybody understood that convulsive political change costs lives, it would be Sacran's daughter. It's not as if your father's hands were clean, is it?"

Sacran snapped forward on the bench. "You shut your fucking mouth. My father had more integrity in his fingernails than you people could synthesize in your whole twisted bodies."

"I imagine he'd be very proud of you, then. Selling out to the same corporate interests you've spent your whole life making vapid speeches against. That is the deal, isn't it, Ms. Sacran?" Madekwe jutted her chin contemptuously in my direction. "You help this ex-corporate piece of shit bring me in to Earth Oversight, they give you a few crumbs and concessions from the COLIN table?"

"That's about it," I agreed brightly. "So how about we all stow the mutual recriminations and live with the terrain?"

Madekwe turned her stare fully on me. "You know, I thought I saw something in you, Veil. Some . . . core, something human that beat the indenture. I was wrong. It's Blond Vaisutis all the way down. They obliterated everything else. You were an attack dog for your corporate masters until they dumped you here, and still all you really want is to scrabble and scramble back into their kennel."

I held her gaze. It ached about the same as the kick she'd put into my balls. "That's one way of looking at it, Madison."

"I told you—"

"On the other hand—COLIN are the ones paying your salary. No Colony Initiative, no interplanetary tax take; no tax take, no Fleet. I'd say we're all in the same kennel when it gets right down to it."

"COLIN is corrupt to the core. On Mars, Mulholland is the result." A weird, taut urgency rising in her voice now. "You know this, both of you do! We can sweep all that away, Veil! Start over clean."

Martina Sacran snorted. I looked at Madekwe, unable to shed a tiny leaking disquiet. This didn't sound like the woman from the Land Rover or the honeymoon suite at the Crocus Lux.

More like the urbane cover identity she'd cloaked herself in when we first met . . .

I'm detecting—

Sharp metallic detonations in quick succession just over my head like rim shots from some running-hot crazy drummer—later I'd count from memory and make it five. Quick, hot drench of blood slapped across my face, in my eyes. The Naspac slewed violently, threw me across the gap into Madison Madekwe's lap. I felt a numbing impact as she brought her cuffed hands down hard on my head behind the ear. A single shocked yell wrung out of Sacran, the crawler nearly toppling on the skid, then the scream of brakes as the autopilot kicked in and locked to a juddering halt across the highway. The counterforce threw me back off Madekwe and into a messy tangle with my erstwhile Crater Critter companions, who'd also tumbled when we skidded. I blinked frantically, trying to clear my vision. Staring upward, saw jagged holes two fingers across punched neatly through the Naspac's roof, sharp metallic petals dipping downward.

And headless corpses all around.

Madekwe was kicking savagely at me—I blocked as best I could. Outside on the highway, my ears caught the nervy scream of performance turbines.

Incoming aircraft. Chatter suggests heavily armed personnel.

Yeah, thanks for the fucking scoop!

"Veil!" Sacran, voice still distorted with shock. "What the fuck is—"

"Counterforce." Wiping blood angrily out of my eyes. "Turns out our SOC pal here has more friends than I thought."

Weapon, weapon—it gibbered through my tumbling head. Nothing on me but my bare hands and the morphalloy knife. I cast around on the floor, grabbed one of the bloodied Norinco assault rifles.

Hack th—

Done.

The gun whined like an obedient dog. I kicked the emergency exit stud on the rear hatch, and it cracked with a soft, controlled hiss. Hinged smoothly up.

"Stay here," I grated at Sacran, and jumped out into the cold and the dark.

FORTY-NINE

THE NASPAC HAD come to a slewed halt broadside across the road. The helicopter was dropping to face it twenty meters off, turbines shrieking. Couple of seconds more, it would be low enough to deploy whoever was inside. I yanked in a quick glance for 'Ris to scan—something vaguely familiar about the aircraft's lines—then ducked back in, close to the crawler's coachwork. Reflexively, I checked the load on the assault rifle in my hands.

So what we got?

Whistler-Hoon P-771 Cloudscout. Personnel capacity eighteen plus optional pilot, in this case deployed.

Yeah. I grinned hard. *They won't want this showing up in machine time anywhere. Is it armored?*

Not really. Civilian specs, retooled for recreational hunting.

Good to know.

I grabbed a breath, popped around the corner of the Naspac, and loosed a burst from the Norinco, ducked sharply back into cover. Clatter-spank of fire hitting home across the matte black carapace, and the whirligig jumped like a scalded cat, tilted, skittered backward away from us, shaking its nose. I spotted the security-netted hunting-platform running boards they'd lowered at the sides, made them for the origin of the kill shots they'd put through the roof of the crawler. Heat-imaging sniper scopes from a discreet height overhead, say, two, maybe four shooters huddled out there in the cold air and wash of the rotors, top-down angles, and five targets shared out among them—even with the tech, that wasn't easy work.

You'd better get Chakana down here. Priority screech, sketch it for her. Tell her to bring everyone.

Dialing.

"Veil, what the fuck are you *playing* at?" Martina Sacran said, scooting out of the crawler beside me, a Norinco she couldn't use clutched in both hands. "These assholes have got infra—you *see* what they just did to Hsu's muscle?"

"See it? I'm fucking *wearing* most of it." I snarled a grin at her. "Good news is—shooting like that, if they'd wanted us dead, too, we already would be. *Come on, you motherfuckers!*"

I popped back out and chased the helicopter with another short burst. Missed this time, near as I could tell, but the pilot was jittery about taking fire now, and he jerked the craft sideways anyway. I ducked down next to Sacran.

"What happened to Madekwe?"

She hefted the Norinco, butt uppermost. "Tried to hit me. I dosed her with this. She'll be out for a while."

"Street fighter, huh? Give me that, I'll trade you. Lock's hacked on this one."

We swapped weapons awkwardly, crouched while I tried to track the whirligig's motion by the sound of its turbines and hoped to fucking Pachamama that I'd gotten the psychology right on this one. The new gun whined in my hands as 'Ris hacked it. I pitched my voice to beat the scream of the helicopter turbines.

"So listen up—they don't want to kill us for some reason, we take that and run with it. Keep these fuckers at arm's length as long as we can. Worst case, we split for the new build over there." I nodded my head out

at the acres of darkened units off the highway on our flank. "Plenty of
room out there to run and hide. I just put in a squawk to Nikki Chakana
at BPD, she'll be down here stat, or someone else will. Probably Gradual's
people, too."

In fact—

Not now, 'Ris.

I gave Sacran another tight, adrenaline-soaked grin. "All we got to do
is hold out for the time it takes. You good for that?"

"Do I have any fucking choice?" Yelling hard now above the sudden
rising shriek of the whirligig as it shot up into the air over the highway,
dropped its nose, and came right at us. I threw the Norinco to my shoulder, got a bead on the cockpit windscreen—

And then something kicked me forward like an emergency deceleration burn, smashed me face-first into the edge of the crawler's hatch. I
bounced off, tasting blood where the metal had broken my lip. I lost the
Norinco from a right hand gone suddenly woolen and weak, folded to the
floor knees first. Big spreading patch of numbness, blotching outward
from somewhere high up on my back, just under my right shoulder, where
belated recall told me the massive kick had landed.

You have been shot.

Yeah, thanks.

Trying grimly to prop myself up on my undamaged side in the gutter,
find out how much functionality my right hand might still have. Waltzing
swoop of the bilious night sky and the towering angles of the stalled-out
Naspac above me, a dull crumpling sound in my ears like puff-down packaging being torn apart and crushed. In the middle of it all, I thought I
heard Sacran scream. The Whistler-Hoon floated by sideways across one
corner of my vision, and I couldn't tell if that was its real motion or just my
stumbling senses.

*Initial tissue response suggests low-velocity antipersonnel rounds tipped
with aminosteroid payload. Most likely military issue.*

I gritted my teeth. *You doing something about that?*

Applying counterinhibitors. Stand by.

Someone booted me hard in the back, rolled me out into the road. I twitched and twisted, as game and agile as the next half-mashed ferrite bug. I got my functional arm under me. Faint tickling buzz against my palm from the nanocrete cultures still active in the surfacing under me—

"Look at this shit," hooted someone, amusement dusted through with faintly admiring disbelief. "Put two caps in him and the motherfucker's still trying to get up."

The boot again. This time the blow rolled me over onto my back. A face appeared directly overhead, peering down. Black watch cap tight to the skull, features swiped dark with antiscan grease, and he appeared to have taken a gash to one cheekbone recently.

I knew him instantly anyway. Groaned and cursed myself for several kinds of fool.

He saw the recognition and grinned, teeth very white in the blood-streaked, greased-up face.

"Hey, Veil, you fucking asshole. Welcome to the A game."

THEY WOULD HAVE made the jump from the running board platforms, soon as they'd confirmed the kill shots on Gradual's muscle. Drop the whirligig to an altitude where you'd walk away from the fall—and on Mars that's not nearly as low as you'd think—then pick your impact point somewhere out in the soft, untenanted Ventura darkness off to the side of the road. Make the helicopter a pure distraction while you close silently on your prey and take out any remaining resistance.

Immaculate cleanup, SOC style.

Still, it looked like Sundry Charms had done himself some minor damage in the fall. That gash on his cheek, and he was limping noticeably as he dragged a dazed Gradual out of the Naspac driver's cabin and dumped her in the road alongside me. His similarly black-clad comrades—two others, as far as I could make out—seemed to have made the jump unharmed. One had Martina Sacran down on her knees in the street, a nasty-looking fat-barreled carbine trained a half meter from her head, while the other had disappeared into the rear of the crawler, presumably to check on Madison Madekwe.

The Whistler-Hoon had settled to the street fifty meters off and sat there, rotors twitching. The turbines had wound down to a throbbing whine. Multiple figures in black combat rig crowding the hatches. Charms hadn't stinted himself on company.

Why would he? He has a whole fucking entourage to draw on.

The late recriminations, stacking up in my soggy head.

Yeah, and you took a whirligig down from the Ares Acantilado with them all, and didn't notice.

Madison Madekwe's words, glinting now in the harsh new light of revelation. *I've organized a low-profile ride into town.*

I never gave it a second thought.

I thought of Ariana's sour postcoital comments, discounting Chami's fannish response to Charms's arrival on Mars—*he's a cheap fucking fake— had so much work done, it barely looks like the same human being anymore.*

Right.

And Madison Madekwe's instinctive covering lie when I showed even the vaguest interest. I heard my own voice as if piped through by 'Ris from recall.

SNDRI Charms. Very good. Never heard of him.

If you had a teenage daughter, you would have.

She'd hesitated on the lie, just a momentary stutter, but there it was, screaming loud for anyone with the training to see. And again, I'd let it wash away in the heat of attraction, the just-maybe accessibility of all that curve-sculpted Earthborn flesh.

Hiding in plain sight. You couldn't fault the methodology. As an ultra-tripper, Charms could go anywhere and access pretty much anything with a smile. Could take *his people,* too, because what ultratripping media star, even faded, didn't have some *people?* It was expected, a function of the role. He could walk muscled and catlike and combat-trained wherever he chose, and everyone would write it off to stagecraft and a hardworking personal trainer. Could even—I played the encounter back in my head, dreary hindsight confirmation—fake a dose of spoiled-rotten-drunk in the hotel bar just to cruise a possible threat to his more exposed teammate on point.

And meantime, his *people* could bring in crates of equipment unre-marked, because a big media blowup like attempting Wall 101 for audiences both here and on Earth requires a whole lot of exotic tech and back-room support.

I had another go at propping myself up. Charms saw it, dragged Gradual up onto her knees, and then came over to look at me.

"You going somewhere, overrider?"

I grinned savagely up at him. "Soon as I get this weak-ass blow-dart shit out of my system, yeah. I'm getting up and killing you. What did you do with the real Charms?"

He shrugged. "Rehab. Some back-side-of-nowhere paradise island clinic, they tell me, all expenses paid. Best thing that ever happened to him."

"Not a fan, then."

"I don't think anybody is anymore. Guy's a fucking has-been—just like you."

I made a noise in my throat. "Like I said—give me a minute."

A wintry smile came and touched his mouth, went away. I looked in his eyes, and this time I saw it, the thing that had been missing in Hidalgo or maybe just lost with all the stranded years. I saw the same dead soul functionality the navy assassins who came after Holmstrom had carried, like something cold and viral ticking down within. This man would snuff me out with less concern than slapping a code-fly.

Question was—why hadn't he already?

Charms—or whoever he really was—went to one knee beside me, open contempt in the lack of care paid to whether I might actually get up. His tone was genial.

"By the way, Veil—just so you know; you bawling for BPD to come and change your diaper? Never went through." He gestured at the Whistler-Hoon. "Got a squelch program running, hundred-meter shadow radius. No one's talking to anybody I don't want them to. So you can dump the delaying tactics—nobody's coming."

He is correct. I tried to—

Skip it. Just get that aminosteroid shit out of my system.

Under way.

Charms's gaze snapped up past me. I heard hesitant footfalls, twisted around, and saw Madekwe being helped down from the crawler's hatch. There was a nasty darker-than-dark welt rising in the skin of her forehead, split and bloody along its axis, but aside from that, it didn't look like Martina Sacran had done as much damage as she thought. As I watched, Madekwe shook off the black-clad figure at her side and stood firm. She nodded at Charms.

"Nice shooting."

"You should have called us in sooner, Colonel. This is a fucking mess."

"You were the last resort, Master Sergeant," Madekwe said tiredly. "This—all of this—is a last resort, and I'm sorry to see it made necessary."

Her eyes fell, finally, on me. Unreadable—I did my best to stare back with the same blank lack of care.

"You quite sure you want this one left alive?" Charms, spotting the shift in attention. He shipped his carbine up across his shoulder in his left hand, drew a blunt black handgun unhurriedly from his battle dress with his right. "Looks to me like he's fighting the takedown chemistry. If he's ex-BV, there's no telling what shit they hardwired into him. We're safer taking him off the board."

"Be that as it may, Master Sergeant, for now I want him alive. Her, too." Madekwe jerked her head at Martina Sacran, winced immediately as she thought better of the motion. She pressed a hand to her injured forehead. "This transition is going to be messy enough. We don't need to saddle ourselves with cheap martyrs before we're even on the horse."

Charms nodded. He saw the sense. "All right. And China Girl here?"

Gradual was still on her knees, lenses gone, thin trickled strip of blood out of her mussed dark hair and down her face, bruising starting to show. Could have been either the crash or a bit of navy pacification when Charms dragged her out—either way, she showed no inclination to get up. Perhaps she'd assessed the situation, seen the futility in trying to fight or run, was quietly trying to call backup from Doriot Broadway on her internals. Or perhaps she was just dazed from the crash.

Madekwe barely hesitated at all. "No. Her we don't need."

Gradual heard. She had time to turn her bloodied face my way, meet my eye as Charms stepped to her. She seemed, I thought, to nod some grim acknowledgment at me that I couldn't decode. Then the blunt black handgun was at her head, and she looked up at her murderer just as Charms pulled the trigger.

Flat crack, echoing out across the roadway.

For a moment, nothing changed. Gradual went on kneeling as if somehow magically unharmed, as if some ancestor spirit had swooped in and shielded her. Then, slowly, she keeled over on her side and lay still. I saw the neat dark hole in the center of her forehead, the pale skin scorched around the entry wound. Her eyes were still open. Charms stepped in and put another shot through the side of her head for good measure.

"Right, then," he said like a man hanging up a casual call. "Let's get this fucking regime change done."

FIFTY

OUT OVER THE crystalline stalagmite city.

That's how some broke junkie poet down in the Strip tried to sell it to me once, anyway. *Piling up all around us now,* she said with a smile that would have been comely and sad if she'd had more teeth. *We came here and planted it all out, but it doesn't seem to need us anymore; just keeps growing all by itself.* I never worked out whether that was some sort of metaphor—on her own admission, she was a poet—for the colony effort in general or she was just talking about the nanotech. Either way, she hit me up for twenty marins, in return for which I got a quick-and-dirty full-on-the-mouth kiss that aroused me way more than it should have and a grubby sheet of kebab-wrap paper doodled around the edges with a blaze paint fine-liner and filled across the center with hand-scrawled, glimmering verse:

> *Under pressures we have wrought*
> *And fires drawn taut across the sky*
> *Crystalline stalagmites retort,*
> *And climb, and yearn, and ask not why;*

A city breathes here now, has built itself,
And cares not if we live or die.

I lost the paper the same night somewhere underfoot in the midst of putting out a bar fight at Maxine's, but for some reason the words stayed with me. As I looked down now from the window of Charms's rented whirligig, that central image came rushing back up at me, hard. Bradbury—jeweled queen of the Gash, rising in eager light-filled blocks and spires as far as the eye could see, thronged and threaded with 6 million firefly lives, indifferent to when or how any given one of them might end.

"Looking queasy, overrider." Charms, grinning at me from across the cabin, voice pitched up a little against the ambient noise of our hurried flight. "What's the matter—all those years on the ground here, you lose your taste for altitude?"

I looked bleakly at him. "You know, Charms, I'd say you'll be less of an asshole when you're older, but I don't think older is something you're going to see."

"Hope not if it's going to look like you."

"Master Sergeant!" Madekwe didn't raise her voice much, but it cut hard across the muffled thrum of the helicopter's engines. "Would you be good enough to leave the prisoners alone now and focus on our insertion?"

As if in response to her words, we tilted hard in the sky and I spotted the pristine, blocky blaze of the governor's mansion below, set apart from the rest of the city lights atop the darkened skirts of its artificial mesa foundation. Executive House boasted blunt neo-Settlement structural lines, already clashing with the conceit of something so elevated rather than hunkered down and then made flatly ridiculous with the massive square meterage of fragile illuminated glass on all sides, the delicate minaret spires spearing upward at each corner. This place hadn't been built for Mulholland—it predated him by a couple of governors—but the brazen architectural incoherence it shouted from its plinth was a perfect echo for the facile shit that came spilling out of his mouth on a regular basis.

It was a fantasy residence to house the high priest of High Frontier fantasy.

We side-slipped and spiraled on in.

. . .

MORE BAD NEWS on the landing pad. Nikki Chakana stood waiting, flanked by the best part of a dozen armored-up BPD tacticals. At her side, cuffed with hands in front of her and looking thoroughly pissed off, was Ariana.

I shouldered my way past Charms's goons as soon as our feet hit the deck, made for the welcome committee while the turbines were still winding down. Heard Madekwe cancel some response from Charms, warn him to let me go. I left them behind in the rotor wash and the engine whine, taking long strides that were starting to feel almost steady— whatever 'Ris had done to the aminosteroid poisoning in my system, it seemed to be working. I got to within a couple of meters of Ariana before the tacs stirred. I stopped short, glaring at Chakana. Shouted over the declining turbine noise.

"The fuck is she doing here, Nikki?"

Chakana's lenses were dialed down to transparent. She looked down at my own plastic-looped wrists. "Keeping you company?"

"Don't fucking start with me. She's got no part in this."

"No, but you do, and until I work out exactly what that part is, I can always use the leverage to keep you in line."

"And what makes you think this constitutes leverage?"

Chakana rolled her eyes. "I'm a detective, Veil."

"You're Mulholland's fucking lapdog is what you are, Nikki—and that's all you are. He tell you what this is all about, or do you just jump on command these days?"

Madison Madekwe rolled up at my side. Ignored me.

"Thank you for the deployment, Lieutenant. I'm hoping it won't be necessary, but it's good to have the extra security."

Chakana inclined her head. "Ms. Madekwe. Welcome back; I'm glad to see you're safe. The governor is waiting for you in the Kernel Lounge. It's the most secure room in the building and has established transmission facilities in situ, as I understand you have requested. I'm to take you directly to him."

"That sounds perfect. Thank you."

"Yes." Chakana tipped a dubious glance past Madekwe at the Charms squad and its weapons. "Governor Mulholland has made no mention of any other participants. Your colleagues are going to have to wait here."

"I'm afraid there is no question of that, Lieutenant."

Chakana tilted her head. Rattle of hardware as the tacticals came to a less formal kind of attention.

"There wasn't a question in it, Ms. Madekwe. I need your squad there to stand down and surrender their weapons. None of us are going anywhere until that happens."

Madekwe's eyes narrowed. "You are aware of who I am? Whom I represent?"

"I can take an educated guess. That's the governor's concern, not mine. My concern is not letting a squad of heavily armed strangers into his presence without his approval. Now tell your people to stand down."

I shot a curious glance sideways at Madekwe. You could see the calculus at work behind her eyes—Charms and his squad might take down the tacs, armor notwithstanding, probably without too much trouble. But that left the whole of Executive House to work through, with who knew how many more of Chakana's troops between them and Mulholland. And with that much gunfire and general mayhem going on, there'd be no telling which way our esteemed governor might jump. If the Kernel Lounge came equipped with panic capsule options, he could seal himself in and nothing short of industrial-grade power tools or a full tech intrusion crew would get him out again.

A lot of headaches, and Madekwe already had one of those, courtesy of Martina Sacran and a Norinco gun butt. She put on a pained smile.

"Very well, Lieutenant. We'll do it your way. My squad will accompany me, but we're happy to disarm beforehand. Is that a reasonable compromise?"

Chakana didn't like it much, but she nodded.

"Get them to come over here one at a time. We'll scan them clean and rack the arms. After that, you can take six in with you."

"I can live with that."

"Let's hope you can. Make no mistake, Ms. Madekwe, I see even one of them make a halfway indecent move, they'll be going back to Earth in body bags." Chakana nodded at me. "I take it you've already searched this asshole?"

"Him, and we have another one." Madekwe gestured over her shoulder. "Martina Sacran—caught abetting criminal elements from the Hellas Crater."

Chakana blinked. "No shit? Thought our Martina was keeping herself out of trouble these days. That your bad influence, Black Hatch man?"

I said nothing. Chakana shrugged, turned away.

"Bring her along, too, then. Let's get these black ops heroes of yours sanitized and fit for polite company, shall we?"

Madekwe beckoned the SOC squad and explained. Charms looked mutinous on it, but he checked his weapons with the tacs and submitted to the scan, and his squad all followed suit. Their weapons were taken, slapped with disabler leeches, and stacked neatly to one side. It made quite a pile by the time they'd finished divesting themselves. Charms detailed three marines to stay with the pilot, and the other six formed up behind him. Chakana peeled off four of her own dozen to stay and watch the newcomers, brought the rest with her.

We all went inside.

In common with pretty much everybody else on Mars who didn't own a high-end uniform or a mansion of their own, I'd never been in here before. It was about as crass as you'd expect. Fake bulkhead aesthetic hijacked to provide the low growl of bullying force in every room and corridor, ceilings vaulted like a burlesque player's eyebrow. Exotic alloy gilt plastered all over everything, complete with garish 'gel display notation to tell you just what each metal was and how much it traded at on the local commodities market—the glowing numerals shifted and changed in real time as we passed beneath them on our way down grass-carpeted halls. Soft, yielding loam underfoot and luxuriant bright green lawn cultures whose growth wouldn't have lasted a day outside in real Valley conditions. Humidifier mist issued from floor-level gratings along our passage, left our boots dewed with moisture. The old governor's mansion at Viking Plaza—the one that got shot up when they deposed Okombi—had boasted a handful of modest fountains in open hallways, but here there were *waterfalls*, guttering down noisily from niches in the walls, smashing promiscuously into broad bowls upheld by gold- and platinum-plated nymphs. Impact splatter from one that we passed put spray on my cheek, like the intermittently failing rain from Particle Slam the night I went to kill Quiroga.

I managed to get myself in step with Ariana. She looked at me but said nothing—her expression was tamped down to a mica-eyed off-duty dancer aplomb; trace flare of long-suppressed old angers but mostly just the habit of weary, anesthetized endurance and contempt.

"Sorry about this," I muttered, shooting a hard glance at Chakana. "I didn't figure the lieutenant here for quite the piece of shit she turned out to be."

"Skip it," Ariana said harshly. "Nothing I can't fucking handle. Been busted by assholes like this enough times before. Fucking BPD, same as it ever was."

Chakana snorted. "The censure of paid killers and pole dancers. My soul is scarred."

"You do know what this is, don't you, Lieutenant? What it's going to turn into."

"Sure." A patented Chakana shrug. "Navy short circuit and a shut-down for Earth Oversight—what's not to like?"

"He's going to invoke Twenty-Seven for these goons, Nikki. And they're going to come down on the Gash like a dose of East End cramping fever. You can pretty much kiss your city good-bye after that."

Chakana turned a slow-burn stare on me. She said nothing.

"It's not too late, Nikki. I left Astrid Gaskell down in Ventura, twisting in the wind. By now she's worked out something's wrong, because these fuckers left chunks of dead Crater Critter all over Upper Doriot Broadway, and that's going to be hard to miss."

"Yes, and that's without mentioning the bodies your Hellas friends ventilated on the Fairchild Loop." Madekwe kept her voice light, but there was a monomol edge of venom in it despite her best efforts. The betrayal had cut deep. "Let's not forget that little massacre, shall we? In fact, I'd say this whole valley is fast turning into a place that needs a little martial law imposed, wouldn't you?"

"It's going to be Okombi all over again, Nikki. Marines on the streets, summary firing squads, emergency powers in all their bloody glory. You really think there'll be a place for you in all of that?"

As if someone had suddenly tightened the bolts on all of us a quarter turn. I saw Charms and Madekwe exchange a look. Saw Chakana's tacticals break step, Sacran stare around in rising alarm. No way to know what was casting back and forth in the air between everyone's headgear or what we all saw in our lenses. I could only answer for mine, and the gestalt readings across my vision were all leaning into the red.

Critical systems, said 'Ris superfluously. *Engaged.*

Chakana barked a laugh. It cut across the tension like a cable snapping, left a sagging expectancy in its wake that you couldn't call either way. She stepped toward me, grabbed the plastic binding on my wrists with a couple of fingers and a thumb. Yanked my hands upward, like some kind of halfhearted toast.

"You know, Veil—you just don't seem to be able to stay out of restraints, do you? Got to wonder what the psychosexuals are on that."

The humor spread, soaked into everyone. I watched the tacticals pick it up first, grins surfacing in echo of their boss. Something hooded in Madekwe's gaze, but she forced a grim smile of her own. Charms stared at me for a moment, then shrugged and turned away. Chakana dropped my hands and turned to face forward again.

"Now shall we just get on with this?" she asked. "Kernel Lounge, up there on the right. The governor is waiting."

FIFTY-ONE

THE THING NOTHING had prepared me for with Mulholland—fucker was charming.

It was a rough charm, sanded down that way to appeal to his constituent High Frontiersmen and -women, pitch-perfect with the long years of deceit. But it was built on something raw that wasn't far off the real thing. You could see it cost him very little to do, see how it flowed naturally from him. He'd gone to seed at the waist and the neck, but it was a faint blurring, and he had the height and breadth of shoulders to carry it off. A long-dead athleticism still haunted his long-limbed frame. The razored silver hair had grown out from the severity of the cut I'd watched him wear on the holding-cell feed screen a month ago, but still it bristled with health. And the face beneath the thick straight hairline was good-humored and well-wishing even as he watched armed men and women file into his presence with cuffed prisoners in tow.

"Ms. Madekwe," he boomed, and came across the lush grass carpet of the Kernel Lounge to kiss her on both cheeks. "It's a real pleasure to finally meet you. I'm only sorry it wasn't sooner. And, well, I have to say— your file photos do you no justice at all."

As if the taped-up gash on her forehead had abruptly become invisible—I guess in politics, you get used to pretending unpleasant things just aren't there. Madekwe smeared him an incredulous smile, but the governor had already moved on to Ariana. With the same airy ebullience that ignored Madekwe's injury, he affected not to notice the plastic restraint cord holding Ariana's wrists together. He treated her to the same two greeting kisses, as if she were just one more honored guest to some corporate soiree his PR people had cooked up.

"A pleasure to meet you, too, my dear. Welcome."

He almost managed not to look down her cleavage, too. Missed the necessary self-control by enough that Ariana, long schooled, caught it and rolled her eyes the faintest fraction. But you could see that some other, less case-hardened part of her was flattered, touched by the way this icon of High Frontier life had treated her with the courtesy and consideration that, day to day, not one man in five hundred who crossed her path would offer. Governor Boyd Mulholland *in the flesh* had reached her and made her feel she mattered. He was in past her tough, laminated dancer facade, courting deeper, older levels, blowing softly on the embers of simpler, more childlike aspects of who she'd once been and once dreamed she'd be.

Got to get them voting you back in somehow, I suppose.

"And Martina Sacran as well." He stood a little back from her, not quite prepared to risk close quarters despite the restraints. He chuckled instead and gestured around us, at what exactly I wasn't sure—the mammoth tusks and hunting guns mounted on the walls, perhaps. Or the floor-to-ceiling 'branegel drapes that hung in place of any actual windows and offered landscape footage from game preserves up and down the Gash. "The daughter of the revolution herself, eh? Here at Executive House. I don't suppose either one of us ever thought you'd see the inside of this place."

"Well, I hear you're leaving. I could always take over for you." Sacran cast her own sardonic glance around the overwrought trappings of the lounge. "Do something about the decor, maybe."

It earned her a pale, dismissive smile, and then Mulholland was moving swiftly along. For Chakana, there was a quick affirming nod—I figure she probably would have decked him if he'd tried to kiss her, and he knew it—and firm handshakes for Charms and his crew. By the time he reached me, he was flagging a little, and I saw him hesitate. Hard to shake the hand of a man in restraints without it looking limp and awkward.

"Don't worry," I told him. "I don't fucking like you anyway."

And for just a moment the mask dropped away, and I saw the real Mulholland, or what was left of him. Like Sandor Chand's face melted back to a screaming skull in the black-site basement, like the tightening gossamer mask of intent pulling Raquel Allauca on to murder me as well—the true visage of the body politic with its back to the wall, all noble sentiment and pretense for the crowd discarded now, like cards you could no longer use to make a winning hand. Nothing left beneath but the grinning bones of power.

"Well, now, son," he said, and put his affable smile back on. "Since you've said it, I don't think I like you very much now either."

I nodded. "We're going to have to do something about that."

"Oh, for *Christ's sake*!" Madison Madekwe, storming across and dragging me away by the arm. "*Enough*. Governor Mulholland, you have our agreed terms laid out. Immediate resignation and exile back to Earth, full immunity from prosecution, a stipend of five hundred thousand marins a year, Earth equivalent, for life, and citizenship resettlement to an Earth nation-state of your choice."

"Yes." Mulholland smiled as if feeling the afternoon sun of his own future on his face. "Kenya, I think. I've heard it's very friendly. Lovely people, well-managed cities. Truly spectacular hunting."

Ariana gaped. Her voice came out faint. "What?"

"He's selling out to the navy, Ari. Handing you all over to Fleet so he can dodge an Earth Oversight trial. It'll be like when they took over from Okombi."

"But—they *made* Okombi step down." Ariana's eyes clung to Mulholland's face as if he might be about to announce a winning lottery ticket in her name—it hit me that she was looking to him for some kind of denial or at least some kind of excuse. "Fucking Earth *made* her. They cut her down when she tried to stop them."

Charms laughed unkindly. "Different model this time, darling. They don't make governors like they used to."

"Master Sergeant." Madekwe's voice was a lash.

Mulholland was turning on Charms with some of the same offended vanity and stripped back anger I'd seen kindling in his eyes before. Charms saw it, too, and grinned back, uncaring. I knew the feeling; I'd stood behind that grin myself enough times. He was operationally locked on, high on the river rapids flow of it all, and not much bothered what specifics came floating around the bend. Mulholland might have been the mission crux, but to Charms he was strictly a package issue, a fat little puff-down payload waiting for the drop. And if the package was coming unbundled a bit, well, it could always be slapped back into shape by whatever means SOC deemed necessary.

Madekwe saw the rising tension and moved in fast. She put herself casually between the two men, smoothed her voice to an alloy of soothing reassurance and firm command.

"Governor, we need to focus if we're going to beat Earth Oversight to the punch. I am lensed internally; assent here will be binding. Are we agreed on the terms?"

Mulholland drew a deep breath, took his eyes off Charms. "Yes, Ms. Madekwe. We are agreed. I accept Fleet SOC's terms in full."

I heard Ariana make a small caught-breath sound, like she'd spiked her finger on something. I raised my bound wrists slightly, gave Mulholland a taunting slow hand clap as best I could.

Felt the plastic bindings give.

IT WASN'T MUCH, a couple of millimeters at most, but it was real. I felt a muscle twitch in the side of my face with the effort of not reacting.

"We are formally agreed, then," said Madison Madekwe, and her voice seemed abruptly distant, tuned out as irrelevant beside the sudden, jagged lift in my pulse. Peripheral vision told me she was steadfastly ignoring me. I stopped clapping, let my hands drop again, hoped everyone else would do the same.

"Yes, formally agreed. I have already said as much, Ms. Madekwe." Rising impatience in Mulholland's tone—he'd probably been taking a lot of questions over the last few weeks and not enjoyed the ride very much. "I'm quite sure it doesn't need repeating."

Across the lounge I caught Chakana looking hard at me like a teacher at a wearyingly useless student. As soon as our eyes met, she dropped her gaze floorward, turned her right hand very slightly to one side.

Purplish discoloration on her fingertips.

Standard BPD debonding agent—no matter how careful you were with those pellets, they always stained a little on discharge. I flashed on how she'd grabbed the restraint binding while we were out in the corridor. The joke about psychosexuals to keep everybody from paying too much attention to what her hand was doing.

"Repeating, no," Madekwe was saying. "But it will need to be announced Valley-wide and as soon as possible. I understand you have the facilities here to do that."

"We certainly do. Lieutenant?"

Chakana nodded and turned away, gestured at the dark wood paneling toward the back of the lounge. Soft hum of motors, and the panels began to concertina themselves away to the sides, laying bare a second space equal more or less to the part of the lounge we stood in. It was the same dark wood and 'branegel footage hunting lodge aesthetic again but marred slightly this time by the tall, skeletal loom of a holo scanner at the far end. A couple of sofas were paired there under the raised and splayed carbon fiber limbs, looking like fat little twinned pupae some arachnoid predator was poised to fall on and devour. A couple of technicians were already busying themselves with the scanner controls, making this or that limb flex higher or angle in tighter. It occurred to me, looking at the arrangement, that this was probably where Mulholland had broadcast from the morning after I was jailed.

"Short and to the point," Madekwe was saying. "I don't think we need anything flowery at this stage. You're standing down with great regret at the realization of how deep the rot of corruption has crept on your watch. Deeply sorry you weren't able to do more to halt it. Time has come, paradigm shift, other men and women, dedicated to something other than the profit motive, so forth, so forth. I now invoke Article Twenty-Seven in full."

Mulholland turned on her, irritated. "Yes, thank you, Ms. Madekwe. I have been doing this for a living for some time now. I believe I'll be able to—"

"Cleansing flame."

Everyone turned to look at me.

"What?" Mulholland snapped.

I ambled a little closer to him, playing up the aminosteroid fug I no longer felt with loose, sloppy steps, keeping my bound hands low in front of me for all to see—look everybody, harmless and chemically hobbled.

"I said *cleansing flame.*" Sneering openly at Mulholland, slurring for effect. "What they called it in the Okombi coup. Go ahead, use it, why don't you? Nice tight asshole phrase, gets everybody ready for when these murderous fucking clowns start shooting down your citizens in the streets."

Mulholland glanced around at Charms, Madekwe, and the others. Tried to radiate detached amusement, failed at all but the most superficial level. The internals read out his bubbling anger clear as a recovery flare in an Upland sky.

"You really do have a knack for making friends on short acquaintance, don't you, son?"

"Not so I've—" Feigning a mild lurch to one side, catching myself again. "—noticed. But hey—who needs friends like you, anyway?"

"Ignore him," Madekwe said evenly. "We've got work to—"

"Yeah, Governor, that's it. Do what you're told, hide behind this navy bitch and her brood. Suits you down to the ground, definitely your orbit. Fucking coward."

Mulholland flinched. His color was up, cheeks mottling, upper lip lifted back from his teeth. He twitched toward me. Chakana stepped in to him.

"Sir." And she put a restraining hand on his chest and shoulder, pushed him back.

I pulled the sneer again, like a blade. "That's it, Boyd. Let the minions handle it. Couple of days, you're going to be riding the ice all the way

home to your Indian Ocean retirement while your loyal subjects stay here
and get shredded with navy ordnance, *you venal fucking cunt.*"

Mulholland roared and lunged at me. Chakana let him brush her
aside.

About as good as it was going to get.

Debonding pellets have a long and dishonorable history in Valley law
enforcement—they don't actually melt the restraint polymer down, they
just soften it enough to snap easily. It's by-product technology and not an
especially efficient way of cutting people loose. It doesn't get much official
use. But down the years, a lot of Valley detainees nobody wanted the
bother of charging and bringing to trial had found themselves suddenly
blessed with what looked like glitching cuffs, and then, either prodded by
carefully set up jibes from arresting officers or on their own not very bright
recognizance, they'd broken jubilantly free and left their captors only one
option, which they, equally jubilantly, took.

Just had to hope Chakana wasn't double bluffing me and *shot while
resisting arrest* wasn't—this time at least—what she had in mind.

I snapped the restraints apart, met Governor Boyd Mulholland halfway.

Left fist clenched, morphalloy blade sprouting . . .

FIFTY-TWO

I NEARLY MADE it, too.

Fourteen years down in the Valley, listening to this waste of chained biomolecules spout self-serving shit about the High Frontier and its joys while he got fat on the proceeds of stripping down the social structure and milking the remains till they screamed. Fourteen years watching nothing get done about it because too many close cronies and vested interests might lose too much from the dislocation.

Fourteen years watching the locals lap up the punishment like it was Pachamama's milk.

Fourteen fucking years.

I took all of that across the gap between us, brought the ABdM knife up in an eviscerating arc, was going to unzip Mulholland from belly to ribs, then slash his throat across and punch the blade in through his eye while he stumbled and clutched at the ruin of his own guts. Catastrophic damage—leave nothing for the crash team if they got summoned in time. I didn't want some supercompetent medic finding a way to bring this motherfucker back. Inti and Supay could have him, play tug-of-war with his shit-stained soul till Pachamama brought on the end of time.

I had Charms pegged; he was too far off to get there in time, and the rest of the squad were quietly locked in on Chakana's tacticals. I didn't figure in their risk assessment at all . . .

Time turned icy crystalline around me, shone cold with the accelerated combat chemistry in my veins. Discreet glowing facades and increments of motion, sliced off moments, held and frozen for dreamy inspection.

Mulholland's face sagging in sudden shock as he realized what he was blundering toward . . .

Somebody yelling, might have been Charms.

Dim wood-oiled light, kissing off the edge of the morphalloy blade . . .

Madison Madekwe hit me from the side like an incoming ValleyVac. She locked up my left arm before the blade could reach Mulholland, stomped hard into my leg behind and below the knee, took me to the floor. On hard flooring, it probably would have sent crippling pain smashing up through my kneecap, but the carpet of grassy loam soaked up the impact. I lashed out, chopping sideways into her belly, heard her grunt and stumble. We went over in a ground-fighter tangle, flailing for grip.

Yells around the room—vaguely, I was aware that Madekwe and I were not the only ones fighting. In amid the chaos, I heard the quick sharp whine of a weapon's user codes being summarily hacked—Charms's soldiers taking away BPD's ordnance privileges. Madekwe tried for a knee to the groin like the one she'd pinned on me in the firefight at Fairchild Loop. I blocked better this time, attuned to the move. Sudden volley of shouts—sounded like Charms and Chakana going at it, stand down, *you* fucking stand down, don't do it, *do not fucking move*—

Two quick gunshots, crisp and flat-sounding across the room—Glock Sandman, you couldn't mistake it for anything else. I heard yelped curses, a body hit the ground, close enough I felt it thump into the grass beside me. The volleyed yelling shut down as if unplugged. Madekwe got to a pressure point on my left forearm, gouged savagely, and my knife hand was abruptly useless. I flailed anyway, hoping to slash her and get free. I heard another weapon, whining weak complaints against the hack, then another. Chakana suddenly yelling something frantic, sounded like *stand down, stand down* all over again, but different this time, all the command gone, helpless rage and pleading in its place.

The heavier boom of a BPD riot gun and a muffled scream. I blocked another punch from Madekwe, angled to get her—

Something ground hard into the side of my neck—it took me a moment to place it as the muzzle of the Glock—and a rough hand grabbed me by the collar. A tight voice in my ear.

"About now, asshole, Colonel Madekwe's the only fucking thing stopping me pulling this trigger." Charms, breathing heavily as he spoke. "So how about you get the fuck off her?"

He dragged me backward, and I let him. Quick peripheral flicker showed me the rest of his squad standing with the weapons they'd poached from Chakana's tacticals. Two of the tacs were down, one pretty permanently by the look of the two neat holes in his face. The other one rolled and groaned, but with a motive force that suggested he'd probably live. The rest stood in awkward poses like children caught out in some freeze-creep game of statues. Their hands were raised palms out in surrender as if trying to hold back something massive. Chakana was huddled back with Ariana near the retracted wood panel partition—looked like she might even have flung herself over Ari in some protect-and-serve thing she'd learned way back in cop basic some other lifetime ago.

Meantime, Martina Sacran lay facedown in the expensive grass—hard to tell what had happened to her—the technicians were cowering near the holo scanner, and Mulholland was still on his feet, now shielded by a marine toting a BPD long gun like he'd owned it all his life. Charms and his squad, unarmed, had taken down Chakana's finest and barely raised a sweat doing it.

Charms dragged me around, transferred the Glock muzzle from my neck to the small of my back and his grip from my collar to low on my left forearm.

"You shut down that morph-blade shit, Black Hatch, or I take your whole fucking hand off at the wrist. Your call."

I nodded, did it. The ABdM knife melted away, the knuckle duster lock broke up.

"Now take off the fucking rings. One at a time, drop them on the floor."

Madekwe reeled to her feet while I was doing it, spit out some blood—I must have caught her harder than I thought somewhere in that mess—and glared around.

"You," she snarled, pointing at Chakana.

"All right." Chakana, rising, spreading her hands. "Enough. It's over, we're done. Stand down. No one's looking to die. Look. Going to take this out, just drop it right there." Fitting actions to words, she lifted one arm and tugged her Glock out of its shoulder holster between finger and thumb, then tossed it to the grassy floor. The marines stood and watched her with hard grins. Charms shot a speculative glance at Madekwe. I saw her shake her head a fraction. Charms pulled a face, wandered a bit closer to Chakana.

"You stupid fucking bitch," he said almost amiably. "Did you really think you were going to get the jump on these guys? We're fucking SOC. You know—Vacuum Command? You were outgunned the minute you let us in here."

"That's enough, Master Sergeant."

"You should be aware I am carrying a second weapon." Chakana still had her hands raised in a warding stance. Something there in her face—I couldn't tell if it was fear, because I'd never seen her scared before. "Got another piece in the small of my back."

"I *know*," Madekwe snapped irritably. "I've had it tagged on internals since we touched down. Lucky you decided to tell me, because if you hadn't, I was going to have you shot. God*damn* it, what is wrong with you people?"

Chakana ducked that one. "I'm going to take the other gun out now—slowly."

"Yeah, you *better* fucking go slow," one of the SOC ninjas growled.

"I already said that I would." Chakana moved her left hand painstakingly to her back, pushed up her jacket, and tugged out a nasty-looking compact gun with a chopped broad-bore barrel. She tossed it farther away, nearly hit Ariana in the leg where she was huddled. Then she straightened slowly up, eyes on Madekwe. "I would like to attend to my injured officer."

Madekwe looked at the groaning tac, now curled up fetally in the grass. She nodded, watched Chakana carefully as she knelt to examine the fallen cop, shuttled a quick glance at Charms, who nodded. She turned her attention more generally to the room. Her voice came harsh and loud, late-stage audio remix for the metamorphosis I'd been watching since the stairs outside Ucharima's apartment four days ago. SOC Colonel Madekwe, now emerged finally and fully from the chrysalis of her Earth Oversight cover.

"All right—listen *up*. You have just been disarmed by very highly trained soldiers who would have preferred to just kill you all."

"Fucking A," someone agreed loudly.

"On my instructions, you are not dead. I expect that concession to be repaid in full. Your comrades outside on the landing deck have been similarly dealt with; there is no help coming. This building is now fully under navy command. You need to let that sink in."

Judging by their faces, it already had.

"Now sit down on the floor, all of you. Hands flat under you. Do it now."

They did it, folded, sat awkwardly on their hands.

"I need a med-kit here." Nikki Chakana, voice raised and strained. "Closers and wound pack, vasodilatory and endorphin boost. If not, he's going to die."

One of the disarmed tacticals freed one of his hands and raised it slowly. Flinched as Charms and one of the other SOCs raised their captured weapons in threat.

"I'm the medic," he said quickly. "Got the pack here. I won't—won't do anything stupid, all right. Just want to patch him up."

Charms hesitated. Wagged the Glock laterally. "Get it done, then. Get over there. You fuck with us, I swear you'll end up making him look like he caught a lucky break."

The tac medic nodded wordlessly, crabbed across to kneel beside Chakana. I caught Madekwe's eye, saw nothing much I could appeal to there. I gestured at Martina Sacran's motionless form.

"Happened to her?"

"I hit her in the head. Have you got a problem with that?"

"Seems fair."

"Yeah." Madekwe stood off, giving the thing between us space. She looked suddenly very tired. "I did my best, Veil. If you hadn't stabbed me in the back, maybe it wouldn't have come to this."

The thing that had gotten in the elevator with us at the Ares Acantilado, the thing that had grabbed us both again like a lightning blast in Cradle City, lit us up and crushed us together in its hands like a potter with recalcitrant clay. The thing that couldn't be blamed for the way we'd fallen apart again after.

"It would always have come to this," I said quietly. "People like us, it always does."

"Are we going to get this announcement made or not?" Mulholland seemed to have recovered from the panic I'd seen spurt out onto his face when I almost killed him. "Because I have to tell you, between Fleet and Earth Oversight, I'm getting pretty sick of having you people line me up and then leave me twisting in the wind."

"Shut up," Madekwe said absently. "We'll get to you."

Mulholland bristled. "I *beg* your pardon, Ms. Madekwe."

"That's Colonel Madekwe to you. And you heard me perfectly well, Governor. Veil, you'd better go sit with the others."

I nodded weary acquiescence, looked sideways at Mulholland. "Hey, asshole—looks like she doesn't like you either."

It seemed to flip some kind of switch inside him. He flushed and swung on Madekwe, blustering.

"Might I remind you . . . Colonel, that without me there is no Article Twenty-Seven. Without *me,* you're just a gang of marauders under license. And let me tell you, you people will have a considerably harder time riding herd on this Valley without my imprimatur. These people trust me, they look to me for leadership. Not Fleet or COLIN or the Charter Assembly. Me. Their governor. You need me to sell this happy horseshit to them, and you know it. So I'd advise you to keep a civil tongue in your head."

Something changed in Madekwe's face. Mulholland saw it and faltered.

"Governor Mulholland," she said formally. "The fact that you're willing to betray your citizens here for the sake of immunity from prosecution and a well-padded retirement on Earth does not fill me with any great desire to treat you civilly. In fact, you make me a little sick to my stomach."

A low spec ops cheer from somewhere, taken up in a couple of throats.

"And if you're implying that you might renege on our agreement, I should warn you against that. One does not betray Special Operations Command on a whim. We are not politicians, and the penalties will be brutal. Am I clear?"

"Got that right," said the same voice again.

I gave Madekwe a crooked smile. "Sure you don't want me to stab him to death after all?"

"I told you to sit down, Veil."

I turned to do it and saw that Mulholland had switched his attention to me. There was a snarled smile lifting his lips, the hard exhilaration of a close call survived.

"Yeah, you talk trash all you want. You had your chance, and you fucked it up. Should have grabbed that moment like a dancer's titties, son, made it squeal like one, too. It's the first goddamn rule. Prime pussy shows up—you grab that action and you squeeze on it, hard. If you haven't—"

"You fucking piece of shit!"

Mulholland jerked as if slapped, then jerked again. Crisp flat echo of the reports, blood blotching across his formal white shirt. He shrieked, staggered backward, flailing arms as if he could ward off the shots as they slammed into him.

And through it all, Ariana's voice, screaming at him like some high-pitched chanted litany of loss—*you piece of shit, we* trusted *you, you fucking piece of shit . . .*

Chakana's second gun, tossed at Ari's feet and forgotten.

Ariana emptied it into Mulholland faster than I could make sense of it, and not one SOC commando was fast or wired enough to stop her.

I SAW CHARMS raise his stolen Glock and pump rounds at Ariana. Doubtful he'd miss.

I charged him, heedless of the rest of the room. He saw me coming, swung his aim too late. I cannoned into him, smothered the gun, took him to the floor. Every fragment of remaining rage crammed into a distraction screech in his face and a short jabbing punch into his throat. He choked and lost focus, I smashed his gun hand aside with one arm, got a thumb in his left eye and buried it down to the second joint. He screamed and thrashed, lost the Glock. I scrambled for it, scrabbling left-handed, felt my right thumb bend and creak on the hard bone rim of the eye socket. Charms, still screaming like something Supay unleashed from hell, punching at me, tearing at my arm, trying to roll me off him. My thumb snapped across in his socket, I felt it go like a rotten tooth. I shut down the flaring pain, jammed the Glock savagely up under Charms's chin, and pulled the trigger.

It took off the top of his head in spray and shattered bone, slapped my face bloody with the gore. His features deformed as the shot tore through behind them like a shift in softening wax. His eyes blew out black. Suddenly he was doll-like and inhuman in my arms. The doll spasmed once and was still.

"Veil!!"

Madison Madekwe, screaming my name. Something hit me in the back with the spread force of a riot gun load, instant crippling damage, and I knew from the feel of it I wasn't getting up again.

The Glock in my hand—I nearly lost it with the shock.

Load remaining?

Eighteen.

Blood in my throat from somewhere, *ohh, that's not good, overrider.* I tightened my grip on the gun.

Target outline.

Locked.

I rolled—frantic I was already too late. On internals, 'Ris threw a limning red glow around the SOC commandos. Rock-solid left-hand aim as she poured shock response chemicals down the arm, into muscles, joints, and nerves. Limbs and lower torsos—the best elevation I could manage. I rolled and locked and fired—bits fell out of me in the grass, searing pain.

I stitched Sandman shells across the room, blew out limbs from under, gut shot the rest, fired the Glock dry . . .

And sudden darkness, webbing in from the corners of my augmented vision, taking out the flicker-bright tools and tallies of the internals as it came. I faded out on yelling, screaming, gunfire, all heard as if distant down the length of a broad-bore fuel pipe—the old tangled chaos of human hurt and rage, the familiar sound of Black Hatch wake-up and everything after.

The mix we've taken out to the stars with us, just like every other fucking place we go.

'RIS BROUGHT ME right back, slapped me firmly awake with a chemical unkindness that burned. Stimulant jolt and a steady, settled pounding in my veins, numbness and agony fighting it out for dominance across my lower back. Bleeding out into the rich man's grass under me, I could feel myself leaching away. Odd sense impression of the Glock Sandman still clutched weakly in my left hand, but when I flexed my fingers, it was gone. The idiot, overwrought decor of the Kernel Lounge's vaulted ceiling floated what seemed like an unfeasibly long way over my head.

People moving around me.

Where are the fucking endorphins, 'Ris?

Risky to re-dose with this level of damage and bleeding—I will attempt to rebalance.

Oh—good.

Voices somewhere overhead, too muffled and distorted to make out words or even identities. Someone tugging at my side, worrying at something in the damage there like an insistent dog with a bone. It hurt, but in a distant, barely important way. I tilted my head, tried to force some clarity. Tried to look around.

"Don't move, Veil." Chakana, hurriedly, leaning over me. Smeared blood down one side of her face from somewhere. "They got you with the street broom. Lot of holes. We cram-packed you from the kit. Crash crew's coming."

I lifted my head again, tried again to look.

"Ari?" I husked.

Chakana hesitated, then shook her head. I made a noise in my throat, tiny keening, let myself sag flat to the grass carpeting again. I felt the blades and the loam beneath on my fingers, indistinct, as if I were gloved with hazmat ultrathins. For dizzying flashback seconds, it felt like I was lying teenaged, face up and drunk in the Harold Boas Gardens back on Earth.

Endorphins inbound.

"Madekwe?" I tried again, staring straight upward this time, fighting the flashback, fighting for focus. Slow, hot leak of tears from the outer corners of my eyes and down my gore-clogged face, because I already knew the answer.

"Yup," Chakana said with nonchalant satisfaction. "Got the bitch for you myself. Double tap. Couldn't have done it without that shin shot you put in her, though."

Modulated endorphin release is under way. 'Ris thought I ought to know. *You will no longer feel any pain.*

CODA

There isn't actually any escape. Once you understand this, you are empowered.

—Enrique Sacran
Notes from a Decaying Orbit

FIFTY-THREE

SOME WOUNDS HEAL faster than others.

Bradbury PD's tacticals, in common with most Valley law enforcement, favor an antipersonnel shredder load in their riot guns, something
that's been illegal back on Earth for longer than I've been alive. The submunition is designed to shatter apart on entry, preventing collateral damage to bystanders and seriously fucking up the target internally. They
picked the razor-edged shards out of my midsection in the emergency
trauma unit at Santa Yemaya, but then they had to put in single-cell alloy
scavenger cultures to run down any remaining contamination. While
those took, they ran a whole mess of rapid regrowth biotech through the
damaged areas, but the scavenger protocols took umbrage, and the whole
thing had to be rebalanced. Twice.

Couple of weeks, they said.

Out beyond the walls of the hospital, a hastily assembled coalition of
Earth Oversight actors and local law enforcement performed similar surgery on the political damage the Valley had sustained. The small gang of
terrorists who'd stormed the Executive Mansion and murdered the governor turned out to be Frocker extremists with military backgrounds,

overreacting to the audit and Mulholland's—in their eyes—craven levels of compliance with Earth Authority. BPD were the heroes of the hour. A valiant tactical swoop operation had managed to neutralize the gang with only minimal law enforcement casualties but could not unfortunately save the governor himself or one Ariana Mendez, a coyly described *personal growth consultant* he was apparently entertaining at the time.

All the terrorists were killed during the raid, some outside on the landing pad by a BPD helicopter gunship but most in a furious firefight during which multiple tactical officers acquitted themselves with great personal valor. Medals and commendations to be announced. The faces and identities of the gang could not at present be revealed, pending the outcome of further live investigations. Meanwhile, a Valley-wide crackdown on separatist fringe elements was under way, together with an exhaustive inquiry into the broader separatist tendency in general. All Earth Oversight scrutiny of Mulholland's personal affairs was mothballed or ruled irrelevant, and in a rare screen appearance, BPD Homicide Lieutenant Dominica Chakana went on record as an eyewitness to praise the governor's stalwart courage and defiance in the face of his assassins. A caretaker governorship under Edward Tekele was instituted with much media fanfare and full COLIN support, to run until further notice.

If Fleet SOC had any operatives up at the Wells navy base, they kept a very low profile.

I WATCHED AS much of it as I could stomach on the screen in my hospital room. Chakana had me signed into Yemaya as an associate BPD contractor with full LEO privileges, so I got better levels of treatment than any resident of the Swirl had any right to expect. That included a convalescence suite high up in the right-hand tower. But it was going to be a few days before I could hobble easily from the bed to the window and enjoy the view, and I wasn't permitted visitors, so the feeds were about all I had to distract me.

And I needed distracting. My ghosts would not leave me alone.

You piece of shit, we trusted you, you fucking piece of shit . . .

And the gunfire crash of it all coming down, burying Ariana in the rubble of a thin air dream she'd never done better than struggle to pay the rent on.

I did my best, Veil. If you hadn't stabbed me in the back, maybe it wouldn't have come to this.

Pinned down in the bed with my injuries, I felt her more than all the others, haunting the shadows of the room around me like the rustle of Earthborn rain in a garden.

I want you inside me.

I want you here, Veil. Right now. I want to feel you come in me.

Chakana swung by a few days after Tekele was inaugurated. She was in a breezy mood. She brought me a single upland rose in a hospital beaker.

"You're going to give me the wrong idea, Lieutenant," I told her as she placed the beaker at my bedside and dragged up a chair. "Unless it's the right idea, of course."

"Stole it out of the bouquet for Hernandez," she said succinctly. "He's next door. And it's not Lieutenant anymore, it's Acting Commissioner. How you feeling?"

"Like I was shot with a BPD riot gun."

"Funny, that."

"Commissioner, huh? Big step up. Haven't seen it in the feeds yet."

"Day after tomorrow. COLIN wants to make it a heavy-duty public announcement, cement the changes. You *could* say congratulations, you know."

"Congratulations," I said flatly. "I guess Tekele and Gaskell need some pretty heavy-duty favors if they wore that for a price tag."

She shrugged. "Safe pair of hands is what they need. Sakarian had a lot of friends in high places on the force. Now that he's busted, Earth Oversight are going to struggle to find anyone senior who doesn't hate their guts on principle."

"That why you changed sides at Executive House? Saw the angle, played it?

"I'm going to take this fucking rose back to Hernandez!"

I didn't smile. "Then tell me why. Come on, Nikki. If it wasn't that, what was it? You were right in fucking line with Mulholland when we showed up, happy to welcome our new navy overlords. What changed?"

She was quiet for a moment. "You said it. Navy overlords. Article Twenty-Seven."

"Come off it. Mulholland didn't lay that part out for you?"

"He lied."

"Boyd Mulholland? Surely not?"

Chakana took off her lenses, pressed thumb and forefinger to the bridge of her nose. "Alright, no, he didn't lie. He fudged, he talked around it. Or—you know what—maybe I just wasn't paying enough attention. No one's been sleeping much these last few weeks, Veil. While you've been away having fun up in the Shelf Counties, some of us were fighting a rear-guard document war against Earth Oversight and trying to nail down the streets for public safety at the same fucking time. We've had riots, demos, building occupations, even a couple of full-on strikes. Navy help sounded like a good idea, to be honest. But *help* was the operative term—not a full crackdown. Fucker never mentioned Twenty-Seven."

She put back her gear, lenses half darkened so the full force of her cobalt eyes was shrouded. She put on a masking smile.

"Plus, you know—here comes the overrider. You showed up, Black Hatch man. Gave me options."

"Oh, what's the matter, Nikki? Big bad homicide cop like you, don't tell me you never killed a man in cold blood before."

Her smile deepened. "Wouldn't you like to know?"

I left that alone. "So you figured why shoot a sitting governor yourself when you can co-opt a gene-engineered corporate killing machine to do it for you? Makes sense, I guess."

"It's BPD, Veil. We like our deniability."

"You know they probably would have let you have Sakarian's job anyway. You make a good plug-in; Mulholland would have vouched for you, no problem."

She pulled a face, mock wounded. "Should have thought of that, I guess."

"You set Ariana up, too, didn't you? That second gun, the throw-down. No user lock, right there at her feet."

The shrouded smile again.

"How'd you know she'd go for it? Pretty long shot, hoping Mulholland would trigger her like that."

"I didn't know. But she was a gritty little kitty, I figured it couldn't hurt to deal her in. Sow a bit of random chaos, see what sprouts. We got lucky."

"She might have shot *you*."

Another patent Chakana shrug. "Nothing ventured, nothing gained, right? Plus—I may not have your spiffy new internals there, but these are Marshal Service lenses. They work pretty good with gestalt. And—as I keep telling you and you keep forgetting, Veil—I am a detective. I do this shit for a living."

Playing the little people—that same old song. Torres, Ariana, Synthia, and a million like them, scattered up and down the Gash like stunted nanobuild seed. They'd spit in your eye and walk away if you called them victims, but somehow that same grit never found its way into any built form better than hardscrabble endurance and nonspecific rage.

And from Mulholland on down, the systems for milking that same endurance and rage were centuries bedded in. Bonded to the available options for abuse, and not much anyone seemed able to do about it.

"What's going to happen to Sacran?" I wondered.

"Landed on her feet so far. I understand she's acting as a specialist witness against Sakarian and Sedge Systems. Something about one of her Sacranite faithful getting contaminated with a bad batch of skin mod." Chakana's posture grew elaborately casual. "I hear that was what the whole Torres thing was about, too. Him and his girl in the wrong place at the wrong time."

"Yeah, something like that." I kept my voice dismissive. Either Chakana knew the exact score or she didn't—if she was fishing, I wasn't going to put Julia Farrant on the hook for her. Let Martina Sacran play out that hand for whatever it was worth. "And Sakarian—he going down for any of this?"

"Remains to be seen. Right now it's strictly *recusal from official duty to assist Earth Oversight with their ongoing inquiries.* If he does time, I doubt it'll be on Mars. My best guess, they'll 'cap him back to Earth and deal with it there."

Earth.

Earthborn weight of one big dark breast.

I wanted to fuck you, Veil. I still want to fuck you, and we only just got done.

I still want to fuck you.

I grimaced at that last echo, because it wasn't Madekwe's voice, it was mine.

Chakana seemed to misread what she saw on my face as pain from the wounds. "Endorphins not cutting it, huh?"

"I'm fine."

"Hey, you want a medal?" As if she'd only just thought of it. "We all owe you for that overrider shit you pulled at the end in the lounge. Hernandez thinks you're a fucking hero, won't stop flapping about it. Can't get you the Service Cross; you got to be in the ranks for that. But there's a Distinguished Acts medal for auxiliaries."

"Does it come with a pension?" I asked sourly.

"Only posthumously. Got to die in the line, and you got to have dependents."

"Pass, then."

"Well, thought I'd ask." Chakana got to her feet. "But like I said, we're all very impressed. Quite a few tac officers happy to stand you drinks when you get out."

"I'll bear that in mind."

"Do that. Oh, yeah, and the Quiroga case? All wrapped up. Turns out some Crater Critter gang did it, trying to move in on his action at Vallez Girlz. But then guess what? Most of *them* get shot to pieces in a firefight down in the Ventura Corridor a few nights back. Barely anyone left alive to arrest. Rival Uplands gang by the look of it, maybe a turf thing. Or some *familias* reprisal for Quiroga." She grinned at me. "Guess we'll probably never know. But you're off the hook, anyway."

"You sure you got them all. This Crater gang?"

"Oh, yeah—they had a whole base of operations down there on Doriot

Broadway. But get this—someone went in there and firebombed it the following day, killed everybody inside. Took out a few others at Vallez Girlz,
too. Real thorough job, no witnesses anywhere. Having a hell of a time
tracing the perps. So far we've had to make do with picking up the pieces,
arresting a couple of survivors, and patching them up. Deporting them
next week, soon as I can get squared away in the new office." Her grin
turned thin and wintry as the wind out of Tharsis. "Guess it'll send a clear
enough message back to Hellas—keep your mucky triad fingers out of the
Gash. Should discourage any collaborative-minded soaks on this end as
well, I reckon."

I looked back at her impassively. "I can see that working, yeah."

"Good," she said brightly. "So look—I got to go brush off a dress uniform for Friday, take some meetings. You stay strong, Veil. Get mended.
Wouldn't have you any other way."

I nodded. Watched her to the door before I spoke again.

"You just got sick of Mulholland in the end, didn't you, Nikki? Simple
as that."

She stood framed a moment in the doorway as it opened. Drew a deep
breath and turned back fully to face me.

"This is *my* fucking city, Veil. BPD owns these streets, and nothing
moves on them without clearing it through me first. Nobody fucks with
Bradbury on my watch. Nobody. You want to remember that."

Then she was gone, boot heels clicking businesslike down the corridor outside, leaving me with my ghosts and guilt and all the tangled pain
the endorphins couldn't take away.

FIFTY-FOUR

MULHOLLAND GOT A full Martian honors funeral—open casket, antique crawler ride through the Bradbury downtown and out to Settler's Point, solemn interment at Luthra Memorial Cemetery thereafter. The city turned out in droves to see it done. There were tears and flags and babies held up for a better view. Edward Tekele made a carefully calibrated speech over the grave, and he even threw in the first fistful of regolith. Sort of a coronation moment. Both of Mulholland's ex-wives showed up, big blacked-out lenses turning their faces into identical tight-mouthed masks of grieving and neatly shrouding any tears they might or might not have been shedding. Neither brought their kids.

Ariana got cremation and an AI eulogy over at the 'Mama's Home Paradiso parlor on Fourteenth Street, then an after-party at Maxine's place. Apparently one of her regulars footed the bill. I was still too badly damaged to make either the ceremony or the party, so I had 'Ris send all the flowers I could afford. One of the girls from Maxine's came by a couple of days later, brought me a memorial disk copy of the proceedings. *It went off real nice,* she told me.

I still haven't watched it.

Meantime, the emergency trauma crew that treated me were right on the money. The rapid regrowth protocols they'd seeded me with delivered pretty much on schedule. Three weeks to the day after the Kernel Lounge firefight, I walked out of Santa Yemaya with not much worse than twinges in the repaired tissue of my liver and some nerve-end fizzing if I swiveled too fast to the left. Residual biosystems glitches, they said, and told me it'd fade with time.

I believed them, because in the end almost everything does.

LIKE ALL THE other moths, I spiraled over and into the Strip. Fetched up at the Dozen Up Club, drinking North Wall Bangers at the bar while I waited for Hannu Holmstrom to get downstairs and join his own welcome back from the dead party.

"Kind of pushing this fashionably late thing, isn't he?" I asked Tessa Arcane as she strained out my third cocktail from the shaker.

"He held off throwing this party until you got out of Yemaya," she said with a steely-eyed focus on what she was doing. "Antivirals we got into him cleaned out the kill codes weeks ago; he's been up and about pretty much ever since. I guess he'll be down when he's ready."

She set aside the shaker, speared a long twist of jalapeño on a cocktail stick, and threw it in the glass. Pushed the drink across the bar at me and moved down to talk to someone else in the crowd.

She still hadn't really forgiven me for getting Holmstrom hurt.

Made two of us.

I watched her go absently, held on to the play of the bar lights on her ebony skin, and gouged myself with the memories it called back. There wasn't really any resemblance; Tess was thinner, slighter built, and had too much Horn of Africa in her features to carry even a faint echo of Madison Madekwe. But there was that skin tone, the way the light clung to it and—

Incoming on Deiss. Standard newsfeed update, recycled to Bradbury City Prowl.

All right, let's see it.

Behind my eyes, unwrapping—the streets of some shithole Upland town somewhere, two police crawlers and a Marshal Service Land Rover pulled up outside some cheap nanofab housing. A breathless young thing did stand up, eyes wide and excited behind his lenses.

Residents of Santa Inti were roused just before dawn by gunfire and shouting from inside this tenement block. One of them told me that's not unusual for this part of town, but on this occasion the police had come for a very unusual man indeed.

The feed shifted. Some grim utilitarian blockhouse of a police station this time, the same Land Rover parked again. The hatch cracked, and two grim-faced marshals brought out Martin Deiss pinioned between them. From the look on his face, either they'd hit him with a twitch-gun earlier or his SNDRI habit had gotten seriously out of hand in the last few weeks.

Martin Deiss, MC for the Ride Home Lottery and known to millions in the Valley simply as the Deiss Man, had been missing from his exclusive Bradbury home for several weeks and was being sought urgently by the authorities. Initially there were concerns for his safety, and some believed he'd been kidnapped. But now it seems the Deiss Man was a victim of nothing more than his own guilty conscience—guilty of years spent faking Ride Home winner tickets for those who could afford to pay the charge, cheating honest frontiersmen and -women of their hopes for the win of a lifetime. An Earth Oversight team, investigating the lottery, tipped off Mars law enforcement earlier this month, but Deiss somehow got wind of the warrant and fled the city. He has been on the run ever since. But here, today, in this hardworking East End settlement, the Deiss Man's luck finally ran out. He can now look forward to—

I shut it off. Relief and disappointment in about equal measures. I hadn't really expected Deiss to be skulking in the shadows of Bradbury, waiting for his chance to strike me down in vengeance, but the fact that it was an outside chance hadn't stopped me wishing for it any harder.

"Hey, overrider!" Slightly slurred tones at my elbow, pitched to beat the low white noise of the crowd. "Good to see you up and walking around again, man!"

"Luppi." I raised my glass at him, didn't drink. "What you doing here?"

"I'm working."

He nodded out across the Dozen Up's dance floor. The glam couple from my early-morning visit what seemed like a lifetime ago were cutting it up in the center, some sexy, fast-moving variation on *huayno* steps, re-mixed for Hard G beats and overlaid with an Okombi speech sample. Flash of long firm thighs beneath a rising skirt as he spun her. Cheers and applause across the floor.

"You just stand there and watch?" I raised an eyebrow. "Kind of work I could get used to."

He knocked back some of his drink and grinned. "Just getting the fun footage now, for framing. She's promised me full face-to-face later tonight. Contract exclusive for Fifteen Famous. Bit of luck and she'll be so cooked by then, she'll spill some real juice."

"That'll be worth something to someone, will it?"

He gaped at me. Jerked a thumb at the dance floor. "You don't know who that *is*?"

"People keep asking me that." I turned back to the bar. "Anyway— would have thought you'd be chasing the Charms thing right now. Sud-den disappearance from the scene days before his big climb. Got to be a good story in that, right?"

He scowled. "Nah. That *medical collapse due to code mismatch* shit? Pure cover-up, right out of the brand management manual. Not what hap-pened. I guarantee you, our pal Charms took one look at Wall 101 and shit himself. Couldn't face it. They're just running damage limitation now, probably already got him capped for the ride home, right next to Sakarian. That's the last anyone in the Gash is going to see of his pretty face, believe me."

"Well, if you say so. I bow to your superior paparazzo instincts." I sipped my North Wall Banger, toasting Pebble Rodriguez in my head for inventing it. "I guess if you want the North Wall climbed, you'd better send a Martian to do it."

"Got that right."

"Speaking of Sakarian—I don't suppose they're letting you write any of that up?"

"Are you fucking kidding me? Sedge Systems and Chasma Corriente is talk-about-it-and-you-go-to-jail right now. They're going to put it straight into closed inquiry lockdown. Why they're shipping Sakarian out to Earth. Probably Deiss as well, now they've caught him."

"You saw that, huh?"

"I'm a journalist, Veil."

Deiss, Sakarian, Julia Farrant. Charms and Madekwe in body bags—the list of people going back to Earth who weren't me was starting to feel like some kind of personal insult. I covered for my seeping bitterness with another raised glass.

"Here's to journalists, then. Long may they sell out."

"Hey."

"At least tell me you bargained that zipped mouth of yours into some kind of halfway decent payoff."

His gaze shuttled back involuntarily to the dance floor. I nodded sagely.

"So. Fifteen Famous got a call from on high, did they? Find something for this guy, we'll throw you a bone some other time. Or don't and we'll close you down." I tipped him another toast, drank this time. "Welcome to the big time, soak."

"Fuck you, Veil. I bled for you up there. I gave it everything I had."

"Yeah. Felt good, too, didn't it—doing the work? Making it mean something. You're welcome, by the way. Shame you've had to quit again so fast."

Low cheers rippling across the room behind us. For a moment, I thought the dancing couple had pulled another particularly risqué move. Then someone turned down the music, and the cheering went on, joined by sustained applause. Luppi slipped away from me, maybe trying for a better camera angle. I glanced around, saw Hannu Holmstrom looming at the far end of the bar on his back-hinged prosthetic haunches and blades. He grinned down at the assembled company.

"So you all heard the drinks were on the house," he rumbled. "That's good. Figured it was the only way I'd get anyone to show up."

Laughter rippled and broke across the room in a wave. I felt it touch my mouth and tried to go with it. More cheers and applause around the room. Holmstrom gestured, and it damped down to a murmur. He raised himself a little higher.

"My friends—and I call you that in the full knowledge that since none of you can do any better than a broken-down old pilot like this, I *am* stuck with you"—laughter boiling up again; he waited it out—"my friends, I thought of you often, saw many of your faces in my mind's eye while I was fighting for my life in cold and lonely places."

The laughter faltered, slid off a cliff into sudden quiet.

"Cold and lonely places," he repeated. "I spent a large portion of a previous life fighting in cold and lonely places before I washed up here in the Valley. At the time it seemed like a bad break for me, an exile of sorts. I thought I'd be leaving soon, I thought of escape. A couple of years, tops, I thought."

He paused for effect, and the laughter rippled again, gentle, preparatory. He had them in the palm of his hand.

"Well, that was the spring of 293." He shook his head. "Still stuck here."

They roared. He let it roll. Someone suffering from too much free bar cupped their hands and shouted *pack a fucking bag, then!* Holmstrom raised a regal hand in acknowledgment.

"The truth is," he said, "that we're all stuck somewhere. And sometimes—"

"Stuck listening to this shit!" yelled someone else.

The goat god grinned fiercely, which is enough to quieten any room, and quieten they did. He gave them a couple of beats to do it.

"*Sometimes,*" he started again, "it doesn't feel that way, other times it does. But it is the truth of it. It is our condition. We're *stuck*, all of us, flailing around more or less creatively, washed up more or less conveniently, depending on luck. But stuck nonetheless, epoxied into life and circumstance, and always with limited options. The only question is what we do with those options, how we move forward into the time we have remaining. And, above all, who else we choose to *stick to* along the way. I look around this room, and I know that I chose exactly the right people and that I have—all right, tell the truth, maybe not with you there, Veil—" The crowd roared with delight, fixed on me, broke out into ribald applause. I rode it as well as I could, grinned glassily, and raised my cocktail high. "—I say again, I know I have—quiet please, guys, quiet—I know I have—apart from Veil there, like I said—I have spent my time on Mars well. If I am stuck here, I can certainly live with the stickiness."

He dropped his voice. He reeled them in.

"And I am humbled that so many of you have stuck, and come here tonight to wish me well—even if it is a free bar!"

Whoops and a thundering crescendo of applause, foot stomping, cheers. I turned back to the bar amid it all and found myself looking into Tessa Arcane's narrow impassive face.

"Could have done without that," I told her.

"No," she said loudly above the noise. "You should consider yourself honored, soak. There's no one else here he would have singled out like that."

LATER, WHILE THE party simmered, he came over and found me. Perhaps he'd had his audio zeroed in and heard my exchange with Tess. Perhaps he just knew me too well.

"Sorry about that, Veil. Speeches, you know how it is. You got to break up all that sincere shit with something. People can't take too much of it otherwise."

"Happy to help." I tipped my latest drink in his direction. "Welcome back. Sorry I got you into that navy fuck-up in the first place."

He shrugged. "I walked into it with my eyes open. Let my stupid ship-hacker pride get the better of me, tell you the truth. Should probably never have gone back in after that first pushback. That was my call, not yours."

"Well." I went through my pockets for something to say. "We both walked away in the end."

An unnerving, glowing green-irised wink. "Both still stuck here."

"Yeah, that, too."

"You had a pretty rough ride yourself from what I can piece together."

"You know what I had, Hannu?" I'd drunk too much, it blotted my voice. I focused hard on the stained and scarred surface of the bar in front of me. I cupped my right hand, as if around a warm dark breast still slick with mingled sweat. I looked up at him, smiling defiantly, feeling the hard brightness in my eyes. "I had Earth in the palm of my hand. Just like that. And I fucking let it go."

I crumpled up my empty hand, made it into a fist.

"Just like that," I said quietly.

He went through the moment with me, stayed quiet. We stood there in the swamping noise of this welcome back from the dead party, and I don't know what he was thinking, but I just ran the list of those who couldn't make it.

He judged his moment, cleared his throat. "Yeah, I guess you didn't come out with too much in the way of revenue either."

I shrugged. "Apparently, I can drink for free at any number of cop bars around the city now. That's got to be good for something."

"Yes—well, I think I might have something a little more crunchy than that for you. I had some time while I was laid up, you see, and the last couple of weeks I've been testing my systems. You know—making sure the intrusion tech is flushed and ready to rumble again. I, uh, I got into the BPD morgue."

I looked up. "You what?"

"Yeah, all those bodies suddenly stacking up—Executive House and down in Ventura before that. Call it idle curiosity, because that's what it was at first, but when I ran the gene codes, I found this weird correlation. Dead guy, multiple gunshot wounds to chest and abdomen, picked up at some fresh-build site on Fairchild Loop—and turns out he codes the exact same way as a certain Hidalgo, whom the Marshal Service have been chasing for a while and for whom certain OC interests in the Shelf Counties have offered a very lucrative bounty—if the body could just be delivered into the right hands."

I blinked some of the alcohol out of my head, stared at him. "You're shitting me. You fucking didn't."

He grinned. Diodes in his piercings winked and twinkled at me. "I had to wait, of course, but BPD signed the local bodies over for cremation a couple of days ago. Simple manifest shuffle, and guess what, one of those caskets winds up on the ValleyVac—express freight for a rental storage facility in Cradle City."

I knocked back my drink hard. Sat staring at the bar, listening to his voice.

"Of course, it still needs someone to go up there with the access codes and take possession. I'd go myself, but the Uplands aren't really *me*. People will stare, you know. I hate that."

I shook my head. "Do you—of course you do—you know how much that bounty is."

"Yes. I thought I'd take a modest handling fee, say, 20 percent. The work wasn't what you'd call strenuous."

"Shut the fuck up, Hannu. You're going to take a modest 50 percent split and like it."

"Ahh . . ." He tilted his head abruptly. "Tess, there you are. Get Veil another drink, would you—a big one. He really is back from the dead, and very welcome, too."

THE PARTY RAN late, flexed and relaxed, eventually began to empty out. I tracked a blurred path through it all, trying to balance the ache of my ghosts with my newfound good fortune and how I felt about it. Half of a hundred and fifty thousand marins wouldn't buy me a cryocap back to Earth; it wouldn't even come close. But there were a lot of other things I could do with it right here in the Gash. Pay off the mortgage on the Dyson for a start. Get my BV physical systems overhauled and jacked to match my new internals. Take out some decent long-term medical insurance. Buy some new clothes.

I washed up sitting alone with my thoughts in one of the raised lounging basins along the wall opposite the bar, watching other people dance. I'd been there a while when someone dropped heavily into the lounger beside me. Proximity alerts twitched, but I knew at several levels I couldn't be bothered to examine that there was no threat.

"So you're Veil."

I caught her perfume, mingled with sweat from the dancing. I looked at her, saw the object of Luppi's Fifteen Famous interview. Dark, delicate Himalayan features, lips the color of plums, and a thick black mane of hair artfully shot through with honey and silver, piled up high and then left to tumble down her back. It clung at her temples in tiny sweat-printed curlicues. Her eyes danced, and the rest of her said it wanted to do the same.

"I am Veil," I confirmed.

"Hannu singled you out. That's *very* high praise. Would you like to dance?"

I shook my head. "Wrong guy, wrong night. What happened to your partner? Looked like he knew what he was doing out there."

"Indeed. But Julian is . . . disenchanted with me this evening." She chuckled throatily. "I agreed to a candid face-to-face with Fifteen Famous here tonight and then reneged rather aggressively on the deal partway through. It's going to be expensive for me, and Julian likes to think he manages that aspect of my life." A pause while she settled a fallen tress of her hair back behind her ear. "He doesn't."

"Why'd you renege?" Interested despite myself.

"Because, Mr. Veil, the interviewer in question was a prurient little cunt and I wasn't in the mood."

I held back a grin. "Just call me Veil."

"Veil. How very *blunt*." She turned herself more fully to face me. "Do you think I was unwise, Veil?"

I shrugged. "Probably. You know anyone around here who isn't?"

She laughed, out loud, and it was the same bright, throaty sound as her chuckle, stronger and more infectious now she set it free. I felt my own mouth twist in response. When she looked at me again, something had shifted in her eyes.

"You won't dance?"

"No."

"Would you like to leave with me instead, then?" She put a hand very deliberately on my thigh, touched her lips with the tip of her tongue. "Would you like to get out of this place?"

I found a smile and put it on.

"More than you can possibly know," I said.

. . .

OUTSIDE ON THE Strip, the night air was raw, but she was warm and loose up against me, nuzzling delicately at my neck with lips and tongue. The Lamina coiled and splotched overhead in bursts of silver and greenish gold. And—miracle of miracles—Particle Slam seemed to have finally wrangled its rain code right. The crowd around us cheered as it swept in and drenched them. A few of them started to dance. My companion laughed delightedly, turned her features upward to catch the droplets on her face and in her mouth.

"Isn't it marvelous?" she cried. "Getting wet like this! Just like on Earth!"

"Something like that," I agreed.

As we cast about in the crowd, looking for the car she'd summoned, I heard the spiteful signature whine of a code-fly zeroing in. I was too drunk and too swamped in the backwash from her enthusiasm to really react or care.

The code-fly hovered and whined a moment longer, as if put out by this new lack of response.

It didn't bite me.

And the icy Martian wind took it away through the promise of the rain.

ACKNOWLEDGMENTS

ENDLESS THANKS, AS ALWAYS, to Virginia Cottinelli and Daniel Morgan Cottinelli for cohabiting with the Creature in the Attic while he flailed and raged and got this book down on the page. You are the fuel that drives me on.

Gratitude, admiration, and awe to the midwives at the birth—Gillian Redfearn and Anne Groell, without whose vast patience, enthusiasm, and painstaking attention to detail, I would never have made it over the finish line. I have been truly fortunate to have not one but two such magisterial editors in my corner.

And, finally, to all those of you who wanted and waited for me to write some more SF—thank you for your voices, they have made all the difference.

ABOUT THE AUTHOR

RICHARD K. MORGAN is the acclaimed author of *The Dark Defiles*, *The Cold Commands*, *The Steel Remains*, *Thirteen*, *Woken Furies*, *Market Forces*, *Broken Angels*, and *Altered Carbon*, a *New York Times* Notable Book and winner of the Philip K. Dick Award. His third book, *Market Forces*, won the John W. Campbell Award in 2005 and his fifth, *Thirteen,* won the Arthur C. Clarke Award in 2008. *Altered Carbon* has been under option for screen development since it was published in 2002 and is now a ten-episode series on Netflix.

richardkmorgan.com
Twitter: @quellist1

ABOUT THE TYPE

This book was set in Bulmer, a typeface designed in the late eighteenth century by the London type cutter William Martin (1757–1830). The typeface was created especially for the Shakespeare Press, directed by William Bulmer (1757–1830)—hence the font's name. Bulmer is considered to be a transitional typeface, containing characteristics of old-style and modern designs. It is recognized for its elegantly proportioned letters, with their long ascenders and descenders.